DATE DUE			

No Laughing Matter

Angus Wilson

NO
LAUGHING
MATTER

The Viking Press

NEW YORK

Published in 1967 by The Viking Press, Inc.
625 Madison Avenue, New York, N.Y. 10022

Library of Congress catalog card number: 67-26185
Printed in U.S.A. by H. Wolff Book Mfg. Co.

Second printing December 1967

FOR GLYN AND JANE

Contents

BOOK ONE

Quentin Matthews
Gladys Matthews
Rupert Matthews
Margaret Matthews
Sukey Matthews
Marcus Matthews

William Matthews (Billy Pop), their Father
Clara Matthews (The Countess), their Mother
Granny Matthews
Miss Rickard (Mouse), their Great-aunt
Henrietta Stoker (Regan), the cockney cook

Husbands, wives, lovers of various kinds, university teachers and undergraduates, Russians, members of Society, politicians, journalists, members of Lloyd's and of the Bloomsbury Group, cockneys, German refugees, staffs of preparatory schools, English residents abroad, Egyptians, actors and actresses, Moroccans, financiers, Scandinavians, and representatives of the Younger Generation.

Before the War

All through that year the kinemas showed scenes from the Wild West Exhibition in London on Gaumont Graphic or Pathé Pictorial (for the cowboys much *largo* to express wide open spaces; but for the little geisha girls the piano sounded a touching staccato). Audiences caught quick jerky glimpses of huge cartwheel hats wreathed in ostrich feathers, of trains dragging in the dust, of bowlers and toppers and peaked cloth caps and little round caps set with their tassels upon the backs of thickly brilliantined heads, of parasols and button boots, of sailor suits and knickerbockers, of pearly waistcoats and choker scarves, of bad teeth and no teeth, of princess petticoats, squirrel skin, sable and beaver, of Neapolitan ices (Oh, oh, Antonio!) and of hot potatoes for the muff, each in its season, of a sari or two, of the Kaffir chief's headdress, of a guardsman's busby, and of a little toque of violets worn on a Great Personage's head (Viking's daughter from over the sea, so splendidly null in half mourning), of the Big Wheel, the Water Chute, the Balloon, the Haunted House, and of diavolos everywhere, of Kaiser Bill moustaches, and above all, of even more imperial moustaches curled like a buffalo's horns, Buffalo Bill himself. Was it S. F. Cody the showman and not the great Colonel Cody at all? Who could tell what came out of America? And true to say, who cared? It was ideal for the children. With their broad-brimmed hats, their fringed breeches, their lassos and their whips. In the wilds of West Kensington the West was now long established.

The Matthews family, as they came that hot July afternoon through the crowds, from the Stadium, might so easily have been frozen and stored away in the files of the National Film Institute. There Mrs. Matthews' chic (Worth or Paquin, it might seem, but

actually the little woman around the corner), or Marcus's pear-
shaped, altar boy's head and great, dark, Greco eyes, or the future
Regan's blowsy, randy, cowlike-cockney Marie Lloyd features might
have caught the attention of the costume designer, the lover of moments of good cinema, or the searcher for social types. But there was
no such camera poised in waiting. And the loss in recall is probably
not very great, since the jerky Colonel Bogey-accompanied life of an
old film news strip would ill serve to dissolve the limbs into that delicious sun-bathed, pleasure-sated rhythm which alone could bring
back the exact feel of that far-off afternoon. In any case, what no
recording machine yet invented could have preserved was the pioneer happiness, the primitive dream that for some minutes gave to
that volatile, edged, and edgy family a union of happy, carefree intimacy that it had scarcely known before and never knew again.
Whatever its origin (alas for the limits of our parapsychological
knowledge), some features were common to all their day-dreams—in
each of which one Matthews played the lead. As a covered wagon,
placidly swaying, lumbers, ambles, or generally browses across the
vast plains (are they desert, are they prairie?). Certainly a wind stirs,
blowing dry reedy grass and sand.

Only the great-aunt, Miss Rickard (Mouse), in *her* dream sees the
grass clearly and supplies the balls of tumbleweed that rollstop, rollstop across the desert; but all see prairie and desert alike as yellowing
through a buff to an almost primrose in the glowing sun. For most of
them the prairie soil turns suddenly to sand (like the East Coast old
Mrs. Matthews, the children's Granny M., sees it, where the spiky
sea poppies and the coarse sea lavender so suddenly give way to
wind-rippled dunes); but Miss Rickard, who once again *knows*,
would (had she guessed at the old lady's English source of comparison) have bid her look up rather to Cromer's cliffs for her vision's
furnishing—she has *seen* this desert and it is not sand but rock—flat
rock—often, it is true, sand-covered rock, indeed always some sandy
shade of yellow, but nevertheless rock.

For Will Matthews himself, bronzed and boyishly smiling, for all
his absurdly young patriarch's Noah's Ark responsibilities, the rocks
have transformed themselves into the Rockies, for something lofty is
always called forth by his muse (can it be Wordsworth's boyhood
lakeside heights—his boyhood reading—that furnish his fancy?).

He gazes up above the solemn peaks (surely there, if anywhere, the Sublime will give us the Ironic Answer) to where an eagle soars, and as he whittles away a stick of wood (for purposes obscure), he shouts out (one less subtly gentle would say "to the very heavens") something of Bret Harte's? something of Whitman's? Bret Harte, no doubt, for Whitman, though more shoutable, seems somehow too fierce for the sunny, easy, ambling roll of that day's wagon ride (English-wise the greatest affirmations are surely made in gently smiling earnest), Whitmanesque acceptant though the day's mood must be. But, however smiling, declaiming, whistling (perhaps a Winander owl's hoot) he is, beneath his lazy summer mood, attentive, vigilant, keen as the moose to scent approaching dangers that may threaten the God-given brood he is leading out of bondage into primeval lands (what bondage can it be? the rising income tax, a bank overdraft, or liability to jury service? Some measure of Lloyd Georgery, no doubt. Most certainly no bondage of servitude, for all our party save Stoker the bondmaid herself are of private means) and on to Eldorado.

As for the older ladies, each has her wisdoms and her skills—never such bread as old Mrs. Matthews bakes, never such stews as she concocts in her billycans, never such improvised mending for her menfolk as this gentle, indomitable old lady, always one to remember, always one to have brought the thermometer, to have brought old Nanny Segram's handwritten book of recipes, to have brought senna pods.

But Miss Rickard needs no book; she is herself their gazetteer and their medical dictionary rolled into one—the wayside, water-filled cactus root, the quamash growing by the sudden spring, the roasted porcupine—all these were her contributions. She it was who found the snakebane and the thorn with which to dig out ticks, and all these she offered with a nonchalant, gracious bend of her ageing, thin, pemmican-dry pioneer's body that disclaimed all praise—as how could she accept it, for despite all her pioneering courage she alone had the sure knowledge that when they arrived at Eldorado it would prove to her, the much-travelled woman, somewhere already familiar—after all, she'd gone through Manitoba to Vancouver in 1898, to San Francisco in 1902, and in 1906 went over the Rockies to Seattle (how wisely not to San Francisco), and no doubt at the last Eldorado would prove to be one of these three tolerably civilized places of interest. So she smiles her old grim smile that acts like steel to stiffen the back of any waverer, and with her old grim (yet tender) wit tempers the wagon's happy family love with a needed austere irony.

Needed indeed now and again by Miss Stoker, who, a good-natured, true serving cockney, will do anything, does do anything for her charges; yet in Miss Stoker's mind is the clear realization that, faced by buffalo, grizzly, or Indians, it is she, the down at the Old Bull and Bush I shall shortly own 'er, walks among the cabbages and leeks, Hetty Stoker who (in her master's version), for all her gallery roaring, heart-as-big-as-the-Elephant-and-Castle loyalty, will panic, take fright, pee her knickers, or otherwise betray her lowly origins instead, as the legend should be, of dying by sucking the poisoned wound of her youngest charge (Master Marcus) when the Indian arrows are flying fast and furious.

Sensing their hidden view of herself, indeed Miss Stoker needs all the force of Miss Rickard's (Sourpuss to her) communicated grim irony to restrain her wish to spit in their bloody faces. But as it is, and so fortified, her version takes in theirs; and Comic Western to the life, she falls over the prickly pear, mistakes the porcupine for a camp stool, and just gets back to the stockade as the growling mountain lion tears through her skirt to reveal the legs of her drawers (chase me, Charlie, lend me one of yours), at once dear, lovable, comical kid to tread on the board that raises the bucket that flies through the air that empties the whitewash slap in her kisser—to the laughter and toffee-paper-rustling of all six of her loving, larking, sticky-fingered charges.

Even young Mrs. Matthews, so beautiful and high and mighty, so very much milady, smiles as she sits at her embroidery. "What would we do without our Stoker and her constant scrapes to keep us laughing," cries milady (but they'd have to in the end, of course, for who but the hickseed cowboy with the freckles and the stutter would carry off Henrietta Stoker, a blushing bride, after a long, comic courtship, and oblivious, even at the end, of the clanking old tin bucket tied to the rear of their wedding buggy. Ah well, if he was like any of the cowpunchers they'd just seen, he'd have a nice packet of meat to him).

And indeed milady, young Mrs. Matthews, does at that moment smile across at Stoker, the conspirator's smile of two young (younger?) women brought close in their pioneer proximity—eating all at one table, no doubt, the shared wash-tub, the shared God-knew-what; but breeding takes such things in its stride (look at Mouse on her outlandish travels) so that some of the outer show of inner differences (maid and mistress right through to the bone) had fallen away like "trunks not wanted on the voyage" when the old country's shores had faded out of sight. But the shared smile soon became more general as young Mrs. Matthews, her great straw bonnet shading her from the prairie's ardent sun, stopped for a moment her plain sewing to day-dream, well-set chin cupped in smooth white palm, large dark eyes gazing absently across the wide expanse, to ponder upon the ties that bound her so closely (her a woman whose febrile beauty, whose voracious love of life might so easily have broken her wings upon the wheel) to all those loved ones in that lumbering wagon, all those whose deep love for her was as warm yet not harsh as the prairie sun's rays.

She stretched out one lovely arm to caress her Billy's curly head (improvident, carefree, hopeless—hush, whisper it not—sometimes prosy, wonderful Billy, whose genius her warming love had still to ignite) and then with her other hand she brushed the crowns (flaxen, ash, russet, chestnut, coal-black) of all her children (Rupert, glorious golden Rupert, a handsome mother's handsome favourite, perhaps), but all, all (yes, even bitter black little Marcus) the extraordinary, brilliant, healthy, handsome, utterly improbable offspring of her own deep hold on life, cherished by her, cherishing her. Jog-trot, jog-trot to the wagon's old everyday motion—she turned back to her plain sewing, wonderingly smiling at this extraordinary world which could cast someone so wild, someone so untameable as herself for the maternal role. But the casting had worked and that was all that mattered.

Of course one day the journey would be done, the jog-trot in sunshine or rain be over, and Eldorado . . . suddenly she walked between the tables, cigarette in hand, hips swaying, skirts frou-frouing, and the men, huge thighed, tight loined, wide shouldered, cheered as she threw down a bundle of notes on the green baize table, or, more suitable to her long, delicate hands, her arms gloved to the elbow, staked a pile of chips to the croupier's call . . . she adored the idea of Monte. But with that named paradise the vision blurred, toppled like the pile of chips on the edge of absurdity; carefully she steadied herself, first one hand on the children's haloed

crowns, then the other on Billy's curly mop and soon she was back
contentedly with her plain sewing, swaying in the happy family
wagon (of Mr. Matthews, the magazine writer—two stories and an
article in the *Strand*, three stories in the *Windsor*; and of Mrs. Matthews, the magazine writer's wife—born hostess for a refinedly successful literary man). She began to hum beneath her breath a silly,
jaunty tune, "Oh, we'll chase the buffalo! . . ."

Quentin, at first, had thought only for the horse beneath him, as
Reuben he rode, proud watch-dog eldest son beside the wagon's precious load, letting the prairie winds blow around him. But another
Quentin was alive within the guardian Reuben, a Quentin if not so
alert, yet more deeply happy, unaccustomedly at ease, lulled into life
perhaps by the unfamiliar rocking cradle of the great cowboy saddle
beneath him. Unity was all to this Quentin—that at last they were all
together, as they had not been since he (he the unwanted, he the
recriminated fugitive to comfort) had left eight years before for
Granny M. and Ladbroke Grove. Now at last he could relax, forgiven for not sharing in shabbiness and sudden violences, could be
caught up and float away in that muddied, strangely twisting, overgrown, smelly, once so familiar family stream that Granny M.'s port-
wine, best plum-cake, solid affluence kept out of her shiny-clean,
patter-neat, timetable-exact, great empty Italianate station of a
house. Keeping an old woman company, it isn't right, Quintus; but
no need for gratitude's denial now, for in the adventures ahead kind,
good, dull Granny M. (Oh, how the Sunday afternoons of stamp
albums and stereoscope with pictures of the Russo-Japanese war
killed the hungry heart) was united with the mad, wonderful,
frightening, undependable parents and best of all with US. But now
behind the happy united Quentin that had grown within the guardian rider, another Quentin peered and quizzed—Quentin the looker-
on. "Good *and* dull," he said, "wonderful *and* undependable," he
said and he laughed to make the reunited Quentin shiver.

Under his quizzing, unity fell away and even the prairie which
had called it forth threatened to dissolve into void, but Quentin, the
eldest son, lean, eager, simple, and straight as a die, forced himself to
feel only the horse beneath him and the wind blowing his hair. I'm
only a schoolboy, he said, no time for looking on, time now only for
tree felling, the lasso and the steers—only fifteen, too much to do to
have time for comment. And if he thought he heard a mocking

sound it was no doubt only the coyotes howling where the winds are free. Oh, bury me deep in this family day.

Gladys, of course, was busy inside the wagon. All the stores had to be checked and double-entered in the great ledger book. With a long quill pen by the light of a hurricane lamp she dipped into the silver inkpot (silver? more likely horn, moose horn, perhaps), counted and wrote, counted and wrote—long bars of coarse yellow soap, packets of candles, loaves of sugar (pyramids, she saw them, in dark-blue paper), red flannel petticoats (use obscure, but an essential item) and beads (like the flannel, of course, for barter—or was that in the South Seas?), huge hams, vast sacks of lentils and chick peas (what could they look like?).

And Father (how cunningly he held the reins, just feeling, no more, the horses' mouths) turned back and smiled. "Well, Podge. Our little manager. She'll make a perfect wife for some lucky devil in Eldorado." She ran up the length of the wagon and, throwing her arms around his shoulders, pressed her cheek against his, and they both looked up (boyishly twinkling blue eyes, solemn little dark ones) through the frosty air to where an All-Hallows 'Eve moon showed its pumpkin form in the great star vault above them. Then he tugged her pigtails lightly. "So that's how it is. But you'll have to leave your little wooden hut one of these days, you know. For some lucky fellah or other."

"Don't tease the poor Podge. Time enough when she loses all that puppy fat. You'll manage the general stores in Eldorado, won't you, darling?" The back of her mother's hand, so cool, like blue-veined marble, stroked against her other cheek, pressed against it.

Instantly his lips were gently finding hers, then pressing hard against them so that she almost cried (it was painful the first time, Marian Sargeant said), pressing as hard as his hard thighs had gripped the black mare's flanks as up and over they went, the black-breeched cowboy with the black stetson hat on the black mare. Mother and father he, and more, as she waited, the girl with the head on her, to run the general stores—so warm to come home to after days of round-up. Horrid Marian Sargeant's nasty whispers sounded in her ear and Marian's grubby little notes passed by a sweaty hand far down the room. Miss Baker looked up and frowned; oh, they would be caught and it was nasty. She forced herself away from Miss Baker's class, away from the handsome black-haired cowboy, back to the account books in the covered wagon. "A plump little house-proud Podge," her father said.

Rupert, the great golden eagle, flew higher and higher up towards the mountain crags and looked down to where the wagon, obese and dropsical, waddled at first like some worn-out pachyderm, a hippo perhaps, stranded far from lakes or rivers, or the last surviving brontosaurus, swollen with thirst; and then, as he soared higher, it scuttled, first like an armadillo, then like the armadillo's dwarf mockery, a wood-louse, absurdly, desperately seeking cover. A ridiculous wood-louse as far beneath an eagle's gaze as a flea to a mousing cat's. But now from the wagon rose the second eagle, smaller, raven-black, fleeter perhaps on wing, yet with only a female's strength. Together they rose and floated, rose and floated, flying above, around, and beneath one another, now coasting on the wind's currents, now battling the full force of the gale, a glorious dance to make the whole prairie sing if there had been anything but a scuttling wood-louse (now almost a dust speck) to inhale this wonderful triumph of mother and son.

Then something glittered in the black eagle's eye, her beak snapped. Rupert made himself the red spaniel at his parents' feet down in the happy, housewarm, family-smelling wagon, and snuffled and licked at their hands, as his honest brown eyes looked up beneath a worried, furry frown. "There's a lovely boy," they cried. And Granny M. and Aunt Mouse and Stoker and All took up the cry, "Our faithful, loving old boy."

Margaret sat on a stool in the shade cast by a wheel of the now stationary wagon. She made an entry in her diary:

> A wonderful, satisfactory day. We made almost a royal progress with little colonies of prairie marmots popping up like so many jack-in-the-boxes from the rocks around us. They would stand for seconds together on their hind legs, their front paws dangling before their white-furred chests, for all the world like a group of village women in their aprons come out to cheer our passing coach. And if happiness is the mark of kings, we are kings and queens now: Grandmother so stately with her piled-up, snow-white hair, Aunt Mouse the embodiment of courtly dignity, and as for Mother and Father, they both look so beautiful and young and so dedicated as they are about to enter their new kingdom. There is no doubt at all that the hardships and high hopes of this journey to a new life have proved their own satisfaction;

united in common dangers we have found the new life before we have even reached Eldorado.

She read through the passage and her mouth seemed filled with sickening sugar and choking starch. Granny Matthews, of course, would pant and exclaim, "What long words for a little girl of twelve and a half! I really think, Will, she's going to be another genius like her father!" But Aunt Mouse—she dreaded to think how Aunt Mouse would look. "Maggie, my dear girl, kings and queens! Where is your sense of humour? Life isn't all icing sugar, my dear." Deliberately she added to the diary's entry:

> At about five as the sun was setting, our two collies, who had been missing all day, returned to the wagon. Their jaws were dripping with blood and out of Trusty's huge maw hung the mangled remains of a prairie marmot, village white apron and all. Life has so many different satisfactions.

She looked up to her great-aunt for a certain grim approval. But then again she had meant to convey the incredible, sudden family happiness of today and now it was spoiled. Deliberately risking a sarcastic gleam in her great-aunt's eye, she turned to the inside cover of her diary. "A Pioneer in the Prairies," she wrote. "Being the Journal of Lady Margaret Carmichael, a Lady of Quality." There, now it was someone else, and Aunt Mouse and all other mice could jeer as much as they wished, it would not touch her. Yet still she had not made these hours immortal.

Sukey fed the few hens they had brought along in order to be sure of fresh eggs, and then sat blissfully for a moment in the prairie sun's warm rays (she had forgotten her bonnet, but never to fuss) watching the fat little puppies (liver and white, tan and white, chocolate and white) grunting and tugging as they fed from old Trusty. That old Trusty should so suddenly and unexpectedly have given birth was the wonderful, supreme surprise of these wonderful, supremely happy days of—at last—a real family life she had always read of in stories, heard of from other girls at school, dreamed of over the nursery fire. No scenes, no "words," no clever laughing at good, ordinary things, no awful disregard of the neighbours here in the prairie. That, if anything, was the tiny, midget fly in the delicious ointment—just for some of their neighbours to know what a happy family they could be! But not the awful neighbours they had in horrid Victoria, in horrid London. She had known things would never be right until they got away from the fog and the smoke and the chimneys. She had thought, it is true, of an English farm like the one in the Quantocks where they had stayed last summer, or of the seaside, all dunes and seaweed beds, like the shore in front of Granny M.'s house at Cromer; but, of course, they were not like other families, the mad Matthewses, a gipsy lot. She should have seen earlier that they would never be happy until they were on the move. All that fighting and bitterness and the dirty kitchen and unmade beds had been just because they had felt caged, their wild spirits bottled up, their wings clipped.

Now that they were as free as air they were happy as any ordinary, nice family and yet, besides, quite extraordinary, clever, talented, unpredictable, lively and absurdly lovable—still, in short, the mad Matthewses. Except, of course, herself—"Sukey, our little changeling, the sensible chicken in the crazy clutch," Father called her. Even now when danger and hardship and sheer wanderlust had brought the best out in all of them, she had her little contribution to make—seeing that some sort of a time-table was kept, if not for their meals, then for the poor hens and the dogs and the horses, seeing that Marcus's bedtime was not entirely forgotten, that Granny M.'s afternoon nap was remembered, that Aunt Mouse took her linctus.

And later when they got to Eldorado and there were neighbours again, it would be she surely who could bridge the return to civilization for this mad, difficult, lovable family of hers. She placed great importance on whether they found nice neighbours. What would Eldorado prove to be like? She could not help thinking it would be like the Quantocks, in which case there would be the rector and Doctor Seely; or perhaps they would reach the Pacific Ocean where no doubt as at Cromer there would be a lot of kind, quiet, retired people with grandchildren. Whatever, her happiness was now complete as, moving away back to join her family in the wagon, another little family began to follow her, each fat puppy wobbling and falling over the other in its eager love. In the country, at regular hours, surrounded by happy little creatures of all kinds.

Marcus sat on top of the wagon, cross-legged; Mother called out,

"Look! Our little black monkey!"—but her words miraculously were without a lash, and she smiled up at him lovingly. He gazed all around at the flat sandy desert, with here and there a palm tree, and he found it sadly lacking. He began rapidly to increase the oases of palm trees so that soon they grew jungle thick, and about them crept great vines with monstrous flowers crimson, purple, scarlet, brightest yellow. In the trumpets flickered emerald, gold, and ruby humming-birds. And soon the flowering trees waving high above the gentle breeze sent down delicious scents of spices to the paddy fields below. Above, too, could be heard the chatter of monkeys and the shriek of parrots; now a macaw's tail flashed blue and saffron and now a toucan's beak showed for a second its livid green.

Beneath him the elephant padded on, all but hidden from him by the richly jewelled howdah in which he sat, with its canopy of fretted ivory; yet ever and again he caught sight of the great beast's trunk lashing through the air as it trumpeted. Around the great elephant his brothers and sisters, led by his mother, danced a triumphal dance, their rich jewelled veils and costly robes churning the incensed air. His father, with grandmother and Aunt Mouse, were borne aloft in litters. Eldorado came in sight; he could glimpse its minarets and towers, hear distantly its splashing fountains. Yet while the others heralded the arrival of this beautiful family by ever more delicious cries and movements, he, high above, crowned by a vast red turban twice his own height, sat, most beautiful of all, cross-legged, black and motionless, a lovely, sacred boy.

At the moment that Marcus in his holy pomp arrived at Eldorado, the communion became complete. Old Mrs. Matthews forgot her everyday goodness, Miss Rickard her wise dryness, Miss Stoker her avenging comicality, Mr. Matthews his sly warmth, Mrs. Matthews her passionate fevers; Quentin became one youth and no leader; Gladys fused desire and orderliness; Rupert was made a boy again; Margaret resolved her formal dilemmas; Sukie forgot the hierarchies of niceness; Marcus's sensuous needs were quenched—all felt only pleasure, affection, and physical ease. Perhaps it was this last that they communicated to the large crowd around them in the Coronation Walk of the Exhibition; certainly people fell away to make room for this family party—husband and wife side by side, flanked by two handsome boys, then two older ladies with parasols, flanked by two elegant little girls, and last a most proper nurse flanked on one side by a solemn plaited schoolgirl and, on the other, a black little imp of a boy.

The family moved forward, apparently unaware of the crowd around them, triumphantly happy, and as they moved, recalling perhaps his wife's earlier humming, Mr. Matthews began to sing joyfully. And soon all the others joined in chorus. It was the ladies who first stopped singing. Men are the egoists of life, of course; women are the conformists. And again, men need to advertise comradeship and ease, women are content to feel it. There are so many ways of explaining the gradual breakdown of the singing, but almost none to explain how it began.

Encouraged by their father's lead, for once oblivious of the adult female example, all six of the Matthews children bawled aloud, even Quentin quite forgetful, despite his school top-hat and tails, of Ladbroke Grove proprieties: "Oh! We'll chase the buffalo, yes, we'll chase the buffalo, in the wilds of West Kensington, we'll chase the buffalo." Many in the large crowd turned with amusement or surprise to see these posh youngsters singing so loudly in public. Mr. Matthews, by now conscious of the public gaze, smiled and swung his walking-stick a little at the attentions of the passers-by; his wife smiled, too, to see him smiling. "Billy loves public notice, don't you, darling?" She put her gloved hand on his white linen sleeve—in the intense heat of that summer day he had got out his tropical suit, relic of their Madeira honeymoon. Herself, she twirled her cream lace parasol a little.

Old Mrs. Matthews smiled, a trifle askance, and kept her eyes intent upon the asphalt; but "The conventions weren't made for Will. And never have been." Miss Rickard, as usual, seemed to see nothing. Turning her head, she made kissing noises with her lips at the knowing green parrot that perched on her shoulder. But young Mrs. Matthews knew her aunt too well to be deceived. "Don't hide your face in Mr. Polly, Mouse. She doesn't want to admit that you've made her smile, Billy. Eccentric Mouse is the really conventional one." She turned to look behind her for Stoker. "And Stoker's singing too." And so the quaint cockney was, if you could call the tuneless drone singing.

Marcus, the youngest, spoke. "But there weren't any buffaloes, were there?"

His father smiled, "Trust His Nibs to have noticed that deficiency." He bent down, and putting his face close to his small son's,
"No, Markie, and a very good thing too. Performing animals can
only be trained by cruelty. Jack London proved that. Not that I
should wish to criticize circuses. A wonderful people, the circus
folk. But wild animals should *be* of the wild. I've often thought of
writing the story of the last great bull buffalo roaring out his defiance of the Paleface on the prairies."

"Oh, you should write it, Will," said his mother, "shouldn't he,
children?"

"I hope," said Miss Rickard, "that if you do, you'll remember that
they're bison, William. Buffalo's an entirely Yankee word for bison.
The true buffaloes are only to be found in Asia and Africa. You see
them wherever rice grows. Great, patient creatures with huge, sad
eyes. What the school textbooks of my day called 'friends to man.' "

Once again young Mrs. Matthews put out her small gloved hand.
This time she turned and placed it on Miss Rickard's grey shantung
arm. "Darling Mouse."

Old Mrs. Matthews blew a little under her veil. "Will's always had
the power to bring places to life, no matter whether he's seen them
or not. Do you remember, dear boy, how you startled them all at
Joppins with your tales of life in Peking? Peking! And he was only
six and a half. You couldn't have been more because Porter was still
with us. Oh, dear! Such happy days! Major Cayley said then you
would be a writer. You must have travelled everywhere, Miss Rickard."

"Enough to have a number of the usual tedious travellers' tales.
Though they are true."

"The places you sent me postcards from, Mouse, when I was little! There was one of cowboys, children; I perfectly remember it.
You must tell them all about that, Mouse. But not till we've found
somewhere for tea. I'm dying for a cup of tea. The dust and the
heat!" Young Mrs. Matthews let her whole hour-glass figure wilt and
even the grey ostrich plumes in her hat seemed suddenly bedraggled.
"Find us tea, Billy. You'd like a cup of tea, wouldn't you, Stoker?"

"Yes, Mum."

"And you enjoyed the cowboys?"

"Yes, Mum."

"Good. Take Master Marcus's hand, will you?"

The square, red-faced woman did as she was asked. Her blue skirt and coat were neat, but her greying carrotty hair crept erratically around the brim of her cherry-decorated hat. "Will you make one of yer drawings of them orses, Master Marcus?" she asked him with grave interest; and very gravely he answered, "Yes, I think I shall, Stoker."

"Our only Pole Star is the Big Wheel," Mr. Matthews announced.

"I don't want a Pole Star, Billy darling. I want tea."

"It's quite difficult to see ahead with this crowd," her mother-in-law observed. "The world and his wife are here."

"This way, then." Mr. Matthews pointed with his stick to where the Big Wheel sparkled and flashed high up against the sky's clear blue. The twins and Rupert began to sing once more as the party moved on.

"Oh! No! Not again, children," said their Mother. "We may recognize the world and his wife but we don't want to attract their attention." But she stopped their singing lovingly.

"I'm afraid we're bound to, Clara dear. It's Mr. Polly. They always stare at him." Miss Rickard scratched the parrot's feathered head. Mr. and Mrs. Matthews smiled to one another.

Quentin said, "I should have thought that *horses* had been trained, Father." He stopped, blushing.

"Of course they were trained. What a rotten silly thing to say!" His younger brother Rupert mocked him.

"I meant cruelty."

"The horses! The darling lovely horses," Sukey cried.

But her twin sister Margaret said, "It was all beautiful. It all went together. You can't *just* say the horses."

"I only liked the horses," Sukey insisted.

"I wish I'd been the man who straddled the two white horses with his arms spread out. Crippen! Didn't everyone cheer."

"Oh, Rupert dear, please don't use that expression. To keep on reminding us of that dreadful little man."

"I liked the cowboy with the black hair. He looked so strong."

"Gladys is being soppy," Rupert told them.

"Not at all. I'm only glad to see Podge has such a good eye." Mrs. Matthews patted her daughter's plump, rosy cheek. "They *were* handsome, darling. You're quite right. And their great chests! How the perspiration ran down them, poor things."

Her mother-in-law coughed.

"So the dust is troubling *you* now, Grannie. Never mind. Here's relief. The Geisha Tea Gardens. Look, children, at the waitresses all dressed in kimonos."

"I hope," said Miss Rickard, "that we shan't be made to kneel. I haven't done that since I was in Japan twenty years ago. My bones would creak nowadays. No, I'm too old for kneeling."

"Except in church," Mrs. Matthews senior amended.

"We don't kneel at the Circle," Miss Rickard told her.

Once again Mr. and Mrs. Matthews were united in smiling complicity; and on this occasion they even extended the conspiracy to include Gladys and Quentin, their two eldest. Later, when the children had finished three stone bottles of pop between them, Rupert and Quentin became restless, despite all the waitresses dressed up as geishas. And even little Marcus showed a sort of lordly boredom. "Such ugly colours," he said. But the twins were riveted to the gaily coloured kimonos until Margaret cried, "They're just dressed up in dressing-gowns, aren't they, Mother?" and Sukey amplified, "Servants dressed up." Then seeing Stoker busy with a bath bun, she blushed. But the spell was broken and now the girls' restiveness was added to the boys'.

"Now just sit still, darlings, and your great-aunt will tell you all about the real cowboys."

"Yes, give us Texas, Mouse," Mr. Matthews agreed.

"Indeed I will not. They don't want an old woman's stories. They want to explore all the wonders here." Miss Rickard gave Quentin half a crown out of her huge Morocco leather handbag. "See that everyone has a share."

Old Mrs. Matthews added a florin. "I think two shillings is enough for children."

"My dear mother, you're spoiling them."

"Yes, Mouse, you're naughty."

But neither parent spoke very convincingly.

"Oh, no," said the old lady, "it's a special day."

And the middle-aged one said, "My dear Clara, when we've all enjoyed ourselves so much it's sheer hypocrisy to deny the children."

Even Stoker intervened. "I'm sure, mum, they've been very good. And we all like to get up to our own larks, don't we?"

Young Mrs. Matthews laughed. "Do we, Billy? Do we like to get
up to our own larks?"

"Yes, my dear, I think we do." He put his hand on hers.

"Oh, what a heavenly summer. Especially here out of the dust.
Oh, Billy, I have a feeling that your Regency boxing novel is going
to be a tremendous success. And we'll have lots of money and travel
everywhere. Japan will be nothing. You haven't seen the half of it,
Mouse."

"My dear, you shall live like a queen yet."

This time Miss Rickard exchanged a glance with old Mrs. Matthews. Her niece perhaps caught sight of it, for she turned almost
sharply to the children. "Well, your father and I are in a good mood
for once. Run off and make the most of it."

Led by Quentin the children wandered across to the great Union
Jack made out of geraniums, white candytuft, and lobelias, and
there, out of the adults' hearing, they argued the spending of the
money. They hoped for the water chute *and* the big wheel, but
prices were against them so, of course, first choice had to be the
wheel—the wheel on which, heavenly thought, twenty-four people
had been stranded all night. But, delicious though it proved to be,
whirled out into the heavens high above the houses and streets of
Kensington, faster and faster until Gladys felt that she had frighteningly swallowed a piece of blue sky and Marcus's laughter had
turned to screaming, they were giddy and white-faced without luck,
for the wheel eventually returned them to the ground.

Now there was nothing for it but the shooting ranges or the for-
tune-telling machines, and over these they were divided equally between boys and girls. A decision might never have been reached if
Marcus had not been seized with one of his screaming fits. That
these were taken for granted at home did not make passers-by the
less curious at the sight of a young boy, in long-trousered sailor
suit, standing apart and uttering a loud prolonged "Aah!" to the
world at large so that soon a small crowd had gathered, and his
siblings became aware that Marcus could prove an embarrassment
abroad. It was Gladys who thought of the laughing mirrors, but
Quentin, the eldest, who agreed rather savagely. "It won't matter if
he *does* scream his head off in there."

He gave the money to the boy with no front teeth in the little
entrance booth, and they filed slowly through a dark corridor, even

"Now, Billy, you must apologize. You've hurt your mother's feelings. Talking like that about the dead! How vulgar you can be."

"I'm sure Will is never vulgar, Clara. He's often very naughty. But I suppose that as his mother I understand that as well as anyone. Once when a Sister of Mercy came to the house, she said, 'What a little angel.' And of course you looked it, Will, with your golden curls. But all you did was to cry 'To hell with the Pope! To hell with the Pope!' I remember it so clearly. It must have been her black veil. A naughty child you were, but everyone loved you. Your own children are far better behaved, Will."

She turned smiling to the children. Gladys was leaning on a nearby unoccupied table and straining her muscles so that her cheeks had turned scarlet with the rush of blood to her head. The other children all stood watching her with evident fascinated delight.

"Doesn't Gladys strain beautifully?" Margaret asked.

"If she goes on longer she sometimes goes purple," Marcus told them.

"She's the purple limit, that's what she is." Rupert showed his delight at pinning down this modish adult phrase by dancing up and down.

"If she went on for ever, she would burst, wouldn't she?" Sukey demanded. Only Quentin said nothing, but he stood by his sister's exhibition of skill with a ringmaster's pride copied from that afternoon's performance by Buffalo Bill. Their grandmother's smile became a little uncertain, but their mother had no doubts.

"Stop it at once, you disgusting girl. Horrible little creatures, all of you. What a way to repay us for giving you the afternoon of your lives!"

"We didn't know we were meant to repay you," Margaret made comment.

"I'm afraid the gel's made an excellent point, Clara. Repayment of kindness. What a sordid idea, worthier of a stockbroker than an artist." Miss Rickard met a silence. "I suppose we should welcome any idea of repayment, really."

"Oh, Mouse, you are the absolute limit. Do stop needling Bill about that wretched loan. If you were a little more generous about it, he wouldn't have to give his mind all the time to shillings and pence."

"I'd hoped so much when Will married you, Clara, that *you* would take over all that side of things. You married an artist, you know, my dear."

"My niece thought she'd married a man and found that she'd married a spoilt baby, Mrs. Matthews. As I could have told her."

"As you did, Mouse, as you did. Don't be modest. Nothing became your guardianship of Clara so well as your taking leave of it. Having neglected an orphan for most of her childhood, except when it happened to suit your travelling fancy, as soon as she showed an inclination to choose for herself you did everything you could to stifle her with a lot of warnings against men. Cassandra on the perils of marriage! But then Cassandra was an old maid. How the human comedy does repeat itself! Thank God for its wonderful humours. What Walter Scott would have made of you, Mouse."

"My dear man, you're welcome to make as much of me as you like, if it will persuade you to get down to some work. Though I can't see you killing yourself paying off your debts like Scott. Smoking a pipe in public and wearing that velvet jacket of yours are more your idea of being an author. But Meerschaum pipes and velvet jackets won't keep a family of six, William, I'm afraid."

"Well, I'm sure Will's family have done all *they* can, Miss Rickard. I was only too happy to take on dear Quintus's fees at Westminster, of course. No one looks smarter in his topper, I'm sure. Though I do wish we still had Hopkins, Will. What a sheen he used to put on your father's hats. But there we are; we can't talk of valets on an annuity, can we? I'm lucky enough to have Edith and Cook and Colyer. Though I do all I can for everyone, I must say."

"Nobody questioned it, Mrs. Matthews. It's a matter of their trying to do something for themselves. As it is I am forever supplementing Clara's allowance. As well as taking on the expense of the gels' clothes and, of course, I'm only too glad to do so. . . ."

"Now, Gladys, say thank you to your great-aunt for your winter coat. And Margaret, you'd better curtsy for your party dress. Will that satisfy you, Mouse?" Young Mrs. Matthews pulled her tall daughter to her feet. "Go on. Curtsy. Show your Aunt Mouse you haven't wasted her kind dancing-class fees."

"Clara, that sort of play-acting's unforgivable. To involve your children!"

"I suppose we were involved anyway, Aunt Mouse. Not being invisible or fairies or anything."

"Don't be impertinent to your elders, Margaret."

"That's all right, Clara. The gel isn't the worse for having a sharp tongue in her head." She beckoned Margaret to her side and gave her a peck on her cheek. "Whatever your disappointments, always try to get your own back, my dear. It's woman's compensation."

Old Mrs. Matthews looked bewildered. "I'm sure the children are *all* as good as fairies. And you're a real little mother, Margaret. A little Wendy."

Marcus looked up and his eyes flickered for a moment over his grandmother's words, but like a snake's tongue the flicker disappeared as quickly.

Rupert did not so restrain his delight. He leaned towards his tall sister and, adopting a special drawl, repeated, "Wendy, our little Wendy, a little Wendy," closer and closer into Margaret's face. Margaret blushed a deep rose all down her long neck, but, "Gladys is the little mother," she said.

"Oh, I suppose so, dear, being the eldest," their grandmother agreed.

But it was the unmentioned Sukey who was suddenly in tears.

"Oh, Lord above," cried Mr. Matthews, "how right was that godly man John Knox when he inveighed against the monstrous regiment of women. What's wrong with Sukey?"

"I think," said Marcus, "that she feels hurt. After all, she's the one who does all the little mothering things for us. Her and Stoker."

Marcus's words diverted his mother from her crying daughter. She turned, seized his wrist, wrenching and twisting his arm. "Will you keep your tongue quiet! Little boys of your age should be seen and not heard. Though who'd want to see you I can't think. Look at the way you wear your sailor suit, all falling out of your trousers. Just like a girl's blouse. Why can't you look like a normal boy? Little girly boy. Apparently you don't even know your own mother. Little mother here, and little mother there. I'm your mother, do you understand that? Though I can hardly believe such a little mollycoddle can be my son." She shook him to and fro by the arm. His face turned white and he stared at her fixedly with his large black eyes, but he did not cry. The other adults protested.

"Oh, Clara, such a little boy."

"Little boy. You don't know him, Granny. He can be a little beast."

But Mr. Matthews leaned back and blew a smoke ring. His soft face set in a contemplative smile as he stared back at his wife. "Oh, cool off, Countess. You don't know your own depths of vulgarity." His wife seemed suddenly all fierce, black gipsy eyes, but before she could answer back, "No, no, my dear. I mean it. Temper makes you look a raddled hag. So much, Mouse, for breeding. Of course *we* can only offer stocks and shares."

"I am not going to be drawn into your quarrels with Clara, William. It's been a very pleasant day, but we're tired now. I suggest we all make our different ways home. I shall certainly take myself off to find a cab. I shall be at my club until the boat leaves on the fourteenth. Perhaps the twins could take luncheon with me there one day. We've a good number of freaks among the members for Margaret to sharpen her pleasant wit upon." She patted her great-niece's neck. Mr. Matthews rose from his chair.

"Help your great-aunt to get a cab, Quentin."

"Good heavens! If I can cross the Kalahari, I suppose I can cross the Earls Court Road on my own."

Her nephew-in-law made her a little bow. "My apologies to you and Mrs. Pankhurst, Mouse."

"I shan't say good-bye to everyone," Miss Rickard announced, but she added, "Good-bye, Stoker, I'm glad to see you look so well. Say good-bye to everyone, Mr. Polly." But the parrot had fallen asleep.

Old Mrs. Matthews indulged herself with only one comment when Miss Rickard was out of sight. "I wonder at her having that creature on her shoulder. Nasty, high-smellin' thing, I should think."

"Now we have no need for pets, Auntie's joined the suffragettes," Rupert recited.

"Oh, dear," said his grandmother, "what a wicked thing to say." But she couldn't help laughing.

"He didn't say it," Quentin informed her, "it's out of a book."

"Quintus knows all the books," she told them. "Well, Will, my dear, I expect Clara would like to have the boy at home now. So if you'll just help me to find the North Entrance; Colyer said he would bring the motor car to the North Entrance. We can talk about Quintus's trunks and things on the telephone later."

"My dear Mother, if you're going to take up every word Clara says . . ."

"Quintus wants to be with his mother, don't you, dear? You've had quite enough of being with an old woman."

"I'm sure Quentin *doesn't* want to be with his mother. Being with me would mean helping in the home for once. That wouldn't suit his lordship at all. No Edith to wait on him hand and foot. No Colyer to drive him to school. Number fifty-two certainly wouldn't be good enough for him, would it, children?"

"Clara, the boy's not like that at all. You'd like to help at home, wouldn't you, Quintus?"

Quentin was gripping the back of Gladys's chair so that his knuckles gleamed white in the sunshine. It was difficult to hear what he said.

"There you are," his grandmother told them.

"A very eager answer!" his mother commented. "In any case it doesn't matter what his lordship wants, there's no room for him unless his father and I are to give up our dressing-room. I suppose even a beggarly author's wife can have somewhere to dress herself, though she's no maid to help her."

Mrs. Matthews had raised her voice, but she found that she had to shout louder, for the children had turned away from Quentin's embarrassment and were singing, "I've got a little cat and I'm very fond of that, but I'd rather have a bow-wow-wow-wow."

"Stop that noise at once! It's like a pack of street Arabs. I suppose you'd rather not hear how your father and I have to pinch and scrape."

"We thought you would rather we didn't hear," Rupert said.

"We didn't want to interfere with what was not our business," Gladys said.

"We thought it was private to you and grandmother," Sukey said.

"We thought it was too public for Quentin," Margaret said.

"We've heard it all before, anyway," Marcus ended.

His mother walked over to where he was sitting on Stoker's lap and smacked his face. Then she turned on Stoker. "I wish you wouldn't make such a baby of him, Stoker. A boy of eight years old sitting on his nurse's lap. We bring you out for a nice outing, Stoker: I think in return you could keep some control over the children. If Stoker's going to encourage you to behave like a baby, Marcus, she'll have to go. And you won't like that. Get down from there at once."

She pulled her son's arm. Immediately he began to scream loudly so that such other visitors to the tearoom as had not yet noticed the family party turned towards their table.

"Never mind, Marcus, never mind," his grandmother said. "Try not to cry like that, dear, you're making such an exhibition of yourself."

"Which is exactly what he wants."

"I don't think he does, Mum. He's tired, aren't you, Markie?"

"I think I know about my own child best, Stoker. And please don't call him by that vulgar name."

Mr. Matthews came over and lifted Marcus in his arms. "You'd like to come with me, wouldn't you, old sonnykins? Turbot and lobster sauce and a nice meringue, how about that? And perhaps Mr. Paul will have some *petits fours* for a stout little fellow."

Marcus looked very grave. "Thank you. Shall we go in a hansom cab?"

"In a chariot, if you wish."

"I wash my hands entirely. You see what happens, Granny. My slightest attempt at discipline is undermined."

"Well, I don't know, I'm sure. If Quintus will just find the North Entrance for me."

"Quentin will go home with you, of course. I've never heard such nonsense. Unless he's to sleep on the nursery floor."

"It might be, you know, that the man's point of view should be heard as well as the clatter of women's tongues. You and Mother seem to think you own the boy. It may not have occurred to you that he's reached the age to appreciate a father's companionship. Well, Quintus, how would you like to live with your dad again?"

Quentin stared at each of them in turn. There were tears of distress in old Mrs. Matthews' eyes. He took her arm. "I think I should go with Granny, sir." But it was still difficult to hear him. Young Mrs. Matthews rippled laughter.

"Oh, Bill, someone hasn't chosen you. You're losing your charms, my dear."

Old Mrs. Matthews said, "I'm sure the boy doesn't mean . . ." But her son turned his back on her.

"It's just as well," he said, in the direction of his wife; "so long as we depend on damned driblets and drablets of charity, someone in the family should keep on the right side of the old lady."

When his mother and Quentin had left, he took his Hunter watch out of his ticket pocket. "Well, I've got an appointment with a man about a dog. I shall dine at the club."

Laughing, his wife said, "I hope the devilled bones choke you, Billy."

And laughing, he replied, "I'm sure you do, my dear. But they won't. After Stoker, Mr. Paul is the best chef in London."

She turned her attention to Rupert. "I wonder if my handsome boy will grow up careless of himself and everybody else, too lazy even to eat his breakfast egg without spilling it down his waistcoat."

But Mr. Matthews did not glance down. Mrs. Matthews put her arm round Rupert's waist. "Of course he won't; he'll be famous, won't he? Entertaining his poor old mother on his flagship."

Mr. Matthews let his hand rest for a moment on Gladys's shoulder. "So she's going to marry a cowboy and leave her father behind." He smiled at her. "Good old Podge."

As he moved off, Stoker called, "But Master Marcus, sir . . ."

Gladys spoke out. "What about Marcus, Father? You promised to take him to dinner."

"And so I will. But some other day, old chap. When we're all more in the mood. And I'll take you, Podge, too." He pulled his daughter's pigtail. "When you lose a little of that weight. A pretty girl is the crown of a good meal." He took a half sovereign from his pocket; then, after reflection, he replaced it with a five-shilling piece. This he gave to Stoker. "Give them all a treat, Stoker, before you leave the exhibition, and see that the littlest fellow has what he wants."

The Countess said, "There, Marcus. Perhaps you'll know in future that all isn't gold that glitters. Now, I'm tired. Rupert, you shall see me home. It's time you learned to be an escort, darling boy. Stoker will take the rest of you on the District Line. You'll like that. And in any case you ought to know that your father isn't made of money, whatever he wants you to think."

Just before South Kensington station Marcus asked Stoker, "Why did they both laugh when Mother said she hoped the bone would choke him?"

"Ah, there's questions."

"Mother laughs to make herself more frightening, like the ogress," Gladys told them.

"She succeeds," Margaret said. "And he laughs to make her more angry."

"He succeeds too."

"Were *your* parents awful, Stoker?" Marcus asked.

"You mustn't talk about them like that to Stoker," Sukey explained. "Must he, Stoker?" But she added, "Most ordinary people don't make people stare at them in tearooms and all those awful things, do they?"

"What were your parents like, Stoker?" Gladys asked politely, for the train had stopped at Sloane Square and they could be heard by other passengers.

"I never knew er. And we never seed much of im. Not when we was little. E was at sea. E paid this woman sometimes. And when e dident, we knew it all right. Then years later when Em was married and I was working along with that Monser Jools at Queen Anne's Mansions—that's the one that learned me my fancy dishes—e comes back from sea. 'I'm finished with it,' e says, 'I can't keep me victuals down.' And e couldn't neither. Well, e goes to live with Em. Barnum and Bailey's it was. E ad a bloomin parrot and a concertina and there was this little Chinee that come regular to play with him a sort of chequers they played. I ad me own room in those days. Dident live in. Tothill Street it was. You could spit on the Abbey. One afternoon I come back tired out after cooking lunches and there e was. 'I've come to you, girl,' e says. 'Em won't let me ave me squeeze box.' Well I gets im a room, but I told im the bird ad got to go, and the concertina, which e called is squeeze box. Well there was a fuss about that all right. 'I'd as well be at Em's,' e said. 'I think you would,' I told im. And off e goes. But then one day ees back again. 'She's sold Polly,' e tells me. Well, I let im stay a week or two. Paid is rent, but I don't know what it was. Em and I was talking about it only last time I see er. 'Things get remembered,' she told me, 'it's only natural.' Anyway, after a bit, I told im I can't ave that Lee Fu comin ere—it gives me a bad name. Well, there it was," she ended, for they had arrived at Victoria.

Walking from the station to the house, Gladys asked what had happened to old Mr. Stoker.

"Seamans' rest," was the answer.

"It wasn't very kind," Gladys said.

"Didn't people blame you?" Sukey asked.

"Kind! Blame! We was too poor for notions!"

They were all silent, then Marcus said, "I expect that's why *they're* so awful. Being so poor."

His sisters in chorus said, "*Ssh!*"

And Stoker said, "Poor! You're the gentry."

"*She* looks like a gipsy," he announced in contradiction.

But when they went to say good night to their mother in the drawing-room, she didn't look at all like a gipsy. She lay on the sofa in her feather-trimmed *mousseline de soie* dressing-gown with eau-de-cologne pads on her temples. Only one small rose-shaded brass lamp was alight in the dim room.

"No good nights, I'm completely shattered. Remember their prayers, Gladys. I'll have a tray in my dressing-room, Stoker dear, after you've got them to bed. And you can brush my hair. Something light—an egg or two beaten in milk and sherry. And bring two sherry glasses. You can make me laugh and then perhaps, by some miracle, I'll sleep."

When Stoker had given them their bread and milk in the nursery, they told Rupert about her treatment of her father.

"She's Regan. That's what she is."

But they didn't understand, so he had to recount to them the story of *King Lear*. Then they all took it up. "Regan," they cried, "Regan," except Marcus who cried, "Dear Regan."

Stoker put her head round the door. "Now then, off to bed, or you'll have yer ma up ere. And you won't like that."

Later Rupert woke to hear Stoker singing one of her cockney songs and his mother laughing. Later still he woke again to see his mother bending over Marcus's bunk.

"You dirty little beast." She pulled him out of the bed and took off his pyjama trousers.

Rupert could feel how dazed his brother must be. She had bent him over the side of his bunk and was smacking his bottom with a hairbrush.

"Little wet-a-bed," she whispered, "dirty little wet-a-bed." And then, "Gipsy, is it? Very well, beware the gipsy." She pushed him back into the bunk. "It'll do you good to sleep in it. Teach you a lesson." Rupert pretended to be asleep when she came over and kissed him on the forehead.

Later still they all heard their father returning. Marcus was still sobbing, so Rupert tried to soothe him.

" '*He*'ll have to sleep in the dressing-room,' she told me, coming home in the taxi. ' "Cool off, Countess!" We'll see who's to cool off. I shall make him sleep in the dressing-room,' she said. It's for always." Then finding suddenly the softest, richest tones of his father, "I don't ask very much of life, children. A book, my pipe, my desk, a comfortable bed, and, is it too much to ask? a little quiet from my loving family." Delighted with his surprising power of imitation, he started to repeat the phrase, when from the corner of the room came his mother's voice, sharp and petulant, and raised to a high peak like the voice of a love-bird. "I hope you'll never know, Marcus," she said, "what it's like to be in love with life and to be cheated of it."

"That's what she says," Marcus explained. "What does she mean?"

"Oh, some rot or other. You do it jolly like."

"So do you."

"Let's try again."

They repeated the same phrases, then they tried out some others. At last they sounded so like that it was creepy, and to break the eerie atmosphere they burst into giggles. Down below, a full row was in progress so that they had no need to hush their delight at their new-found game. Giggling and imitating, it was some time before they fell asleep.

BOOK TWO

1919

"So," said Quentin, "we're all agreed." Expecting the response that should surely have come in rapid fire, he covered the silence for himself, as he had always done when waiting for volunteers, by prolonged play with pipe and pouch and matches.

Sukey looked in turn at the others, mute in their private concerns —Gladys re-threading her ambers; Margaret soaking her feet luxuriously in the hip bath; Rupert lolling on cushions, long legs loosely dangling, hand aimlessly waving the limp Pierrot doll beside him. She put down the monthly tradesmens' books, her toil for the family, very deliberately.

"Yes, thank you, Quentin," she said, "we're all very grateful to you. Without you things would have dragged on interminably. Coming from outside you've seen the whole thing so clearly."

Marcus's small puckered white face, his huge dark lemur's eyes, appeared above the sofa.

"*I've* seen it clearly for at least two years, ever since my voice began to break."

"It hasn't," said Gladys.

"It hasn't finished," said Margaret. "We should be exact even about small boys."

"*You* ought to be especially grateful to Quentin, Marcus," Sukey told him.

"He ought to be in bed." Rupert with his plectrum plucked three notes on the Hawaiian guitar on his lap.

"I left my love in Avalon," Gladys sang.

"That was not remotely the tune I sounded."

"I think if it hasn't broken," Marcus said, "it's because Gladys did more than her family share of voice breaking."

"Praise heaven for it," Rupert cried. "Do Dame Clara Butt singing 'Land of Hope and Glory' before we all go to bed, Gladys."

"Oh, yes, Gladys, do!" said Margaret. "It'll send us away with high hopes."

"Dame Clara Butt's real name is Mrs. Kennerley Rumford. There's glory for you," Marcus said.

"Kids of that age," Rupert remarked, "think everything funny."

"He's encouraged at school as a wit and aesthete," Margaret explained.

"And shall be for three more years if all your plans for me work out. Remember that. If I am to stay at school, and of course Quentin's right—I ought to want to—then you'll all have to put up with my being precocious."

"Precocious to the grown-ups," said Rupert, "a wit in the playground. But to us a pimply little squirt."

Since the others paid no heed to Quentin's busy pipe-sucking, Sukey said, "Please don't think we're really against Marcus, Quentin. It's just that he mustn't be encouraged."

Quentin stopped sucking. "The sharpness seems general."

"Oh, dear, does it? I suppose it does. It's just a rather silly way we've got into. Under it all there's a lot of loyalty. We've had to stand together so often, you see, in the last years when you've been away."

Marcus hid behind the sofa. Rupert strummed. But Margaret took her feet from the mustard bath's luxury and spoke out.

"If *you* had been more of a little mother to us, Gladys, we shouldn't have to put up with Sukey talking like that in public. It's your fault. You're the eldest. *You* should be our substitute for the Countess's failure."

"As a matter of fact," Marcus spoke from behind the sofa's safety, "Sukey was right. We've kept up a front and we really are united. If anything's wrong this evening it's because we're shy of you, Quentin. You've been away so long."

"Keeping up another, more important front," Rupert murmured.

"Talk about school-kids' bad taste!" Gladys said.

Sukey broke in. "The only thing I'm worried about is this relying on the old women. They just aren't to be trusted."

"We're not going to *rely* on them. We're simply going to see that they know what's what."

"Quentin means we're going to *use* them," Margaret explained. "Actually we had all understood that except Sukey. You mustn't expect her to understand things quickly, Quentin."

"It has been a help, Quentin," Gladys said, "knowing that we don't seem to you to judge *them* too harshly."

"Oh, no. The war is on."

"Against the white slug," said Rupert.

"And the black bitch," whispered Marcus.

"Names don't help, do they, Quentin?" Sukey asked. And repeated her question, for, as they all often found so disconcerting, he seemed to have fallen away from them into a black chasm of his own thoughts. But now he answered, in the brighter tone he used when he returned to their world suddenly.

"Battle-cries are a bit out of date in modern trench warfare conditions, but we might allow them as a special ration for young hotheads."

Margaret said, "As a returned soldier on demob leave bitterly pledged to end all wars, Quentin, you offer us a straight diet of jolly military metaphors."

"I'm disgusting."

"Oh, no, no. I didn't mean quite that."

"Your tongue, Mag," Sukey said reproachfully.

"I was only thinking of Rupert."

"Thank you, Maggie." Rupert put his hand on his sister's bare leg where, shapely, it protruded below her kimono. "As a matter of fact, I do rather resent being put in with the schoolboys, Quentin. After all, I have been dingily winning bread for the house in my awful clerk's job. Though I'm grateful to you for releasing me under The Plan."

"I'm sorry," Quentin said. "I salute you as an independent artist of future fame."

"Salute!" Marcus said. "Margaret's caution has not been very effective."

Gladys picked up an empty rubber hot-water bottle and threw it at Marcus's head.

"I think," Marcus said, "that by extending our sharpness to Quentin we show him that we're more at ease with him."

"Oh, the ghastly child! But we are, old boy, we really are." Sukey put her hand on her eldest brother's stooped shoulders.

Margaret looked at Rupert and he unfolded himself from the cushions to tower above them in his six feet one. Elocution-wise he cupped his ear, elocution-wise he put his finger to his lips.

"Hist! I hear creaks. 'Tis now the very witching hour of night."

"And witches may well be abroad at any moment." Margaret used her cracked, cockney, pantomime dame's voice.

Marcus peered round the sofa. "Children! Children! Dismal faces! I don't want dismal faces. I've been dancing all the evening and I want to go on and on."

"Bandmaster, give the lady a tune," cried Rupert.

Marcus rose and continued, "I'm in love with life, children. And so must you be. Come on now. Stop looking sleepy, damn you! Let's raid Regan's larder."

"Cups of coffee and *La Bohème* and talk, talk, talk," Margaret said dryly.

"Till any old hour," ended Gladys in her gruff voice.

"I thought we weren't to play The Game tonight," Sukey said. "Quentin said . . ."

But Rupert was beaming at them now. He had made himself small and cosy-looking. His voice was infinitely mellow. "Pardon an old white slug for creeping out from under his stone. Back from his club. An old white slug but with a young slug's heart. But midnight, you know, midnight."

And maunderingly, mumblingly, they repeated the words, first Margaret, then Marcus, then Gladys—"Midnight," "Midnight," "Midnight." As the solemn, empty voices rolled around the room, they all began to laugh, even Sukey, who, at last, in a thick suety voice that she knew would reduce them to final delirious giggles, said, "Midnight." Then she glanced nervously at Quentin, but he too was laughing helplessly.

Gladys was the first to pull herself together. "I thought it was to be plans, not games."

"Come," Rupert cried, "be bloody, bold, and resolute. And let me tell you all that nothing may quicker break our resolution and our unity than a sudden little young-hearted, brave-hearted, paternal pathos at this time of night."

"Unless," said Margaret, "it be a young-hearted mother's sudden brave gaiety. Scolding . . ."

"Flirting," said Rupert.

"Confiding," said Gladys.

"Cajoling," said Susan. "Is that a word, Mag?"

But to their surprise Quentin ended it for them in imitation of Gladys's deep voice, "Till any old hour!" And then in his own voice, "No, we can't run that risk. Off to bed, everyone."

Marcus stood up in his striped pyjamas and old plaid dressing-gown. "Neither of them would have the slightest effect on my resolution."

Gladys lifted him up, all five feet five, and pressed him to her plump bosom. "Oh, yes, they would. In the small hours."

"When *their* energy is highest," Margaret said in a dark, ominous voice.

"And ours is lowest," Sukey remarked as a matter of fact.

"For the small hours are *their* time," ended Rupert in the falsetto genteel tones of a pantomime fairy queen.

Gladys, puffing, set the struggling Marcus down on the floor.

Quentin gave the boy a light tap on his bottom. "Off to bed with you!"

The others all looked at their eldest brother. He seemed to be one of them again. And all, except Rupert, who was to sleep there in the fug and debris, filed out of the nursery.

At half past midnight, negotiating with uncertainty both the door and the step of the taxi, conscious with some lust but a good deal more nervousness of a peroxide-haired tart hovering a door or two away, he overtipped the taxi driver. "Dear old London," he said. "You'd never know she'd taken such a plastering." The driver—though clearly the chap was a cockney—drove off without reply. Counting-mounting the front steps and relievedly-wistfully ignoring the tart, he added, for his own benefit, "London, thou art of cities a per se." The lock he found ill fitted to the key, but, by great care and concentration, he joined the two. He let himself into the house, remembering the argument at the Club, moving, as man's talk will, from wines and France to women and poetry—"I have been faithful to thee"—and, at last, to God, does He exist? and if so, which of all the inspired chaps were right about him? Now as he came through the hall to the stairs, he saw clearly how he should have ended the evening's argument (great horsehair chairs and balloon glasses of Martell). "Give me a lever," he said, lifting his handsome head determinedly, "and I will raise the world." But nobody gave—no one had ever given him that lever; hence he cherished a sense of pathos.

Gladys, by instinct, turning gingerly in her too-narrow bed, knew at once, with a moment's intense panic, the step on the stairs. Then relaxing her solid limbs, she let herself out of the nightmare memory by means of a now familiar comic vision. Like a Punch drawing she saw it; herself, enormous in boxing kit, her gloved hand raised by the ref, he, and the little white slug, flat on the canvas, stars rising from his forehead, and beneath, the words, "A knockout."

"What's wrong? Is my little girl too grown up for a good-night kiss?"

She had pushed him, and he had fallen, sprawling over the pile of trunks. He had begun to cry.

"God forgive me, I am drunk." Raising himself by one arm, he had smiled his old, bleary, daddy's smile. "Promise me something, Glad Eyes. Promise me never to let this put you off . . . well, the real thing. Don't punish me too much. Promise me that. In time to come there'll be heaps of decent chaps after you."

At least he'd never call her Glad Eyes again. And Daddy, dear, you foul little beast, there have been heaps of decent chaps, and I haven't been put off men, even when something as beastly as you "happened" to me. Anyway, men! Who wants "men"? I have a man so wonderful that even if you really knew what "decent" meant, it still wouldn't have anything to do with it. He doesn't have to be "decent," he's above your "decent" chaps. He has so much strength and power and he's not afraid to love. He's made his life for himself and so, unlike you, you lazy little fraud, he's not too scared to face his feelings. As, with increasing anger, the perspiration began to run down her neck and breasts, she felt Alfred's arm come round her shoulder, his hand patting her cheek. "My darling girl, you must never let things that are past have any hold over you. That's fatal in life, if you want to be one of the world's big people. And you can be, Gladys—sweet Gladys."

So that for you, Billy Pop, billygoat of fathers, bleating and ruttish, women don't all have to be your little grateful Glad Eyes, nor like HER turned tigress by your failure, a mock tigress to be mocked. If the world was just little Glad Eyes and HER you could sit tight in your cosy chair at your important-looking, useless desk and laugh at women, God bless them, dear ladies. But it isn't going to be like that now. We shall be bosses just like you (if you ever had been one, that is), not bossy, but doing the job, running the show and running it well. Deserving a man like Alfred who's a natural boss himself. Equal partners—no claims made. If it seemed far off, well, there was Alfred's help, and Alfred's arms. Relaxing, cradled in them, Gladys, soft Gladys, sank softly back to sleep. And the hard bed she lay on didn't matter, she knew, one damn.

One o'clock. Turning the corner, away from the late tram's clatter, an Aussie and a Canadian, desperately homesick, were sick into the gutter. Out of the shadow came the peroxide tart Trixie and bubsy dark French Fifi, and all four together, arms linked, made off down the street, singing, "Jazzing around, painting the town . . . after they've seen Paree!"—pausing only for the Aussie to be sick once more, into the area of No. 52.

Quentin woke crying. All music, all singing, all out-of-tune singing, all drunken out-of-tune singing still brought proportionately these shameful tears dribbling slowly down his cheeks, as the fat slow tears had plopped noisily, disgustingly upon the hospital sheets in the weak, muzzy-headed days after his second go of dysentery. And every tune still bawled at him as then, "There's a long, long night of waiting, until my dreams all come true." But his shame for this weakness was at least so strong that, in fighting it, he only glimpsed the fearful memories that lay behind the tunes. Never again, never again should men be crippled and blinded by talk and boasts and lies, never again made weak as women to weep at sugary songs. He tried to stretch, but in Rupert's bed his long legs had no room to uncoil; nor indeed, surely, nowadays could Rupert's. And Marcus in the corner in some sort of home-made cot! Well, all *that* sort of crippling also must go. Whoever or whatever it meant fighting. To hell with England, Home, and Beauty if they got in the way. To this he, like others, would lend all his tested strength and discipline and trained intelligence. And, do not forget, you Parents, Brass Hats, and Hard-faced Men, that we don't believe a bloody word you say. Spitting out the words half aloud, he savoured the hardness of them, and,

dried and thinned almost to leather and bone, he fell into firm sleep
on the hard mattress in the narrow bed.

Half past one, tense, bitter, yet weeping, she had refused his escort, and now unaccustomedly but quite firmly she opened for herself the door of a taxi with her long, elegant, white-gloved hand. The
breeze caught her gold-embroidered black evening cape for a moment. It billowed outwards and she shivered. Rapidly she paid the
fare, and refusing a demand for more, cut short the unequal wrangle
by taking out of her silver-gilt evening bag her silver police whistle.
She had hardly put it to her lips before the taxi had gone. Even so
small a triumph made her for a moment forget her terrible mixed
grief and rage. She walked up the front steps quite gaily. Only the
usual temptation to slam the front door made her remember how
angry, how desperate, she was. Yet to enjoy a banged door brought
an intolerable risk of facing in her terrible mood anyone, anyone at
all who might wake, but worst of possibilities—Billy, woken from
sleep in the bed in his dressing-room. She took off her silver dancing
shoes and carried them in one hand as she mounted the stairs.

But however gently you come, my darling, however softly you
tread, my love, I shall hear your bitch's steps. Rupert counted them
as she climbed the two flights to her bedroom, heard the door click
to, and bitter-sweet smiled to think how, undressing, she would caress her own body where her lover's hands had stroked. Good luck
to her, since the white slug had never given her what she needed.
And damn her too for cheapening the name of my mother. Sensing
the shape of his own limbs in the bed—hard calves and thighs, long
legs, small hips, hard flat belly and wide shoulders, and now a proud
erection—he thought how at last he was grown her equal in
beauty, and soon (for the last shall be first) would outstrip her,
aged, hagged, and dried. Meanwhile they were almost a perfect
match.

" 'Lord, Sir, to think my great lubberly son should grow into
such a one as you, as pleasing and wanton a young fellow as a gentlewoman (somewhat past the spring-time) could wish to keep her out
of the draughts on a cold December night. . . .' But the triumph of
the evening was Mr. Rupert Matthews' playing of the young bully
lover; it was a rare theatrical experience to watch the man grow
from the boy as the evening progressed, even his frame seemed to fill

out, and his step to announce an ever firmer resolution. Miss Madge Titheradge brought her usual experienced playing to the part of the older, desperate mistress, but it was Mr. Matthews' evening. There was an autumn pathos in Miss Doris Keane's ageing actress, warming herself sensually in the last rays of love's sunshine, but Mr. Matthews, as the young musician, anxious to free himself from a hopeless passion, determined not to act caddishly towards the woman whose infatuation is strangling him, gave us the more terrible pathos of spring in his portrayal of youth's first realization that life will not always allow us to be noble."

CHARMIAN: It was that moment in the dressing-room when you suddenly looked at me and saw that I was almost an old woman, that was the moment that you fell out of love with me, wasn't it, Derek? Answer me, wasn't it?

DEREK: Don't torture yourself, Charmian.

CHARMIAN: Answer me. How dare you treat me like a child? You're insolent.

DEREK: I shall always love you, Charmian. Always. I have told you so a hundred times.

CHARMIAN: Yes, as you do your mother.

DEREK: God forgive me, no. Not like that. My mother left me with my heart frozen. And you with your love and your experience have warmed it into life again. That I shall always remember. . . .

"And we in the theatre that night will always remember Mr. Rupert Matthews . . ." Mr. Rupert Matthews . . . Mr. Rupert Matthews, a handsome, passionate Romeo, stepped on to the stage and on to a banana skin and fell on his arse, the silly sod! Pleased by his own sudden self-mockery, Rupert fell into a sweet sleep, cocooned in his blankets on the nursery floor.

Half past two. And down the road she comes. With a too ral, too ral, aye, does your ma know you're out? Swing, swing, how the bleeding pavements swing. Steady, me little cock sparrer. Hold on to the railing. Whoops, she goes! All to feed the fishes. Christ, what's that? There he comes, my own little Bobby, swinging his truncheon, helmet and all. Smash his helmet over his bloody nose, crying, "Wotcher, cock?" Only she didn't; holding herself very refined and speaking all la-di-da, "Goodnaite, constable," she said. And all the answer clatter, clank echoing down the empty street. Blasted swine couldn't have the manners to reply, eh? Oh, absolutelah, don't cher know? Archibald? Certainly not. With his hand in his pocket too on duty. Ma, look at Charlie, whoops, ees at it again. Not that she'd say no, herself. What about it, cock, lend us the end of your finger? But they wouldn't lend you a sausage, not one of them, the bleeders. Not if your name *was* Henrietta Stoker, mother unknown, probably titled, six years with the Honourable Mrs. Pitditch-Perkins, French cooking trained with Monser Jools what had been at the Savoy. Oh, Lord, up she comes! Oh, Jesus help me, Jesus help me, Let me to thy bosom fly, While the gathering waters roll . . . yes, and five years going to the Stockwell High Road Sunday School. Treated like dirt by the lot of them. Regan do this, Regan do that. Lend us a quid, Regan. Regan, darling, have you got a pound handy? My name's Henrietta, I'll thank you. Forty-six. Forty-eight. Tradesmen owed everywhere, the guvnor boozed every night, and SHE can't keep her legs shut. Oh, the Yanks are coming, the Yanks are coming. Well, they came every night up *that* street. Fifty-two. Home in port. Who says there's not a God to answer prayers? Oh, who done that? One of them filthy tarts, most like. On the steps of our home too. Filthy, trollopy lot. If that constable done his job instead of . . . Oh, if Madam were to see.

This is the home of Mr. and Mrs. William Matthews. And the young ladies. Their eldest a major and wounded but not decorated. And Master Rupert, handsome as Lewis Waller, handsomer. And Master Marcus that goes to Westminster School regular, or nearly. And they call me their old Regan, bless their hearts. A regular old cockney I am and one of the family. Make them laugh a caution sometimes. Oh, Ria she's a toff, darn't she look immensikoff, and they all shouted, waatch Ria!

The singing disgusted Sukey before she was fully awake enough to distinguish what it was. Well, living in this sordid little street they had no need to worry about neighbours. It was to be hoped that all the family would be wakened by it, by their beloved cockney character, whose filthy hands and drunken breath they appreciated so much all over their food. At least from what she learned at the cookery school—although with fees unpaid she was little more than a scullion to Miss Lampson—she could occasionally prepare a clean,

healthy meal at home when that drunken old creature had taken
herself off for the evening. French cooking! Horrible, rich, greasy
stuff, and unpatriotic, too, with butter from heaven knew where and
hoarded sugar. Really, sometimes she'd thought of telling the police
about the dirty old creature, if it hadn't been that the family would
be involved. But, of course, the family wouldn't be involved—not
them, at any rate. They'd lie black that they knew nothing of it and
let the dirty old wretch go to prison for them, for their greed.

And suddenly she found herself sobbing uncontrollably. She
buried her face in the pillow so as not to wake Margaret. Margaret
who understood people and would put Regan into a book as a comic
cockney charwoman, but who did not wake up when the poor,
dreadful old thing came lost and stumbling down the area steps, singing some ghastly tune once recognizable no doubt when, as a girl, all
ostrich feathers and boa, she'd sung it up in the gallery, but now the
tuneless dirge of a drunken old crone. Sukey's limbs began to tremble and totter as she felt Regan's must do, lost and stumbling, on the
scrap-heap. The physical sense of being Regan disgusted her. It was
this that she couldn't stand any longer in this sordid home, this terrible pity to no purpose, pity for people who were on the scrap-
heap, in the dust-bins, the drunken, dirty old Regan, and HIM rambling and maudlin in the evenings to forget failure, and HER in her
rage for the loss of her body's youth.

She wanted to give love and pity where it could be used, where it
could make things grow. To a real family where you never felt
alone. To a husband with his life before him, to children asking to be
shaped, to plants, to animals, small animals. She thought of the kittens that she had watched sleeping under the stairs before she came
to bed, her kittens, the kittens she had rescued, and from the memory of their curled-up innocence, she found herself stepping out
through the French windows and across the lawn, followed by small
things of all kinds and down into the kitchen garden to cut the let-
tuces for tea, and then, putting on gum boots and jackets and scarves
in the lobby, to set off in the frosty moonlight to aid the cowman at
calving time. Reverently competent with the new-born calves, practical with the sensible cowman, she turned to receive the faithful
parlour-maid's message: "The master says, Madam, will you be
long?" Oh, he who can't be left alone! Turning, she went back in

smiling woman's conspiracy with Ada (yes, that would be her name) to the house. Smiling, she snuggled over on to her side and slept, the little ones of all kinds following.

Four o'clock, the Aussie at No. 51 woke from a drunken sleep to find French Fifi going through his pockets. Leaning across the bed he hit her once very hard with the flat of his hand across her face. Her scream rang out across the street.

Marcus woke suddenly, soldered tight with terror, powerless to move or utter. Yet surely it was his own scream that had woken him. For some seconds the gipsy's dark, bony laughter still menaced him, and around her the soft grey mist sweetly offered him escape to treacherous safety. Then the threat of her raised arm faded before he could tell what horrid club she held above him. But the fading nightmare did not at once release him; he could not so soon turn his head to assure himself of his bunk's familiar safety. At last the wheezy breathing of his stranger brother lying across the room in Rupert's bed relaxed his muscles.

He followed the beams of moonlight to where they bathed Granny M.'s old screen of varnished scrap-work in a shiny pool. In the sudden light he could distinguish nothing, but knew the two splashes of red for the robin in the top left-hand corner and the bunch of cherries in the bottom right. How the robin had changed for him over the years! At first just a robin who visited a wren. Then, in turn, a robber robin (straight from Grimm), a robin rag-and-bone boy (slum chum he sometimes dreamed of) a Regency roué robin (straight from the *Scarlet Pimpernel*), and now again—parody of a Victorian screen Robin—the robin who visited crippled little Jenny Wren, who would never grow quite strong enough to quit the nest.

From these scraps of colour in the colour scraps he followed the cold light back again to the window, where, reflected on the ceiling, it revealed, in all their now-fading outlines, the Double-hooded Crow and the Woman with the Club-foot—visitors that had appeared when the cistern above had burst a week before his sixth birthday.

The chain of stories these two shapes unfolded was longer and far more intricate than the sagas of the screen, for here he commanded all, source and ballad too, so that the crow in certain lights could become the Bearded Emperor and the woman's club-foot turn into *a* mermaid's tail; but as so often now, he put childish tales aside and dwelt only upon the forms themselves, making wilder and wilder arabesques, ever more involuted spirals, draping the room in sables and furs and crimson velvets, adorning it with domes and minarets, until at last it was Scheherazade's room and not his own at all, except that there in the centre of the gorgeous East he sat, cross-legged, round-eyed (a page, a mommet, Scheherazade herself, slave-master-mistress), crowned absurdly, fantastically, wonderfully with a vast jewelled tiara almost his own height again; and there, like Venice, he held all this splendour, this gaiety, this nonsense in fee. Until he could build his own world, the familiar ugliness of 52 must be his plasticine. Stretching his small, thin legs and arms, feeling his own wiriness against the hard wire mattress of the small bunk bed, he turned on his side to meet whatever the nightmare world had ready for him.

Six o'clock. Billy Pop tried every position of cosy warmth he knew to counteract the increasing pressure of his over-full bladder, but at last he was forced to get up and make use of the chamber-pot. He did so, as always, kneeling beside his bed; this and saying the Lord's Prayer at night in the same kneeling position were rituals he had maintained from his childhood. He had first been made conscious of their absurdity by the Countess's mockery in their early married days when they still shared the double room.

On this coldish morning, in the solitude of the little dressing-room where he now slept, he thought of it again, because in returning from the club last night he had managed to bruise his left knee. It would have been more comfortable to pee standing up, but he somehow felt unable to do so, for he connected the kneeling position in his mind, as he did the Lord's Prayer and bowing whenever you saw a piebald horse, with good luck. And God knew he was a man who could ill afford to dispense with any luck that might be going. Not but that good luck might well be running his way again, for last night at the club Murphy of Locke, Harrap had spoken to him for the first time since that unpleasant business in the war over the contract—"When are you giving the world another, Matthews?" he had asked. Noncommittal, of course; these people were fundamentally business-men. Murphy had added that historical romances were two a penny these days, but good historical novels were as precious as rubies. He had said, of course, that he was busy with his memoirs.

But the conversation was pleasant to dwell on. After all, we can all
do with a fillip now and again; the confirmation of talent, the belief
that we have the goods to deliver. We bring nothing into the world,
and it is certain that we can carry nothing out; maybe, but in between, man, being the sort of animal he is, does need a little coddling
now and again.

Relieved by urination, warmed with the thought of recognition,
he set down the chamber-pot and decided that his new luck must be
followed up. He never felt too well in the mornings these days;
indeed a persistent sort of ill health—nothing you could put your
finger on—had a lot to do with his small output in recent years.
Headaches and a little giddiness were not a help to morning concentration; all the same he'd feel better out of this fusty little apology
for a bedroom. Vaguely it seemed to him, too, that if he got down
to work early on this morning, Sunday morning, luck might reward
him tomorrow in the shape of a cheque for unexpected royalties, or,
after all, as he suddenly remembered, the old lady was coming to
lunch today . . . Musing, he knocked his button-hook off the dressing-table.

Her voice sounded from the bedroom, "Billy, Billy." He had not
heard her call so softly to him, he thought, for years. Something so
unexpected was, on top of the throbbing pain in his temples and the
sudden big-wheel revolutions of the room as he stopped to pull on
his socks, more than he could cope with if he were to keep himself
fresh for a morning stint. He hummed a few bars of that pretty
thing from *Les Cloches de Corneville* to cover his inattention. But,
of course, her voice came more sharply, "Billy, stop making that
horrid noise and come here." Holding his brown brogues in his
hand, he opened the communicating door. "I hoped you wouldn't
wake, Countess. I was creeping about in my stockinged feet."

"Of course I was woken up. You wee-wee like Niagara Falls."

He looked wistful. "I'm glad I can still perform some sort of wonder in your eyes, my dear."

"Oh, don't be so coarse, Billy." She lay back on the pillows with
her eyes closed. Then she patted the bed. "Come and sit down here."
He sat very gingerly at the end. "Have you minded it all very much,
Billy?" And when he didn't answer, she opened her eyes and looked
at him. "I don't believe I've hurt you at all. What a ghastly little
piece of nothing you've turned into."

He picked up the brogues and moved back to the door. She clenched the sheet tightly in both her hands. He thought she was going to scream. He said, "My dear girl, that won't do any good."

"He's going back," she shouted at him. "He's going back. Next week. I hate every bone in his body." He looked at her primly.

"I suppose so. But you'll get over it." He became aware suddenly both that he was smiling broadly and that his sudden, involuntary sincerity had goaded her into fury. He added, "The children will miss him." He sought for other benevolent phrases to restore their usual relationship. "We shall all miss his wonderful Yankee directness."

She seized the ivory box of cigarettes from the night table and flung it at his head. He ducked, and it crashed against the wall, showering the floor with black, gold-tipped Turks.

"Oh, Lord!" He mocked her antics, but all the same he turned tail and fled. Her screams followed him, "Take your filthy smirk out of here. You gutless swine!"

A crash below her bed woke Margaret suddenly. And then came the Countess's screams to make her at once, as always, tense with renewed childhood terror. Slowly, practisedly, she relaxed by means of the familiar stringing together of words. "If a certain cacophonous crying is the hallmark of Greek tragedy, Sophie Carmichael qualified for Clytemnestra herself, a role which she would dearly have loved to play if only in order to shock the bridge-club gossips. Her adulteries, though suburban, could perhaps have passed for something more regal if only her husband, James, had been more worthy of Agamemnon's role. As it was, thought their daughter Elizabeth, rudely awakened by parental quarrelling, their noise might as well be mice as Mycenae." Margaret relaxed, but she was hardly content with the words. The long analogy was altogether too cumbrous, and the pretension of someone of her half-education scribbling about Agamemnon and Clytemnestra made her blush. Then through the words came a sudden intense vision of her mother's bare shoulder, and with it the sensation of rubbing her cheek against it, of being squeezed in her mother's arms, stroked by her mother's cool, long-fingered hands. It was when she had fallen down on the rocks at Cromer and cut her forehead (the scar was still there, but hidden under her fringe); her mother had responded at once, had whispered and kissed away her fright. Pity, if not love, nagged her. But she

would never be able to reach them, never. At least she could bring
them to life again in words that were more complete, more understanding, more just to her own comprehension of them than the flat
self-protective ironies of her Carmichael writing. But first she must
get away, far enough off to be fair and just and creative. In a room
perhaps in the Adelphi (a real writers' world, from what she could
tell) she would sit at her desk, and words, exact and living, would
flow from her pen like the river flowing past her window. Exactly,
definitely, she relaxed her long, immature body enough to fall into a
light sleep, not so fully that she would fail to awake in time for her
early morning duties.

At the sound of Regan's retching in the basement, Billy Pop almost cut off Teddy's long tail. Instead, he so jolted the scissors that
the blade pricked his left thumb. He searched for a wad of cotton
wool that he had put away in one of the drawers of his desk. He
could ill afford such a loss of precious time. Gingerly dabbing the
tiny drops of blood, he reflected on how often work, certainly over
the years his work, had been interrupted by trivia. Regan's regular
drunken Saturday night visits to her family in South London, for
instance. He'd written something about it during the war, "Our
Cockney Cook Goes Over the Water," but for some reason or other
he'd abandoned the essay unfinished. He thought to look for it now,
but to find things was always such a business and a half. Also, hunting for something, he might make a noise and wake the Countess
again. And then Regan banged the lavatory door. Oh, Lord! that
would put the cat among the pigeons.

But the Countess, half-dozing, was jolted into drowsy speculation,
not into anger. How did Regan get back to Victoria, tipsy, and with
those poor old swollen feet, stumbling along through silent early
morning streets, lurching over Westminster Bridge? Why didn't the
police charge her? What must it be like? She had been a bit squiffy
herself once or twice after parties with Milton and some of the other
American officers—suppers at the Waldorf or the Savoy. The next
morning the back of one's throat seemed stretched so dry that it
ached, one's eyeballs throbbed with each step one took. But every
week! Why *did* she do it? Stretching her legs down to the cool of
the untouched sheets, stroking her thighs, she supposed that it must
be, poor old cow, a consolation, an oblivion for years and years of
never having had a man's arms round her, never a man inside her.

Poor old Regan, poor old cow! To have been ugly always and now to be old. "This isn't important to you, Countess, don't let it get under your skin. You've got a lovely home and a fine bunch of kids. And well, if Pop's no great shakes . . . you're still a beautiful woman. And so what? Bed isn't everything."

She twisted the sheets in her hands as though they were his rotten neck. How dare he offer her, her own children, as compensation, vulgar little Yankee. And to tell her what was everything and what wasn't. I can tell you, Milton J. Ward, that muck like you wouldn't *be* everything to me if I hadn't made a mess of it all, of everything that really matters. And you're not, in any case; there'll be others. Yes, worse and worse muck. And the end of the road couldn't be far off. With her right hand she took the fingers of her left and twisted them until she cried out against the pain. Stop dramatizing, she told herself. Don't be soft. And then the memory of Billy's scared rabbit face as he bolted down his dressing-room hold came back to her and she shook the bed with laughing. If they didn't care they could at least be frightened.

And relaxing, she remembered that it was Sunday morning. Everyone at home and under orders. She had decreed that the children should take it in turns to bring Sunday breakfast to her so that Regan could sleep off her Saturday orgies. It was such a benefit for them, instead of wasting half the morning lazing in bed! She savoured the word "benefit." Smiling gently at her own hypocrisy, at the hypocrisy of all the world—we humans really were too absurd!—she stretched again luxuriously, and forgetting, fell into dozing thoughts of Milton's strong legs straddling her.

Before Margaret could knock on the door of her mother's bedroom, the Countess called to her, her babyish drawl a little sharpened in tone.

"Don't knock, Wendy. Bring my tea straight in—I can't stand the slightest noise this morning and your knock isn't exactly fairy-like, darling."

Propped against the white, lace-edged pillows between a mass of mauve *crêpe de Chine* night-gown and a mauve muslin boudoir cap, the Countess's thin face was all darkly smudged skin and Pharoah-sized black eyes. She'll tell my fortune, but it won't be a pleasant one.

"Dancing with all those little brats is giving you a permanent stoop. If you're like this at seventeen, you'll look like a battered lamp-post before you're twenty-one. Dear little Wendy."

With the bed table arranged and the tray set on it, Margaret felt free to skirmish.

"My name is not Wendy."

"Well, darling, *I* didn't give it to you. It was your sensible Granny M. who found you *that* name. But it is rather irresistible. Oh, Margaret, have some sense of fun. 'Wendy' applied to a great gawk like you! If you can't laugh, take Billy's breakfast down to him in his study. I'd only just got to sleep after all the noise you children made upstairs last night. Toing and froing! Did Regan put senna pods in your pudding? I've never heard such a noise."

Margaret made no answer, and suddenly her mother shouted at her.

"No one's to pull that chain at night. No one. Do you understand? No one!"

Margaret's attention was so intent upon her mother's expression that she showed no reaction. The Countess returned to her usual drawling ennui. "Oh, really, Margaret! If you can't laugh at *that*! 'The Forbidden Chain!' Why, the whole idea's too delicious. Sanitary inspectors descending upon us. 'Mother's Inhuman Order' head-lined in the West London *Gazette*. Heaven knows what absurdity! But perhaps with such constipated children as I have . . . Yes, you *are* constipated, mentally and physically, all of you. . . . Oh, go away, Margaret. I'm tired and I can't bear you so early in the morning. And tell all of them I require absolute silence. I mean it. Not a sound until eleven. You can call me then. And now give me one of my *cachets fièvres* for my head. Oh, and Wendy, you really must learn to consider others a little. I've told you again and again to use lavender water when you've got the curse on. Poor Sir James! Poor Peter Pan! Wendy indeed!"

As Margaret handed her the tablets, the Countess sank back on her pillows, mopping the tears from her eyes with a little lace-edged handkerchief, then she put one long elegant hand to her head to ease the pain that so much laughter had caused her. Her voice followed Margaret out of the room.

"Now, don't go being hurt. And, Margaret, silence means your father and Regan as well, please."

Making her way downstairs to her father's study, Margaret fixed accurately the little stream of frothy spittle that had run from the side of the Countess's mouth. Later she would make a phrase about it, connecting it perhaps with snakes and venom, and write the phrase down in her notebook. Yet with venomous spittle alone she would satisfy, she knew, only today's resentment, to give full shape to the Countess . . .

The smell of stale tobacco smoke halted Margaret for a second when she opened Billy Pop's study door. Through the blue-grey haze she could see him like some soft-toned impressionistic sketch by Whistler—a symphony in grey: grey, curly hair, neat grey moustache, grey tweeds, grey foulard bow tie, dove-grey cloth waistcoat, and dove-grey cloth spats. And, to bring the picture together, of course, two dancing, gay points of colour—the amber stem of his curved pipe, the rosy pink of his peach-soft cheeks. "Mr. Carmichael thought of himself as a symphony, his children knew him to be a nocturne." Phrase-happy, Margaret was sucked into his soft grey cloud-kingdom and let herself be kissed on the lips.

"I'll have two fried eggs and bacon, Mag. Marcus's and Sukey's— shall we call the two eggs? And your sister Gladys's butter ration if my own has been used. It's hard to believe that a child of mine can fail to distinguish butter from margarine, but so Gladys says, and she must pay for her Philistine boast. Golly, early work makes me hungry."

Margaret, determined to remove the twinkle from his eyes, looked fixedly at the mass of cut-out Bairnsfather Old Bills and *Daily Mail* Teddy Tails on his desk, but when he saw her expression he only twinkled the more.

"Don't be censorious, Mag. In any case I'm not as idle as you think. Memoir writing's an oblique art; this is my hobby, and the roots of art and play lie very close together. And then again trifles— the humour of an eye—like these stir the memory."

She could not help saying, "Oh! the memoirs!" He spoke through her exclamation and so did not seem to hear it.

"Besides, cuttings like these will be of great interest to my grandchildren if I'm vouchsafed any."

"Gladys's twenty-first birthday should be still fresh in your mind, Father."

"Oh, yes, yes, I know. Oodles of time yet. Oodles of time. Especially for you. Especially for my Mag."

He took her hand. She did not withdraw it, but she said, "At seventeen I suppose so. But not more than for Sukey, I imagine, since we're twins."

"You shouldn't wear brown, Maggie, with your dark skin. Besides, brown's old-maidish. Take a tip from the Countess. Wear gorgeous reds, old golds. Nothing drab or dull."

"Old gold means that it *is* dull. *Mother*, by the way, wants complete silence this morning. We all disturbed her sleep last night, especially you."

"Oh, Lor! Is she still awake?" He crumpled for a moment, then triumphantly cried, "And she shall have it, bless her heart. Your mother's energy and wit shine like a steady flame all day to illuminate this house; we mustn't be surprised when now and again she's burnt out and low. People suffer from being sensitive. I don't suppose anyone will ever know how much the war took out of your mother. And the Armistice, for that matter." He chuckled.

"I'll get your eggs."

As she prepared Billy Pop's breakfast in the kitchen, Margaret was assailed by the whistles and snores of Regan's drunken sleep. She wrote a note. "Her Serene Highness hasn't slept. The mere dropping of a teaspoon may mean death to her in her present anguished state." Then she tore the note up and wrote another. "Mrs. Matthews has slept very badly; please make as little noise preparing lunch as you possibly can." They had agreed last night that in this war there were no allies; besides, there was no point in talking over people's heads.

When finally she returned to the top floor, her eldest brother was already running hot water into the bath, the door wide open.

"Mother hasn't slept, Quentin, we're none of us to make any noise."

The battered old geyser reverberated fit almost to wake the dead. The dead and the dying lay all around, teeth grinning vilely white through gas-blistered, greenish lips; Harrison's guts all spewed against the wire, Johnson's brown eyes, that he had known and answered to, liquefying into no meaning. Only when the thin, dark-haired schoolgirl turned off the tap and made a sudden silence did he see her.

"Mother wants absolute quiet."

"So did so many and they've got it. Let's hope they like it."

If his meaning was lost to her, he could see that he had alarmed her by his fierceness. There seemed no way to speak to them, for he had nothing to offer them as yet that was speakable and he could only guess to what absurd stereotype of the returned soldier they believed they were speaking. He tried as usual to banter his way through the thick walls that divided them.

"Surely such orders don't apply to wounded heroes."

She seemed to give his words serious consideration.

"I think they do, Quentin. Anyway, you'll soon be demobbed. And then you'll see how little you'll be indulged."

"Oh, I'm not asking for favours. God forbid! No black-legging. Unity is strength."

The reference to unity—subject of their last day's discussion—got through to her.

"To bother about our childish troubles after all you must have been through! The least you should be able to ask is reasonable comfort. But in this house! Are you sure there's enough hot water there? I can boil some kettles in the nursery. Sukey and I did it last year when the Countess had her no-bath campaign on."

"No, no, that's enough, thank you."

But to refuse anything might break what fragile links he had forged. To show intimacy, he began to unbutton his pyjama top. For a moment the girl's eyes were riveted on him. Then she was gone. Too late he remembered angrily his shoulder wound. Looking down at the pale hairs fringing the shiny, smooth-sided pink pit like an arse-hole in the wrong place, he fell once more into his waking nightmares.

"You're too thin, Margaret. The beast isn't giving you enough to eat. She can't be or you couldn't get in here when I'm out of bed. Not even she can do that. There isn't room for two in here."

"It's the room that's too thin, Gladys. They've no right to put you in this box room. What *are* all those great trunks, anyway? I do think at least that the place might have been cleared."

"Oh, they're some old trunks of HER father's that Mouse sent up from the country. They couldn't possibly be parted with, of course, although she's never looked to see what's in them. But as SHE said they *do* provide a washstand and dressing-table."

"Washstand and dressing-table!"

"Well, there weren't any before."

"And they have the cheek to charge you for it! What's the good of you going to the Food Ministry place every day and having independence. You might as well be supposed to be still at school like Sukey and me."

"Oh, I save a bit for the future this way. Give us a chance. I don't want to cut up ration cards forever."

"And now with The Plan it will all go on Marcus's school fees. We've treated you like a burnt offering, Gladys."

"Well, the eldest girl, you know. Didn't they all get smitten hip and thigh or something? Besides, there's more liberty here than in some of those ghastly digs. You should hear the girls at the office. Sally Shepstone has a notice in her room saying, 'No wovens to be washed in the bathroom.' I ask you."

"No wovens! Gladys, I must make a note of that."

"How *is* the writing, Mag?" Gladys touched her sister's elbow, but the arm was at once withdrawn.

"The Countess didn't sleep last night and she wants absolute quiet until eleven."

"Oh, Mag, was she foul to you?"

"Only fairly. She didn't make me cry. She hasn't managed that for two years now. I suppose with that awful Milton going back to America we're bound to have a frightful Countess time."

Gladys didn't answer.

"You mustn't stand up for her, Gladys."

"No, of course not. Only it must be rather hell for her. All the same she'll have to put up with my ironing, if that counts as noise. I dropped jam on my organdie blouse and I must have it for dinner. It's my only wearable day-time garment."

"You *are* a bit stingy. Surely you don't have to save as carefully as that."

"The last two weeks I have. Billy Pop was trying to borrow off poor old Regan. The beast. So I had to step in."

"You *lent* to Billy Pop?"

"Only a couple of quid."

"You lent to HIM."

"Well, only to help keep up appearances."

"That's just it, Gladys, to help *them* keep up *their* appearances. You deserve to pay them to sleep in a box room."

"Look here. It's my money. So shut up and hop it, twin squit." But immediately she'd said it, Gladys felt her thighs pressing together with embarrassment and shame. "Oh, I'm sorry, Mag. I didn't mean to talk elder sister stuff."

"You're fat, foolish, and faithless, Gladys."

But Gladys could see from Margaret's eyes that she wasn't really altogether joking. "Honestly, I want to pull my weight against them. The team can do with a heavyweight." She could hear her own gruff voice pleading absurdly like some schoolboy who asks to be let into the gang. Damn them, she thought, damn them, I am the eldest. Guying her part desperately, she leaned backwards, pretending to pull in a tug of war. She fell heavily on to the bed, her fat legs waving in the air. She sat up, red in the face. "What about that, Mag? Collapse of stout party."

But Margaret had gone.

To where Rupert, with small hand-mirror propped over the nursery basin, was busy lathering his chin. He turned at the sound of his sister's footsteps, his body bowed with age, his beard of white lather stuck imperiously forward; with his right hand he waved the shaving brush, regally he addressed the heavens. "You sulphurous and thought-executing fires, vaunt-couriers to oak-cleaving thunderbolts, singe my white head!" His sister interrupted him.

"Our present business is general woe. Sir, the Countess, your mother, commands a general silence. She has slept but indifferent well."

Rupert threw off his senile posture. Towering above her, he was trembling with anger. He stamped hard on the floor. "Would it were not so, you are my mother," he shouted. They waited for some reaction; then as Rupert seemed about to stamp again, Margaret intervened quickly.

"Alas, he's mad."

Her comic tone relaxed him. Absurdly he thrust out his slender chest bosom-like, and swelled his pale delicate face to a turkey cock's trembling red.

"Send no compliments to my mother. She deserves no such attention. I am seriously displeased."

"Displeased in *this* prettyish little kind of a wilderness." Margaret displayed the familiar nursery with a sweep of the hand equally familiar from their childhood theatricals. "Oh, Rupert, you've never done Lady Catherine before. I didn't know you knew Jane Austen well enough."

"Just a matter of obliging the audience's taste. If any other lady or gentleman has a request . . . " He broke off and flung his arms round her neck. "Oh, how I love us all. But especially you, Mag, especially you."

He saw her wince, withdrew his arm, and plunged once more into pantomime of Billy Pop. "And so she *shall* have silence, bless her dear old heart. No one but me knows, Mag, what suffering the war has cost your mother. Yes, and the peace."

He was delighted with her delight, and he repeated with sugary solemnity, "and the peace, Mag, and the peace."

"You've been listening at keyholes."

"No, no, Billy Pop's too easy."

Margaret put her head round the boys' room and called, "Marcus!" Only Rupert's bed, tumbled as Quentin had left it, confronted her. She walked to the corner of the room behind the large cupboard and looked over the partition of the "contraption."

"Oh, you're there. Well, you're not to make any noise."

"I can't very well while I'm here, unless I drum on the boards, and I gave up doing that years ago. It's so boring. Anyway, Quentin says I'm to have a proper bed. It's part of The Plan."

"The Countess'll never agree. She'll say what about sleep-walking?"

"I haven't slept-walked, or whatever it's called, for at least four years."

"The bunk bed your old Billy made for you all those years ago!" Margaret said in the Billy Pop voice.

"It'll do for his coffin."

Margaret edged away from her brother's place of sleep. "Well, you're not to make any noise. SHE says so. SHE's in one of her states."

Marcus made a face at her. "All right, grown-up." He clambered agilely from his box bed and, running to the dressing-up trunk, he rummaged out a scarlet silk ribbon and a long necklace of red beads. The ribbon he tied round his head, sticking into its side an old feather duster for an aigrette. He threw the rope of wooden beads round his neck and shook his striped pyjama jacket off one shoulder. Catching sight of Margaret's expression he said, "It *is* like the famous photograph, isn't it?" Before his sister could comment, he thrust his bare shoulder forward, holding a long pencil in one hand to serve for the Countess's cigarette holder, while his other hand toyed with the beads.

"I'm blue, Milton," he cried, "blue, dawling. You haven't given me the lurv I need. Latelah."

Margaret's face flushed as red as the ribbon and the beads he had chosen. Delighted, he took off the ribbon and beads and sat cross-legged on the ground as he had for Puck in last term's photograph of the house play. Demurely he looked at her from under his long eye-lashes.

"It *is* like, Margaret, isn't it?"

"Yes. But you're not to make any noise."

Completing the performance, "No lurv," he said. "Poor old bitch." Then his own dark cheeks flushed red as mulberries.

Finally Margaret returned to her own room. Sukey was busy tidy-ing up, but she immediately sat down in front of the dressing-table and seemed absorbed in putting on her little coral ear-rings.

"I don't *mind* your tidying up, Sukey. Really, after all these years of sharing, as if I hadn't got used to it!" Margaret laughed.

Sukey avoided comment. "I shan't be a jiffy, old thing. And then you'll have the room to yourself for your famous meditations."

"Meditations! I have to mend a bit of *broderie anglaise* for the Countess." Margaret stared out of the window for a moment, then she turned. "You'll have to be quiet. The horrible Milton's gone and she's in a terrible state. She looks a hundred, Sue. It must be awful having it at all if it makes you feel like that."

"It's only temper. Anyway, how could anyone let someone like that dreadful man kiss her?"

"I think there was more."

Sukey didn't answer.

"Do you think you would want a man to ask for more, Sue? I mean being naked and so on."

"Oh, it would just happen, wouldn't it? With the really right per-son."

"You mean like Billy Pop and her."

Sukey only said, "Then think how wonderful having babies."

"Like us?"

"Mag, I don't think we should talk about it. Just because they've made a horrible mess of things doesn't mean we would."

Margaret sat down on her bed, made most neatly by her twin. "Probably with some men it would be lovely. Jimmie, for instance, if it was half as good as his kissing, and when he's playing tennis you can see just how . . ."

"Mag, your Mind!"

"Perhaps it's yours. You don't know what I was going to say. Anyway, I'm sure you've thought of some boy in that way—Larry Hughes or Geoffrey Upcott."

"I haven't."

"I bet you have. What about him?" she waved a postcard.

"Oh, Mag, don't be silly. Owen Nares is just a crush. I'd love him as an escort, of course."

"An escort! Really, Sue. I'm not going to let you get away with that. What about Jon Crowe? I bet he has muscles like Tarzan."

Sukey saw her escape.

"And what about Colonel Vivian. His muscles . . ."

"Ugh, Sue. How can you? An old man like that! You might as well say the piano-tuner."

"*He* has ginger hair in his ears."

"Or the baker's roundsman."

"Oh, Mag, you can't think of common people in that way."

"No, I suppose not. Well, what about Doctor Croker?"

"Say ninety-nine. In that case, what about Mr. Hargreaves?"

"A little wider, please, Miss Matthews."

They both collapsed into giggles.

"But seriously, Sue. She commands strict silence."

"Oh, she is the limit. She goes on exactly as though she was a real countess."

"That *was* the origin of the nickname, dear."

"Don't be sarky, Mag. Anyway, I don't think it was."

"What was it, then?"

"I can't remember. Ask Rupert. His remembers everything to do with HER. She's sort of sacred to him. Yet he sees through her completely. I can't understand it."

"I shouldn't try, Sue."

"But I like to think we all know what the other thinks."

"How very disagreeable."

"Why is it disagreeable? How can we be a team if we aren't of one mind?"

"We're not a team, Sue. We're a coalition. Like Mr. Bonar Law and Mr. Lloyd George. For limited practical purposes."

"Mag! How can you compare anyone you love to that awful Lloyd George? But you're only talking for effect, like you did in Miss Coulton's English class. I know you are."

"Yes, I suppose I am. And, of course, we *are* all united. But it isn't a thing to *say*. Rupert's just as bad. You're both so sloppy and unseemly sometimes. And Gladys too. It blurs the line and makes *us* seem like *them*. It's much worse than talking about naked men. But I do love you, yes."

"Dear Mag." Sukey kissed her sister on the cheek. "I hate sloppiness too. Well, down to the infernal regions. I've been ordered to help Regan. Lunch *must* be on time with Granny M. and Dearest coming."

"Sue, we mustn't put ourselves in the wrong today, whatever happens."

"Well, I can't promise about noise, because old Regan loathes having me in the kitchen as much as I loathe being in the filthy place. She always clatters and bangs as much as she can to show her disapproval."

"You'll *have* to stop her this morning. The Countess mustn't be able to make any complaint against us if we're going to speak out."

"Do you really mean us to? It's easy enough for Quentin to *say*, but . . ."

"You're not funking it, Sue?"

"Of course not. All right, I'll suppress the horrible Regan even if I have to put her head in a saucepan."

"Yes, do, please. And see that that food's just right. You know how greedy the old ladies are."

"I'll try."

Sukey hooked her right-hand little finger with Margaret's.

"Till lunch time, then."

In the nursery, Marcus, acutely aware of being hungry, mixed a subtle peacock green in the paint-box lid and listened to the near

silence of the house. The sensation carried a memory of a sensation
that carried a memory of a sensation on and on back to his dimly
remembered baby years. The periodic thump of Gladys's iron in the
next room sounded deadened and dull; Margaret muttering crossly
over her sewing was a mere punctuation of Rupert's continual whispering repetition of his words. Different actions each year, but the
same actors producing the same subdued noises. And always, as long
as he could remember, he had felt hungry.

" 'Peaceful slumber meek and mild, meek and mild. Never would
my nights be wild.' No, blast it. 'Peaceful slumber *sweet* and mild,' "
Rupert said.

I expect you were thinking of Gentle Jesus. What is *Chu Chin
Chow* about?" Marcus asked. "It sounds nonsense."

"It is rather tripe. We're only doing it because Morrison, the ac-
countant, is a baritone and fancies himself as a comic. Myrtle James
and I wanted to do something really passionate. Myrtle's hot stuff,
you know."

"Is that the young lady with red hair who came to tea with you
and licked the butter off her fingers after eating a crumpet?"

"Don't cheek. In any case no one said she was a lady. She's a
typist. All the same she's had a jolly hard time at home and she's a
good sort. Hot stuff, too. If the Countess hadn't been sitting there
like a basilisk, I'd have asked her up here and I believe she'd have
come too."

"Into the nursery? It wouldn't have been very comfortable."

"No, into my room, of course, you idiot."

"Oh, I see. *Our* room actually. I'm very glad you didn't. She was
soaked in a most disagreeable scent. I shouldn't have been able to
sleep."

"*You* wouldn't have been able to sleep. People think it's a pretty
shocking state of affairs that I should have to share a bedroom with a
school kid. Of course, I don't usually let on. You can't let the world
know your business in a family like this. And then to be turned on to
the nursery floor. At nineteen!"

"You aren't quite that yet, are you? I'm very hungry. But I'm
sorry if sharing embarrasses you."

"I expect we all are, but it's a special dinner today."

"That doesn't mean *I* shall get any more to eat even if you do. It'll
just be Sukey's bread-and-butter pudding and there's never enough

even of that. You'd think they'd know that growing boys need feeding."

Rupert fished a bar of chocolate from his pocket and broke it in half. "You can have this if you like. But don't make yourself sick. We mustn't any of us be in the wrong today."

"Thank you very much. You needn't worry. I'm never sick."

"You still wet the bed."

"You oughtn't to mention that. Just because we share the same room ought to make you more respectful of privacy than ever."

"Oh, ought it?" Rupert peered over his small brother's shoulder. "That's jolly good. I thought you were drawing those boring women's dresses. What is it? Ali Baba for the pantomime?"

"No. Strange as it may seem to you, I'm not still concerned with pantomimes. It's Harun-al-Rashid's palace."

"It would make a jolly good set for *Chu Chin Chow*. We might use it. Wait a minute, though, what's all that going on up in the corner? That looks a bit thick."

Marcus giggled. "It's the grand vizier in hot pursuit."

"And hot it looks! I hope you haven't got a foul mind, Marcus Matthews. All the same I think I'll take a closer squiz at those fleeing nymphs of the harem."

"They're not nymphs. At least I don't think so. Nymphs are always girls, aren't they? Those are two beautiful boys. One's my idea of a yummy boy called Rampion who's up Grant's. Of course, I've never seen him naked."

"You filthy little swine. Just you shut up. I should think you *have* got a foul mind. It's worse than that, it's like a sewer. I ought to punch your head. You'd better watch out. That kind of thinking can easily land you in the loony bin. It's worse than playing with yourself. I'm not sure I oughtn't to talk to Father about this."

"You won't, Rupert."

"Oh, won't I?"

"Because first you wouldn't be able to get the words out. Secondly, we mustn't upset them at the moment. Thirdly, it's none of your business. Fourthly, if it really sent people mad everybody at school would be in a lunatic asylum, and anyway Billy Pop would never allow himself to hear it. Come to that I bet you had a crush on somebody at school. Much worse went on when you were there— I've heard about it."

"Oh, crushes. Of course there were those. House tarts and so on. Actually, if you must know, I kissed one kid once. But only a few complete beasts were foul."

"Oh. Then it's different now."

Rupert stretched out on the nursery rug, his hands locked beneath his head. He stared at the ceiling as he talked.

"Look, you'll grow out of this. Everyone does. So you don't want to worry. But don't give way to it. I mean if I could draw like you can I should make some top-hole pictures of girls. I've seen some. Atkinson had them at the office. Saucy oo-la-la stuff like Delysia. One was wearing nothing but a feathered garter. Try and think about girls as much as you can, Markie. That's my advice."

"Thank you. But I don't think I should like to."

"But seriously, you've got to. It's a question of growing up. Otherwise people would never get married. And what do you think would blooming well happen to the world then?"

"I don't intend to marry. I don't see how any of us could. After seeing *them*."

"Every woman isn't a virago like the Countess. In any case, she'd be all right if she'd married a proper man."

Marcus considered. "Well, he can't be a eunuch, can he? I've thought about that. Unless you think we're all bastards."

"No, of course we aren't. But there's such a thing as the art of love."

"I know there is. It's by Ovid. I'm sure Billy Pop must have read it. He's read most of the boring books there are."

"Ovid! God, you are a kid. No, I mean some men know how to make love to women and some don't. That's all there is to it."

"I see. Well, I don't think I should want to. There's always something wrong even with the nicest of them. I mean that Myrtle friend of yours having that scent."

"Better than a pimply boy. Anyway, shut up now. I've got to learn these lines. But I'm warning you. If you go thinking all that filth, something ghastly will happen to you."

Marcus tried to concentrate once more on the peacocks and apes with which he was filling Harun-al-Rashid's fountained court. But the pleasure had gone from it. He remembered that when he had caught a glimpse of Rampion's bottom as he was changing it had

been very spotty. He looked with disgust at the familiar nursery.
Once he had believed that if he yelled loudly enough he could magic
into any scene that he wanted, even Harun-al-Rashid's Baghdad. But
now he knew that even were he to yell the roof down, there would
be no elegant fountain-cool palace, but simply roofless old hideous
No. 52, and around him would be not only the debris of the raised
roof but all the mess of Sunday morning Victoria—pages of *The
Pink'un* flapping against walls, paper bags, banana skins, pools of
vomit. Surely there were other things somewhere, things both comical *and* elegant. Not that it mattered. For the wind had got up and
was blowing above and under and around every draughty door and
window. No need to scream, for soon the dust would cover all;
would silt up in the basement and stifle Regan's snores; would cover
grey Billy Pop with thicker grey, and all his paper-weights (the see-
no-evil monkey, the Lincoln imp, Mother Shipton) that made his
desk a toy town; would bury the drawing-room under a sandy film
thick upon the water in the black china bowls where the Countess
floated marigold heads; and moving on up above, would strike the
Countess's bed like the Annunciation's beam, but stifling, not awakening. Finally he, too, would surrender to the tender death of dust's
embrace, would give himself . . . But something sneezed—loudly
and clearly, something in the box room under the water-tank
sneezed and mewed. Marcus came to and laughed at his day-dreams.
The dust no doubt had reached the kittens. And soon they were
setting up a chorus of jerky, competitive wailing, not so shrill as a
nest of birds, but more urgent—calling perhaps for their dead
mother. Sukey had put them in the box hole after the taxicab had
hit Leonora, when they had all agreed that the small creatures must
be preserved from the Countess's unpredictable love and Billy Pop's
spite-laced maunderings. "We'll *all* look after them," Sukey had said.
But they all knew that she meant them to be her particular care.
Sukey, then, must act, or their mewing would disturb the Countess.
Softly Marcus called, "Sukey! The kittens!"

Quentin, too, was stirred from soothing warm water. "Sukey,
you'd better do something." Yet, receiving no answer, he fell back
into contemplating the greasy brass-maker's plate on the geyser.
"The Heats-All, Manufactured in York"; from these letters he tried to
make words—he had played this game with the same letters on the

same geyser when he was seven. He tried to make "Change All" or "Renew All," but could find only "Ruin All." Yet the water still lapped him deliciously.

And now Marcus, getting no answer from Sukey, paid his tribute to the kittens. He painted broad tiger stripes of brown and yellow into a *mousseline de soie* ball dress he was designing; and the stripes in turn gave him the model's name: "Zaza." He scrawled this in dashing scarlet ink across the bottom of the cardboard sheet. He turned to Rupert, seeking what should be done to hush the crying kittens, but Rupert was saying to himself, "We are the dust beneath thy feet, O Chu Chin Chow." Marcus watched his brother saying it cringingly and then saying it with a mocking smile; then he walked out into the passage and found Gladys already busy giving the kittens milk from a fountain-pen filler.

"I say, I wonder how Sue gets them to open their mouths. They shut up as soon as this fearsome-looking thing comes near them."

Margaret peered into the basket. "Their heads are enormous and their bodies are like snakes. They're liked diseased weasels. I can't think why one should feel so protective towards them."

"Never mind what they're like, Margaret. Pick up the little tabby blighter and see if we can get him to open his mouth."

The kitten cried out happily as Margaret held him in the air.

"Can't they all be fed together?" Marcus asked, taking up the beautiful little ginger one and giving his finger to its sharp teeth as a nipple.

"No, they can't," said Gladys. "Why?"

"Oh, just because they make such beautiful patterns in the basket. But held up separately like that they *do* look like weasels, or something. Perhaps just kittens."

"They are each of them just that," said Margaret. "How self-centered you are, Marcus." She tickled the tabby kitten's ears. "This little beggar's done very well. I won't give him any more. He'll get wind. Pick up the white one. That's the little blighter that's been raising the roof."

By now Quentin had put his head solicitously round the bathroom door. "Are you sure you're doing the right thing?"

"Well, not sure. That is, if you know better, old boy."

"I don't. Poor motherless little things."

"It's hardly for us to condole with them on that score," Margaret said.

Rupert loomed through the nursery door. "No, indeed, I suspect that's why they look in such healthy shape."

"Oh, you mustn't," Marcus cried. "Leonora would have been a wonderful mother."

To their surprise Quentin said, "Dead mothers tell no tales." Perhaps to his own, for he immediately returned to the bathroom.

"We must make up to them for what we've never had," Rupert said. He bent down and stroked the tortoise-shell kitten. "This one's a girl. Tortoise-shells always are."

Gladys announced: "Sue oughtn't to keep milk in your room, Mag. If the Countess knew, there'd be blue murder."

"You flatter Sukey. I'm sure her blood isn't blue like the Countess's. It's probably pink like Billy Pop's." Marcus's sisters laughed at his remark, but Rupert went back to the nursery.

Gladys said, "It's a shame Marcus never has any school friends round here at week-ends."

"If you remember the way she went on the last time he had a friend here . . ."

"I wasn't at home. Was she awful? Rotten luck, Marcus."

"I shouldn't let her prevent me from asking friends here, thank you. It's just that this is hardly a house I want to entertain in."

Gladys burst into a guffaw, but a second later the Countess screamed from below. "Who's making all that unnecessary noise? Margaret, didn't you give my message? You wait till I come upstairs, you'll wish you *had* been born Wendy. If your father had any . . . Billy, Billy, leave those old papers for once and give me a hand with your children. Come upstairs."

"There *is* going to be murder," Margaret said. She put the kittens back into the basket. Gladys shut the box-room door and stood before it like a sentry.

"Oh, don't be such funks." Leaning over the banister, Marcus called, "It's the kittens, darling."

The Countess's face peered up at him. She had taken off her boudoir cap and her thick black hair streamed over her shoulders.

"Medusa," Marcus murmured.

"What did you say? It was some impertinence, wasn't it? I know that smug little smile. Anyway, what are you doing on the landing? What kittens?"

"Dear Leonora's."

"Leonora?"

"Our darling cat that was killed last week, that's all."

"What do you mean 'that's all'? It was perfectly dreadful. Only a morbid child like you would want to dwell on it. Anyway what do you mean '*our* darling cat.' *I* was the one who looked after that cat. And old Regan. She doted on it. You children take old Regan far too much for granted. She's a human being as well as a servant. What she did for that cat! She and I did everything for it. As far as you children were concerned, it might have died."

"It did," said Margaret.

"There you are. The poor creature! It was an adorable cat, too. A real alley cat. An independent cockney street cat. That cat and I understood one another."

"But you couldn't remember its name," Rupert called from the nursery.

"Learn to speak without shouting or shut up. You're not acting now with the Mincing Lane Mummers. Names! That cat was a street Arab. Street Arabs don't have names. Well, where is the shameless gutter-snipe's brood?"

"You shouldn't insult the dead."

The Countess turned for a moment to stare at Marcus's pear-shaped face and large dark eyes. Then she struck him a sharp blow on the cheek with the palm of her hand.

"You're talking too much."

She bent over the kittens, and picking up all five of them at once, she disposed of two in the wide sleeves of her Japanese kimono, the others she pressed to her flat breast.

"They are a mongrel brood! Every colour of the rainbow. Adorable vulgar waifs of the London streets."

The black-and-white kitten, alarmed by the swinging of its sleeve hammock, caught for a moment at her bare arm; but this did not check her sweetness.

"*You'll* have to be tamed! You Seven Dials kitten! They're apaches. That's what they are, they're apaches! But who put them in *this* black hole of Calcutta? It isn't fit even to be a box room. It wouldn't be one if our wage earner didn't insist on a room of her own. I suppose they were shoved into this hole because they weren't pure-bred Persians. Oh, dear, what snobs I have given birth to. But I must say you're beautiful-looking snobs, the lot of you. Even my barber's block, Rupert, and Gladys is becoming quite a handsome matron."

"And as for you, Countess," said Rupert, "is it Bernhardt and dog, or dog and bone?"

"Yes, I know the joke, darling heart. But it is a silly one for you to make since you never saw the divine Sarah. Anyway, my sort of figure will have its day, you mark my words. And you're not going to stop me being a doting mother. You're all quite beautiful. Every one! Except, of course, snotty-nosed little schoolboy Marcus. But then schoolboys shouldn't be beautiful. That wouldn't be quite decent. Except for you, Billy." Turning, she addressed her husband's head as he appeared, blowing a little, above the stair rail. "Your father was indecently pretty as a schoolboy. I have an enchanting photograph somewhere of him just at Marcus's age. In his mortar-board. A little angel face. Weren't you, pet? Oh, you don't know the half of your father. Look, Billy, these adorable kittens!"

"The poor little kittens have lost their mittens."

"Oh, don't be so whimsical. Anyway this little ginger is going to do a number one if we're not careful. Take them away at once, Marcus. But don't put them back into that black hole or we'll have an inspector or somebody fussing. Get a basket from Regan. Not that awful old thing. Where *did* you children find it? Oh, it's Rag's basket! Whoever kept that? How disgusting and sentimental! That's your fault, Billy, you've taught them sentimentality. Now remember, all of you, when someone dies whom you love—it doesn't matter who it is, animal or friend—don't hang on. Love them and forget them! It's so much more healthy. Marcus, you're going to drop them. Don't droop so. You're not holding a lily. Sukey had better deal with them. She likes being the little mother."

"You sent Sukey to the kitchen."

"*Sent* her to the kitchen! What do you mean, Margaret? She's gone to help Regan. *Sent* her to the kitchen! Well, of course I did. We don't pay expensive fees to have her taught cooking if she's never going to cook. Call down to her, Billy. She's your daughter." She paused to hear Sukey's response from the depths of the staircase well, then she went on. "You, Wendy, what's your name, since

Sukey can never be where she's wanted, look into the next-to-the-bottom drawer of my chest of drawers and you'll find a square of scarlet velvet. Put it under them in the basket. It'll go with my red curtains in the dining-room. For that's where the kittens must live, of course. Not all the time. They must have a box of sand in the kitchen. Regan will explain to you about emptying and filling."

"Leonora used to go outside."

"Yes, and got killed as a result. No, thank you. If you don't really care about them enough to bother, then you'd much better wring their necks now."

"It's more usual to drown unwanted kittens, Countess."

"But they're not unwanted, Billy. Not by the children and me, anyway. Their games are going to be so amusing. Gladys, you can get a ball or something for them tomorrow and then . . ."

"You're not to touch them. You're not to. They're my kittens!"

The Countess turned to see a red-faced Sukey shouting at her. Would she rush at her mother, who stared fixedly at her? Billy Pop put a hand on his daughter's arm.

"Steady, Sue, steady."

"That gold band has done nothing for that child's teeth, Billy," the Countess remarked. "So they're yours, are they, Sukey?" She came closer to her daughter. "Sukey, the little mother, who shut them in a cupboard. Do you have any idea of what a long, slow death stifling is? Gasping for breath. Do you, Sukey, do you?"

The bathroom door opened and Quentin came out in an old mohair dressing-gown. "They're *our* kittens, Mother. We're all responsible for them. And, by the way, Margaret didn't forget to impose silence on us."

"She'd have been perfectly justified if she had, wouldn't you, Mag? I was absolutely beastly to her when she brought my breakfast. Remind me to be nicer to you all day, darling heart." The Countess went up to her eldest son and kissed him. "A nice long bath, darling? You always loved to soak. Acting Major Matthews and his kittens! No, Quentin, I can't have your dignity demeaned like that. An acting major going up to Oxford is enough . . ."

"London, Mother."

"So you keep telling me, dear, but they don't have universities in London, or if they have they shouldn't. Anyway a major at a university is bad enough, but a major with kittens . . . All right, Sukey, you've said your piece. Don't ruin the lunch as well. And speak nicely to Regan about putting a sand-box in the kitchen."

But Sukey disregarded her mother. She was intent upon apology. "I'm sorry, Quentin. Of course, they're *ours*. I didn't mean to be possessive. I should never have said they were mine."

"Indeed you shouldn't, Sukey. Anyway they're mine now." Looking at her children the Countess felt quite warm towards them. "You shall *all* look after them for me. And now enough of kittens. What have you all been doing this morning?"

"Look," Billy Pop held out a book he had taken from the shelves. "A first edition of *Virginibus Puerisque*. It oughtn't to be here with these old review copies. I remember so well finding it on a junk stall in the cattle market at Stirling when I was on a walking tour of the Midlothian."

"Oh, how can you be so selfish, Billy? Just the same rambling egotism as your mother. 'Do you remember that picnic on the Island? Do you remember, Will, when you forgot yourself at the Christmas party, dear little boy?' At least she has the excuse of being senile. But you! Can't you live in the present for a moment? Don't you want to know what your children are doing? You'd have done better to *write* a few more books instead of *finding* them. Life isn't just to be found, you have to work for it. There's nothing to laugh about, Marcus. Your father's a brilliant man. If he didn't lack application, he'd be somebody. And now I've no time to hear what my children have to say, because I have to dress up for your mother. If Granny M. didn't insist on sitting up to table, we could all have a nice nursery picnic. *You'd* have liked that, wouldn't you, Quentin?"

"I dare say Quentin picnicked quite often enough at the Front," Margaret said.

"Nonsense. You none of you remember Quentin. You've forgotten him while he's been away defending his country. He has the simplest of tastes, haven't you, darling heart?"

But Billy Pop was clearly in an interrupting mood. "Just to get the record straight, I'd like to remind you, Countess, that the formal occasion is as much on your aunt's account as on my mother's."

"Billy darling, I do love you when you're touchy. But if I can't have my picnic, I shall have my revenge. I'll wear a hat at luncheon just to see your mother's bewildered face. She can never remember whether I'm doing the right thing or the wrong." She began to laugh as she thought of Granny M.'s old head shaking with the difficulties of etiquette. Blowing a kiss to her family, she went downstairs to her bathroom to dress.

Billy Pop was absorbed in *Virginibus Puerisque*, but he could feel that his waiting children expected some remark from him.

"If only Stevenson hadn't whoremongered after that French harlot, the novel, but had stuck to his ane fair Scots bride, the essay! He was a natural rover, you know. When he could get away from fixed forms and let his fancy wander, he was superb. Listen to this."

"We are listening, Father."

The sound of Gladys's voice coming distantly made him look up. They had all gone back to their rooms. He decided not to read the extract. Instead, he said, "I doubt if it's true. Your mother as usual was being generous. I didn't really have it in me to be anyone." Getting no reply, he added, "But I've tried to be a friend to you children." In face of their continued silence he decided to take his treasure trove down to his study. As he went downstairs he called, "When I eventually have to pay Charon his fare, you will look back on me as a grey man. Not memorable like your mother. But perhaps you may say to yourselves, 'He wasn't such a bad old stick.'"

Rejecting all old sticks, bad or good, the Matthews children began to use their Sunday morning leisure. In the nursery, Marcus, craving for the newest and smartest, began to paint in a chic *Vogue* background for his models. In the nursery, too, determining on a new world where reason and humane feelings would reign, Quentin set himself to the recommended book *Self-Government in Industry*.

In the bathroom, Rupert, rubbing lotion into his hair, thought of a new sort of play where all would happen naturally in a natural setting—lovers' quarrels, for instance, in a bathroom, but not of course an old squalid geysered bathroom like this, a scene all jazz design and gay silk dressing-gowns and hairbrushes, bottles of scent and of expensive hair oil flying across the room in a lovers' witty battle of words. Beatrice and Benedict brought up to date in a Riviera villa, perhaps, or a suite at the Ritz, or a gay Paris atelier.

Gladys, checking her Post Office savings book as she balanced on the edge of her bed, thought of the new world lying open to girls, a new world that with such interest she would open to them in her brand-new employment office with its brand-new punch-card system of classification, and the newest portable typewriting machines in Kingsway, she and her one or two sensible bachelor girl aides. And Alfred had offered to invest a hundred pounds for every fifty of her own capital.

Margaret, sitting at her dressing-table, wisps of dark hair brushing the virgin pages of her exercise book, worried and frowned over this new story that would at last have its just proportions.

Sukey, who was trying out a new eggless recipe, turned from mixing batter for the toad-in-the-hole to see Regan lift each of the pheasants in turn and sniff at them. The light for a moment caught at some bristly featheriness left by incomplete plucking of the largest bird and then glanced on to the dark hairs that protruded from the mole on Regan's chin. She looked away and concentrated on whipping the batter. When she turned again to make her plea for the kittens, Regan was flicking into her mouth a speck of raw giblet from the kitchen table.

"The cock bird's the igh one," she said. "That'll do for your Granny Matthews. She's one of the old school. She likes er birds gamey. Miss Rickard's got a weaker stomach for all er travelling. She'll take the breast of one of the ens. Or as much as *eel* leave for er." She chuckled.

"Oh, Regan, the things you remember about us."

"That's part of bein in service, Miss Sukey."

"You've spoilt us, you know."

In the great roomy farmhouse kitchen from whose speckless tiled floors one could eat one's breakfast any day, Ada laughed. "Oh, I gave him a piece of my mind, Madam; 'The garden isn't yours,' I told him. 'Asparagus like great pillars. The idea of it! Just for your old village show! When you *know* that the mistress likes the early spikes as thin as her little finger.' It won't happen again, you can assure the master of that." Sukey said to this tall country-woman, so neatly dressed in her uniform, almost handsome with her direct, self-respecting gaze, "Oh, you've bullied him, Ada. The poor man! And you know he's in love with you." "Oh, he's all right, Anderson is, Madam. But every man needs to be put in his place now and again. It doesn't do to spoil them. You know that." "Indeed I do, Ada." Then laughing—two women together—she looked up and saw Regan's greasy old apron, a hairpin hanging over her ear.

"And *we've* spoilt *you*, Regan," she added softly. And then, not to upset the old creature, no, rather, surely, to be fair, "*They* have. This house. It spoils everything." She looked ahead trying to catch sight of Ada, even of the kitchen garden, but there was only the grocer's gift calendar still announcing June and marked with a bloody thumbprint.

"Too stiff for your wrists?" Regan came towards the bowl of batter. "Ere, let me."

"No, no, it's quite all right. Oh, you are a darling, Regan, putting up with us all."

"Now what's this you want? All over me, aren't you?"

The woman was in a rare friendly mood. Sukey, drawing back from a blast of cooking-brandy fumes mixed with onion, determinedly separated real warmth from maudlin alcohol. Determinedly also she replied to Regan's warm self.

"Dear Regan, you always see through us. I do want something. Yes." She made her request.

"Kittens messing all over my kitchen floor. No thank you. Never eard of such a thing. Insanity, that's what it is. Insanity."

"But think of the mice we'll get if we don't have a cat to take Leonora's place."

"Leonora! That taxi was a dispensation, if you ask me. Besides, you won't get no mice in my kitchen. The idea! And if there was, mice droppins is better than cats' mess. Why, there was an old geezer once sent down to the kitchen to thank me for the sponge cake with chocolate flutings. I said to Monser Jools, 'Chocolate flutings! She's barmy!' It was only after, I thought of the mice. Mice droppins, why when I was working for Mrs. Pitditch-Perkins . . .'"

"Oh, Regan, darling! What an absolutely glorious story!" Sukey turned and there was the Countess "framed," as she no doubt thought of herself, in the kitchen doorway. Sukey saw in her mother only a means of stemming Regan's tide.

"So you're going to challenge poor Granny's cherished ideas of etiquette." She looked at her mother's small toque of pansies and violets.

"Well, she shouldn't cherish them if she's so vague about what's the done thing."

"All the same, a toque's rather a timorous challenge. Especially with Granny's short sight."

"A timorous challenge! That's quite witty for you, darling. I used to think Margaret would be the wit, but she's getting so sour. Perhaps you will be. I hope one of you will inherit. After all, I'm here as a constant example, and better still you've got Regan's *natural* wit. And so you've agreed, Regan. I knew as soon as I heard that wonderful mouse story. You're going to give my kittens a warm home near the boiler. And for party occasions they can come upstairs to the dining-room and be looked at by visitors. You mustn't let them be a nuisance, Regan. Sukey will see to their feeding, won't you, darling? And one of the others can empty the sand-box. Marcus, I should think. It will be good for him. No schoolboy should have such clean white hands as Marcus has."

"I don't fancy kittens in the kitchen, Madam. It's insanity."

"Insanity!" The Countess laughed down the scale. "You've been got at by Miss Sukey and all those awful school-of-cookery ideas; sanity, that's what they teach there. And look at the result. Those terrible potato-flour scones! Thank goodness, Sukey, you cook only for the nursery menu. But you, Regan, you made even the Zepp raids an orgy! Do you remember those delicious little woodcocks the night the bomb fell in Covent Garden? But you will take my kittens, won't you, Regan? I need an awful lot of consoling today. My friend Major Ward has gone back to the United States. He sent a special message to you, Regan. Your praline ices will live with him forever."

The Countess was in tears. Sukey turned away. But Regan responded.

"You ad igh old times together, didn't you? And will again. If not with im. There's others. You've never been content with one."

"Oh, Regan, you're a shockingly bad influence on me. Thank heaven for you! And my kittens?"

Regan clicked her tongue. "Oh, all right. You can ave your muck box. But don't blame me if you all get the bellyache. And now off you go if Miss Rickard's to ave er *crème brûlée*."

"Dear Regan," the Countess said. She went over to Sukey. "There you are, darling. The kittens are provided for. And I want *you* to look after them for me. And Sukey," she whispered, "do see she doesn't take another nip. She's had just enough to produce a superb luncheon, but we don't want her paralytic. The kittens are *called* mine, darling, but, of course, you're the one to care for them. The idea of your sharing with the others was absurd. Do remember, darling heart, that Billy and I have special reasons for wanting to please the old girls today."

"Yes, Countess, I understand." Sukey felt quite conspiratorial in the irony of her answer, like Mazarin or someone in one of Billy Pop's historical stories.

She poured the batter mixture into the greased baking tin. The mixture, cascading smoothly white from the smooth white bowl, seemed to carry her along with it without thought or care. Regan, too, was whistling gaily, not in her usual sad, off-key drone.

"Why are we so happy when she gets her own way, Regan?"

Regan, busy clarifying the sugar, said nothing.

"I suppose it's a relief to have her in a happy mood."

"Oh, drat you, Miss Sukey! Don't keep on talking. Your ma's aving a bad time. Let's leave it at that. Anyway she don't know what a real bit of fun means. You none of you do. The gentry, or those that goes by the name. She ought to come over to my sister Em's place of a Saturday night. I couldn't let *them* know what I've come down to." She poured herself out a glass of cooking brandy. "But there, you've got to kick the bucket somewhere. And one filthy ole's as good as another."

Sukey concentratedly spread margarine thinly on the bread scraps for the pudding she was preparing. So concentratedly that she found to her annoyance that she had prepared more bread scraps than the baking dish would hold even if she left out the always optional fistful of currants. She turned round with released fury when she heard Billy Pop's voice.

"Well, Regan, well?" he was asking.

"It isn't well at all, Father. It's very bad. She's just called the house a filthy hole."

"Oh, dear," he began to lick the cream from the blades of the whipper that Regan had used. "Oh, dear! Well, there it is. If you know a better 'ole, Regan, go to it, as Old Bill said."

"It isn't only Regan who wants to go. Don't make any mistake about that. We all of us hate it here. Not just the dirt but the way you've let everything slide. Look at you dropping cream on your waistcoat now."

Regan dipped a dishcloth in boiling water and rubbed Billy Pop's waistcoat vigorously. "There!"

Billy Pop poured himself out a half glass of the cooking brandy. He took a mouthful and made a face. "Not a good brandy." He hastily swallowed the rest. Sukey's full bottom lip was trembling; she brushed tears from her eyelashes with the back of her hand.

" 'April, April, laugh thy girlish laughter, and the moment after, Weep thy girlish tears, April.' Nothing seems so terrible again as it does when one's young, eh, Regan?"

Regan did not answer him, and as Sukey started to cry, he went over to her. "If you're trying to compete with your mother's mercurial moods, my dear, don't. Remember she's a Mrs. Siddons, a Bernhardt. You're not. Or probably not. You're peaches and cream." He pinched her cheek, but this did not stop her sobbing. "Well, you've brought all this on, Regan. You'll have to deal with it," he told her. She was balancing the baking dish against her knee as she basted the ducks. He went over and broke off a piece of well-toffeed skin.

Sukey shouted at him. "Oh, yes, anybody but yourself. And what have you brought *her* to? Faithful old Regan."

"You're saying hurtful things, Sukey."

With this rebuke he faded out of the kitchen like the steam from the brussels sprouts boiling on the range. But something moist remained with them—for Regan a kiss in the cellar before the All Clear, for Sukey the watering eyes the day his last manuscript came back "no sale" from his agents. They also conjure up who only fade away.

James Carmichael lightly touched his gay blue-and-white-spotted foulard bow tie. He was out of his seat in a second to greet her. "My dear," he asked, "how do you contrive to look so lovely? Like champagne to the thirsty traveller." But her black eyes were contemptuous. "James, if you're going to make speeches, think first. Champagne doesn't quench thirst." His body became bowed, his knees sagged, he resumed his seat before she sat down. Ash fell from his cigarette upon his waistcoat. "I don't seem to sleep. This shortness of breath. But still, who cares?" he mumbled.

Margaret put down her pen, satisfied that Billy Pop had been nailed on paper. The speech was less rotund, perhaps, less pompous; but then James Carmichael was an idle stockbroker, not a failed writer. His speech *would* be more truncated, less flowery. But the Countess wasn't there at all. She was neither herself nor Sophie Carmichael. True, Sophie was intended to be less "bohemian," but this dialogue was that of a dowager—"think first"—it was an old woman snapping; without the Countess's laughter and mockery, the words were dead. Complexity was gone and complexity was the heart of the life she sought to convey. How to put it on paper? Her fingers itched to tear up all she had written, to find the one magic word that would say everything. If she could convey the surrounding atmosphere of No. 52 perhaps:

> From below stairs rose the familiar, humiliating smell of cabbage a-boiling, and with it Charles's tremulous tenor singing some ridiculous, sugary tune from *Chu Chin Chow*.

"A-boiling" was too affected and "cabbage" too obvious. Why not use the immediate, the familiar and real "brussels sprouts coming to the boil"? But where to put the phrase, "Like champagne to the thirsty traveller"?

> From below stairs rose the familiar, humiliating smell of brussels sprouts coming to the boil, etc.

Margaret sat back with a smile. It was pleasing, placing irony. And yet, and yet, by ironically placing so carefully it somehow failed to capture the contradictory whole. She flattened the nib of her pen against the blotter until it broke. Now at least she had the respite given her by the task of replacing it.

"Youth is the time for loving, so poets always say." Maybe they did, but Billy Pop felt a resistance to the couplet when offered to him by the flirtatious mingling of Rupert's tenor and the Countess's contralto floating out from the drawing-room. He felt isolated by it and decided to seek feminine assuagement from his daughters on the top floor. Meanwhile, as he climbed the stairs, he covered the unwanted duet with his own bawled solo: "I cobble all night and I cobble all day. *Tum tiddy tum, tum tiddy tum.* I am Chu Chin Chow from China, from Shanghai China." The "Shanghai" was a mistake, inartistic. Particularity spoils art. Some important chap had said it. Probably at the Thursday Bookmen Luncheon. Gosse or Q.

But the great features did not emerge at all. Probably not great at all, probably Smith, Brown, or Jones. For after all, exactitude, the *mot juste* and the cherished fact, artistically cherished of course, was the key to art. For example, "I cobble all night and I cobble all day." Everything exact. The last, the stretch, the awl. The cobbler gives his awl. No, excess of wit destroys simplicity. Just "The Cobbler," that crystallized gem, the short story—surely crystal gem, most unfortunate to crack one's teeth on a sugared ruby. Every word as hard as a diamond. The last, the stretch, the awl. All, but not perhaps enough. Well, any trade would do when starting from scratch. A printer maybe. A more familiar world. César Birotteau. But then, Balzac really knew. No, damn this splitting head, stick to your last. *Ars longa* and needs endurance.

Arnold Bennett, generous old vulgarian, "to those of us who still care for the precise image your little masterpiece of the cockney cobbler's day out at Margate . . ." Cockney? Ah, perhaps Regan's brother-in-law was a cobbler. Exactitude, that was what one needed. A writer's notebook. And then selection. Life can't be put on paper in all its complexity. "True art, as you show, lies so much in the selecting gift of eye and ear." Arnold Bennett, generous old vulgarian. "The generosity of your encouragement, needless to say, is a more satisfactory stimulation to fresh work than any perfunctory praise from run-of-the-mill critics. If my little story has passed your exacting . . ." Composing his generous but quite unvulgar reply to Arnold Bennett and humming "The Cobbler's Song," Billy Pop paused in contented dreaming mood for a moment on the top landing.

What children they all were. The doors ajar of each room, a continued, habitual practice from the Countess's ban on childhood privacy. There at her dressing-table, Margaret, frowning over some scribbling; there, with pad balanced on her knee, Gladys intent over a letter she was writing. His Grub Street Grubs. There was an article. Between Margaret's fine-edged art and Gladys's rough simplicity, where did the greater feminine solace lie? True art, after all, is simple.

"My darling," Gladys wrote, "I don't want to shock you but you *don't* have to worry about my finding it difficult to accept the loan you're offering me. When we became lovers I told you that for me this meant *total* acceptance of *everything*, good and bad, that followed from it. Well, this is one of the good things. Good because it means, old thing, that you really care for my plans, that you're *not* just pleasing me as *some* men would please their mistresses by humouring them. Hark at me laying down the law about the ways of this wicked world of ours. Anyhow, *we're* going to be equal partners. And I shall have my *own* life. I know sometimes you think I'm spouting women's rights and all that, but I'm not, you know. It's just that *our* kind of love means each having their own thing in life and respecting the other's. For instance, you sometimes worry about Doris getting hurt. But I *honestly* don't believe it will happen. Of course, we can't be *quite* as above-board as we should like to, because that's how the world still is. But I shall never barge in on your life with her because I've got *all* of you *all* the time whether you're with me or not. And I can't wait for *anything* else but that you should feel happy. Fussing you about D. could only be if I was *jealous*, but then if I was jealous we shouldn't *truly, truly* be *absolutely* in love with each other. As it is, it's all so *frightfully simple*, really."

Hearing his steps, she covered the letter with her accounts book.

"Surely 'tis so, you ought to know. Any time's kissing time." Alcolom, gaily she sang, a faint but true contralto to his Ali, a caressing yet tremulous tenor. "Youth is the time for loving, the poets always say." She hit the keys in angry discord.

"Damn them, damn them, Rupert. But they're right, darling boy. Even this silly song tells me I'm being a fool."

"Oh, no, Contessa. Surely 'tis so. You ought to know. Any time's kissing time."

"Not for me, Rupert, not for me. I know I've always seemed young to all of you. I've tried to be. I didn't want you to have a frump for a mother. But I'm not any longer. My kissing time's over. Oh, don't let's cry over it. It happens to every woman. And it's not the end of the world, they say."

"How can *I* speak, Contessa? But surely no world could end because of Milton. We owe him a debt for christening Billy Pop, but surely . . ."

"I can't have you talk to me about it, Rupert. Your own mother. It isn't proper. But then I've lost the right to stop you. Billy and I have made you all grow up too quickly. But I have so terribly needed sweetness, Rupert. And you haven't always, all of you . . ."

"Well, we could hardly give you what Milton . . ."

"Oh, my dear boy! You've grown so cynical, but it's true. And poor Milton—he was a common little man but he was rather sweet to me."

"Poor Contessa." He kissed her forehead. "I suppose that's how love is. A cruel thing. But very simple."

"Simple! Oh, Rupert, how much you've to learn. It's cunning, cunning, darling heart, cunning all the time. It's two people and one of them's going to be hurt. That absurd little Yank thought he'd got me on a string, but I played him like a fish, Rupert. And now that it amuses me, I've thrown him back into the Atlantic where he belongs. Don't think I'm grieving for him, my dear. I wept for a moment for my lost youth, but not for him. I long ago learned to treat empty trifles for what they are. You'll have to learn to do the same, Rupert. One's either born into this world as a conquerer or one's not. You and I were. But it isn't simple, darling heart. It's a battle, a very old battle. In which we conquerors don't get hurt. The casualties are the little things, people like that red-haired girl you brought back here. Mona or Myrtle or something absurd. But you'll be a Conqueror. You're like me, dear boy. You carry your head high. Where were we? B-flat. 'Love has no charm, no meaning, till man has reached his prime!' Oh, that's horribly true, darling heart, I'm afraid, though youth can never believe it. There! Sensible poets at last."

They had no more to do now than to wait for luncheon to be cooked. Regan sat at the kitchen table poring over "The News of the World," running a licked finger along the lines of print. Sukey just sat. She wanted to mend the boys' things, but she was determined to apologize, and she feared that if she started on a new task, she would make it an excuse not to speak. She had done the unforgivable thing of insulting a servant, someone who couldn't answer back. No matter how good her intentions, she had not respected the pride of someone who had served them loyally and faithfully since they had been children; there was no possible way out of it but a direct, unshirking apology. It was what she would expect of her own children. "They have their responsibilities to us," she told her children, the oldest boy in his snotty's uniform on leave from Dartmouth, the eldest girl in her first evening dress (white), home for the hols, and all the smaller ones, on and on, to a rather indefinite blur, "but we have even greater responsibilities to them."

"Regan, I'm very sorry I spoke to you like that. I hope you will forgive me."

"Ah, you take em all too seriously, Miss Sukey. It was the left luggage ticket that done for im, you know. They couldn't identify on burned legs alone. Not to satisfy the jury."

"If it hadn't been for you, Regan, when we were little, I don't know what would have happened to us. From the very start they had no intention of being real parents at all."

"Met in Eastbourne. Quite the young lady she was. And she didn't know im two days, before she was out there in is bungalow."

"From the very start. No intention at all."

"Oh, drat it, Miss Sukey. Talk never stopped the fire of London nor brought the boys back to Blighty, them that was killed. Intention's easy enough, but doin's more difficult. When I first come to er, she was carrying Miss Gladys. And a better mother you never see. Nor an appier couple. Eed just ad is little stories out and everything in the garden was lovely. Then more and more come till it was you lot, the twins. And it about broke them. They ad'nt the money anywhere. Then the old lady takes Master Quentin. She never forgave im for that. To let is boy go like that without so much as a finger raised—'Stoker,' she said to me, 'I don't want nothin more to do with im.' But e made er. I don't blame im. It was is right. All the same, when Markie come, e was born in ate. As far as love from er goes, Master Marcus was better born dead. 'No intentions.' I've no patience with you. Intentions they ad from the start and good ones. As good as any of yours, Miss Sukey, with all your ideas aving fifteen kids and raisin them easy as cuttin butter. But intentions need a bit of splosh to back em up. And that they ad'nt got, not to live as their fancy told em."

"But thousands of poor people are wonderful parents, Regan."

"Ah, so they say; well, I've lived where they're very poor and I never seen it. You don't want to believe all you're told."

She turned back to the newspaper.

"It seems er sister ad seen it all in the cards only the week before she go down to Eastbourne. Everythin. Right down to the boiling of the ead."

"Any time's kissing time." Her laughter, her jaunty humming mixed with Rupert's caressing high notes to make him shudder. He put down his paint brush. He rolled Harun-al-Rashid's palace into a ball and threw it across the threadbare hearth-rug into the broken wicker basket. "Not all the perfumes of Arabia will expunge that sickly noise."

As Ali's voice against Alcolom's, so the sucking of Quentin's pipe against the popping gas fire. Sunk deep into the old nursery basket chair, his knees crouched high as a lectern for agreed wages and workers' management councils, Quentin spoke from far away, from a decent world of shared profits and consultations at every level. Gravely the Man Mountain addressed the odd Lilliputian (was he perhaps going to prove artistic? The craftsman has an honoured role).

"I'm sorry?" he asked with formal politeness.

His brother's young subaltern courtesy was like a kissed hand to Marcus's irritation. "Only," he said smiling, "that terrible sugary song. And happy Quentin not to hear 'Chu Chin Chow.'"

"I'm tone deaf, added to which I need to know this book for pre-lims, added to which it's one of the books which may change the face of everything."

"It ought to change its own face first. I've never seen such a horrible mud-green little book. Like slime off a crocodile's back."

"I'm more interested in the contents of books than their covers, to be quite honest, Mark."

"If you really don't care what books look like I should think you'd better not be quite so honest about it. Ugly books ought not to be allowed."

"Perhaps not. But there are more important things to get rid of first. Ugly conditions of life, wars."

"I can't see why you have to connect them. Anyway we had all this conversation with Tucker in form the other day after Thucydides. Wars and plagues are worth it to have Praxiteles."

"I didn't think we had much Praxiteles."

"I meant then, as you jolly well know. Anyway, I don't care much about Praxiteles. I mean just a way of living—like Louis Quatorze and Lorenzo de' Medici . . ."

"And men torn in four by horses and half the population dying before they are your age and hundreds crowded into hulks and dying of thirst before they reach the slave plantations."

"That doesn't make it any less important to have Michelangelo or the gardens at Versailles. Anyway, history shows you can't change human nature. Mr. Tucker said so. What are you proposing to do about it?"

"Let human nature try to change itself, that's all. Try this out, for instance." He slapped his book.

"*Self-Government in Industry*? I can't think of anything more awful. All I want is idleness. Anyone can govern me who likes as long as I can be idle and have time to live an elegant life."

"Like Billy Pop?"

"Billy Pop! A nice idleness he's got. See-no-evil monkeys on his desk."

"What's wrong with them?"

"What's wrong with whimsical, machine-made, plaster-cast monkeys painted chocolate and squashed plum! And you talk about altering the world! You'll make something like those terrible Bolshies."

"Don't believe everything you see in the *Daily Mail*. Why are the Bolsheviks awful?"

"You think I'm going to say because they've killed a lot of countesses. Well, I'm not. It's because the ballet, which is the one really new and exciting and beautiful thing we've created these days, had to leave Russia."

"Who said?"

"Nobody has to say it. It's obvious. That's why they're in France, that's why they're coming to London. And when they do, I mean to go to *Sleeping Beauty* twenty-four times at least. And *Scheherazade*, if it's done, a hundred times. Which is something to thank Lenin for."

"You don't know how I ached, darling one, for some beauty in my life after all those corridors and dormitories and hideous clothes and nuns. An author. And an author who had a house and an independence. An independence! That's what he told me, Rupert! It makes me laugh now to remember how I thought it would all be a miracle of beauty. I've tried all I can with this dreadful house. Especially here in the drawing-room. You do like my room, darling heart, don't you? Oh, Rupert, I saw such wonderful new lampshades last week. Like great turbans. So exciting and new. *Ballet Russe*, really. Oh, Rupert, I do hope you'll always care for beautiful things as I do. But you will. You're indecently beautiful for a young man. Do you know that, darling? And you *will* cram hard at your languages and go to those awful night classes, and give up this silly amateur acting and these awful Myrtles and Monas. Rupert, the overseas manager. Does it sound very pompous and grand to you, dear boy? Never mind. Be a bit grand for my sake. You've got to be rich. I need beauty so much, and beauty needs money. Billy will never make any. So I've only got you to rely on."

Actually, Quentin said, the dilemma isn't such a real one as would appear. Before you're an old man the problem's going to be how to provide for people's leisure. All the disagreeable jobs will be done by machines. The problem of the forties and fifties will be education for leisure. That's where you aesthetes will come in. I see, said Marcus, meanwhile I've got to stay on at school and get School Cert. and Higher Cert. and everything else so as to be sure of a job. Doing the Medea. It's all very confusing, isn't it? I mean, you wouldn't think the Medea was such a two-purpose education.

I think you're living in the past, Regan. Things are changing. A lot of board-school boys can get quite a lot of schooling nowadays if they want to. What with night schools and so on. The old ignorance is disappearing. Oh, we was ignorant all right, Miss Sukey. But we ad our bit of fun. And we knew ow to come in out of the rain. We wouldn't ave ad our eads boiled. Not owever good-looking e was.

Any time's kissing time. If you must be in these terrible amateur productions I do wish you could choose something a little less monotonous. I promise you, Countess, very soon no more amateur theatricals. There's a dear boy. Once in a way, if you must. Perhaps *The Chocolate Soldier*. You'd look so much more handsome as a hussar. But not too often, they take up so much time. Precious time when you ought to be at night classes getting on. I shan't be any more. I'm going to be a professional. Professional what? An actor. The only sort of pro a man can be. Oh, Rupert, don't be so absurd. Have you any idea of what it would be like? Paid a pittance and cheap theatrical digs. The selfishness, the vanity of it, Rupert. Just because you're passable-looking. How many become famous do you think out of the thousands of silly boys who join the back row of the chorus every year? And at least they can sing. You, my dear boy, hoot like an owl. I don't intend to listen to such conceited nonsense. And now let's play something pretty. Here you are. "At seventeen he's got it, oh, so badly with eyes of a tender blue. At twenty-four he's flirting, oh, so madly with eyes of a different hue." I hope you won't wait for twenty-four to find something better than that Myrna. Not that her eyes were blue. Green cat's-eyes like all red-heads. *And* she had a cast in one of them. I did think you'd have better taste. A professional actor! You won't get far if your leading ladies look like that. *She* won't make you money.

Do the figures add up? You lucky girl. They never have for me. I wanted to talk to you, Podge. I needed to talk to a woman. The twins'll be more sympathetic than I am. Not about this. The twins are virgins. Virgins are always prudes. They're bound to be. Especially where other women are concerned. But you won't be. I don't know what you mean. Oh, that. Oh! I'm not making any judgments. It's just what I've sensed. Remember I'm a man as well as an artist, and a man who's lived. I shan't say forgive me if I'm wrong, for I'm paying you a compliment. Virginity's a tight, ungenerous state of affairs. Anyway, I'm appealing to you for your understanding of another woman. Another woman? Whatever it is, I don't want to hear about it, Father. I'm the last one to be your confidante. My dear girl, as if I should. No, the woman's your mother. She's going to be so desperately unhappy in these next weeks, and she'll need another woman's understanding. We may not have liked him but he meant youth to her. And there won't be another. I don't think I want to hear what *you* have to say about the Countess. Now you *are* punishing me, Podge. That and the fact that I can do so little for her. Almost nothing. She needs the illusion of youth and I'm not good at supplying illusions. I thought perhaps I could give her the bright lights and the jazz that would help her to forget. The Piccadilly Hotel and blue trout. Did you know that she's like an excited child when she can net her own blue trout? I confess I shall get pleasure myself from seeing that again. It'll take ten pounds, Podge.

On their daughter's entry, the Carmichael parents instinctively doubled the fierceness of their battle. "Oh, to be mean about money!" "You leave me no money to be mean about." Elizabeth just walked on and out through the farther door which she closed behind her with her usual distant politeness. For a moment Sophie and James continued their exchange; then as Sophie was screaming, "Money for cigars, of course—but you can't find even ten pounds for your wife," she caught her husband's eye. In a moment both were in fits of laughter. They laughed until they were forced to sit on the sofa, holding their sides. "Oh, the sidey little prig." "Putting us in our places," Sophie answered. They could hardly speak for laughter. Then, "Darling," Sophie asked, "how can the young be so solemn?"

Through a palimpsest of ink and straying hair Margaret began to see some shape emerge from her ardent, sweating labours of imagination. At least between the elder Carmichaels stretched now a line of communication. The first of the more complex strands was woven.

Ten pounds, ten simple pounds, three rubbers at three a hundred up, partner, on the first rubber, and four hundred on the second, and game and third rubber to us, partner, three hundred up and two fifty for the rubber at five shillings a hundred, that's . . . (sums are so difficult to the tired head, so hard and refractory like a brick wall to the literary imagination) and an unexpected bonus declared on the Rubber Bearing shares; have to inform you that your quarterly balance stands at three hundred and thirty-three pounds fourteen and sevenpence, no reason at all why not three quid or even ten quid on, know you aren't a racing man, Matthews, but put your shirt on Meg Merrilees, as a humble admirer and imitator of the great laird of Abbotsford can hardly refuse a tip, fifty to one, five hundred pounds, here you are, Podge, your bread has come back over the waters quite a sizeable loaf and your mother can net blue trout until her arm aches, but everything depends on that first ten pounds, ten little sovereigns, I wish I had ten quid, two hundred quid, two hundred and fifty, in a box, a black box. Getting, getting we lay waste our powers. The power of the word. A small beginning, that was all he asked—to use his eyes and ears each day on the familiar, to find all heaven in a shell. (Or was it a petal? or again a rainbow? But a rainbow was less easily come by.)

As he passed the dining-room door (if he couldn't be sure of ten pounds, then at least there would be pheasant) he heard the mewing of the kittens. Helping himself to sherry from the cut-glass decanter on the mahogany sideboard, bending with one moment's acute giddiness and an aching knee (art is no easy mistress) he examined against the scarlet velvet the exact colours of the small animals, and as usual the artist's true eye applied to the simple, the ordinary, the wayside pimpernel revealed a miracle: the black on the flanks of the black-and-white kitten was in truth a rusty red, and there where the fur was thickest on the tail a cock-feather bottle-green, but where black patches ran down its small feet they proved the darkest Prussian blue; as for the ginger kitten, it was to careful scrutiny a blend of apricot, yes, and, by Jove, rose pink. With canvas and paints the miracle could at once be recorded, but as it was, the details could only be stored away. If he but had a writer's notebook, the entry would go under K for kitten—to await inclusion in the wider vision. Nevertheless detail was the thing, art was a simplification, a selection and an exactitude. The tortoise-shell kitten mewed loudly. "Poor little devils," Billy Pop said aloud. Then straightening up, he felt refreshed. A moment's compassion is worth volumes of theory to a writer.

There was one chap, Markie, who couldn't write at all. I'd told them to put their names, numbers, and platoons on the top right-hand corner of the test paper. His was a total blank. Of course the Colonel fumed and created hell. The chap had been sent back for special instruction. Probably the company commander had got the bumf just as they were going up the line and so he recommended the first name he could. And the chap didn't say anything; he wasn't going to refuse a Blighty leave, why should he? But the Colonel felt he'd been made a fool of. We want officer material here, Matthews, and they send us cannon fodder. So the chap was packed off back to France. With luck he'd have missed a spell of front-line duty.

Something he said stuck with me though. He was talking to a group of other duds before they entrained. They were standing there in the great court of Trinity with the sun shining on the russet brick and grey stone, and the fountain sparkling, and some spring flowers or other in the beds. I shouldn't think most of them knew where they were or noticed for that matter. Just another kip and a place to booze in. Across the yard came two or three dons in their

gowns and mortar-boards. And this chap said, in his country accent
—Somerset or Devon, I should think—"Look at they rooks." Then
he pointed to that figure over the great doorway—Henry the Eighth
or whatever it is. "Oh, no use putting up scarecrows. Rooks don't
scare easy if they've found a tidy field of barley or oats. And I don't
reckon there's a better field of oats than this in all the bloomin'
land." It was the relating of one experience to the other that struck
me, as much as the fresh country language. The Colonel couldn't
have done it to save his thick, red neck. But the man couldn't write
his name, so he was cannon fodder. I knew then what I wanted to do
when the great day came. Don't think I'm sentimental. They must
all be given a trial, but of course many will never profit from it. The
half literates are usually no good. There was one chap in that very
intake. He could write his name all right, but after that he'd written
a lot of nonsense—fittoon, foottoon, fottoon, fattoon, and God
knows what. Trying to write platoon, I suppose.

"I should have thought that was original enough," Marcus said.
But Quentin, having made his testimony, had returned to workers'
representation in socialized industry. Marcus painted fittoon and fottoon in green and then interwove them with fattoon and futtoon in
purple, then with black India ink he wrote beneath these strange
words, "on foot," "on fat foot," "on hot fat foot," "on hot fat foot
in India." But at last he wrote again, fottoon, foottoon, fittoon, fattoon, and he liked them better, with their suggestion of baboons and
spittoons and feet and fits that needed no overt expression. Looking
at his brother so solemnly intent on crocodile slime, he felt quite
sure that of the few who would ever see what was new, he himself
would be one. He laughed with sheer pleasure at this certainty.

Gladys laughed as Billy Pop folded the two five-pound notes and
placed them in his waistcoat pocket. He hummed a few bars of "Chu
Chin Chow." He smiled a warm, humorous smile at her before he
left her room. "And people say that Micawber's an impossible character. They haven't met me, you know. I always believe that something will turn up. And it usually does!" When his observation drew
no laugh from her, he looked to see if at least it had angered her, but
she was staring at the wall, smiling and apparently entirely forgetful of his presence. He hummed more jauntily and went away. For a
moment his parting steps brought her back from Alfred's kisses,

from the tip of his tongue tickling an entrance between her lips, but only for a moment.

What you get out of it anyway? Kids! When Emmie ad er second they ad to crush its ead with the forceps; it was either er or im and they took away four pints of blood. Old arry Tate's got the proper word for that—very nice, I don't think. Oh, you'd soon be sick of them. Nappies, rubber teats, and up every night like they was with Master Marcus bed-wetting and sleep-walking. I don't think I should, Regan, I'm very used to it. How does Marcus get these huge holes in his football socks? To hear him you'd never think he moved an inch on the field. Ah, you put a good face on it becos you don't want to see things untidy, but you don't like it. Like it? Of course I don't like it, but it's got to be done. Look at these cuffs of Rupert's, somebody's got to turn them. And anyway it wouldn't be the same. They'd be my own children. And the man I loved would have given them to me. Well, fancy you to talk like that, Miss Sukey. Still waters run deep, eh? But still, what's marriage? I was a MUG. Oh, Regan, how absurd you are, every woman, every natural woman anyway wants a husband and children. Oh, I didn't mean, I didn't . . . You think I've never ad me chances. Well, you're wrong. There was a Canadian come after me. French e was. Well, I've always ad a taste for a bit of oo-la-la after Monser Jools. And then me cookin the French way drew im, I expect. Anyway, e was all right—to look at, I mean, and e was well supplied where it matters. But . . . well, she asked me not to, warned me against im. I'd be ungrateful, she said, after they'd took me in without a reference. Mrs. Marshall wouldn't give it on account of the drinkin. Where'd I be, she said, if it wasn't for them? So I promised. And now I'm past it. I didn't like tellin im though. But there you are. I expect she was right. There were hundreds let down by them Canadians and Aussies. There was I waitin at the church, waitin at the church.

And when he fancied he was past love, it was then he met his last love, and he loved her better ever than before. I suppose you will one day, dear boy. Will what, Countess? Meet your last love. You can't just have an old mother, you know, to grace the end of your table when you're rich and famous. But do choose someone with style, darling. A woman can make or mar her husband's career. I've thought about that. I don't believe it would do unless she was professional too. Marry a professional! Well, you've started all right. Bringing that tart what's-her-name home here. I could see at once what she was. And if I'd turned my back for a minute you'd have had her up in your bedroom. You've begun your filthy tricks early. She's not to come here again, Rupert, do you understand? She's not to come here again. I won't have filthy harlots in the house. I've been so careful to bring up the twins as happy, healthy-minded girls. And Marcus is only a boy. She's not to come here again, do you understand? Oh, shut up, you silly strumpet! You've paraded your cheap adulteries in front of your children until . . . If you do that again, I'll smack your face, Countess, and I can hit harder than you. Do you know what you've done? You've hit your mother. Yes, and if my father had done it long ago . . . Leave me alone, how dare you? You're hurting my arm. Rupert, you've hurt me. Go up to your room. I don't want ever to speak to you again. I'm not pretending either. You've horrified me. Oh, wonderful son to astonish such a mother. For I have astonished you, haven't I, Mother? I *was* pretending, you see. Perhaps you'll believe me now that I can be an actor. I believe that you can be a rough, foul-mouthed lout. I'll tell you this, Rupert, you'll go on the stage and you'll fail. You smell of failure like your father with all your sloppy good looks and your weak mouth and your chocolate-box smile. They'll throw things at you and I hope they throw them hard.

Elizabeth rejoined her sister in the sewing room. Jane looked up for a moment from her book. "Were they throwing things, Liz, or was it only nasty words?" "Nasty words, of course, they stepped them up for my benefit." "But you didn't show, darling, I hope?" "Of course not." From below, their mother's laugh came, a jangling treble scale. "Oh, dear, hysteria." But now there followed their father's raucous bellow. "They can't both . . ." "But what . . ." "I think," said Elizabeth, "that perhaps they're laughing at *me*." "Oh, Liz! you've brought them together. You're a little healer. A go-between. A peacemaker." Jane commenced that series of gulping sounds which always evidenced her delight at her own occasional sharpnesses; and soon Elizabeth, in recollection of so many previous occasions of Jane's self-delight, began to laugh also. Their giggles punctuated the laughter of their parents. A child of ten might have guessed that it was a happy home.

Margaret wrote the last sentence with care and satisfaction; then she read the whole passage over. It was the final sentence that gave shape, of course; and yet the shape irked her. All the patterns of conflict and cohesion were present in the laughter. The last sentence was the master stroke, was herself scoring. She flushed red at the thought, erased the sentence, and sat back. For the first time for months she felt contented.

The front doorbell rang. Regan, hearing it, said, "About time. We don't want the ducks dried up." "Oh, dear, Regan," Sukey cried, remembering the hour and the importance of it to well-fed old girls, "you must put them into a cooler oven. We can't have anything go wrong."

Billy Pop, hearing the bell's tone and remembering all that depended on his mother's amiability, gave himself another sherry. "I am Chu Chin Chow from China," he bawled. Gladys thought, Of course I was right to lend, and if it comes to a battle I shall tell the old girls about it. Quentin had said war's foul; but Alfred: war's a bad business, old girl. And there's only one rule—make sure you win. Quentin, looking up, said: "Beginners, please." And Marcus answered: "Five minutes, please. How lucky," he said, "that Rupert has told us all about the rules of the theatre." The Countess seized a new music sheet from the piano top. "I left my love in Avalon," she sang. "Have I got the ragtime rhythm right, dear boy?" "Yes, Contessa darling." "And sailed the sea," sang Rupert.

The bell rang again. "Whatever it is," Elizabeth Carmichael thought, "whatever it is that's coming—a sudden fortune from an unknown uncle in Johannesburg, a mysterious letter from an unknown quarter, a fair young man from next door, a dark young man from over the sea—I'm open to it." Exulting, Margaret reached the bottom step, crossed the hall, opened the front door. There was Mouse—in her pepper-and-salt tailor-made, a severe tricorne pulled down over her pepper-and-salt hair.

"How ever long have you been there, Aunt Mouse?"

"My dear Margaret, when you get to my age you'll cease to count the minutes. In any case"—she kissed her great-niece—"it's your job to keep time, not mine. How is the dancing?"

"There's so much noise I didn't hear the bell."

Indeed the cacophony of voices raised in song appeared to overwhelm Miss Rickard a little, for she stepped back from the front door. A gust of wind blew among the green feathers of the parrot that sat on her shoulder and set it shrieking.

"Hush, Mr. Poll, don't you add to the noise. At least one can make no mistake about its being a happy home." She set her lips in a twisted, ironic smile.

The Family Sunday Play

Act 1

SCENE: *The first floor drawing-room of Mrs. William Matthews at No. 52 Gillbrook Street, London S.W.1. Left, a fireplace with coal fire burning; right, a door leads on to landing and staircase; backstage, casement windows with curtains (through which a revolving light may show the falling leaves of late autumn, swirling in the high wind). A deep sofa and two deep arm-chairs in flowered cretonne, with many cushions, round and sausage-shaped in bright primary colours; a pouffe in the same cretonne; two or three Victorian imitation Hepplewhite chairs and two Victorian imitation Louis Seize tables on which are black bowls and Wedgwood blue jugs filled with bronze and yellow chrysanthemums; a rose-pink Wilton carpet; at one end of the chimney-piece a late Dresden figure of a shepherd with a goat and at the other a shepherdess with a lamb; in the centre a pewter mug filled with cape gooseberries and honesty pods. Above the chimney-piece there is a copy of "The Holy Family." A grand piano on which is a white Spanish shawl with red and green embroidered roses and on this some silver-framed photographs and a china bowl containing potpourri. At the piano Mrs. Matthews is seated on a piano stool playing and singing "I left my love in Avalon." She is a slim, dark, gipsy-like woman in her late forties, smartly dressed in a blue gabardine coat-frock with patent-leather appliqué and a toque made of artificial violets. Beside her, facing upstage, is her nineteen-year-old son Rupert, tall, handsome, and fair-haired; he joins her in the song, both are almost guying the ragtime rhythm, and their gaiety becomes more hectic as the sound of voices and steps outside the door grows nearer. It is clear they have recently been quarrelling violently and they are now putting on a show for visitors. (Amateur producers, whose cast finds it difficult to make this "clear" state of affairs clear, may decide that it is easier for the curtain to go up on the actors quarrelling in mime; the doorbell should then ring, and the actors start to play and sing.) The door opens and Margaret Matthews, a tall girl of seventeen, with dark untidy hair and a general air of having "come down to earth" somewhat uncomfortably (a testing air for the young actress to assume) enters with Mouse, an elderly woman of sixty-five or so dressed in a rather mannishly cut grey tweed skirt and coat and a tricorne hat. On her shoulder is perched a green Amazon parrot. (Unless a well-trained bird is available, it would be wise to substitute a stuffed parrot, but one that is provided with mechanical locomotion and speech—"Polly, what's your name," "Scratch a Poll," etc., form all the simple vocabulary that is necessary. More ambitious producers, or less well-equipped ones, will no doubt prefer to dispense with any parrot, live or stuffed, and leave its appearance to the imagination of the audience.)*

MRS. MATTHEWS JUNIOR: Should I vamp here, dear boy?

MOUSE: I have never known her to do anything else when men were about, Rupert.

MRS. MATTHEWS JUNIOR: Mouse! Really! Before my own children! But how lovely to see you, darling! It's so nice that you've been able to spare time for us before you go off again. Where is it this time? Patagonia?

MOUSE: No. Nothing so exotic. Just Constantinople. Though after being cooped up for those four miserable war years in this overcrowded island I should be perfectly justified in seeking the Kalahari Desert. But my desert days are over. The small taste of Tunis after the Armistice told me that. Keep to the tourist beaten tracks from now on.

MRS. MATTHEWS JUNIOR: I don't believe it for a moment. And I'm sure Mr. Polly looks as though he could cross the Sahara unaided. Would I be wrong, or has he lost a few feathers on top?

MOUSE: Wrong. I'm the only one that's going bald. Well, Mag, you haven't answered my first question. How's the dancing?

MARGARET: My left foot is less painful than the right, Aunt Mouse. Somehow the little boys of Claremont School seem to tread on it less often.

MOUSE: Little boys? What little boys?

MARGARET: The boys of Claremont Preparatory School. They come to Miss Lamont's for dancing class each Saturday morning.

MOUSE: You don't mean to say Miss Lamont . . .

MRS. MATTHEWS JUNIOR (*interrupting*): And of course, as you may suppose, Mouse, all the little boys are desperately in love with our Mag—notes and *billets doux* and, no doubt, a bunch of roses from the head prefect, the stems a little sticky from the sticky little fingers, but no less a genuine offering of love. Oh! I can imagine it all.

MARGARET: You do.

MRS. MATTHEWS JUNIOR (*more desperately interrupting, sings, playing the little tune on the piano*): Sir, she said, sir, she said. Your face is your fortune, my pretty maid. (*She breaks off singing and rattles on in speech.*) But your *feet* are *your* fortune, Mag. Well, of course, seventeen can hardly be expected to care about the broken hearts of thirteen-year-olds. She wants to break older hearts, Mouse. I tell her that if she would get out of these old maid's browns and greys . . . (*Rupert smiles.*) No, I know what I'm saying, Rupert. I don't make gaffes so easily. Mouse *chose* the single state. That's not old-maidish; it's just being less foolish than other women. But don't you think, Mouse, if she wore warmer colours? She's got beautiful eyes. You have, Mag. But you don't give them a showing.

MOUSE: Warmer colours won't help her feet. Her feet are the source of her art, Clara. Like a painter's eyes.

MRS. MATTHEWS JUNIOR: I don't agree with you at all, Mouse. If Mag has one really good feature—and everybody has one—it's her eyes.

MOUSE: If she lets her feet get misshapen, she won't get a showing anywhere. What can Miss Lamont be about, letting a ballet dancer . . .

MARGARET: It's been decided that I shouldn't go on with ballet . . .

MOUSE: Decided? Who's decided? What do you mean, decided?

MRS. MATTHEWS JUNIOR: What indeed? Nothing's decided, Margaret. You know that.

MARGARET: Well, then action's been taken without decision.

MRS. MATTHEWS JUNIOR: Action? That's just what we need. All this can be discussed later, but at the moment poor Mouse is dying for a glass of sherry. Take some action, Rupert. Stir your stumps. You're not there just for your beauty. What do you think this ridiculous boy wants to do, Mouse? Go on the stage! And with a wonderful business career ahead of him!

MOUSE: One thing at a time, please, Clara. What's this about Margaret giving up ballet? Why haven't I been told?

MRS. MATTHEWS JUNIOR: My dear Mouse, the girl's whole future is hardly something one could discuss through Coutt's Bank and the camel post, is it? If you *will* go to the ends of the earth . . . I intended to have a good long chat with you this afternoon. About that and all sorts of other things that just wouldn't do in letters.

MOUSE: You could find time to write about your own money difficulties, Clara.

MRS. MATTHEWS JUNIOR: They were very pressing, Mouse. I hope everyone's not going to bully me. Today's not a very easy day for me, Mouse. *You* understand, dear boy, don't you. Well, then, do something. If Mouse doesn't want a sherry, I want a cocktail. Mix me a Bronx like Milton showed you. Oh, we've been so American, Mouse, these last months. (*Playing and singing feverishly*) But it's all quite over, over here. Oh, well. Oh, Rupert, do something. Act, dear boy. Now's your chance to show us. Prove you can act.

RUPERT (*to audience*): Prove that I can act! I've had one feeble line since the curtain went up. And now I'm to play the butler. (*Exits as Mouse speaks.*)

MOUSE: Why has Margaret given up her ballet?

MRS. MATTHEWS JUNIOR: If anything, ballet's given her up. Look at her. We've always known that if she grew too much . . .

MARGARET: That's not fair. We agreed that if I outgrew Pavlova . . .

MRS. MATTHEWS JUNIOR: Outgrew Pavlova! Outgrew Pavlova! I'm sick to death of hearing that parrot cry. Oh, not you, Mr. Polly. You've been very good. He's lost almost all that shrieking, Mouse. He's quite a grown-up parrot, now. Outgrown Pavlova! Anyone would think Pavlova was a bad habit like nail-biting, instead of a very great dancer and a very beautiful woman.

MOUSE: But if it's really so, Clara, does the girl want to go on with dancing? Do you, Margaret, ordinary ballroom dancing?

MRS. MATTHEWS JUNIOR: Now, Mouse darling, you mustn't judge everyone by yourself. Not all girls are bluestockings. Why, at seventeen I could have danced all night. In any case she's got to think of earning her living. We can't support these children forever. That's why I jumped at Miss Lamont's offer.

MOUSE: What offer?

MRS. MATTHEWS JUNIOR: For her to do a little teaching.

MOUSE: I don't think that's quite straight of Miss Lamont. I'm surprised at her. She receives my Bankers' Orders regularly and then . . . (*Rupert reappears with drinks, bottles, and a shaker on tray.*)

MRS. MATTHEWS JUNIOR: Oh, darling heart, heaven-sent boy. And with a perfect Bronx! Isn't he clever, Mouse? Give Mouse a sherry. And so handsome! And the silly boy's covering those wonderful features with yellow paint when he ought to be a hussar with glorious whiskers.

MARGARET: Aunt Mouse, I think you ought to know . . .

MRS. MATTHEWS JUNIOR: Don't be so egotistical, Mag. For once the conversation wasn't about you. But now you've begun, we'd better tell Mouse, shall we?

MARGARET: Please, Mother.

MRS. MATTHEWS JUNIOR: She's embarrassed, Mouse, because after all the money you've spent on her dancing, she's been wasting a lot of time writing stories.

MARGARET (*interrupting*): But that isn't it . . . my writing's nothing to do . . . you know very well . . .

MRS. MATTHEWS JUNIOR: But Mouse won't mind. She might even make a little pin-money by it, mightn't she, Mouse? Who knows? (*Margaret has tried to interrupt her but her mother has talked over her.*)

MOUSE: Perhaps the girl would prefer to take some course in writing, or what about going to the University if she's too tall for ballet? I should like my great-niece to be a writer. It's a fulfilled life. Mrs. Belloc Lowndes . . .

MRS. MATTHEWS JUNIOR: Oh, really, Mouse. She's got to *earn* her living. Why, *Billy* can hardly make a living out of writing.

MOUSE: He's almost made one out of not writing.

MRS. MATTHEWS JUNIOR: Now, that's not nice. Just because he's a perfectionist like you, Mouse. I won't have my poor Billy abused in his absence. (*She goes to the door, opens it, and calls*) Billy! Billy! Leave your old books and come down and talk to Mouse.

MOUSE: It's Miss Lamont I've got to talk to. She has no right to take

full fees and then use the gel as a teacher. It's very near to false pretences . . . (*As Mouse talks, Mrs. Matthews, who is beginning to
despair of deflecting her from the fatal subject, makes a last desperate effort, by addressing her remarks to the parrot.*)

MRS. MATTHEWS JUNIOR: Well, Mr. Polly, I hope you're taking a
nice supply of nuts to Constantinople. Or will they convert you to
Turkish Delight? Will they, Poll? Will they? (*She puts out her
finger and withdraws it only just in time.*) You bloody bird! No,
no, Mouse. Mr. Polly and I were just talking Pygmalion talk!
Swear at you, Mr. Polly? Not bloody likely!

MOUSE: Has Miss Lamont given you no explanation, Clara?

MRS. MATTHEWS JUNIOR (*at the door, calling*): Billy! Billy!

MOUSE: Will you listen to me, Clara, please?

MRS. MATTHEWS JUNIOR (*apparently defeated, in a resigned voice*):
Yes, Mouse. (*The front doorbell rings.*) Saved by the bell. (*She
sinks on to the piano stool exhausted, and as Billy Pop appears
at the door she begins to play and sing with imitated piety, "Safe
into the haven, guide, oh, receive my soul at last." The others form
a tableau of astonishment on which the curtain descends.*)

Hearing the front doorbell, Quentin laid aside his book. "Second
Act, beginners, please," he said. Marcus painted a great eye to the
peacock's feather that Narcissus held in his hand as he gazed into the
pool; then he laid down the brush. "We're on," he said, getting up
from his chair.

Gladys, too, put aside her writing. But before leaving her room,
she took Alfred's snapshot from behind the photograph of her parents which stood in a red Morocco frame on top of the trunks. She
kissed it. "Wish the Matthews brood good luck, old man," she said.
"We're going over the top."

Sukey put aside her mending. "I suppose I must go and make myself beautiful for Granny." She looked up and caught a sudden
glimpse of Regan's eye that recalled the young Stoker of their early
years; but that placid eye was set now in such disgusting and gro-
tesque contours of sagging grey flesh and deeply scored wrinkles,
beaded with blackheads, that she felt a momentary terror of being
alive beside such a memorial to the corruption of the flesh. Then,
ashamed, she put her hand on Regan's shoulder for a moment as she
went out of the kitchen. She felt an impulse to bend down and kiss

the mole-marked cheek. "Dear Regan" was all she would say, or rather, whisper; and then, perhaps, "Dear Regan, do you remember the slide we made at High Bank and Gladys splitting her knickers?" As suddenly, she felt that she had no right to organize Regan's memories.

As she came up the basement stairs, the bell sounded loudly again. She called up to the drawing-room, "Can't somebody let Granny in? I'm not tidy yet." But only chatter and the piano replied. She went to the front door herself. As she opened it, the wind blew a strong smell of camphor from her grandmother's sables into her face; but almost as though in revenge a strong smell of rich gravies drew the greedy old woman eagerly indoors, yet set her black Pomeranian bitch, less gross in her tastes, yapping frantically at her heels. She said, "Gran," and kissed the old woman's veil-netted cheek. She murmured, "Noise and kitchen smells and not properly ready," but the old lady turned to the uniformed man still at the door of the Packard with its swelling, gas-balloon top. "That will be all right now, Colyer. You'll see to your own ale, won't you?"

"Colyer will be welcome below stairs," Sukey said. But as though in answer, a whiff of pheasant, too gamey almost for the old lady, made Sukey wince, Pom yelp, and Colyer touch his cap respectfully. "Thank you, Madam," he said. "About three." Then, as Regan's voice came droning, "The little nipper turned to me. Ain't mother goin to av none?" Mrs. Matthews Senior said, "Stoker fidgets Colyer, my dear. He's a bit of an old maid. He likes everything just so." Sukey frowned at the justice of the implied criticism and turned away to shut out her grandmother's distaste for their home. Mrs. Matthews drew her hand out of her muff and put it gently on her granddaughter's shoulder, impelling herself and Pom finally and irrevocably into No. 52. She bent down and kissed Sukey's cheek. "Dear Sukey, do you remember 'I'se made scrambubbled eggs'? Oh dear, all those lovely farmhouse eggs wasted. But you *had* made toast, darling. How *is* the cookery, Sue?"

Act 2

The curtain goes up on the same drawing-room scene. It is ten minutes later. The whole household, except for Regan, is present

to meet their two intimate visitors. Down left Miss Rickard
(Mouse) sits upright with Mr. Polly on her shoulder and a sherry
in her hand; near her stands Margaret Matthews. Then towards
backstage Mrs. Matthews Junior at the piano with a refilled Bronx;
backstage Rupert Matthews, leaning on the piano. Centre back-
stage Mr. Matthews Junior, a handsome, boyish, curly-headed man
in tweeds; only a slight pot belly, over-rosy cheeks, and constant
belching reveal how sedentary is the life of this outdoor-looking
man; he is seated in an arm-chair, whisky and soda in one hand,
the other hand held dramatically to his forehead. Down centre stage
Quentin Matthews stands, his back to the audience, addressing the
family. His loose old tweed jacket is bound with leather at the el-
bows. His thin body is stooped at the shoulders. By him Marcus
Matthews sits cross-legged, looking up at Quentin, his back to the
audience. Down right Granny Matthews, a tall, handsome, ample
old woman, all sables and black velour hat, sits in an arm-chair
holding a handkerchief to her eyes with one hand and a glass of
sherry in the other; on her lap sits Pom (unless a highly trained
Pomeranian dog—now an unfashionable breed—can be obtained,
it will be sufficient to employ a clockwork dog). By her side
stands Sukey Matthews, an upright, flaxen-haired girl. The whole
grouping should be reminiscent of (i.e., not exactly like) a con-
ventional family photograph. As the curtain rises Quentin is speak-
ing, but his voice is drowned by Mrs. Matthews Junior's loud play-
ing of the chords up and down the length of the keyboard.

MOUSE (*half rising, angrily*): Be quiet, Clara. Control your temper. We want to hear what the boy has to say.

MRS. MATTHEWS JUNIOR: We! I have no intention of listening to
another word of his priggish conceit.

GRANNY MATTHEWS: How can you talk of your own son like that?
When he's been wounded, too.

MRS. MATTHEWS JUNIOR: And haven't his words wounded me? His
own parents cheats and liars. These are the sorts of wounds that
don't heal.

QUENTIN: Now, Granny, my wounds have nothing to do with it at
all. We must keep to the point.

GRANNY MATTHEWS: But we're so proud of you, Quintus.

QUENTIN: Thank you, dear, but what's more important is that Rupert and Marcus and the girls shouldn't have their lives crippled from the start.

MRS. MATTHEWS JUNIOR: Crippled! (*She plays a loud chord in the bass.*) We've clothed and fed and educated you. What more do you want? (*She addresses the audience.*) Every year when they were children I made them give to the Barnardo's homes out of their money-box. But the lesson's been wasted.

MR. MATTHEWS JUNIOR (*rising and crossing over to his wife, he puts his hand with dramatized affection on her shoulder*): No, old dear. They believe that we've hurt them somehow. God knows how they've come to think it. But now they must say their say. Wounds are bad enough, but festering wounds!

MARCUS (*turning to the audience*): If only one of my sisters were ambitious to be a field-hospital nurse, she could learn from all this.

QUENTIN: We've absolutely no wish to be unfair, Father. We know you and Mother find it difficult to live on your income. How you deal with that is, of course, entirely your own affair. But we have a right to defend ourselves, to consider our own lives. Careers, professions, what we're going to make of life.

MRS. MATTHEWS JUNIOR: Careers! Professions! I don't want to hear another word about it. Is that what my children think life means? Then we *have* failed.

MR. MATTHEWS JUNIOR: She's right, you know, as usual. Getting and spending! It's not enough.

MOUSE: Spending alone seems to have been enough for their parents. And money that they had no right to. (*She puts her arm round Margaret's waist.*) This poor girl's precious feet ruined!

GRANNY MATTHEWS: My little Sukey no better than an unpaid kitchen maid! (*She puts her hand on Sukey's arm.*)

MOUSE: It's being made a fool of that I shall never forgive, Clara.

GRANNY MATTHEWS: It's the lies, Will, that have hurt me so. The unspoken lies. (*The twins disengage themselves from the two old women.*)

MRS. MATTHEWS JUNIOR: Unspoken lies! What nonsense all this is. You've condemned Billy unheard, Granny. On the basis of a lot of spiteful children's tittle-tattle.

MARGARET (*to herself*): If he had been heard, the lies would have been spoken.

MRS. MATTHEWS JUNIOR: What did you say? What was it? Come on! Some more of your spinsterish spite. Get out of here! Go on! We've no place here for malicious old maids. No wonder your father can't work with all this stifling sourness around him. What children for a creative man! Get out of here, all of you. Do you hear me?

MR. MATTHEWS JUNIOR: No, no, my dear girl. Don't let their hysteria touch you. You're too clear-headed for that.

MOUSE: *Their* hysteria!

MR. MATTHEWS JUNIOR: Yes, Mouse, I'm afraid so. But of course Clara and I are to blame. We've let them live in a fairy-tale nest up there in the nursery for far too long. We should have pushed them out into real life long ago.

RUPERT (*to audience*): Mr. Darling reproves Wendy.

GRANNY MATTHEWS: Oh, Will, how can you say that about Quintus? All the best years of his youth spent out there in the horror of the trenches.

MR. MATTHEWS JUNIOR: My dear Mother, Quentin's been a hero. God help me, how do you think I feel criticizing him? An old crock like myself that they wouldn't take. But it has to be faced that in a sense, in an important sense too, he's only just learning what reality is. War has its fineness, its heroism, and its horror. Young chaps like Quentin must plan to see that it doesn't happen again. But everyday reality's much more grim. It has neither heroism nor horror. And Maggy wren, leave wit to your mother, my dear. You're a hedgerow bird.

GLADYS (*roaring with laughter*): Maggie a wren! Do you know what a wren looks like, Pop? Go on, be a wren, Mag.

(*Margaret stands on one leg pretending to be a stork.*)

RUPERT (*joining her, does the same*): Where shall we make our nest, Mrs. Wren?

(*They make a giant one-legged tableau centre stage.*)

GLADYS: Let's hope there aren't any nature passages in your memoirs, Pop.

(*The children laugh and are joined by the smiles of Mouse and even Granny Matthews*)

MRS. MATTHEWS JUNIOR: How can you encourage them in these feeble, childish jokes? You say you want them to grow up. What sort of example are you setting them, Mouse? And you, Granny?

(*Laughter continues and she bangs the keys.*) Will you stop it at once, you stupid children? (*The noise sets Pom yapping.*) Get that old bitch out of the room.

RUPERT: Now, really, you go too far, Countess. Poor Granny!

MRS. MATTHEWS JUNIOR: You think every woman uses a harlot's language. There's the sort of career your precious grandson wants. On the stage with tarts. (*She shouts at Granny Matthews and Pom yaps again.*) I said, put that old bitch out, did you hear me? Sukey? Put the dog *out*. (*Aroused by the shouting and Pom's yapping, Polly begins to shriek.*) And that filthy bird! There'll be fur and feather flying all over my Wilton carpet any moment. I will not have animals fighting in my drawing-room.

MOUSE: They are not fighting, Clara. And no one says what Polly must or must not do but me.

GRANNY MATTHEWS: I'm sure you wouldn't fight with pretty Polly parrot, would you, Pom? And you're not old, are you? Though your mistress may be.

MRS. MATTHEWS JUNIOR: Well, if she's not old she's got mange and I won't have that in my drawing-room. Will you take those creatures out, Sukey? You're so famous for your kindness to animals.

GRANNY MATTHEWS: Sukey wouldn't put a little dog out of the room, would she, Pom? Please, Sukey, Pom says, don't put me out.

MOUSE: My dear Mrs. Matthews, don't encourage Clara to act like a spoiled hysteric. There's no question of anyone touching our pets unless we wish it.

MARGARET: But do wish it, Aunt Mouse. This is so important to us, and we shall never be able to discuss it while the Countess is issuing royal decrees.

QUENTIN: I think Mag's right, Granny. Pom'll be all right on her own while we thrash all our problems out.

GRANNY MATTHEWS: Well, I don't know, really. I don't see why poor Pom should suffer. But if you think it will help, Quintus. Tuck her little handkerchief under her collar, Sukey, before you leave her. How our little mouth does water nowadays, doesn't it, since we lost our teeth?

MOUSE: I'm not at all happy, Quentin, at giving way to your mother's ridiculous moods. But since it was my spoiling her as a girl that's at the root of the trouble, I mustn't let you children suffer. Don't put him on any family heirloom, Sukey. He's a bit erratic where he does his biggies, now he's a grown-up parrot.

SUKEY (*with Polly on her shoulder and Pom in her arms*):   But where shall I put them, Countess?

MRS. MATTHEWS JUNIOR: Oh, on the landing, anywhere. They're such good friends, it seems. I suppose they can manage the stairs, being so young and agile.

(*Sukey puts the parrot and the Pomeranian dog outside the door and returns to her place by Granny Matthews.*)

MOUSE: Well, now that you've spent your ugly temper on dumb animals that can't help themselves, Clara, perhaps you'll let us hear what Quentin has to say.

(*Quentin is about to speak when Mr. Matthews Junior feels that he should assert his place as paterfamilias.*)

MR. MATTHEWS JUNIOR: Fire ahead, old man. Give us the glorious revolution. I'll promise not to chuck the Great Seal into the Thames.

QUENTIN: Look, Father, you fought a battle to be a writer. You've said yourself how Grandfather opposed . . .

GRANNY MATTHEWS: Oh, Will, how could you say that? Your father took the greatest interest when your first story came out in the *Strand*.

MR. MATTHEWS JUNIOR: Oh, yes, when the meagre allowance he greeted my marriage with forced me to write for popular magazines, the old boy was delighted. But I would remind you, Mother, that my first published story appeared in *The Savoy* alongside something of Lionel Johnson's. That was the sort of promise that the Guvnor's meanness nipped in the bud. If he had ever heard of *The Savoy* you may be sure that he'd have thrown any copy he found on the drawing-room fire, even at the risk of putting it out. To give him his due, his prudery always defeated his parsimony if only by a short head.

(*Granny Matthews subsides into tears.*)

QUENTIN: Well, whatever the rights or wrongs, Pater, can't you listen to our hopes and ambitions with sympathy? Three of us are grown up now, and the twins and Marcus soon will be. We're trying to understand what that means, what life is.

MRS. MATTHEWS JUNIOR: That's all very well for you, Quentin. Of course we know that you must make your own life. Nothing's too good for our returned soldiers. But you must have a sense of proportion, my dear. Marcus and the twins are children. They can't be considered in the same terms.

SUKEY: But that's just what Quentin is doing. If you and Father don't care what happens to the family, Quentin does. He's going to stand by us until we can all make a start together.

MRS. MATTHEWS JUNIOR: Make a start together by keeping Marcus on at a school which he hates and where he learns nothing. You're making a good start together, aren't you? No, you're all just trading on your brother's generosity, sheltering behind his misplaced kindness. If Quentin had had more to do with children, he'd know exactly how selfish they are.

MARGARET: But Gladys isn't a child.

MRS. MATTHEWS JUNIOR: Girls! As if boys and girls have the same life in front of them. Whatever cranks like your aunt may say, I'll tell you girls what growing up should mean for you, what life is for women—marrying, and if they're wise, marrying well.

MR. MATTHEWS JUNIOR: Yes, marry well, my dears, and if you can't, well, marry. There are lots of different ways of marrying well, not all of them bringing material comforts, but that's where growing up begins. And not only for girls. After that, life takes its true shape. Companionship, sharing the rough with the smooth . . . it isn't just a cliché. Your mother and I have proved it. We know its reality. Comradeship of any sort. But the best, of course, is marriage. How could I have done my work or your mother have given to the world so much of herself unless we'd helped each other out of the cold? (*Mouse snorts.*) Well, Mouse, what have you got to offer the children?

MOUSE: I'm not unaware of what I've missed, William, nor of how considerable it is. And I'm not so simple as to think that however shoddy a marriage or any other relationship may be, it can't be a real relationship. But relationships are as valuable as their results. Clara and William have pandered more every year to each other's weaknesses. When William calls that companionship, it is right that his family should see it for the cant it is.

MRS. MATTHEWS JUNIOR: And what will you offer them, Mouse? A lonely, bitter, sharp-tongued old age?

MOUSE: I shall tell them that growing up means self-reliance, Clara. A lesson Quentin knows a great deal better than any of us pampered civilians.

MRS. MATTHEWS JUNIOR: Self-reliance. As if the universe was self. Responsibility for others, that's the only kind of growing up that doesn't kill the heart.

MOUSE: And irresponsibility towards others is the kind of childishness that kills others.

MR. MATTHEWS JUNIOR: There are more kinds of responsibility than you ever envisage in your narrow, gilt-edged world, Mouse. You'll grow up, Rupert, when you see that life could have a meaning just in giving your mother some of the things I ought to have given her and haven't.

RUPERT: She's already made that indecent proposal. But then, what of my responsibility to my own wife? Or is it mothers we owe our responsibility to? Has Billy Pop's failure been to you, Granny, is that it?

GRANNY MATTHEWS: Oh, my dear. I don't understand you all. I'm not a clever woman. But perhaps it's just as well. Life isn't all cleverness.

MARGARET: Granny gives us only a negative definition of life. The other definitions have all been positive.

SUKEY: Yes, Granny, what do *you* think growing up means?

GRANNY MATTHEWS: I don't know, my dear. That's such a big question. Now if only your grandfather had been here to answer it.

MR. MATTHEWS JUNIOR: One comfort at least I can feel is that the Guvnor is not here to offer his penny-wise, pound-foolish version of life to my children.

SUKEY: *Ssh!* Father, *sssh!* What *do* you think, Granny? After all, you're the one who really cares about family life.

GRANNY MATTHEWS (*patting Sukey's hand*): Thank you, my dear. Sometimes it seems as though I had failed so badly. I suppose, really, growing up is when you can first see that life's all one thing, that however silly you have been in the past it's all part of you, you can't refuse it. There, I can't express what I mean. But I remember that when I was your age I used to suffer agonies of embarrassment thinking of the silly things I'd said as a child. And then suddenly one day I saw that it was all part of my life; I couldn't turn my back on any of it. I think that's when I grew up.

MR. MATTHEWS JUNIOR: Having a sense of the past you mean, really, Mother.

GRANNY MATTHEWS: You put it so much better than I can, of

course, Will. But laughing too a little, dear. Not too serious. Remembering all the funny things that have happened in the family.

MARGARET: Like looking through a photograph album.

MARCUS: Or going through the bits and pieces in the dressing-up
box.

GRANNY MATTHEWS: I expect so, dear, yes. But enough of my silly
notions. We want to hear from Quintus. What is it you propose,
dear? When your mother and father have heard it all clearly and
had time to think about it, I'm sure they'll find some way of arranging things . . .

QUENTIN: Well, their way of arranging things is perhaps what we're
trying to avoid, Granny. For example, as an absolute necessity to
start off with, the money you and Aunt Mouse have given for the
twins must be used for them . . .

(*The scene slowly darkens as Quentin speaks until at last nothing
can be seen. His voice fades until no words are clearly audible but
its low sound can be heard in the background until Act 3 begins.*)

The ginger kitten rasped the fur of his left thigh again and again
with his small pink tongue. He had been carrying out the same washing exercise now at short intervals for over half an hour, but still he
could not rid himself of the strange disturbing smell from the few
drops of sherry that Billy Pop had spilled on his coat. The muscles of
his lithe little tongue ached, yet hardly did the kitten decide to rest
them when the unfamiliar odour would again draw him back to his
cleansing ritual.

The black-and-white kitten had found a new and delicious posture
in which to drowse—front paws bent backwards and tucked beneath
the chest, tail curled round and under the left flank, head forwards
and ears cocked outwards. So it would stay for many minutes at a
time, its head now and again nodding gently like some palsied old
woman's. But then, feeling its folded-in paws cramped under the
pressure of its body, it would leave its precociously adult drowsing
position, and stretch and roll on its side in a kitten-like sprawl, only a
few moments later to feel its way into the sensual delights of grown
cats once more.

The eyes of the tortoise-shell kitten closed to a slit, then opened,
and again closed to a slit, then opened wide to the sight of an earwig
that had travelled long desert distances across the dining-room floor

from the Countess's bronze chrysanthemums. The kitten sat up and lazily stretched out the claws of her front paws, then deciding not to bother to strike, lay back in the basket. She closed her eyes again in simulated sleep, but through the slits she was all the while following the earwig's mountain climbing as it tottered its way across the thick pile of a rug; and so she lay discomforted between sleep and the lure of a moving object.

The white kitten's ears pricked up momentarily as odd squeaks and creaks sounded from the room above where Granny Matthews and Mouse and Billy shifted angrily or distressedly in their chairs; once the kitten raised its whole head as a sudden high vibration came from below, where by chance Regan scraped a knife edge against the side of a saucepan. Even the mother-of-pearl Japanese screen placed before the near-shut dining-room door, and the red cloth-covered, sawdust-filled sausage laid across the window ledge did not shut out periodic freezing draughts that made the kittens wobble on their small legs and shiver and huddle together as one body for warmth. For the rest, even when they crawled and stretched and tottered across one another like a tangle of furry caterpillars, each remained encased in its own dominant sense.

It was thus natural that the first kitten to detect far-off invasion— sinister, Martian—should be the sharp-eared white. A rapid tick-tacking tapping sounded in the distance, so fussed and busy, so loudening and abating turn by turn, that the kitten could not tell at first whether something was approaching or going round in circles; but at last the sound came always tack, tack, tapping nearer. Now all the kittens cocked their ears; and soon the ginger's white streaked fur was near bristling round his chunky neck as an acrid, dangerous smell came to him, half smothered in another pungent scent familiar from human hands that now and again so wildly lifted him in the air, so deliciously caressed him, so brutally dropped him back into the basket. When all the kittens were tautened and bristling and the tack, tacking had changed to a pettish scratching by the door's open chink, it was the tortoise-shell who glimpsed long, coarse, black fur through the gaps in the screen's hinges that made her arch her orange, black, and gold-brown patches in prompt defence. And now Pom inched her sharp nose through the chink and squeezed her little frou-frou, Kiki's-mop of a body into the room. Four kittens stood like trembling croquet hoops in the basket, when Pom, scenting their dangerous acrid smell, began to prance forward and back across the room, yapping with delight as the kittens reacted to her presence in sharp contrast to Mr. Poll's teasing, unperturbed indifference on the upstairs landing. There was soon such a preliminary challenge of hysterical yapping and desperate spitting that Mr. Poll's more sedate tap-tapping entrance went unheeded. Only the ginger paused for a moment even in his alarm to sniff a sweetish, cloying scent as exotic as the sudden flash of green that a moment later, to the accompaniment of two awful shrieks, blew overhead in a daunting wind that for seconds silenced both dog and kittens.

But Mr. Poll, once clear of the feeble battle below, resumed his crablike tapping of inturned claws across the table and on to the sideboard. Here he paused for a moment, cocked his head and rounded his button eye, stretching the wrinkled parchment of the lids, so that he seemed to listen to some far-off faintly disturbing hum rather than to the deafening skirmish below. Even this soon failed to distract him from a few almonds that he found lying amid the decaying dust of their outer skin in a small cut-glass dish. But it's a long, long while from May to September and even further from September to the previous Christmas; Poll, having taken each almond in turn in his left claw, snapped it in two with his coal-black crackers, and spitting out its staleness from his purple tongue in a trail of mess upon the genuine Turkey carpet below (ironically a wedding present from the bride's aunt), began to search for some fresher food. The little yellow-red worm that wriggled and reared on the basket's edge was both bright and lively. With a crescendo of shrieks Poll fluttered down and caught the morsel neatly in his octopus beak.

Act 3

Scene: as in Act 2.

QUENTIN (*raising his voice against the animal noises below*): Very well then. And what do *you* propose to do with him?

MR. MATTHEWS JUNIOR (*shouting even a little louder to be heard*): Quentin, you're made of heroic stuff. And you mix well. Not that ⁺he two things always go together. The shyness of heroes is proverbial. But you're the exception. I was an athlete, yet I hated school. You played games not because you could play but to conform.

QUENTIN: I played in the colts.

MR. MATTHEWS JUNIOR: Never mind colts. That you should be familiar with such terms demonstrates the difference between you and Markie. Markie could never distinguish between colts, lambs, calves, or kids as far as the football field is concerned, though he might find words to describe the wonderful movements of those young creatures in the fields of clover or trefoil. He has his own originalities, his own special touch on life. But like me he's a non-mixer. We belong to the frankly-we-didn't-like-school brigade.

GLADYS: As long as Marcus doesn't join the frankly-I-don't-like-work brigade.

MR. MATTHEWS JUNIOR: A palpable hit, Podge. But all the same he may. And it won't do any harm if he does. He's clever and original but not made to be hemmed in.

QUENTIN: What rot you do talk, Father. If he were to work he could win a schol to the House.

MR. MATTHEWS JUNIOR: There again, my dear boy. Your aims are so much worthier. But your vision's narrow. You probably despise my pass degree. But I can safely say that my true education at Oxford came from the books I did not read when I wasn't working.

MARGARET (*to the audience*): His was the epigrammatic age of youth.

MRS. MATTHEWS JUNIOR: University! You seem to think we're made of money. We're taking Marcus away from school to save our pockets.

MOUSE: From the look on your face, Clara, anyone would suppose you had said something elegant instead of something cheap and cynical.

MARCUS: She has said something realistic. I must be grateful for that. I shall call her Motor. It's the fashionable companion to Pop at school. And she deserves fashion as much as he—more.

GRANNY MATTHEWS: But what will a little boy like this do at home all day?

MRS. MATTHEWS JUNIOR: At home! Good heavens, he's fifteen. Three-quarters of the nation are earning their living at that age.

He can start at the bottom, can't he? That's the way Americans get to the top. And whatever else we may say, they're real men.

QUENTIN: You pick on every social evil and treat it as a virtue.

MRS. MATTHEWS JUNIOR: I pick on nothing, darling boy, except that your father and I can't afford to go on paying out and paying out. We shall all be picking oakum if . . .

GRANNY MATTHEWS: But such a little boy . . .

MRS. MATTHEWS JUNIOR: Oh, good heavens, he doesn't have to go to work at once. We're not turning him out of his home into the snow. He can stay at home here and be useful to me while he looks around for something to do. You none of you realize how talented Marcus is. He's eccentric, of course, but it would be a poor world if we were all the same. He's got great talents. He arranges flowers beautifully.

SUKEY: But he's a boy, mother.

RUPERT: You're the absolute limit, Countess darling. You complain that Marcus is effeminate and then you want him to arrange the flowers. What do you want to make of him?

QUENTIN (*to Mouse and Granny Matthews*): Surely you see now how wrong it would be for Marcus to leave school.

GRANNY MATTHEWS: You know, I really do think Quintus is right, Will.

MOUSE: Of course he is, Mrs. Matthews. It's unheard-of selfishness.

MRS. MATTHEWS JUNIOR: Very well. If that's how you see it. But I should like to know where the money's coming from.

GRANNY MATTHEWS: Well, it's a mercy your grandfather didn't tie down all the capital. But I suppose I must help out temporarily. If Miss . . .

MOUSE: Oh, yes. If it meant selling out capital, mind you. But luckily there's no need for that. However wrong it may be to encourage this irresponsibility, we can't let these children suffer. But we must do it on our own terms.

MRS. MATTHEWS JUNIOR: Well, it's nice to hear that there's so much money to throw around. When I think of how Billy and I have to scrape and save. I ache with money worries. And how he's expected to write books with such a burden round his neck . . . However, we must be sacrificed, even if I haven't a rag to my name. You're to stay at school, Marcus, whether you like it or not.

On your grandmother's charity and your great-aunt's bounty.
And if the big rough boys frighten you, then little man must run
to his granny in the future and not come blubbering all over me.
They'll be paying your future term's fees.

MARCUS: They'll have to pay last term's and this term's if I'm to return next week.

MRS. MATTHEWS JUNIOR: What do you mean?

MARCUS: Only that the last letter from the bursar said that I could
not continue there if the outstanding bills were not paid.

MRS. MATTHEWS JUNIOR: Nonsense. How insolent of them. Anyway, how do you know?

MARCUS: I shouldn't have done so if I hadn't found the letter in
Billy Pop's handkerchief drawer.

MRS. MATTHEWS JUNIOR: How dare you look in your father's
drawers?

QUENTIN: How dare Father risk his being sent back from school
next week in such a way?

GRANNY MATTHEWS: I expect he was looking for a handkerchief.

MARCUS: Well, actually, I was doing what the Countess calls "just
going through his things in case."

MR. MATTHEWS JUNIOR: Whatever we've done wrong, Clara, we've
reaped our reward. We've taught them to be prigs, to sit in judgment on us.

MRS. MATTHEWS JUNIOR: If they can't face life's unpleasant truths,
then . . .

(*She is interrupted by the eruption of a hot, panting Regan, who
bursts in at the door. She is disheveled and a bit drunk.*)

REGAN: Look, I've shouted and I've beaten that gong till its own
mother woodent know its dial from its bum. Dinner's ready. And
if the duck's dried up don't blame me nor if the pheasant's burnt
to a cinder. Talk talk talk. That won't fill yer bellies. (*To Granny
Matthews*) Ow are you, Madam? And you, Miss Rickard?

MR. MATTHEWS JUNIOR (*with an amused worldly chuckle*): She's a
character, Mother. But a real *maître de cuisine*. With the artist's
temperament. We owe you an apology, Regan. We've probably
ruined a poem. You must forgive us, but we've been discussing the
root of all evil.

MRS. MATTHEWS JUNIOR: Now here's someone who knows what
Billy and I have to go through. It's one financial crisis after another

in this house, isn't it, Regan? Who else but Regan would wait *days* for overdue wages.

REGAN: Wages! Bugger wages! What I want to know is oo took the three quid out of my piggy box? Come on now, which one of you was it? Oh, I don't mean you, Madam, of course. Or you, Miss Rickard. For you're the upper ten, too, tho' one of the cranks.

MRS. MATTHEWS JUNIOR: Are you accusing my children of stealing?

REGAN: Children! Come off it, it's you or im. Now which one of you was it? I just wanter know.

MRS. MATTHEWS JUNIOR: Come, Mouse! Granny! I believe there's your favourite chestnut stuffing. Billy, take your mother down. Rupert, give Mouse your arm. Sukey, dish up, will you? Quentin, please cope with this drunken creature, darling boy. I'd ask Margaret, but I think the situation calls for a man. Come, children, let's see what smells so delicious, shall we?

QUENTIN: No, Mother, this is not good enough. I'm sorry if Regan's upset you, but don't you see that this is only part of a situation that cannot go on. We must bring some order into this squalid chaos.

MRS. MATTHEWS JUNIOR: If you're not man enough to do what your mother asks when she's been so horribly insulted, then you may do what you like. I'm going to forget all these vulgar melodramatics and remember my duty to my guests.

QUENTIN: I'm sure Granny and Aunt Mouse . . .

MOUSE: Well, Quentin, dear, I *am* a little hungry. And I'm certain we'll all discuss better for Regan's delicious cooking. (*Whispers to Quentin*) If I know anything of your greedy parents they'll be much more amenable when feeding time's over.

MR. MATTHEWS JUNIOR: Have you uncorked the Pouget, Regan?

MRS. MATTHEWS JUNIOR: Billy, don't speak to the wretched creature!

REGAN: Pouget! Parrot's piss more like by the time you get it. From what's goin on down there. (*She throws open the door and a confused noise of animals fills the room—then she sinks to the floor in a drunken haze.*)

SUKEY: Oh, the kittens! My darling kittens!

MOUSE: Good heavens! I never allow cats in the same room as Polly.

GRANNY MATTHEWS: Pommie, poor Pommie! Never mind, his mother's coming.

(*Exit all three, squeezing each other through the door.*)

MRS. MATTHEWS JUNIOR (*to audience*): Thank heavens for the distraction. (*To Rupert*) Come, my dear boy, take me down. If the others have lost all sense of the *convenable*, let us at least keep *our* manners.

RUPERT (*bowing low to her and offering his arm*): Contessa.

(*As they walk out with stately formality, he turns his head back and winks broadly to the audience.*)

MR. MATTHEWS JUNIOR (*to the audience*): A very tricky corner turned, I think. At least we may save the wine from the general debacle. Marcus, come and help me with the Pouget. No, on second thoughts, I prefer Maggie for my cup-bearer, my little Hebe. (*She takes his arm and they exit. But she drops her handkerchief by the door, and, returning, addresses the audience.*)

MARGARET (*imitating Billy Pop*): My little Hebe! His actions are dross, but his words are pure gold. Such may be said to be the compensations of living chez Carmichael. (*Exit*)

GLADYS: All right, old boy, I'll give you a hand with her.

(*Gladys and Quentin lift Regan on to a chair, where she opens one eye and looks at them like a malevolent Mr. Polly.*) What ho! She bumps.

QUENTIN: Now come on, Gladys, let's get this time-wasting meal over and pin them down to a definite and satisfactory arrangement before they all become drowsy. Sunday gorging! Disgusting Victorian institution!

GLADYS: Oh, I don't know. (*She pats her plump stomach.*) My tum's rumbling for a slice of pheasant. (*Seeing Quentin's expression*) Sorry old boy, I didn't mean to fool. Come on, Marcus, time to be fed, if you want to grow up to beat the Hun. (*Exeunt Quentin and Gladys.*)

MARCUS (*to audience*): Grow up to beat the Hun! I really must apologize for the language used this afternoon, but you can't slice life up without making some sort of indecent mess. (*To Regan, all little boy*) Do I have to grow up, Regan? It's not a process that's encouraged by example. (*She merely smiles vaguely.*) What do you think life is, Regan? (*She does not answer—he shakes her by the shoulder.*) What do you think growing up means?

REGAN (*sleepily and drunkenly*): Always keep in with the nobs and the upper ten. Go where the splosh is. Don't mix yourself up with the muck.

(Regan nods off for a moment, then wakes herself up with a peculiarly loud snore, then nods off again. Exit Marcus in a reflective mood. The lights go out and light up again immediately upon the lower half of the divided stage to show a few minutes later the dining-room in wild chaos. Mouse, standing behind the dining-room table, is with some difficulty holding a shrieking parrot with one hand, while with the other she dabs its head with a table napkin which she liberally souses in vinegar from a bottle on the sideboard. Granny Matthews, seated on a dining-room chair moved away from the table, has Pom on her lap while she binds up her small paw with her handkerchief. Pom also bleeds from the head. Billy Pop on hands and knees mops up with a table napkin the wine from a broken bottle and squeezes it through a handkerchief spread over the top of a decanter. Gladys has the tortoise-shell kitten on her ample lap; Margaret holds the white one in her arms; they are both stroking and calming their charges. Rupert holds the black-and-white kitten and dabs at its bleeding eye with the tip of a handkerchief dipped in water. Marcus is kneeling at Gladys's feet and talking to the tortoise-shell kitten; Quentin stands behind Margaret and every now and again strokes the white kitten's ear. Centre stage stands Sukey, white-faced and trembling as she holds out towards the audience the ginger kitten, bloody and lifeless. Next to her and in even more dramatic posture, the Countess holds out the kitten's basket with its scarlet lining.)

MRS. MATTHEWS JUNIOR: Poor little objects! The home we provided has hardly proved a castle.

MOUSE: What I shall never forgive or forget is that you all thought of nothing but yourselves. Mr. Polly came down here—poor innocent—to a den of little hell-cats. Mr. Polly, who always goes his own little ways and isn't a bother to anyone. And now look at his poor tail!

GRANNY MATTHEWS: And Pom says, "Please, Mother, I'm trying to be a very brave little dog but those kittens *have* hurt me!" Never mind, Mother'll give her a little VC all to herself. I don't know that I oughtn't to go straight to the vet. Nasty high-smelling little things. Heaven knows where their claws may have been.

GLADYS: I'm sure you needn't worry about that, Granny. The kittens haven't been out of the house since they were born. They can't possibly be dirty.

MOUSE: Good heavens, girl! Where's your nose? The smell in this house!

GRANNY MATTHEWS: A lot of stray kittens from heaven knows where. I'm surprised at you, Will, having them in here.

MR. MATTHEWS JUNIOR: For various reasons not too subtle even for you to understand, Mother, the house is somewhat dilapidated, but shabby as we are, we don't turn away strangers from the door.

GRANNY MATTHEWS: Look after your own, my dear. That was your father's motto. He never trusted vagrants—men or animals—not one of them if they hadn't a place to call their own. Your father and I always took pride in what was ours. I didn't want to let little Pom out of my sight, only your children knew better.

QUENTIN: Granny, how can you? That's why the world's like it is. Because Grandfather's generation couldn't see farther than their own property and their fat noses. Beware of a closed heart, Granny. No government debentures will make up for that.

MOUSE: Good heavens! Stop moralizing, boy. And you talk about Victorians!

MARGARET: Quentin was talking about *false* moralizing, Aunt Mouse. Weeping over little Nell and then letting little matchsellers die. Like Grandfather's generation.

GRANNY MATTHEWS: What a wicked thing to say, girl. How can you speak like that? Your grandfather was the kindest of men.

MARGARET: Oh, I didn't mean Grandfather himself, of course. It was an attitude of mind of a whole generation.

MOUSE: You should be more careful of what you say, Margaret. Uttering generalities about something you know nothing of. And all because two lonely old women object when their pets are savaged by wild cats.

GRANNY MATTHEWS: Anyone of sense would have had them put away.

QUENTIN: That sort of sense decided on the use of mustard gas.

MOUSE: Oh, don't be so absurd, Quentin. First Margaret accuses your grandfather of being sentimental and now you accuse your grandmother of being without heart. Use a little logic.

RUPERT (*dramatically*): He does, Aunt Mouse. Easy tears and a stony heart are not strangers. Empty postures. Hypocrisy. That's what we charge the past with.

MOUSE: You charge! My dear boy, you want to watch your words. I thought you were seeking our help. You don't go about it very wisely.

QUENTIN: But Aunt Mouse, you can't ask us to let self-interest affect what's right and wrong. Everyone knows where secret diplomacy led to.

MOUSE: Secret diplomacy! It wouldn't do you any harm to learn a little tact. Tact is only another name for kindness, you know. (*The parrot shrieks.*) Oh, shut up, Mr. Polly, I'm talking. (*The parrot shrieks again.*) Now look what you've done. You've made cross words between me and Mr. Polly, when the poor old man's in pain. And all over a bunch of beastly stray cats.

MARCUS: The kittens were not stray. They were Leonora's. This is their house. Mr. Polly and Pom are only visitors. Uninvited visitors, too.

GRANNY MATTHEWS: Pom uninvited! Did you hear what the little boy said, Pom? That to the little dog, Marcus, who let you pull her tail when you were only a baby. I'm sure if Pom's unwelcome, her mistress is too.

MARCUS: Anyone's unwelcome who savages our kittens. If I had my way I should put a millstone—if I knew where to find one—round Mr. Polly's strong neck and little Miss Pom's slender one. And I'd cast them into the uttermost depths. And then pull the flush. And yet when one thinks that the beautiful Elagabalus suffered a similar cloacal death, it seems too good for them.

MOUSE: You use too many big words for a small boy, my lad. That's the trouble with all you children. Too many words.

SUKEY (*stepping forward and holding out the dead ginger kitten*): You complain of our words. What about your actions? You don't seem to realize what's happened. This kitten is dead, Granny. Savagely killed, Aunt Mouse. Murdered by both of you. And you complain of our words. (*She lays the dead kitten reverently in the basket.*)

GRANNY MATTHEWS: Poor little thing! But I dare say it's just as well, Sukey. Motherless kittens, you know. Nobody wants them these days, living in flats and all the contrivance that's asked of one. Anyway, even if it wasn't for Pom, I could never have a cat in the house. They upset me.

SUKEY: We shouldn't let the cats come to your house, or to anyone else's. *This* is their home.

MOUSE: I can tell you this, my dear, if this house is going to be filled with cats you won't see your Aunt Mouse here. Though that can hardly be important as long as she stumps up with cheques when asked.

(*There is a silence as no one answers.*)

MOUSE: That's clear enough. As long as I know. (*Again there is a silence.*) I'm surprised you don't show more spirit, Mrs. Matthews. We're evidently not wanted here.

QUENTIN: Aunt Mouse, you've no right to blackmail us.

MARGARET: My dear Aunt Mouse, of course you're wanted. But so are these poor unwanted kittens.

GRANNY MATTHEWS: I'm afraid, my dear, Miss Rickard is right. At any rate as far as I'm concerned. I can't come to a house where there are cats. Apart from Pom, they give me asthma. But I dare say they're only a passing fancy—what do they call it nowadays? —a craze. They'll be gone the next time I come, I expect.

SUKEY: I'm afraid they won't be, Granny. We're sorry about your asthma, of course. But you can't ask us to turn the kittens out into the street because you don't like them.

MOUSE: Of course not. Take them to a vet and have them put away. The Poor Peoples' Dispensary for Sick Animals will do it free. There's one in Fulham Road, if not nearer.

ALL THE YOUNG MATTHEWSES: Put away!

MOUSE: Yes, put away. I'm not an old sentimentalist, as you think; if it's Mr. Poll this time, it may be me the next. They're danger-ous. Clara, are you going to bring these young idiots to their senses? I hope you all clearly understand: if those cats remain in this house, I do not set foot in it. (*Silence again.*) Well, Clara, are they going to be got rid of?

MRS. MATTHEWS JUNIOR: Now children, do you hear that? Remem-ber, your aunt and your grandmother are used to having things their own way. They can afford to. Shall I tell them the kittens are to go to kingdom come? (*An embarrassed silence.*) Very well. My dear Mouse, whatever else I do with the children, I do not bully or blackmail them. They've decided, and so it must be. But I hear Regan's footsteps. And steady footsteps at that. You've obviously done wonders with her, Quentin. I knew it needed a man's hand. Forget all this nonsense, Mouse, and remember there's your favourite *crème brûlée.*

MOUSE: I'm not to be blackmailed through my stomach, thank you, Clara. Mr. Polly and I can do perfectly well with barley water at the Club.

(*She goes to the door. It opens and Regan totters in bearing at last the roast ducks and pheasants on a vast dish.*)

REGAN: Well, you children are a fine lot. If I adent woken up from my snooze, there'd ave been no luncheon on the table at all today. Madam comin all the way ere. And Miss Rickard too, tho shees used to travel. But no arm done. (*In a loud stage whisper to Mrs. Matthews Senior*) Ave the duck, Madam, I should. The pheasant's a bit on the dry side. (*To Mouse, who has heard and taken more offence*) Now sit down, Miss Rickard. I shan't be a jiffy gettin the etceteras with Miss Sukey's elp, and then you can tuck into a nice slice of breast of pheasant. (*Exit*)

MR. MATTHEWS JUNIOR: Yes, do that, Mouse, tuck in instead of flouncing out. You'll forgive the sartorial pun.

(*Mouse turns and stares at him with disgust. She goes to the door, opens it, then turns back.*)

MOUSE: If I get an apology, Clara, before I leave the country on Friday, I shall forget the whole incident. An apology and a promise that those animals will be disposed of. Good-bye, Mrs. Matthews. If you take my advice, you'll back me up. You should have remembered, my dears, that who touches an old maid's pet touches her. And old maids, like cats, have got sharp claws.

(*As she goes out, Mr. Polly shrieks, "Good-bye, good-bye, good-bye!"*)

(*A moment later, Regan comes in with vegetables, sauces, and plates.*)

REGAN (*to Granny Matthews*): Now, Madam, turn around and sit up to table. Miss Rickard'll be back in a jiffy, that's for sure. Just gone to you know where. All these old maids are the same. No sooner is food on the table than they must excuse theirselves.

GRANNY MATTHEWS: Thank you, Regan, I don't fancy anything. My asthma's come on and I don't feel at all well.

MR. MATTHEWS JUNIOR: Now, Mother, don't fuss. A piece of gamey toast from under the bird.

GRANNY MATTHEWS: Gamey toast for asthma! Really, Will. And I don't know what you mean—fuss! Miss Rickard is quite right. The least you can do is to get rid of those nasty little creatures. I don't ask much. You ought to tell the children, Will.

MR. MATTHEWS JUNIOR: My dear Mother, we're not living in the pater's autocratic times. We don't set up to be respectable here but it is a place of freedom. The children have turned their thumbs up. I'm certainly not going to play emperor and turn them down just to give you a Roman holiday.

GRANNY MATTHEWS: I don't want any sort of holiday. The children get me here to ask for my help, though heaven knows an annuity's difficult enough. They show no feeling for poor little Pom. It's all those horrid creatures who nearly took her eye out that they care about. I don't say it's not for the best, either. If there's not your aunt and me to pay for you all, you'll have to make shift for yourselves like your grandfather and I did. And many's the laugh you'll have together when you look back on the so-called hard times. (*Then, taking a tin from her muff, she places it on the table.*) I'll leave the toffees I brought. I know Quintus likes Mackintosh's. Well, if they can't do the little thing I ask . . . Oh, I do wish Colyer hadn't gone off. I want to go home. No, don't try to persuade me, Will. I shall go and sit outside in the hall until he comes. Come on, my little unwelcome Pom.

(*Exit Mrs. Matthews Senior. Quentin makes to follow her and then returns.*)

QUENTIN: Oh, Lord! That ought to make me feel bad. But we can't possibly give way. Anyhow Colyer and Edith will fuss over her and she'll get over it in time. If they hadn't been so self-righteous . . .

GLADYS: Poor old things! Did you hear Mouse say "lonely old women"? But really, if they will go on as if they owned the earth, what do they expect?

MARGARET: Poor Aunt Mouse! I know she says sharp things. But I never thought her heart had shrivelled up so.

SUKEY: Of course Granny was upset about Pom, after all she's *her* dog. But to act as though this wasn't the kittens' home.

RUPERT: If only they hadn't relished making a scene so much.

MARCUS: And being so solemn and self-important and rich.

MRS. MATTHEWS JUNIOR (*sitting down to table*): So you've learnt about the rich man and the camel and the eye of a needle. My dears, that really is growing up.

MR. MATTHEWS JUNIOR (*sitting opposite her*): I couldn't be quite sure how it would go. My heart was in my mouth once or twice. But I should never have been in doubt; I ought to have known that my children would follow their hearts as soon as something touched them deeply enough.

MRS. MATTHEWS JUNIOR: How could one be sure, Billy? After all that horrid talk upstairs when everything was plans and careers? I felt stifled by self-importance and office desks.

QUENTIN: Everything we said upstairs was completely serious, Mother.

GLADYS: And important.

MR. MATTHEWS JUNIOR: Of course, Podge. Your mother and I learned a great deal from it. We've improvised, you know, all our lives. We've had to. Always avoided Gladstone and speech-making where a little bit of bright chatter would get us by. Perhaps you've seen something of the reasons for that today. We, too, were children once and made our own rebellions. Little Nell and the starving match-seller—I liked that, Mag. But you're asking us to learn a new seriousness, my dears. I laughed with Oscar, you must remember. Or with those who had known him. He must have a heart of stone, who cannot laugh at the death of little Nell. . . . But now it seems we must learn new ways, your mother and I.

MRS. MATTHEWS JUNIOR: No, not new ways, Billy. New objects. The children's lives are not going to be ours. Their ambitions are bound to be post-war ambitions. New to us. Not that I'm exactly an antimacassar mother.

MR. MATTHEWS JUNIOR: No, my dear, you're ragtime. (*Seeing Marcus and Rupert smiling*) Or whatever's the new thing.

MRS. MATTHEWS JUNIOR: We respect you so much, Quentin, dear boy. But you mustn't be too sane, darlings. It really won't do in this family. Surely we can all get these things, the real essence of life for you all in our old happy-go-lucky stick-it-together-with-secotine way. Surely we don't have to go back to "mine is mine" and gilt-edged securities and "money talks" and all those horrors. And please, Quentin darling, especially not a lot of smugness and pretending.

(She gets up and puts one arm round Quentin and another round Rupert, kissing them in turn. Then bending down, she kisses Marcus on the forehead. Billy Pop puts an arm round Margaret and another round Gladys. He tickles their waists. Releasing them, he goes and holds Sukey to him for a moment and kisses her. The Countess cuts up some duck on a plate and puts it down for the kittens.)

MRS. MATTHEWS JUNIOR: There, they shall have the lion's share. Now that the roarers have left us. They won't learn any lesson from it all, of course, poor old things. *(She giggles)* But that odious Mr. Polly and the horrible Pom are balder than when they came here. *(She sits and begins to carve)* Oh, we're all together again. Billy, this calls for a celebration. *(But Billy Pop has already brought out a bottle of champagne from the sideboard cupboard. He opens it and when the cork pops everyone cries "Oh!" As he pours out the champagne, they hear the sound of the doorbell and of Granny Matthews' departure in the car. Regan appears at the door.)*

MRS. MATTHEWS JUNIOR: I know, Regan, Madam's gone. Have a glass of bubbly, Regan darling. You couldn't be *more* squiffy. *(Seeing one of Mr. Polly's green tail-feathers on the carpet, she picks it up and puts it in her hair)* Oh, you darlings, all of you, you've made me feel so much better. I feel quite ready for any battle. With my war paint and my tomahawk. I know, Marcus, I know . . . *(Imitating him)* Whatever a tomahawk may be.

(All the family watch to see how this teasing overture from the Countess to her most ancient enemy among the children will be taken. The boy smiles and speaks.)

MARCUS: It means the sharpest of axes, Motor. But, as befits you, the most gaily coloured of axes too.

(All the family feel free to laugh and the curtain comes down on their happy laughter.)

End of Act 3 of the Family Sunday Play

Quentin said: "Of course this means going about things the hard and slow way. I hope everybody realizes that. We're not to suppose that the parents have changed their spots overnight. We'll have to put up a fight for what we believe in. But I admit that I feel happier this way. It isn't as if we don't all know what's wrong with the ethos of number fifty-two; we've all suffered from it. But Billy Pop had a point when he spoke of *their* revolt. His, at any rate, I can imagine. I lived at Ladbroke Grove and I know. You've none of you felt its full force. Dividends, roast beef, and the Great British Empire used to stifle me. It was Granddad's legacy. Of course Granny's all right. She's a fine old stick. But it was part of his system that she should be a reflection. And from what Aunt Mouse said this afternoon, she appears no better. Their failure this afternoon was the failure of a class. But that's another matter. We couldn't have acted in any other way. We'd taken on the kittens and we were committed. Luckily commitment to action is a wonderful tonic. One found that again and again after a long spell of trench stalemate. It happened just in time. If we'd gone ahead with our plan we'd have given hostages to the barbarians. As it is, whatever we achieve will be without strings."

He talked on like this for some time. At first, with the unfamiliar champagne inside them, the others listened with a sense of inspired certainty, of high will that knows no obstacles; and at last, with the unfamiliar champagne still inside them and the familiar cosy nursery warmth around them and the familiar fairy-tale Gothic storm outside, they fell into various fitful sleeps. And Quentin, too, eventually droned his way into slumber.

At about that time his mother awoke from her after-lunch nap. Awoke with the clearest impression of her father's hand laid upon her shoulder. Father, those strange dark flecks on the flesh of his cheeks, which in his last years was alternately wrinkled and stretched like the skin of a tortoise's neck, but never pale except in the final, unfamiliar death (how angry Mouse had been that the nurse had taken her, a five-year-old, into the bedroom), always sunburnt from his years abroad, and with his dark restless eyes always bright (though that must be sentimental distortion, for no eyes could have remained bright with all that pain and wasting). Father, who smelt so nice of lavender water and heather and cigar smoke and leather.

She sensed that she had netted some true beauty from the depths
of her childhood when she realized that the words had come to her
in rhyme. And now this frowsty bed, and the *crêpe de Chine* nightdress she had put over her petticoat, smelt of stale sweat and, God
knew why, faintly of onions. But surroundings are nothing; memories, feelings, these are one's true self, despite all life's mischances.
Knowing this, she returned resolutely to the past. If Father had
lived, she would have gone with him to his foreign stations, for he
refused all the old Indian conventions and Mouse was like butter in
his fingers; indeed, he had promised her that there should be "no
boarding-school for his motherless girl." She would have sat on the
verandah with him, he reading aloud, while she sewed, for even
the nuns had to grant her the sewing (especially fine stitching), and
the Indian servant coming out with delicious drinks at sundown, and
a letter from Mouse from Turkey or Nepal or somewhere mountain-
ous, telling them of a new tulip species discovered or a row with
some Orthodox monks over photography, at which together they
would have looked solemn and then burst into laughter at the same
moment, but kind laughter, for who would have minded Mouse's
madness while he lived?

But he hadn't lived, damn him, and so she hadn't married one of
his subalterns, a regiment at her feet, but Billy Pop and a smelly
house and a sour bed. What right had the old beast to come back and
haunt her in her dreams, making her remember the crocuses at the
foot of the elm where he sat in his wheel-chair that sun-filled March,
and the tadpole he showed to her in the pool by the cow-houses? In
the last weeks that he was wheeled out in that chair, it must have
been, for it was hot late May or June weather—she could smell roses
—and by August he was dead. And a good thing, too, probably an
old bore like most army men. Yet his hand, rough-skinned and bony so
that the flesh slid upon the veins and sinews as one touched, had been
so gentle as it held hers and guided her fingers over the inside of his
crocodile-skin cigar case, to help her not to mind putting on gloves,
for the uncured side of the leather set her teeth on edge. "A pair of
gloves are the making of a beautiful woman's hands, Clarrie. And
hands and feet . . ." he had said. She had drawn in green and red
chalks a picture of him shooting the crocodile; in the Sudan it had
been, near Wadi Halfa or some such place. And now Marcus drew

and she must sacrifice good gloves to help him do so. Or so the world would say.

Milton had loved her hands. Now stroking the back of her hand against the pillow, she seemed to be once again caressing his cheek where the pillow threads had been unpicked and it was rough to the touch, as occasionally his chin. She buried her face in the grubby linen and—memory stronger than fact—his smell came back, something very expensive he rubbed in after shaving, from New York, and masculine sweat. She stretched and moulded until Milton held her, when suddenly her father was with her again, but now with no hand on her shoulder, but in his wheel-chair staring at her gravely until she was frightened and forced her eyes to open to escape him. It was all very well for him, the dead don't feel, so what the hell right have they got to reproach with their eyes, cutting off sleep—sleep which was the only remaining escape? And come to that, he was probably as lecherous as the rest of them, only that she'd been too small to recognize it. Disgusting they were in his day, groping their way through all those layers of undies and whalebone. That girl in grey who came to see him, fifteen years younger at least, and Mother only dead a year. Miss Karton, or Keaton. Filthy old beast.

But at the thought of Keaton she had slid off the bed, put her kimono on, and a few minutes later had tiptoed down to shake the sleeping Billy Pop in his study swivel-chair. Though he stared at her in bleary dismay, yet he seemed at once to know what she intended, as though they had been two illicit lovers of long standing and secret night couplings. She said, whispering, "I'll go to Mouse's club and see her tomorrow." And she smiled, but not, as he might have thought, in anticipation of money received, rather because she had decided to wear her grey coat-frock with the lemon leather trimming.

"You go to your mother's at tea-time. Don't take flowers. I've got some of that honey which Edith believes cures her cough. Your mother always likes you to think of the servants."

"But you'll come . . ."

"No, Billy. She sees you alone so little."

She almost laughed as she said it, because he reacted at once with a little sentimental, vain movement of his head which she had anticipated. But now, having spat out the phlegm which seemed to trouble

his afternoon awakenings, he buttoned up his cardigan and was
ready to act. They tiptoed upstairs without a word said of their
immediate intent. She motioned him to lift the basket and herself
placed a cushion on top of the sleeping trio, but the white kitten
moved and she hadn't the nerve, as she'd meant, to press the cushion
down. Perhaps he had expected her to do so, for when she relaxed
her weight and, taking up the cushion, put it under her arm, he
stumbled and almost upset his burden.

"Oh, don't be clumsy, Bill. It's hopeless to ask you to do anything.
Give me the basket," and she snatched it from him.

He now carried the cushion and downstairs they crept. For a moment, coming from the dark staircase into the light of the hall, she
stood blinking.

"What's wrong? Seen a ghost?" Then peering at her, "You look
ghastly. Are you all right?"

"Dreams," she said. "I dreamt of my father or someone very like
him. It upset me. I don't know why."

"Duck and stuffing," he said. "I've got the filthiest taste in my
mouth. But I thought your father was a hero. Now if it had been my
guvnor popping back from the dead . . ."

"Oh, shut up, Billy! You talk too much."

As they crept down the stone stairs to the basement, she said angrily, "He was a soldier. At least he wasn't scared."

"Anybody could massacre Afghans or Zulus. I don't suppose his
duties often called on him to drown kittens. Who knows what gur-
gling and struggling there'll be?"

"Oh, Billy, don't be so horrid. Keep your writer's imagination
until it's over. When it's done you'll have seen it and have something
real to write about for once."

"And what if I muck it all up?"

"Well, then, you'll muck it all up. But of course, you won't."

Between the two versions of what was to be she couldn't decide.
But of one thing she was sure: standing with her back to the kitchen
door, barring his entrance, she said, "And 'muck it all up'! You used
to speak such wonderful English, it was pleasant to listen to. But
now it's like all the rest, you've let everything slide." And when he
smiled, she added, "No, I mean it, very seriously. If you don't pull
up, you're done for, my boy."

As he seemed about to defend himself, she pushed the door open and impatiently urged him on. Taking the bucket from the pantry cupboard, she knocked over a broom but the noise seemed of little concern, drowned as it was by Regan's loud snores from her bedroom. Nevertheless the tortoise-shell kitten mewed and the Countess started, almost dropping the bucket.

"That damned dream," she said, "if it hadn't upset my nerves I'd have done all this myself. I know what you are, Billy, all talk and no do."

"Well, this time, the quicker it's done the better."

She noted with satisfaction that what she said seriously still influenced him even under stress, for he added, "I readily grant that this is no occasion for protracted parleying."

She filled the bucket. He took the black-and-white kitten by the scruff of its neck and plunged it into the water, holding it down with his hand. But a few seconds later he fished it out again, a squealing, struggling object, monstrously embryonic, its head more than ever abnormally large above its thin, fur-flattened, dripping little body.

"I'm sorry," he said, "I can't."

"Oh, give it to me." But at the touch of its soggy fur she was revolted. "Get Regan," she said. "Servants always understand how to do these things."

Regan, indeed, took longer to wake from her heavy sleep than, once woken, grumblingly to drown the kittens.

The Countess remarked, "Well, that's soon over."

But Billy Pop must have found the time had passed more slowly, for he said, "Who would have thought such little blighters would have such a kick in them?"

"Well," Regan demanded, "what's to be done with this lot?"

And she thrust the bulging, dripping sack beneath the noses of her employers. (She had seen at once the need for a sack. Had she a peasant granddam somewhere back in history, this apparently wholly Rowlandson-Hogarth woman, or did the basic folk-lores still bind country and town at that level in those days?)

"What's been done with the other?" asked her mistress.

"Miss Sukey's wrapped it in a andkerchief and put it by the back door. They're burying it under the tree in the back yard."

"Burying it! I've never heard such nonsense. What's wrong with

the ovens?" The Countess spoke prophetically, then changed her
mind. "No, put them in the dust-bin. Good heavens, when I think of
the huge Christmas box we give each year to those men."

And the bell rang.

"Oh, my God, who can that be on a Sunday afternoon? Your
mother perhaps, or Mouse, come back to apologize?"

The Countess went to the kitchen window to peer up the area
steps, but with the kittens' death the wind had died also and fog was
thickening outside in the growing dusk, murky, smoke-thick, dun-
coloured, so that viewed through the grubby, fly-blown glass the
world outside was crepuscular, passers-by mere shadowy moths.

"I'm out, Regan. No, see who it is. And tidy yourself up, Billy,
while I dress. Be sure you wash all that muck off."

Who could say what muck?

Not Regan who, left alone, set out to finish the job started, bell
or no bell—and the effing thing rang and rang. Shovelling muck into
a dust-bin doesn't take all day, not, that is, if your head doesn't ache
to beat the band. And then again, if you've had a couple at midday,
especially watery, vinegary stuff like champagne, number one comes
first. So like Marie Lloyd she walks among the cabbages and pees.
Oh, ring, ring, ring your bloody head off. What silly sod will call in
a pea-souper. More like night! And sure enough it *was* a foreigner.
One of her Yanks, though not the usual. "Mrs. Matthews?" And,
"Come on in," she told him. In the hall, in the light, he seemed a nice
boy. Young, younger than the other. Does your mother know you're
out, Sonny Jim? But you couldn't help fancying him. Probably the
champagne; there's other things it brings on besides peeing. "I've
been ringing that bell a pretty good while. I reckoned the Matthews
family was away from home. Were you hitting the high spots last
night or what?" "We were sleeping." "Sleeping? Come to look at
you, you seem as though you had a pretty thick night." But she
wasn't having familiarity. "What name, sir, shall I say?" A randy
laugh he'd got, but she smiled to show there was no offence. It
sounded like Lootnant Iced Pratts. Well, he'd certainly come to the
right shop for them. If that was the way he wanted it . . . So she
shouted the name loud and clear up the stairs.

And there was milady, quick as your finger, standing at the top of
the stairs. "Oh, Lestah, how lovelah to see yah." Have a banana!
And, "You wicked boy, you've brought mer flahs. My favour-

ite . . ." chrysanthe-old-enough-to-be-your-mums. And, "I thought maybe that now Major Ward has gone, you wouldn't object to a plain lootnant!" Object! You'd better move quick, Lestah, or Her Highness will have come in her drawers. And, "Oh, no, I can't let you spend your pay on little me, but Billah, Billah, come and meet Mr. Iced Pratts, and while I slip into something a bit more suitable (what about your birthday suit, Madam?), see if you can touch this poor mug for a couple of quid? And where shall it be? Oh, ai know, the Piccahdillah. Did you know you can net your own trout thah?" Yes, and he's netted an old trout here while he's about it. "Let me mix your highballs before I go up to change." Oh, milady, how can you talk so dirty? And now we come tripping down in our black-jet bodice, apache skirt, velvet tam, cigarette and all. "How do I look, Regan, darling?" Like a young girl going to her first ball, I don't think. But, oh, Gawd, a short life and a quiet one, not in this house. Here they come and up will go the bloomin balloon. Who's going to answer this one? Not yours truly. Not on your nelly. I'm off to finish my kip.

But Sukey was the one, despite all her convention and love of respectability, to make a public scene.

"Where are they? Where are the kittens?" she asked, going straight into the drawing-room from her vain visit below.

"Sukey, dear. Lieutenant Eispratz. One of the twins, Lester."

"How do you do? Where are the kittens, Mother?"

"I don't really know, dear. She's the animal lover of this family. Have you seen the kittens, Billy?"

"Lost their mittens again?"

"Oh, don't be silly, Father."

"Oh, dear, the lack of respect of the younger generations for the paternal parent. Of course it's all the fault of you Americans. Ever since Milton christened poor Billy 'Pop.' Perhaps they've gone for a walk, Sukey. They're getting to be rather big kittens."

"They would hardly walk out of the dining-room when the door's shut."

"Well, ask Regan, dear. She's probably done something with them."

When Sukey called over the banisters to Regan, "Are the kittens in the kitchen, Regan?" the old girl just bawled out, "I ave a little cat, and I'm very fond of that, but I'd rather ave a bow, wow, wow,

wow, wow," so that, comical kid, even the most po-faced would have had to smile.

Sukey gone, the Countess was quick to urge her swain abroad.

"No, no, it's not necessary. There's a taxicab rank just round the corner. I love to get there early and see the people. Yes, why not? A restaurant is a sort of theatre. Oh, no, I know my way blindfold. We cockneys, you know. You should see our wonderful cook. It's only the dirt I object to in fogs. How can one ever get one's hands clean? Yes, what a night, wasn't it? Roof gone? My dear boy, as long as you're here to tell the story. Yes, I know. Well, of course, this is such a noisy street and with the wind voices carried so. You little know the wicked street you've come to. Billy and I keep meaning to move but we love our little house and it's all so gloriously central. But the noises last night! Of course it's quite an apache quarter and when these terrible whores beat each other . . . Horses eat each other? No, why should I? What a gruesome idea!" And with this she had brought him to the front door but not, alas, out of it by the time that Sukey appeared.

She held in her hand the horrid sack and for a moment appeared about to fell her mother with it. But instead she called hysterically (hysteria was all you could call it when a visitor new to the house and one at once so unexpected and so welcome was standing in the hall) up the stairs to summon her brothers and sisters. And soon there they were, craning and crowding from the landing above—Rupert like Georgie Giraffe looming above the rebellious boys gathered at Tiger Tim's call. But if Mrs. Bruin had gone too far this time, Billy Pop Porky Boy seemed in most danger as he stood at the foot of the stairs, rotund and blinking (frabjous owl), marooned between his retreating, errant wife and his advancing children. However, he suppressed his *OoooGooroos* and his *Oh, my stars* bravely but somewhat tritely to say, "The Countess is going out with Mr. Eispratz. Have a wonderful time, my dear."

The Countess smiled at all of them (yet she looked—who would not?—in need of an Abdullah) and the lieutenant's perplexed look cleared. Seeing her smile, he smiled too in a warm friendly grimace of his rough-tough, ugly-handsome, young India-rubber Chicago phiz. A smile that appeared finally to enrage Sukey, for, dropping her horrid evidence, she rushed at her mother, and placing her strong plump fingers on those scrawny shoulders, she shook her until her long jade ear-rings swung like gibbets in the wind. But the Countess stifled her royal rage and decided on helplessness. A self-restraint that paid, for the lieutenant seized Sukey in turn by her shoulders and swung her away. Gladys called in her deep voice, "Leave my sister alone!" Quentin took a menacing step forward; but Marcus, who had crept to the bottom of the stairs, acted—he spat very fiercely and very accurately in their visitor's eye. Startled, Mr. Eispratz (his family immigrants from Frankfurt two generations back, his great-grandmother, *Scheitel* and all, a rare friend of old, old Gutele Rothschild, legend said) moved his hands from Sukey, who immediately smacked him hard across the face and then sank upon the hall carpet sobbing. The Countess quickly opened the front door. Touching the lieutenant's slob-green sleeve to urge him to his escort's duty, she said, "I'm so terribly sorry all this should have happened here." "Too bad in any house, lady," he replied. For a moment the Countess stood framed in the doorway, her fringed black evening cape billowing flittermoth-like against the yellow world beyond.

"It was either that, my dears," she said, "or killing the geese—for your grandmother and Mouse are silly geese, that I grant you. But when you get to your father's age you'll know that nothing ever, ever must be done that could prevent the golden eggs being laid." Smiling with childlike glee she added, "Never mind, darlings, all the righteousness is on your side and that's what the young enjoy so much." Then putting her hand through her bewildered escort's arm, she was gone.

Trapped, Porky Boy snorted a little and then, coming up with a luxurious truffle, said, "The awesome nature of memory! I remember so well my own distress in a similar circumstance. I say similar, though the curious thing is—and the thing quite typical of memory's random, useless charm—that I'm quite unable to recall what the circumstances were. I have only a hazy sense that my parents were the instruments of the blow. But what I do remember is the awful sense of injustice I felt. It was some days before I realized that this was in fact the impact of life's unpleasant reality. Life *is* unjust. The Countess and I today have only been dusty instruments. I don't say you'll come to thank us. You won't. But you'll see the inevitability of our being used by life to illumine her painful way."

If his last words seemed a trifle incoherent, it was perhaps that he could sense Quentin's growing angry disgust, although with good taste he turned his head away from his children's painful reactions to the truth, for he did not wish to bear unpleasant witness against them in time to come. He seemed not to notice, yet, apart from his incoherence, his side-stepping movement suggested that he knew the danger and sought good sense in escape. But before Quentin could hit his father, Gladys held back her brother's arm.

"Not that I care if you knock his chump off. The beastly little bounder! But I don't want you to go back on your beliefs, old boy. He's not worth having on your conscience."

To Gladys, Billy Pop said, "You *would* feel it most, Podge, because, God bless you, though the least suited by figure, you're the family's true idealist." And to Sukey, "We must get you a nice, dependable husband. That'll put a stop to all these tears and rages." Then taking his green homburg with the broad band from the hatrack and his Malacca cane, he departed. "I have need of serious sustenance after this episode in *la comédie humaine*," he said. As with the Countess's farewell smile there was something childlike in his humorous twinkle as he left them. But then "except ye be converted and become as little children . . ."; although also, of course, "whosoever shall offend one of these little ones . . ." But Rupert was six feet and Quentin five feet eleven inches and Gladys weighed ten stone, so the offence had to come sometime perhaps. And it came now—all his pretty chicks at one fell swoop, but not his dam.

Not until Billy Pop's mixed aroma of cigar smoke and eau-de-cologne had quite faded did Gladys remember. "What about my tenner?" Then bitterly, "Serious sustenance! He'll blow the whole lot in one go."

Rupert walked to the door that Billy had left open and, before shutting it, cried bitterly into the night, "Oh, for God's sake, get out of our lives."

The Game

The Game began quietly that evening at about half past eight. It started as usual with some spontaneous exchanges between Billy Pop

(Rupert) and the Countess (Marcus), founders of The Game, born of their need to relieve their pent-up shame, distress, and anger in histrionics, to heal their hurts with mimicry's homeopathic sting, and no doubt as well to indulge some sexual urges. So much for the casual, conventional beginning as it might be: MARCUS, THE COUNTESS: Oh, for God's sake do up your flies, Billy, when you come into my drawing-room. What will visitors think? To which RUPERT, THE BILLY POP: I dress, my dear, to accommodate your friends' conventional ideas of the artist. I'm sure they will forgive such little sartorial peccadilloes as part of the Bohemianism they've come to see. MARCUS, THE COUNTESS: Well, if that's where they're feasting their eyes, they needn't worry. There's precious little by now to feast on. (Collapse of stout Billy Pop.) Or: MARCUS, THE COUNTESS: Oh, for God's sake do up your flies, Billy, when you come into my drawing-room. RUPERT, THE BILLY POP: Drawing-room! What drawing-room? This is our old free-and-easy, hugger-mugger, argy-bargy den. MARCUS, THE COUNTESS: Nonsense. We still live *comme il faut*. We have servants. Where are the servants? Gladys, your cue. And in comes old REGAN, THE PODGE, sliding on the parquet floor, laughing to beat the band, holding on to her maid's cap. REGAN, THE PODGE: *Oooh!* I went and fell over, Mum. Just look at me batch of scones. I've flattened them out like pancakes.

But in fact all six had sensed that The Game would go further that evening, played as never before. They awaited some ritual.

Quentin, the eldest and the newest, the most experienced in life, the most innocent in the life of No. 52, appropriately marked the occasion, gave the word of command, opened the show, launched the boat, and offered up a sacrifice by at last rounding out his own part, often tentatively suggested in the few weeks since he had returned home, but now finally declared to be that of Mr. Justice Scales, the dispassionate, objective outsider (appropriately a returned hero) who, by eliciting the facts, reveals the moral pattern, sets all to right, undiscovers the riddle.

First as a stickler for principles, a getter-down to basic facts, a young chap, necessarily questioning everything in order to rebuild, he examined the fictions, though they had already been intuitively agreed, by which The Game, now tacitly understood to require the form of a trial, was to be played. Was the man or the woman able to be another also the most suited to defend that other's interest? Yes, for simulation, whatever its motive, demands identification. But was he or she sufficiently detached to be able to offer a defence intelligible to others, as defending counsel should, without the confusions and blurs of subjective statement? Yes, for simulation and mimicry also demand observation; in them compassion is tinged by mockery or mockery by compassion, and identification is distanced by the demands of technique. But could this simple mixture of opposites, which mimicry requires—of affection with distaste, of respect with contempt, of love with hatred—be justly defined as a sort of reasoned apology? Yes, if passed through the tempering fire of the scrutiny of Mr. Justice Scales (Quentin). The rules established, The Game could now proceed.

Call Clara Madeline Matthews, born Clara Madeline Rickard. Objection from MARCUS, THE COUNTESS, that such a call was prejudging, for, first, the name by its stiff unfamiliarity meant the trial of someone else—of a birth certificate, or a shoplifter of that name, if such has ever existed; secondly, Marcus pleaded, the first names were unfair ironies for she, the Countess, never pretended to the purity suggested by Clara nor to the repentance suggested by Madeline; she should be tried in all her familiar glory as "The Countess."

Question by MR. JUSTICE SCALES.

Would not the sobriquet prejudge the issue by suggesting the horrid fates of the Countess of Salisbury and the Countess Du Barry? No, for the Countess *tout court* was something much more tra-la-la than the frightened, beheaded ladies, however virtuous, however light, however high-born, however low. Even the Countess Porgi Amor (send back, send back, send back my Milton to me) to *e dico di si* (I can't say no to you, Iced Pratts), only superficially suggested all the overtones in that title. Would she please name some of these overtones? Impossible, the range is altogether too rich. Then the Court must seek evidence in history. General suggestion that Mr. Rupert Matthews, as so emotionally close, should testify.

RUPERT, THE BILLY POP: The name was a little whimsy of mine thrown off . . . But objection. The intention had been to call Mr. Rupert Matthews in his own right. No evidence could be taken from Rupert the Billy Pop as a witness not yet sworn in. MR. RU-

PERT MATTHEWS then gives it as his own opinion that the name is a genteelism of Cuntess, established for the benefit of the nursery. To the judge's horror a lady in the audience, notably Gladys, reveals by her flushing that she understands.

MARCUS, THE COUNTESS: How inexpressibly vulgah you are, deah boy. It must have taken generations of Matthews trade to produce such vulgarity.

RUPERT, THE BILLY POP, insists that he be sworn in to answer such a slur on his line. He will forego his rightful name, William Ackerley Matthews, if it please the Court; or his proud pen-name, W. A. Matthews, author of, etc.; or his once used pseudonym, Long-Stop, author of a series of articles, published in *Blackwood's Magazine*, on "Cricket in Literature," from Dingley Dell onwards, with a special appendix discussing Mr. Jingle's West Indian tour; or again, homely Will, Shakespeare of his mother's eye, and with the modest, tweedy, pipe-formed smile that declares his Englishman's birthright—the ability, nay the privilege, to laugh at himself. He will accept the name given by his family; however it may have originated in mockery, bitterness, unfaithfulness, or almighty dollar vulgarity, he can take it, chuckling, on the chin. Rupert, the Billy Pop—so he will testify. Request accepted more to accelerate the proceedings than to satisfy any ignoble desires for martyrdom of witness-accused. Very well, what does he wish to say?

RUPERT, THE BILLY POP: Only that by trade, England is great, her coffers full.

MARCUS, THE COUNTESS: And by arms has that greatness been preserved, the dear King sent victorious.

RUPERT, THE BILLY POP (scornfully): Gentlemen and officers!

MARCUS, THE COUNTESS (equally so): Merchant princes!

RUPERT, THE BILLY POP: Legalized murderers!

MARCUS, THE COUNTESS: Authorized thieves!

RUPERT, THE BILLY POP: Scum of the earth!

MARCUS, THE COUNTESS: Money-bags!

MR. JUSTICE SCALES, ordering the two accused to cease their recriminations, urges them to remember how only by combining had the professions and the trades been able to form that great middle class which had prevailed against both aristocratic arrogance and the madness of the mob. The great middle class will be proud, he said, that its daughters and sons, however they may

have strayed into the Arts or into Bohemia, should recognize the
sources of their greatness; but there should surely be no quarrel
to divide them. We who have returned, he says, have no doubt
of what part the City played in sending us there nor of what part
the General Staff played in seeing that millions of us remain there,
in some corner of a foreign field that is forever . . . But united in
checking further comment by their Judge, MARCUS, THE COUNTESS
(now with shoulders bare and feather-duster egret in his hair), and
RUPERT, THE BILLY POP (now with velvet smoking cap and his
old one-inch Ramblers' map, source of "Rambles through Surrey"
and "Walks around Box Hill," alas, never written), join in happy
duet—I brought the breeding and you brought the dough (to the
tune of *Il chittarino le suonero*).

Come to that, cries REGAN, THE PODGE, somersaulting into the
centre of the court (who knows, deep-voiced and muscular as
Gladys was, what centre court she might have walked into if it
had not been for a glandular imbalance that in a pre-endocrino-
logically minded decade had swollen her in adolescence, that and
the enforced resignation of Billy Pop from Queen's Club for un-
discharged debts to fellow members at the time when his daughter's tennis zeal was strongest), come to that, it was her hoity-toity
ways and that what got her called the Countess. It was him that
called her . . . But the stout, lovable old cockney clown was herself called to order. I'll accept this evidence, the beak said, when
the witness is sworn. Witness-accused number three, he added,
nasty-like. Henrietta Pubbles Stoker, he said, giving her her mon-
iker in full. But to their surprise, cook-in-a-million, faithful old
war horse, their own, their only childhood friend, she elected to be
sworn as REGAN, THE PODGE (jokers that they were, both of them).
It was them give me the name, she said, and I'll stand by it. On account of they thought I killed me da, she explained. But the judge
asked her to consider the wisdom of this admission. Apart from
anything else, he said, those who have fought on the Western
Front did not do so, I must tell you, to hand over the Western
World to playboys; or to playgirls, for that matter. There's a
world waiting to be solved, he said, describing a large circle with
his hand; a world waiting to be remade so that never again . . .
But MARCUS, THE COUNTESS, could stand it no longer. I refuse, she
said, to have my butter rationed again for anybody. I want fun,

she said, gaiety, laughter. I want to dance round the clock. And so she did in the arms of RUPERT, THE BILLY POP. With the old nursery tablecloth with bobbles for a skirt, she danced with him round the old nursery alarm clock, in slow fox time. "Do you remember, Billah," she asked, "when we bunnah hugged till dawn?" "Not all the old fire has died down, has it?" RUPERT, THE BILLY POP, observed. "We can still teach the young 'uns a thing or two, eh?" But MARCUS, THE COUNTESS, sprang away from him. "Your breath smells, Billah," she said. "Oh, God! You've let yourself go to pieces." "Come to that," said her ex-partner ungallantly, "you stink like a whore's knocking shop."

At this point whispered representations to the judge showed a certain public impatience with this marital bickering. "Your failure to keep alive any of the ideals, any of the love, any of the hopes that presumably inspired your days of courtship is your own concern. We are here . . ." But MR. JUSTICE SCALES was rudely interrupted by MISS MARGARET MOUSE. In acid tones she told him, "Ideals, love, hope." She cried, "If you're talking of my nephew-in-law, the eminent writer whose ink has run dry, you've chosen your words most aptly. His ideal was to live on other people's cash, his love was for himself and for no one else, his hope that the rest of the world would believe that it owed him a living." "And so it does," said GRANNY SUKEY, beaming goofily, "so it does. Everyone always loved Will. Everyone wanted to do things for him. He was such a lovely little boy. If only he'd married little Mollie Spooner. Oh, dear, I can't help laughing when I think of that picnic on the beach—If I gives her a ring does we have to have a big bed like you and Dadda? And he was only four years old. Dear little Will!" "Dear little fiddlesticks. He caught my poor silly niece when her pretty little head was filled with some silly romantic notions about love in a garret. 'We'll be poor but happy. There'll be bread and cheese lunches, Mouse,' she said to me. Poor little fool!"

"Bread and cheese lunches when Will always needed something solid midday! He was lucky with her if he got bread and cheese. It was servants here and servants there or milady dined out. But *she* never thought she was going to be poor. I'm afraid she told you terrible lies, Miss Rickard. She certainly did to us. We understood there was to be a proper dowry."

"And you fell for the bait, my good woman?"

"There's no need for name calling. And I should choose your words more carefully. Bait indeed, with a name like Mouse." GRANNY SUKEY blew out her cheeks and puffed and huffed and then gave a characteristic earthy chuckle. "How we laughed when we first heard that name. 'Clara's Aunt Mouse,' Will said. 'A hole-in-the-wall sort of crowd they sound,' my dear husband answered. But it's your own life, my boy. You must make what you can of this business. Those were his very words in our dear old morning room at Roehampton."

However often Sukey "did" Granny Matthews, the others never expected their conventional sister to succeed so well, and her sudden inventions always brought the house down. Gladys was rolling in her seat, fit to burst, Marcus jumping up and down till his shirt threatened to slip more than *décolleté*. Rupert tried hard to preserve a professional's condescending smile, and Quentin put down in laughing despair the nursery bell he was ringing in vain to bring The Game to order.

For now Margaret, not to be outdone, stretched the skin of her face to Mouse's thin parchment and tightened the posture of her long thin body so that it seemed to recall a hundred wary tent slumbers—a woman alone among sand and Berbers and camels. MISS MARGARET MOUSE laughed the dry laugh with which she turned clubs and hotels and pensions the world over into desert.

"A generous disposition of a young, parentless gel of eighteen. It's a pity your husband never lived to see how his son fulfilled his kind licence. A young gel of beauty, attainments, and breeding reduced to a shrill drab!" "If Clara had been anything of a wife to him . . ." "She'd have let him land her with twelve unwanted children instead of six." "She's not been unwilling to grant her favours elsewhere, if these terrible stories are true." "My dear woman, would you give yourself happily to a jellyfish?" "It's easy to see why she has no morals, no warmth." "And he no stamina, no will. Your will-less Will!" MISS MARGARET MOUSE laughed dry sand in GRANNY SUKEY's face. "How can you laugh at such a time, you godless suffragette!" And now the two old beldams had come to hair-pulling and slaps. "One expects no better than brawling from Mrs. Pankhurst's crew." "You ignorant woman!" . . .

"Oh, dear," Margaret broke away, panting. "What is that name Mouse is always boasting? Her leader! Some dowdy old battle-axe. Oh, I know, Mrs. Fawcett . . ." She engaged in physical battle once more.

"You ignorant woman, my leader was Mrs. Fawcett. We never used violence."

But whether because of Margaret's momentary fluffing of her lines or because he was impatient to take the stage again, MARCUS, THE COUNTESS, lay back across the nursery table, egret-duster flopping over one eye, long bead necklace flying wide. "Don't force it, Billah, for God's sake, don't force it," she shrieked. And as though from a long way off, from memories of some half-forgotten game, RUPERT, THE BILLY POP, said sadly, bewilderedly, "I don't know any other way of doing it, my dear."

For a good two minutes there was silence, then Quentin, catching Gladys's eye, took brisk control. JUSTICE SCALES said: "All five accused are charged with deceit, with bad faith, with cruelty, and with negligence. In addition, the defendants, the Countess and Billy Pop, are accused of being accessories to the crime of murder. The defendant Regan is charged with murder. What have you got to say in your defence?"

MARCUS, THE COUNTESS, smoothed upon her thin white arms a pair of elbow-length white kid gloves and turned her head to look haughtily at the judge over her shoulder. She said, "Guilty to producing a generation of horrible little prigs." She added, "Am I a *ci-devant comtesse* now, Quentin?" To which Quentin, warming up, finding a childish desire to emulate, answered, ringing his Fouquier-Tinville bell, "Who slanders the younger generation with opprobrious epithets attacks the principles of the Revolution. You condemn yourself, Citizeness."

"I am an old man," RUPERT, THE BILLY POP, said, "a very old man, my lord, a very old writing man. I played for Thirsty Scribblers against the Cheshire Cheese Chaps, an annual village green shandy-gaff fixture, in aught six. Even then I was out for a duck."

"Age and incompetence were the pleas of Methuen, Moltke, von Falkenhayn, Joffre, and Fisher in a greater crime than yours. The plea is insufficient."

"I was poor but I was honest. And when I wasn't, it was because it slipped out of me ands like," said REGAN, THE PODGE, attempting a ridiculous hand-spring and falling bump, bump on her you know where.

"A plea of diminished responsibility is accepted. In seeking to cling to it you are your own class's worst enemy."

"I'm sure I was only looking after my poor little Pom."

"A dog-in-a-manger attitude. A nice thing for a respectable churchwoman, monthly communicant at Saint John the Evangelist, Ladbroke Square, to put such an animal in that holy birthplace. Guilty."

"I am in no way morally obliged to sustain the younger generation in sentimental illusions. That the wretched animals were subsequently drowned in an amateurish fashion only shows the good sense of my recommendation that they should be disposed of by a professional veterinary surgeon."

"Real polly talk! A mouse should be careful how glibly she disposes of cats. Guilty.

"I find," he added, "none of these justificatory pleas adequate. Have you got anything more general to urge in your defence?"

"He understood once when I was frightened of the dark after Regan had been telling stories of Jack the Ripper. When I screamed She came and smacked me, but He rebuked Her and carried me down to His study in a blanket, set me before the fire, fed me with the ginger sticks out of the tin of Edinburgh Rock."

"Why," asked THE JUDGE, "did you do this apparent kindness to your youngest?"

RUPERT, THE BILLY POP, seemed quite bemused by the question. He hummed and ha-ed—a kind of noise that few men produced so exactly. "I was concerned for the little lad. Literary man," he said, "more imagination than Woman. God bless her. I've written one or two ghost stories, they're not perhaps my finest. Unmarketed, in fact. But . . ."

"Will hated to be alone as a little boy. We never left him," said GRANNY SUKEY.

"Ha," commented THE JUDGE.

"Getting back at his 'old trouble-and-strife.' That's what it was," REGAN, THE PODGE, cried. "I know im. Men are all the same. Just like our old man. Use us any time it suits em."

"All the same," said Marcus, "he needn't have given me the ginger sticks. He likes them himself. I know because he usually wolfs them down and leaves the horrible strawberry ones."

"The plea is dubious," said THE JUDGE.

"She knew when I first got fat how much I minded. He wanted me to go on with the tennis lessons altho' I knew I was no longer any good and that people laughed. She cancelled the lessons and took me to San Toy instead."

"Explain your unexpected kindness to your elder daughter," THE JUDGE said.

MARCUS, THE COUNTESS, laughed harshly. "I had no intention of letting Billy waste the money just to show off at his club."

But MISS MARGARET MOUSE intervened. "Clara was a much shyer girl than you would think. Perhaps I made her do things on her own too much as a girl. But I've always believed that shyness must be overcome. Perhaps she was thinking of her own girlhood."

"A sort of transferred egoism," said THE JUDGE.

"But she needn't have taken me to San Toy," said Gladys.

"Did you want to go?"

"Well, not very much, but it was nice when we got there."

"Another dubious plea."

"When I played Wolsey at school *She* forgot the afternoon and *He* arrived late and squiffy. But the old lady came in time and applauded and prevented *Him* making a fool of *Himself* in front of the House. *And* she gave *Him* a terrific talking to afterwards."

Here JUDGE SCALES rang his bell furiously. "I cannot accept any of these exceptional, quixotic, and inexplicable acts as pleas. They run contrary to the well-known personalities of the defendants. We're concerned with general influences and over-all trends in judging our elders. In any case these are your children's memories, not your own. You have filched enough from them already without barefaced robbery in the Court."

His words left them bewildered, then RUPERT, THE BILLY POP, said, "Only today we offered our children advice, valuable advice for life's journey ahead. I seem to remember that your mother said, 'Marry.' She addressed her advice to the girls. The Lord save us from spinsters. But I invite you, my boys, to come with me to my club and watch the bachelors sitting there spinning out the hours, holding on to us luckier fellows like so many ancient mariners with their glittering eyes. No, God forbid! Marry, all of you, marry!" At which MARCUS, THE COUNTESS, put her hand on his arm in silent thanks for this tribute to her wifely virtues, and then, smilingly, slyly, lisped, "But, oh, Billy, do see that they marry *well*."

Rupert whispering in Quentin's ear, the COMMENTATOR-JUDGE banged on the table and called, "Ladies and gentlemen, I give you your own, your only, your oonique Rupert Matthews." At which Rupert, tripping across the room, seeming all feet and no body, sang, "Cash in the bank she said she'd plenty, I was a MUG."

"But," continued RUPERT, THE BILLY POP, "it was the companionship, the often laughed at but the very real comradeship of marriage that I particularly stressed as the real staff for you children to lean upon in life's uphill journey."

"If you please, Mr. Chairman," said Rupert. And as THE JUDGE banged once more upon the table, Rupert the incomparable coster, white silk choker round his neck, billy cock set jauntily on his head, waltzed with arms folded towards his dear old Dutch. "We've been together now for forty years, and it don't seem a day too much. (Bowing to her) There ain't a lady livin' in the land as I'd swap for my dear old Dutch."

His Lady making him an awkward curtsy, he trips her up and smacks her bottom. He then goes off singing, "My word, if I catch you bending, my word, if I catch you bending."

To recover the proceedings from yet another of these marital knockabouts that seemed to threaten all orderliness, THE JUDGE reminded the court that not all the advice they had received had been parental. At which RUPERT, THE BILLY POP, seemingly irrepressible, intervened once more. "Ah, no!" he said. "My dear old mother gave you her bit of wisdom. God bless her! True to the good old days and the good old ways as usual, she told you, if I remember rightly, to cultivate a sense of the past."

At which GRANNY SUKEY, settling her hearth-rug sables round her shoulders and spraying the room as her teeth rushed forward cheerfully to correct him, said, "Not too serious, of course. Just remembering all the funny family things."

This time, before THE JUDGE could bang upon the table, in came Rupert the Wrecker carrying a small stepladder and a pot of paste and after him his mate Ghastly Gladys with a roll of paper, and My Mate Marcus with a broom. After some screamingly funny acrobat-

ics and some witty backchat, they joined together in chorus—
"When Father papered the parlour . . ."

But now MISS MARGARET MOUSE claimed their attention. "In all
this welter of comic sentimentalism, may I pour just a little cold
water to restore a little common sense. If you remember, I urged self-
reliance upon you children. You would have done better to have
taken notice of what I said."

THE JUDGE allowed himself a comment here. "At least you took
good care by your subsequent action to see that we could not rely
on you," he said bitterly.

"You have to look after yourself in this world." MISS MARGARET
MOUSE said, "for no one else will."

And in cakewalked Rag-time Rupert, straw boater all ajaunt, playing upon his old ukelele cane. "I love me, I love me, I'm wild about
myself. I wrote myself a letter . . ."

"Self-reliance," said MISS MARGARET MOUSE acidly, "is not always
self-love."

So Rupert the Baritone threw aside his boater and his cane, and
thunderingly gave it to them. "The top of the hill hasn't room for
two, but sure the one that gets there must be you."

MARCUS, THE COUNTESS, smiled. "Yes, darlings, and who was the
one who pointed out that self wasn't quite enough? Your cynical old
mother. Responsibility for others, for . . ."

"For your own dear self," said RUPERT, THE BILLY POP, "that was
what I advised them. As some little return for all you have done."
And in a second, putting on his bowler hat again, he was Rupert the
Cheeky Chappie (a prophetic role at that date). "And now I'm in
the money, and I've lots of L.s.d., I'm looking after my old mum as
she looked after me."

"So it seems," said THE JUDGE, "that only Regan had no advice to
offer us."

"Most proper. Knows her place." GRANNY SUKEY smiled benevo-
lently. "Her broad wisdom learnt in the school of the streets," said
RUPERT, THE BILLY POP, "needs no words to express itself."

"To expect advice from a servant owed wages," began MISS MAR-
GARET MOUSE, but Marcus was whispering in Gladys's ear. And now
REGAN, THE PODGE, rolled forward. "I've got me a little word to say.
It was master Markie I give it to. I'm careful who I talk to in this
ouse. But between these four walls ere it is for the lot of you. Keep

away from the muck. Get to know the upper tens. Get yerselves asked to their ouses. All them weekend goins on." Broadly she winked at them.

Marcus, the Countess, laughed delightedly. "Adorable, delicious Regan," she cried, "of course she *would* be the one to teach us. She's right, my dears, she's right. Go for the fun and the beauty in life and let all the solemn duties fit in where they can."

And now at a signal from Mr. Justice Scales (their own, their ownerly Chairman and MC, acting Major Quentin Matthews, wounded but without the MC), she played at an invisible piano and Rupert the Lothario, all whiskers, light tenor, and a smile's caress, sang to his Bohemian girl, "I dreamt that I dwelt in marble halls with vassals and serfs at my side."

When the singing faded away, Regan, the Podge, could be seen polishing the floor. Sweat pouring from her, she looked up at the company. "Doin' the floors is fersty work. Wot about a pint of wallop?"

"The advice—such as it is—offered by the defendants is accepted," said the Judge, "in mitigation of their actions. But we also note the comment on that advice offered by the musical reflections for which we are particularly indebted to that fine old favourite of the Halls, Mr. Rupert Matthews. Before I deliver judgment, I shall retire for a moment in the approved fashion."

It was notable that in the Judge's short absence a marked bifurcation of personalities occurred. Marcus, the Countess, said, "Give me a gasper, Billy." But when Rupert, the Billy Pop, presented his silver cigarette case, Gladys intervened: "He's not to, Rupert." Meanwhile Margaret, asserting her Mousehood, got away with smoking, though only by forcing an unwilling Sukey into the act, who with natural giggles and little puffs miraculously produced a perfect Granny Sukey coy exhalation. "Oh, I don't know if I ought, but after all one's only on trial once in one's life." "How lucky you are, Mrs. Matthews, most of us have been on trial all our lives," said Miss Margaret Mouse, as, old campaigner and rough sleeper-out, she smoked a "Wild Woodbine" from a battered old square tin, just like the Tommies in the trenches.

"Oh, God!" said Marcus, the Countess. "I wish there was some fun, some gaietah, some beautah in meh life." Then Marcus, putting aside his pencil cigarette holder, helped himself to three toffees from the Mackintoshes' tin. Cheeks bulged, words swallowed, he said, "I must say, Quentin makes the game pretty grim. He's so solemn." Gladys looked shocked. REGAN, THE PODGE, said, "I'll catch you one over the lug ole if you're narky about the Judge, me lad." Gladys added, "Surely you're not too young to realize how much Quentin is doing for us all these days." "Yes," said Rupert, "put a sock in it, bed-wetter. And put your shirt on properly. Actually," he added, "I should think it's jolly bad for you pretending to be a woman."

MARCUS, THE COUNTESS, said, "You cad, you're twistin meh wrist."

Whereat RUPERT, THE BILLY POP, twirling imaginary moustaches and grinding his teeth, cried, "Ho, ho, my pretty maiden, I have you in my power."

"Have you ever heard the Billy Pop trying to imitate?" Rupert asked. "It's absolutely putrid."

The flushing of the water next door caused Margaret to remark, "I can't think what happens to prisoners when they're taken short, can you?"

But GRANNY SUKEY, beaming, said, "The dear boy. He's always so regular. That's Ladbroke Grove training."

So that when Quentin opened the door they were all in fits of giggles.

"I shall now pronounce sentence," he said as he sat down. The five accused trembled and shook until their teeth chattered. MARCUS, THE COUNTESS, lovely white arms outstretched, went down on her knees and cried, "Remember you once loved me, D'Artagnan."

But all was to no avail. "I thought," said THE JUDGE, and it could be seen from his manner that he did not intend to forego any part of his role. "I thought when I retired that I should have to condemn you as a generation, or rather as two generations, indeed as all the older generations, perhaps as the embodiment of accumulated history. You are, after all, all we know of the past. It's you who've put us in the soup and don't seem prepared to help us out of it for fear of scalding your fingers. Not to put any pretence upon it, you are a guilty lot. But as in my moments of retirement I reflected, I soon saw that this business of generations just would not do. Here we have a system and a class in decay. Granny, you with your large annuity, your servants, your house property . . ."

Sukey said to Margaret, "Miss Lampson wanted me to wait on customers on Thursday. I may be an apprentice teacher, but I drew the line there . . ."

". . . And Aunt Mouse," THE JUDGE was saying, "is just as much part of the system. She may go to Kamchatka or Tierra del Fuego but she only does so on what she inherited. . . . And with her non-violent tactics, what will she do with her vote? Why, vote for her gilt-edged, of course, or the occasional safe gamble like . . ."

Margaret said, "Penelope Skinner gets relief by bathing them in boiling water and washing soda when she gets home, but it's so hard to tell whether they were always rough-looking or whether it's the soda that's doing it . . ."

". . . As to Regan, she's a pitiful victim of the system, but now so pitiful that it's hard to imagine the system without her. She flatters our . . ."

Gladys frowned hard in order to appear to give adequate weight to her brother's words. She thought, If I took six guineas out it wouldn't be a lot and I could buy that black taffeta evening dress for when we go to the dinner dance at Maidenhead, but then probably Alf'd say I was dressing old just to fit in with him. But the white does make me look a size!

". . . As to our dear parents, they have been entirely destroyed by the economic system in which they have been brought up. They have learned to expect its benefits automatically. Some greater emancipation of women might have been allowed Mother. . . ."

Rupert thought of the months ahead of him. He was to start in a Christmas season at Liverpool and then on to Edinburgh with a reportory of *As You Like It, The Merchant, The Dream, Monsieur Beaucaire, Ghosts,* and *The Rivals.* Perhaps he would have two lines in *The Merchant,* and two in *Monsieur Beaucaire,* that at the most, but he would double perhaps in *As You Like It.* Even though Stratford had finished, Lady Benson had said, they would carry on, though poetry and religion were like dead in this futuristic world. And then there was always Spanish flu—the boon of understudies. Resolutely he decided to give notice at the office in the morning. They would be glad to see the last of him. Moving his lips and his eyebrows in suitable notice-giving manner, he suddenly said aloud, "I shall not easily forget the months that I have spent here."

Surprised, THE JUDGE brushed aside such unsolicited gratitude. He leaned forward with his elbows on the table and compelled their attention by his suddenly menacing gaze—hawk's, eagle's, stout Cortés's, Father Bernard Vaughan's. "All this sounds very nice, very comfortable, very warming to our little vanities. Everyone else is to blame. Only, unfortunately for us, it isn't so. The most rotten part of this rotten set-up is us. Yes, you all and me. Especially me."

Margaret thought, As Robin Carmichael grew older he fell into the habit of making the most disagreeable sound. He called it "thundering." With shame, she stored the passage away for future use. Sukey blushed, because the pitch of Quentin's voice suggested that they had all failed him. And Gladys shifted in her seat because she understood that she could not have been pulling her weight. "I'm a lazy great porpoise," she announced. Rupert reddened with prepared anger, for his brother might be about to demand sacrifices. Marcus was just embarrassed.

"We've all enjoyed ourselves very much being funny or witty or whatever we like to call our performance at their expense. But we've never considered for a moment that we have only ourselves to blame. We've taken it for granted that the system which has produced them will work for us, only decently of course, because we're such decent people. Well, it won't. Or at any rate not for much longer. Crumbs from rich men's tables, or rich widows', or rich spinsters' for that matter, just won't be falling our way or anybody's soon. And so the quicker we make up our minds to depend on ourselves the better . . ."

"Self-reliance," said Miss Margaret Mouse. "Can I hear aright?"

"You can call it what you choose. But it's not the old cut-throat selfishness. Co-operation."

"Each for all and all for each," said Marcus.

"Not a bad idea," his eldest brother told him, "though hardly for the same aims as the Three Musketeers."

"They couldn't be really," said Marcus, "because we don't know any cardinals to frustrate."

The Judge frowned; and the others straightened themselves. Rupert, withdrawing his chair a little from where Marcus sat:

"If our despised parents in their decadence can take action, then surely . . ."

"Do you mean," asked Sukey, "that we should make our peace with Granny and Aunt Mouse? For *they* will tomorrow, I'm sure."

"Yes," said Margaret, "Mother in a new hat to Mouse's club, and Father on his own to Ladbroke Grove to make it just the two of them together, like it used to be before he married."

"Well, after all," said Rupert, "now the kittens have gone . . ."

Quentin put his face into his hands and gave a groan. "We cannot compromise," he said. "That's their rotten system, parasites on parasites. For God's sake don't let us add to it. Let's get on with the delousing. I'm the most to blame, for I have had a chance to stop still in the last months and to read and to consider. And then before that I . . ."

They sat listening now as he spoke of the trenches and the war. Everyone knew that it was his or her duty to do so.

". . . But ghastly although the whole thing was—something I can't and never shall be able to speak about—it didn't happen out of nowhere." Sukey tried to stretch her legs without interrupting. "It came from the diplomacy of secret treaties by frightened men who didn't understand the world around them. It came from the natural result of years of Grandfather Matthews"—Margaret quickly wrote something in her pocket diary, then tucking the little book under her knee, she looked absorbed—"who now saw that it was the time, if his income was to increase, to send Grandfather Rickard to fight a heroic battle. And of course"—Gladys stared ahead, but her lips were counting (hours before she saw Alfred? pounds necessary to start out on her own?)—"if he were wounded there was always Great-Grandfather Rickard, the surgeon, to cut him up and patch him up if he could. Oh, for heaven's sake, I'm not thinking of myself and my famous hero's wound. Eight million were killed, let alone the wounded." Only just audible at moments was the hum of Rupert's "Any Time's Kissing Time." "And of course I don't just mean Grandfather Matthews but Grandpère Mathieu and Grossvater Matthäus and all the rest of them. The thing was the logical outcome . . ." Marcus twisted the egret-duster into a feather boa. Quentin laid his arms upon the table, the palms of his hands flat on the wooden surface, UP-Jenkins, smashems, nothing hidden. He seemed to relax, then speaking suddenly in a whisper, he said, "And I, God help me! (but He won't) dictated to you who had asked me for help. No, that's not true. I came in as Mr. Panacea, a President Woodrow Wilson whom nobody had invited. And my fourteen points were not like his, something to offer us a ray of hope, but an encouragement to you all to fight the same old wars, the tedious, pointless battles that have shaken this family to its decaying old roots ever since I can remember. I who should above all have known better than to have suggested that the old world of alliances and counter-alliances, secret treaties and open pacts, in short, of balance of power, could lead to a positive result, could lead to anything but war and wicked waste."

They were still now, as his voice grew louder, staring at him fixedly, Sukey's neck even suffused with red. Only Marcus moved once or twice, knocking his knees together rapidly, whatever emotion had roused in him having made its greatest impression upon his bladder. Quentin sat back and smoked his pipe. As he did so, he looked for a moment frightened, as though, losing their attention, he might be left all alone. Then, wreathed in infernal smoke, his thin face creased to reveal Mr. Punch, the Imp of Lincoln, "Good God! As if it mattered. As if any of you mattered, or less still a broken-down skeleton like myself, fit only to hang in the wind and let the bones rattle to scare the birds away."

The sudden change in his features, the fierceness with which he spat out his words, above all the cackling contemptuous laughter with which he accompanied them, now at last compelled attention. "I've seen enough rotting, green corpses and young flesh that had barely time to live to suppose that it matters what happens to the clever young Matthews kids who've had a hard deal, especially to the soap-box orator, know-nothing, returned hero Quentin Matthews."

Margaret tried to look away, but her brother's tufted eyebrow, as he looked through the curls and loops of his satanic smoke rings, held her. Sukey tried to think of something else—the family, her own future children, England, the Quantock Hills, the North Sea waves breaking against the cliffs at Cromer—anything by which she could be justified; but as they all failed, she waited with fear for his next words. Gladys saw only Quentin's eyes where points of light danced and glittered in mockery of all her hopes—Alfred was an old lecher, their love a hole-in-the-corner squalor, herself a fat bladder of lard for a clown to burst as a joke on an ass's head. Rupert wanted to give forth in rivalry, to howl, "Blow winds and crack your cheeks! Rage! Blow!" or to volley forth, "You common cry of curs, whose breath I hate!" But he knew, as his brother's voice lashed him, that however he swelled his chest there would come forth no tenor

Caruso, he would drown no stage with tears, for his croaking would show him to be not Rupert of Hentzau but the bullfrog Prince. Marcus's dark eyes stared, yet not as usual, ikon-like from a varnished yellow skin, but more ghostly, like holes in a white sheet on All-Hallows' Eve.

"If we rotted and stank like the wretches who are sleeping out tonight in ditches or under the Adelphi arches, what would it matter?"

As they now sat without stir or sound, he stretched his legs a little, relaxing before he sprang at them again with flash and cackle. But into this short silence came a noise they had not heard for six years or more, a sound that had not ventured even to vie with the zeppelins and the anti-aircraft fire. Marcus began to scream. He was shaking with hysteric sobbing: "The kittens are dead, the kittens are dead."

At first they were silenced by surprise. Then Gladys, big sister with the longest memory, bent across Rupert and smacked her little brother hard on each cheek, first with the palm and then with the back of her hand. When his screaming subsided in a choking struggle to recover his breath, "He's only a kid. It's been a long day for him. This hasn't happened for years," she added in explanation to her elder brother, Quentin.

"Oh, Lord! I'm dreadfully sorry. It's all my fault."

"No, no, old man," Sukey told him. "Really it isn't. We all of us feel a bit all in, I think."

"A basin of nice smooth gruel, thin but not too thin," said Margaret, "that I could recommend. I'll go down and make some Bovril."

"No, let me, Mr. Woodhouse. You've got a rotten day ahead, I know," Rupert suggested.

"Do you think Mr. W. ever had rotten days?"

"Yes, when doors were left open or governesses married." Chattering they went downstairs together.

Marcus, wiping tears from his eyes, announced that he would go to bed.

"Not a bad idea all round," Gladys counselled. "Monday's always a bit of a let-down."

Later, seeking a mislaid handkerchief, she tapped on the nursery door after Rupert was in bed. She seldom spoke directly to this younger brother, but now, "I'm afraid we've missed the boat this time. Poor old Quentin meant to be a great captain . . ."

"Oh, I don't know." Rupert spoke comfortably from under many blankets. "That Yank's face when Marcus spat at him will always remain to cheer my weary hours."

"Yes, but you haven't got an unpaid school bill, Rupert. Oh, I'm sorry, old boy. I know you must be feeling rotten about giving up this acting job. Perhaps you won't have to . . ."

"I won't. I've already given notice at the office."

"Oh, I say. We'll have to see how everything works out, Rupert; I mean what Quentin and I can afford."

"Whatever you can or can't afford, I can't afford to miss this chance."

"You mean if Margaret and Sukey have to go on . . ."

"Whatever happens, I'm going to Liverpool. But it'll all fit in. Life does. It's more of a joke than we can see at the moment. You'll learn, Gladys."

Gladys looked down at her brother. "I've always thought you were a rotter," she said. He closed his eyes. "Just because you're the maiden's dream of love." But she paused at the door. "Said the ugly sister," she added, and laughed to make it all a joke. "If you hear an elephant bedding down for the night, it'll be me. Pleasant dreams." Thumping in mockery of her elephantine tread, she went to her room.

Sukey put down her emptied cup on to its saucer by the bedside. "If we'd used a spoonful of Bovril for the gravy," she announced, "instead of all that rich stuff, things might have gone differently. I shouldn't have gone to sleep after dinner, and the poor little kitties would be alive still."

"Perhaps," said Margaret, trying to concentrate on her few nightly pages of *Persuasion*. "Perhaps it was the poor quack-quack's revenge for your eating him."

There was a silence, so she put down the novel. "I'm sorry, Sukey. I think I've had as much of today as I can manage."

"Oh, that's all right. Anyhow, I expect we shall look back at it all in years to come and smile."

"I hope," answered Margaret, "that I shall grow into a more pleasant woman than that."

Through the darkness Marcus could hear Quentin trying to stretch in his cramped bed.

"I'm very sorry, Markie. I'm afraid I upset you with all my talk. I wasn't much use to any of you."

"Oh, I don't know. You showed that you too have a sense of humour like the rest of us. It's obligatory, you know, in this house. Only yours is of a fiercer brew than we're used to."

"Well, whatever we decide tomorrow, today's over. That's one comfort."

"I see. I thought you at least had enjoyed yourself considerably, Quentin."

From the sound of his brother's body tautening, Marcus could tell that his words had hurt. He lay awake for some time, for when firing the arrow, he had forgotten that his brother had already an all but open hole in his shoulder.

BOOK THREE

I ꗈ 1925

Oh, in the old days that was quite another thing. Time and time again when they'd had a more than usually violent row, when he'd been more than usually impossible, less than ever a husband to respect, something would snap in her and she would hit him. Nothing could excuse such a thing, of course, that she full realized; nothing, that is, that others, outsiders, could understand—a sudden awful feebleness would ooze out of him as he talked and talked, like cheap sawdust out of a cracked jack-in-the-box, and there seemed no way out but to smash the rotten toy she'd been cheated into buying. Sometimes she would really hurt him, more than just physically; and then he would hide himself, locked in his study. But at other times he would play the spoilt child. Packing into his old cricket bag two pairs of socks and, God knows why, his black dress braces, he would walk out of the house, slamming the door, shouting as he went that he would bloody well never return, calling her names, adding the usual hope that his father was burning in hell for leaving the money tied up. For a few moments, of course, she would respond weepingly, distressedly, to his going, for in these rows one got keyed up to take everything seriously. But then her sense of humour would break through, as often as not brought to life by Regan's cockney common sense. "Ten past twelve," the old girl used to say, or whatever time it was, "e'll be back in alf an our. I'll pop over to Overtons and get im a nice Dover sole. Don't you worry, Madam. E'll just fancy that when e comes in ungry." And sure enough, they'd hardly have time for a laugh over his previous dramatic exits before there he was back again, tail between his legs. Into his study to sulk, where Regan or one of the children would take him his grilled sole with a double lump of butter deliciously melting into the solid white flesh.

And later, over a glass of sherry, neither of them would allude to it, or ever again. Unless, of course, laughter failed to ignite and her anger went on smouldering in rows with Regan, with Marcus, with Rupert, with any or all of them. In which case he might well come back from his little temper-trot not to find grilled sole but instead a tumbler or an ash-tray or an old book flying through the air. But eventually even then it would be all China tea and Regan's scones and Sukey sent round to Fuller's for his favourite walnut layer cake, and everybody sorry for what they'd said, although a bit sorry for themselves.

That was the way they had always lived, the kind of odd-job lot they'd always been.

But now she stood in the dark little hall by the telephone, refusing to panic. He had been gone five days, had stormed out with one of these new expanding suitcases given him by Margaret for his birthday. And the cut across her upper lip where he had hit her still bled at intervals; not even witch-hazel seemed to clear the yellow-and-black bruises around her eye. This time, too, Regan had brought no sole, played no consoling role. "I don't want to fuss the children, Regan," she had said when she heard he was not back for dinner. "I should ope not. They don't come ere so often that you can afford to go makin use of em." Such a horrid Bolshie spirit there was in the air, everywhere.

The Wedding (a Carmichael Story)

"The ironies of Miss Margaret Matthews' stories expose our most cherished evasions."

> . . . Mrs. Culmer talked of Derek when he was small. "He was always neat and tidy, Miss Carmichael," she said. "Where the others collected just stamps, he had his chosen field. He couldn't have been more than six when, 'I shall only collect the stamps of Europe,' he said. 'It'll be harder, but that will make it more interesting, won't it, Mummy?'"

And her head shook, was it with pride, was it with the unaccustomed champagne that gave quite a rose flush to her cheeks, white and wrinkled as old kid leather?

Through the shimmering amber haze of the paradise feathers that surmounted the high crown of Mrs. Culmer's hat, Elizabeth had a misty, shimmering picture of the wedding party, a picture that jerked and trembled as the woman's head suddenly swerved—like some of the early bioscopes that she could just remember. The Carmichael family on parade! Or rather, really, in hot pursuit! And she had to admit, they made a most impressive showing; not that the Culmers—poor rabbit-toothed, pop-eyed warren—were an elusive quarry. Mr. Culmer's double chins wobbled as James told him stories of what Frank Harris had said to Leonard Smithers, leading him always to the brink of the sort of thing they did not say at 165 Mimosa Road, Dulwich, and then re-prieving him with, "But Frank's observations on women were never of the kind, you know, that can be uttered in the presence of ladies!" From where she stood, Mr. Culmer, a red turkey seen through his wife's magnificent crest of exotic feathers, seemed to be literally gob-bling his thanks for what he was spared from receiving.

As for poor Derek himself, the happy bridegroom (and happy he should be, carrying off darling Jane), even in his wedding-day ecstasy (and she gave him credit for some real ecstasy that day, for what man would not be seized with a spasm of divine fury who carried off Jane as his prize?) he paled a little before his new mother-in-law's relentless pressure. He stood there, poor thing, champagne glass trembling ever so slightly in his hand (or was that the tremor imparted by his mother's paradise feathers through which she saw him?), gazing hypnotically at Sophie's emerald-green shoes, her emerald-green stockings showing below her elegant monkey-fur-trimmed dress, and let himself be pa-tronized into nothingness.

"James and I went to Madeira for ours. It was quite divine—the mimosa, the bougainvillaea, the little boys diving for pennies! Of course we don't expect *that* in these hard post-war days, but I did think you'd be a little more enterprising than the New Forest. Poor Jane, sur-rounded by honeymooning bank clerks! But how silly I am! She won't notice the bank clerks while she has you there." Her eyes selected for exemplary compassion Derek's clerical collar below his weak chin as she said it.

Elizabeth could hardly keep from giggling, for at that very moment Mrs. Culmer said, "Jane and Derek make such a splendid pair. It seems the Bishop saw them at the church fête and asked who were the Vikings? It's their being so fair," she explained. Elizabeth could still hear her mother's voice, "But perhaps you'll become chaplain at Monte. They do have an English chaplain there, don't they? And then I can spend my winters with you and Jane. But shall I tell you something very shocking?" Derek's teeth protruded even farther now in his alarm. "I like vulgar Nice better than Monte, isn't it awful of me?" Then she added loudly, "I do hope you're going to be a nice, worldly, ambitious clergyman." Even Mrs. Culmer turned at the sound of her son's nervous giggling; she stared for a moment at Sophie's green-and-black outfit, her emerald-green turban, her long, tasselled, green cigarette holder. "Your mother," she said, "can wear things that other people . . ." "And does," Elizabeth said. "Let me assure you, Mrs. Culmer, does." The wretched woman jerked back her head as though the weasel had at last struck. Weasels and stoats, that's what we are, Elizabeth thought, with these rabbit Culmers. But there it is, she decided, I've tasted blood too.

She tried to make reparation by urging the woman to take a *foie gras* sandwich. Claridge's, footmen, and the Fragonard Room! "How shall we ever recoup?" Sophie had wailed. "But Jane will like a Claridge's reception. And if she doesn't, I shall." Truth to tell, there would be no recouping necessary, for Granny Carmichael was footing the bill. And there she stood, now repaid in sycophancy, diminutive yet Madame Mère by virtue of her sables and her lorgnettes, and still more because of the Sèvres and the large cheque she was known to have given.

Such of the Culmer guests as were not overwhelmed by the Carmichael opulence stood in a cowed semicircle before Sophie's Aunt Mildred who, severe but smart, gave an account of the noseless boy's head that had been her gift, noseless antiques being beyond the usual aesthetic range of the Culmers. "I picked it up in a lamp shop in Trebizond," she said. "It was some recompense for a sprained ankle that kept me from seeing the *tulipa sprengeri* I'd been after." Derek's Aunt Ella, the bank manager's widow, clicked her tongue as an appropriate commiseration. But Aunt Mildred clearly misconstrued the click. "Oh, it's not a masterpiece," she said defensively. "It's provincial workmanship, of course. But at least it has the archaic feeling. Nothing of the Parthenon about it, thank heaven. Or are you a Parthenon devotee?" Poor Aunt Ella, Elizabeth thought, for if she had been devoted to anything it would have been the spirit of the Parthenon, flickering still in Alma-Tadema or Lord Leighton—in oleograph, of course. Oh, it was a rout. The ferrets had properly cleared out the warrens. Elizabeth felt a wild elation. She could have cried Yoicks or Tally Ho!

Just so long as Jane didn't sense it. But she wouldn't, she couldn't, for extraordinary though it seemed to tell it, Jane, their own Jane, their one conventional pretty duckling (though she could give a devastating comic quack when she chose), Jane, so beautiful there in her veil, her train, her blossoms (Oh, how the conventions worked on her side!) carrying roses as pink and gold and soft and utterly, absurdly English as herself, was in love, oh, but head over heels in love with this superior rabbit Derek. So that for her, long quivering ears and pink quivering noses and two teeth just perceptibly ready to nip the lettuce leaf were not only the required human look but the perfection of male beauty. To Jane at this moment of solemn, absurd happiness, Elizabeth knew, Adonis and Don Juan, Hercules and Valentino himself all had long ears and quivering noses and, no doubt at all, white scuts. Un-Carmichael-like, Jane today, it could be seen, would see, speak, and hear no evil.

Suppressing her laughter, Elizabeth made excuses to the bird of paradise, and whispering to her tall musician brother Gerald, took him, ostensibly, for a piece of cake, but really to gaze at the bridegroom's backview, where, sure enough, some handkerchief or piece of shirt or heaven knew what showed white so that, giggling into their own handkerchiefs, she and Gerald had to take refuge in the pretence of viewing once more the presents. "But it doesn't matter," she whispered to him, "doesn't matter a jot, for if all her babies are born leverets, Jane's much too miraculously happy to mind."

And Gerald agreed—so imposing and handsome, now he *was* a Viking! The Culmers scattered before him like pitiful puny Picts before the glorious Northmen as he advanced to the piano at his mother's request and gave them "La Cathédrale Engloutie." "I say, jolly good fingerwork," said Derek's tennis sister and her own sister's bridesmaid. Aunt Ella said, "Charming. So light. Is it your brother's composition?" And down went all the rabbits, drowned with the cathedral.

Meanwhile Selwyn, their lean, clever brother Selwyn, was giving Mr. Culmer apoplexy by being pro-German. "Reparations as Clemenceau and the French conceive them are not only wrong," he told the old gentleman, "but much worse, they are stupid." If only, Elizabeth could see Mr. Culmer gobbling to himself, this dreadful young Bolshie hadn't been wounded. As it was, the rabbits sustained all the wounds; the Carmichaels just tasted blood. Even dear Louie, so handsome, yet somehow cramped in a picture hat and grey charmeuse frock, had joined the attack. "Yes, I'm opening a branch in the spring," she told Mrs. Culmer gruffly. "Putting in a young ex-officer as manager." "A man's going to work under you!" "If he doesn't, he'll soon get his marching orders."

But it was Ronnie, looking so absurdly decadent with a vast gardenia in the button-hole of his hired wedding clothes, his lips and cheeks, as Elizabeth, if no one else, saw, more carmine than mere nature had fash-

ioned, who put the rabbits to their final rout. "Putney?" he answered
Derek's tennis sister, and the waves of heavy scent that came from him
spoke of exotic blooms as much as his shrill voice suggested exotic
birds. "How amusing! Well, yes, I *have*. Once a metropolitan train,
you know—not the deep kind where you expect to see miners with
lamps, but the other sort that pops up above ground now and again for
air—took me by mistake to somewhere called Putney Heath. Well,
naturally I adore heaths, with all the gruesome gibbets and handsome
highwaymen, so I thought, how amusing. But, my dear, it wasn't amusing *at* all. The whole place was covered, but covered, with the most
sinister tramps in old burberries—I expect they were trench coats really
that they'd worn out at the front in both senses—who indulged in the
most impudent, not to say improper, mendicancy. Well, I am only a
boy, so I thought discretion was the better part of valour, to use a tiresome cliché—and fled."

Of course it was all wrong at seventeen and living at home with
nothing to do. God knew what he would become, but all the same she
would back him, for he had—and to a degree—the Carmichael hunting
instinct when confronted with silliness and mediocrity.

Gerald began to play again, this time Falla. But Elizabeth's attention
was distracted from the nights in Spanish gardens, however cool, however fountained, by the bride's sudden discreet movement towards the
door. Elizabeth whispered to Louie, but her elder sister from the corner
of her mouth said, "Travelling dress. Room hired. *Ssh!* Mother's putting on her Chopin frown." It was clearly what they all thought, that
Jane had gone to put on her travelling dress. But no, no, it wasn't that;
she wanted to cry to them all, can't you see she's distressed. Some blun-
dering Culmer has trodden on her toes, no doubt, hurt our beautiful,
our rare Jane on this of all days.

The room grew cold and the footmen shrivelled into mere mummies;
the cake crumbled into dust; the bubbles died in the champagne; the
paradise feathers drooped; Falla indeed became Chopin, his funeral
march. And nobody noticed except herself—and why should they, for
none of them were as close as she to Jane's sweet candour and simplicity. There in the Abbey Cloisters the tablet read, "Jane Lyttelton—dear
child," and she wanted to call to them all to stop their chatter—murderers, worldly, trivial murderers, you've sent her to the block, our nine-
days Queen, dear child.

But more to the point was to go after her. Slipping past the footmen,
she inquired softly for her sister's tiring room. And there it was at the
end of the corridor—the ridiculous room, all Pompadour and Du Barry

and powder blue and satin ovals and mirrors, no doubt, that would have to serve for their last heart to heart, their final sisterly confab, instead of their own attic room at home shared over so many years of secret laughter and secret thrills and secret diaries. A hired room at Claridge's must stand proxy at the last for the whole of their girlhood.

Hearing Jane's choking sob—oh, dear! all the times that she had heard it in protest against falsity and cruelty—she slipped in without knocking. "Jane, darling Jane, don't," she cried. And was greeted by Derek's rabbit nose, almost, as it seemed, sniffing at her. "I think," he began. But her sisterly sympathy swept right over him. "Jane darling, don't, don't," she cried. "It's not as if you were going a thousand miles away from us. Besides you're going to be so incredibly happy." She lied firmly, for she realized that darling Jane in her heart found the whole rabbit wedding as absurd as she did. But over Derek's shoulder Jane's blue eyes blazed at her. "Oh, go away, Liz, go away! Haven't you all made me unhappy enough?" And Derek, suddenly, yes, she could see it now, not a rabbit at all, but a noble though gentle hare, said, "I think, Elizabeth, that it would be better. You mustn't care about it, Jane darling. But you have all been a bit unkind, Elizabeth. We *are* the family Jane's marrying into. And we are human. But it doesn't matter," he added.

She rushed from the room. Oh, it was too terrible. She felt so ashamed. Stoats and weasels indeed! Vulgar, self-centered, attitudinizing brutes! As she came back into the Fragonard Room, Sophie was giving orders to the photographers. "Ah, there you are, Lizzie. We're just going to have a Carmichael photograph." And her elbow firmly brushed Mrs. Culmer out of the way to make her point. "Where's Jane, Lizzie?" "With Derek, of course." And James, in a special warm, bumbling voice, "Well, let our Jane put off her cooing if not her billing to join her family for a last photograph." Elizabeth stamped her foot. "Oh, how can you be so blind and selfish?" And when Aunt Mildred took her arm, saying, "Stand by me, Lizzie. The two giantesses together," she wrenched herself away. "I wouldn't think of being in the damned photo."

She stared at her family drawn up in close phalanx for the photograph; as James so often said, they were nothing if not striking-looking. In the older generation, indeed, the cult of personality might well be said to have strayed into eccentricity, or what her mother called "looking interesting." For such seasoned campaigners Jane's distress, even if she told them of it, could only, like her marriage to the ridiculous Derek, be a weakness, a fit of the vapours. But Louie and the brothers, were they also determined to prove themselves the surviving fittest? Alas, she felt, they were. Ronnie, for instance, how in his pretty butterfly flight could he be expected to take account of a dowdy sister's mothlike marriage? Elizabeth saw this elegant, gaudy young brother of hers, so mysteriously lost for hours of the night among London's bright lights, as flitting from flower to flower, gathering little honey perhaps, but oh, so enjoying his winged arabesques and *pas de chat*. What should such as he do risking his beautiful wings in the dim candlelight of marriage? No, poor Jane Culmer, you are no longer, perhaps you never were, a Carmichael, she thought.

"Well," said Sophie, "it's been a good wedding."

"She's made a good marriage, our little Jane," said James.

But Sophie burned him with a look. "Don't be sentimental and false. *We've* made the best of it. That's all. As we all well know." And she looked around at her family.

Elizabeth, alone of them, refused her mother's smile of complicity. "Jane has the best of it, I think," she said.

And as she said it, much of the day's guilt fell away from her. For, however late, she at least had felt and seen reality. Oh, she felt a wild elation! She could have cried Yoicks or Tally Ho! as she hunted her heartless family on behalf of the ordinary, the decent, the simple.

In the little stuffy parlour a bee, trapped between the pots of Busy Lizzie and the never-opened windows, buzzed a *continuo* to Quentin's impassioned explanation. Every now and again he would glance across at it angrily, but he was too eager and too voluble to spare time to put an end to its interruption. The noise of the others, consuming the ample spread the pub offered, also made him stop his discourse two or three times with an impatient look that settled, now upon Vernon Seymour stirring into his tea, now upon the chap from Balliol cracking his eggs unnecessarily loudly, now upon John Ballard chewing crisp lettuce, at last upon Marian Powell, who for some annoying woman's reason had started to stack the disused plates. While he was still out of breath from their long tramp over hilly country, he had eaten voraciously and in record time more than his own share of boiled eggs and of the slices of bread and butter and jam, and of the rock cakes that the landlady had set before them. That his heart beat so fast and so irregularly had only made him more impatient with the idea of slow eating or of any relaxation; it was always so when he was forced to remember his wound. Now as he talked he covered a series of rending belches with the sucking in and blowing out of clouds of pipe smoke.

"I only tell you, of course," he ended his recital, "because it means that the discussion groups will need a new convener. I suggest Marian."

"Oh, no." The young woman was quite determined. "I'm glad to come along, of course, but as you all know, nothing I say in this field has authority. I'm a historian who's strayed into contemporary issues, not a trained political scientist. In fact, I'm really only here as a chaperone for Valerie."

He turned away at the laugh with which she accompanied this last remark, and knocked out his pipe on the mantelpiece edge. The tobacco ash fell and scattered on the clean, tiled hearth.

"Oh, the poor landlady," Marian said.

"Yes, really, Quentin . . .", Valerie began.

"I thought we chose this place because it was homely."

"Of course, and it is." Valerie pulled off her red tam-o'-shanter and shook out her dark bob to confirm the words. "But whatever sort of home can you have had? You'd get what-for all right in ours."

He imagined with distaste her own home's neat front parlour; the thought helped him to take his eyes from the shining flesh colour of her crossed knees where they protruded below her tight check suit.

"My family are *lumpen* middle class, to risk a Marxist heresy." Dismissing applause easily as he always did when it came, he pointed at them with the stem of his pipe—"If you should want to become an official society at some time, statutes require, you know, that your chairman should be a senior member of the university. You're the only one who qualifies, Marian."

"I do not. And you, as an exploiting male, should remember it. We don't exist. We're just a place in the Woodstock Road that boards and teaches young women like Valerie. But Ballard could."

"No, no. Ruskin's in the same position. Working men, like women, don't exist. We don't even board in a posh, respectable street like you do."

"We could invite Wicksteed as honorary chairman or Cole or one of the Left Wing dons?"

Valerie leaned forward on her little hardwood chair, showing the outline of her small firm breasts as they pressed against her green woollen jumper.

"Oh, not Wicksteed after the way he's let Quentin down."

"He hasn't let me down at all. He warned me that they might not renew if I went down to Wales. Don't get it wrong. I went down to encourage men in a strike that should—would, in any logical, continental country—have been the spark to set off revolution. St. Ebbs don't want revolution—most of them want port, and medlars after dinner, the undoing of the Revolution of Sixteen Eighty-eight, and the abolition of votes for women. I was the odd man out, not them, as Wicksteed said."

"Yes," said Seymour, "urging you, I suppose, to toe the line. He's no guts, you know. I don't know why you stand up for him."

"You might have the charity to remember he was in Maidstone jail for two years as an objector. The swine deliberately ruined his health."

"Well," said Valerie, "and you were wounded."

He glared back at her admiring look and noticed with satisfaction that she blushed and looked down. He did not, as he knew they expected, fill the silence. The black marble clock on the sideboard ticked loudly. Staring at the wall opposite he suddenly took note of the dismal oleograph behind a fly-blown glass. A ghastly mid-Victorian sentimental picture of a young man bending over a young woman with a baby in her arms in some rosy arbour. Across her shoulders, around the baby's neck, and on to the young man's wrist hung some flowery creeper. The lovers, if such they were, were dressed, God knew why, in Regency clothes, or something of the kind—cravats, breeches, hoop petticoats, and wigs, what Granny M. had always called "costumes of the olden days," in fact, the stuff they used to have in the nursery dressing-up box. The title he could just read through the stains and the dirty glass: "The Daisy Chain That Binds Them." He shivered and withdrew his gaze. Valerie was smiling at him. He frowned. Picking up his cap, his ash-plant, and his macintosh from the wooden bench by the window, "I'll pay," he said. "We'd better push off while it's only drizzling."

As they came out the sun suddenly shone for a moment over distant Oxford. Only Marian remarked on it.

"So you're never going to be a scholar again, only a gipsy," she said, and smiled amusedly as she saw the others look down on the ground or away from her. Quentin realized how ill-suited she would be to lead them in his absence. Valerie pulled off her tam-o'-shanter, rolled it up, and put it in her macintosh pocket; then taking off the macintosh she folded it neatly over her arm.

"I dare say you don't want testimonials from your students, but you can't surely give up *all* teaching, with your talent for making people think for themselves."

This time he returned her smile.

"Not the talent most commended at the universities."

"Not here, perhaps," she cried, "but join Ballard at Ruskin. Or in London. Good heavens, to work under Harold Laski! Just think! Or at Manchester."

"No. I don't want any of it."

The man from Balliol said, "Of course, free-lance journalism will leave you time for WEA work."

"No! No!" cried Quentin. "That's extensionism. For God's sake, let us confine the plague while we can."

The blurred wave of his hand seemed to suggest that the centre of infection lay somewhere around Tom Tower, now hidden in thick grey rain clouds.

"I shall give courses at the labour colleges if they want me. There one can teach as one likes."

"As they like," said Marian quietly.

"University teaching within the present class framework of education must end in perversion or sterility."

"But—*laying* the seeds for socialist infiltration in the higher levels of the bureaucracy?" Seymour asked.

"That's an evolutionary illusion. In any case, whatever you stuff into their heads here, the machine will corrupt them three years after they've gone down. Besides, I want to test all this theory against the facts of industrial life."

"Empiricism," said Marian, "a grave if not infantile disorder."

He noticed with gratitude that Valerie didn't laugh with the others. Even so, despite the fact that they were rapidly being swallowed up by the growing domestication of large houses with drives and gardens and shrubberies that sucked them back gradually into urban life, he felt isolated on an empty, bare hillside. A sudden cold breeze blowing his macintosh tightly round his thighs made him conscious of his legs, his body; he knew himself naked, scrawny, and damaged before the world at large, before the great city stretched out there, sophisticated, sure of itself, and unfriendly.

Hitting with his stick at the well-trimmed hedges of the large gardens they passed, he sought to draw all his companions in with a net of words, that, rescuing them from their withdrawal, he might gather them around him again, a warm screen to keep off the blasts.

"It takes a tough bourgeois background to resist this soft, insidious, misty charm, to see through the bonhomous invitation to join the club, and the cold heart, the indifference to a rotten world's pains that lie behind courteous passing of the port. *You've* all had warm family backgrounds. Oh, I know that the genteel poverty of mine is a feeble joke beside the poverty you've known as the norm of daily life. But your homes were warm with necessary generosity, the neighbourliness that's born of no hope. I was farmed out, you know, pretty early, to an indulgent grandmother. But the family existed all right with the unusual pretences of bourgeois family morality spread so thin that the cold heart and the ruthless claw showed through all the time."

A few large drops of rain were falling, but he could feel that he was holding them, for no one hurried or protested about the coming storm.

"That's why it's so much easier for me to renounce Oxford and all her false works."

Ballard said, "Ruskin's hardly part of the club. However, maybe you're right. I like to believe that what I enjoy here is not part of . . ."

Marian interrupted, "You mean, Quentin, that we're snobs." And she added, "Not that my family ever *was* poor."

The rain coming faster now seemed to find some gap through which to strike him, cold and sharp.

"Oh, God," he said, "it's me, Marian, who's the snob. Always seeking some argument or other to advance my rotten gentility, to make me out superior. No, Ballard, you're right. *You* can make Oxford accept you on your own terms. But I can't. I must get away or be damned."

He could not quite tell what effect his words had upon them, and a moment later the rain pelted down so hard that they must run for such shelter as they could get beneath some overgrown, ornamental hollies at the entrance to a rich man's drive. As they stood there silent, Quentin felt a hand on his forearm. Looking up, he saw her fresh face, her cheeks red from the wind, her dark eyes glittering like the raindrops that ran down in streams from her sopping black fringe.

"You've done the right thing," Valerie whispered.

"Oh, you've done the right thing all right," Doreen cried. With tears and rain at once pouring down her face, with her scraped-back, lively yellow hair, now dark and dead with water, she seemed to look more than ever for the pity due to someone saved from drowning. "Oh, yes, you've done the right thing. But how can I bear it if I can't be sure that you've done it because you love me?"

As she spoke she levered herself up a little from the floor of the barn by her hands; then sinking back, she beat upon the hard ground until her palms were bruised and scratched. Quentin took off his knapsack, and clambering down beside her from the sacks of chicken food on which he stood, held her in his arms and kissed her mouth until her crying was silenced. Then, forcing his tongue in, he pulled her towards him fiercely, yet he knew that his hands were still stroking her back with a gentle, controlled touch. Pressing himself against her thigh he noted with relief that despite her hysteria he was stiffening. But as his left hand moved round to her breasts, she pulled herself away and lay back, her head upon the sacks, her eyes closed.

"Well?"

"Oh, of course. I suppose. Good God, I don't want to doubt you. I love you so much," she began to cry again.

He sat back on his haunches. "Why, then, do you refuse to believe me?"

"Oh, I don't know. Yes, I do. When we made the mistake, you couldn't hide your shock from me. You talked about our marrying as though it was some inevitability that you'd learnt from a Victorian novel."

"My darling, how anyone can do such good work on Bentham and have such a sick Romantic imagination, I . . ."

"No, no, Quentin, please. Don't act. I know what I've just said is true. Your face went white and sickened when I told you. And then came the conventional words. There was no connection between them."

"All right. I was shocked. You don't seem to understand. Of course, I don't believe in it, but the old conventions have their hold on us. You are *in statu pupillari*, you know."

She motioned impatiently.

"Oh, I know they've no right to farm out pretty girls to young research fellows. Even with chaperones in the shape of hideous girls like Hilary Notcutt."

"*That* isn't what frightened you. You know it wasn't."

"All right. It was all kinds of shock. I was unprepared, though it was my own monstrous carelessness. I've so many plans, there's so much that needs doing, I don't leave much room for personal revolutions. And then perhaps I did feel a bit of a hero of a three-decker novel! But now it's all digested. Surely you can see how I want you. I'm not going to live this hole-in-the-corner existence any longer, creeping down to Herefordshire, meeting in a barn, and even now who knows whether those awful women on your reading party or some busybody farmer's wife may have seen us? You must let me announce our engagement."

"Oh, no, no, *you* must give me time to think about today, about . . ."

"Whether you believe me. Oh, for heaven's sake."

But she was crying again.

"You know what, Doreen, you're working too hard, my girl. I want a beautiful body, not an emaciated corpse."

And when she still sobbed, he started to sing in an imitation cockney.

"Oh, comrades all, come rally round, our cause I fear is dying." He nudged her, "Come on, comrade." And singing with him she began to laugh.

"What a blasphemous way to bring me to my senses," she said, but she continued laughing so that her face lost its haggard, hysterical, pinched look. The pressure of erection was becoming intolerable, and he put her hand on his crotch.

"Please," he said, "I promise I won't let you run any . . ." But he saw he was talking too much and felt in his pocket for the proof of safety he had brought with him.

The principal of her college telephoned him with the story before he saw it in the Oxford *Mail*, so that he was forced at once to produce a moderate seemly grief.

"It is very tragic. She seemed so full of life. And then I can't help thinking of her brilliance. She had a real chance of getting a first."

"I'm so very much afraid that this was the cause. We women, you know, alas, are taking a long time to learn a sense of proportion," the principal said.

When, then, a week later her parents, visiting the college to pack up her things, called in at his rooms, he was able to control the incredible vitality that seemed to have possessed him since her suicide.

"My husband will never forgive me," Mrs. Collett said, "for wanting Doreen to come up here. But she was so clever and it was something I'd missed."

"No man has a right to blame his wife for serious decisions," said Colonel Collett. "That's the first rule of marriage. But then I'm old-fashioned."

Quentin got up and offered them sherry, and when they refused, he walked over to his pipe rack and took out a new pipe.

Coming back across the room, "She was very happy with her work. That I am sure of. As far as a tutor can tell."

He sat down and began to light his pipe, then stopped, asking Mrs. Collett's permission. When this was accorded, he said between suckings and lighting of matches, "I don't feel that you should think you did wrong in letting her come to Oxford. At least that's my judgment." He added the comment, "She paid the temperamental price that most clever girls still pay in our society."

He got up and collected an ash tray from his desk. He could hardly control his enormous sense of energy.

"If she'd been frustrated she would have been much more unhappy."

He could see that even Mrs. Collett thought him jumpy; Colonel Collett looked at the end of endurance.

"Well, whatever it may be for men," he said, "I'm certain it is no atmosphere for girls."

As they left, Quentin knew that he hadn't been able to help them, yet the energy in him almost escaped into a jig.

As they approached Oxford, Quentin found Valerie's nearness at once so exciting and so intolerable that he talked without cessation —about his famous luncheon with the Webbs, about the Spartacists, about state railway finances in France, about the new town hall in Oslo, about Cobbett, about Hyndman, about Sorel, about the plans for creating some new school of modern subjects to offset Greats, about his interview with Horrabin and the articles he would do for *Plebs*. As they came under the Railway Bridge, excited as always nowadays by half-light, he brushed against her; but before she could respond, he abruptly excused himself from accompanying the women and Ballard in the direction of Worcester, and kept on with Seymour past the castle.

Seymour said, "What a bunch of egoists we are. I'm afraid we didn't show up in a very good light. Not a word about how serious this is for you."

"Oh, I think I've made it plain that I couldn't have stuck an academic life."

"All the same, it's a big wrench. And how are you going to live on what the reviews will pay?"

"I can live on tea and bread and dripping, thank the Lord, with the greatest of ease."

It was true. Even when his scout had woken him this morning to porridge and kidneys and Oxford marmalade, he had known that, though he could hardly look out into the Quad without crying, one thing he would never miss would be scouts and High Table and medlars with the port.

Seymour said, "Well, you can add this unction to your soul. There's not one of us, however big we talk, who'd have the courage to give it up . . ."

But Quentin did not answer. When they reached Carfax, he went away with no more recognition of the young man than a curt nod. In the Cornmarket the shopgirls were pouring out of Elliston and Cavell's store after their day's work. He took in their cheap scents, their underlying women's smell, their bright chatter, their tight, short skirts, their faces mysterious under their bell-shaped hats, the glitter of their odd bits of cheap jewellery. One girl in a blue woollen tammy turned back and smiled at him—cheeky, black-currant eyes. He smiled back.

"Good evening, sir," she said, giggling to temper the address, but he froze. The bloody social system of this stinking country! And he had been about to join the exploiters. Suddenly he felt that far worse than a pound or two left on the dressing-table would be his emotional exploitation, to use that slim healthy body to purge his own disorders. Disgusted with himself, he turned off down Market Street to his college. Here in the Corn he could only feed his randiness. Better go back to his rooms and sit on it.

"This way," Alfred said, as they passed through the turnstiles. It was his invariable announcement on their arrival at any new place of note—and in the last two years they had visited so many, mainly in England, though they had also passed four blissful days in Bruges and Ghent. After three years of prudently confining their meetings to her small flat, the sense of being in the open had proved a wonderful stimulant. He was so well groomed, handsome, and mature; and herself, she truly believed, not disgracing him—always well turned-out (good gloves, good shoes, good stockings), fine figure (if not to fashion's taste, yet to his), at any rate what *he* said a young lady should be. Which was all that mattered. If they could not enjoy social life together, they could at least look all that society could require. Anywhere, they had finally settled, that was not enclosed, any open space where face to face meetings could be evaded. The decision ruled out museums or art galleries or concert halls "for which relief," Gladys said, "much thanks." Freedom was what they sought. Yet Gladys knew that half her pleasure lay in having come back full circle to the conspiratorial scenes of their first hastily snatched, clandestine meetings on Blackheath, or Putney Heath, or Wimbledon Common—before she had finally left home for a place of her own.

"When in doubt," Alfred said, "always follow the crowds."

And so they mixed with the main stream of Sunday visitors moving towards some sort of pond or lake or something.

"You wouldn't say that if it was a business decision, Alfred. You forget that I've heard you on the dangers of investing money that way. 'The butler told the bishop, and the bishop told the barmaid, and the barmaid told her boss. And that's how bucket shops were born.'" She laughed.

"Did I make that up? I'd forgotten. It's rather good." He took her arm to help her avoid one of the protruding patches of grass that got in the way of the gravel. "Winding paths here, aren't they? That's business. I shouldn't be in doubt there. But relaxation means relaxation for me, not losing my way and landing up miles from anywhere. When Doris and I were first married, she was always being told of plays to go to. As a result we nearly always spent a boring evening. Often in half empty theatres. Then I took over. I just went to the Keith Prowse ticket agency people and asked what was the best thing on. If they had only two seats left, we always found it was something worth going to. That's one of the saving graces of Doris's illness: we neither of us need pretend we want to go out in the evenings."

The houses were of glass and the sun's reflection on them shone like a ball of fire; the blaze caught Gladys's eye for a moment, but happily she was not easily distracted from her pleasure in being with him. And they were walking now on the pleasant, familiar, paving-stone surface of the terrace.

"What do you do in the evenings when you're on your own, Gladys?"

She realized that he had never asked her before; they seldom spoke of empty time, there was so much to say about their busy days . . .

"Well, thank goodness there *are* only five."

He took her arm and squeezed it. She knew that he felt the same secure happiness that she did.

"And Wednesdays I usually stay late at the Agency. Then Fridays I go out to Clapham to go over the books with Larkin. I *was* right, by the way; he's hard-working and good. Tuesdays and Sundays I'm with you. Other nights I'm often very tired. By the time I've eaten and had a long hot bath, I'm only fit really to take a book to bed and sleep over it."

He put his arm round her shoulders and stroked the firm smooth flesh under the silk.

"To love a happy woman. It's a miracle. Really it is, darling."

"Oh, it isn't all roses. I try to spend one evening a week at Fifty-two."

"I don't see why. After all you've told me of that bastard, your father."

"You mustn't remember that, Alfred. I don't. I've tried to chuck out all that awful past. And mostly I've succeeded. They're merely a

day-to-day problem to me now. But just at this moment, when Marcus has finally left home, they are in such a mess."

"You do enough. Good Lord, at your age! You're already making
them an allowance."

"Sort of. Driblets. I daren't trust them with more. Though it's
worse, really. As a result, of course, they bleed all of us now. I'm so
afraid they'll worry Marcus. Just because he's secretary to a rich
man doesn't mean he's got money to spare."

"They're impossible. You should cut off from them completely.
In any case there's no love lost between them. I can't think why they
don't separate."

"I think they may any day now. Billy hasn't been home for a
week."

"Well, there you are. It's not a real marriage. Best thing they
could do. Anyway, you make up their income. That's quite enough.
It's not as if they'd given you a family life."

They had left the firm stone terrace far behind and were walking
on gravel. The trees seemed well arranged to give shade, but their
leaves made a lot of litter. Now, turning a corner of the path, they
arrived in what appeared to be a clearing in the bushes.

"We're getting off the beaten track," he said.

So they began to retrace their steps. She saw now that the masses
of colour they had passed earlier were beds of roses.

Reminded, she said, "I like your button-hole, Alfred. It's kept
very fresh."

"Yes, I told the girl at the shop, 'I want something that'll last over
Sunday!' And she gave me this. A moss rose, she said it's called. See
all this mossy stuff on the stem. I had to put it into a glass of water
last night. But she was quite right, it's kept all day."

"Alfred! Mrs. Livingstone's on to me again. She wants me to put
money into her typing agency."

"Mm. Well?"

"I don't know. I send ever so many girls there and she's doubled
her business in the last years. But . . . oh, I should like your advice."

"Tell her to give you the books. I'll look them over."

"Oh, I've done that. They're all right. No, it's her. I just don't
believe she's steady. I think she may let the thing run downhill sud-

denly. I haven't time for salvage operations, now that I've got the Clapham office as well. I wish you'd meet her. Say just for a cocktail. I trust your judgment so much."

He stopped, and pausing, she had time to look round her—some of the trees were such a dark red, they seemed almost black. People said they had every plant and tree in existence at Kew.

"I'm sorry, darling, I can't. We've taken some calculated risks, but we did promise ourselves firmly that we wouldn't meet other people together. No matter who or how much we wanted it."

"Yes, but that was friends and family. Mrs. L. doesn't know anybody you could possibly know."

"I can't take any risks with Doris's ignorance. It's not only that she's an invalid. But, well, I've said it a hundred times, marriage is marriage. And then I've all my past with her before she was ill. I owe her a lot for that. You've had such a dragging up, darling, that quite reasonably you don't understand how the past can hold people."

From her grunt he knew what to expect. Already he was thinking of their return to her flat—of the upward curves each side of her firm white belly taking him on to the stiff, upturned nipple stalks to the full pears of her breasts—and on up by the lines of her ample throat to kiss her upward-turning wide mouth set between her plump cheeks; but if he did not arrest her mood he would turn to find downward pouting lips, leading—it was always his superstitious fear—to sagging, hanging gourds, and a swollen, dropped belly.

"The Colman thing's going through. *I* was right in thinking that the shares would come on to the market. But *you* were right about Master Norton. He's a wrong'un."

"I felt it as soon as you told me about him."

"Woman's intuition!"

"Well, *you* have intuitions, why shouldn't I?"

"Yes, but I *trust* my own."

She took his hand and swung it as she always did when she revealed that she had been teasing him.

"Oh, but my intuition was based on information. One of my girls worked as a private secretary for him for over a year. And . . ."

"You mean she told you his affairs?"

"Oh, no! Don't be alarmed. Good secretaries are discreet. Or most of them. No, I read between the lines of what she said. He made advances to her. As she said, 'Father of a family!'"

"I'm not surprised," was Alfred's comment.

"Well, perhaps you'll believe a little more now in woman's intuition."

She laughed and every curve was upward now. He could tell that just from her voice.

"You're a shocking leg-puller."

She immediately found herself thinking of the strength of his thighs, of the black curled hair on their flanks. Looking at him, she could guess *his* thoughts. But now the people they had been following had thinned to a line and ahead of them was the door to the great glass-house.

"Oh, Alfred, I don't think we want to go in . . ."

He looked back at the queue behind them.

"We can't turn back now, Gladys, not without a fuss."

"But we might meet . . ."

"Nonsense. In point of fact it's probably a short cut through," he said decisively.

Inside it was difficult to walk comfortably for the press of people and the plants that swung above them, to the side of them, all around them.

"They haven't planted these things with much thought for the public, have they?" she said.

Even high above she could only faintly see the glass roof for the tangle of great leaves and for a sort of rope plant that hung from tree to tree with ferns and even sometimes flowers growing on it.

"Exotic plants," he explained.

But the heat was stifling.

"The heat, Alfred!"

"It's a glass-house, darling."

"I know that. Granny had a conservatory. But it wasn't like this."

"Well, I daresay it's a bit up with today's sun."

A plant with great pink trumpet flowers and long yellow spikes hit Alfred on the nose. Gladys read the label.

"*Hibiscus rosa-sinesis*—what a name to go to bed with."

Above them towered the endless spiral of an iron staircase. The noise of people clattering up the stairs was deafening. They looked up and saw some girls, frillies, suspenders, and all.

"Ere! Eyes front. We'd better get you out of ere, my lad, before you're in trouble."

Her cockney as usual set him laughing. Perhaps it was the heat, perhaps it was happiness, but soon they were in convulsions of laughter. Seeing a path to the side, they turned to get out of the queue's pressure.

And there straight ahead of them was this awful, sweet-smiling, hag's dial.

"Good heavens! Alfred Pritchard, of all people."

Gladys tried to turn back, but the way was too narrow, and the people behind who had followed their example, too many. When she looked round again, Alfred said, "Miss Matthews" and immediately the sweet, toothy smile froze to a what's-that-the-cat's-brought-in disdain.

"Please don't insult me, Alfred," she said; then red in the face, she turned to Gladys, "I'm an old friend of Doris Pritchard's. Everyone who knows her, loves her. It's women like you who make one disgusted with one's own sex."

"That's quite enough of that, Mrs. Armytage. You seem . . ."

"It is, indeed."

Pushing her way through the crowd with the ferrule of her parasol, the awful female left them.

With sweat pouring down her neck, her cheeks dryly burning, Gladys followed behind Alfred's broad, grey-tweed back as he bore down upon the crowd in front of them and clove a way out. She longed to call to him to take her into his arms, on his knee, to kiss and to fondle her, to tell her she was forgiven, to ask her forgiveness, to make up a bawdy song about the hag or, best of all, some phrase from a serial she'd read in the *Daily Mail*. "It's all as if it had never happened"—why couldn't he say that? By the time they had got out of the glass inferno, tears had begun to ooze up under her eyelids. Fat tears from a fat girl. That's what she'd have said in the old days at home—laughed it all away. But she wasn't a fat girl now; she was a well-turned-out fine young women who couldn't be taken into the arms of the well-groomed, florid, big man in front of her. Not in public. People of their kind shouldn't need such things at such times. What price, then, diet and Marcel waves and always the best stockings and gloves? She felt ashamed of her own bitter egotism. It was he who was hurt, despite the firm, strong set of his shoulders ahead of her. She hurried after him and took his hand.

"It doesn't matter a bit, old boy. We've always got them beat."

But the comfort didn't appear to reach him. He walked on disregarding. Suddenly, if not fat, she felt completely whacked. She sat down on a bench.

"Collapse of stout party," she said.

Before the Week-End

Upstage left at the writing-desk, young Freddie Manningtree begins to write a letter, then tears it in two and throws the pieces on to the desk. Begins a second letter, this time rolls it into a ball and throws it on the floor. Begins third letter, then unrolls second letter, and pieces together the first, compares all three. Finally rejects all three. Sits facing light pouring in through French window— man in attitude of dejection. Takes cigarette case and matches from dressing-gown pockets, lights a cigarette. Mother's voice from garden, "Getting along all right, Freddie?" (Some laughter as usual from the audience here, but quickly suppressed when with bitter, angry gesture he batters out his cigarette in the ash tray and with fierce, jerky gestures writes and completes a new letter.) Enter LADY MANNINGTREE *through the French windows, carrying a flat raffia basket containing freshly cut roses and delphiniums. She goes to down right, places basket on table.*

LADY MANNINGTREE: I've never known the delphiniums so heavenly as this year, Freddie. The soft blues and mauves. No wonder the dear Queen . . . (*Moves up right to collect in turn a small can of water and two vases.*) Now if you want something lovely to paint! The subtlety of these colours! (*Begins to arrange the flowers in the vases.*) Well, have you finished?

(*He waves the finished note towards her.*)

FREDDIE: Here! You've got what you want.

LADY MANNINGTREE: My dear boy! Have you quite lost your manners? (*After hesitation walks upstage to him.*) I'm not surprised. You can't touch pitch . . . (*Takes the note and reads it.*) "I've always known that if I was to be serious as an artist I couldn't let myself fall in love for many years to come. That's why I'm writing to you now . . ." Serious as an artist? You have the most ingenious way of putting things.

FREDDIE: It happens to be true.

(LADY MANNINGTREE *shrugs her shoulders.*)

LADY MANNINGTREE: My dear boy, we're all delighted that you enjoy painting, but the vital point was that she was quite impossible. A provincial dancing-school teacher. Thank goodness, we saw her in time. Even your father . . .

FREDDIE: Father's manners with Violet were perfect.

LADY MANNINGTREE: As if that helped. Anyhow, you've done the sensible thing. And you're looking very handsome, too. That scarlet dressing-gown suits you. It's the greatest absurdity to think that scarlet should only be worn by dark people. (*She puts her hand on his shoulder.*) Dear boy!

FREDDIE (*shaking her hand off him*): Oh, for God's sake, Mother. I'm your son, not your lover.

(*From the audience, as usual, a shocked intake of breath, while* LADY MANNINGTREE *walks deliberately and with great dignity to her flower-arranging. As often, one or two bursts of applause from Alma Grayson devotees.*)

LADY MANNINGTREE (*in casual, conversational tones*): I've got a fascinating party for this week-end, Freddie—the Cantripps, Lady Celia, the Wickendens, Francis Morell, Sybil Stutterford . . .

FREDDIE: Francis Morell?

LADY MANNINGTREE: Yes. You admire him so much.

FREDDIE: He's only our greatest painter. How did you manage to persuade him?

LADY MANNINGTREE: Oh, I have my little methods. I haven't been a hostess for twenty years . . .

FREDDIE: You're wonderful.

LADY MANNINGTREE (*beaming*): They seem like daubs to me. However . . . I wanted it to be a surprise. You deserve a reward for doing what I asked you.

(FREDDIE *scowls.*)

LADY MANNINGTREE: Oh, and I've asked the Carnaby girl. (*She looks to see the effect of this. He shows no interest.*) She's very pretty, Freddie.

FREDDIE: And the Carnabys are the right sort of family to marry into. That's it, isn't it?

LADY MANNINGTREE: Who said anything about marriage? Really, you young people today sound more like Victorians sometimes. Flirt with her, my dear boy, amuse yourself. Why, at your age I broke a different young man's heart at every house-party. But then we were civilized . . . before that dreadful war.

FREDDIE: And Douggie Lord? Is he coming?

LADY MANNINGTREE: Oh, I expect so. I really hardly notice him.

FREDDIE: Then you won't notice his not being there.

LADY MANNINGTREE: What do you mean? (*She stands with a vase of roses in her hand.*)

FREDDIE: Simply this. (*He takes out of his wallet and waves a sheet of a letter at her.*)

(*She gives a little scream and drops the vase of roses.*)

FREDDIE: Only this, Mother. An eye for an eye. Violet for Douggie Lord. I can't stop you seeing him, but if you ask him here again, I shall show this to Father.

LADY MANNINGTREE: Your father! What's he got to do with you? How dare you? (*She rushes forward to seize the letter, but something in his expression stops her.*)

FREDDIE: I'll ring for the maid to clear that mess away. (*He walks to bell left and rings*)

LADY MANNINGTREE (*stares silently across at him, then speaks slowly*): I believe you hate me, Freddie. Oh, my God, I believe you hate me. (*As she speaks and during his answer to her he shows his disregard for her emotions by quietly clearing the rejected letters from his desk and putting them in the wastepaper-basket, which he moves into its original position at the side of the desk.*)

FREDDIE: No. Shall we say only that you've destroyed every atom of love I had for you?

(*Knock, and enter* MAID *down left.*)

FREDDIE (*smiling*): Ah, Lady Manningtree has dropped a vase, Parsons. Will you clean up, please? What a shame, Mother. You'd arranged them so beautifully.

(*As the curtain descends* LADY MANNINGTREE *still stares at him in horror.*)

The applause, as every night, was tremendous. Alma Grayson took four curtain calls on her own, one with the whole cast, and one with Rupert.

Eating his usual chicken sandwiches, drinking his regulation whisky and soda in Alma's suite after the performance that night, Rupert wanted as always to burst into laughter at the absurd lavishness of the management's idea of Louis XV—all these mirrors and satin ovals and little gilt tables and china bowls of rose petals. Such laughter was only relaxed nerves, of course. And the object it attached to varied from place to place.

Here in Liverpool, from the very first night, his hilarity had fixed upon Alma's excessively Pompadour setting. He had learnt by now not to release his laughter until he knew her mood; and to this, even after three months, he never had the smallest reliable clue. "They've certainly put you in a profusion of Pompadour. It's like a bad setting for *Monsieur Beaucaire*." And he called her the Beauty of Bath. She had taken the joke up and nursed it with her strange cooing laugh; even saying when she came back from the lavatory, "My dear, the noise of that cistern. It must date from Pompadour's days. *Après moi le déluge*." This with one of her rare, coarse chuckles that so delighted by their contrast to her ethereal, lily-like grace. But on another evening she had cut him off quickly with, "It's the principal suite in the hotel. Everyone one's ever heard of has stayed here at some time or other. But, of course, I oughtn't to expect you to know that at your age." And yet again, she had revived the joke herself when they came back on the Wednesday night. "Are you reboff by Meestaire Nash, Monsieur Beaucaire?" she asked. "I am no Beaucaire, Lady Mary. I am a French gentleman. The hotel insult me with imitation French fashions." But then, swiftly turning against him, "They've done their best. Look at these lovely sweet-peas they've put in here for me, and this delicious fruit. It is never in very good taste to sneer when people have tried to be civil."

Sometimes Hope Merriman gave him a little comradely smile to help keep up his spirits under Grayson snubbing, but she never said anything aloud, and Ronald Rice always made a noise in his throat somehow indicative of support for Alma; it was only one of the many sounds that Rupert had christened his gentleman-player noises. Not that she needed support, for everyone—cast, management, stagehands, hotel staff—all united to line a cheering route for her; not a puddle uncloaked where she walked.

This evening, at full length of elegance with her feet up on the chaise-longue, she said, "Heavens, how glad I shall be when Sunday comes along and we leave this grey, sad town." She smiled up at Rice, who was pouring out her usual glass of Graves. "Dear Ronnie," she said. "Though it isn't the same. Now, at the Cavendish at Eastbourne they give me white wine *and* oysters."

"Not, I hope," said Rupert, giving a teasing smile, for there was still time to charm her out of her mood, "in July."

"And why not in July? Oh, we are West End, aren't we?" she had put on what she called her knut's voice, "No oysters, dear boy, unless the R's in the month. If you swallow much harder to sound grand, Rupert, you'll swallow your tonsils. Anyway, I really can't be expected to spend my time remembering what month it is. In good hotels they do that for me. Here, I doubt if they know what season it is. Chicken mayonnaise on a chilly night like this. Even a bowl of soup would have . . . However, Liverpool's the home of early closing and all those terrible Bolshie things. But, I'm forgetting that Rupert loves it here. He finds all this heavy French furniture killingly funny for some reason. I never find ugliness funny. I wish I could. Cities like this must be one long laugh to him."

"I often think," Hope said, "that the great warm heart of the north of England is overrated."

"Do you, Hope dear, really. I've always found the greatest kindness in the north. But then people are what you make of them, aren't they? North, south, east, and west you'll find that. Even Liverpool, though it's not my favourite town to play. After all, we're all reflections of the Divine Mind. What you give out, you receive back. And we've been giving them this horrid, ugly play."

Ronnie, as always when the play was mentioned, shivered and said literally, "*Brr!*"

"So how can there be an atmosphere of love?" Alma asked them.

"They've applauded the horrid ugly play loudly enough and filled the theatre," Rupert said.

"No, darling, they've come to see me and they've applauded me. Oh, I don't mean they haven't had a lot else to applaud. Darling Ronnie, who's the most wonderful, dependable actor, who never puts a foot wrong. Yes, you are, Ronnie. You're always too modest. And Hope . . . I thought tonight, Hope dear, when you came in, in the second act, looking so perfectly lovely, that there ought to have been a round of applause just for that. And they've the excitement of the critics' famous new find—Rupert Matthews. But now, darling, I'm going to talk to you seriously about those little bits of fussy business you've started putting in. They'll be a disaster with the London critics, that you can be sure of. What you did to that poor play's ending tonight! Surely, you can see that this is a moment of agony. She's been rotten, God knows, and hard and thoughtless. It's a horrid, cruel play. But at this moment the author does rise above his cynicism a little."

She explained the play to them with characteristic little fluttering gestures of her left hand, swivelling on a rigidly held wrist, emphasizing the important climaxes with nods of her head.

"It's a terrible moment for her when she sees that even her spineless, spoilt son has turned against her. The audience is riveted. They despise and dislike her; the author and I have seen to that. But then suddenly they can't help pitying her. And we must play on that, Rupert, for all we're worth. That moment of pity is the only excuse the play has. And you, dear boy, what do you do? What does he do? Hope, Ronnie, I appeal to you! He moves a wastepaper-basket. The whole tension, the whole tension that both of us, Rupert—for up to this point you sustain the awful young man's odiousness beautifully —the whole tension is broken by that stupid move of the wastepaper-basket."

"But Alma, darling, I move the wastepaper-basket as a deliberate refusal to take your misery seriously. We fixed all that with Gerald in Edinburgh."

"*You* may have done, darling, I never did. I should *never* have agreed to such a thing. One of the things you'll learn as you have more experience in the theatre is that we have very solemn obligations to our authors. Now, here's this play: it's cruel and clever and modern and everything else, but this young man has had one moment of tremendous insight into a woman's essential loneliness. We can't, whatever we do, let him down there. The London critics will be quick enough to see that the whole thing's brittle, but if we can really put over that moment of sincerity, who knows, when the cleverness has worn off, we may be responsible for launching a new, a more solid Maugham. But we won't, if you move wastepaper-baskets."

"But if I don't, I shall appear to be accepting my mother's emotions at her own false valuation. We argued all that out with Gerald."

"You and Gerald never stop arguing. And it's all very clever, no doubt. But I know one thing. And that is that you can't fool around with a moment of sincerity. Audiences can tell. I felt it tonight. The applause was there, but the moment had been missed as surely as if you'd fluffed the lines."

He was about to argue further, then, catching Hope's eye, he said, "I'll think it all through again."

"And now, darlings, I'm going to send you all off to bed. Apart from tomorrow night's performance, we've all got to be very amusing and loving for Nina's tea party tomorrow. Nina McKinley was a very great actress. Please, all of you remember that; now she's old. Beyton's a darling, too, and very handsome. If she wanted to marry a peer she couldn't have done better. Oh, dear, if our clever author could meet a few real aristocrats like Beyton, what much better and nicer plays he would write."

Out on the terrace at Beyton, after admiring the heavenly roses and the quite glorious peacocks (how mad people were to be superstitious about any of God's creatures, especially birds so lovely), Alma gathered rather more than three quarters of the Beytons' house-party around her to form her court. She told them how Lady Macbeth had to be played from a tiny, tiny little piece of hardness somewhere deep inside you, because, when anyone obstinately refuses to reflect God and all the beauty He has given us, hardness is all that is left—a little nugget of hardened will, a tiny patch of darkness that refuses to reflect the light. But for herself, she told them, she always preferred to play in comedy, for when the comic spirit came to life on the stage, it was like ships flashing signals to one another across the sea, signals of laughter and happiness, so that she fed the audience with her vitality and they fed her back with their laughter. Playing in a successful comedy run, one often seemed to need less food because of this feeding back and forth. And then, more seriously, she told them of those mysterious times when she had known for certain that the fun and the happiness she was giving out had been sustaining some particularly poor, unhappy love-starved soul in the audience; and how these intuitions had always been confirmed later. It was such a thing that made all the hard work seem worth while, for acting was, of course, mainly hard work—as old John

Hare had taught her, thank goodness, work and work again, then work again. Here she broke off to tell Rupert that he ought not to be standing there idle.

"You've heard all my stories before," she said. "Besides, now that you are a celebrity you have to sing for your supper. Good heavens, here you are in the same company as the great Nina McKinley and you're not hanging on every word she says! Go and listen. That's theatre history. She's the giant. We, God help us, are the pygmies."

Ronnie Rice was telling Lady Beyton of his century in the Actors *vs.* Authors in the first year of peace.

"I hadn't touched a bat the whole time I was in Mespot and yet I played like an angel. I haven't topped thirty-five since. Cricket's a mysterious game."

Lady Beyton gave him a mysterious smile, but she seemed pleased to change her devotee. To worship, Rupert found, was not altogether physically easy, for Lady Beyton, though flat and square as a playing card, was very short—the top of her head just above his crotch. Yet it was not a simple bend one must make to talk to her, for she held the world off with a very large square bosom. This was not all, for she wore an enormous, floppy, rose-decked hat, the brim of which, from his height, appeared to be resting on her bosom. He took a step back, bent forward, then sideways, and from this agonizing position he confronted a very, very old, enamelled face out of which stared wildly two very round, cornflower-blue eyes. He took a listening position, but he was soon to learn that he was a courtier at a much more ancient court than Alma's, one with different courtesy books.

"Have you been looked after?" she asked. "Good. The fig jam is our only real boast at Beyton. The trees are very old. Andrew's great-grandfather brought them back from the foot of Vesuvius. And they've always thanked us for rescuing them from lava by bearing profusely. Now I want to know all about you. The young man the critics are raving about."

There was no mockery in her voice, which indeed was all on one note, and her eyes begged for some message from the world outside to one so old.

As Rupert talked, he felt increasingly aware of the difference of these two generations—Alma's so claiming, so loquaciously uncertain, Nina McKinley's the great age of theatrical certainty, of kings

and queens for all their ham and rabbits on the stage (or perhaps
because of them). The great eyes looked up at him; occasionally the
famous voice said, "Oh, that's so clearly put" or "If you act as well
as you talk, young man, you'll go far." Quite soon he hardly felt the
crick that had come into his back from bending so low.

"And now, what of this part. What are you making of that?" she
asked abruptly while he was still speaking, so that he wondered if he
had been talking too much; but it was clear from her eager eyes that
it was just an old woman's impatience to keep up to date. All that he
had forborne to say to Alma, all the points that he had left for Gerald to make at rehearsals, all that Hope or Ronnie would have been
bored to hear, he now poured out to this famous, yet sympathetic
woman.

"Technically it's superb melodrama and many of the lines are
really witty. But, of course, it's not a great play. Only it is something
absolutely fresh. Part of a new willingness to say what we really
think, to face the fact that there's something rotten about the smart
set and that there's a real hatred beween the generations nowadays.
Maugham got near to some of it with *Our Betters* and, of course,
The Vortex last year was a real break-through. But I think *Before
the Week-End* is better because it's truer and more bitter. More how
my generation feels," he added with a boyish laugh, for he didn't
want to seem pompous. "And above all it's got a great fat part for
me."

He stopped, for really he was doing all the talking. There was a
silence for a moment and Lady Beyton still stared at him as though
to make sure that he had finished.

"Well, you mustn't let them fob you off with a mingy part like
that again. Who's your agent? He's the one to blame. But never
mind, the critics have noticed you. That's the main thing. My
daughter was telling me before you arrived. She read something out
to me about you from *The Morning Post*. I don't go to the theatre
now much myself because I'm a bit deaf. And they put on so many
unpleasant things. Mothers and sons drunk and shouting abuse at
each other, and now I hear it's sons blackmailing their mothers.
They'll get nobody to come to see such things, of course."

For a moment he was nonplussed, but then he thought that since
once she had been so great, it would be monstrous to agree with her
like a small child.

He raised his voice. "I think it depends on your experience," he said. "My own family is a very rackety one. I don't believe my parents ever cared for their children. And so I suppose we've never really loved them. Certainly my mother's been far worse at times than any Lady Manningtree . . ."

Now that she heard she cut in impatiently, "Oh, dear, oh, dear. That *is* bad. For an actor too. I used to rely so much on coming home to a hot supper and everything laid out for me by my dear mother. This poor boy," she told Alma who came across to them, saying loudly that she must pay her respects, "this poor boy has been telling me about his home. No family life at all."

"Oh, I'm sure he has," Alma said. "We all know his hard-luck story. But you mustn't be so proud of your awful upbringing, Rupert. We all suffer agonies when we're young. Children have an extra sense that makes them so vulnerable. I can remember now as well as anything my own mother coming downstairs with a telegram in her hand—I couldn't have been more than three at the time, all frills and bows as I stood at the bottom of the stairs watching her. I'm doing it again now as I tell you. She seemed to come so slowly, and every step as she came nearer was like a little death for me because I could see that my darling mother was suffering. Of course I didn't know that the telegram was to tell her of her own mother's death. I didn't even know what a telegram was. But I could feel her suffering in every tiny bone of my body."

Lady Beyton put her hand on Alma's. "I don't believe a word of it," she said laughing. "Not one word. You were always a great fibber. And now you've got this clever, handsome young man for your lead. That's just what we all need as we get on. Young blood."

Alma shouted angrily, "He's had a lot too much praise. He's still got a great deal to learn. Now if you want hope from the young, look at that pretty girl, Hope Merriman."

Once again Lady Beyton patted her hand, laughing loudly. "And your puns," she said and she winked at Rupert. "They've given him a rotten part, he says. You must bully your agent. Tell him to get you into *The Three Musketeers*. They're sure to revive. You're taller than Lewis Waller, of course. But you'd make a fine D'Artagnan."

"D'Artagnan!" Alma laughed her scorn loudly enough to make

even Lady Beyton jump. "D'Artagnan has to have fire and gaiety. When D'Artagnan comes on the stage every woman in the house knows that a *man* has come among them. This boy's got a long way to go yet before he can play D'Artagnan. D'Artagnan isn't just a question of clever ideas about wastepaper-baskets."

Rupert felt too angry to remain even within earshot. Although in his rage he could see nothing, he pretended to be looking at the flower beds and so wandered away on his own into shrubbery. The evergreen bushes and his own sense of isolation reminded him that he was in "a prettyish kind of little wilderness." "I send no compliments to your mother," he said aloud, and hearing Margaret answering with delighted laughter, he realized to his surprise that his detestable, for ever renounced past had for once brought him relief. He sat down on a wooden seat that encircled a huge beech tree. "I am seriously displeased," he said aloud a number of times, trying to assess what emphasis would most completely crush Alma Grayson. After the last attempt, Ronnie Rice's voice interrupted.

"And so is somebody else, old boy. I've been sent by Alma to tell you to return at once to the glittering throng or for ever be accounted one of the lesser breed."

"Damn her. Damn her blasted impertinence. What's she picking on me like this for?"

"I haven't the least idea, old boy. In any case I shouldn't think of being mixed up in it."

"If you know, you ought to tell me. If she continues like this, there'll be a row and that won't help the play."

"Ah, now, for the sake of the side, of course, that's quite a different matter. I don't *know*, mind you, but as a shrewd guess, I think she's needled because you haven't told her the old bedtime story."

"But I couldn't possibly. She must be over fifty. It'd be a kind of incest."

"All right, keep your wool on, old boy. Anyhow, you've rather yourself to blame. It isn't as though you haven't kept stoking the fire under her kettle."

"But she's the sort of woman one naturally flirts with."

"Nothing natural about it, as far as I can see. You asked my diagnosis and I've given it. That's her usual trouble."

"Well, I'm afraid she won't get any relief from me."

As they moved back towards the terrace Rice whistled, then, "To be Alma Grayson's leading man may not be a sinecure but it's not to be sneezed at, you know."

But, whether because of the pollen from the flower beds or not, that was exactly what Rupert then did very loudly.

Every head on the terrace turned towards him, and among them, to Rupert's great surprise, was that of their producer, Gerald Crace. Alma threw out her arms to the assembled company.

"And now we know that our juvenile lead hasn't drowned himself in the lake because I don't love him. We can face tonight's audience without fear of disaster. Darling Nina, you've chosen the better part." She waved one hand towards the park, the other towards the Wyatt mansion. "To live with such dignity and beauty."

Perhaps Lady Beyton thought that the allusion was to her husband who, panama in hand, was hovering around Alma. At any rate she produced an unexpected, vulgar chuckle. She put her old, ringed hand on Rupert's arm.

"You haven't done too badly for yourself, Alma."

Alma turned to Lord Beyton and at the top of her voice said, "I'd no idea she'd got so deaf. Almost nothing gets over now, does it?"

Lady Beyton moved away; over her shoulder she gave her husband his orders. "See they all get into their right cars, Andrew."

Alma sought to pass it over by an account of how she would spend her next hour.

"Fingers and wrists quite loose," she told Lord Beyton, "and the mind absolutely receptive . . . I fill my thoughts with a colour. But it must be a positive colour like blue."

Rupert found that he was to travel with Gerald in his touring Wolseley, but before he could put his foot on the step, Lord Beyton drew him on one side.

"A word of advice. If you're going to marry one of the stars, as they call them now, you must get the upper hand early on."

Gerald asked, "Well, what are we going to do about it?"

Rupert was uncertain enough of what he was talking about that he felt it fair to assume an expression of ignorance.

"Alma. She was on to me by trunk call for half an hour at half past midnight. You're ruining the magnificent curtain, you're keeping the audience away, you and I have been sophisticated and clever with something natural and lovely and sincere. In short, we've ballsed-up her big moment and blowed if she'll stand it."

To give himself time to control his emotions, Rupert said casually, "Ah, the wastepaper-basket."

"Don't," Gerald shuddered. "That rather silly combination of words came over the telephone to me fifty times between half past twelve and one this morning. And I went on saying them over in my head until three. Have you heard three such words repeated like that? Well, they sound damned silly."

"The bitch! Shunting us off to bed and then telephoning. But anyway you and I had agreed. You said yourself we can't afford any sentimentalization with a play like this. It's telling a new truth . . ."

"Indeed, yes. But what we also can't afford is to do without Alma."

"You mean that she's actually threatened . . . but that's nonsense; she's under contract."

"Only pre-London with options. Her agents are very tough. In any case, if she goes to the management . . ."

"But you're the producer."

"My *first* production for them? Oh, we can fight her. But it could be a very nasty shambles for us. If you could manage to look a bit touched by Lady Manningtree's naked fight against the world's cruelty, help to give old Alma the one moment when the audience loves her . . ."

"But they're not meant to."

"Perhaps the w.p.b. is a little bit obvious. Yes, that's what I suggest cutting."

"And if I refuse?"

"I don't see how I could support you against her."

Rupert found a voice that seemed to come from far off, mellow, caressing, with a touch of acceptant chuckle.

"Well, I suppose . . . life's full of rum necessities. All right."

"Thank you. I promise I'll support you if she goes too far."

"I'm not going to bed with her, if that's what you mean. I'll tell you that."

"I should hope not. For the Lord's sake don't try anything like that. She's a tremendous prude, is our Alma. Kharma and Christian Science and heaven knows what. Sex is just an untrue thought to her."

"But Ronnie Rice implied . . ."

"Ah! I should have warned you. Never believe a word Ronnie says. For all that hearty cricketing manner, he's a shameless old gossip."

It was only when he had begun to put on his make-up that Rupert's anger returned. He went straight along to Alma's dressing-room and walked in without knocking. She was lying on her day-bed with her eyes closed, thinking of blue, no doubt. He stood over her.

"You had absolutely no right to ring up Gerald behind my back. We agreed to discuss it all on Saturday. I'm not willing to give way. You know very well the play can only work if we're true to it. I'm grateful to you for all that I've learnt from you in the last months, but I'm not going to learn fake things. You know that this play could be my big chance; you also know that you would wreck it. It's up to you. But so long as I'm playing it, I'm not going to sweeten the end."

She had opened her eyes as he started to speak and he expected a tirade but she only stared at him. When he finished, she swallowed once or twice as though considering; then she spoke in a voice of artificial gaiety.

"Oh, my dear boy. Don't let us sugar things over. Not after that pathetic spectacle. A great, almost a terrible woman she was. But how could *you* tell that, who only see her now when the terror has gone soft and pappy. Poor Beyton! But I've been waiting and hoping for this from you. We'll give error its innings. My dear, I've caught that awful cricketing language from Ronnie at his most boring. I only wanted to know whether you cared enough to stand up for your own views. But, thank God for it, you're big enough."

She held out her long elegant hand to him.

"So be it," she said in a comradely voice. "We'll go all out for the hard, bitter ending."

He bent down to kiss her hand, but then he decided to kiss her cheek.

"Thank you, Alma. You're a darling," he said, and then he found himself kissing her passionately on the mouth. She seemed to push him away for a few minutes but then she held him. He felt like a victorious army gone berserk.

That night he almost overplayed the wastepaper-basket business just to show her who had won. But the applause was still terrific. Gerald after the show appeared puzzled and apprehensive, but Alma settled that.

"It all works so beautifully, Gerald, now that this boy understands what I want."

They were settling all three into the plushy comfort of the hired car that took her back to the Adelphi Hotel each night.

"He's a very clever boy," she said, and she emphasized each word by tapping his cheek.

It was the beginning of their highly successful partnership on and off stage.

P.S. was asleep in his pram on the front step. The soft down on his veined little head flashed gold when, from moment to moment, the sun's rays caught it as the breeze blew the fringe of the pram's hood. Of course children are often golden before their hair gradually darkens, but with herself for a mother P.S. might well keep his little golden fleece. He had Hugh's rather small mouth, and the comforter accentuated it. By the corner of the privet hedge where the builders had left their debris, Senior and Middleman were constructing something from the lumps of solidified cement and the broken bricks. Sukey, who was pegging the washing on the line, asked, "Is that the Tower of London?" She spoke softly for P.S. was going through a phase of light sleeping in the day-time.

"No, of course not," said Senior in his gruff voice, "it's a bungalow just like ours. Only it's got a proper name. It's called Thomas."

"Domus isn't a proper name, darling, it's Latin for house."

"What is Latin?" asked Middleman. He was hardly at all babyish in his speech.

"Latin is what Daddy teaches," Senior said proudly. "He's going to teach it to me, when I'm bigger."

"Well, maybe." Sukey smiled as she always did when she modified the children's statements in a way that they couldn't understand.

"Keep an eye on P.S., Senior. I'm just going to get Daddy and Mr. Plowright their eleven o'clock tea. If you come with me, Middleman, you can get a cake each for yourself and Senior."

"Oh, can't *I* come, Mummy? Can't I come? He'll choose the wrong thing."

"I won't."

"I bet you will."

"I won't."

"*Sssh!* Both of you. You'll wake P.S." Sukey rebuked them with a smile, "Anyway, you don't know what there is."

"What is there?"

"There's Queen cakes which are still hot. And there's raspberry fingers that I made on Monday. Now you're in a fix, aren't you? Which is it to be?"

She watched with enchantment the pantomime of solemn frowns and pursing of the lips that accompanied her sons' choice.

"Can't I have both?"

"No, you can't, you monster of greed. Now, hurry up or the Middleman will choose for you."

Horrified, Senior said urgently, "Raspberry fingers."

"So icing sugar wins over freshness." Taking her second son's little hand, she went laughing into the bungalow.

When she came into the sitting-room-cum-study, Hugh and Mr. Plowright had spread exam papers all over the floor. Mr. Plowright jumped up as soon as she entered and offered to take the tray from her; and when she refused he still stood up, fingering his tie—as a gesture of respect, perhaps, but no, probably only out of nervousness.

"I think we can allow 'a big African bird' for ostrich for the juniors," Hugh said.

"Oh, yes. We're marking the general knowledge, Mrs. Pascoe. We're nearly finished."

"Don't worry about me. I must drink my tea and go. I've got to put the stew on, and then Senior tore a hole in his knickers climbing a fence yesterday. I'm not sure I like them going up Toad Lane by themselves."

"I shouldn't worry . . ." Hugh came out of his papers, but she smiled him back to them.

"I was only talking to myself, dear. Have one of the Queen cakes, Mr. Plowright. I made them this morning."

And, of course, what does the ridiculous man do but drop the raspberry finger he'd picked up and take a Queen cake instead.

"Ooh, er, jolly delicious, Mrs. Pascoe."

She'd hardly done this imitation in her own mind, before he said it, *and* with his teeth all protruding in a jolly smile. She thought for a second how Margaret or any of the family for that matter would laugh at her imitation of him, but she never did it aloud because Hugh didn't like one to make fun of friends. And Mr. Plowright counted as a close friend. Anyway, the children liked him, and he hadn't got a wife whom she would be expected to visit or ask to the house. No, on the whole, Hugh was very good really in not cluttering the house up with a lot of strangers. Moved by his goodness she went over to him and put her arm round his shoulders.

"Anything amusing this term, darling?" she asked, for the General Knowledge Exam always produced some howlers Hugh liked to tell her.

"Plowright has a good one."

While she was thinking that Hugh could never forbear trying to show his friend to her to the best advantage, Mr. Plowright had told his joke, which was something to do with Henry VIII and Anne Boleyn. It could hardly have been unsuitable, coming from him, so she laughed loudly; indeed she suddenly felt rather warm towards the boring little man because he made Hugh happy, and supposing it had not been him, Hugh might have become friends with the Great Man. And then, she could hardly bear to imagine it, she would have been taken up by the Great Lady, which would have meant going up to the School House at the word of command.

Hugh said, "Fitchett thinks that the Guadalquivir is a kind of tropical jelly. Something to do with guavas, I suppose."

They all laughed. With the Great Lady it would be jokes like that all the time, if they weren't talking about the boys, or worse still, parents. As it was, she really got involved with the school only on Sports Day, Play Day, and the match against St. Hildebrand's; as for those dreadful, termly dinner parties, she still had P.S. as an excuse. And yet Hugh, who had it all day from nine to seven, still wanted to bring Plowright back to the bungalow. But men were a tribe apart.

"Wichelo's become very high-brow," Mr. Plowright said. "Name one living author. Margaret Matthews is his choice. Who on earth can have told him of her?"

Hugh chuckled. "I expect his parents have got on to the fact that she's Sukey's sister."

"Oh, I am most frightfully sorry, Mrs. Pascoe."

"You don't have to be. Although Mag isn't as vinegary as those books of hers suggest. We have an aunt, a tremendous *poseur*, who always encouraged her to be the clever one of the family, and now of course these literary critics . . . But I'm hopeful she'll marry and settle down. If she doesn't get too much into the arty set."

"Sukey thinks marriage the cure for everything. Actually I thought the little story she based on our wedding party was very cleverly done."

"He just says that, Mr. Plowright, because he doesn't want to admit how annoyed he was. He was quite right to be furious. The whole thing was complete nonsense. To begin with, she made Hugh a curate. Hugh, who always tries to cut school prayers when he can! And then she talks down about Hugh's family as though I ought to have married into the aristocracy or something. Imagine me with broad acres and faithful retainers! It's such nonsense because my parents never knew where the next penny was coming from."

"I suppose if one knew a lot of these writers, even chaps like Galsworthy or Hugh Walpole, one would be surprised how they'd twisted facts."

"I never have time for reading, so I don't know; but I can't believe they make things more depressing than they really are, like Mag does. It's so pointless. There's a story of hers about a visit we all made as children to that exhibition at Earls Court. It was a completely perfect day. You know how children love exhibitions, and we saw real cowboys and went on the Big Wheel. Oh, all sorts of delights! And glorious sunshine. Everything glittering. The Big Wheel shining high up against a blue sky. The prettiest of Japanese lanterns swinging in the breeze. I can remember now seeing an ostrich swallow a stone, it seemed as though the great lump would never finish its journey down that long neck . . ."

"*You* should have been the writer, Mrs. Pascoe."

"That's what *I* tell her, Plowright."

"And how do you think I should find time to write? The children would thank me. No. But what I meant was that all Mag can find to say is, 'And then it rained.' That's how she ends the story—'And then it rained.' In fact, it was very dramatic. A great black-and-yellow thunder cloud . . ."

But now P.S. had woken and was crying.

"Good heavens! What ever did you get me on to all that dead and buried nonsense for on a busy morning. Coming, angel, coming!"

When she had persuaded P.S. to sleep again and had put on the stew, she sat by the pram mending Senior's knickers and watching her two boys at play. Senior had all the patience, setting one piece of brick on top of another, however often it fell off; but Middleman had the ideas.

"This will do for the bicycle shed. We can put the boot cupboard here. We must have a fence to stop the neighbours seeing in."

Hugh and Mr. Plowright came through the front door, talking loudly.

"It seems to me," said Mr. Plowright, "that if the Third are ready for algebra they're ready for their Latin grammar. I'll back you up at the meeting if you say so, Hugh."

It was kind and typical of him to be on Hugh's side, but he spoke so loudly that she had, frowning, to say, "*Ssh!*" She pointed to the pram to soften her admonition. Mr. Plowright went over to the two boys.

"I've got a few more of this celebrity set for you. Let's see. What have we got here? Sir Thomas Lipton. C. B. Fry. The Aga Khan. That's rather a good caricature. And lastly the great Steve Donoghue. I wonder whose colours those are he's wearing."

Senior was really trying to listen, although he obviously wanted to get on with building his bungalow; Middleman took no notice. But the silly little man wouldn't stop.

"I had a feeling I'd got Dean Inge in a packet the other day. Have I given you the Gloomy Dean already, John?"

Senior was blushing; he hated to be asked questions he didn't understand. Sukey felt that she must intervene.

"Just give them to me, Mr. Plowright, will you? They'll like them so much later, but they're a bit young for them yet."

The Gloomy Dean indeed! and, of course, the wretched little man nearly fell over.

"Oh, I say. I'm, er, most frightfully sorry. I just thought they might be interested . . ."

She would have reassured him if his protestations hadn't woken up the Postscript.

The daffodil, fish-tasting soup was delicious and even more the bread soaked in it; but the pieces of fish were glutinous lumps attached to long, menacing bones. In the best bouillabaisse *langouste* meat was used, Madame told her, *"Mais ça serait en supplément."* So, despite the wonderfully favourable exchange, Margaret had commanded the inferior, non-crustaceous variety. What she had not bargained for were the griping pains that began when she was sitting far out on the jetty that afternoon about four. At first she relied on the absorbing problem of disguising, without cheating, the heroine's blindness until the end of the short story in such a way that the reader would say, "But, of course, why ever didn't I realize that?" The problem absorbed her but insufficiently to prevent the sudden spasms from doubling her up; then strange muscular twinges made her shiver; she sweated now not just from the delicious heat of the sun but with some burning fever. Simple caution told her she must get back to the hotel, especially when nausea added a second danger. She thought of Granny M.'s favourite "Penny wise, pound foolish" and wondered if the French said, *"Centime sage, franc fou,"* when suddenly she knew by sensation the meaning of that unattractive expression, "It kept me running all night."

Of the two *outré* garments she had chosen for her Mediterranean visit—two garments which caused such looks of disapproval among the many respectable black-clad widows of the little town—the wide beach pyjamas rather than the flapping sandals impeded her as she ran back along the cobbled quaystone to the hotel. Her great, floppy straw hat she had to carry attached by its elastic to her arm to prevent its blowing away. She rushed past Madame in her glass-enclosed desk and past young M. Roger, all napkins and smiles at the *salle à manger* door; she clattered up the stone stairs and was halfway down the tiled passage towards the cupboard-sized little cabinet at the end, when from the other converging passage stepped this tall young man with curly black hair and a pipe. An agonizing new spasm made her run quickly enough to reach the door just as he was about to lift its winged-shaped brass handle. She had no time for blushes and politeness; to his *"Je vous en prie, Mademoiselle"* she merely replied by pulling the door open so that he was wedged against the wall; then shutting herself in, she loudly clamped the bolt. She could hear, as he moved away down the passage, that he was overcome with laughter.

She was indeed kept "running all night," but by lunch time the next day she felt restored enough to occupy her table. She supposed that the other place laid there was for show. (Sunday lunch, as she had learned last week, was a very showy, crowded time when the *pensionnaires* had to wait patiently to be served.) As usual the thread that tied the paper envelope containing her serviette had become complicatedly knotted; she bent her head down to give it her full concentration, when M. Roger said, "*Cela ne froisse pas, Mademoiselle. Elle connaît bien la maison.*" And there, of course, hesitating to seat himself opposite to her, was he. It was her turn now to say, "*Je vous en prie.*" Indeed she must, for every place in the room was taken by Sunday visitors from Marseille or Toulon and, though Madame and M. Roger had been "lovely" to her, she knew that their love would hardly survive her losing them custom.

As though to reward her for her complaisance, M. Roger, after whispering with Madame, brought her *rouget* (*spécialité de la maison* as well as *supplément*) instead of the pension fare of sardine and olives. To combine gratitude with excuse, and both with the request (on a busy *dimanche*) for a special plain omelette, made heavy demands on the emotional pantomime with which she eked out her merely serviceable French, and required a more full declaration of the state of her health than she would otherwise have given, in fact a frank statement of her suffering from diarrhoea. As she said it she became aware that the young man was trying not to smile. There was nothing else for it but to make a joke—waving her hand in his direction, "*Comme Monsieur connaît trés bien,*" she said. However imperfect the French, he caught the echo and gave her a little mock affirmative bow of the head. It was M. Roger who looked bewildered and at this they both at once burst into laughter. That was how it all began.

Looking back on it, Margaret could find no other than this hackneyed expression to fit the events of those hot September weeks. For if "all" suggested more than indeed occurred, it was in fact her first real affair. She'd been in love of one sort or another innumerable times, or so it seemed; and then in these last two years since the success of the Carmichael stories, "more" had happened once or twice: a literary agent exploring her body with feverish fumbling hands when she was squiffy at a crush; passionate embraces from a married host at a week-end house-party; a young Jewish painter almost staying the night at her tiny bachelor flat—but this was the first affair that had meant anything.

If he had been French, or indeed any foreigner, she would have been scared, although she had come prepared with the excuse that on her first visit abroad alone she had "no intention of doing anything as commonplace as being seduced by a Frenchman." If he had been English of any class or area that she knew well, she would have shied away with alarm, saying "really" she hadn't come "all the way to the Mediterranean for that." If he had been a business-man or a tea-planter on his way back East, or any other "lowbrow," as the Americans said, she would have avoided him for "one can't make love like Rosita Forbes or some other lady explorer adventuring into unknown lands." On the other hand, if he had been literary in any sense that she understood, that is, had known at once who she was, she would have run fast from his embraces—"the London literary world is both small and cruel-tongued." All this she knew in advance, for she had sketched out a short ironic story about exactly such a timorous virgin as herself who would make just these excuses, though for disguise she intended to set the scene in Italy and to make the girl a young abstract painter. She had even chosen the title, "Nothing to Write Home About." But Clifford Arbuckle defied all these prohibitions. He came from Consett, Durham (his was not even the Yorkshire accent of "pleasing broad A's" that she knew); his father was an ironmonger. He had come straight from the University of Durham to the University of Aix-en-Provence; he intended to give his life to the study and teaching of literature; his particular knowledge was of the changing reputation of Corneille through the centuries; of modern English literature he knew almost nothing, although he professed to know her name very well. It was almost a perfect fit. And then he was so improbably romantic-looking, the young Byron. But this, too, had its counterpart apparently, for he said before luncheon ended, "I suppose I ought to have known you were in the Bohemian set. You look too much of a gipsy, too romantic for what I've seen of the posh London crowd you talk like." He was perhaps a trifle too emphatic in his assertion of provincialism, of northernness, as he was in his adoration of all things French; even as she grew more talkative, let herself go, allowed his attraction to work on her during the meal, she made, out of habit, a little caricature in her mind of his excessive trait. "Francophily" the story might be called, or more vulgarly "Our Fred's Gone Froggy." Trying to feel blind that afternoon out on the jetty, she banished successfully the black-and-white wheeling gulls, turning them to monstrous, strident cats mewing; and as to the green-blue sea with its puffy waves, nothing was left of it but a smell of brine and ship oil and salt-caked rope. But one visual image persisted, blotting out all traces of the blind girl, so that even though she invented and said a number of times the phrase "a board-school Byron," she was forced in the end to close her writing-book in despair.

She woke quite suddenly. It must have been early in the morning, half past four perhaps, certainly not yet five, for there was hardly any light, yet the early fishermen were clattering their carts across the cobbles. Gingerly she felt for the little swivel switch by her bed, for it had come loose from the wall and she was always afraid of receiving a shock. She turned on the light and then, opposite, high up near the ceiling, where a pipe crossed the wall in the lofty room, this huge thing suddenly ran, this horrible thing with a tail, this great rat. Her heart beat as though to burst through her ribs, but otherwise she could not, dare not, move, even to turn her eyes away. Finding no opening under the ceiling, the creature—she could see now that it was old and foul, grey-muzzled and with two protruding teeth—turned at right angles in its tracks and began to scuttle down another pipe towards the floor. Margaret put the bedclothes over her head, but still her screams came very loud. Someone moved in response in a room along the passage; she thought she heard Madame's voice for a moment. The nauseous rat—frightened, no doubt, people would say—disappeared below the floor board. She almost knew that the tap on the door was his. He was dressed in a sort of schoolboy's piped grey dressing-gown and, beneath it, pink-and-white striped flannel pyjamas. He left the door open; even in her terror she registered this.

"What's up?"

She wanted to dismiss it all as the noisy awakening from a nightmare, but she was too frightened, that, once in the darkness again, the rat might return.

"It was a horrible great rat." She began to cry.

"Good heavens, they're more scared of you . . ." He was laughing; but then his tone changed; "What did you come to a dump like this for? I suppose you thought you'd get local colour or whatever it's called. You ought to be at Nice, or at least Bandol or Cassis— those are the new smart places for your set, didn't you know?"

His sudden anger touched her loneliness. She sobbed uncontrollably. Clifford, she could sense, was alarmed. He went to the door, she supposed to abandon her, but really to shut it. Then, sitting upon her bed, he took her into his arms, stroked her hair, kissed away the tears that were running down her cheeks. At last when she had come to the hiccoughing end of her hysteria, he said, "I'll go and dress. Put on some warm clothes. You can't lie here anticipating rats. We'll walk over to the Bec d'Aigle."

In the early morning light and mist they had passed the fat-faced, whiskery old women who, in grey printed dresses and black straw hats, sat like ancient tom cats, except where here and there a lower eyelid had fallen to reveal red-flecked eyeballs like those of a blood-hound, guarding their *rougets* and sea-spiders, their *langoustes* and that squizzling, wriggling, indeterminate grey mass which would appear on the hotel menu as *poissons du golfe* from the slinking, darting, voracious, half-starved cats which could be seen like jackals' lean shadows here and there by the harbour's edge. On the deck of a tramp steamer stood a young Negro in drill trousers and a sparkling white vest, cleaning his teeth with a piece of sugar-cane. From the tenement buildings on the hill leading away from the harbour, Armenian dock-workers were crossing the cobbled street, slippery with trodden-in debris from the vegetable carts, to wait at the broad, wire gates of the naval dockyard for the siren to sound its summons to work.

Looking back, Margaret remembered all these scenes as quite separate from one another, from herself. Their only unity lay in Clifford, his talk, his presence, his movements, the swing of his body, the turn of his head, the inverted triangle that his dark hair formed on the nape of his neck. Perhaps happiness, she thought, is entirely disjunctive, love so powerful an emotion that the scrabbling of human reason busily making patterns and corrections is momentarily stilled. Indeed, when a month later the memory of this happiness became too painful, she set out consciously to piece together, to unify, all these sharp-edged pictures with a thread of irony. The mists and the early morning light, where had she got them but straight from a score of Impressionist paintings? The fisherwomen were surely not real to her but little Boudin figures imported into the Midi from Normandy. As to the cats, she had reason to know that the fish-sellers of La Ciotat were lavish in their disposal of fish-

waste to these animals; the implied battle was the conventional
nightmare of some English spinster in Rome. The Negro, too—
Conradian figure—sprang all too easily to life, for what sugar-cane
would have kept its savour from, at the nearest, India or the Sudan?
As to the Armenians—creatures of a chance word of Madame that "*il
y a beaucoup d'Arméniens dans le quartier ouvrier*"—how clever to
recognize such ethnic distinctions in that Boudinesque light! But all
this tissue of mockery came later, as she very well knew. At the time
and for all those four weeks (a lie, it was only three) she had never
seen the world around so clearly as when it needed no explanation,
since Clifford was the meaning of it all.

Weeks later she could have stood examination on every step of
that walk: on the froglike shape left by the peeling stucco of a white
outhouse in the first farm they came to; the green lights in the farmyard cock's feathered neck as it stretched to crow; a row of maize
that marked the change from tomato plants to eggplants; the first
myrtles of the *maquis*, the first brooms; which step in the steep
descent to the *calanque* had kept its wooden support, which had lost
it and was crumbling. Yet every object they came to was only a
setting for Clifford's talk and Clifford's presence. Then they reached
the last step and looked down from jagged rocks into the deep, clear
blue water flecked with floating weeds and sticks and a sudden glint-
ing shoal of sardines caught in the sunlight.

"And now I suppose we salute the deep waters with our bodies'
splendid nakedness," she said.

But he had not seemed even to hear her, let alone to find cause to
laugh or smile. And this was exactly what they had done, diving
from the rocks into the deep, clear water, unbearably cold, instantly
livening. It should have been absurd but it wasn't, for his body, at
any rate, was splendid as he plunged and surfaced and swam around
her, and she felt herself a necessary part of his pattern.

When they lay together in a warm, sandy hollow among the aro-
matic undergrowth and he put his stiff, veined rod into her hand to
guide between her opened thighs, it should have brought easing,
mocking words into her head, but they weren't needed. When at last
she lay back, the pain only a remote memory amid a delicious muzzy
languor, his tongue licked the sweat from her thighs and her belly
with a wonderfully agreeable faint rasping, and all the store of irony

she had saved over the years against this moment seemed too absurd to remember. It was he who commented as they were coming back into the town.

"Well, at least your readers can only call you Miss Matthews by courtesy now. Unlike that awful old maid you call Miss Austen."

But they bubbled with jokes and giggled like ridiculous children as they hungrily devoured the *noix de veau* and carrots at lunch. Clifford ordered two plates of *pintade rôti* as well, *en supplément*. They ate all the white grapes and all the figs and more of the Brie than was really their pension due. And this delight in herself, in him, in everything continued for the whole four, or rather three weeks that they were together. All the bogies were banished. M. Roger caught the rat in a huge, old-fashioned cage trap (or so Clifford told her, for thank goodness she never saw such horror caged); and if there were others, she did not see them, for she slept ten or twelve hours solid after the strenuous days.

Only a hole in Clifford's left pre-molar came as the smallest intimation of mortality. He must go to M. Pertuis, the dentist, who lived in a verandahed villa behind a large acacia. She would buy the two almond-paste boats that they ate each morning after bathing in the *calanque*, and await him in their sandy hollow under the tamarisks, where merely by sitting up straight she could see little green lizards motionless in the sun on the outcrops of rock fifty yards away.

She blew up the air cushion, arranged it among the shrubby undergrowth, inhaled the scent of the rosemary that she had crushed, settled herself and pulled her knee-length lime linen skirt well up her thighs to get the sun's full warmth. She was aware only that he would be with her in less than half an hour. She needed no more than this assurance to make the waiting into bliss.

Meanwhile she took out her notebook and fountain pen. She felt no present inclination for the new volume of stories. Editors, publishers, agents all could wait. There was enough money, just, especially now when he had given her the knowledge that the moment was absolute. She had begun something fuller, something that, instead of putting a sharp line under life's episodes, would capture the fusion of all the moments, happy, unhappy. A Carmichael novel in which the surface absurdities and conflicts and bitterness were only one theme in a much larger symphony, where the faithfulness, the

enduring affection of the seemingly comic and vulgar Sophie and
George were the real, still centre of all the little storms.

The Countess and B.P. [she wrote], seeing each other still as they
did thirty years ago on their Madeira honeymoon. They pretend to see
each other in more hateful or ridiculous images for public consumption, so that they shall not seem to have failed to notice the stress and
storm of the years. But this is only the surface, the public picture they
offer to us, their children . . . your mother's aged pathetically, your
father's lost all sense of pride . . . but behind that, when they're alone,
or even in company, the old wedding photo remains as fresh as ever,
ready to pop up at the most unexpected moments. Not realizing this
basic continuity, we are dissatisfied with the disjunctive joys and sorrows, and seek to impose other patterns—the C. resents B.P.'s failures,
we say, or B.P. cannot forgive the C. for seeking warmth with other
men—but these imposed patterns falsify, blotting out both the lifelong
vision and the immediate joy. Are these in fact the same? Is eternity
experienced in the split second? If B.P. and the C. had this great possibility I now have of standing still in the silence and receiving,
wouldn't . . .

Suddenly, like the clamours of the knights breaking in on Becket's
sanctuary, voices sounded, carried to her on the light wind. People
were coming down their steps. Not the little children who sometimes lost their way there, looking for errant goats, but intruders.
Men's voices and women's—"*C'est tout ce qu'il y a de . . . C'est la
petite plage où Jean-Louis a cherché trouver . . .*" Determined
never to know more of these monstrous Saracens—intent no doubt
on sacrilege and plunder—she buried her head deep among the
myrtle and sought escape in the shrubby scents and the shrill monot-
ony of a cicada settled somewhere on the bark of a near-by pine tree.
But a strange animal sense made her feel the invaders' presence although she could no longer hear their voices; equally, she suddenly
knew that the danger was ending. Allowing herself to surface for a
moment, she could hear the voices disappearing up the steps, no
longer, after this desecration, "their" steps. "*O, je dirai à Jean-
Louis . . . dangereux et un peu puant aussi . . . Non, après tout,
c'est évidemment un petit coin pas du tout agréable.*"
Taking up her note-book, she turned some pages and wrote:

I think he would not have minded that intrusion as I did. First, of course, because it was French and for him everything French has a special claim for consideration. Which seems to me nonsense, and sentimental nonsense at that. Anyhow, his picture of French life is a confused and contradictory one, although he doesn't seem to know it. First there's all this *clarté* and civilization and the idea of France as the only classical country of restraint and of honour. (Oh, dear, the tedium of that awful *Cid!*) And then there's a much more conventional sort of thing for an Englishman—the only country of sexual maturity. When I point at the black widows, he says: Ah, the provinces! I think he sees Paris as a world of love-making and good talk and wine-drinking . . . And so it may be, for all I know. I know nothing about it. And, of course, he *would* forgive the intruders for intruding in French because he really knows French and is interested in its idioms and forms. And anyway, none of this matters in the slightest, or in any way makes him less than the most enchanting person I shall ever know.

She read through what she had written and wrote above it, "Some differences between us."

Then she started to write a few lines farther down the page:

At three and twenty, with experience behind her of quarrelling parents and a disordered household, Margaret Matthews had nothing further to learn either of the world or of its ways. What she could not attribute to selfishness she put down to stupidity, and where neither of these conveniently pervasive qualities of mankind seemed to apply, she frequently discerned motives of greed or lust. It was not surprising, therefore, that Margaret was considered universally as a most alarming quiz, and that the young gentlemen at the Assembly Rooms absented themselves . . .

But then she wrote:

All the same it *is* a deficiency that he could read P and P and see only snobbery and concern with money. "A narrow world"—as if all life were consumption and moorlands. The *awful* thing was when he said, "I should have thought your family life would have been a nice change from the deathly upper-middle-class respectability of the south of England. After all, you're a bit of a Tessa Sanger." *Tessa Sanger!* That dreadful sentimental book. The woman can have known nothing of so-called "Bohemian life" if she could portray it like that, all sugary and sweet. The Sangers could only have been allowable if treated with due irony—and much irony was due to them. Irony was not, as he said, swank. It was discipline for oneself and others. Discipline that wouldn't allow one to have had *The Constant Nymph* as one's only modern reading in the last two years! "You catch them without their bathing trunks, don't you? I've never read a writer who can do it like you. But I suppose you'll be working towards a sustained novel now." When he says such things, and puffs his pipe, and looks like a little boy pretending to be his own father, I can't tell whether I want most to hug him and kiss him, or to smack his hand.

She looked at her watch. Heavens, that dentist was keeping him a long time, but, of course, anticipation was one of the best parts of their times together. Deliberately relaxing her legs by burying her feet in the sand, she took up her pen again.

At four and twenty, Clifford Arbuckle felt that the world lay at his feet. Time and the temporary convenience of others were obstacles that he did not allow seriously to incommode him. He had felt so at ten years of age and the events of the intervening years had not given him reason to revise his estimate. Nurtured in a humble home, early imbued with strict denominational principles that forbade all frivolities, including dancing and Sunday travel, he had yet been indulged from his first years by his mother, a system to which his affectionate sister soon learned to subscribe. Absolute male authority was the principle of the Arbuckle household; subordination of all female claims to consideration its inevitable result. The manners of Mr. Arbuckle and his son Clifford were simple, almost rude, their diet was frugal, but in all else their whims and caprices were as much indulged as those of the most effete and luxurious caliphs or sultans.

Endowed by nature with a clever disposition and an agreeable person, the young Clifford soon learned to explain the system of his upbringing as the reasonable expectation of his exceptional talents and graces. A system of state scholarships continued the indulgence which the fond mother had begun. Born in the ruder north, he feared the established society of London and the surrounding counties, lest a more polished code of manners would accept less easily the primitive claim to male superiority.

His admiration, his attentions, his studious enquiry, all were given to our enemy across the narrow seas. To be received by the French was a delight, to be thought French was bliss. To this end he smoked a pipe, so, by a complicated whim, imitating those anglophile young French-men who supposed themselves to appear English by filling the drawing-room with clouds of coarse smoke. To labour to study the French sys-tem, the French manners, the French history became all his pains; yet the endurance of more childish pains—a sick headache, a toothache, a disordered digestion—he found impossible, fretting about them with a petulance that might rather have been expected from a small child. To such a state had constant and excessive maternal indulgence reduced this young man of parts, so that if he had not possessed . . .

But Clifford's saving graces remained forever unrecorded, for Margaret's attention was distracted by a young girl's cries. Looking up, she saw on the farther side of their path a girl of twelve or so—one of the goat-seeking children whom they had encountered previously. It was impossible to tell from her nasal accent and patois speech what was wrong, but she clearly required help. The day seemed fated to be one of interruptions and tediums, so Margaret, climbing over the rocks and through the undergrowth with some difficulty, followed the girl's lead, sometimes helped by her hand. At last they came in the growing heat to a widely spreading old fig tree. Here stood a small boy of nine or so, whom Margaret remembered to have seen with the girl before. At once both children pointed to the ground, and there to her horror Margaret saw a brood of young snakes lying basking on the dead leaves and leaf-mould. At first she wondered if some child had been bitten, and tried to recall stories of Mouse about first-aid for snake bite; but at last she understood that the children were offering to sell her the snakes. To her frightened disgust, when she had made her refusal perfectly clear, the young boy began to beat the small, delicately marked coils with his goat-herd's stick, and within seconds both children were dancing bare-footed like African savages, reducing the dying snakes to a squalid pulp.

Margaret turned and fled. Hysteria overtook her. She was tripped by the undergrowth once or twice, cut her hand, and bruised her knee before she returned tearful to the sandy hollow. Her book lay open as she had left it. Fear that Clifford's toothache had been a more serious symptom than they had thought, conscientious anxiety that she had mocked, both determined her to return to the town. I shall meet him on the way, she thought, and all will be all right again. She picked up her book. Beneath her own writing, she read in his:

The tooth extraction was bloody. The man is a maniac. How pleased you will be! Seriously, I don't see how we can maintain a real relationship if I (and other human beings) are so totally unreal to you that you can love them when they're with you and write this sort of thing when they're away from you an hour. I apologize for thinking that your upbringing had any advantages; it has clearly left you without the confidence to make any deep and sustained relationship in life. You have not commented on the selfishness of my ambition, but one of the side effects of the male dominance that you so dislike and which I know to be natural is that I do not intend to be saddled with a neurotic wife. Best of luck with your stories for which you have got very great talent. I'm going back to Aix. Thank you for everything.

Her first anger was for his total lack of humour, her second for her own selfish frivolity. For two days she stayed on at the hotel divided between these furies; then she telephoned to him. At last he agreed to pass a night with her at a hotel in Marseilles. Perhaps it was an insufficient remedy for a deep malady, but they parted next day, agreeing to be good friends.

The only permanent legacy he left to her was that she always remembered that Corneille was a Norman "*qui patoisait*," whatever that implied socially in seventeenth-century France.

Letting the curls of his wig fall around his shoulders, Marcus unpeeled one layer of disguise, changing from Lady Caroline Lamb's vengeful page to the lady herself. He had taken off the page's neckcloth and embroidered livery-coat, and lay on the big bed, naked to the navel, below which an orange sash was wound. This, with his baggy pink Turkish trousers, was presumed to be Lady Caroline's somewhat extravagant idea of a page's uniform.

"*I* don't think Mary Clough either attractive or intelligent," he said, and, shaking his Turkish slippers from his feet onto the floor, he curled his legs up on to the bed.

"No. But then you're not qualified by nature to judge either the attractions of women, or intelligence." Jack took off his full-bottomed wig to rid the reproof of the triviality of travesty. Yet in eighteenth-century undress and in his controlled anger, he seemed much more like the vitriolic Mr. Pope than he had when rather clumsily fox-trotting at the ball.

"And you, of course, are a connoisseur of cunt."

"No. I simply don't find it necessary to sum up the qualities of my friends. That someone is a friend naturally means that he or she is attractive, intelligent, and so on."

"Don't sum up! You're the biggest set of gossip-mongers I've ever met."

"I should hope so. We're not politicians or public servants trained to avoid reality. My friends are people. Their concerns are humane."

"Pulling to pieces Lady Westerton."

"Lavinia Westerton is only doubtfully humane. Anyway, only people who have no capacity for friendship talk vaguely about speaking ill of no one."

"Well, it wasn't very humane of Monty Golding to make fun of me because I mixed up Masoch, or whatever he's called, with the Italian painter."

"First of all, you're using the word humane in a loose, colloquial sense that is hardly helpful." Jack tightened his thin lips. His delicate, bony, Jewish face, his wide-nostrilled nose suited the eighteenth-century undress, if not exactly the role of Pope. Marcus knew that this precision, this pedantry, were meant to try him; he only hoped that Jack didn't know how nearly they exasperated him. "Secondly, your confusion of Sacher Masoch with Masaccio led to some ludicrous misapprehensions which it would have been affected not to pursue. Instead of primping and pouting you might have assisted in furthering the joke, as you very well could have done if you'd tried."

"And what about Mary's pouting? I suppose that was aesthetic disgust."

Jack was clearly set upon aggravation, for he did not immediately answer the question. He stared, instead, at the Bakst drawings he had given Marcus on his birthday.

"I can't remember why you wanted these."

"Because they're the prettiest pictures I can think of. And the most decorative. Also, for good or ill, I first saw you magnificent in your box from my gallery seat at the *Sleeping Beauty*. Years before you picked me up at the Coliseum."

"You said . . ." Jack left it. "But sentiment apart, you should have a good painting in here. After all, it was you who chose the Delaunay and the Gris still-life. In six months you've improved the collection enormously."

"Thank you. But I don't want the good pictures in here. I just want fun things like the Bakst. Gorgeous. To go with my wonderful, vulgar, ornate bed. Oh, how I wallow in it after years of Fifty-two."

"I'm not sure that it's quite decent for you to wallow in my parents' bed. And they not so long cold. To return. If Monty wasn't disgusted with you, I was. Vulgar malice and spite! You sounded just like your awful mother. And to Mary, who's always been so civil to you."

"Civil! It's impossible to tell with your friends whether they like one or hate one."

"Being my friend they're naturally disposed to like you, as you should them. Anyway, all this hangover of lack of self-confidence. It isn't much of a compliment to our six months together."

"If only Monty hadn't got on to that bloody wedding story of Margaret's."

"Your sister's stories are limited, but they have real merit. They appealed to Monty. He praised them. Surely it's as simple as that."

"It isn't simple at all. I've suffered from that awful wedding story of Margaret's before now. It always upsets me when people talk about it."

"Oh, don't be so tiresome, Mark. A work of art is a work of art. That's what Monty was talking about. Nobody knew it was by a sister of yours. Or would have cared if they had. Now that *is* gossip. Anyway, it was only because you'd been sitting there ever since the dancing finished, looking like a very pretty, constipated chinchilla, that Mary out of misplaced kindness asked what you thought about it. You're very decorative, my dear, but . . . And why couldn't you have just said it was written by your sister and that you thought it false and left it at that, if you wanted to. 'I don't think you and I are ever likely to know much about weddings, Miss Clough.' "

Jack's imitation, Marcus knew, caught exactly his own prissy, high-pitched petulance.

"Poor Mary! You knew bloody well that Oliver had just walked out on her after all these years. And to marry some flapper. It was foul of you, Mark, and cheap. And it hurt her."

"There wouldn't have been much point in saying it if it hadn't. Anyway, shall I tell you why I didn't rush to claim Margaret for my sister? Perhaps it'll make you and your friends a little less quick to

sum human beings up in phrases. 'So mysteriously lost for hours of
the night among London's bright lights . . . Oh, so enjoying his
winged arabesques and *pas de chat.*' You see, I know the passage off
by heart. It was easy enough for Margaret and all the rest of them to
fancy me as 'flitting from flower to flower.' They'd left home. Do
you want to know what I was doing, lost among London's bright
lights? I was flitting from one sordid old man to another trying to
sell my bum. How disgusting! Not yet seventeen! Well, I couldn't
always get extra work at the film studios, that's why. And when I
couldn't and Regan was drunk or the Countess was in a rage, I didn't
get enough to eat."

Marcus was crying now; not with the old hysterical screaming of
his boyhood. Tears ran slowly down his face; but his hands were
shaking. His anger was as great as Jack's had been. Jack went over
and tried to put a hand on his shoulder, but Marcus pushed him
away.

"All right," Jack said, rather wearily, "tell."

He sat back in a little tub chair, one leg thrown over the other,
finger-tips of one hand pressed against those of the other.

"You bloody judge," Marcus said, but he nevertheless began to
talk.

"I don't think you can imagine what Number Fifty-two was like
after I left school. At first there were my fashion drawings. But then,
as every paper from *Vogue* down sent them back, I gradually knew
that all that was a sort of dream. One woman was nice enough to
write and what she said seemed to sum it all up, 'Your designs show
a nice sense of fantasy, but you appear to be living in a vacuum.' I
was. I just used to sit and think about sex all day. Not that I don't
think about it most of the time now. It was the only thing to do;
Fifty-two really had become an awful house. The Countess had no
one else to pick on but me and then she'd got the change coming on,
so she was at her bloodiest anyway. That probably made me put on
what she called effeminate airs, just to spite her. I was supposed to
have an allowance until a job came along. Billy Pop did give me ten
bob once. In return I was to help with the housekeeping. I must say
there wasn't much to do. Arrange some daffodils for the Countess
and then I used to do the shopping, when there was any money to
shop with or we'd got credit again at the Army and Navy Stores.

What I must have looked like among all those colonels' wives and admirals' widows at the grocery counter! A boy of sixteen.

"I put red on my cheeks and my lips from my paintbox, and sometimes blue on my eyelids. And then I had a sort of grey sombrero that I'd bought second-hand in Soho; and I used to stop all the time in front of shop windows and tuck my gorgeous black curls in on the other side. And my walk! I took so many little delicate steps that the muscles of my thighs used to get cramp. Of course all the men who sold flowers or newspapers down at Victoria Station used to call out after me, 'Look at Angela,' 'Puss, puss, puss.' Terrific dishes, some of them were! Anyway, the more they called the more I did the nance. I was terrified of them, of course, partly because I was hoping they would pick me up and partly because I honestly thought they might knock me down. Once when I'd pinned a small bunch of violets on to my overcoat a man came up and said, 'Bloody little pouff! They ought to pole-axe the lot of you.' I was so scared I peed myself, but I only put on a more queeny act. I held the collar of my overcoat together as though it was the sables the grand duchess had smuggled out of Vladivostok. I just longed to be noticed. It didn't matter how. Then, of course, lots of the boys at the agency and down at the studio at Cricklewood when I did extra work were just the same. You should have seen us tripping over our togas in *Ben Hur*. I became used to picking up people then, if there wasn't any work going at the agency.

"It was in Windmill Street and when the awful little man put his head through the hatch and said, 'No work at the studios today, boys,' there I was right on top of Piccadilly, so there wasn't much else I could do. At first, of course, I just got picked up myself having tea or a poached egg at the big Lyons and other cafés round there. But later I started trolling, though I never went up West specially for it at night until I was eighteen at least.

"At first I used to take them back to Fifty-two. For some reason I was terrified of going to strange houses. And I used to make awful social conversation—you know, 'Yes, those are all my father's books. He's tremendously learned,' or 'I'm afraid my room's a bit old-fashioned, but I'm hoping to do it up myself soon. Scarlet and black, or something amusing.' Can you imagine? When there was only one thing in *their* minds. However, I must say most of them were very kind and polite. I think they were bewildered, poor things. You see, I looked more than my age and they probably thought I was an old pro who would take them back to some squalid bed-sitter near the Station. One or two just took off and fled when they knew it was my parents' house.

"And then once I was lying there, hoping it would be over quickly. I'd shut my eyes because it was so painful. And when I opened them the door was very slightly ajar and I looked straight into *her* eyes. Of course she was gone in a second. But I *know* it happened. The man—a huge great brute of a Scotsman—hadn't seen a thing. So I said nothing, but I don't know how I ever had the courage to get him down those stairs and out of the house. For some reason I thought she'd gone for a policeman. I was an awfully daft mixture of sophistication and childishness. The only sign she showed was when I gave her money that week. We didn't even pretend about allowances by then, but I often earned two or three pounds in the week, what with film work and the clients, and I always gave her a pound or thirty shillings. This time she threw the notes on the drawing-room floor with her most tragedy-queen look. 'How dare you offer me that filthy money?' and so on. Of course I should have had it out with her then and there, but I was too scared. I just picked up the money and spent it all on seats for *Giselle*. But after that I had to take my courage in both hands and go back with *them*.

"Even then I used to go into long social explanations. I can remember it happening on that occasion I wanted to tell you about. I'd tramped all the agencies from Oxford Circus to Villiers Street and back. And my poor old feet, dear, well, lor luv you. I'd relied on a call for more Roman citizens to cheer on Ramon Novarro. But no, they weren't shooting that day. It couldn't have been more tiresome, for I wanted to go to *Sylphides*.

"Suddenly I saw this sort of dashing guards officer in Jermyn Street, a bit red in the face and corseted, but still I'd known far worse. I stopped and looked in the window of the cheese shop. And which cheese was *I* going to buy and did I keep house for myself and was I musical? So I said, yes, I was, but I found it difficult to get the money to go to concerts, which was to make it clear to him the whole thing was rent. Well, you know all that, because that's what I said when I met you that evening after the *Three-Cornered Hat*. And then, I can hear myself now—'I would so tremendously like to entertain you in my own studio.' Studio! ark at er. 'But the awful thing is I still live with my people and so I'm afraid it's rather out of the question.' So we went back to his place in Mortimer Square or somewhere like that behind Selfridge's. Me talking all the way in the taxi, 'Didn't he just adore Marie Tempest?' 'And did he like the Impressionist painters?' and 'Could I be right and was he in the army?' And I was right. And he was called Major Mooney or Moody or something, and he got tremendously fatherly with me, and called me young feller, me lad, and told me it was a damned shame to see a young chap with obvious artistic talent at a loose end and he was rather an artistic cuss himself despite the army and I must come with him to Covent Garden, did I like opera?

"But of course it didn't stop him taking me straight up to the bedroom and making me strip. All I ever wanted with them was to get it over, but the major started a horrible catechism. What did most men expect from me? Who was the first who'd done it to me? Had I had it from the front? I stood there naked and wished the floor would swallow me up. And then, as though sent from heaven, I saw a copy of Margaret's book. So I tried to say casually, as though I was in the habit of saying such things in the nude, 'Oh, I see you've got my sister's book of stories. One or two are rather terrific, aren't they? Actually she's caught me rather well in that wedding story.' And posing with one hip stuck out in what I hoped seemed like Donatello's David, I read aloud—'Oh, so enjoying his winged arabesques and *pas de chat!*' I drawled it all quite brilliantly. I suppose I hoped to stop the major in his tracks. I certainly did. He stood quite still and stared. Then he walked to the bedroom door, opened it, and whistled.

"A few moments later another major appeared, only thinner and more wooden-looking. Then *my* major said, tremendously formally, 'Seymour Dunlop, my housemate.' Waving his hand at me—the Michelangelo made flesh—he said, 'This silly little bitch has been lying like stink. Says Margaret Matthews is her sister.' 'I *don't* think,' Major Dunlop said. 'Rotten little twerp.' 'I didn't bring you back here to hear snobbish rot and lies,' my major said, and picking up a hairbrush, he caught me a nasty blow on the buttocks. 'That's what's interesting about you, or would be if you weren't so spotty.' No, don't protest. It was probably true. I only got rid of that awful acne about six months before I met you. 'Go to hell,' he said. 'Get your things and get out of here. Back to the rectory.' I think trying to keep some dignity while I dressed and got out of that room was about the most awful moment of my life. I was determined not to cry."

Nor was he crying now. Most of his tension and anger appeared to have vanished as he became absorbed in telling his experience. Then he laid his head back on the pillow. Jack sat on the side of the bed and stroked Marcus's cheek with the back of his hand.

"Poor sweet," he said. "By the way, I've managed to buy the Modigliani portrait of Bakst for you. Though why I should encourage you to have any father figures before me, I don't know."

"If any major tries to insult you again, I'll kill him. All the same," he went on, "that major did have an eye for the essentials."

Parents at Play: A Lesson in Lamarckian Survival

The dining-room of the residence of William Matthews, Esq., gentleman and author, at about half past three of an autumn afternoon in the year 1925. The room, though clearly originally furnished to give an air of warmth, of opulence worn with gentlemanly ease, and solid but not heavy comfort, has now acquired, through years of over-indulgence on an insufficient income, an appearance of draughty penury, ill-concealed shabbiness, and vague but pervasive discomfort. For those with sharp eyes and noses, stains, mildew, and stale gravy have taken possession of the room. Centre, the long mahogany dining-table is set out with plates of sandwiches and biscuits; tumblers, whisky, and siphons of soda adorn the sideboard; seven chairs are placed at the table: it is clear that company is expected, but not for a formal meal.

Enter by door to right WILLIAM MATTHEWS, *aged fifty-five, a small man, once boyish, pink, and cherubic, but now a trifle motheaten, harassed, and with an incontestable air of slyness difficult exactly to pin down. He is dressed in well-worn tweeds and floppy bow tie, and carries a vaguely "artistic" old, shapeless, green homburg hat. He might be a minor portrait painter, a land agent to an indigent nobleman, an amateur antiquarian, the harassed tutor of*

*the unruly son of a millionaire, or an Asquithian Liberal candidate
for a safe, Conservative rural constituency; he is, in fact, an un-
successful author, who maintains himself by a diminishing private
income and an even more diminishing stock of journalistic small
change. A moralist would soon label him self-indulgent, weak,
evasive, and lazy; in fact, by far the most interesting feature of his
character is the highly developed cunning by which over the years
he has survived the disaster the moralists have predicted for him.
To this survival, of course, the snobbish reverence of the English
tradesman towards paraded gentility has greatly contributed.*

After him follows his eldest son, QUENTIN MATTHEWS, *aged
twenty-eight. He is a tall, very thin man who appears from moment to moment as a young man prematurely aged and embittered
by pain and failure, and as a middle-aged man with the boyish
smile and movements of someone in whose breast hope springs
eternally, if a little fatuously. He is, in fact, a journalist and newspaper columnist who has in a few months had sensational success
with his trenchant, hard-hitting attacks on the government's supine
industrial policy—sensational success, that is, within very limited
circles of I.L.P., Fabian, S.D.F., and various minute groups of
Marxist and anarchist readers; but as this is the only world that at
the moment he recognizes, he feels his power to be infinite. His
butcher-blue shirt, chrome-yellow tie, and mop of fair hair through
which he runs his fingers when excited have become a well-known
feature of most left-wing platforms during the last months, and he
clearly speaks in ordinary conversation as though addressing a
meeting. Nevertheless, despite this air of theatricality, Quentin
Matthews is a young man to be reckoned with, for he has the disconcerting habit, hardly known among politicians, industrialists,
trade unionists, and other men of action, of on occasion actually
doing the things which he has announced that he is going to do.*

WILLIAM MATTHEWS (*going at once to the sideboard and the
drinks*): It seems unsuitable to be offering my own son a drink in
my own house. But until such time as you have all finally decided
that it would be impractical and unethical for me to live on my
own property and with my own wife, have a whisky.

QUENTIN (*ignoring the offer*): By the way, in relation to any economic agreement that you and mother may reach, I think it only

fair to point out that while the survival of private property into 1940 at the latest is highly problematical, the continued toleration of run-down housing, whether by the landlord's negligence or because of his inadequate capital funds, is something that will hardly continue into the next decade.

WILLIAM MATTHEWS: Oh, my dear boy, I'm far more of a Socialist than you think. If the Government want to do up this house, I've no intention of objecting. Of course if it becomes your mother's, I can't say. Women are so much more snobbish about these things.

A FIRM, CLEAR WOMAN'S VOICE OUTSIDE THE DOOR: What things, Billy? *Enter* CLARA MATTHEWS, *a good-looking woman on the edge of fifty. The short skirts, flat chests, and slim hips fashionable at the time suit her well. She has legs of which any girl might be proud. With her Eton crop she might indeed be a boy from that school playing the heroine in a house play. But no boy ever had that woman's instinct for getting her own way by as devious, illogical, and seemingly irrelevant course of words and action as Mrs. Matthews. With her children, in particular, she has the great advantage that, having brought them up to expect her to act with consistent selfishness and egotism, they are always totally disarmed when she seeks the same ends by sudden shows of generosity and concern for others. She has made her entry carefully, flanked by her two younger sons—on her right,* RUPERT MATTHEWS, *twenty-five, tall, fair, handsome, dressed in lilac Oxford bags and a bronze high-necked sweater. He looks too theatrical to be taken for a successful young actor, but those who know the limitless "hammy" qualities of the contemporary theatre will have rightly reasoned that no one could look so actorish without being in fact an actor. Being an actor, however, of our own day, and not of the vulgar, robust era of Irving or Tree, he has all the necessary manners of a gentleman, i.e., he makes a good deal of play with lighting cigarettes for himself and his mother, moves chairs very "realistically," speaks with a clipped accent as though unwilling to communicate in words, and generally follows the vogue of our contemporary actor-knights, that "realistic" apparatus of manners which the English, with their infallible gift for the trivial and inessential, have made their special heritage from the great art of Ibsen. However, since, with the social shake-up consequent upon England's pyrrhic*

victory in 1918, "gentlemen" in general take their manners from
the stage, RUPERT MATTHEWS *is well on the way to being as suc-*
cessful a gentleman as an actor. His brother MARCUS, *who supports*
CLARA MATTHEWS *on her left, is within a month or two of twenty-*
one, or manhood. His good looks, however, are of the kind that do
not give promise of the masculinity demanded conventionally in
our own day of those who call themselves men; nor do his wide,
skirt-like pleated trousers, tight black coat, and tighter black
double waistcoat assist his masculinity. His short black Valentino
side whiskers bring out the Spanish in him, but again not somehow
the Spanish man. His intermediate type has never perhaps found a
satisfactory social niche since Saint Paul, interpreting Jesus Christ's
social revolutionary views in the light of his own peculiar sexual
temperament, brought to an end the long-lived sexual morality of
the Romano-Hellenic world. In 1925 he stands between the na-
tional scapegoatism of Oscar Wilde and the national obsessive at-
tention of the later decades. Given England, he has no choice but
to be "artistic"; but a certain firmness of chin and fierceness of eye,
not unlike his mother's, suggest that MARCUS MATTHEWS *will de-*
mand a more important role in our capitalist society than the
artist's—perhaps even aspire to that of artistic hostess.

CLARA MATTHEWS: What things, Billy, are women more snobbish
about?

WILLIAM MATTHEWS: Quentin tells me that the Government will
step in and do up our home, my dear. Someone from the Home
Office perhaps. (*He laughs delightedly at his own joke.*)

CLARA MATTHEWS: What a revolting idea! Some dreadful little
town clerk choosing my wall-papers. Over my dead body. If that's
your socialism, Quentin, I can soon tell you it won't work. Taste
is a matter of fashion and whoever heard of town clerks being in
the fashion. Not that I don't want to see this dining-room re-done.
I can't quite make up my mind . . .

RUPERT: I think it should be beige. Tallu's new flat is entirely beige.

MARCUS: Beige is hardly new, is it? Now Lady Melchett has done
something so amusing with her small drawing-room. It's all sand
pink and off-white.

CLARA MATTHEWS (*looking in turn with admiration at her sons*):
Well, at least Rupert and Marcus have learned something by go-

ing out into the world. Now what you think you're doing, Quentin, giving up that most suitable job in Oxford, I can't imagine. What *are* you doing?

QUENTIN: As a matter of fact I've just been asked to do a series of articles for *The Daily News*.

WILLIAM MATTHEWS (*now, in his turn, impressed*): *The Daily News*, eh? I used to know old Callcott there, but I should think . . .

CLARA MATTHEWS: Dead, of course, bound to be. No one has made so many influential friends who die easily as your father. Articles about what, anyway, Quentin?

QUENTIN: About the unemployed, Mother. Even you, I suppose, may have heard of them.

CLARA MATTHEWS: Even I! Why, I'm almost an expert on unemployment. I've lived with your father for over twenty-five years. Now there's something for your father to do. He can help you with your articles. I'm sure nobody knows more about the subject than he does.

QUENTIN MATTHEWS: This happens to be a serious subject, Mother. Some of the men in the Rhondda have been unemployed since the war ended. There's a real danger that they'll become unemployable.

CLARA MATTHEWS: Then your father *is* the man to write the articles. But enough about why *you've* been so silly as to leave Oxford. We're met here because after all these years *I* have got to leave your father. While you children were young and needed a home, a mother, a nominal father, then I was prepared to make any sacrifices, I was prepared . . .

RUPERT: As you know, Mother, for many years, we've all thought . . .

CLARA MATTHEWS: Don't interrupt me, Rupert. You're not playing the lead here. Now, at last, I can't go on. Physical brutality, desertion, infidelity with the lowest of the low . . .

WILLIAM MATTHEWS: She was from a very respectable family in Tooting.

CLARA MATTHEWS: Tooting! You could hardly sink lower, Billy. (*They both share in laughter at this.*) It isn't even picturesque like Stepney and Whitechapel. And how can you eat sandwiches at a time like this?

WILLIAM MATTHEWS: They're very good sandwiches, my dear. They make me realize what I'm missing without Regan's cooking . . .

CLARA MATTHEWS: You must pay *some* price, I suppose, for acting like a brute. However, I'm glad you like them. The children won't appreciate them. They've never known the difference between blinis and bully beef. But I told Regan—*foie gras* and smoked salmon. After all, we don't bring twenty-five years of marriage to an end every day. Give me a *foie gras*. Well, as I say, brutality, desertion, adultery. I suppose even the English law won't ask for more.

QUENTIN: I think you have every ground for divorce, Mother . . .

CLARA MATTHEWS: Divorce! My dear Quentin, I'm not a Bolshevik woman commissar. Nor a low-comedy actress (*looks at Rupert*) nor a God knows what (*looks at Marcus*). No, I don't intend to end my days as a notorious divorcee, however little my children care. I want you to arrange a legal separation for me. Unless, of course, I might later meet someone responsible and distinguished to pass the evening of my days with. In which case I should look to you boys to see that it was all regularized. But the important thing is the financial settlement, and that's where you boys can help. Let's hear what settlement you children propose so that your father and I can live separately without too much diminution of the little standards we've tried to build up to do credit to our successful children.

WILLIAM MATTHEWS: A very sound point, my dear. You're all doing so well now, you can't afford shabby genteel parents. It only proves what I've always said, that the more you neglect children the better they'll fare later on.

CLARA MATTHEWS: Don't be absurd, Billy. We've never neglected the children. We taught them early to be adult and responsible and as a result they're responsible adults. Now what exactly do you all propose, Quentin?

QUENTIN: Well. First of all we want to make it perfectly clear that we're not taking sides. I've made some notes here about the usual form of bourgeois separation settlements . . .

(*Curtain as he speaks. When the curtain rises again it is clear that the financial consultations are over.*)

QUENTIN: I suspect that that's as fair a settlement as we shall devise.

I think Mother would be wise to have certain clauses written in that would protect her from Father's importunities in the event of Aunt Mouse leaving her any considerable legacy. The women's suffrage movement largely completed the emancipation of the bourgeoisie from the last vestiges of feudalism, but woman has kept some of the subordination of a chattel even under enlightened capitalism.

MARCUS: I suppose that the Countess will only be happy if she knows that Billy Pop is living in some kind of decency. Every woman's first concern must be for her man.

CLARA MATTHEWS: How very curious! Marcus of all people is the only one who shows any understanding.

MARCUS: That's the advantage of being a "God knows what," darling. They have their special insights.

QUENTIN (*interrupting impatiently*): I think we'd better leave it to the two of them to talk it over.

RUPERT: Yes, let's all go up to the nursery and regress for a quarter of an hour.

(*Exeunt children.* WILLIAM MATTHEWS *helps himself to another whisky.*)

CLARA MATTHEWS: Oh, I do hope you won't take to drink, Billy, on your own. (*She waits impatiently for a few seconds.*) Well, you might at least offer me one.

WILLIAM MATTHEWS: I thought you wanted to be independent. (*However, he helps her to a whisky and soda and lights her cigarette.*)

CLARA MATTHEWS: I want men always to be chivalrous to me.

WILLIAM MATTHEWS: I doubt if most men will respect a separated woman. I only hope I don't hear too much about their insults, or I shall find myself involved in a lot of fights. And I'm getting rather old for that.

CLARA MATTHEWS: It would have been better if you had stood up to other men sometimes instead of hitting a defenceless woman.

WILLIAM MATTHEWS: Don't reproach me with that again. You know that I was disgustingly drunk, Cootie.

CLARA MATTHEWS: Cootie! You can't get round me that way, Billy. You haven't called me that since our honeymoon. And what about that awful woman?

WILLIAM MATTHEWS (*pathetically*): Awful she was! She soaked herself in cheap scent. Though I still say she'd made herself some very smart hats. But that scent! Ugh! The lower classes, you know, Cootie, scent themselves to disguise, not like us, to enhance.

CLARA MATTHEWS: Oh, poor Billy! How you must have hated that. I will say you've always been fastidious. But we must be practical. What about this scheme of the children's?

WILLIAM MATTHEWS: An appalling impertinence, if you ask me! However, I suppose if we sell the house we've always lived in we can afford a couple of bijou flats—I believe there are such things. What worries me is what's to happen to Regan?

CLARA MATTHEWS: Regan! But she'll come with me, of course. How could I dress without her? And then nobody else can cook delicious meals for someone who's banting.

WILLIAM MATTHEWS: I doubt if you could cope with her drunkenness in a small flat. You need a man for that. Besides, my digestion has been ruined since I left here. Have you ever been served with undercooked fish?

CLARA MATTHEWS: Oh, you! A man can always eat at his club.

WILLIAM MATTHEWS: No, I can't. I've just been asked to resign. So many of these new members make such a fuss about card debts. I suppose they think it gives them the claim to be called gentlemen.

CLARA MATTHEWS: Oh, Billy. We'd better go and talk to Regan. She's so sensible.

(*They leave the room. A few seconds later their three sons return. They appear surprised at the empty room; however, they seat themselves at the table. They have hardly sat down when their parents return arm in arm, looking a very smart and gay young couple.*)

CLARA MATTHEWS: If you children want to have supper here, you may. Regan will knock you up something. Your father's going to take me out to the Maison Basque. Only a little spoiling can help me after all I've been through today.

RUPERT: Now if you've been silly, Countess . . .

QUENTIN: We haven't got time to waste, Mother . . .

MARCUS: Oh, really, it's too tiresome . . .

CLARA MATTHEWS: Don't say anything more children, please. For your own sakes. I was sparing you any allusion to the awful way in which you've worked on an unhappy woman's feelings. To come between your father and me after twenty-five years!

QUENTIN: Now, understand, Mother, if you go back on this we shall never intervene again, whatever Father does . . .

WILLIAM MATTHEWS: That's quite enough of that, my boy. You've bullied your mother enough. I dare say you all meant very well. Yours is a hard generation. They say the war's responsible for that. So I'm not going to point out to you that you've ignored some of the deepest and finest instincts in the human race. But . . .

CLARA MATTHEWS: Oh, come along, Billy, I'm ravenous. By the way, did you say that dreadful woman made hats?

WILLIAM MATTHEWS: Yes, she's a very clever milliner.

CLARA MATTHEWS: Oh, Billy. And you're a very clever man. Just when Miss Millington's died so inconveniently after all these years. Really, children, to try to separate me from a man who's clever enough to find a new milliner for me just by walking out of the house.

(*Exeunt* WILLIAM *and* CLARA MATTHEWS. *Enter* REGAN.)

REGAN: Oh, lor. Now don't take on abaht it. Wot did you expect? You carn't break bad abits like nail-biting in a few weeks, let alone worse ones like marriage. Besides, the only way *they've* got of livin in the future is lookin back on the past. That's always ow the gentry as survived. Separashun indeed! After they've brought you lot up.

QUENTIN: ⎫
RUPERT: ⎬ That's all very well, but think of all the trouble we've been to.
MARCUS: ⎭

REGAN: Lor luv a duck, you don't know when you're well orf. Now, look, you're going to be payin out to them for the rest of their lives. At least I ope so, or I shan't get my wages. With them together you can keep some check on what you're all sendin, but if they're apart . . . Well! But I'm surprised at you not knowin that, Mr. Quentin. It's in The Book. Centralisashun, e says, is one of the keys to modern society . . .

QUENTIN: What book? Who says?

(REGAN *goes up to the bookcase and takes out a large book. She presents it to Quentin.*)

REGAN: Why! The Book, of corse!

QUENTIN: *The Intelligent Woman's Guide to Socialism,* by Bernard Shaw! Good God! That Mussolini-loving old heretic!

RUPERT: So *démodé!*

MARCUS: So tiresome!

ALL TOGETHER: Except, of course, for *Saint Joan*. Whatever do *you* know about Bernard Shaw, Regan?

REGAN: Nix me dolly. But them's the lines I was given.
(*Exit* REGAN.)

QUENTIN: *The Intelligent Woman's Guide to Socialism and Capitalism. I* ought to know that title. When was it published? (*He turns to title page.*) Nineteen twenty-eight! But . . . but, that's not for three years yet. It must be some mistake.

MARCUS: Oh, no, it's just one of those tedious Shavian jokes.

RUPERT: Thank goodness, there's unlikely to be a revival of *his* plays.
(*Curtain. The actors, recovering from their paradoxical feats, fall into the relaxing intimacy of The Game.*)

QUENTIN AS JUSTICE SCALES: Not the least repellent feature of capitalism in decline is the degree to which the cynical exploiters become victims of their own sentimental shibboleths. The sanctity of marriage, the inviolability of the home can at such times take in even the most clear-headed idolators of the cash nexus.

MARCUS AS THE COUNTESS (*patting her Eton crop into place*): Exploiter isn't a very nice thing to call anyone, least of all a mother. (*Turning to* RUPERT THE BILLY POP) I don't think we ever really made the children understand the joy of living. But let's forget them, darling. Do you know, I don't know whether it's the change or not, but all I really want now is just to be a comfortable old Joan to your Darby.

RUPERT THE BILLY POP (*taking her hand sentimentally*): However the change may change you, dear, it hasn't changed you for me.

JUSTICE SCALES: Marriage! Sense of the past!

QUENTIN: Oh, Christ! It's too disgusting to go on, isn't it?

RUPERT: Yes, we're not children now.

MARCUS: I think I *am* a bit. But I don't like Rupert holding my hand. He does it so fraternally.

RUPERT (*dropping Marcus's hand quickly*): Though after six years in the theatre I could pretend to press a cod's fin with passion if the producer told me to. Well, I must be off. We're playing a matinee this afternoon.

people, I suppose. But 52 was so ugly. Not like Chekhov's *dachas* in their birch woods. So we had to get out. We so desperately needed some beauty in our lives. Beauty with elegance. The Matthewses were only potential Prozorhovs. If I can only get back to that potential past, though—the long, stifling, nursery afternoons, the long talks about ambitions and schemes which at times *did*—even for me— seem almost dreams.

The clue is Billy Pop. If only I could shed some of the layers of contempt and hatred which she made me feel for him. But he's so awful, the fat white slug. Fat white sluggard whom nobody loves. Perhaps I can begin from there. First he isn't really fat, only run to seed. And then he's certainly not white, on the contrary, and heaven knows why, he's always rather bronzed and pink-cheeked— russet apple. And then his mother loved him deeply. And *she* love- hates him enough to be unable to leave him. And he loves himself dearly, oh, so dearly, that he'll preserve himself until Doomsday.

There I go immediately in disgust and dislike; and probably there would go Sofochka and Bobik about Andrey if we could have the "T.S." twenty years later. But the fact is that Andrey is an irritating man and an absurd, comic man. (This is essential to Chekhov, for to him, Willie tells us, all failure is comic. *N.B.*—read Nietzsche, Scho- penhauer, etc., etc. There must be abridged versions. No. Better accept what Willie says here, for the *feeling's* the thing. Acting is feeling. We're not, thank God, playing Shaw. So we can take all these ideas for granted as simply the atmosphere we breathe.) But also a mov- ing, a pathetic, even lovable man. B.P. has irritated me and I've laughed at him. But I've never loved him; I couldn't. Why not? Well, he's more active in defending himself than Andrey, his whole life is a sly defence of himself. But Andrey survives. If I could get that touch of survival into him—not sly, of course, with him, but surviving.

But B.P. and his hopes of being a great writer, there we have An- drey—"Just think—I'm secretary of the local council now . . . and the most I can ever hope for is to become a member of the council myself . . . I, who dream every night that I'm a professor in Mos- cow University, a famous academician, the pride of all Russia!" Well, B.P. was more than a member of the local council. He had been an up-and-coming writer. But how much I can't really say; it had already gone when I remember clearly. No, that's not true.

When I was still at my prep, oh, before 1914, he came and spoke to the school about "Cricket in Literature"—later, in the twenties, he still did it at a guinea a time for local literary societies—but at that time he created a tremendous impression and the master who introduced treated him as a terrific pot. I suppose he'd had his *beauty* with the *Yellow Book* and the *Savoy* and playing cricket with Stephen Philips. And no one interested later. Of course he sees himself as Shakespeare or Tolstoy. His humour, his acceptance of life, of its joys and sorrows. I must get that in Andrey. That's what makes him lovable. But not with B.P. That's all sly bunkum with him. Acceptance of his own joys and of others' sorrows. That's his humour. But if I can remember him pushing the twins in the pram, sent out by her to do it. Me walking, or rather running, breathlessly beside. Oh, years ago. They were building. Yes, of course, Westminster Cathedral. And me so tired, asking if we can go back. And his dead, mechanical pushing of the pram, humming some little tune, not even hearing me, dreaming. Yes, that's it. That's Andrey in the Fourth Act. What was it he said? Suddenly, and I didn't understand. "We must all grope our way. As best we can, into that complete darkness." Self-pitying bunkum. I used it once later in The Game. . . .

From the terrace the whole world seemed to shimmer, then to tremble, then to heave, and at last to break again and again, on and on down over the Heath and across the wide river of London's dancing lights to misty beginnings in the Surrey Hills, where the primeval monsters crowded at Crystal Palace, or perhaps even as far as the death place of our ancestor at Piltdown. All green—sea and evening sky, shagreen, malachite, turquoise, emerald, jade, celadon, beryl, opaline, and aquamarine. Here you could not tell young men from the grass they lay upon, or young women from the leaves of the trees. In one great mass Marcus had created a kitchen garden of living dancers who, as they danced, put now cabbages against lavender, now spinach against peas, now lettuce against parsley. Greenfinch ladies chattered with matrons dressed as Amazon green parrots, peacock young men paraded before voluptuous snake-green debs. As for the lounge lizards, they were dressed in their natural lizard green. "My dear," said one, "Marcus tells me it's the green of cheetahs' urine," and "Mine, darling, is the green of turtles' fat." Green! green! everywhere green. But predominant tonight the yellowish it was *grande dame* to fart loudly. Perhaps it was. Oh, damn. There was never any way of getting back at people. He sat repeating, as Jack had taught him, "Malice is dreary and disfiguring, malice is dreary and disfiguring," until his face, at least, must have been less contorted than his body felt, for Ivo Latham, passing him, snapped his crocodile jaws and said, "I have no intention of swallowing anything as delicious as you in one go. Is it too early to ask you to dance with me?"

"Much. We can't hope to get rid of the respectables until two."

On the other hand some of his peevishness must have stuck, for when he was still sitting there, merely thinking what a success it all was, and how right he had been to make the explorers and conquerors—from Pizarro through Cook and Mungo Park to Stanley—come in a green version of their period costumes, Mary Clough came over and said:

"Why are you looking so sulky? Is Jack being unfaithful, or something?"

And at that very moment Jack came by, garlanded with green orchids, followed by a group of debs, all green humming-birds, who darted and swooped at him. From the cascades of waxy blooms he looked out like the most delicately Syrian of emperors, exalted with the thoughts of the Mesan ceremonies.

"I *think*," he cried, "that they're trying to suck my nectar. A *new* experience."

And he winked broadly at Mary and Marcus.

"Jack winking!" Mary cried. "Now that *is* good."

"Don't you mean vulgar?"

"Oh, do leave off. You are an Edwardian. You fish away like my Aunt Rose. You know very well that all his friends care for you so much just because you've made him happy. In bed and out. And don't ask which is more important, because to distinguish between those two sorts of happiness is one of the real sins."

"Well, haven't I made him vulgar, too? All this!" He waved his hand over the entire ball, Hampstead Heath and farther.

"You haven't created all London yet. Besides you know very well that when it's on *this* scale, words don't apply."

"And *I* thought I was a snob, minding Lady Westerton snubbing me."

"Oh, is *that* what you were sulking about? How tiresome you are to mind such things! Anyhow, if it's a question of being grand, my Great-Aunt Sybil, who was a dreadful old thing but the biggest of bow-wows, had the Westertons only on her big crush list."

"Oh, I know you've got hundreds of throw-away grand aunts and uncles, Mary, but that doesn't help me. I *could* order her out."

"You're lucky she came here. The German Embassy's her usual stamping ground."

"The German Embassy!"

"Yes. Surely you've noticed her stuffy Brahms look? So many of that generation have it."

"The old bitch! If only she'd brought some German attaché along uninvited, then I could have told them both to leave."

"Marcus, aren't *you* being a bit stuffy? Gate-crashers. Why, even dowagers back in the twenties—Oh, I see. Because he was a German. Oh, Marcus, how awful. Don't, please. You don't remember the war like I do. That was the most wicked part of it. Oh, no, my dear, you really mustn't say things like that."

"It's nothing to do with wars, Mary. Jack is Jewish. That at least makes me responsible for who comes into this house or not."

"Responsible! Marcus! What words! And why do you think about Jack being a Jew? I think that's terrible. None of his old friends ever do. Oh, Marcus, look at all the *fun* you give us just when everybody thought that sort of thing was coming to an end. Well, if you want me to use grand words, all the *beauty!* Look at what you've done with this house, to make a Lutyens house look so elegant, *and* with Marlcote! Grand and beautiful, darling, if that's what you want me to say."

"But I don't understand you, Mary. You speak as if fun and beauty were somehow not responsible things. Anyway, while everything's so un-beautiful and so un-funny in Germany for Jews like Jack, I've got a responsibility to *them*."

"Oh, dear, Marcus! You of all people! Of course it's all dreadful and wicked and hateful and incredible. And none of us could ever, ever compromise with it. That goes without saying. But let the politicians deal with it. Not all worldly people are like Lady Westerton. Look at Baba's husband; he's killing himself getting this wicked Baldwin policy changed. And there are dozens of others. That's their job. But we've got positive things of our own to give. Oh, you do make me feel old! Poor Jack, if you treat him to this sort of thing."

She stopped speaking abruptly, then:

"I like the polly cage you designed for me. I do think it's clever. Does it become me?"

"Enchantingly, Mary. You always ought to wear feathered crinolines. Come and talk to my sister Margaret."

"What, is she here? Well, naturally I had heard she might be, but I didn't dare ask because you were so cross once when we spoke about her."

"Oh, wasn't I awful in those days! Let's go and look for her. I'm not sure about her new husband, are you? He's rather a dish but bloody male, I'm afraid. Anyhow it wouldn't do, would it? One's sister's husband. I think it's forbidden in the Prayer Book. To talk to, he's the bore of all time. But she adores him—well, anyway, makes noises as if she did. You can never tell with Margaret. Did you know he was a tremendous archaeologist—King Tut and things? So he's almost in place here just as himself."

With difficulty they resisted snakes that wound round them, peacocks that raised whirring arcs to stop their passing, alligators that snapped; for a while they were caught up in a leaping dance of frogs. Across the entwined bodies of web-footed young men and women, Mary shouted to him:

"Now what *was* naughty was your stopping Jack buying that Pevensey painting of Lionel's. Monty's furious. It's one of Lionel's best. And you know how well he's been painting lately. You *must* have read what Monty's been saying."

"He's praised Lionel's work every week for as long as I can remember. And it hasn't got any better or any worse. He still paints without imagination, let alone a spark of genius. *And* uses three shades of shit to do so."

"Oh, colour! You live in such a schoolgirl's dream of Bakst. Lionel's such a subtle and expressive painter. Expressive of plastic values, I mean, of course."

"Subtle! Really, Mary! Lionel's one of the most pleasing friends we have. He's a real person, intelligent, civilized, and absolutely without nonsense. His paintings are exactly like him. But they aren't any good. I mean any real good. And I *won't* have them here with real paintings. That terrible Chanctonbury Ring with the Picassos and that bit of fake Cézanne of the Downs right beside Braque's 'Homage to Bach.' It's too impossible."

"You speak as though you were the only person in England who did justice to Picasso or Braque. You *know* what Monty's done to make people realize that Paris exists, and against what opposition and from the start."

"Yes, and then praises Lionel because he makes Pevensey Marshes look like the Camargue and Firle Beacon like a sea-sick memory of Cézanne's Provence."

"You're talking about an old friend, Marcus."

But the chain of frog dancers now surrounded him in a ring from which she was excluded. "Betty Co-ed's a smile for old Northwestern," the band vocalists sang at them through their megaphones, "Her heart is Texas treasure, so 'tis said."

"Whatever can it mean?" Mary mouthed at him.

But although laughing, he was not to be deflected.

"I'm talking about his *painting*," he shouted. "That's the trouble, you've mixed up friendship and art, the lot of you."

He wasn't sure whether she heard or not, for she cried:

"Jack's always been one of his most important patrons."

Now they were thrown together again and he clung to her—jungle parasite.

"If he's short of money, you know that Jack will help at once."

She threw off his exotic embrace.

"Now that *is* vulgar," she cried, "ineffably vulgar."

"Well, I'm not giving way. Jack's buying two wonderful Kandinsky compositions this year. And a marvellous, inventive, sad Paul Klee. And if there's anything over he's promised to buy those Cardinals in a Vault of Magnasco that Sachie found. To go with all the lovely fun pictures in my bedroom."

"Oh, really, Marcus. That awful religiosity and dead elegance. It's just snobbery. And Klee too, for that matter—all that whimsey, and then you talk about a real master of plastic values like Kandinsky in the same breath."

"Plastic values! It's his wonderful vitality, his rich colour."

They stood still, facing each other beneath a sombre holm-oak; against the dark foliage her delicate, high-cheek-boned face shone a furious shiny red beneath her wide crown of parrot feather and soft grey hair like any cook's, like Regan's. He wanted to kiss her but he realized the patronizing affection that prompted him, so, waving his arm in what he thought of as a haughty *ancien régime* manner, he asked:

"Do you still want to talk to my sister?"

She leaned forward and kissed him on the lips. She laughed.

"Oh, you are absurd! No wonder Jack's got it so badly for you. Why, why, why, just because at heart you've got the taste of the nineties, should I not want to talk to Margaret?"

And now here was Margaret advancing upon them.

"I know you'll think I'm making fun of Ethel Smythe, Mary," she said.

"Oh, no, Ethel's so robust. Anyway there's nothing tropical about her. I thought you were a sort of Lesbian Robinson Crusoe with that parrot."

Marcus and Margaret began to giggle.

"Well, Mouse *did* love deserts, Mag. It's a private joke really, Mary. Quite vulgar families have them, you know."

"I think it's in rather bad taste," Margaret's husband said. "The aunt in question's only been dead a few months. *And* she left Margaret all her money."

"That just shows how little outsiders understand, doesn't it, Marcus? Aunt Mouse would have been tremendously honoured, Douglas. Oh, I do think this is a wonderful ball, Marcus."

"Yes, it is, isn't it, Mag? Do you think I ought to have asked the Countess?"

"Of course not. There's no 'ought' about such things anyway. And especially when she was such a beast to you always. She'll be green with envy."

"Oh, I do hope so. 'Marcus has given a green ball again, Billy. I'm green with envy.'"

He threw a liana root around his neck for a sable stole. Margaret bent over him and produced Billy Pop's muzziest tones, to which she added a slight brogue.

"Ye need no ball at all, me darlin', for 'tis as green as the shamrock ye still are."

"Oh, Mag, an *Irish* Billy Pop! What an appalling thought!"

"Yes, there were things that Divine Providence thought too unspeakable to visit even upon the wretched Matthews children."

She said: "No, darling, if you'll forgive me, I really won't. I'm sun-
drunk and lazy and happy. And although I know it will be quite
wonderful, I'd rather come again and see it all, not sticky, not with a
glare like this. And there is a glare even though it's nearly five. But
then if there weren't, this wouldn't be the solar paradise that's getting me ready for Gide and Malraux and Mann, and all the other
ferocious peace-and-freedom lovers in Paris. As for dinner, have
something there, dear, so that you can poke about until the last boat
leaves. And then I needn't go to the saloon. I shall just put on a dress
and eat that delicious lobster out here on deck, with a slivovitz or
two, to complete the sun's bacchic rout of a decorous English
gentlewoman."

"It isn't only the temples, Maggie, and the peristyle; there's some
very fine Romanesque in the cathedral and a riot of baroque pal-
aces dilapidated and crumbling enough even to satisfy you."

"Please don't make me, Douglas. This is all working out so very
well. And it isn't as if we shan't have time to do a hundred splits
together in the coming years."

"A middle-aged couple doing the splits. It sounds worrying."

"Oh, you've no idea the energy I shall have when middle age
comes. A second Mistinguette. Once we've brought that beast to his
knees. That's the only thing that worries me here. I almost feel that I
can hear him bull-frogging away over there in the Palazzo Venezia."
And she waved her hand vaguely to the west. He bent down and
kissed her, and ran his hand along her thin, sunburned arm.

"Ow!" she cried.

"Sorry. Now you're *not* fussing about that speech?"

"Oh, no, that's all composed. Peace, freedom, art, all put in their
places. And an encouraging word for the Lion of Judah thrown in."

"Nor those reviews? You knew what Desmond MacCarthy would
say. You gave me his review, word for word, the afternoon you
finished the novel. And look how understanding that chap Muir's
been. And that great long piece in the *Literary Supplement*."

"No, no. All the reviews are forgiven and forgotten, thank God.
And for all praise I'm duly grateful. Now go along, or they'll close
the Museum and you'll never be able to tell me what Diocletian's
wife looked like."

Grey rock it had been all day as, lying in the sun, she had travelled up from Dubrovnik; grey rock except for the short call at the island. Limestone, the guide book said. But change a letter here and there and it could as well have been timestone or lifestone, for it seemed to Margaret all that day as she lay there, and still seemed as she sat back in the deck-chair, to offer her some place of refuge between the cruelty of those words written, printed, and not now by any means to be recalled, and the terror of those other words not yet spoken, not even finally formed, but hardly less, by any means that left a shred of decency, to be evaded.

She sat on the deck and saw only cursorily the town walls, the cranes, and the custom-house all losing their outlines in the dying sun; for she was watching herself, a tiny figure, a modern primitive, a schoolchild's pin-head woman, a lilliputian—yes, a lilliputian—for every finger, every hair, every nail was there in little, enough to delight Queen Mary—some sort of human ant scaling these endless cliffs, a mere speck seated on one of the huge boulders, absurdly standing on the sheer vertical cliffside or clinging to an ugly, twisted, windswept pine tree precariously growing in a rare cranny: a Pearl White of the cinema series of her youth. Yet leap from the deck and swim in the green sea as she would, she could not become one with that minute Margaret Matthews, left to die in shipwreck, falling from heights in a nightmare, for there remained all the while, inert and heavy with despair, her own real body here on the deck.

Do your characters sometimes come to life, Miss Matthews? Yes, but not real life. You know I'm not a dissociated schizoid. Oh, to be just that, to melt this lean flesh and take on cliffs or wrecked boulders, a dwarf, nightmarish incorruption. Mind what Desmond MacCarthy wrote! She wondered at how little Douglas guessed what was tearing at her vitals. And yet, at a moment's notice, if she switched on to him—lay in his arms; went over his exquisite photographs of Luxor with him; read aloud with him turn by turn the poems and sermons of Donne; saw peristyles and Gothic *voussoirs* and baroque cupolas in his company, under his enlightening, teasably pedantic guidance; or simply sat with him at café tables or on public benches staring at Spanish nuns, at Arab water-sellers, or at Serbo-Croat gentlemen reading newspapers on bamboo frames—in a second the despairs and their fuzz of surrounding depression would disappear, become one with outer darkness, where they would wait to spring at her in the night, or as she came downstairs at Holland Park to re-

ceive friends for dinner, or as she waited for a bus, or in the hotel
lobby buying postcards, at any time when her guard was down.

This very Douglas, her refuge, her hand that stroked the forehead,
her voice that banished the lingering shreds of nightmare, her water-
wings, and her "excellent, you only want confidence in order to
achieve the highest . . ." Douglas, who was all these, a very present
help in time of trouble, thought that she had been upset by Desmond
MacCarthy's warm, burring, avuncular reproof, by Uncle Desmond
regretfully chiding her attempts to spread her wings and asking her
to repeat again the little pieces she used to say so well, the little
pieces that had allowed him and her other literary aunts and uncles
to see what a clever little girl she was.

> I cannot help wishing that Miss Matthews had never heard of God
> and Tolstoy. She was surely so much nearer to saving us and the world,
> if that must be her generous concern, when she remained content to
> feed us periodically with those cool, astringent doses of life as lived by
> the fascinatingly disagreeable Carmichael family. After all, Jane Austen
> did not feel it necessary to show Wickham regenerated by death upon
> the field of Waterloo, nor Mr. Darcy's spiritual enlargement by con-
> templation of the Derbyshire peaks. And we are grateful to her that
> she did not.

How to mind such a kind, irrelevant reproof?
How could Douglas fail to see the brutal thrust with which the
Literary Supplement's flatteringly long review had pierced her!

> We do not believe as so many of Miss Matthews's admirers would
> seem to hold that she has extended her range too far, nor, in aiming too
> broadly, missed her mark . . .

And on and on through hundreds of flattering words of clever, considered criticism to end:

> The simple think that Miss Matthews "hates people." The more so-
> phisticated believe that she loves them, and quarrel only whether she
> has been wise to attempt to express that love positively. The truth is
> that she neither hates nor loves human beings; she is indifferent to
> them. And considerable fiction, even perhaps considerable art of any
> kind, cannot be born of human indifference.

And it was with this judgment, these words ringing in her ears, that she must now sit down and compose stirring words to rouse a congress to defend the liberty of the artist, and, in so doing, affirm the vital importance, the final significance of each and every human being, and of man in general as the centre-piece.

If it hadn't been for the limestone cliffs she would simply have given this anonymous creature (a well-known face, no doubt, red and blustering or white and smirking, seen very often all smiles behind a cocktail glass) the direct lie. From girlhood she had been the amused and loving observer of human quirks and oddities. Every face in the street as she shopped or travelled to work by bus posed problems for her, haunted her, pursued her. Each boy, each girl in dancing class had demanded her attention as a potential sketch or story of adult tragedy or farce. Catching the exact word, pinning down the phrase, these had been as much her constant pursuit as imitating the exact nuance of voice had been Rupert's. For year after year, for twenty years now, yes, since she was fourteen or less, she had been straining herself, tearing herself to pieces to put together human mosaics, to give movement and purpose and relationship to the creatures of her imagination, to set them working backwards and forwards in time, round and about in space; and now this anaemic, constipated, bad-breathed, underpaid failure, lurking behind anonymity, told her that all she had been doing was playing a glorified game of chess.

If it had not been for the limestone cliffs, and last year the vast, rolling, empty plains of La Mancha, or again and again over the years mountains, deserts, marshes seen in flashes from trains, seen and longed for, she would have dismissed the little flutter of fear that responded to the Grub Street jackal's whine as a seemly but oversensitive humility. She who enjoyed life so much—travelling, talking, walking, eating, dancing, sleeping, making love, reading, writing, and painting in oils, too, if that meant doing nothing in glorious contentment! But why then did she long to become that little Pearl White figure, Andromeda chained for ever alone on that rock, Crusoe before he was troubled by Friday's faithful service?

Of course, she had known despair: before the divorce she had looked at the white tablets by her bed hopefully and then, picturing herself with vomit pouring from her mouth and nostrils, turned away; she had smelt eagerly the gas fumes in that room in Onslow Square but, seeing herself a mindless, empty patient year after year in a hospital ward, had turned off the tap and had gone out to the cinema. Certainly in those months in Cassis, after that boy from Durham when she had first found the easy trick of bed without love, she had been very near once or twice to "contemplating suicide," but that did not mean that she had not always been tempted back to life by hot fresh rolls and French butter, by the way the sea lapped around a rock, by a new evening dress, by the muscle of a man's arm stretched on the sand, above all by fusing on paper Adela Takeley (that dreadful artists' model) and Geneviève Rocquetin (that caricature of a *jeune fille bien élevée*). There had always been more than enough in life to spare.

And yet how the limestone, the marsh mud, and the desert sand drew her to them! For every human assertion there are hundreds of inanimate negations; it was those, their stillness, their quiet, their nonexistence which she so desperately needed. They were the other side of life, the nothing side, denying which everything was an empty boast, a silly whistling in the dark. She was not in love with easeful death, not at all, if that meant surrendering to the grave's embrace; but she did need the refreshment of negation, the refreshment of bare, dead rock if she were to have the strength, the endurance, to receive human noises. The great tenor arias that she would hear in humanity's defence in Paris, how to bear their inevitable vulgarities? The small, private noises, sharp and astringent, that she, perhaps, or Mr. E. M. Forster might contribute. How to bear their occasional cosiness? How to endure the millions that exulted in the boastful, empty lies that came from Nuremberg and Bayreuth and Rome? Or the little, dirty, cheapening talk of everybody every day? For these she must keep her imagination frighteningly yet deadly clean of the non-human—of the snow blowing through centuries in the icy blizzards of Antarctica, of the sand collecting endlessly in the Gobi Desert. But Mouse, who had died amid such refreshment, would have urged her to snap back at the world. This she would not do, comfortable, easy though it would be, delighted though the world was to be snapped at. Relying upon that other side, that clean, inanimate world to be there when she needed it, she would return as warmly as she could to men and their doings, and offer them, if not certain love, at least the devotion of all her will. She would start to build once more upon these new foundations. The name of Geneviève Rocquetin had brought memories that pressed.

She got up from the deck chair and returned to her cabin. Undressing, she put on her pyjamas, took a fresh exercise-book, got into bed, unscrewed her fountain pen, and wrote:

> Andrée (Geneviève's sister Adele, Sukey as she used to be at Cromer before she knew her vocation was marriage) living near Aigues-Mortes (that château of the Rocquetins) has a life divided since girlhood between the marshes (those hours of my riding in the Camargue, the egrets white against the black cypresses, suddenly coming on the flamingoes, the popping sound of crabs bubbling below the mud surface) and the frigid Protestant *haute bourgeoisie* of Nîmes and round about (Madame Pipard, 'Ours is the clean France, Mademoiselle Matthews. In more than three centuries—Monarchy, Empire, Republic, what does it matter? The others have got their hands dirty'). Reacting against this glacial social world of her parents, she becomes friendly with . . .

When Douglas returned she was busily writing. Seeing that he was ready for her attention, she made some rough notes—

> a continual dialogue between Andrée, alone on the marshes, and Andrée, the dutiful daughter, the secret mistress of Patrick, the secret diary writer, is the only solvent of the *absurd* beauty of *life* (satirical scenes) and the *futile* need for *death* (the solitary scenes). Being alive means a responsibility to solve this.

Then she added quickly:

> Much of the solitary Camargue nature side to be treated with irony too, a young girl's first reactions to nature, to God, etc. Almost a compendium of the absurdities of nineteenth-century romanticism. On the other hand the full-felt tragedy of this ridiculous, dead, ingrown, provincial Protestantism. Balance on both sides so that life isn't mocked.

"We leave for Rjeka in five minutes. I wish you'd seen the cathedral. It was benediction. The singing was surprisingly good."

"I've started a scheme for a new novel."

"I know. I saw. You were bound to. It was the only thing. But don't suppose I don't realize the courage it's taken. I could smash that MacCarthy's jaw."

Naked he lay beside her, taking from her the book and the pen.
He held her and kissed her. She couldn't respond immediately. With
Ralph she'd always been able to; he could touch her physically as
though she were controlled by an electric button, but then with
Ralph daily married life had been an unloving blank. Douglas was so
good to her, made her days so happy that at these times she owed
him sincerity.

"All this is only a substitute, you know."

"Good Lord, yes," he took it for teasing. "I'm well aware. Close
your eyes and think of Robert Taylor."

She couldn't carry sincerity on into cruelty, so she made no further remark, but with pleasure, almost with excitement, she responded.

At midnight she woke to the wind outside the porthole and to
Douglas's light breathing. But these Protestants from Nîmes would
speak in French. All her main gift for dialogue would be valueless.
The whole novel, she saw, was an absurdity.

Rupert came in from the stable-yard invigorated, warm, pleased
with everything, although a little breathless. He took off his top
boots and left them in the passage, but his trousers still shed a few
flakes of mud, a little sawdust on to the parquet floor when he came
into the living-room. He carried a heavy basket of logs and, bending
down, set it beside the already blazing open fire. When he stood up,
his shoulders in their peat-smelling tweed still seemed a little bowed.

Deborah's aunt remarked on it: "You're not holding yourself so
straight as a year ago."

"I'm not as young as I was a year ago, Aunt Annabel." And then,
before she could reply, "Oi be very old. Oi be one undred and foive
come Martinmas. In the archives of Vladivostok is certificate. Born
seventeen hundred eighty-five. How much is? One hundred fifty.
Then I'm one hundred fifty. But nothing appen to me. Not even
Emperor Napoleon. I sit in my chair. When is Emperor coming? I
ask. Emperor is not coming. Emperor doesn't come. In Vladivostok
nothing ever appen."

He sat back dejected on the pouf. Aunt Annabel laughed a little
nervously, but at that moment Debbie, holding little Tanya by the
hand, came in through the French window.

"Have *you* done all that sawing? Bless you, darling. The moorhens are on the pond again."

Tanya said, "Boorpen."

Rupert snatched her up in his arms.

"Oh, by garnd be ko to Bosgow? By garnd be, Darnyer?"

"He's been like this all the morning, Debbie. Sausages for breakfast, that's what it is, I can see. You should never feed men meat before luncheon, my dear."

Rupert gave a lion's roar. Deborah, seeing Tanya's lip tremble, took her from her father's arms and set her on the floor.

"Daddy's happy," but as the lip still trembled she quickly took the teddy bear from the piano top where someone had left it and gave it to the child. Then she knelt on the rug, throwing logs on to the fire.

Tanya cooed over the woollen animal.

"Now if you appeared in the *Daily Express* every day, darling, like Rupert the Bear, you might receive some respect from your daughter."

Rupert lifted his wife from her kneeling position. She put her arms round him and he kissed her, working his lips against hers until she broke away, patting her hair, pulling down her tweed skirt.

"Oh, the Sundays are wonderful!" she cried. "Dear, lovable Jimmie Agate. I could kneel down and kiss his shoes."

"My dear, the *pee*culiar things you say."

"Well, if what our Doris says, and she's not one to tell a lie, the *pee*culiar things dear Mr. Agate does."

"Apart from the delicate presence of your Aunt Annabel, I will not have the greatest dramatic critic of our time besmirched. That's rather a good word, Aunt Annabel, isn't it? Besmirched. Besmirched or be-anything else in this house. The man who can write, 'Never has the meaning of Chekhov's play come over so completely to me as in Rupert Matthews's performance of the brother Andrey. Watch him in the last act as he comes up for the third time, clutching that depressing pram, and goes down for ever to the insensitive scolding of his vixenish wife. For this is what *The Three Sisters* is about—drowning. And seldom have I seen an actor drown so piteously and yet so comically as Mr. Matthews—an Andrey that combines the pathos of Danleno with the lovable absurdity of Mr. Pooter.' "

"Darling! Really! To have learnt it all off by heart. At least you might have fluffed a line here or there out of modesty. And *do* remember when Willie comes that *some* of the critics haven't been all that favourable to the *production*."

"Some of the critics have been bloody well right. When I think how often I've argued, and so have Beatrix and Stella, about the pace of Act III. But no, 'Act III goes down into smoke and ashes with the fire. It ends on a brown note. Its colour is brown.' We were lucky the whole audience wasn't browned off. With Beatrix and Stella going down a key or two and *più lento* as the last words of the act die away. 'That's only a rumour. We'll be left quite alone then . . . Olia! Well? Olia darling, I do respect the Baron.' "

Rupert's voice became slower and more suety until it came out a mere trickle of shaky deep notes. "Poor Stella! She said once to Willie at rehearsal, 'Darling, why do I have to go into the bass register when I agree to marry the Baron? I know she isn't awfully happy about it, but I don't see why she has to change her sex.' But you know what Willie is. He just ignored it, and at his most schoolmasterly, he said, 'Very nice, Stella, very nice. Beautifully brown.' Beatrix got the giggles and hiccoughed. 'I'm terribly sorry, Willie,' she told him. 'I oughtn't to have had the brown Windsor soup for lunch. But I thought it might help.' Oh, there *were* rows!" he ended, shaking his head like an old, gossiping charwoman.

"Of course there were, darling. There always are. It's all the rows and bitching that I miss most since I left the theatre to become a loving wife and mother. Anyway, no rows today. You deserve an absolutely wonderful Sunday."

"What I believe I *do* deserve is pink champagne. What about a glass of bubbly, Aunt Annabel, before the others come?"

"Well," said Aunt Annabel, looking at her watch, "since it's after eleven, yes. But who are the others?"

"Oooh, my dear," Rupert in an old pansy pro's voice, "we must ave *er* in the play. She's the playwright's dream. Can't you imagine. Act I. Everything ready for the exposition, but how to make it natural? Then up speaks Aunt Annabel, 'Who *are* the others?' and we're off."

"You'd have made an absolutely enchanting actress, Auntie." Debbie bent down and kissed the nape of her aunt's grey shingle. "And as to who the others are—well, there's Rupert's producer, Willie

Carter, who's got a week-end cottage near-by at Ascot and he's bringing a party, God knows who *they* may be . . ."

"Behold," said Rupert's voice, loud and clear, "one black-haired trollop of uncertain age and dubious morals. Come in. Don't bother to knock."

"Trollop, darling, yes, and four years older than you. But I've got where I am entirely by talent. Not that you haven't talent too, Rupert. Your wonderful notices, darling," she kissed him. "We've been making waxen images of you all morning. And we've run *out* of pins. Debbie, dear, I'm just taking him down a peg. Actually he deserves every word. How can he be so moving and so absurd at the same time?"

"It's the great clown's art," Rupert struck a posture. "I had it from Grimaldi's fancy bit on her death bed. Champagne, Stella, darling?" And he kissed her.

Debbie looked rather worriedly at Willie. "Well, we *are* all rather pleased," she said.

"Don't look at *me* like that, dear," Willie answered. "I'm not going to contradict you. You thought I was going to bitch Rupert, didn't you, lovey? Just because he got the plum notices? Well, I'm not. He gives a very nice performance, as the old ladies were saying between chocolates last night in the Upper Circle. 'I always say Rupert Matthews gives a very nice performance.' And you thought I was going to bitch, Debbie Matthews. Somebody always thinks I'm going to bitch," he told Aunt Annabel. "Introduce, dear."

The blond young man who had come with Willie said, "I wonder why."

"Carry your spear in Henry Five and you'll find out," Willie gave a little snigger which he seemed to realize cut him off from the others, for he said again to Debbie, "Introduce, dear."

There were introductions all round.

"Stella played Irena, Auntie. You're terribly *good*, Stella. And the bit where you and the Baron can't speak before the duel. *So* touching, darling! I honestly was crying. But then I'm one of Willie's toothless matinee ladies at heart."

"Nonsense, you're just a loyal wee wifey."

The blond young man said: "Perhaps everyone thinks you're going to bitch, Willie, because you bark so much before you bite."

Rupert, perhaps to ward off any scene, asked the blond in a specially loud, man-to-man voice:

"What's your college?"

But Willie replied for the boy: "He's doing P.P.E. Whatever that may be. It sounds very un-housetrained."

The young man disregarded him: "I'm at Exeter, actually."

Rupert appeared to have nothing to say to this. But Willie explained to Deborah the backgrounds of his young men:

"Mr. Garner," he said indicating the blond, "and Mr. Peploe"— indicated a speechless, dark young man in a blue suit and horn-rimmed spectacles—"are respectively President and Secretary of the O.U.D.S. They've come over from Oxford because I might, if they're very good, produce *Henry the Fifth* for them."

"You *will* be producing *Henry the Fifth* for us," said the blond, "and it'd better be good."

"He's the privileged one, dear. He's been at it all morning. It's chronic," Stella whispered loudly to Debbie.

Willie glared at her. "When all you pampered players were tucked into bed at Oxford, I had to go to the young men's smoking concert. The loo lewdery! The lavatorial levity! My dear, I nearly died of boredom. But these two were some compensation. They did a completely splendid Jack and Cis together. Do," he said to the young men; "the jealous lady doesn't believe."

To oblige, the blond stuck out his upper teeth and waved his arm soldier-wise in a Courtenidge gesture; the dark young man did no more than remove his spectacles and stick out his lower jaw. Although Willie clapped his hands, none of the professionals seemed very entertained. But Aunt Annabel found it very amusing. She laughed loudly.

"What a marvellous imitation of Jack Hulbert," she said.

The blond young man was ready to sulk, but luckily at that moment some business neighbours arrived—Mr. Packer, all Savile Row tweeds, Mrs. Packer, all tweeds, Jacmar scarves, and diamond rings.

"Rupert, *we* thought you were marvellous. Honestly, I can hardly bear to look at you. I keep seeing that poor little man pushing the pram. And yet one laughed."

Rupert, introducing, explained that the excellencies belonged to Willie, the producer.

"Ah, so you're the producer!" Mr. Packer cried. "Congratulations! Though I must say that, as with conductors, I rather wonder what it is the producer does."

"Willie would love to tell you," Debbie said, but Mr. Packer had walked over to Rupert.

"You were very good, you know, you blighter! It's not the sort of thing I'd have gone to in the ordinary way. Too much talk. Strictly between the two of us I found all that Russian gloom very irritating. But you did something with it all as soon as you came on. Especially pushing that pram. Useless, wet sort of fellow." He lowered his voice, "Wanted kicking up the arse. But you made me feel sorry for the chap, though I wouldn't have employed him as an office boy. That's what I call great acting."

Rupert was about to answer this praise, but Mr. Packer changed the subject, or rather, as so often, he resumed his analysis of their last game of golf.

"I ought never to have risked the brassie. If I'd have used the spoon I'd have had the ball clear away down through the gulley and on to the apron. But . . ."

Rupert caught Debbie's eye. They exchanged their social look. All Sunningdale, golf, and week-end host, he settled down to listen to Packer, while Debbie, re-filling everyone's glass, assembled the rest of the party at Willie's feet—almost a class in production, she thought.

Yet, for Rupert work was always more magnetic than play. Again and again his attention strayed to *The Three Sisters* conversation. At last he gave up listening to his neighbour with anything more than his eyes.

"The most difficult part in tempo *and* in colour," Willie was telling them, "is Anfisa. It's a perfect Chekhov paradox that the only positive value in the play should be embodied in an eighty-year-old peasant woman. And even *she* isn't positive in the first two acts, just old. Then . . ."

"Oh, the old servant," Mrs. Packer said. "I *did* think she was well acted."

"Mmmm. She wasn't as bad as the critics made out, but . . ."

"I feel a bit guilty about that"—Rupert joined in. "Maybe Alma *could* have done it, but . . ."

"Alma Grayson! Of course she couldn't. She'd have been terrible. She'd have given it a sort of false spiritual thing," Stella said.

"Well, that's what I felt and what I told Willie, but all the same I do feel a bit guilty."

"Very touching and proper, Rupert, but unnecessary. I make my own casting decisions. She's played in rubbish far too long. She'd have patronized Anfisa. And that would have been fatal."

"But I do feel responsible . . ."

"What I think Rupert means is that he feels a natural responsibility towards the play and that he may have let his personal feelings . . . But I'm sure you haven't, darling. All prejudice apart, Alma just isn't made for a Chekhov servant. It isn't in her. But, of course, whatever Willie may say, every actor should feel responsible for what happens to the play he's in."

Willie said, "Dangerous egalitarian rubbish, dear."

"And," said Aunt Annabel to them all, "when you've given such a lot of fun and beauty as you obviously have to everyone."

"I know she's a silly old cow. And you're right; she's played in rubbish for years because the audience flatters her. And she's lazy. But what she *can* do! I know. I worked with her all those years. And she *wanted* so much to do this."

"My dear," Willie said, "for heaven's sake! That's life. It's bloody for some people all the time. For poor old Alma it's only getting bloody now. But that's it. That's what it's all about. And thank God for it. Without light and shade we shouldn't have any art."

Rupert put his handsome head on one side. He smiled a kind of all-purpose smile that included everybody equally benignly. He made a mellow humming sound. Then, as suddenly, he drew himself up, drank off a glass of champagne, kicked a log in the fire.

"No. That's not good enough. That's the sort of stuff my father used to give us. *I* feel bad towards *Alma*. That's the point. Nothing to do with loyalty to the play. However much the play might have suffered from her. She started me off. It's true she was silly and a bitch at times, and when I met Debbie in the Acland play she was like all hell let loose. But she taught me a great deal and we had a lot of fun together. And she's a very good actress. I *ought* to feel guilty and I do."

The party feeling was destroyed by his outburst. It drifted on for a while in desultory conversation, and then the Packers left. Soon after, Willie, looking at his watch, said:

"Din, din, all. I'm famished."

As they, too, were leaving, the dark young man in spectacles came up to Rupert. When he spoke he had a very bad stammer.

"I just wanted to say," he pronounced with great difficulty, "that you were marvellous. You've taken in all these people and the critics. You've made them think that that filthy parasite Andrey, that fat white slug, is pathetic and lovable. Which is just what he obviously made his sisters believe. And the wonderful oily slyness and cunning with which you do it . . ."

Emotion and his stammer made further words impossible.

When they had gone, Rupert stood brooding over the fire. Then he said quite sharply to Aunt Annabel:

"I haven't really begun to stoop, you know, but when one acts a part with any degree of intensity a lot of the characteristics follow you around. Certainly for the length of the run."

Before dinner at the Trocadero, of course, they were to have their usual *tête à tête* drink at the Monaco—scene of some of their clandestine meetings in the old days before Doris—so much more of an invalid now, it seemed—had accepted the situation. They knew all the barmen there and had long agreed that it was the most friendly place to wait for each other in. Gladys had in fact to wait half an hour this evening; well, not just this evening; if you love someone very much it insults them not to admit their minor faults; and Alfred lived on the end of a telephone nowadays. Indeed, when he did arrive, the *soigné* effect of his Anthony Eden double-breasted charcoal pin-striped suit, poor old boy, was a little spoiled by his breathlessness.

"Sorry, girlie," he said. "What are you having?"

But she had it there before her—a gin and it. He ordered a double dry Martini from Victor, and then excused himself to her.

"I must put a call through to Bratsby," he said. "Old Evans has agreed to sell, but only after delivering us a lecture on changing conditions in the City. As he was probably the original negotiator for Dizzie in buying the Suez Canal, it took rather a long time. That's why I'm late. Bastard, aren't I? But I've got some good news when I come back."

"It'd better be short news, Alfred," she called after him as he made for the telephone. "We're due at the Troc in ten minutes."

"He's a shocker for time, isn't he?" Victor said. "You didn't train him properly, Madam."

"You can't curb the faults of great men."

They both laughed. When Alfred came back, she told him, "Victor's noticed the shocking way you keep me waiting. I've excused you on the ground that you're a Napoleon of finance."

"Napoleon! Didn't he march on his stomach? I don't fancy that. By the way, your tip for the three-thirty was lousy, Victor."

"But he gave *me* Baccarat Boy last week at Kempton. And it romped home. I never thanked you, Victor."

"Baccarat Boy?" Alfred laughed. "It was red-hot all over the City. You want to freshen up your tips, Victor."

He dismissed Victor and the conversation with his laugh. "Bratsby's tickled pink. So he ought to be. He'd be negotiating with Evans until Doomsday if we'd waited on his methods. *Now* look, kiddie . . ."

"Now look you, Alfred, as the Welsh Druid said to the king, you must not call me kiddie. Girlie I can just about carry off. After all, Bessie Bunter was a girl. But I'm five foot nine, nearly ten stone, and I shan't see thirty-six again. If you associate me with scooter and hopscotch I can't promise to make the right impression on your important customers. You should have found some little girlish piece all giggles and chiffon."

"You giggle until the fat shakes, you know you do."

And because it was true and he'd never before admitted to noticing it, she began to giggle just that much. Which set him off. To put an end to this unsuitable public sight, he kissed her.

"Thank God this joint's going bust. It means their electricity bill's been cut. Oodles of privacy."

And was it really, she asked; and of course as always he knew everything, what the debt was and who the creditors.

"Oh, dear! *Our* little place!"

But he wouldn't allow nostalgia.

"If things go on as they are, I'll buy it for your birthday present next time it comes on the market. Anyway, what do you mean, chiffon? What's that round your neck?"

"It's not chiffon, darling. It's a real lace jabot. Much more suitable for my mature years." Gladys was pleased, but impatient. "I know I look terrible in these halo hats with my big face," she said. "Anyway, darling, what about your surprise?"

"Ah, I'm coming to that. But just you look this evening at Frau Garmisch. I only met her once at Frankfurt when I went to little Willy Garmisch's house. They've got a beautiful place, everything that money could buy—but *she* looked like a missionary on a Sunday outing. And Sylvia Heathway will probably be got up like a tart. No, you're the goods as far as I'm concerned, as old Arthur Roberts used to say. Long before your time. And now that your face is suitably suffused with blushes, we must beat it, or we'll be late."

But Gladys insisted on getting out her compact. "Good Lord! You've made my nose blush. Who is Sylvia Heathway?"

"You remember I told you about little Tubby Heathway who cut his throat. Well, she's his widow. I want you to be very nice to her, girlie. She's a lady and all that, but she's rather let things slide, I think, since the shock. I got her along for this Dane, Andersen. He's potty on antiques and she used to collect old furniture apparently before Tubby crashed. Good God!" he said. "Huns and Danes! What an evening! Just to carry you through it, what would you say if I told you my surprise was to set you up in business on your own again?"

She stood in the entrance to the Monaco, breathless with excitement, until Alfred had to take her arm to make way for some new customers.

"Oh, I couldn't," she said as they moved off.

"Not when I was the bastard who borrowed your business off your back?"

"I've told you so many times, Alfred, it was you who gave it to me in the first place. So naturally I was glad to help you."

"Out of my own stupid mess."

"No, darling, it was that awful Depression. Thousands were in your position."

"Well, for God's sake, now I'm in a different position . . . Not that I can always lay my hand on ready money, but that's big business everywhere. What I can do and I'm going to do is to put you in business on your own again. If only not to have you hanging round my neck in your old age."

He squeezed her arm to emphasize that he was joking. There he

stood at the curb of Piccadilly Circus, a handsome, portly, well-to-
do man in danger of being knocked off the pavement by the crowds.

"You've got to accept," he said, "or I'll stand here until you do."
He had raised his voice.

"Oh, don't make a show of yourself, Alfred. A couple of clowns
we must look! All right. And thank you, darling, more than I can
say."

But she did try to say it as they were held up on the narrow island
in Shaftesbury Avenue. "Oh! Alfred, to be mistress of my own business again. Of course, they've been very good and left me a free
hand, but . . . I shall start a black-list of bad employers. Some of
these women treat their people abominably. Times are changing.
You know what, Alfred, I'm going to get rid of this idea of 'ladies.'
That was all right in the twenties when I started. Not that most of
our type of employers don't want ladies now, but they want the sort
of ladies who've forgotten what the word means. And a night telephone service! Oh, there are so many things that I've been longing to
do. I shall take Kempie and Miss Sutton with me. That's not just
sentimental . . ."

"Christ," Alfred said, looking at his watch, "we're going to be
late, and old Willy's always punctual. You know what Germans are.
That's what makes them such first-rate business people."

But luckily the traffic came to a full stop and they squeezed
through between two taxis. In the swing doors of the Trocadero,
Gladys really thought she was going to be sick, she felt so excited
and happy.

During the *hors d'oeuvres* and poultry Alfred was summoned
three times to the telephone on business. But to Gladys's amusement
he refused a fourth call when they'd reached the sweet. She could
almost see his mouth watering as his guests helped themselves to the
ice pudding.

The great *omelette surprise*, its meringue fortifications surmounted by a vast bird's-nest of spun sugar, had already been
opened and had revealed, apparently to the genuine surprise of Frau
Garmisch, if the widening of her empty blue eyes in their empty
expanse of natural, untouched girlish skin was any measure of sincerity, an inner treasure of combined vanilla, chocolate, and raspberry
ice cream. That inner treasure had been despoiled and almost con-
sumed before the band changed from a blaring medley to a softly

played "Love Parade" that introduced Maurice, the waltzing *maître d'hôtel* in his imitation of Maurice Chevalier. "Eyes of Delphine, charm of Josephine, the cuteness of Pauline, that's in you displayed," he sang.

"He's genuine French, you know," Alfred explained to them.

"Oh, yes, he makes that quite clear," said Herr Andersen.

Gladys, who found Maurice a great bore, smiled at the neatly dressed, bow-tied Dane, though she thought it a pity that he had learned his English from a Welshman.

"Unfortunately what's always clear to me," she said, "is that he's the headwaiter."

Hr. Andersen laughed delightedly, but Alfred remonstrated.

"I know it's only a stunt, Gladys, but he hits Chevalier off beautifully. And those tunes are a delight anyhow."

"I'm enjoying myself, Alfred. We all are. Alfred has a feeling that any criticism means that the evening's flopped. I never feel that."

Gladys had addressed the Dane, but Frau Garmisch, coming up from her ice cream for a moment, said:

"I suppose that Mr. Pritchard feels that little of good comes from constant criticism. We learned that so much in Germany in the years after the war."

Gladys said: "Did you really?"

And Alfred said, "I bet."

But neither comment seemed helpful. Bright, bald-headed little Willy Garmisch obviously saw the need to lift them out of the silence that his wife's remark had produced.

"No, surely the *French* are the perfect cabaret entertainers," he said. "We have good artists and so have you. Do you know our Comedy Harmonists? But the French have the perfect art of amusing at the end of a day's work. From Offenbach to Mistinguette, let's give them credit for it, they are great entertainers."

"The French have a fine culture," Hr. Andersen said.

"Governments that change every week? Barricades in the street?" Frau Garmisch asked.

"Oh, I do so agree. I simply can't take Paris any more," Mrs. Heathway said, stubbing out a third cigarette end amid the melted ruins of her ice pudding.

She's in too much of a state to notice what's said, Gladys thought. Then she thought affectionately of Alfred's simple view of women.

Sylvia Heathway used a lot of make-up, so she looked like a tart; she put on that make-up carelessly, so she had begun to let things slide. She felt warmly, too, towards the woman herself, not only because she had called forth Alfred's simplicity. But Frau Garmisch, who had looked away from so much make-up until now, gave Mrs. Heathway a special nod of encouragement.

"I was thinking of literature and art," Hr. Andersen said.

"The literature and art of a great nation in decline," said Willy. "That's rather sad, I think. When the birth-rate goes persistently down, nature is surely making her comment."

"It could be other things than nature, old boy," Alfred tried teasing, but he shifted uneasily and caught Gladys's eye.

"Are you going to do any shopping while you are here, Frau Garmisch?" she asked.

"I shall look for some of your excellent wools and leather goods. Yes."

"I think for wools you can't do better than Bradley's. What do you say, Mrs. Heathway?" She almost perceptibly winked at the woman, for Hr. Andersen had grown pink now, in addressing Willy Garmisch.

"Denmark, then, I should tell you, is also one of these decadent countries, by your ruling."

Sylvia Heathway did her best. "If I can take you to Bond Street or Regent Street any morning this week . . ."

But Frau Garmisch had left the ladies. "Oh, but we're not talking of little countries like Denmark," she said, laughing; "they have to do as they are being told." Her laughter seemed to clatter across the intervening tables to the cabaret floor, for the girls dressed as powder puffs abruptly ended their routine by sticking their fluffy behinds in the air. Alfred, supported stoutly by Gladys and Mrs. Heathway, clapped loudly. Their visitors followed suit.

"Now that's something more like chiffon," Gladys said. "Alfred was telling me this evening that I should wear chiffon. Can you imagine? The elephant at the circus."

"If I may compliment you, the cut of your suit has extraordinary elegance . . ." Hr. Andersen began.

"There you are, Gladys. And I may add that she finds time to run a business as well with extraordinary efficiency."

"I wonder how long England will be able to afford this luxury of her women doing the men's work?" Frau Garmisch pondered. Now that she had finished her ice pudding she seemed ready to renounce any show of sweetness.

Gladys stifled a furious sense that her whole life was being swept away with the crumbs from the table. "Black, please," she said, and added brown sugar. "Alfred tells me you have an absolutely beautiful home, Frau Garmisch."

"My husband is happy there. That I have tried to make. And the children, too. I don't know what else a woman should do."

She smiled, and although her face lost none of its frumpiness, it seemed less sour. But Hr. Andersen was not softened. He appeared to aim his cigar smoke at her as he exhaled.

"Nevertheless, for many women the choice of a career is a great social achievement, I suppose."

"What kind of women are they, wishing for such choices, Hr. Andersen. Poor things! One can easily tell that you are a bachelor. You know so very little about us. Would you like your Danish women to have the choice of working on the roads and the railways? That's the choice the Bolsheviks give their women. The *Berliner Tageblatt* showed recently some pictures of them. More like animals than women."

"One cannot believe all that one sees in the newspapers, dear lady, I think."

"Not in foreign newspapers. We know that." Frau Garmisch's hands were trembling.

"Now, Gretel," her husband said, "we mustn't talk politics on this pleasant evening with our good friends. All the same, you know, Alfred, when are you English going to stop some of these absurd stories about us in your newspapers? That's no way to do business. We've had to kick one or two of your newspaper chaps out this year."

All Gladys's anger was released in that moment.

"Look here, Herr Garmisch, I've got a bone to pick with you there! You turned my brother out of Germany a couple of months ago. I don't agree with his politics, but he's the most honest chap living."

"Are you the sister of Quentin Matthews?" asked Hr. Andersen.

"Oh, I admire his articles in the *News Chronicle* immensely. A little extreme, perhaps, but what a brilliant brain!"

Herr Garmisch countered the Dane's enthusiasm with a show of contempt.

"I'm afraid I don't remember the names of all these chaps."

Before Frau Garmisch could speak out her fury, Alfred said, "You don't see him often, darling, though, do you? Anyway your parents are enough to have turned any son into a Red."

He clearly saw no easy passage between his German and his Danish trade routes. Gladys merely repeated:

"Quentin sometimes loses his head, but he's as honest as the day."

"Unfortunately on these big issues today we cannot afford to lose our heads." Willy Garmisch allowed himself no more comment.

At first, Gretel seemed content to dwell with distaste over Alfred's lapse into "darling," on which she had pounced with a little bitter smile, then she said very slowly and with great fierceness:

"Your newspapers are mostly owned by Jews, aren't they?"

"Well," said Willy, "I wish you could have seen the concern *our* newspapers showed when your king was so ill. That's all. And the German nation as a whole. We admire your Royal Family. And the Prince of Wales! What an asset for England. Britain's best business representative, eh?"

Gladys had seized these moments to deflect Hr. Andersen on to Sylvia Heathway and antiques; now Alfred called her finally to guide the German trade out of the choppy seas into smooth waters.

"*You've* got some good stories of the Prince of Wales, Gladys, haven't you?"

"Well, yes, as a matter of fact, I have had to supply secretarial and domestic staff for Fort Belvedere sometimes. You'll be surprised, I think, to hear how much the Prince knows exactly what goes on in his own household. For instance . . ."

The attentive faces of the Garmisches showed that he at least had not lied when he announced the German admiration for the Royal Family. As Gladys spoke of the Prince's mixture of boyish irreverence and sudden hauteur, Sylvia Heathway was saying, "Oh, as far as provincial France is concerned, Hr. Andersen, of course you're right. There are the most extraordinary treasures still to be picked up. But even there the enormous amount of imitation in the last century means that you've got to watch like a hawk. I am sure you know that so much of the genuine Louis Quinze came over here with the *émigrés* during the Revolution. I remember . . ."

Fair weather at last. And then when dancing time came, Gladys found to her delight that Willy Garmisch was a beautiful waltzer. He too had obviously not expected her to be so light and rhythmic. And now she was quick-stepping "I'm putting all my eggs in one basket" with Alfred—always for her the culmination of the evening.

She was concerned that he might be angry, but he said, "My God, what a sour Kraut Willy's missus is. I'm only sorry you had to cope with her. Though funnily enough she doesn't dance half badly."

Indeed, dancing seemed to lubricate all the Anglo-German friction; and as for Hr. Andersen, he and Sylvia Heathway would have been yapping about Louis Quinze and Louis Seize until the cows came home, if Alfred hadn't broken the party up.

Later that night (or rather early the next morning) as Gladys knelt by the bed massaging Alfred's feet, for he paid a price whenever he indulged in dancing, he pulled her towards him and he held her head against his chest.

"I'm going to give you a bit of a shock, darling, but you mustn't start objecting until you've heard me out." He held her away from him and looked into her eyes, "Promise?" he asked. "Promise?" Her heartbeats came painfully fast, but she promised.

"All right, then. You only had to feel the undertones of tonight's conversation to see where we stand with Germany. For myself I think there's quite a lot to admire in Hitler. And, as a business-man, I genuinely believe that war would be madness. As a matter of fact, I think our government will keep us out of it. But you can't be sure."

"Oh, I don't think we could be so stupid, Alfred. Anyway, they couldn't call on you again, darling, after all you did last time."

"Good Lord, no! But it isn't that I was getting at. I've been thinking a lot about your agency business. I know how you love the work, but one thing's certain: if we get even a near-to-war situation there isn't going to be any more choosing jobs and that sort of thing. Especially for the young. They'll be directed where they're wanted. And that goes for girls, too. Quite right, I think. Lack of discipline is one of our troubles. But all that's theoretical stuff. I'm a practical man and what I'm worried about is where does that put a job like

yours? The days of private employment agencies are probably
over."

"Oh, I don't think so, Alfred. The employment situation's improved a bit. And then more women of our class are earning their
own livings . . ."

"Now wait a minute, girlie. You promised to hear me out. I
kidded you earlier on about retirement. And, of course, I shall see
you're left all right if anything happens to me. But you're an independent cuss, you know . . ."

"I have my insurance, Alfred. It's not large. But I'm not in the
grave yet . . ."

"Of course, if you're not going to listen . . ."

"I'm sorry."

"Well, then. Shall I tell you something I'm doing myself? I'm putting a whole lot of my property into portable assets. I've bought a
hell of a lot of jewellery for Doris. Not that she can wear it, of
course, but as a security. And so on. Now I think that you couldn't
do better with this new business of yours than to go into antiques."

"Antiques! Are you mad, Alfred? Why not pigeon fancying, or
nursery gardens, or some other thing I know absolutely nothing
about? Antiques! I'm interested in people. Surely you know that."

"Well, you'd get a very interesting crowd to deal with in the antique business, all sorts of eccentrics . . ."

"Very eccentric they'd have to be to trust my judgment about antique furniture."

"I'm not suggesting that you'd want to run that side."

"And who are you suggesting should?"

"Now don't start making a hullabaloo before I've finished. I happen to know that Sylvia Heathway has been very near to a complete
breakdown. The one thing she must have to save her from going
over the edge is a real interest in life . . ."

He paused, but Gladys said nothing.

"If she were to start up again in antiques on her own, as she's
talked of doing, she'd probably go bust in half a year. She's got no
business sense at all. She doesn't even begin to understand what hit
Tubby. All the sharks in the business would be round her in a
week."

He paused again and Gladys said, "Are you having an affair with
her?"

"Oh, for God's sake, kiddie. Even if you don't understand what I feel about you, surely you don't think I'd go after a haggard crea-ture like her, got up like a tart?"

She asked again, "Are you having an affair with her, Alfred?"

He looked at her so directly that she had to believe him.

"No. I am not."

"Well, then, whatever . . . Of course, it's very sad. But you're not a charity organization. Nor quite honestly am I. You told me yourself that her husband had only himself to blame."

"Did I? Then I was lying. Tubby Clayton killed himself because I ruined him. Oh, no, it wasn't as dramatic as that, of course. All legit-imate business. But he was a competitor and I deliberately undersold him. It was fair business and I'd do it again. But I had no idea he'd panic and shoot himself. Now, do you see why I want to help her?"

"Yes, but . . . Oh, dear, Alfred, how can you have made me feel so happy and it was all a trick?" Gladys could not stop herself from crying.

"It's not a trick. I'm not even asking you to leave the agency if you feel so strongly. I'm just buying the business in your name. Let Sylvia do all the work. So long as you keep an eye on the books. You can do it in your spare time in your head. And the profit's yours."

"If I ever did such a thing, I couldn't do it like that. I'd have to learn the business and go into it properly. I'll only suffer for my own mistakes."

"Well. All the better. It'd be the greatest help to me. You saw this evening with Andersen, and he's by no means the only one. It would help me a lot if I could advise clients where to buy and sell old things. Antiques are all the thing nowadays, you know."

"I don't believe you know anything about it."

He pulled her on to the bed next to him, then he lay back and laughed. "My God! You do make a chap work hard, don't you?"

She laughed also, but she said, "Well, this is important, Alfred. It's my life."

"Gladys," he began again, "when Doris agreed a few years back that she could never be a full wife to me, she said, as I told you, that she understood how I needed you in my life. But she said a lot of other things. Above all, that you were obviously the woman who understood my temperament and my ambitions . . ."

"I don't think I want to hear what Doris said."

He sat up and groaned. "All right. Skip Doris. Very well, I'm beat. I can only say that I'm asking you to do this for me. I've given you a hundred good practical reasons. But if *they* don't appeal to you, just do it for me."

"I'll think about it and let you know."

He lay back again and chuckled like a small boy. He mopped the sweat from his forehead.

"If working hard for something deserves success!"

He rolled over on to her and began to kiss her. From beneath his mouth she mumbled, "I haven't said I will, you know."

"That's all right, you will."

She mumbled again, "Now why do you think that makes me love you? And why are you right?"

"Perhaps because I know women."

He looked at his watch. "As usual with our evenings, darling, it's all gone. The fun's over. Tomorrow you have to go back to responsibility and the treadmill."

She looked at him in amazement, but he obviously spoke as he saw the situation. So there seemed nothing to say.

For over a fortnight he was too busy to see her, so that she had plenty of time to think it over. It was such a delight when she did see him to be able to say yes. After all, he had given her such good, practical reasons; then again, as he pointed out, she would make her own hours now, could help him out more with business lunches and so on, see more of him in short. She remained unsure of why he set so much store by the scheme.

"But *you* have been here before, haven't you, Mr. Matthews?" Sukhanova called to him as they poured out of the delegates' charabancs into the courtyard. She added, "Mr. Matthews is an old friend of ours."

M. Garcin, in his Midi accent, asked of the man who interpreted for the French, "*Qu'est-ce qu'elle dit?*"

He spoke, as always, even about the most trivial matters, in an ironic, self-protective tone, and his little black eyes glanced suspiciously at Quentin. To the interpretation of Sukhanova's remark, he said: "*Ah! Très bien. On l'a déjà dit,*" and he converted his suspicious glance into a half-smile that might or might not have implied more suspicion.

"Paranoids' Pantomime!" Quentin thought, and this valuation took in all but a few of the large crowd streaming across the court-yard. He did not exclude himself, but he must attend to his now rather stale little battle with Sukhanova, so, as gaily as he could he called back, "And I never cease to envy the girls who once boarded in this beautiful building! But last time I was here with my old friend, Professor Yudenich, Sukhanova. Where did you say he was?"

"Oh! Mr. Matthews. Always Professor Yudenich! Where is he? Why is he not here? The poor professor has been ill. He's gone away to get well. Sochi? Yalta? I don't know. We don't have to leave our addresses when we go on holiday, you know, in the Soviet Union."

Sukhanova's voice moaned away at him in light badinage which yet implied, as it did to all foreigners, a sad patronage of their ignor-ance. Her eyes looked as tired and depressed as she no doubt felt. For a moment Quentin almost desisted in his little game. Poor woman! If she found all this sightseeing with social scientists as tir-ing as he did. And on top of that, the vanity and self-regard of all the delegates! It seemed too hard to try her with this little baiting game as well, one that might so easily be dangerous for her. For she, like the others, was glassily, stickily frightened, for all her maddening mechanical jollity. Of this he was more convinced each day of the Congress; almost all their hosts lived in terror, not just the sad, con-stant alarm that he knew and accepted as the price of a great Revolu-tion's necessary vigilance, the price of the capitalist spy system, but some special fear that came at them down corridors, round the cor-ners of streets, behind every connecting door of every room. What-ever was happening, he must not further it by being frightened off, even out of pity for their hostage hosts. He must register his knowl-edge and condemnation.

Then he asked himself, had he come here after the unspeakable-ness of the Führer's heroic land expecting in his relief far too much; or, perhaps, bringing some infection of a dark, irrational fear within himself?

The disquieting answer came as always from the Russian side. "But if you have not got your friend Professor Yudenich here, dear Mr. Matthews, we have a new friend for you in Professor Weiss-heim, the great authority on the gipsies. Did you know that here in the Soviet Union we have many different groups of gipsies with most colourful and interesting customs. But in Germany, it seems, the National Socialist Fascists are getting rid of their gipsies, and Professor Weissheim has come to us from Marburg."

Always the same answers—look at Germany, look at Mussolini, look at the Fascist beasts. He smiled across at Erwin Weissheim, whom he liked, but he returned to the charge.

"And Mrs. Rakitin, I miss her, too."

Sukhanova disregarded this.

"Mr. Matthews has also been turned out by Hitler, Professor Weissheim. No one must dare to tell the truth in the Third Reich."

Quentin thought that Erwin Weissheim's blue eyes grew a little clouded, a little weary, at this repeated introduction.

"I know Comrade Matthews' work. I know what he has tried to say for the forces of freedom in my country in the English newspapers. I know . . ."

"We know and respect each other well, Professor. I wish you could have met Mrs. Rakitin. In her work as a child magistrate she had no doubt a lot to do with gipsies . . ."

But now Sukhanova, in desperation, spoke to the guide. "Come on, Comrade, tell the delegates about the Smolny Institute. You're not here to go to sleep."

She beckoned her English-speaking flock around her so that they might hear her interpretation of the guide's words. The French-speaking delegates gathered on the other side of the entrance hall around their interpreter.

"Now we are here in the Smolny Institute. Catherine the Second added this building to provide boarding-school for girls. But, of course, in those days, only the daughters of the nobility received such a fine education. The importance of the building lies else-where. It was here that the Soviet Government sat, until the capital became once more Moscow, as it had been in the days before the Romanovs. Here V.I. Lenin lived and worked and directed the Revo-lution in the fateful days of November 1917. The room in which he worked has been preserved as it was then. We shall now go to see that room. Turn to the left, if you please, along the corridor."

Miss Amy Taylor, the Co-op expert on distribution, ran a comb through her bobbed hair in readiness for what was clearly to be an impressive moment, but she could not forbear asking one of her questions.

"Did you say, Miss Canova, that this was only part of a larger building?"

"I am Sukhanova," their Russian friend, with a sweet smile, told her wearily. "Yes, this building is an addition to the earlier building, the former Smolny Monastery, built in the baroque style."

"By the great architect of Petersburg, Rastrelli," Quentin added. He felt at once ashamed of himself. What importance had baroque architecture beside Lenin's achievements, what the hell did he care anyway for baroque architects? And Miss Amy Taylor, as could be seen from her blank, rather pretty, freckled face, cared less. To descend to needling with points of minor aesthetic interest was to have sunk pretty low. Then ahead among the crowd he saw the short white hairs and wrinkled flesh of the nape of Zemskova's neck. She was walking on her own, but as some delegate pressed forward upon her heels, she turned. He smiled and gave a little wave of his hand. Her old grey eyes went completely blank, although her nicotine-stained mouth twitched slightly; she had aged enormously, as he had seen in their one conversation, but he had noticed then no signs of senile twitches. He felt a new resolve not to give in.

It was difficult, however, in the stuffiness of the corridors, with tired feet and bored mind, with the close pressing of stout, over-dressed men and thickly clad women, all too human in the great summer heat, not to relax into vacuity if one was to avoid claustrophobia. He concentrated on placing and naming the delegates, but now as they queued up to go through to that little fateful room, he realized again that of the Russian delegates he knew only a handful. In his own field of housing, old Kursky was there with his wife, and there was an unpronounceable penologist, and Melgunov, the transport man, and a few others, mostly subordinate people. Of the Leningrad University people only Professor Polovtzev and Doctor Breit were there. The numbers who were not . . . Now, suddenly, the little room itself, the desk, the chairs, the stove, the small, Spartan bed—he remembered how, when he had seen them before, despite his dislike of political emotionalism, he had been forced to swallow again and again to prevent tears coming into his eyes. At the sight of such dedication, such clarity of purpose, such inflexible will, all the

ruthlessness, the undoubted chaotic absurdities of some of the early
Revolutionary decisions, the megalomaniac traits were so swallowed
up as to become as nothing. He had felt an overpowering admiration
for the man who could force millions of human lives and wills and
all the chance events of this so vast a country into one dogmatic
bottle as small as the room he organized the bottling from. But now,
as Sukhanova's cooing tones took up the tale, he revolted from the
whole thing as though he had been told of a very neat but brutal
rape.

"On the morning of November 7, 1917, Vladimir Ilyich Lenin,
deciding that the moment had come for action, left the villa where
he had been staying since his arrival from Finland . . ."

"The villa that used to belong to the Czar's mistress, the ballerina,
wasn't it?"

Sukhanova paused for a moment. "Yes. But please do not interrupt, Mr. Matthews. Now I shall lose the guide's words."

She appealed with a look to the audience, many of whom frowned
at him. A picture came into his mind of beautiful young girls in
tutus, dancing towards him on their points, arms waving. Catherine's
young noblewomen. Hardly in *Swan Lake*. He shook his head to
keep awake in the stuffy atmosphere. After all, those girls, beautiful
young creatures in hoop petticoats and powder (did young girls
wear powder?), with their ripening breasts, were also leaders in a
revolution. Boarding-school! Experiment of the Enlightenment. A
long step to woman's emancipation, to the bob of Miss Amy Taylor,
or the boyish crop of that attractive bitch, Andrée Paulhard—she
would have suited Lenin's ruthlessness.

"And, of course, Krupskaya was with him all the time, cooking
upon that stove you see there, acting as his correspondent, his secretary."

Sleeping with him in that narrow bed? He wanted to ask, but, as
they moved on out of the room, they were pressed almost to stifling
point. Since he could not ask his question, he moved close to Madame Paulhard, letting his hands accidentally press for a moment
against her thighs. To his surprise the soft smoothness that he
touched rubbed against his fingers. True, the press of the crowd was
considerable, but . . . His fingers itched for a moment to give her
buttocks a sharp tweak, but why spoil the chance of a beautiful
friendship? Instead he let his hands travel deliciously down her

thighs. The pleasant pressure continued until they had left the holy fastness, but when she turned, her little delicate face bore its usual angry scowl, like a schoolboy afraid of appearing soft. Now he found himself next to old Kursky's wife, an imperious, handsome, elderly creature who always reduced him to the sort of social banality he reserved for old ladies.

"So they had the telephone even then?"

She was quick to register his fatuousness, but not in the words he expected.

"Nineteen seventeen? Well, of course. My parents had the telephone in nineteen hundred."

You old snob, he thought. Then he remembered her pre-Revolutionary bourgeois social origins; that was why she had that vague aura of bourgeois chic that irritated him so, made him address her as if she were an old fool.

"Where was your parents' mansion, Sofya Petrovna?" he asked, delighted to remember her patronymic.

She looked down her Roman nose at him. He realized suddenly that since those he trusted were not here, he had come quite illogically to see all who were there as enemies. Yet his intuition, perhaps because it was usually so strictly bridled, had its head in full canter today.

He heard himself say, "I am most disappointed not to see Mrs. Rakitin. Her name was on the list of speakers. She gave such an interesting paper three years ago. Do you know why she's not here?"

Mrs. Kursky paused a moment.

"Mrs. Rakitin? I don't think I know her. What does she do?"

He knew at once that this must be a lie, but he registered no surprise.

"She's a child magistrate."

"Oh, I see. Well, my husband isn't a lawyer. And we have no small children. But I'll ask Sukhanova for you."

He should have stopped her, but he didn't.

"Sukhanova," she called. My word! he only now saw how grand her manner was. "Mr. Matthews wants to know why a friend of his, a child magistrate, why Mrs. Rakitin is not here."

This time Sukhanova turned in real anger.

"Mr. Matthews, I have told you twenty times. Mrs. Rakitin is not

here because she is busy. The courts have to continue, you know.
The Russian people don't stop living because all the clever social
scientists from abroad are discussing the best ways to live."

In her annoyance her voice sounded sarcastic enough to startle a
number of the delegates—even Miss Amy Taylor pursed her lips.
Mr. Kursky, large, portentous, yet more managerial than his grand
wife, said something to rebuke her, which Quentin could not hear,
but Sukhanova seemed unwilling to listen.

"Come along now, everyone," she cried brightly. "If we don't get
into our coaches soon we shall miss the treasures of the Winter Palace. Or our lunch. You don't want to miss your lunch, do you?" She
said this quite sharply to Miss Taylor, who had, as Quentin remembered, a rather small vegetarian appetite. He got into the charabanc
feeling relaxed. He had achieved his purpose: both Kelvin Douglas
and Mary Parr had, he saw, registered at last his insistence upon the
absent delegates—and these were the two English visitors who held
any really big guns.

So much had Kelvin Douglas observed that he came to sit next to
Quentin, his vast bulk flowing flabbily all over his neighbour. With
his huge head, hair *en brosse*, conventionally, almost Victorianly,
clad huge body and his plummy, pompous voice, he was hardly dis-
tinguishable from Kursky or many other Soviet delegates. Only the
burr of his *r*'s gave to his academic solidity a peculiarly smug,
homely aroma of high teas and a distant Free Kirk childhood.

It was no surprise when he said, "I think perhaps, Matthews, we
ought to drop this question of some of the Russian delegates not
being here, eh? Quite frankly I have the impression that there may
be some little domestic quarrel that's divided our friends and some
have preferred not to attend. It's very understandable. I often feel,
when we disagree at home, as we so often do, that it would be much
better for the minority to stop away from meetings. Controversy
and disagreement do impede any sort of decision. And decision must
be ultimately what we're after."

"With the first of your suggestions I agree, though I doubt if any
of the absent delegates I know have chosen to stay away. With the
second I entirely disagree. This is not a revolutionary situation, nor
are the decisions we are reaching binding upon anyone, nor are they
indeed, in any but the most academic sense, political. As I understand

it we are an international meeting of more or less professional people connected with various branches of social organization and the theory of social organization, all Socialists, designedly chosen on a very broad definition of that term to include as many of us as possible who are committed to the furtherance of a Socialist society. Our purpose is to exchange ideas and experiences in our various spheres in order to facilitate social planning in Socialist communities of every size, from the Soviet Union down to the mayoralty of Marseilles, or the Borough Council of Clydeside. Am I right?"

"Oh, perfectly, perfectly," Kelvin Douglas paused, and taking a very small lozenge from a small tin, placed it very slowly into his vast mouth and began even more slowly to suck it. His voice sounded like that of an eminent hippopotamus underwater.

"Oil of clove. Very soothing wherever there's any little roughness of the throat. You don't however mention two things which, though not part of our agenda, are, as is so often the case, almost more important than any published aim. I'm thinking, of course, of the very valuable work we've already done in demonstrating against the Fascist claim to any serious social planning. Understand me, I see our meeting as only in part an exchange of ideas. At the present crisis all meetings of Socialists, whatever their concern, must serve primarily as demonstrations of our determination to resist by all means in our power the naked aggression of fascism. And to deter whatever right-wing reformist elements in our own countries . . ." He glanced at Quentin, and appeared to decide on a new sentence to express his views. "Whether we necessarily accept our Russian friends' definition of Social Fascists for some of the more backward of the Social Democrats is perhaps a matter of literary taste."

He smiled in naughty complicity at Quentin, who managed not to respond. "But the language apart, and it has a certain shorthand value on these occasions, we are united in sentiment. Which puts upon those of us who have differences of view from our Russian hosts a peculiar duty of preserving our disagreement for the most private occasions, since the aim of the reactionary forces everywhere today is to drive a wedge between the Soviet Union and the Western democracies. This really mustn't happen, or, to be very English, appear to have happened."

"There could be no possible reason why it should appear to have happened if the conference were to stick to its educative purpose and not to attempt to turn itself into an international demonstration."

Kelvin Douglas shifted his weight from one buttock to the other, pinning Quentin against the side of the coach in the process.

"I must say that these concepts of professionalism and academic discussion seem to me the sheerest petty bourgeois illusion." He added, "Sukhanova does a very hard job extremely well. I think we ought to buy her some little gift before we leave—the English delegation, I mean."

"Certainly."

"And meanwhile perhaps we can all make her job a little easier by not pressing her with questions which, as those of us who are old hands know, she is not in the position to answer."

He had made his own position quite clear, yet Quentin felt perhaps that if he could force the man more into the open they might at least argue out their duty.

"If you mean that such questions make her job more dangerous, I . . ."

He was indeed open to argument on this ground. But Kelvin Douglas was not. He receded.

"Dangerous?" He laughed. "Well, no, even at their worst, most trying moments, I doubt if any of the Anglo-Saxon delegates are literally homicidal." He left his seat and joined a Ukrainian authority on social hygiene. "I've just been telling my colleague Matthews that I'm extraordinarily impressed by the reports you gave us of the rapid and efficient isolation system in the event of epidemic."

Sukhanova had to translate, but the Ukrainian answered emphatically and immediately.

"Yes, we act very quickly."

Later that evening, following an afternoon of speeches on crèche organization and child care, Quentin tried to relax in the sitting-room of his hotel suite. The grand piano with its flowered shawl, the high Japanese pot, the ebony table with mother-of-pearl inlay, all reminded him of 52. And so, of course, every decorative object in the city—that was not a treasured antique—should, for all bourgeois decoration had been put to sleep in the city like the princess's castle at that bourgeois moment when the Countess was braving the Zeppelins. And these *art nouveau*, early *Ballet Russe* objects, would re-

main in that sleep, no doubt, for a hundred years, until they crumbled. But what then would they use to embellish the rooms of
bourgeois sympathizers from abroad, for they had evolved no decorative style of their own? No need, he would have said a few years
back, for long before then there would be no more bourgeois sympathizers, world revolution would be complete. But now he only
hoped that for this reason alone he would not be cut off from the
U.S.S.R., for if anything warmed his heart it was this lack of triviality, of luxury, of effort and skill wasted in designing fashions and
modes to keep running a world of high profits and pitiful doles.
Grand pianos and pots and portraits and all the rest of it, if they
must be, let them be as shabby as possible; and for the rest, the plain,
the simple, and the dowdy.

All these girls with their cheap printed frocks in the streets, even
though they did look tired, tore the balls out of him. That was why
he was always so randy here—none of that awful cash display which
made bourgeois women into profit charts, none of that superfluous
display which choked the life out of sexual desire, making women
whores without the harlot's honesty. Now here . . . He went to his
private bathroom. He turned the worn-washered brass tap of the old
wooden-cased bath; tepid water groaned and gurgled and gushed in
spasms as fierce as if it had been at boiling point. This was the only
luxury he ever craved, for here, as a well-known friend of the Soviet
Union, he could indulge it. He lowered himself into the lukewarm
water so delicious on this sticky evening. But not for long; mopping
his dripping body, in his old Jaeger buff dressing-gown, he answered
the knocking at the door.

"It's me, Mary Parr."

As he looked at her standing there with her heavy amber ear-rings
and amber necklace, her dyed black hair done in ear-phones so dead
and scurfy that one felt that if they were lifted moths would fly out
of them, her dreadful arch smile as she took in his dishabille, he almost shut the door in despair. But then, for all the absurd artiness
and girlishness of her manner, which made listening to her interven-
tions at the Congress more embarrassing than watching the posi-
tively last appearance of some grisly old worn-out opera singer, she
had yet produced since 1898 (yes, 1898; God, she must be quite
sixty) a series of books of somewhat excess enthusiasm but remarka-
bly good sense on that stamping ground of bores and cranks—

woman's role in society. Now she sat herself firmly in his solitary chair so that, standing, he felt more the silliness as well as the discomfort of being wet and naked beneath his old gown.

She fussed as usual with an absurd cigarette holder and lady-spy black cigarettes, so that he began to shiver as much with impatience as wetness. But then she surprised him.

"I'm their special star, you know," she said. "Not really political. Just what they call a modern thinker. My name adds a whole colour band to the anti-Fascist spectrum. And I'm glad to do it. We intellectuals can't stand aside any longer. But I don't want to add a band to the wrong rainbow. That's why I want to know why you're surprised at these absences. I don't know the place like you do, but I came prepared for some, what shall we say, disappearances. And these aren't even that. Just non-appearances. Or am I being naïve? What do you know? Why are you fussing?"

He looked around the room. He must have seemed more worried than he realized, for she said: "What's that about? I've got you out of your bath, haven't I? Is that face 'cause you're wet or because there's some sound equipment in the room? Well, if there is, I'm glad they should know what I have to say. And if there isn't . . ."

"I've not felt happy in Leningrad this time, Miss Parr, though it's my favourite Russian city. I've missed many friends at the conference and many more whom I've wanted to see in their private homes. Of course, as they say, it's August. It's pleasing to see how the success of the second Five-Year Plan is making possible the summer holiday habit. It wasn't so when I was here two years ago. On the other hand, the telephone system is not so good. I've been cut off many times and so many numbers appear to be unobtainable."

"I see. More non-appearances than is reasonable even in revolutionary circumstances. Well, I envy you having so many unavailable friends. However, I must judge as I find. I don't think I've ever been so charmingly entertained. As Kelvin Douglas said to me, 'What other nation in the midst of one of the world's greatest economic experiments would have time to think of baskets of fruit in their guests' bedrooms?'" She winked at him. As she talked she was writing. "And this *is* the nation that's had this charming little thought. There is, you know, a little ticket on my basket of fruit, 'in admiration from the Russian people.' So that proves it, doesn't it?" Her voice sounded more than ever like a little girl trying to sound sophisticated.

She passed to him what she had written.

"That's my London address, by the way, for that article you promised to send me."

She had written her address and some lines lower had added: "I want to know for myself, if possible."

"And," he said, tearing off this sheet from her pad, and writing on the next sheet, "this is the name of that book of Maurice Dobb's we were speaking of in case I forget to give it to you." He wrote the title indeed, but beneath, "No one will speak, they're all too frightened."

To his amusement, she tore off this piece of his message and swallowed the tiny piece of paper.

"I'm a great reader of light fiction," she said, laughing. "Insomnia, you know; but who can sleep well with Hitler on the doorstep?"

She got up from the chair, "Well, you've not really convinced me. And I suppose we'll all be signing a joint statement tonight."

"I *will*," he said, and added immediately, "I *won't*."

She seemed to understand, for she stopped at the door, her many bangles jangling. "I expect you to squire me to this delicious banquet tonight."

Before he got back into his bath, he took her address from his dressing-gown pocket and tore off the message. He was about to flush it down the lavatory, when he divided the small strip into two and swallowed both pieces. He laughed and said under his breath, "Infectious paranoia." But he thought with disgust as he splashed in the cool water that they were mockingly parodying the same scene that people were enacting in mortal terror from Tokyo through Moscow to Munich.

The long eighteenth-century gallery with its baroque carving, its mirrors and chandeliers, was like the scene of some Victorian academic banquet. So, with similar pomposity, jocosity, verbosity, and hideosity, must Carlyle and Tennyson, Herschel and Huxley, George Eliot, Miss Nightingale, Baroness Coutts, Mrs. Lynn Linton, Sir Theodore Martin, Matthew Arnold, and Ebenezer Prout, or any Victorian mixed bag of worthies have degraded often and often, with their tedious hypocrisy, solemnity, and greed many and many a beautiful English eighteenth-century drawing-room. The men, in particular, in their drab dress and huge bulk, were a Lytton Strachey sketch for a circle of Inferno; and the tables groaning with caviare and sturgeon and blinis and whipped cream and crayfish and fruit from the Crimea and ice puddings and pies of pigeon, pies of duck, pies, for all one knew, of Russian bear, all waiting to be washed down with Georgian wine. The whole banquet united Queen Victoria with her Tudor ancestors. That indeed was what it was; for despite the short hair and dresses of the women, the talk of hydro-electric dams, and the great scientific and industrial projects of the twentieth century, the conformities and the hypocrisies of these social gatherings were mid-Victorian, while the appetites, the terrors, and the vast empty laughter that hid the terrors, belonged to the court of bluff King Joe.

Mary Parr, who appeared to have met the banquet's sartorial demands by exchanging amber for jade, twisted and swayed her skinny old hips for all the world like a Mata Hari playing out her last brave act. She came in on Quentin's arm, the great spy coolly flirting with her handsome firing squad. As he listened to her, he despaired. Even her supposedly sophisticated remarks were imitations of what had been said a hundred times at the functions during the week. "Caviare again," she drawled. "Isn't it naughty of me, but do you know I get a tiny bit tired of caviare." And, "Oooh! Do have some of this sturgeon. It's so deliciously tender. I think it must be virgin sturgeon." And so on.

Seeing Andrée Paulhard farther down the room, drinking her champagne with such seductively sulky contempt, made Mary's stale gushing twice as intolerable; he needed all his sense of duty to remain by her side. At last, after what seemed an endless series of flirtations between her long jade holder and the cigarettes of Soviet notabilities whose eyes were on younger women, she consented to be taken away from the buffet, shrugging her shoulders and smiling as though she were humouring Quentin's jealous passion.

Zemskova was standing at one of the long windows that looked out on the courtyard where lamps caught fitfully the open mouths of the great stone dolphins.

"Zemskova, this is Mary Parr."

She who, two years ago even, would have been excited if a little amused by this contact with a famous figure from outside the bars, turned towards them, now a little apprehensive, as she shook hands and expressed her admiration for Miss Parr's *Life of Mary Woll-stonecraft.*

"A friend of mine, Mr. Dorchenko, translated it into Russian. I think he did a very good job."

"Oh, I should so like to meet him and thank him. Translations of one's work into languages one doesn't know are so mysterious. What a pity this is our last evening. He's not here, I suppose."

"Oh, no, Mr. Dorchenko lives in Moscow."

"Can you give me his address? I'll write to him."

"I think he is away now, Miss Parr."

"Oh." Mary paused for a second, then took it in her stride. "Like Mrs. Rakitin and Professor Yudenich?"

"A little," said Zemskova, very quietly, but she looked as though she would like to cleave her way out from between the two English guests. Mary had met half the test by herself, but nevertheless Quentin decided he must complete it for her.

"Perhaps Miss Parr should keep asking for her translator as you told me to ask for our absent delegates."

He had expected some alarm from Zemskova; it was the sorry price he reckoned on in order to secure Mary's credence. What came was a moment's open terror. Mary realized the cause before he did.

"Yes," she said, drawling loudly, and putting her hand on the old woman's shoulder, perhaps to steady her, "the thing is to have a large spray of artificial flowers, or some women prefer leaves, just pinned across the shoulder here to the bosom."

"Oh, we should think that *too* artificial. Shouldn't we, Sukhanova?"

She had been there out of nowhere as he had put his question to Zemskova.

"I am sure whatever fashions Miss Parr follows are becoming. But we prefer simple lines, you know, Miss Parr. We are a very simple people, aren't we, Mr. Matthews? Will you all come please to the other reception room now? Our dear friend Mr. Kelvin Douglas is going to say a few words."

The few words were many. Unctuous, Quentin thought, and devious. But, at least, Douglas was consistent with his morning opin-

ion: ". . . These have been only some of the problems and of the
answers that happen to have stood out for me in a week of invigorat-
ing talk. I think that too many of us who have been brought up in
the atmosphere of Western social democracy with its individualistic,
laissez faire liberal roots have an ingrown belief that only disagreement, what we tend to call 'healthy disagreement,' can be invigorat-
ing. But I wonder how many of my colleagues from Britain and the
United States, from France, and from German democracy in exile
have felt with me this week that when we Socialists and progressives
have a chance to get our thoughts in order in the atmosphere of
Socialist achievement, of socialism in action which we breathe here
in the U.S.S.R., then what becomes the source of good health is not
disagreement but concord, for many of us the concord that comes
from humility in face of Socialist solutions tried out and proven."

   Quentin, looking round, saw that to their Marxist hosts the shape
and tone of Douglas's words were as unfamiliar and meaningless as
that sermon of a Free Kirk minister which they resembled. The util-
ity of Kelvin Douglas, however, they recognized and honoured with
a variety of lively, high-minded, and sometimes surprisingly sentimental expressions on their large, smooth, very naked faces.

   "We who come from the Western democracies have every day
before us the tragic experience of seeing how the peoples' determination to throw back the Fascist aggressors in Abyssinia and China,
to destoy the infamous racism of Hitler and his crew, is constantly
weakened and cheated by the self-interest, the vacillation, the stupidity, and the treachery of our own capitalist governments. We social
scientists know what a Socialist world could be like. Here we see
much of it in action . . . Fascism, whatever its cause will never
conquer against the implacable will of the people. It is above all,
comrades, the spectacle of our unity here that we offer as a demonstration of the determination of intellectuals everywhere to unite in
rejecting the return to the Dark Ages . . . to offer defiance to Hitler, Mussolini, and the Japanese warlords and their jackals Mosley,
De La Rocque, Doriot, and the rest . . . and to make a last appeal to
our own rulers to show themselves in action what they profess to
be—lovers of peace and freedom . . ." Quentin, to make clear his total commitment to the defiance of Chamberlain and Co., clapped
loudly.

   Kelvin Douglas said, "I'm very glad to have the support of my

good friend Quentin Matthews. Most of us academics and adminis-
trators would consider his expert knowledge of housing a lifetime
work, but Matthews has to take on the world of foreign affairs as
well and enrich our daily lives with his courageous, stimulating
newspaper articles."

Here there was some special applause from Mr. Kursky, his wife,
and other Soviet representatives; Sukhanova even patted Quentin on
the back.

"Bravo, Mr. Matthews," she said.

He cursed at having caught his foot in so obvious a trap. But now
they were silent as Kelvin Douglas, selecting a lozenge, indicated
that he was approaching his peroration.

"Mark the occasion indelibly . . . not only a blueprint for the
foundation of a new organization . . . many steps yet to take for
the formation of a secretariat and administration . . . for myself,
can think of no happier headquarters than . . . generously offered
by our hosts . . . suggested name, World International Federation
of Social and Allied Scientists . . . have heard the Russian but will
not insult that beautiful language . . . no doubt fated to go the way
of all fine names . . . already accustomed to the familiar friendliness
of WIFSAS . . . but the charter to which I now appeal to you to
subscribe is above all a challenge to the Fascist dictators . . . a fit-
ting and memorable conclusion to . . ."

The applause was long and loud; and the silent, very neat, slightly
scowling young men and the talkative, slightly grubby, always
smiling young women who had done all the donkey work at the
Congress began to bring round copies of the new charter for the
delegates to sign. Quentin tried to engage Mary Parr in trivial conversation, but she walked out on to one of the little balconies that so
absurdly decorated the palace's great bulk. It was he, in any case,
who had to testify first.

Quietly he read over the document and he refused it, as one might
refuse to contribute to an offertory for some unsympathetic cause in
church. Quietly the solid, yet feline, high-cheekboned young man
went away like a polite but outraged sidesman. He spoke to Sukhanova, who in turn spoke to Kursky, Doctor Maximov, and some
others.

So here it was at last. But he would fight for his visa, for his living,
for his power to influence. Russia added to Germany would be near

castration. Perhaps with evasion and duplicity he could win this round.

It was Sukhanova they first sent to try to induce him.

"Mr. Matthews! You don't *sign?* But this is the document for publication in *Pravda* tomorrow. Everybody's signature is needed."

"Mine won't be there. I don't feel that such a manifesto is desirable. In any case the terms of the document are not, in my opinion, either sensible or truthful."

"You would like something changed? Oh, you certainly are one of the men Comrade Kelvin Douglas described, a believer in healthy disagreement. I'm afraid you must argue it out with Mr. Kursky and the experts. No," she went on, as though he were attempting to discuss it with her, although, in fact, he had remained quite silent, "it is no good arguing with me. I am only a poor interpreter."

Now Kursky invited him over to a sofa in the banquet room among the broken meats and lees of wine, where through the half-open, communicating door they made most successfully an appearance of intimate and serious debate for the rest of the party to observe, when, in fact, they were only two men seated side by side, disagreeing.

"To begin with," Quentin said, seeking a means of avoiding the showdown, " 'the peace-loving democracies of the West': I don't like that woolly phrase. As Mr. Douglas suggested, a good number of the members of the English and French governments have no concern with peace whatsoever, except the peace that will allow them to continue their exploitation of the working classes."

"But we are speaking here, Mr. Matthews, of the united working classes, intelligentsia, and peace-loving elements of England and France."

"Why don't we say that, then?"

"Oh, come now. You are an informed journalist and a Socialist. You know very well that at this phase of the workers' struggle we must seek to carry the governments of the West with us even against their wishes. If they do not respond, then we must expose their evasive tactics. We are bringing pressure to bear upon your ruling classes at this very moment, to fulfil their obligations to the Covenant of the League of Nations, to resist the aggression of Mussolini against the Ethiopian people . . ."

Perhaps, Quentin thought, they would give up before too obvious an exposure of tactics. "Do you remember what Comrade Lenin called the League of Nations? Mr. Matthews, you know as well as I do that changing historical conditions demand changing policies. Then the Revolution was threatened, now . . ."

"Nevertheless there *are* people who would say that sanctions against Italy are only an aspect of the Imperialist policy of Great Britain . . ."

"Who would say? Trotskyites, and other dupes, willing or unwilling, of the Fascists. Do *you* say so? Surely not."

"No. But perfectly honest, intelligent Socialists, for example, Cripps in England. You can hardly call him a Trotskyite. I simply give the example to suggest that to cover a multiplicity of progressive views in these formulas is unfitting."

" . . . And I am only asking you to give your name to this declaration—the necessary foundation for the World Federation on which so much future international planning for . . ."

Quentin saw that to avoid a night of words, of relayed persuaders, he must relinquish all hope of an evasive victory.

He said: "I don't think that my government can be called peace-loving. That's the first point of unnecessary rhetoric. The second is more important. I am increasingly unable to speak as the document does of the Soviet Union as a freedom-loving country in any sense that can be intelligible to a Western Socialist."

After this it was all an absurd pantomime, as he should have known. He had accepted so much as necessary in the past, he could hardly hope to appear other than a fool or a hypocrite in refusing to accept more now. Nevertheless he knew that something much more terrible, much more complete was happening here than on his previous visits, but to reduce it to an argument of quantitative persecution was an absurdity. And the quantity he chose! He found himself ridiculously asking for personal contact with twenty-nine named persons whom he had failed to see in Leningrad during the week— he could not even quite remember how in the heat of the argument he had fixed on the figure of twenty-nine, but he heard himself repeating it again and again with a histrionic force that would not have shamed Rupert. Luckily he could have named up to fifty without involving one person whom he did not know already to be too en-

dangered to be harmed by his questioning. He felt elated, too, when
at last Kursky, joined now by Maximov, declared that all these persons were on holiday or on business.

"I can wait to see them."

"But the delegations are leaving tomorrow."

"But I am remaining a week here in Leningrad."

Their answer to this was made clear when they got up abruptly
and returned to the assembled company. But he had not signed. That
at least.

When he walked back into the main reception room, people already appeared to avoid him. M. Garcin demanded of his interpreter: "*Qu'est-ce qu'il a fait, le délégué anglais?*"

She shrugged her shoulders, and when he repeated his question,
she said crossly: "*Il n'accorde pas sa signature.*"

"*Il a raison. C'est un manifeste trop politique.*"

Perhaps, Quentin thought, he had gained an unexpected additional
convert by his refusal; but no, the Frenchman added, "*Moi, je re-
grette déjà ma signature.*"

He glared with peculiarly venomous suspicion at Quentin.

Now Sukhanova called, "Miss Parr! Miss Parr! Ah, you are taking
the air. We are looking for you, naughty Miss Parr. We need your
signature."

Here it came, Quentin thought. At first Mary Parr also sought
evasion; he heard her say: "But I don't see Mr. Matthews' signature."

"Matthews? Oh, Quentin Matthews the journalist. But this is only
for the social scientists. Imagine the great Kelvin Douglas's name
along with a lot of journalists. Or that of the great Mary Parr. That's
what we all wait for now."

But now Mary, too, and more quickly, chose her own direct tac-
tic.

"No, I'm awfully sorry," she said, a little bewildered girl. "I never
sign anything political. I don't understand politics well enough."

"But, Miss Parr, there is nothing political here, only the declaration of the undying hostility of progressive people to Fascist aggression. You hate fascism, I suppose.

"Undyingly," came Mary's drawl, "but my hatred is much too
well known to need publication in a document that contains so much

that I find ambiguous. Peace! Freedom! Do we all of us really mean exactly the same things by those words?"

There was something so determined beneath her drawl that Quentin relaxed. They would press, perhaps even allow themselves in desperation the pleasure of being offensive to her, but she would not give way. They would dismiss her as a fool, of course. But in England and the United States, where her name stood for sanity and broad-mindedness and "advanced thinking" among a vast number of often foolish or ill-informed, but basically decent, people, her signature would not now subscribe to the statement that freedom reigned in the U.S.S.R. at a moment when terror, he felt sure, was triumphant. He had won a victory. As to how they would dismiss him, he was to learn later that evening.

First from the concierge of the fourth floor of his hotel to whom he went for the key of his room.

"But this is not my key. My room is 410."

"Your room is needed." Could the old woman really feel such personal pleasure as her vindictive look implied? Instead of the suite, a room, almost a box, without even a washbasin. He felt too tired to protest against this absurd being stood in a corner. But the disappearance of all his notes on the Congress—and there had been two addresses of real interest—his notes for an article he was composing on the relations between the Nazis and the Catholic Church in Bavaria, the draft of the first three chapters of his book on his year's experience in Hitler's Germany, all were gone. About these his weariness vanished, as he proceeded through various officials to try to contact the manager. The hotel staff assumed the forms of cretinous troglodytes who only left their caves to man the hotel at night, but understood no language of the day-time, had no cognizance of the affairs of the day. His papers, the manager, his change of room, all these were day matters at which they could only bark or yelp or nod in incomprehension. He sought the help of his hosts in interpreting to these night people. Some members of the Congress secretariat had disappeared to their homes irrevocably—"The Congress is over, Mr. Matthews; we have *private* lives, you know," a voice—could it be Sukhanova or one of the many pseudo-Sukhanovas?—told him. Others were friendly and vague, promising to ring back and not doing so; others again were cold and definite, no, they could do nothing, copies of all the proceedings of the past week's Congress would be posted to him when published, no other papers concerned them. At last, when speaking to what sounded to be a near illiterate porter, he found himself angrily declaring that a country which claimed to be in the forefront of the fight against fascism acted strangely in hindering the publication of three chapters of a book that revealed in damning terms the brutalities and lies of Hitler's government. It sounded to him as though the porter, in all his near illiteracy, had answered him with the sophisticated, mocking laugh of the stage villain. He knew then that exhaustion was producing absurd fancies and he reconciled himself to sleep on the hard bed with his papers still missing, until, at least, the morning.

But he was woken from a deep sleep at three o'clock by one of the neat young men of the Congress secretariat who returned him his papers, as it seemed, complete. The guest who now occupied his former suite—an important guest from India—had found them in a drawer. He was grateful, Quentin said, for their discovery and re-turn, but not at all for the hour of return; and he went back to his bed in as rude dismissal as he could convey.

But the young man would not be dismissed. Could he see his pass-port, please? Certainly not. How long did his visa last? His visa had been extended for a further two weeks. He regretted that Mr. Mat-thews would not be able to make use of it. A complaint had been made against him by a woman delegate, a complaint of a most deli-cate nature. A Soviet colleague, another young woman, had indig-nantly confirmed that she had seen his behaviour. Such public con-duct under the revised Soviet Law . . . but the girl was willing not to press the charge. However, he must leave with the delegates by boat tomorrow; it was the least return surely that he could make for the hospitality of his hosts. He would not wish surely to smirch the name of social science; accommodation had been found for him on board.

But Quentin seemed all for smirching. Who was this woman? Since she was not preferring a charge, his hosts were not at liberty to say—but the young girl (Paulhard appeared to have regressed to pre-puberty) was a respected French delegate. They hoped he would not insist on making such an unpleasant incident public. After all, he might wish to return to the Soviet Union . . . He did not seem to be himself on this occasion. No doubt, next time he came to the

Soviet Union, where as always he was a good friend, he would be in better health, less liable to sick opinions. These sudden mental illnesses were not uncommonly the result of overwork. If he could offer advice Mr. Matthews would be wise to leave aside writing for reflection for a while; and, of course, to see his London doctor. And now, as it was already half past five, he suggested that Mr. Matthews dress and pack and occupy his cabin on the ship. He should introduce himself, Mr. Garamedian, yes, from the Armenian Republic, no, not a social scientist, an observer only at the Congress.

When he returned to London, responsibility and fun and games did not seem so sadly in conflict. He spoke in a debate at the Conway Hall, where his fierce attack on the ILP delegate's anti-sanctions warning was strongly supported from the platform by a Liberal Lord and a Trade Union leader, and loyally cheered by the Communists in the audience. Afterwards, in a continued debate with some of the audience in a Holborn pub, he picked up a young student from an art school and took her back to his flat in Brunswick Square. As the next day was Sunday they had a lot of time for fun. When, late next morning, about eleven, she stood, enchanting little waif, lost in the voluminous folds of his so-much-too-big-for-her spotted dressing-gown, inexpertly cooking sausages over his little gas stove, he got on beat all over again. And when she said, in a naïve schoolgirl's downright way, that, for her part, she couldn't see how it was possible to be anything but a Party member, to be anything else was a failure to comprehend the logic of history, he forced her into bed again, almost brutally. He thought with excitement of her reaction when she read his article the following Friday in *The New Statesman*, giving his analysis and his prophecies concerning hidden events in Russia.

The article, in fact, was inevitably conjectural, and its effect was not helped by editorial disagreement with its pessimistic forecasts. But when the full-scale news of the purge broke, his reputation was considerably enhanced. True, he was unable to report any of the subsequent trials firsthand, and even his most anti-Fascist speeches were coolly received by Party members in the audiences, but he was among the first to receive a top assignment from the *News Chronicle* when the Spanish war broke out. Above all, this double row with authority—first, like everyone else, with Germany, then on his own with Russia—gave him a greatly renewed vigour, an increased energy which seemed to him to be reflected in sexual potency—but that probably was just superstition.

At about the time when Quentin and Sally Sloman, art student and declared supporter of the CP (she never actually got round to asking for a card) were resting after their second orgasm, Regan was knocked down by a taxi in Victoria Street, up towards the Westminster Abbey end. She said later that it came at her sudden from behind out of the darkness like a blow from the Heavens; but the taxi driver said the old girl swerved off the pavement like she'd been knocked off with a hammer, and he couldn't brake in time. Whether, as the doctor thought possible, she might have swerved as a result of a slight stroke remained uncertain, for her injuries called for prior attention—she had suffered concussion, a broken wrist, multiple bruising, and a wound in the thigh that required five stitches; she was also very drunk. She was taken to Westminster Hospital. Her absence from 52 provoked an immediate crisis that was only settled temporarily when Marcus arranged a three months' cruise for his parents to the Canary Islands and to the Cape, and when all six of the Matthews children combined to send Regan for convalescence to Hastings after her discharge from hospital. As her sister Em said, thinking of the monstrous series of Regan's Saturday visits that had before the accident seemed only likely to end with life itself, "That taxi was a dispensation, really, for she'd got too old to be so lively."

The Russian Vine: An English Play

Scene: the back garden of No. 52, the house of Mr. and Mrs. William Matthews, a warm late September morning in 1935. CLARA MATTHEWS, *a smartly dressed woman of about sixty, is seated in a deck chair under a plane tree whose leaves are turning yellow. A rickety garden shed is weighed down by a vast, overgrown Russian vine which has clambered over the wall into the next garden. For the rest, the garden consists of weeds which throughout the act periodically shed their seeds in the breeze (this may be effected by means of bellows blown offstage) and two or three cane garden*

*chairs and a garden table in the last stages of desuetude. The back-
cloth represents the back façade of the house, from which a central
door opens out into the garden down a small flight of steps. Inter-
mittently the scene is punctuated with whistles of trains, screeching
of brakes, hooting of motor buses, and the noise of cats fighting. Mrs. Matthews is writing a letter, with her back to the audience. Although her figure is young, when she turns to face the
audience we see that a pair of youthful, glowing dark eyes look
out from a thin, ravaged face almost clownishly disguised with
make-up.*

CLARA MATTHEWS (*calling*): Billy! Billy! (*No answer comes from
the house and Clara Matthews gets up, when we see that her movements are agile and young. She is fashionably dressed, only her
greying shingle stamps her with the previous decade. She calls
again*) Billy! Billy!
(*A middle-aged, rather beery-looking woman puts her head out of
the door.*)

WOMAN: Ees barthin isself.

CLARA MATTHEWS: Bless his heart! He loves his long morning baths!
He gets inspiration in them, you know, Mrs. Hannapin.

MRS. HANNAPIN (*uncomprehendingly but darkly*): Ah! (*After a
pause*) Lady Alice Montague Douglas-Scott. That's her name. Ah,
well, it's better than foreigners, isn't it, mum?

CLARA MATTHEWS: Oh, nonsense, Mrs. Hannapin. Princess Marina
has wonderful style. (*She sits down and Mrs. Hannapin comes
down into the garden to gossip. On further appearance she proves
to be a slummocky, heavily breathing fat woman in a dirty old
apron and a woollen hat that seems like a dead cat.*) If they had
their way the poor boy would have to queue in the mornings for
his bath. And my dear little garden! Where would we get that
again in London? Has that Miss What's-her-name gone?

MRS. HANNAPIN: Oh, yes, mum. And the taxi man didn't arf grumble, carryin all that luggage down.

CLARA MATTHEWS: "Do we dress for dinner?" I ask you! I expect
they sat down in full evening dress to half a cutlet each at the
bishop's palace. Bishop's daughter indeed! Miss Gladys must be off
her head! I can just imagine the sort of cheese-paring we'd have
suffered. As well as the airs and graces! She'd only been here one
afternoon when she said that we didn't need cut flowers as well as

chrysanthemums in pots. I didn't say anything, Mrs. Hannapin, I couldn't. For my own daughter to send me someone who doesn't love flowers!

MRS. HANNAPIN: She took those chrysants you done in Miss Stoker's room and throwed em away. She said the water wasn't ealthy. "Don't worry, love," Regan told er, "I never drinks water."

CLARA MATTHEWS (*laughing down the scale*): Of course! Silly fool! She would get as good as she gave from Regan.

MRS. HANNAPIN: Well, mum, she didn't understand er. Or pretended not to. I don't know which. Not that I understand Miss Stoker too well these days. Not now er mouth's all gone crooked.

CLARA MATTHEWS: Oh, nonsense! I understand every word dear Regan says. The same dear old clown, she is! And they imagine we could live in this house without her! But you're all the same. You all exaggerate that accident. If it hadn't been for Mr. Matthews and me the poor old thing would be buried by now.

MRS. HANNAPIN: It's not the accident, mum, it's the stroke she ad at Astings that done it.

CLARA MATTHEWS: Hastings! How any children of mine could have been so mad as to choose Hastings. I knew before I opened the letter. There's something very psychic about the atmosphere of Cape Town. We were staying at the Mount Nelson. It's so charmingly situated under the mountain. And the view over Table Bay! The native boy always put fresh chicherinchees on my dressing-table. Oh, I wish you could have seen those chicherinchees, Mrs. Hannapin! Though they're not as beautiful as my dear old Russian vine. Miss Margaret used to call it the snow vine when she was a little girl. She'd already inherited her father's pen, you know. As if I could live without my Russian vine!

(*She pauses and sighs. As she seems to have lost the thread of her discourse,* MRS. HANNAPIN *feels it necessary to comment.*)

MRS. HANNAPIN: Ah! Dear old 52. I said to my usband the other day, for all that I've only been goin in daily for two years come March at Mrs. Matthews, I feel as though I've known that ouse a undred years.

CLARA MATTHEWS: You've been very loyal to us in all our tiresome upsets. Of course August was far from the month for Cape Town. Quite cold winds at times. *I'd* never have arranged to go there at that time. But Mr. Marcus would have it. He's in the smart set now, but that is not the same as being travelled. I know because my dear old Aunt Mouse was a *real* traveller! Do you know that ridiculous woman would have it that the piece of rock from Sinai came from Ararat! And there it is labelled in my dear aunt's own hand. Just because her father confirmed a lot of little boys with sticky heads in Jordan water or something. But I'm not going to get angry about her. She's gone. And, where was I? Oh, yes, such charming people—Sir George Latham, who'd been Governor of St. Vincent, and Mrs. Harcourt-Wemyss, who was quite an old friend of the Duchess of Buccleuch. And—so amusing—Renée Lamont; you remember she starred in *Going Up* and all those pretty shows. She lives permanently at the Mount Nelson now. But when I saw that letter on the breakfast table something told me. I said to Billy, "The children have done something silly." I couldn't eat my pawpaw. There was always pawpaw for breakfast. And there it was—a letter from Mr. Quentin to say they'd all got together and sent Regan to Hastings! To Hastings! I was nearly frantic. With that buoyant air and the cliffs! Of course I wasn't a bit surprised when we got the news at Las Palmas that she'd had this stroke. How is she getting on with luncheon?

MRS. HANNAPIN: Well, er legs drag somethin terrible and then all them grunts and groans. It's ard to know whether she's in pain or not.

CLARA MATTHEWS: Good heavens! No. All those grunts and groans as you call them are just Regan. Oh, dear, I don't know what I'd do without them. Those and Mr. Matthews' humming round the house. Heavens! There's eleven striking. Do pop down to the kitchen, Mrs. H., and make some coffee, there's a dear. I've got my three daughters coming. Quite an occasion! Although I'm afraid Miss Sukey and I are going to have words. Interfering with Regan's family life like that. But there you are—a schoolmaster's wife. I don't see her often, but she's got very bossy. (*As Mrs. Hannapin moves indoors, Mrs. Matthews calls her back.*) Oh, just before you go. What do you think of Mrs. Sankey's work? Is she thorough?

MRS. HANNAPIN: Oh, I wouldn't like to tell stories out of school, mum.

CLARA MATTHEWS (*grandly*): And I shouldn't want you to. But you
and she are working as a team now and it's only right that I should
know how you find her work.

MRS. HANNAPIN: Well, she does er best. But of course I appen to
know er ome circumstances. It's not only that Mr. S. is in one job
today and out the next. But there's the son . . .

CLARA MATTHEWS (*delightedly preparing herself to hear gossip*):
Ah, now, what about that famous son of hers?

MRS. HANNAPIN: Well, if you arsk me, ees a nasty piece of work.
My usband . . . (*But a ring on the bell interrupts them.*)

CLARA MATTHEWS: Oh, dear! That must be one of the girls! And I
was *so* interested. But another time. Go and answer the bell, will
you? And hurry the coffee up.

(*After Mrs. Hannapin goes out, Mrs. Matthews gets up, picks up a
handful of gravel from the path and with surprisingly youthful
agility throws it against one of the first-floor windows. The sash
window goes up slowly and the still handsome and boyish but now
very lined and red face of her husband* WILLIAM MATTHEWS *appears, his grey, curly hair dripping.*)

WILLIAM MATTHEWS (*singing loudly*): And we've fought the bear
before and we've fought the bare behind, and the Russians shall
not take Constantinople. We don't want to fight . . .

CLARA MATTHEWS: Billy! Billy! What will the neighbours say? (*But
at the idea of the neighbours he pulls a solemn parsonical face, and
they both burst out laughing.*) Oh, Billy! You're impossible. One
of the girls has arrived already. What will they think? You don't
want to appear lazier than you are. Still in the bath and the morning half over. And, oh, Billy, it's so beautiful out here in our dear
garden. The Russian vine's still a mass of flower and the plane
tree . . .

(*As she speaks her eldest daughter,* GLADYS MATTHEWS, *a fortyish
woman, handsome, well proportioned, in a black suit with a silver
fox fur over one shoulder, appears at the back door*)

GLADYS MATTHEWS: Who on earth's that terrible old creature who
answered the bell, Mother? All the faces seem to be changed these
days. Where's Miss Agnew?

CLARA MATTHEWS: Oh, my dear Gladys, she didn't do at all. I dare
say she's very good at harvest festival and that sort of thing. But

neither your father nor I have ever been church-goers. No, I should take her off your books, dear, if I were you. Just look at our old plane tree, Gladys. Do you remember how Rags used to chase the leaves at this time of the year? Some people think autumn a sad time, but I've never felt that. To me it's always been a coming-home time. All those holidays with old Granny M. at Cromer, everything so stiff and formal, all you children hushed at the least thing—how glad we all were to get back. I used to have a phrase for it—we'll loosen our stays. That was in the days of stays. (*She calls up to the window*) Do you remember, Billy? Loosen our stays? Billy! Billy! (*But Mr. Matthews has shut the window again.*)

GLADYS MATTHEWS: No, I can't say I do. I always enjoyed myself at Granny's. Anyway, what *are* you sitting in the yard for? And what do you mean you've sent Miss Agnew away?

CLARA MATTHEWS: Just that, dear. Sent her away. Oh, quite politely. Anyway, I think she saw as well as I did that it would never do. She's a semi-evening, dear. And I could never fit in with that class. For me it's either real evening dress or any old thing that's comfortable.

GLADYS MATTHEWS: Really, Mother, this is not a question of clothes. I was trying to get you a first-rate housekeeper to take everything off your hands now that Regan's no longer with you.

CLARA MATTHEWS: Oh, but she is, darling. Your father and I went down to Clapham two days ago and fetched her back in a taxi.

GLADYS MATTHEWS: You've brought her back here?

CLARA MATTHEWS: Where else, dear? This is her home.

(*While they are talking, Mrs. Rootham*—MARGARET MATTHEWS *—has appeared in the doorway. Tall and thin, she has already developed her own individual, eccentric manner of dressing at thirty-five. Her high black turban, shaped like a chef's hat, has magenta tulle hanging from it—forerunner of the snoods to come? Her long, black Indian-lamb coat has a military cut. She wears magenta gloves.*)

MARGARET MATTHEWS: Whose home, Countess? For heaven's sake, there's enough people to support here without succouring the strangers from the street.

CLARA MATTHEWS: The stranger from the street! You call the woman who gave her whole life to you children a stranger!

GLADYS MATTHEWS: It's Regan, Maggie. They've brought her back here.

MARGARET MATTHEWS: Oh, no! But she's an invalid, Mother. What were her family doing to let her go?

CLARA MATTHEWS: Her family were doing what I told them. I've never liked that sister of hers, but she's a respectful creature when it comes down to it. I hope, by the way, dears, that *you* two were not party to Susan's cruel idea of sending Regan away like that.

MARGARET MATTHEWS: I didn't think of it, but I approved.

GLADYS MATTHEWS: It was Sukey's idea. And it was jolly good of her to go down there and arrange it all.

(MR. MATTHEWS *appears at the door, dressed very neatly in grey Harris tweeds, grey foulard bow tie, grey spats, and tawny brogues, but he walks a little arthritically and uses a Malacca cane to aid him down the steps. He sings as he comes, but as his wife begins to speak, he stops.*)

CLARA MATTHEWS: Billy, these girls were part of the plot to shut poor Regan up in that horrible little house in Clapham.

WILLIAM MATTHEWS (*starting to sing again*): And the Russians shall not take Constantinople. Morning, Podge. (*He kisses Gladys.*) You sent us a dragon, but your Mother's slain her. Morning, Maggie. (*He kisses her.*) I got your last from *Mudie's*, dear, but it was too long. Condense your narrative, my dear. Read Maupassant. *Bel Ami*, there's your model. Or that old fraud's "Esther Waters." You try to put in all this atmosphere. That's all right for the big chaps, the Russians, Chekhov, Tolstoy, but we lesser fry must stick to hard work and art. So you thought it was your duty to take a poor old sick mare out of the sweet hay she's been stabled in all her life, and dump her down among a lot of strangers who happen to bear the same surname. And you're supposed to be a fighter against convention, Maggie. Why, poor old Regan . . .

(*Mrs. Hannapin appears in the doorway with her tray of coffee.*)

CLARA MATTHEWS: *Pas devant les domestiques*, Billy, *s'il vous plaît.*

(*Billy Pop stops talking, but as he drinks his coffee, he hums loudly through their conversation.*)

MRS. HANNAPIN: The other lady's gone to tidy erself.

CLARA MATTHEWS: Oh, how like Susan. Thank you, Mrs. Hannapin. You and Miss Stoker have got cups of coffee, I hope?

MRS. HANNAPIN: Oh, yes, thank you. And she's gettin on ever so nice drinkin out of the cup erself now—with a guidin and, of course. (*She goes.*)

(*Mrs. Pascoe—*SUKEY—*appears in the doorway. She is dressed in a pepper-and-salt coat and skirt with sensible shoes, under her coat a navy-blue jumper, a string of pearls, a small navy-blue hat with matching eye veil—her "visit to London" clothes.*)

SUKEY PASCOE: Mother! Father! It's disgraceful! I've seen her. She no more ought to be in the kitchen than she should be flying an airship. And that old creature who opened the door to me is nearly as bad. And after all the trouble and tact I used to get her family to take her in. Haven't you any sense of responsibility?

CLARA MATTHEWS: I thought you were meant to be tidying yourself, Susan, not spying in my kitchen.

MARGARET MATTHEWS: Now, Countess, you know very well Sukey's never been called Susan.

CLARA MATTHEWS: Don't interfere, Wendy. Your father and I were the ones who christened her Sukey. Now I'm calling her by another name. Responsibility! It's you girls who've forgotten all you owe to that woman. To dump her down in a back street in Clapham. After all the years of fun she's had with us here. And the ugliness of that dreadful little slum house. It almost makes one understand why Quentin went Bolshie. Why here she's got the garden. All this beauty! Do you see that your snow vine's flowering, Margaret?

SUKEY PASCOE: Mother! Don't be absurd. What is going to become of this house with old creatures like that looking after it?

MARGARET MATTHEWS: Yes, Mother, really, you know, you cannot run a house this size on a half-paralysed cook and a slummocky charwoman.

GLADYS MATTHEWS: And we'd all arranged to pay Miss Agnew. She'd have taken the whole thing off your shoulders.

CLARA MATTHEWS (*a little daunted by this triple attack*): There's an excellent woman, Mrs. Sankey, who's to come in and get Regan's supper. W're not expecting Regan to cook more than once a day. And if your father and I don't feel like going out, we can always have a lobster mayonnaise or some oysters sent over from Overton's.

SUKEY PASCOE: The place will get like a pigsty.

GLADYS MATTHEWS: Miss Agnew said Regan herself really needed a nurse.

MARGARET MATTHEWS: You'd much better let us sell up and get you a good suite in a hotel.

WILLIAM MATTHEWS (*singing*): And the Russians shall not take Constantinople! We don't want to fight, my dears, but by jingo if we do . . . (*Kissing his wife*) You've fought the bare behind, my dear, haven't you? No, my dears, we're not going to be tidied up. We love our old 52. "I love it, I love it, and who shall dare to keep me from my old arm-chair?" Your mother used to recite that when I first knew her. In drawing-rooms. Brought tears to my eyes.

CLARA MATTHEWS (*giggling despite herself*): I never did, Billy! You dreadful liar. Anyone would think I was born before the Flood.

SUKEY PASCOE (*bursting into their flirting*): Well, I've never known anything so irresponsible. And cruel. Poor old Regan! I'll tell you this, both of you, even if you get into such a state here that you have the Council condemning the house, I'm not going to involve myself. The trouble I took. Coming up to town, then all the way down to Clapham, when P. S. has been frightfully seedy.

CLARA MATTHEWS: I see no reason why you interfered, Susan. You don't help your father and me like the others. No, Margaret, I must speak out. We know your husband only earns a pittance at that school and then you've the boys, but the fact is you contribute nothing, so you've no call to interfere.

GLADYS MATTHEWS: Oh, Mother, really. We all do what we can.

CLARA MATTHEWS: It's hardly your father's fault or mine if the government has reduced our income to nothing. (*She is almost tearful.*)

WILLIAM MATTHEWS: Now, now, my dear. They all mean well but they've none of them the feeling for life that we have. We knew the world as it was before the crash. Feelings have coarsened since then.

SUKEY PASCOE (*explaining on the side to Margaret*): I'm glad to say the time hasn't been entirely wasted, Mag. Hugh's buying a partnership. I've at last got him to see that it's impossible to go on with the awful Great Man. I didn't mind Senior and Middleman. But P.S. is very highly strung and I couldn't have anyone telling me how we should educate our children. But with our own school, P.S. won't live with the other boarders. He'll be like a day-boy. I've been to Gabbitas, the agents. And there's a school in Kent. It just suits because the present head's wife doesn't want me to be involved with the school at all. So there's no question of my having to fuss with other people's children. On the other hand, Mr. Carver, that's the head, quite understood that I should want P.S. living at home. Hugh may fuss, but Senior and Middleman are away as boarders at public school now, which is quite enough. Don't ever marry a schoolmaster, Mag. One has to spend so much time keeping them in their place. Not that Hugh isn't an old dear. But he's such a stick-in-the-mud. Just because he's been at St. Aidan's so long. Men are such sentimentalists!

CLARA MATTHEWS: You've the money to buy schools then. Have the Pascoes suddenly become so rich?

SUKEY PASCOE: If you want to know the truth, Mother, hard though you may find it to believe, I've saved the money out of what you call Hugh's pittance. That's one thing 52 did for me. It taught me how to save. Hugh's quite happy with pocket-money for his old tobacco. And then there was the little that Granny left me.

CLARA MATTHEWS: Which should have gone to your father. Well, it should, Billy. I never was so upset as when I heard about your mother's will.

WILLIAM MATTHEWS: Never mind that. My old mother left me something almost as precious as money. All the family albums. They've proved an invaluable mnemonic for my memoirs. You girls haven't seen them yet. A world without eternal talk of doles and dictators. (*Exit.*)

CLARA MATTHEWS (*looking round the weeds and rubbish*): And your father was so upset at the time. But troubles to him are like water off a duck's back. When I think of what a happy, free home this was for you all. London children brought up in all this peace and quiet. We must have been a family in a thousand! All this talk about self-expression nowadays. Your father and I had discovered that for you children years and years ago. And now . . . I can't think how things have gone with you as they have.

SUKEY PASCOE: Oh, don't talk such nonsense, Mother. I know I've only brought up a family, though that's something too. But all the others have done very well. Maggie and Rupert are quite famous.

Hugh's friend Trevor Plowright has a sister who reads all your works, Maggie. And anyone who's employed matrons knows of Gladys's agency.

GLADYS MATTHEWS: It won't be mine much longer.

CLARA MATTHEWS: It hasn't been for some time, has it, dear? I mean not your own.

GLADYS MATTHEWS: Well, no. But in any case, I'm leaving. I'm starting up my own business with antiques.

MARGARET MATTHEWS: Antiques! Gladys! How fascinating!

GLADYS MATTHEWS: Well, I'm getting to be a bit of an antique myself.

CLARA MATTHEWS: Chop and change, chop and change. And Margaret's divorce!

MARGARET MATTHEWS: There's no question of divorce, Mother, only . . . Oh, you mean my divorce from *Ralph*. Darling! That's ancient history.

CLARA MATTHEWS: It doesn't make it any less sad, Margaret. And then Rupert. What does he want to appear in this miserable Russian play for? Anne Faulkner White went to a matinee and she said with the best will in the world she could hardly sit through it. And the theatre was half empty. A few terrible cranks in beards and beads. When I think how fine he looked in those amusing plays with Alma Grayson. Things one could really recommend to one's friends. That first night of *The Other Menage!* I shall never forget it. Lady Diana Cooper and Lady Louis Mountbatten! I really felt one of you had arrived. Of course, Marcus is apparently in the so-called smart set. It amuses me to see his name in William Hickey's gossip column. Your father and I went through all that when you were children. And our dear old plane tree would soon be cut down if Quentin's Bolshie friends had their way. To make way for some wretched crèche or other. No, I don't think Billy and I could possibly have seen how far away you all would drift from the simple, happy way of living we've tried to give you. (*Although the three sisters have once or twice caught each others' eyes during their mother's speech and even had to suppress a giggle, as the yellowing leaves flutter down over them and the smoke from a near-by bonfire drifts across the garden a mood of sadness settles upon them. Margaret sighs, Gladys shifts uneasily in her rickety chair, even Sukey shuts her eyes in an unwonted moment of tiredness.*)

CLARA MATTHEWS (*observing them with satisfaction*): Oh, I didn't mean to depress you girls. You've had your own lives and you've chosen to live them the way you have. You mustn't be affected by my feelings for a quieter, more spacious way of living. It's only an old woman's mood.

SUKEY PASCOE (*pulling herself together*): And a very stupid one! Ugh! sitting in this falling-to-pieces old yard! (*She shivers.*)

(WILLIAM MATTHEWS *has come down the steps again. And now he puts in front of his three daughters a large photo-album open at a particular page.*)

WILLIAM MATTHEWS: Do you remember this? "I shouldn't have paid a guinea for *this* fowl. It's jolly tough." And you were quite right, Podge. A guinea fowl's a beastly table bird.

GLADYS MATTHEWS: Was I really as fat as that?

CLARA MATTHEWS: You were a Glaxo baby.

SUKEY PASCOE: You always looked so neat though, Gladys. Do you remember, Mag, how we used to call her the sleek rook? And we were the scarecrows.

MARGARET MATTHEWS: It was because you had that black coat, Gladys. Terribly sophisticated for a girl of ten!

CLARA MATTHEWS: Not at all. Black coats were in for little girls. Besides, it had a white fur collar. I should never have let a child of mine be dressed in too grown up a fashion.

GLADYS MATTHEWS: Look! Marcus after that party when he was sick at Cromer!

WILLIAM MATTHEWS: My dear old mother's idea of food for children was not exactly . . .

(*The scene fades as the falling leaves and bonfire smoke turn to a delicate rose pink. We hear the voices, excited, nostalgic, reminiscent through the haze. Then gradually the sound of a barrel organ playing the dear old tunes grows louder and with it the mists clear to reveal the group still bent over the album.*)

MARGARET MATTHEWS: Mouse was tremendously elegant, you know. It was part of an immense sureness about our culture and our right to take it to any desert or jungle we chose.

SUKEY PASCOE: Dear Granny! No old ladies would wear those black velvet ribbons round their necks now. Everyone's too frightened of belonging to the past. But Granny M. never cared. She was much too sure of everything she believed in.

GLADYS MATTHEWS: Look! A photo of poor old Regan in her Sunday best. She was really jolly good-looking, you know, when she was young. And the cheeky look in her eye. They may have known their place in those days, but Lord! what fun they had with the antics of their lords and masters!

WILLIAM MATTHEWS: And here. Look at that! In this very garden. A family photo. Don't we look a rare old rickety rackety crew. I've got an amusing story about Phil May in my memoirs, by the way. But *this* must have been about the time of the Wild West Exhibition. We still had a rockery then.

CLARA MATTHEWS: Yes, and the laburnum was still living that we'd put in when we were first married. Oh, Billy!

WILLIAM MATTHEWS: This calls for a celebration. I'll open a bottle of Bristol Cream. (*Exit.*)

(*The barrel organ grows almost deafeningly loud.*)

CLARA MATTHEWS: There they go. They're Welsh miners. I always give to them. Soon there won't be any unemployed. And we shan't have our gay little tunes in the morning. I hope Quentin and his friends will be satisfied. Oh, I must take them some coppers before they get too far down the street. (*Exit.*)

SUKEY PASCOE (*turning over a page*): What a revolting little creature with that common smile! It's that awful little American of hers. What was his name? You know, the one that Marcus spat at.

MARGARET MATTHEWS: Sue, did you know he made a pass at me? It was her fault. She would make me teach him the slow fox. And then she saw and she was in one of her rages with me for days.

GLADYS MATTHEWS: Look, there's Marcus with that poor cat that was run over.

SUKEY PASCOE: Leonora! Oh, I don't think I've ever been so unhappy as I was over those kittens.

MARGARET MATTHEWS: Will really does look disreputable, doesn't he? He's put on what we used to call the "patting" smile! The one he used when he patted our friends from school.

SUKEY PASCOE: Did I ever tell you that he patted Mary Crowe's bottom and she slapped him? She did! Thank goodness being his daughters kept him away from *us*.

GLADYS MATTHEWS: It didn't save me.

SUKEY MATTHEWS: Gladys! He never!

MARGARET MATTHEWS: Really? Oh, Gladys, darling, how absolutely hateful. And how typical of his slyness and your courage that we never knew . . .

GLADYS MATTHEWS: Wet Sunday afternoons I used to feel as though I were in prison.

SUKEY MATTHEWS: The dirt had worked into the grease in corners of the kitchen in a way I shall never forget . . .

MARGARET MATTHEWS: Trying so desperately always to make some sense of those rare moments of beauty when one came up for air . . .

(*The smoke seems to close in again and through it we hear the three sisters' voices as when they were girls.*)

THE THREE SISTERS IN CHORUS: Now we shall never get away from 52.

GLADYS: Alfred in apologetic secrecy will make up for a spinster-hood of cutting up food cards.

SUKEY: I shall stand in the squalid kitchen clearing my little space for fresh vegetables and greaseless meat and I shall dream of manor houses and ordered voices and little creatures properly cared for.

MARGARET: They will tread on my toes, my feet will ache, my back will burn, but my fancy will be mocking their clumsiness, their platitudes, their vulgar genteelism.

(*From the house behind them we hear the voices of their parents.*)

BILLY POP: Humour's the great leaven in life's heavy dough.

THE COUNTESS: And wit gives sparkle to the flattest wine.

(*Encouraged, the three sisters respond and through the mist we hear new voices.*)

OLD GRANNY SUKEY: There's such a lot to smile at as one looks back and even tears have their own salty tang.

MISS MARGARET MOUSE: Elizabeth Carmichael liked at times to think of her father and mother as an inexhaustible treasure house, but artistic honesty forced her to admit that even their store of vulgar pretension, unbridled selfishness, and capricious affection was ultimately limited.

REGAN THE PODGE: What price Gladys Matthews Limited as a name? Limited? I don't fink. Twice round er once round the Albert all.

(*She ends with a pantomime dame's exit laugh. Then all at once more sighs. But now the smoke and fuzz gradually clear. The sisters shake themselves, open their eyes, and rub them.*)

SUKEY PASCOE (*getting up briskly*): I ought to be at Harrod's . . . Senior's decided he must have a lounge suit and if I'm not there, heaven knows what terrible garment he'll choose.

MARGARET MATTHEWS: But, darling, John's nearly sixteen, isn't he? Surely . . .

SUKEY PASCOE: My dear Maggie, he's not French, thank heaven. English boys are never grown up until they've left school.

MARGARET MATTHEWS: I wonder if they ever do. Well, I've got an agent's lunch.

GLADYS MATTHEWS: And I, believe it or not, have to go to a museum to learn the difference between Chelsea and Bow.

(*Exeunt.*)

(*A moment later Billy Pop returns bearing a tray with sherry and glasses, followed by the Countess. They look at the empty chairs in surprise.*)

THE COUNTESS: Well! It couldn't be, Billy, surely, that they've actually decided to run their *own* lives instead of ours.

BILLY POP: I think, my dear, that for once the piper went on strike. And we're calling our own tune. That surely demands a celebration.

3 ⊕ 1937-1938

"The Comic Spirit is indeed wonderful and mysterious in her workings. To hear something that has been a familiar feature of one's youth hailed by the younger generation as a startling modern phenomenon is one of those recurring situations that bring a discreet twinkle to the eye or a hastily suppressed twitch to the risible nerves of the lips of most septuagenarians at one time or another. Such is the present . . ." But supposing the twitches were no longer under one's control, supposing they came and went not at the mysterious dictation of the Comic Spirit but as the physiologically explicable decline of senescent motor and vascular systems. Then surely one ought not to be alone. Autumn, sad autumn, the autumn of one's life, season of mellow fruitlessness—and in truth he had seldom been writing more smoothly, more easily; but autumn was only a prelude.

At the end she had lain down there in that little room with but one eye still alive in that cheery, cockney, little body. Oh, *she'd* have battled on even if *they'd* thrown in the sponge and let the authorities cart her off to hospital, for she had had the tough self-reliance of the streets.

"Such is the present crude wave of anti-Semitism in Germany, released by him who must surely be the world's most tedious and offensive house-painter, Adolf Schickelgruber. To hear the young of today talk, persecution of the Jews would seem to be a peculiar and virulent disease of the nineteen thirties instead of one of the oldest plagues man is heir to. In my own young days, we were not without the croaking warnings of Mr. Hilaire Belloc and the most rumbustious doubts of Chesterton. Splendid, gifted writers—masters indeed of the essay form, witty polemicists, acrobats of paradox—yet they had bees in their bonnets, bees, as it seemed, with hooked noses and

Ikey Mo gestures. The material wealth of our far-flung Empire, the Kimberley Diamond era, the Mammon of High Finance, even the vulgarity that surrounded Edward VII's court were often unattractive, and with this world the names of Joel and of Cassel were closely associated and have to bear some of the odium. . . ."

Written words echo round an empty house and give off hollow reverberations which make it hard to keep going, hard to forget that you could lie here for days—no, in fairness to Clara and not to let one's imagination become fevered, not days at all, but hours—before she came back from her blessed bridge parties. "I shall only be gone for a few hours, Billy. We cut for the last rubber at half past ten." But that was all very well; those were the hours that mattered.

The room was hot, almost stifling, but August was cold this year like autumn. It must be something else than the room that was oven hot. Who knew when the oven's heat, flooding through the veins, would send the blood pounding to the head, when the room—his old study desk, the see-no-evil monkeys, the *Encyclopaedia Britannica*, and the bound copies of the *Savoy* and of *Wisden*—would fly round in the crazy fireworks revolution of a Catherine wheel, to stop at last in black darkness, sudden and complete . . . "the odium that undoubtedly attached to a mammon-worshipping City of London and a meretricious high society in what Henry James, in one of his more unreadable later efflorescences, called *The Awkward Age* (if only the Master's words had had half the pithy wit of his titles!).

"But with or without its grain of truth to feed it, anti-Semitism certainly flourished in some circles of pre-1914 literary London. Foremost among its exponents was T. W. H. Crosland, the now almost forgotten but able and picturesque editor of *The Academy*. I first met Crosland when he was editor of the short-lived *English Review*. He struck me at once as a most plausible ruffian, but then the reader who has borne with me so far in my reminiscent peregrinations will have realized by now that I have a very soft spot for ruffians. Crosland was . . ."

He was dead, and forgotten, though there was probably a widow about the place somewhere. How would she like it, when someone else in fifty years' time (perhaps also in the supporting degradation of crutches) wrote of W. A. Matthews that he was dead and forgotten, though there was probably a widow about the place somewhere? A widow might be about the place, but a wife wasn't. Well, who could tell if this furnace were to burst . . . "Mr. W. A. Matthews, the author, was found dead today . . ."

"Crosland was a born journalist but less evidently intended by nature for an editor. I always thought that Crosland and Alfred Douglas were about the most ill-assorted partners since Codlin and Short. Yet both, even Douglas whom I never cared for, had guts, could stand on their own. They had one trait in common—their love of abuse. And it was on the libel suits that resulted from this love that *The English Review* foundered. Nevertheless their partnership, while it lasted . . ." was a good one.

It wasn't only self-pity that made his imagination fill the empty house with the sudden swish of her skirt as she turned, with her usual nimble rapidity, even now at damn near sixty-five, round some corner, and entered through the door of some room. He could hear the peculiar silky quality of that swishing sound as he had heard it now for over forty years, like no other woman's. He could see at intervals the quick flash of her legs, never perhaps again so excitingly shapely after short skirts had revealed them to other men's eyes. He could smell her scent, something French—he couldn't remember its name —that had never changed over the years, although now and again in recent times he had smelt tiredness, age, death in her wake, or was it his own smell he put on to her? Did he seek to take her with him? To break such a partnership after so long would be the cruellest side of it. He didn't want to go alone into an emptiness—or to be left behind to the mercy of others, not knowing his lore, for a man acquires his lore over the years. He banished the thought by calling her up from every corner, not only the swish of her skirt and her perfume, but the occasional, increasingly frequent click of a joint, the little cough that nowadays accompanied the tick-tack of her heels up the stairs, the turning of taps, the flushing of the lavatory cistern, the half-click of doors to be followed by the louder sound of their closing, the *arpeggios* with which she prefaced her piano playing. Oh, why didn't she come home?

"Yet their particular partnership while it lasted was fruitful for English letters if not for the writers who contributed to their journal. My own first contribution to *The Academy* was an article on the Surrey of Meredith's novels. After long waiting there came a rather grubby reply from Crosland asking me to visit his offices— somewhere in the City, near the then fairly recent Queen Victoria

Street, if I am not mistaken. Apart from meeting a few literary cronies every week at the Cheshire Cheese in Fleet Street, I did not as a rule penetrate London east of Temple Bar, to me the very symbol of the Forsyteism of my childhood—though of course, like most young writers of the time, I had been lured to look at Limehouse and at Stepney by Jack London's God-given prose and had peeped at the Jewish East End brought to life by Zangwill's colourful pen. I therefore climbed the stairs on that particular afternoon with a certain resentment, which was not decreased when a stentorian Yorkshire voice from within the office answered my knocking by 'Come in, blast you.' "

And there was her key in the Yale lock; he would have known it from all others—did in the days when the children had their own keys—she seemed to take more time to insert it, to scratch around the lock almost as if she'd had one over the eight. Of course, a woman all over, she wouldn't confess that she needed glasses. But that she was home, that was the main thing; he was no longer alone. There it was, that rustling, an inexplicable noise that set you speculating and made concentration on the page before you impossible. If he asked her, of course, as he often had, she would reply, "What noise? I was just coming in at the front door, that's all. You speak as though I were the piano-remover." This, when the piano had not been moved since they entered the house a quarter of a century ago, so that she couldn't know what noises such a man (if there were one) made. This feminine absurdity, this inconsequentiality was what made her so special. And now she was home and he wasn't alone. He pushed aside his manuscript book and was about to call her when he heard her heels tapping on the floor-boards of the landing above. What had she gone upstairs for? Probably to pee, of course. Her bladder wasn't what it was, though she wouldn't admit it. She had a tiresome genteel side. But no noise of water flushing came. Perhaps she'd lost badly at cards and was about to seek refuge in playing the piano. He steeled himself for the *arpeggios*, but they did not come. He determined to put her out of his head, to live as though the house were his alone, only so could he write with the flow that memoirs (bears all its sons away) demanded.

"The man that stood before me was not prepossessing. He was tall, well over six feet I should think, with a corporation and the familiar heavy moustache of those days. To crown all, he was dressed in what seemed (and probably was) as incongruous a collection of second-hand garments as could have been purchased from the street markets of London so much more evident than today."

But now she was tapping her way downstairs. She could hardly have given a more exact aural account of her movements if she had been blind with a white stick. For a moment, with the word "blind," some fears he had not known since a child came to him. Someone would open the door, but it would not be she; it would be a hideous creature with black glasses and a tapping white stick who lured children. He shook himself. These tedious background noises! No wonder he had written "the man that stood before me," vulgar journalese, and "corporation," a tired piece of facetious verbiage. With such pervasive noises! And now that cough! *Uck uck. Uck uck.* If she'd got phlegm on her chest, why couldn't she hawk it up and be done with it? All this gentility. She had reached the kitchen now. He tensed his body to resist the clashing of crockery, the banging of saucepans. To relax his tension he carefully shut up his manuscript book and capped his fountain pen. No noise came. And a moment later she was with him.

"Here's your hot toddy," she said.

"Did you have a good evening?" he asked and he smiled up at her.

"I won the last two rubbers," she said. "I cut both times with a Mr. Isaacs, a new member. I'm not fond of the chosen race as a whole, but they always play a very good game of bridge."

Margaret woke to the sound of an aeroplane overhead.

Her first thought was that whatever they all said—comforting newspapers, well-informed old clubmen, ladies with nephews in the diplomatic service, family solicitors seeing one to the door, poets who respected the Germans as fighting men, above all, Douglas acting nanny-comforter to her distressed senses—there *would* be war. She tried to say, without fear, "And so there ought to be. Against such evil." Then, banishing all unreal seeming certainty of war, the book's problem came full before her. Its form; but its form was its statement. She had lived too long with Alice Cameron and her attendant nieces, so that now greedy expectancy seemed also justified hope of reward, as the pitiable anxious concerns of old age seemed often a hideous selfishness. Self-pity was pathos; hardness, noble pride. In the light of old Alice's sterling bawdry her nieces were genteel rubbish; in the light of those fading spinsters' sensitivity old Alice was a vulgar, greedy harpy. Upon who narrated certainly depended everything.

The figures properly related would give the answer. Yet it was not the easy balance of a bit of A and a bit of B, and if that seemed too simple, the addition of a little C to blur the too-hard outlines. All voices meant no voices; an all-round view looked out on a blank wall. Supposing Jessica were to narrate, and yet, through her report of Nancy's reactions to old Alice, the ironic truth of the old woman's view should itself emerge—no, that would not do, for then Alice, the bullied old woman, would be the central victim and all her past bullying of the faded, genteel nieces would be ignored. If each of Alice's humiliations were balanced by the recall of her past despotic insensitivity, then . . . but flashbacks were no answer, for past and present must be made one. When the nieces cruelly kept the bedridden, witty old sinner from company, then they suffered again *and at that moment* her mockery of their first girlish pangs of love. In time-structure B *was* A, A *was* B. But these letters had once been three full human beings whom she had slowly and at such cost brought into existence. Now in this formal search they were being petrified into figures and lettered proportions. She banished A, B, and C and set all her thoughts, all her feelings, painfully to make the three women joyously live again. Thus: Alice Cameron, now seventy-five, rich, arthritic, property in Birmingham, South African mining shares, Argentine Railways, once the actress-mistress of the Duke of M., then of Barney Woolf, millionaire . . . No, that was only another kind of figures.

Letting her bed-jacket fall from her still well-shaped shoulders as though she were settling into her box at the opera, she picked up the silver-backed hand-mirror from the side table and found everything surprisingly well. A very small touch of eye shadow—her left pupil had always been a fraction larger than . . . but now, well, for an old woman of seventy-six greeting her solicitor . . . But he was more than that—he had been very . . . not handsome but *soigné*, amusing and worldly, and he'd been madly in love with her. Oh, that had been clear at that dinner at Romano's, though he'd tried to hide it for fear of being hurt. She would tease him a little now. Her hands trembled at the . . . But would they never bring him up? She rang and rang furiously. "Where's Lionel?" "Oh, Auntie, did you want to see him? I'm afraid . . ."

She began once again to feel the anger of the lively old woman who had so much to say—stinging, witty things about these soft-shoed, whispering, genteel ghost women—who could hear voices downstairs—"Who was that? Why am I not told?" "Only the post-man, Auntie, nothing for you." Oh, yes, she could feel it all again now. She could put it on paper if wanted, where it would flow—but to where was it flowing? She was back then to form and figures and moral shapes. Old Alice was the victim, but the victim of her own victims—so what could one do but stand outside, an ironic, Godlike judge? Yet to do so seemed to ignore the fact that the old woman suffered—and so did the nieces. A victim was a victim. To be one alone was to uphold one's right to the inner poetry, yet to be one alone was also to be an insufficient human being. To be two was the start of all human fulfilment; and also of all gangs and conspiracies. Once again she was drifting from old Alice's powder-thick flesh into abstractions. Books were not written in the insomnia of the small hours, or at any rate, not hers.

Deliberately she thought of the speech she was to make to Gladys's professional women. Should the appeal be the usual warn-ing of the totalitarian menace? If professional women were like business-men, abstract liberty would not be their rallying cry. Per-haps like herself, like Gladys, they would be childless, then she must reach the same sentiment in them for these refugee children that she knew was in herself. If she could let herself go for once, not to be afraid to wallow a little, avoid the barbed remark. Surely if ever irony was not called for it was in the cause of these wretched, refu-gee, Basque children. Why not? Mockery was the best weapon . . . If now she could show old Alice mocking her nieces, and yet some-how mock the mocker, for goodness knew perpetual irony had its own absurdity. But how?

Oh, she must sleep. Sleep as Douglas's gentle breathing showed that he slept. Every night in that divan bed not two feet away from her he slept the gentle sleep of a gentle man; and she the victim of his gentleness. How could she bring the conflict, the anger, the cru-elty of these trapped women to life while he smoothed out all wrin-kles, turned away all wrath, negotiated all tricky corners, smothered her in the softness of his feathered decency, her dear old goose, her murderer. She felt the flush and trembling of anger that came over her nowadays with sudden consciousness that she was the victim of a victim. With Ralph there had been no smothering kindness, but a constant renewal of the body by battle. There was no end to the passion *then* in her writing. What was she trying to kindle some old woman's embers for? She should be writing about men, about their bodies, about the way our bodies answered theirs, about the courage and heroism that lay in the line of a man's shoulders or the curl of his mouth and set the heart beating, the blood rushing to the head—no matter how he treated one. The real values lay not in words and emotions and memories but in the movements and responses of the bodies, of two bodies—a man's and woman's. All the rest was old woman's talk and old maid's defences.

"Oh, no doubt there was a very undesirable element in the early days. Mostly in the S.A. A friend of mine tells me it came as the greatest shock to Herr Hitler himself when he . . ."

"I've no doubt at all of the fairness of the *Lebensraum* argument. Besides, I always look back to the visits of courtesy I used to pay as Commissioner into Togoland before 1914. The whole place was a model of what a colony should be. If one compares the shambles of the Portuguese or the Belgians or even the French . . ."

"Of course, you have to realize that they're quite different to the sort of Jews we come across here. In Frankfurt, or in Vienna, for that matter, since Versailles, you've had to be a Jew to have any hope of . . ."

"Yes, Tony's at Westminster with the ambassador's son. We met the father at the Latin play. A very distinguished man and a connoisseur of wine. I felt that he was *personally* so very upset by the tone of some of our newspapers . . ."

"They're largely the creation, of course, of men who had no understanding whatsoever of Balkan history."

"I only wish our young people were anything like the same good ambassadors for us . . ."

"No, in the original *Mein Kampf* there's no mention of any *British* colonies. The English translations are all *very* unreliable."

"Shared their plum pudding and holly across no-man's-land. Of course that didn't suit international finance at all well."

"Had the cheek to ask our Prince of Wales, as he was then, to sit down to dinner with this Jew who'd robbed the Post Office at Tiflis. We should never have recognized them after 'seventeen."

"I went prepared to scoff but I damn near stayed to pray. The extraordinary piercing blue of the man's eyes—I happened to look his way as the torch-bearer came into the arena . . ."

"It seems there was a slaughter-house for cattle near-by. That was the simple origin of this righteous Boston schoolma'am's story. But, of course, torture of the Jews is probably half round the United States by now. There's nothing the Americans like better than moral indignation."

"Oh, Professor Crawford's so interesting on that. Genealogy's his subject. The Churchill stock is at least a quarter Jewish. Didn't you know? Oh, they don't all advertise themselves with names like Leopold Amery."

As Marcus elbowed his way to where an ancient maid was pouring out drinks, these bursts of conversation came to him from every corner of the large, stuffy, Edwardian room—from among the pretty-pretty blue of hydrangeas, from behind Japanese screens, from out the faded charm of Hokusai prints, from under innumerable gilded rococo tables . . . He, so unpolitical, so undereducated, could hardly have understood them, but, aesthete, he found the noises most disagreeable. He felt himself among overfed toads and elegant, spitting snakes, each giving out its own kind of venom. The snakes were tall, emaciated women, of the kind called "society," with too much rouge and long ear-rings, or thin, well-groomed greying men of military or diplomatic appearance; the toads were fat, double-chinned old women whose heavy make-up ended abruptly in thick, yellowish, grubby necks, who flashed too much jewellery and dripped too much mascara, or stout, pink-cheeked, white-haired, doctored-tom old men who looked like prosperous sidesmen at a fashionable church. Among them went old Lady Westerton herself. Obviously now rather gaga, she groped her way from group to group, presenting a Hollywood English diplomat—a tall, thin, fortyish man with a small military moustache and a suggestion of corsets about his elegant figure. Whoever this notable snake was, Lady Westerton did not introduce him to Marcus. Indeed, when Marcus had arrived at the cocktail party—and if it hadn't been for poor Ozzie's pictures he would never have thought twice about the invitation—she had shown in her embarrassment that she had invited him only through senile absent-mindedness.

"I'm afraid Jack couldn't come. He's on a business trip in New York."

He didn't offer details, because, although he approved of sending the pictures away, he was uneasy and troubled about their own suggested emigration. But the old woman had chuckled quite rudely in answer—she'd obviously become a trifle touched in the head since he'd last seen her two or three years before.

"Oh, it wouldn't be Jack's party at all. In fact, I doubt if there's anyone here *you* know. Although it may not do you butterflies any harm to hear what responsible people are up to. Let me see who's young. I know. Dulcie Stewart."

She had taken him over at once to a smartly dressed blonde girl.

"Dulcie, here's Marcus Matthews, a rich butterfly who might be most useful to you if he wasn't under the worst of influences. Get him along to your club."

She had made one of her Edwardian grimaces and waddled off.

Dulcie Stewart said: "Oh, yes, well, do come. I mean if Lady Westerton vouches for you. I mean we do have to be a bit careful because new ideas scare the pants off people, don't they? After all, that's England's trouble."

She spoke to him in a bright but condescending way, laughing quite irrelevantly, as though she were running the coconut shy at a garden *fête*.

"It's not exactly a club, really. But we get together once a week and discuss in a room over a pub in Shepherd Market some of the absolutely necessary questions. For example, last week two or three chaps who knew about that sort of thing put forward their ideas about how to stop the unemployed going to pieces. I mean, after all, even those of us who don't actually do jobs have got a duty to stop the rot if we can. Of course we're only the younger crowd. You'd be rather a grandfather." It was clear from her smile that she thought he would like this observation. "But we do get people along to talk to us who matter—people like Colonel Deniston."

"I don't know who that is. He's never mattered to me yet. Should he have done?"

Her expression as she looked up at him, disgusted by this conven-

tional flippancy, was so stupid and self-satisfied that he felt compelled to go on annoying her.

"Oh, don't think I'm against colonels. Some colonels are very
beautiful," but then, from the collapse of all her smiles, he had almost feared there might be a tiresome scene. Luckily a very over-
dressed, double-breasted, waistcoated "city" young man, who it
seemed was in Lloyd's, joined them and Dulcie gave all her attention
to him, swinging about in a sex-hungry way as she talked that Marcus found peculiarly off-putting. Immediately he had excused himself to bring her another medium-sweet sherry. As he made his way
back through the crowded room he began to feel that these little
poisoned darts of talk would lay him dead on the floor before he
could give Dulcie her fresh drink. He kept his eyes resolutely on the
two paintings that he had come to see.

Amid the faded mass of *japonaiserie* and fake *dix-huitième*, in a
drawing room that had clearly always been too drained of colour
even before the sun and the dust had done their worst, the Bonnard
and the Segonzac flaunted their purples and blues and greens. How
could Ozzie have been so mad as to leave them to this old trout?
They weren't by any means his sort of paintings. True, he'd vowed,
apart from an odd Laurencin, or some other bit of "fun," not to buy
anything but abstracts for the next two years. But yet to leave those
Bonnard peacock curtains and the red of the Segonzac sitter's dress
in those dead surroundings! To leave them to the old trout just because she was his aunt. That was the worst of these aristocratic old
things, even ones as nice as Ozzie, on their death beds and other
solemn places they reverted to the most stultifying conventions. But
still, if what he had heard was correct . . . Excited by thoughts of
possession, he gave Dulcie her drink and immediately interrupted
the ardent conversation she was holding with the young man from
Lloyd's.

"Do you know if it's true that Lady Westerton is wildly in debt?"
Even through his longing for the paintings, he could see their horrified expressions. Quickly he amended his question. "Is the poor old
thing really very hard up nowadays, do you know?"

"I suppose most people one knows are hard up so long as we have
to maintain an army of idle men," said Lloyd's.

Marcus could not immediately think what this army was. Was this young man one of those insane people who wanted to go to war for some cause or other?

"It's the appalling effect on *them*," Dulcie said, "that *we're* concerned with. I say, I suppose this sherry does come from the Nationalist territory? I'm horribly vague about Spanish geography, despite all the news one's read in this last year. It must do, the Reds hardly hold anything now except Madrid, do they? Young men in their teens and twenties losing all self-respect, hanging about street corners, when simple physical exercise could keep them in decent condition."

Marcus was completely bemused. He could only guess that the political signposts he knew of from his politically minded friends would be of no help to him in Dulcie's land, whatever it was.

"I'm not political in the least," he said, "and I'm not going to apologize for it. But if you mean that that sanctimonious old horror Chamberlain should be ashamed of the dole, I quite agree. But then what can you expect of an awful old provincial. He gets all his orders from the mayoress of Birmingham. Oh, it's quite true. Didn't you know that?"

Dulcie didn't smile at all, but the Lloyd's young man gave a smirk.

"Chamberlain's tied down by more than Birmingham, I'm afraid. He has to sing to the tune of his international paymasters."

Marcus was surprised at such scandalmongering from such dreary "nice" young people; he awaited further details with interest, but Dulcie took up the conversation.

"Of course, a decent system of labour camps would solve the whole thing. A friend of mine who knows says there're masses of forestry work that needs doing. Work of real national importance. And they'd be able to drill and play organized games."

"Who would?"

Dulcie looked at him as though she now understood that his strange manner had been a symptom of the imbecility that too often attacked the very rich.

"You *do* live out of things. What's your job?"

"I collect paintings."

She turned to the Lloyd's man: "There you are, you see, Lionel. That's what Hamish said at the last meeting. There *is* still an idle rich here and until we've got rid of it, we can't really curse the rottenness at the other end of the ladder."

Once again the Lloyd's man was more polite. "You're too dog-matic, Dulcie. There are heaps of valuable chaps who simply don't know what's what. You'll learn a lot from the Colonel this evening," he told Marcus. "He will give you an idea of what the papers simply don't tell us. *And* of what needs doing."

All that Marcus now felt was a strong dislike for Dulcie. He gig-gled in her face.

"I hope you don't think you're going to make *me* drill."

"Actually," she replied, "I was talking seriously. About the unem-ployed. Labour camps are the only answer."

It was the almost dotty, starry look in her blue eyes as she made this judgment that brought home to Marcus exactly what political company he was in. He felt ashamed to have believed, in his inno-cence, that such views were held only by black-shirted bruisers and corner-boys. He must at least show some fight.

"And what if they don't want to?"

"Beggars can hardly be choosers," said Lloyd's. "No national work, no national dole. That's fair enough. But in fact, you know, they'll welcome it, if the case could be put to them without agitators getting at them first. I believe the Colonel's going to tell us quite a lot about what they're doing in Germany in that way. What they call the *Arbeitsdienst*."

"I've never heard anything so disgusting. People through no fault of their own are out of work. You pay them a pittance. Then not content with that you want to make them do physical jerks."

"Well, it's that or watch decent Englishmen turning into degener-ates," Dulcie cried. "A friend of mine who knows the seamy side of the West End says that most of these pansy-boys start as unem-ployed."

"Which," said Lloyd's, "suits the Reds and their friends beauti-fully. There's nothing they'd like better than a degenerate England."

"Who are their friends?" asked Marcus, while he contemplated whether he could hit Dulcie and get away before Lloyd's hit him.

"The Jewish bankers and financiers, of course."

He could see that Dulcie had been forbearing not to add "silly." Trying to control the trembling that his anger had brought on, he said in a voice that he intended to be loud and bold, but which came out as high and hysterical, "I think you'd better know that I'm a pansy-boy. And the man I live with is a Jew."

Some people near-by turned in shocked disgust towards them.
Lloyd's and Dulcie were too overcome with embarrassment at being
seen with him to react more violently. And now a croaking filled the
room as Lady Westerton announced:

"Will all you people take your glasses through with you? You
know the way. Colonel Deniston is ready to begin his address."

Ostentatiously Marcus moved against the tide of scented old Jeze-
bels and debollocked generals, but he could feel by the chafing of his
thighs, to his chagrin, that his retreat was of the most mincing kind.
However, at last his feeble little protest was over, and released by a
seedy old butler, he found himself in the autumn sunshine of Cado-
gan Square.

Sitting back in the Daimler, he stared at the pits in Prescott's neck
that no doubt would bear witness throughout the man's life to the
acne of his youth; but he could think of nothing but Jack. There
were English people—ghastly, awful English people, it was true, but
people not absolutely marked as criminals or thugs, people whom
one might meet at boring Belgravia cocktail parties—who would insult Jack, imprison him, for all he knew kill him, just because he was
a Jew. He agreed that, if there was to be the least danger of war—
and there clearly was—the pictures should go to New York and go
now. But he had tried not to listen to Jack's occasional hints at their
own emigration. It seemed hysterical; and after all, if war came, they
would all be killed within the first week by poison gas or some other
horror. The paintings must be preserved, that was a basic duty, but
you can't live life thinking all the time about your own skin. He had
developed a hatred of pampering himself, much though he loved
luxury, from the days of 52 onwards, when he'd been on the streets.
But now he saw that this stoicism was a silly nonsense for Jack and
all Jews who could get away. He hated not to judge other people by
his own rules for himself, especially just because, like Jack, they had
circumcised cocks or had worn ridiculous little tassels and caps as
small boys. But when "nice" people revealed the obscenities of their
minds and wills, such easy moral rules were no longer possible. Now
he saw suddenly that people were going to get in the way of things
that mattered, of the Kandinskys and Baksts. Jack, to begin with—
he would have to manage Jack, to make the prickly, sensitive, rude,
loving, guilt-ridden man whom he cared for above everything not
ashamed to run away. At the thought of "managing" Jack's safety he

felt exhausted; at the thought of these disgusting, ordinary people, who out of envy or stupidity or vulgarity hated Jack, he felt sick.

The car was held up to allow a small group of demonstrators to cross from Byron's statue to Apsley House. He could not see who marched in the procession for the press of onlookers and the linked policemen, but he caught sight of a banner that read, "Scholarships not battleships," and he heard voices shouting, "Stop Hitler's war on children," or so it sounded. He could make no sense of it. Almost before Prescott spoke, he had some premonition of what he would say; at the very same moment he caught the eye of this stocky young man in a faded purple suit and white silk choker who was standing, picking his nose, on the island.

Prescott said, "Giving the police trouble again, sir. They're holding some sort of meeting down at Trafalgar Square. Lay-abouts' paradise. Of course, it's foreigners behind it."

Disgust and lust fought for possession of his bowels. "Don't talk nonsense, Prescott. And you can drop me here. I'm going to walk in the park. Tell Dempster I shan't be in to dinner after all."

He waited until the Daimler had passed well on its way to Marble Arch before he smiled and beckoned with his head to the young man to follow him down to the Dell. He had remembered picking someone up there in his own down-and-out days.

"Rabbits! What appallingly silly faces they do have, don't they?" he had said then by way of an opening.

But the purple young man said, "You wouldn't think you'd see them—wild rabbits right in the heart of London—would you?"

Ah, well, in England, differences of technique like most other things could be traced back to class.

The northwest wind blew strong but fresh across the heath, over the downs of the main course and into the dip where the small course lay concealed in warm intimacy. Here, coming slap up against the members' stand, it whirled around, stirring up dust, blowing newspapers and ticket ends to dance in horse-dung-scented air, destroying the cosiness of the little informal meeting. Gladys, seated precariously on her shooting stick, had to hold on to her wide-brimmed straw hat. That came of Alf's insistence these days on her dressing Ascotwise for the most unsuitable occasions. She put her hand on his arm to steady herself.

"I'm too big-bummed for these things, Alfred."

But he looked up from his race-card and frowned disapprovingly at her words. He never used to worry about being genteel. Seeing his anxious, frowning red face bent over the card and hearing his usual stomach rumble, she felt ashamed to be criticizing the poor, overworked, clever old darling. The more power he got each year the less he slept and the more he burped. Fumbling in her bag, she found a bottle of soda mints, and patting three or four into her hand she handed two to him.

"Oh, for God's sake, kiddie."

But luckily now they were off and she could think of nothing but gold-and-green hoops. And there they were—gold-and-green hoops down the course.

"Oh, Marie Stellons or whatever your name is! Oh, you blighter, you've let me down."

"I'm always telling you not to throw your money away on these outsiders." Alf sounded really cross. But now gold-and-green hoops were gaining, past purple-and-yellow stripes, past red-and-grey hoops, and, oh, God, coming up to second place, coming up to flush with maroon and black.

"Stella Maris, Stella Maris, Stella Maris wins."

"Oh, Alf, I've won a hundred quid."

But he hardly did more than grunt.

Of course, if he'd lost money himself, well, that would be different, everyone hates losing. But he hadn't. He'd won on the first two races, it seemed; and he hadn't even laid a bet on this race. Not even to congratulate her; she'd never known him like this before. She decided to disregard him and climbed up the steps to the Tote to claim her money. As she folded the notes away into her bag, she thought, if I didn't have these little bits of excitement, these little bits of luck, I don't know that I could stand him sometimes. Clearly her luck was in. She made a little prayer to the luck provider to let it flow over from today into tomorrow. If my luck holds, she thought, I'll get those two Chelsea figures at the sale tomorrow, and Sylvia'll get that marquetry table she's after (hideous thing!). But she willed for it strongly because you must wish for others if you're to hold on to your own luck. Then casting round for others to wish luck to, she said aloud: "*And* for Mr. Ahrendt," so that a man with ginger moustaches and a brown bowler stared at her. Lucky that Alfred wasn't there. Oh, but wouldn't it be wonderful if old Ahrendt's picture *did* turn out to be by this chap Grünewald; he and the old girl looked so thin and they'd obviously sold every bit of porcelain, every stick of furniture they'd managed to bring over. She agreed with the luck god to undo her own luck, and Sylvia's, for that matter, if old Ahrendt could get all that money. Ten thousand pounds, the Christie's man had murmured, noncommittally, of course. The old pair would be all right for life.

Coming down the steps again she saw suddenly a heavy, red-faced old man with a desperate look in his eyes making his way to the telephones. Then she realized with horror that he was Alfred. And she had never even thought to wish him some of her luck. She firmly opened her race-card and began to study the form of the horses for the next race. So Daffy Down Dilly had been carrying a couple of pounds more last time out . . . That was the only way of doing it. Look how she'd mugged up her porcelain over the last two years— first English and now, though only for background, continental. Everything, as Alfred said, should be systematic. Luck was superstitious. She felt almost ashamed of the twenty new five-pound notes in her bag.

She was still studying form when she felt an arm round her waist and, looking up, saw Alfred, his eyes smiling, the lines of his face all upturned in laughter.

"You're getting to be an obsessive punter. Just because you win a hundred quid by picking a winner blindfold with a pin . . ."

"But I'm trying to be more serious, Alf. I'm studying form."

"No, put it away, darling. I can't have *you* becoming a gambler. Let's go and have a plate of cold salmon and a bottle of bubbly. They've got a very good Heidsiecker here."

"Come on"—he smothered his fish in mayonnaise—"tell us the best news from home. What happened about that old girl's Chelsea Neptune?" But before she could answer, "I think it's in the bag. I think I've pulled it off. I'm almost certain of the collateral now. If only the bloody bank manager hasn't got an attack of Hitleritis."

She supposed that he meant the new trading company, but his affairs moved so rapidly she was not always sure.

"Oh, Alf, I am pleased. Tell."

But no, he said, much better to wait until we're past the post.

Meanwhile, what news of the shop? what about this sale? where was this big pot's place? at Bottisham? where was that? and so on. She told him about the two Chelsea figures; she explained about the *commedia dell'arte*. He seemed delighted.

"Clever girl. How you've learned it all! I might start buying myself, one day, you never know."

"Oh, I wish you would, Alf. Anything that would give you a hobby."

"You're my hobby."

"At rising forty, Alf! Don't be silly. No, honestly. If you would only just slack off a little. You've provided for Doris. You've no need to work so hard."

He took her hand. "Don't nag, Glad. I'm doing the job that excites me most. There are big possibilities. How can I stand aside and let them go by? But you do help me, Glad, you know, in times like this, when things get on top of me, just by chattering away."

"Well! If that's all I do."

Yet she felt delighted. She described to him the chances at the sale; she told him of her luck in identifying the Harlequin.

"And Sylvia has a rich lady from Detroit if we can secure her the Louis Seize marquetry table."

At Sylvia's name, as usual, he made a face, but this time, since he was so happy, a droll rather than a glum one.

"Oh, shut up, Alf. You can't sulk about a three-year-old snub. And she's proved to be the greatest asset to *me*. *You* wouldn't have been paid back if it hadn't been for her efficiency. When I think how nearly I sent old Ahrendt away with that medieval wood-carving of his. If it hadn't been for Sylvia . . ."

But two mentions of her name proved too many, or else he had not liked to be reminded of having been repaid—it had been their nearest moment to a serious quarrel—anyhow, he began to frown, so she decided to tell him of the Ahrendts' possible luck, it was such a happy-ending fairy story that it couldn't possibly fail to cheer people up.

"But you mustn't mention it to anyone, Alf, in case it doesn't prove to be genuine. I think the excitement might kill Mrs. Ahrendt. She's very frail."

"My dear girl, you can't get anywhere in the City if you talk out of turn. How much would it be worth if it was by this chap?"

"About ten thousand pounds."

"A nice little pile of spondulicks."

"It would mean the difference of life and death to those poor old things, I think. It can't be right, Alf, for us to sit by and let that dreadful little man push wretched people around in that way. And as the old boy said to me, '*We* were the lucky ones that got away, Miss Matthews.' "

"My dear girl, whatever you do, don't start a lot of war talk. The market's only just bearing up as it is."

"War! It's simply a question of decency, Alf."

He patted her hand. "You're a good girl. Well, let's drink to good luck for your Yids." He looked at his watch. "Look, I've got to phone a man. Cut down to the course and lay me a tenner on Archimandrite. But don't take less than a hundred to eight."

The race had been run and Archimandrite had come in second before he returned.

"It's all right, darling. I backed it both ways for you."

But his renewed gloom had other business causes.

"Priestley's ratting on his previous offers. He's got war nerves. Some fool called Vansittart has been saying that we've got to have a showdown with Germany. And Priestley's impressed just because the chap's been an ambassador or something. These politicians! Lecturing other countries all the time. Why can't they get on with the job of running England properly? No wonder a lot of these unemployed chaps are putting on black shirts. Get business going. Give men jobs, not the dole. Then you can start lecturing Hitler about how he should treat his Yids, though even then you'd much better mind your own business."

Carefully making no answer she gave him his tote card.

"Go and get your money, darling. And then why don't we go back to the Rutland Arms? You ought to have a rest before Sylvia comes. Otherwise you two will row the whole evening."

"I've no intention of seeing the stuck-up bitch. I've got to get back to London."

"Oh, Alfred! I'd so looked forward to tomorrow. You've never been to a sale with me. And *you* were looking forward to it, too. I know you were."

"My dear girl, I only happen to have the most important business deal of my whole career in the balance."

"Oh, don't be so pompous. You get worse and worse. It wouldn't hurt you to give one day to doing what I want."

"I'm afraid, you know, Gladys, that you've always had things far too much your own way. Now if you'd known what it is never to have had anything you wanted in life, like Doris . . ." But he stopped, for in her anger Gladys seemed about to hit him with her shooting stick.

"Damn you, Alfred." And she spoke so softly and casually that she frightened him. "After twenty years to treat me like this."

"Oh, go to hell." He walked off.

Later that evening when she and Sylvia were half-way through their roast pork and cauliflower *au gratin,* she was called to the telephone. He spoke from London.

"You must forgive me, kiddie. I've been worried to death. But I've seen Priestley personally. I think he's going to play ball."

When Gladys returned to the dining-room, Sylvia said: "That's better. I like you to look happy."

Gladys knew that it was true. Sylvia really liked her. So many women did. And she liked them, too, cared what happened to women, but she never let them into her life.

"Oh, no, Hugh, it would be quite impossible in term time."

She stared across the front garden over to the distant golf links for a moment, while she particularized her objection to suit her husband's schoolmasterly love of fact.

"Your mother will be staying here, for one thing."

"Mother's visit will only overlap by one day, and that can surely be got round."

She had gone back to sewing the stripes on Middleman's uniform.

"I'm so glad he's got his Cert A. He's corps mad at the moment and it means the world to him."

He spoke mumblingly with his pipe in his mouth, and, as so often in the holidays, completely slumped in his deck chair.

"God save us," she supposed him to say, "it may mean the world to more . . ." but his mumbling died away.

He was sulking, she felt, because she hadn't discussed this ridiculous proposition. She looked instinctively for one of the boys to call on to distract him, but as so often this summer holiday they were all out. If she and Hugh were to be left together like this much in the years to come! Now there was something for God to save them from! They were never cut out to be Darby and Joan.

"Well," for the best thing was to carry straight on, "with Senior being head of the sixth and Victor *ludorum* and so on, I do like Middleman to have a look in."

"He won the fives' cup."

"Yes, despised fives! You know I felt quite ashamed, Hugh, with this term's mag. If it wasn't Pascoe I on one page it was Pascoe II on the other. I told them both that they'd better watch out because when Pascoe III came along next year, they won't get another look in."

"There won't be a Pascoe I by the time that P.S. gets there."

"No." She took it quite calmly. "I must remember to look out a second-hand arm-chair for Senior's room. After all, he'll be our lodger when he's articled, and lodgers always expect arm-chairs." She waited for him to laugh, then, "I said that about the magazine on purpose when P.S. was present. I'm doing all I can to get him excited about going to Radley, but, of course, he's been so happy here. What a wise move it was, Hugh. The best decision we ever made." When he didn't reply: "Where else would you have found a golf course to suit you like this one?"

He didn't reply directly even to that.

"Yes, the Carvers have certainly done a good job on P.S.," he said.

Sukey put down her sewing and patted his hand.

"Darling, only you could fall into an unconscious pun like that. Making him sound like a little joint of meat." She took her hand away. "The great thing was getting him away from that terrible Great Man of yours. But you're right. Even if Daisy Carver will never set the world on fire, she's got a basically kind nature. And P.S. is the sort of boy who sees straight through any surface silliness to the kindness beneath."

He picked up an ant that was running across *The Forsyte Saga*, which lay on the lawn, paused with it between his forefinger and thumb, then set it down to scuttle away in the clover-infested grass.

"Couldn't you see your way to repaying her kindness by having Mrs. Liebermann here?"

"Oh, really, Hugh. Filling the house with old women during the boys' holidays!"

"I think they're always very glad to see Mother."

"Oh, of course they are. They're loving, beautifully behaved boys. If we so much as mentioned this Frau what's-her-name, they'd urge us to have her here. But I won't have them traded on. They only have one summer holiday in a year."

"Sukey, darling, Frau Liebermann hasn't seen her small son Arnold for two years. Also it's very uncertain whether her husband or her elder boy will ever get out of Germany."

"Don't start exaggerating, Hugh. You and James Carver have accepted I don't know how many Jewish refugee children free at the school this year alone. And quite right, too. But that does show that it's not all *that* difficult for them to get out. That awful man's only too pleased to get rid of them, I believe. Besides, the last thing she'll want is to have a whole mass of people round her when she sees her boy again after so long. I know how I should feel if it was P.S. And a household like ours, too, that's so full of incomprehensible family jokes."

"Perhaps we should try to make ourselves a little easier to understand."

"Darling, you said that just like Margaret. You'll have to write books and be praised for your ironic style, or whatever it is they say about Mag."

She saw that he had begun to suck the knuckles of his right hand.

"You're annoyed with me. Of course, if the poor woman had nowhere else to go . . ."

"She hasn't, Sukey, that's the point."

"She was invited to the schoolhouse to be with her boy. And very well it would suit. There's only James and Daisy Carver there. And James speaks German which is more than any of us do. It was Daisy's idea and a very kind one. But now she suddenly has this absurd notion about going to France. That's Daisy all over. Kind-hearted and muddled. That sort of thing can be very selfish. And I'm not going to have the boys' holiday sacrificed to it. What does she want to go to France for, anyway? A great deal of all the trouble the world is in is due to French selfishness."

Hugh picked up his book.

"That's right, dear," she said. "You bury yourself in that awful old Soames. Why *should* you be worried with all this in the summer holidays? It's very naughty of Daisy and I shall tell her so when I see her."

He closed the book and threw it angrily on to the grass again, but she took P.S.'s blazer from the basket beside her and held out each sleeve in turn to discover if any buttons were missing. He had put his fist into his mouth, but now he relaxed enough to withdraw it and to say:

"Darling, a woman who's been very kind to our son wants to go to France for a couple of weeks because she thinks it may be one of her last chances of travelling in the country she was educated in. She asks us to help her out of an obligation she's already . . ."

"Thinks it may be her last chance! Oh, I do think it's wicked, all this war talk. Don't they realize what war means? I saw my brother Quentin come back wounded. It isn't a sort of game."

"No, darling. You forget that I was in it . . ."

"Well, then, how can you . . . ?" she broke off in dismay at the irresponsibility of people.

He was about to argue further, but in the end he decided in favour of Soames's difficulties with Irene.

Sukey had finished her mending and was reading over some old diaries she had kept from past family holidays, when Hugh, looking up, said:

"Why one wastes time on detective stories. His extraordinary sense of what people are like! I'd forgotten Winifred and Montague Dartie. They're your parents to a tee." Either Sukey's inattention or the word he had used reminded him, for he said, "Isn't it time that Rose brought tea out to us?"

"I told her to wait until the boys get back."

"Oh!"

"They've gone on one of these treasure hunts. They'll be ravenous when they get in."

"Surely they'll have tea with some of their friends."

"Not while there's my home-made marrow and ginger to come home to."

"Darling, this last year or two you have got very . . ." But he changed his course in mid-stream. "How would you like to live in the West Country?"

"Now that really *is* strange, Hugh. It almost would make one believe in second sight and all that, like old Aunt Mouse. Here am I reading about that trip we all made to Cheddar Gorge in 1933 and you suddenly say that. And it's not as if you're the imaginative kind of person who would have psychic gifts."

He laughed. "I don't quite know what that proves. But you haven't answered my question. *Would* you like to live in the West Country?"

"With a caravan and a Dartmoor pony! Darling, if you want to get away these holidays, you must just go. But I can't leave Rose to housekeep for the boys. It's too much for her. And they just don't want to leave their beloved Kent. After all, now that they're away half of the year . . ." But Hugh began to pluck at the grass and she looked up at him, "Oh, Hugh, what have you got into your head? You haven't gone back to that old dream of running your own school? And in the West Country! Just when we've got Senior articled with Jarvis in Canterbury. The holidays are always bad for you. You get restless without those wretched little boys to fuss about."

"It's not me that's restless. It's the world. I don't want to worry you, and you *must* keep this to yourself. But James has had a serious hint from a high-up chap in the War Office—General Tyler, whose grandson was with us two years ago. He says that in the event of war the whole of Essex and Kent are likely to be in the line of German air attacks on London. Of course, we've had the odd parents worrying before; but this is a bit more serious than that. Mind you, he's very keen to point out that it probably won't come to war. But he must take it reasonably seriously because he ought not really to make his view public . . ."

"I should think not indeed. Spreading alarm!"

"My dear girl, it's only a warning. Prepared is . . ."

"Well, then let them make their preparations without putting wretched mothers into agonies . . ."

She took a pair of Middleman's socks from the mending basket and began twisting them round her fingers to control her mounting misery. She looked to Hugh to see her distress and to reassure her; he only stared at the ground. But then, answer to an unspoken prayer, to banish her anxieties and to end the horrid talk, the three boys came into view, just dimly through the thickness of the elder-bushes, then their heads appearing above the wall, their bicycles invisible as they sailed in silhouette before the distant golf course.

"Don't say a word to the boys," Hugh said as they came whizzing and circling up the gravel path.

"As if I should. I don't want to hear any more about it myself. Well, did you win any prizes?"

"*I* did, Mummy, *I* did." P.S. made figures of eight, wobbling precariously on the brink of the laurels, calling to them across the lawn, exulting in his success.

Senior was too grand to notice this exhibition, but Middleman caught his mother's eye in affectionate amusement at the younger boy's antics.

"Jolly good!" Sukey cried, but Hugh, seeing that Senior was going indoors, said quietly:

"Tell Rose we're ready for tea, will you, old man?"

"Who was there, darling?" Sukey asked Middleman.

"Oh, John Beamish. And the Philpott girls have got a German boy staying. He was awful . . ."

But P.S. was too excited to let the others describe what was, after all, his victory.

"I bet you wouldn't have got all the clues, Mummy. For instance, 'To keep out Boney it succeeded. Let's hope it won't again be needed.' "

"Oh, that was an absolutely obvious one," said Middleman.

"Mummy hasn't got it."

But Mummy had clearly got something, for she was holding the old diary in her hand as though she would squeeze the past from it, and she was biting her lower lip. Hugh, glancing at her, said:

"Could it be the Martello Tower, old man?"

"Yes, that's right, sir," P.S. cried. "Jolly good."

"Daddy, not 'sir,' " Sukey said, and with this familiar correction she recovered some of her usual poise. "It's not term time. Tell us some more clues. Yes, you and who else, Middleman?" Then seeing her eldest son coming back from the house, she called to him, "Was that awful Eileen Dowsett there? And did she make eyes at you, darling?" To Rose with the tea, she said, "Master Philip's won the Treasure Hunt prize. What was it, by the way, P.S.? I hope Mrs. Roeburn didn't spend a lot of money. They're very badly off. Oh, look, Rose has made jumbles. Now, is my marrow and ginger to your taste *this* year, my lord?" she asked Senior. "Well, come on, give us some more clues, P.S."

"How can I when you talk all the time? There was one jolly good one. How did it go? You know. *That* one," he nodded at his brother.

"No, we don't," Senior said.

"Yes. About you know what. I can't say or I'll give it away." P.S. looked very earnest. "Wait a minute, 'Where the hangman's gibbet stood.'" His voice was the perfection of dramatic elocution, "'There within the . . .'"

"Look, darling," Sukey cried, holding up Middleman's corps jacket, "is that what you meant me to do?"

"Oh, Mummy!" P.S. protested.

But before Middleman could reply, Sukey had found a tear. "Oh, drat your old corps, darling, and I never saw it. Yes . . . hangman's gibbet," she began to thread her needle.

P.S. took a moment to recover from his annoyance at her fresh interruption. Hugh, to smooth the situation over, started to hum and then to sing, "And the soldiers dum dum dum dum said they'd rather sleep on thistles than wear the shirts that sister Susie sewed."

Billy Pop's tuneless voice came mockingly down the stairs to her. It was the last straw of an intolerable day. Bursting into tears, she threw down the sewing and brought her fists down on to the tea tray, scattering milk, jumbles, marrow and ginger, and all.

"Stop it, stop it!" she cried. A bony, florid-faced woman with fair hair streaked with grey, she ran like an angry young girl into the house.

Senior looked down at his plate, Middleman busied himself picking up the debris; only P.S. cried after her, "Mummy, Mummy."

Hugh, lighting his pipe, said, "Your mother's having a rather worrying time."

Middleman and Senior both looked very serious. Senior said, "We quite understand, Dad. Is there anything we can do?"

P.S., watching his brothers, tried to make the same sort of face. Hugh said, "No, I doubt if there's anything any of us can do at the moment except to hope for the best."

Half an hour later, smelling of eau-de-cologne, Sukey came out of her bedroom, where she had been crying in the dark. She went to Hugh in his study.

"I want us to have Frau Liebermann here, darling."

"Now, my dear, are you *sure*? I've never seen you rattled like you were at tea. You ought to take things easy."

"Take things easy! It was nothing. Good heavens, as a girl I . . ." Then more quietly and deliberately, "If she gets here in September, your mother will be staying until the fifteenth, but I'm sure if we asked her. Yes, if she goes on the fourteenth that would give us a day to get the room ready. And when term starts Arnold can come over from the schoolhouse for Sunday lunches."

"Promise you won't knock yourself up, Sue."

"No, no," she cried, "I *want* them to come here."

"No," said Marcus into the telephone, "I don't think the Soutine or the Dufy, do you? Certainly not the Dufy." He made a face at Jack. "But the Klees are what we specially want. The landscape with the sea anemones and the Bauhaus one—Study, what's it?" Jack could hear the expected expostulations at the other end. He was peeling himself an orange in an elaborate but to him immensely satisfying manner so that it looked like a water lily. The headwaiter at the Mamounia in Marrakesh had shown him how, and he, who could do nothing manual, was greatly proud of the skill. He gave one segment to the blue Persian cat, who happily doted on all exotic foods.

"Yes, I do understand, of course, of course. The Dufy's tremendously decorative. Perhaps the best in the English collection. It's just that in this exhibition . . ." "Oh, no, you're quite wrong. I *adore* the Soutine pageboy. But it's more of a fun picture—all that decadent elegance." "Nihilism? Oh! Mm. I see. I didn't know he had a message. Anyway, that's not relevant, is it?"

Jack whispered in his free ear, "You'll never get anywhere with Vernon with charm."

Marcus said into the telephone, "Jack says I'll never get anywhere with you with charm. So I won't go on trying. We want the Klees and the Miró, because even though you think they're amusing, they are in fact superb paintings. And we don't want the Dufy, because it's a pretty poster, or the Soutine, because fun's fun but we can't smile all the time. Now have your heart attack and agree because you know you'd rather die than not have the Corkoran collection represented." Jack was right, for a deep intake of breath at the other end was followed by rather snappish agreement.

So that was settled. And now Marcus was charming again, saying, "Yes. Yes. How amusing. We'll certainly think about *that*. No, I'm entirely amateur as far as arranging exhibitions goes, so I shall be grateful for any advice."

When he put the receiver down, he said at once: "I must have a drink." And when Dempster appeared he ordered a very cold Chambéry. "I must freeze my temperature down, Jack, after a morning of talking to fools. Only half of these people know what's good in their collections. And half of those wouldn't know if they hadn't been told. Anyhow, I've got everything I want. It's going to be a good exhibition. And it's not, by the way, going to be called *Kultur Bolshevismus*, even though Lucy Ainley took the trouble to translate. 'It would serve Hitler right. It's what he says, you know. He calls all serious modern art culture Bolshevism.' " His imitation, as of all women, except deep-voiced Lesbians, was exact. "Do you know that Vernon Corkoran was the tenth person this morning to suggest that witty piece of sarcasm. Can't you imagine Hitler's little moustache withering under our cruel irony?"

"And all this you are doing," said Jack, "for the little *yiddische Kindchen*. Mr. Matthews, allow me to tell you, you're a damned nice chap."

"Oh, God! Where did half these refugees learn their English? It's not really funny, Jack. Can't you explain to that sad little man about it? I'm sure he doesn't sound so awful and hearty in Germany. Did you know he was one of the early producers of Brigitte Helm? Oh, yes, he was a great silent director. But that won't help him to get work here. Especially hitting people on the back and saying 'old chap.' Or perhaps it *will* in Denham and all those studio suburbs, who can tell? Certainly my very unhearty manner got me no further than crowd scenes. Though I was splendid in those. But as to the children. I am only too well aware of the shame of it. Children and good works! Beastly little things masturbating in their handkerchiefs. I could kill Hitler for dragging me into all this. Anyhow, I'm going to have a glorious afternoon just being poked."

Jack frowned as he took the Martini from the tray Dempster offered. He had never reconciled himself to the way that Marcus imposed his private life and language upon the servant's susceptibilities.

"Your *other* good work?" Jack said casually when Dempster had gone. His beautiful, etiolated Semitic face seemed frozen in camel-like disdain.

Marcus walked over to him and looked into his large, liquid eyes. "See any green, dearie?" he asked himself, and answered, "Yes, one or two flecks."

"No, I'm not jealous," said Jack, "merely realistic. *You* were unemployed when I met *you* . . ."

"I was *not*. A gentleman had asked me to model for Saint Sebastian. And another gentleman had said he might be able to get me a walking-on part in a production of *The Miracle* at Alexandra Palace."

"As I said, you were as good as unemployed. A lot of heavy father rescue work I had to do."

"Oh, rehabilitation! You should have tried dumb-bells. You and that awful Dulcie woman! But I had my hidden talents. Ted's one of those workers who has nothing to lose but his balls. Oh, all right! He's a nice, boring, kindhearted, weak-willed creature of low intelligence and moderately good intentions. *And* I shall treat him well. But there's strictly one reason why I'm seeing him. He keeps that between his legs. And I'm quite willing to forgo that delight if it fusses you. After all, I've been faithful or almost so for more than ten years. You said you didn't mind when I told you. But if you do, say so. Is *that* what this is all about?"

"No." Jack spoke meditatively. "No, I don't mind. Or rather I should mind if I thought that you might walk out on me in a fit of claustrophobia."

Marcus looked around the room. His eye lighted on the Klees, the green-and-pink Mondrian, stayed quite a while on his own portrait by Tchelitchew.

"With those!" he said. He went up to Jack and hugged him. "And you. Oh, yes"—with a tragedienne gesture—"this golden cage stifles me. Give me cold water and fresh air."

Dempster received the melodramatic order quietly.

"Luncheon is served," he said.

As they walked in, Marcus observed, "Having it off may make you feel very good but a diamond bracelet lasts forever."

Crumbling his toast Melba and drinking the lunch of lemon juice that kept his figure so slim, Jack said, "All the same there must be some pressure on our partnership, otherwise you would never use a stale quotation like that. Even in your dirty version."

"You play him along, really, don't you?" Ted commented with a worldly look in his empty blue eyes.

He was lying full length in his shirt on the divan bed in the recess of the one-room flat Marcus had rented for their meetings. When Marcus showed no recognition of this cynicism, Ted assumed a more serious look.

"Ees all right, isn't e? A lot of blokes wouldn't take it so easy. I mean your goin with me. A lot of blokes like im would be like wild cats about it. Proper bitches! No, ees all right, your Jack is."

Still Marcus made no response, but contrived to wash up the tea things in the cupboard-like kitchen.

"Oh, well," Ted said. "What's e matter to us? You're all right, you know. I mean larks apart. I don't know I've met another bloke I've liked as much as you."

He stretched and scratched his thigh, and as he did so his shirt moved up. Marcus almost buried his head in the washing-up lather. This bloody randiness always threatened to suck him down into the vast, empty, emotional gulf of Ted's shapeless life, a fluid mess of random thoughts, chance feelings and appetites, half-formed words, glottal stops that took mould only as now from a desperate attempt to suit the mood of the person he was with.

"I was lucky meeting you. *And* you can cook."

He offered the joke to Marcus perfunctorily, but then, perhaps remembering the number of pick-ups to whom he had said it when it had no meaning, he added, "No, I mean that. That fish you done for tea was as good as Lyons. Better." He belched to show his appreciation. "I don't know anyone who cooks better. Well, cept my Mum did, of course."

But Marcus knew that big, tough, lost-boy look, so he kept his eyes on the iridescent bubbles. Ted stirred uneasily.

"And my sister-in-law, Madge. You and er ought to meet, you'd like er. She's a proper caution. You two could talk about cooking."

Already a note of defensive sarcasm was creeping into his voice. Marcus knew he must find soothing words or face a quarrel.

"Anyone ever tell you you've got good hard tits?" he asked. The soothing remark was at least sincere. The element of therapy irked him but it worked.

"Oh, a few," Ted said, soothed. He added, "Well, I think I'll take a kip."

Thank God, Marcus thought, for to watch the sleeping figure was one of his best rewards. But Ted's need for affection was too great that evening for sleep. In less than a minute he opened his eyes.

"What you watchin me for? You *like* me, don't yer. I mean more than just screwing. You like to play tough, but I know. I like you too. You given me a lot I needed. I don't mean just money. Madge saw it. She's quick. I told er what you said. You know it's not being out of work that matters, it's when you don't care. Madge was quick on that all right. Ees right there, she said; of corse she was thinkin of Arthur as much as me. Your bloke's right, she said. Look at Arthur, e was only stood off once, and e never rested till e got work. That's what you've got to do."

Ted looked for Marcus's approval and when there was no response, he added, "I dunno. Talkin's easy."

The repetition of the facile moralizing he had used in his first meeting with Ted sickened Marcus with himself.

"I need a blike like you. It's not my fault, yer know. I go regular to the Labour. But it's like they say, one alone can't beat the system. Friends and family help though, don't they?"

In Marcus self-disgust swelled into intense irritation that burst upon Ted.

"For God's sake, shut up. I've taken on the Jews. I'm not taking on the unemployed. Not even you as a sample. I've been rent myself once. But at least I was honest about it. I just gave what they paid me for. I never asked any of them to hold my hand or wash my nappies. And I'm not going to do either for you. Just because you're cinema sodden you needn't imagine you're Spencer Tracy. Your butch looks don't go with baby talk. Or not for me. So for God's sake let's not have any more love on the dole. You're here because of one thing, and one thing only. And you know what it is."

"You fuckin bastard. All right. If that's ow your ladyship feels, you can fill your own ole. I'm off."

Ted even went so far as to swing his legs down on to the floor and pick up his socks, but bewilderment, depression, lassitude prevented his going farther. By chance, however, his choice of words resolved his dilemma for Marcus, for he heard the echoes of his own voice in the room and recognized them with horror.

"I am very sorry. I was screaming like a vulgar, self-centred bitch. Like my mother, in fact." Seeing Ted's shocked look at his abuse of the sacred name, he said quickly, "She's not really. She's a poor old trout, in fact. And my father's far worse, if that makes it better. In any case, for God's sake, don't let us talk about *that*. I shouldn't have said what I did and I apologize. Of course I like you. I mean to do all I can to help. Only let's not talk. It breaks your wonderful strong-silent-man image for me, I suppose."

He smiled to remove any bite from the touch of sarcasm he had indulged to help himself through his apology. He could see Ted searching anew to respond to what he did not understand. At last he said, "That's all right. I'm not much a one for talk anyway. I just wanted to show that I'd appreciated . . ."

Marcus put his hand over Ted's mouth to indicate that there were better ways of showing appreciation.

"No," said Madge, "if e goes slidin on them mats again, eel wear out the seat of is knickers. And we can't av im goin around without them. Not when winter comes. Damage im for life, that might." And she gave one of her fortissimo laughs.

So little Stanley couldn't go again on the Jack and Jill, but Marcus and Ted took him between them on the Giant Dipper.

"Well, what do yer know?" asked Madge. "Two and a tanner each to bring up yer tea."

"Yeah, it's a racket all right. Boy! Is that a racket!" Ted often spoke in his idea of American when he was with his family. He said it made the kids laugh, but Marcus had not heard this.

"E done all the screamin," Stanley said, pointing at Marcus.

"*E did, e* did. Oo did? You want to learn to talk proper," Madge cried. "What if e did? E paid for it all, didn't e?"

Shirley had finished her sno-fru and was insistent that Ted and im should swing her, which they did several times, her white knickers gleaming in the bright, crisp, ozoneful air. She was quite red in the face when they had finished, but her affection for Marcus seemed only stimulated, for she clung to his leg. Stanley, not to be outdone, hugged his arm.

"Good old Shirl," Madge said, "she won't pay no two and a tanner for *er* bit of fun."

And then after more shrimps and cockles it was time to return to

London. Shirley cried and Stanley announced firmly that he was
going to stay on.

"Where'll you sleep, then, daftie?" his mother asked.

"On the beach."

"What'll you do when it gets cold, eh?"

"Go in one of them otels. E could buy one of them. Could you
buy all Sowfend?" he asked, round eyed.

"No," said Marcus.

"There you are," Madge told them. "So that's it. You can always
tell it's time for em to go ome when they don't want to. Not that I'd
stop any poor kids from doin what they like." She often announced
such things about herself, as though she thought nobody noticed her
many virtues.

So to the train they went, for Madge had been firm against the car.
On their earlier trip to Hampton Court, Prescott's stillness and silence had spoiled her fun, she said. "Looked on us as if we were dirt,
e did. You could see it from the back of is neck." Chauffeurs were
out, like presents of money to the children: "I don't mind treats, but
not tips. I've got my rules. That's ow Arthur and me make out. You
ought to teach *im* a few rules," she had told Marcus, pointing at
Ted.

Although it was the end of the season the railway carriage was
quite full. Marcus read aloud to the children from *Rupert the Bear*
he had bought for them, and they remained quiet for the complete
journey. When they were bored by Bill Badger's advice to Rupert,
they revelled in the consciousness of being the centre of attention of
the whole carriage, for Marcus, who loved reading aloud, let himself
rip with mime and expression. At first Ted, and still more Madge,
shifted uneasily, but when they found that Marcus's voice, far from
arousing derision, produced on every face a sweet, reverent expression, they felt free to share in the credit for the performance. Madge
even leaned across to the old lady opposite.

"E reads beautiful, doesn't e? Rupert the bear! Makes you laugh,
doesn't it? Still, the children love it. That's the thing."

"Dear little mites," the old woman said.

They had a talk in loud whispers about Princess Marina's big hats,
that threatened to drown the reading. But all the same, reading aloud
was clearly to become one of the permitted treats.

At Fenchurch Street Station, Madge said, "Well, we'll all say ta then, unless you want to come over the water for a cupper. You're welcome. But you won't want more kids' row for today."

When Marcus seemed hesitant, she looked towards Ted, surprised. "Yeah, why not?"

"Well, then, if I'd av known you was coming . . ."

The children finished the line for their mother.

"You like to get shut of all that posh stuff, don't you? "she went on. "Ees gettin to be like one of the family, isn't e, Ted?"

"You'd better watch out, Madge. E may get kicked out of Buckingham Palace one of these days, so ees got Devon Mansions, Tooley Street, in mind as an ome from ome."

"No, I can't this evening," Marcus said. "I've got an engagement, I'm afraid."

The change in his expression was so complete and sudden that Madge stopped to think.

"If your engagement's with Ted, you don't ave to be bashful. I'll op it with the kids."

"Yeah, we aven't been . . ."

But Marcus said, "No, I'm awfully sorry, Ted, I must go home. I'll see you soon."

As he left them, Ted called in a hurt voice, "Well, don't forget little Stan's birthday on the ninth."

As he made for a taxi, he could hear behind him, above the station's din, how Madge's anger at this reminder clashed with Ted's grievance.

Margaret had been listening to the young-faced woman with blue-rinsed hair seated next to her. One of the last war's tragic girl-widows, she was now one of England's rare, successful women solicitors. Question by question through the grapefruit, the meagre fillets of sole Dieppoise, the cutlets *reformés*, and the mocha *bombe*, she had built up this life of male and still more of female prejudice overcome, the "not the clients I should have chosen" that gave the start, the family clients wooed and retained, at last the spectacular case won, and then, thought Margaret, no doubt the "not the clients I should have chosen" (poor shady creatures) dropped. Gladys had interrupted once: "Watch out, Monica, she's preserving you in vinegar."

But Monica had said, "Libel's my speciality. I'm quite safe," and with laughter Margaret had continued her fascinating jig-saw game. "And do you still feel that you must go down to Mrs. Seymour-Clinton's house? Or can you command her presence now at your office?" For listening is an art and part of it consists in feeding back proper names, dates, and other facts to show the speaker that you are inside the story. But now with the coffee and Turkish cigarettes (though most of the halo-hatted ladies with eyes as hard as their diamond clips preferred their own Players or Gold Flake) she began to feel the usual tiny scratchings in the depths of her insides. As they grew she could do no more than smile fixedly at Monica, and finally (for even those very thin, bright green peppermint creams could not save her, though she adored them) had to become intent on making pyramids of crumbs around her plate. At last Monica noticed (as they always eventually did) and turned to her other neighbour. Margaret knew just that humpy, glum look that she must be wearing, for even Gladys was drawn to say, "I say, I'm afraid Monica's bored you horribly, Margaret. I'm afraid none of us are intellectuals. But Monica's rather bright as a rule."

"No, no, it's been fascinating. It's only that I'm going to speak in a few minutes. I always die the little death. Aren't you worried, Gladys?"

"Me? I'm only going to make an announcement and the rest is you. You don't realize what a big figure you are. Most of these women will have read a lot of your stuff. You mustn't judge by a Philistine like me."

"But don't you ever feel nervous before speaking?"

"No, I can't say I do. Ought I to?"

Out of her deepest beliefs about luck and humility and atonement Margaret wanted to say, yes, yes. But she thought instead—none of this is important, my writing's all that matters. Suddenly she saw how to develop the story—Alice would try, of course, to play the nieces off one against the other. And they maliciously would encourage it, comparing notes. The irony would . . . but, if she thought of this, she would lose touch. She made herself attend to Gladys.

She was surprised when her sister, despite the muffling disadvantage of a huge wide-brimmed hat, spoke clearly and easily. So surprised that some minutes had passed before she realized how even more unexpected was what Gladys was saying.

"I don't know how many of you know Cromer, but it's cliffs and east winds. At any rate it seemed to be so when we were there as kids. Perhaps that's why I used to feel particularly out of it all there, out in the cold, as they say. That and the fact that I felt so useless. At home, as I was saying, things were so hopeless that I could try to be a little mother and flatter myself that I wasn't cut off from all the rest. But down at my grandmother's there were competent servants to look after us and regular meals, and the old girl herself, though rather a fuss-pot, was kind to us all. But just because of that I suppose I felt desperately lonely always on those holidays. Of course it was just as bad for the rest, but I had this special difficulty of being the eldest. I think that's why I used to love *Little Women* so . . ."

Margaret felt a wave of resentment. It had been good of Gladys to let her make this appeal to her business-women on behalf of the Basque children, but she had no right to use the occasion to make this tear-jerking appeal for herself. "Little mother" indeed—it called up pictures of Little Nell and Little Dorrit and all those awful horrors that made Dickens so impossible to read. She looked around at the hard, well-made-up faces looming like so many painted moons from beneath their halo hats and was even more furious to see that their hard-boiled expressions had softened into mawkish blurs. And Gladys seemed determined to press upon this sickly and irrelevant *vox humana* stop.

"I must have looked a disgusting object, legs too fat in long white cotton stockings, and a sort of straw bonnet that girls had to wear then, just like the bonnets the donkeys wore on the front, and out of it a great fat face like a kid's drawing of the moon. It wasn't exactly the face to win friends and influence people, but then as a kid one doesn't realize that. You can imagine then how bucked I was when this couple by the high-falutin' name of Tankerville-Jones took me up. A fat girl of twelve whom nobody much wanted to know. It must have been down on the beach one of the few sunny days we had in frozen Cromer. The Tankerville-Joneses had a hut near Granny's. I am sure if she had seen them, she'd have said they were most unsuitable people, but she never came down to the beach. And as for the parents, they didn't notice anything that we did. Nobody noticed, in fact, that for more than a week I was away from the family most of the day. Mr. Tankerville-Jones had hired a pony and cart and took me and her out into the country for farm teas. He used to call her his missus, though I doubt if the poor thing was. And she used to tell my fortune again and again with the cards on a woolly green chenille tablecloth—you know the sort I mean, Margaret, what we used to call caterpillar muck—in the dingy room they'd rented. I loved that, for she was a romantic creature and was always marrying me off to Lewis Waller. And as for Mr. T.-J., he was a perfectly splendid mimic—and I know about mimics with my brother Rupert at home, a brilliant actor already, even though he was only a small kid. But Mr. T.-J. could do Little Tich so that you wouldn't notice he was six foot and all his height seemed to have gone into his feet. Oh, they were wonderful days!"

Gladys sighed, and Margaret came to, realizing that she had long forgotten the Soho dining-room, the paper carnations, the hard-faced women, the Italian waiters, and the litter of coffee cups and *petits fours*.

"And I knew," Gladys said, "as sure as eggs were eggs that they were an illusion. I remember thinking one day as I came into that stuffy little parlour and Mr. T.-J. looked bilious and Mrs. T.-J., for all her rouge and her feather boa and her little laughs, was tearful, that I was in a balloon and soon someone would prick it and it would go bust all round me. Which was something I hated. At Christmas parties I used to stuff my fingers in my ears. I suppose it was just to cheer them up that I told them how Granny would be giving us each a five-pound note that week, as she always did every summer holidays. I remember now that as I told them about it, I knew that the five-pound note would be theirs. I could see all around Mrs. T.-J.'s eye that she'd powdered it thickly to hide where the skin was bruised, and something in *his* eye frightened me as much as it did her. I think that's why she cultivated me, looking back, because she was scared, and to have anyone around, even a child, was better than being alone with him. I shouldn't be surprised if he did her in, in the end. But I never saw it in the papers if he did. And why *he* bothered with me, I never like to think. But back I went next day with Granny's fiver. And of course he borrowed it. And the day after, when I went round to the lodgings, my friends had done a moonlight flit. And, honestly, that was all I could think about. Not the money, although I had to keep on lying all that summer and went without sweets or anything for months, but all I cared was that I'd lost the only friends I'd ever made. It all came into my mind in the taxi coming here. And here are these Basque kids turned out of their homes. Never mind for what reason. As I told my sister, we're not political here. But it's awful for kids to be lonely. It makes them so dependent on any bit of love they can pick up here and there."

Margaret, looking at the women around the table, saw that their hard little smiles, their conscious competence, and their conscious chic had melted as completely as the little pools of mocha cream that remained in the ice-cream glasses. She felt a wondering admiration for Gladys and with it a faint, grumbling envy. I don't *want* to have sentimental, middle-brow, story-telling powers like that. But still, melted faces meant lots of money for Basque children.

Although not, perhaps, for Gladys. Her speech continued: "I say, I've just realized that I've as good as said that we don't want your money because lonely kids shouldn't be dependent on strangers. Just the sort of floater I would make, babbling on. But anyhow, there it is, and Margaret's the clever one, she'll tell us why we've got to fork it out. The only thing I ought to have said is that plans are going ahead and I hope that when we meet next year we shall do so not as a lot of nameless women but as the Association of Professional and Business Women—what a mouthful! That is, if certain objections to our using the title from some ladies in Burlington Arcade and Bond Street can be got round. With which bad joke in poor taste I'll sit down and let you hear a real speech from your favourite novelist, Margaret Matthews."

She sat down with one of her clownish bumps—surely there must be a jam tart stuck to her sit-down-upon. Why *did* she have to clown? Looking at the melted faces Margaret saw that they too had hardened again into their usual lines of boredom, crossness, egotism, and fear. Well, *she* couldn't revive their fleeting tenderness. They must be content with facts and figures from her. Such she gave them, for, after all, they expected a dry note from so ironic an author.

In the taxi on the way back for a cup of tea at the shop in George Street, Gladys said, "Honestly, Margaret, I do apologize for waffling on like that. Thank Gawd you were there to save the day."

Margaret was about to snap back, when, turning, she saw that this stout, handsome woman in the smart black suit and the silly hat was genuinely afraid of her reaction.

"It's awful, Gladys, that we all seemed so close to one another as children and yet we knew nothing really of each other."

And despite the oath she had taken on Sukey's wedding day that after all these years of sharing a bedroom she would never in her life again touch or let herself be touched by another woman, she put her arms round her sister, and refusing to allow even the absurdity of the brim of Gladys's hat pushing her own Astrakhan cap askew to deter her, kissed her full on the lips.

"If you knew, darling, what a heroine you've been to us all, always."

She wanted to say sacred cow, but it would offend; and it was true, whatever else they felt about each other, Gladys's courage and simplicity and lonely success had stood above all their bitchery or moralizing.

"And as to your hold on all those women," she added. "Darling! And *you* talk about loneliness!" For it was true, for those few minutes they had obviously adored her.

"Oh, well, you must remember a whole lot of them got their first jobs through my agency."

Then she stopped the taxi for a few minutes at a fishmonger's and returned with a huge bag of prawns for their tea.

That, thought Margaret, is the secret of her charm. Here they sat in the little office at the back of the antique shop, she and Gladys and this rather nice, faded woman called Sylvia, drinking strong Indian tea and peeling prawns as though it were some dormitory feast. Imagine strong Indian tea and prawns at home! She would never allow herself such coarse indulgence, such threats to her digestion; and if, in some moment of madness, she did so, Douglas's good sense and forethought for her health would banish them at once. Yet here she was trying covertly to take two prawns to every one that Gladys ate, while this most genteel, faded Sylvia was probably getting away with three. Of course they started off the occasion to a happy tune, with heartening news that some impoverished old refugee couple possessed a Grünewald without knowing it. But Gladys had made the most of that. Then and there they had debated about how and when to break the news; her own opinion had been asked and regarded as though she'd been in on the story from its very beginnings; so much so that it looked in the end as though she were re-

sponsible for the final decision—that nothing should be said until the
letter from Christie's confirmed the telephone call to Sylvia, and
that then Gladys and Sylvia would go up to St. John's Wood, and
Sylvia would say *this* and Gladys would put *that* face on, and so on
and so on until, at the last, the moment would come when the good
news could burst forth. And the old gentleman's thin, bearded face
would crease into incredulous smiles of happiness, his nicotine-
stained fingers would tremble with excitement. And as for Mutti—
strange little bent, witchlike lady! "Oh, what a good thing you were
here, Margaret! That's absolutely the best way to go about it."
When really, of course, she had played no part in devising such a
children's surprise. It was gross sentimentality. That awful Dickens
again. Scrooge and Tiny Tim. But it was entirely acceptable, for
unlike Dickens, it obviously came to Gladys naturally; there was no
faking, no told to the children.

Then from toasting the old couple in strong tea, they had passed
now to prawns and intimacy. Sylvia was telling them of a ridiculous
boy with huge ears who had fallen madly in love with her at seventeen—the sequence was a natural one, for the boy's father was a
picture restorer, as Gladys commented, "of all things." Margaret
wanted to say, Why shouldn't he be? but somehow the atmosphere
was unpropitious for such dryness. As Sylvia's story unfolded she
seemed to Margaret's ear, even for a girl, to have encouraged the
wretched boy in a heartless, genteel fashion. But under Gladys's influence—at least that was what it must be—the story appeared quite
different—absurd, droll, a tremendous lark. "Oh, those ears!" Sylvia
ended. "Wouldn't it have been terrible if I'd married him and produced a whole brood of bats?"

And it did seem comic, and Margaret found herself laughing with
the others, for all the world like three schoolgirls drunk on pop and
doughnuts. She had an extraordinary sense of loving women's company as though it were a happy world of innocence from which the
old Adam had been temporarily shut out. Fighting against this irrational view, she thought, I know what it is, for all that caddish-
looking man of hers, Gladys is really Lesbian, that's why women
respond to her. But looking at her sister, she knew the idea to be an
absurd, sophisticated platitude, plainly inapplicable to this simple,
easy woman. She heard herself saying, "Believe it or not, I should

never have had my first affair but for a rat in my bedroom. It was the most absurd thing . . ."

But of course she knew it wasn't absurd at all, that for very good reasons she never let herself think of the business with Roger . . .

"I screamed and screamed and this very presentable young man . . ."

"The age of chivalry was not dead *then*," said Sylvia, but what might have been bitterness sounded like light-hearted comment.

"Oh, yes, a very parfitt gentle knight. But I'm afraid I was a horribly scared damsel in distress. You see, I'd had no experience . . ."

Margaret thought, why don't I talk more with other women in this open way. She was really enjoying her story when the telephone rang.

"Oh, hullo, old dear," Gladys said, and, "Oh, Lord! I thought that was all settled . . . Do they, the blighters? . . . That's steep, isn't it? . . . Oh, Lord! So do I . . . No, I didn't mean to. Of course, I see it's frightfully serious . . . I don't know where we're going to get that amount from . . . No, of course, my dear. No. We'll just have to try . . . No, I'm not, Alf. Honestly, I'm not. I blame *myself*. I ought to have known." At last she said, "All right. The Piccadilly. American Bar. I'll come straight away."

Margaret had tried with Sylvia's help to cover this strained conversation with vague chatter about the shop—did people really pay good money for Victoriana? How many people knew a fake from the real thing? Not to underline their unconcern with Gladys's private alarms she went straight on with her story.

"He was an awfully nice boy, really. And only a bit less innocent than me."

But Gladys said, "Sorry, Margaret. Some other time. I must dash. Will you shut up shop, Sylvia? I shan't be back this evening."

And when Margaret, in her annoyance, invaded her sister's privacy by asking, "Whatever are you going to the Piccadilly Hotel for? That was where the Countess used to net trout. You *must* remember," Gladys said impatiently, "I can't say I do. This is a damned sight more important than anything Mother ever did." And was gone.

They saw her through the shop-window, fat and ridiculous, agitatedly flagging a passing taxi.

Margaret exclaimed, "Well! Is that old flame of hers always so importunate?"

She regretted the question, for, looking at this thin, anaemic woman, she realized that she liked her as little as she knew her. She regretted it more when Sylvia answered, "I know nothing about Gladys's private life. I never think that sort of thing does in business."

Margaret rose. "I must say antique buying's as good an excuse as any I've heard for an afternoon's gossip. How much is that?"

She seized upon the first tolerable object to hand as she walked through the shop—a hollowed Seychelles nut set in an ornate gold salver.

"Twenty pounds. It's not genuine. It's a Victorian imitation in gilt of the sort of baroque stuff you see at Waddesdon."

"It looks pretty. That's all I mind."

As Margaret made out her cheque, Sylvia said: "I hope we gave you lots of material with our gossip for one of your wonderful, nasty short stories."

Along the last five hundred yards of the bridle path, brambles stretched out at every level, to sting the face, to catch the arm, to tear stockings. As Frau Liebermann hesitated, Sukey stepped out on to the stubble.

"It's quite all right," she said, "the harvest's in weeks ago. Such as it was, this dismal summer." Then she cried, "Oh, of course, your shoes! I should have thought to warn you. Or perhaps you don't have these stout brogues in Germany. They're hideous, but they're awfully convenient in the country."

"Oh, no, we have them. But I can walk easily in these."

"No, Middleman! No, you mustn't! Where are your manners? Darling, really! Hold back the brambles for Frau Liebermann and then she can walk on the path."

Sukey would have liked to protest at the woman's total lack of any sense of economy. Ruining good shoes in her position. Coming on a picnic in that good, real wool three-piece and with high heels. But tact was the only thing that mattered for these next three weeks.

When they reached the grass clearing, Senior set down his picnic basket, looked at his watch, and said, "I say, it's pretty late, Mum. I should think we'd better do our blackberrying stint before we have tea. Give everybody a basket, P.S."

Sukey made faces at him to be more tactful.

"I'm not going to apologize, Frau Liebermann, for treating you like one of the family. We'll leave you here with the picnic things while we go off blackberrying. Rugs for Frau Liebermann, Middleman."

Behind her, in a scarcely audible whisper, Senior said: "Frau L.'s not Granny to be left with the basket."

"No," whispered Middleman, "nor a maid."

"I thought at one time," Sukey said, "that my offspring looked like avoiding the tiresome state of growing up. Now I see that was a fond mother's delusion." She laughed in order to give the rebuke a flavour of teasing. But if Frau Liebermann tactfully did not hear the boys' words, she responded to their sentiments: "Oh, no, I shall be glad to pick fruit."

"We don't usually say 'pick fruit' for blackberries and things that grow wild," Sukey told her.

"But we could," Middleman said. "It would sound rather nice. I vote we do."

"I'm trying," Sukey explained, "to help Frau Liebermann to speak English correctly."

"Thank you so much. You are very kind."

"You speak jolly good English already," Middleman told her.

"Jolly good, jolly good." Sukey laughed. "Well, you'll be equipped with schoolboy lingo anyway, Frau Liebermann." But she put her arm round Middleman's shoulders. "And I wouldn't have it otherwise, darling."

"Do you have blackberries in the Harz, Frau Liebermann?" Senior asked. "These ones here?"

"Oh, yes. We call them *Brombeeren*. But more usually on the ground. *Heidelbeeren*. How are those called in English, Arnold?"

The little boy's swarthy features flushed with red as usual when his beloved mother questioned him, and as usual he answered in a mumble, "I don't know."

"Could it be heathberries?" P.S. asked. "Heide is heath, isn't it?"

"Jolly good," said Middleman, "except that there aren't such things as heathberries."

Sukey frowned at him.

"There could be," Senior said. "I should think they'd be what we call bilberries or whortleberries. We don't get them round here."

Suddenly Arnold had flung himself down on the ground, crawling on his stomach, as so often quite unrestrained in his imitations. Sukey looked towards P.S. and gave him a comforting smile, for she knew how much this feeble fooling by another boy of his own age embarrassed him. At the same time, remembering Frau Liebermann's position, her evident devotion for her hideous little son, she cried:

"Oh, that's just right, Arnold. What a nuisance they are to pick, aren't they? And what a strain on the tummy muscles! But they're delicious with cream. And they remind us of our darling Quantocks, don't they, boys? The west of England is so beautiful, Frau Liebermann. You and Arnold must . . ."

But as strands of hennaed hair blew across the thick orange make-up with which Frau Liebermann apparently loved to cake her face, Sukey broke off. The clash of the two reds, and then again the dark oiliness of Arnold's skin, the precocious black hairy growth on his upper lip simply did not fuse with the brown coombs and the purple heather of the Quantocks.

"Well," she said, "each to his own direction. And back here, in what? Half an hour? But do remember your lovely stockings, Frau Liebermann. The thorns are terrible."

Arnold pulled at his mother's sleeve.

"Look, Mummy, that way are the best. Shall we go there? Mummy, *auch sprachst du?*" She ran her hand through his thick, straight, lifeless black hairs. Then she gave him a little push. "You go there, Arnold. I shall go another way. So we shall be getting more fruit for Mrs. Pascoe than if we go together."

Sukey smiled, but she felt herself now forced to take the opposite direction from that P.S. proposed.

Blackberrying was something that she truly enjoyed. To find a bush covered with shiny, fat, ripe berries, patiently and systematically to pick every one, never by any chance allowing an immature, still partly red fruit to fall unnoticed into the basket, to hook down with the crook of her stick clusters swaying high up in the air, to bend low for single mammoth berries growing almost over the hollows of rabbit warrens, above all, sighting a fruitful bush deep within the thicket, to fight her way through and emerge a little scratched and dishevelled, to repeat the despoiling of another hoard—all this called for sufficient physical endurance and agility, enough demands on her constant awareness to excuse the indulgence of half an hour's day-dreaming. Better still, it was usually an occasion for the peculiar pleasure of sharing day-dreams with P.S.—spoken or unspoken, for their bond was too close to need words. But today this tiresome woman had deprived her of P.S., worse still, had intruded herself into all reverie. Today she picked and picked and scrambled through briars and knelt on rotting leaves and sticks until a cruel cramp seized the muscles of her calves, not in order to excuse her roving thoughts but by concentrated action to keep Frau Liebermann out of them.

Of course one felt desperately sorry for her—a bit absurd with her hennaed hair, but that was Continental, or even more likely Jewish; indeed it only made her stories of neighbours' slights, that had turned overnight into bullying, the desperate fears for her absent husband and her grown son more horrible, more pitiable because so unheroic. A human being after all that one could not but want to help; yet not someone to include in the family circle, no, not at all, for she neither fitted in nor stimulated by her challenge. She was just there, living in her own feelings, with her thoughts quite somewhere else. And naturally so, she would have been the same herself in some foreign land without the family, without the boys, without P.S.; but then Frau Liebermann *had* her Arnold with her. Somehow the woman made them all feel as though the happy life they had built up was not quite . . . Sukey heard the word "nice" echoing in her thoughts, but it was hardly meaningful, no, as though their life, the world they had made, did not matter. She refused the idea at once; she had never accepted the view that merely because people were unhappy or poor or ill, they should be considered before others. Hugh at times spoke in that way about some wretched small boy who couldn't fit into the school, but then that was his job. For the rest, health and happiness every time—without them all was muddle and dirt.

People like Quentin—clever, if cranky—disapproved strongly of individual charities, said they only scratched the surface of the world's troubles. Certainly the Frau's coming to them did not seem to have put off this foul war scare one atom; God had not answered . . . With her stick to the ground she levered one long spiny branch packed with luscious berries, then held it in place with her foot and picked, telling herself not to be a complete, dotty fool. She must read the papers more often—she had never had time for such things in her busy life—but that article of Garvin's last Sunday had been most reassuring, and he *knew*.

No! She suddenly accused herself, for she saw the real truth—she was jealous, of all absurd things, jealous, that was it. Despite her streaky hennaed hair, her orange make-up, her dullness, her abstraction, Frau Liebermann was one of those bores who yet had charm; an unconscious, odd, uncaring sort of charm; but it had conquered Senior and Middleman, there was no doubt of that. And she, their own mother, was becoming jealous. Stirring the blackberries around in the basket with the palm of her hand, making patterns, picking out here a green, there a red interloper, she gave herself very bad marks indeed. It was well known that boys of seventeen or eighteen fall in love with older women, women old enough to be their mothers. It was only a question of understanding, perhaps of a bit of teasing. She felt the hot, late September sun waking her after the disappointing, cold, wet summer; she looked with pleasure at her full basket. That she had beaten down so many brutal thickets, smashed so many thorny, lacerating branches, and braved her hands, and had come through victorious made her body, now that she could relax, seem to her young again, younger than her thirty-five years, certainly young enough to laugh a bit at all her own solemn mother-of-a-family-bowed-down-with-care stuff. Returning, she slipped easily through a gap in the bushes here, noticed a trodden branch there, noticed indeed more than her own former pathway—a new place for picking primroses next spring, and surely, yes, it was, a weasel's skull to tell P.S. of—lively, observing, with a swinging walk, with a sure sense of direction, she returned to the family, and catching her foot in a bramble sucker, fell. Most, though not all of the blackberries were scattered, yet she could only think—pride came before a fall. And, for some reason, the old maxim made her giggle helplessly. If only P.S. were there to share the fun. She picked up the scattered fruit one by one. But, as for those berries that had rolled into the dense, thorny scrub, damn them, they can stay there; what do I care if they have escaped me? On the stretch of open downland the others had already started their tea, or rather they took her appearance as a signal to begin. Only P.S. waited for her to give the usual word.

Yet she felt no desire at all to rebuke them. Sitting down on the same rug as Frau Liebermann, she asked, "Do you have sausage rolls in Germany? Oh, they're delicious, you must try them. Look, have half this one with me to see if you like them. And for goodness' sake, help yourself. I shall. We can't afford to be ladies with these great louts about."

And stuffing her mouth with food, she imitated Senior at his greediest until they were all laughing.

"Well, *you* drop crumbs everywhere and get butter on your chin when there's buttered toast," he told her. It was his old retort.

"All perfect ladies do eat messily, don't they, Frau Liebermann?" Sukey asked. And they had to laugh because Frau Liebermann really had made a terrible mess with her sausage roll.

"Anyhow, she's collected a perfectly wizard basket of blackberries, Mummy," Middleman said.

But P.S. wasn't having that. "Mummy's'll be the biggest, I bet. It always is."

The two baskets put side by side showed Frau Liebermann was an easy winner.

"But mine fell over," Sukey said protesting. "It did, really it did." She began to giggle helplessly again. "You don't believe me, do you? You think I'm just saying that to save my wounded pride. Oh, dear, how funny!" She could hardly get the words out. Then she saw Frau Liebermann's glance of surprised curiosity. "Congratulations, Frau Liebermann. We ought to shake hands."

But she could not stop laughing. "You know what," she said, "I'm going to seize this rare sunshine to have a delicious snooze."

She lay back with her head on an ancient molehill and soon fell asleep in the warm breeze.

When she woke, the sun was still shining, but it might as well have been smothered in cloud, for she felt cold and cheerless; and she must have eaten the sausage rolls too quickly for they lay on her chest like sharp-edged stones. Her cheeks burned, sour bile filled her mouth, she felt too tired to move. Their talk went through her like the movements of some animal, of a dog or a cat licking one's face when one wished to sleep. All she could do was to let it lap over her.

"But you see we did not notice at first. The people who turned their heads from us, we had never liked. So naturally we were not so sad. If you do not like some people, if they are pigs, you are glad when they do not speak to you. But then Arnold was sent back from the school and he was crying and his eye was cut. I did not know what to do. I was so angry and frightened. But after again it was better. We heard from the Friends and he came here to Mrs. Carver and your father. And Sigmund was still away in Italy, so for some months it was only I and my dear Herbert who must face these things. And with Herbert it is always so easy to laugh. He is so brave. But now I shall tell you something to shock you. There was in our—what do you say—house of apartments a girl, quite young, seventeen, eighteen, I don't know, something of your age, who for many years cannot walk. She has been quite ill with poliomyelitis and must be in a chair. So, I have never liked to be with ill people, or what do you say, cripples? Yes, that's it, thank you. But each morning she is there at her window and so I found the habit—can you say 'found the habit'?—to say to her, good morning, and sometimes, because her mother is old, to make some shopping for her. One day when I ask, 'What do you want me to buy today?' Fräulein Kissinger she turned her head away and would not speak. At first I was finding tears in my eyes—how shall I bear it if the poor cripple girl will not speak to me? And then I think I am very happy—I don't like cripples, I don't want to speak to them, I don't wish to make their shopping. I am free from all that. So, you know, staying here now with you in this beautiful country I sometimes think in such a way, what do I care about Germany, I am free, but then . . ."

There should be no "but then" to it. Sukey had up to now let the words flow over her, but the monotonous, level voice depressed her spirits, flattened the world for her. The boys said nothing; with her eyes closed she could not tell their reactions, but she guessed—knew —hoped them to be bored; what sort of stuff to serve up to boys of that age! And she could not have this woman boring them all, boring and depressing *herself* with these tales; she must assert their strong happiness, the happiness of nearly twenty years to banish these treacherous, pervasive mists of sadness. Sitting up suddenly, she said:

"Do you know, that's exactly what I used to feel on the houseboat? You didn't know *we'd* been exiles, too, Frau Liebermann. But we were, in Cairo, on the Nile. Hugh had pneumonia some years ago and one of our parents was a rich Egyptian currant merchant and he lent us this boat for Hugh to convalesce. I know exactly how you must feel. The strangeness of making orders for lunch that first day, because of course P.S. was too much a baby to eat rice. And just being on the great river with the strange little fishing boats that might have come out of the beginning of time. Do you remember Ali, our little cook, Senior? 'Yes, I tank you.' And the geese that swam round the boat as we breakfasted? I thought I shouldn't be able to bear it all at first, but then Hugh had an absolutely beastly headmaster, a proper Hitler. I'd had terrible rows with him. And suddenly I remember thinking, just like you, that I was glad to be away from it all. Senior was only five then but he made a little garden on the bank of the river with just a packet of seeds and, of course, with the sun and the fertile soil we had flowers in a few weeks. I think I was as surprised as he was. Do you remember, Senior?"

Senior gave a slight smile of recall.

"But *you* don't, Middleman, you were too small. You might just remember the great captain of the boat, such a huge man in his turban and blue coat, quite dark, a Sudanese. Do you?"

"Perhaps I do, Mother, I'm not sure."

"Well, I am sure if he's alive he remembers you. He was for ever saving you from drowning. I shall always be grateful to him. Like a very lovable gorilla. And then the old carriages, the victorias, with their drivers calling to us whenever we came on deck. The noise, the bustle, the sheer life of the Nile. Oh, I shall never forget . . ."

"Mummy! Mummy!" P.S. shouted. "Do shut up! Who wants to recall that old stuff now?"

As a rule he just sat and let the hideous, whimsical advertisements break up in the rattle and speed of the journey into a pleasant, trivial, Dufy-decorative mass of points of colour and light. Appropriately reminded by the many toothpaste names that shot at him from every side, he would feel himself encased in a grey steel tube rushing through time to what? To Sunday afternoon family fug, the smell of the baby's nappies, of washing up and of Madge's old dad's incontinence—but why? why? Easiest for the moment just to say, over the water to Ted. But this Sunday afternoon bodies pressed upon him, threatening to crush him against the glass partition—more and more of them at every station, blotting out the specks of colour, obliterating even the swinging bells made by the hanging straps. At first he

distracted himself with Jean's letter. Then came a sharp pain, as with
the swaying of the train a high heel dug deep into his foot and made
him drop the letter and then scrabble for it among the pillared maze
of legs. Jean's spidery elegance was defiled by the criss-cross imprint
of a rubber heel by the time he retrieved it; but like all his posses-
sions it was in any case due for a crumpled existence, wedged amid
combs and pocketbooks and other old letters in his inside breast
pocket. He amused himself until Camden Town with Jean's accompanying sketches of *les boxeurs et les boxophiles*, but always the feeble lines—here of a young man's tapering hips, there of the crooked
mouth of a drooling old satyr—annoyed him by their total failure to
measure up to Jean's power of words, his wit, his charm, his wonderful physical presence. Stuffing the drawings away with the letter,
he looked up to see an enormous black, cloth-clad bottom sharing his
line of vision with thinner, meagre buttocks, their outline lost in
shapeless, almost threadbare, grey flannel. As he let his eyes rove,
these nearby spheres and hemispheres seemed to stretch out into an
infinite series of circles, semi-circles, ovals, as white faces gleamed
against heavy breasts bursting out of their dresses, and vast bottoms
gave place to tree-trunk thighs and bottle calves. With the swaying
of the train the shapes changed their patterns until suddenly, with a
violent lurch, the huge black bottom fell upon his face, threatening
to cushion him into extinction.

Here at his changing point, Charing Cross, there were rifts and
eddies in the crowd, but the patterns no longer fascinated him, had
suddenly become nauseating. The press, the noise, the human smell
were more powerful than his vision. Satisfying abstractions were
now replaced by a vile, expressionist, nightmare army; a threatening
insensate world turned vengeful was led all the way to the Borough
by two jellied breasts, two ripe bursting fruits that with another
lurch of the train might at any moment cram their mellowness into
his mouth and stifle him with soft-scented female flesh.

He came out with the crowd (who could they all be? and why
was London Bridge Station closed?) on to the narrow platform,
shot up, wedged in the lift, and emerged into Long Lane, half fear-
ing to find the road as jammed as the carriage had been. But even a
large crowd is soon swallowed up and lost when unconfined; so in
the street he found, not, it was true, the usual Sunday, empty, grey-
brown desolation of poverty, litter, and decay, but a curious bustling

Brueghel-like scene in which little brightly coloured knots of people gathered here and there for a moment and then broke only to reform in some different pattern upon the other side of the road. Policemen, papersellers, now, as he looked closer, badges and lapel buttons, here and there a small group busily unfurling a banner. He must have arrived for some minor political demonstration, some dreary slogan-shouting do. Fortunately, in his many visits to Devon Mansions he had come to know every side lane that led into Tooley Street, so that he could easily avoid whatever tiresome nonsense might be going on. He refused *Soviet Weekly*, the next day's *Daily Worker*, and some disconsolately offered peace leaflets, also *Freedom*, and set off down the broad, sad road of endless, decaying artisan rectangles, whose decently regular shape, thank God, disguised their monstrous misery. "Or was it," Madge said, roaring her jolliest cockney *fortissimo*, "that that lot were all right; the more the bugs the warmer in bed." And Ted said, "What you want to come by them back streets for? I don't like it. They'll get you one time in Long Lane or Abbey Street. One of the mobs." He came that way of course because Madge also said, "Look, honest, we can't av that shover sitting out there for all the neighbours to see, can we?" and Ted also asked, "What you want to keep a taxi checkin up outside like that, Markie? It don't look right."

Not because of anger, righteous anger—God blast the rich—but because of "What will the neighbours think?" That was why he travelled over the water (or under it) to Ted by the tedious, smelly tube train; why he walked through the dead streets past houses that he wanted to level like nursery bricks with one angry blow of the hand, yes, and all the poor who lived in them, the helpless poor who gave you only disgusting alternatives—to freeze your heart, Countess-like, into a useless icicle or to weep cheap, Billy Pop tears. Now he found himself swallowed up by a small group of men, capped and blue-suited, with a banner (talk about Longfellow's strange device!) which they carried so uneasily that he could only guess at some noble Puvis de Chavannes figures beneath an ornate scroll. Battersea, was it? No, Bermondsey, of course, Trades Council. Another home-made banner of white canvas said in red letters, "No pasaran. Yiddisher boys know what to do." Some young men were singing, "Bye, bye, Black Shirt." But only one or two of them looked Jewish. At any rate they were on the right side and he found himself

humming the tune of "Bye, Bye, Blackbird," and even joining in the
words, "as we come the Black Shirts go." Embarrassed when he
heard his own voice, he rapidly crossed the road only to realize that
he was leading this small procession. The crowd on this far side of
the road had swelled to such numbers that he slowed almost to a
crawl. Impatiently he turned off down a side lane, but here the
throng of people was thicker still. Although its movement was rapid,
its progress apparently purposeful, he felt suddenly that he was
being held back, sucked into a pace and will that he refused. He had
to dodge and skip among the crowd to make his own pace. Cutting
through a gap between two groups, he bumped against a stout
woman and she cried, "There's no need to push, mate. We're all
together."

A young man in a sports-coat, his neck enveloped in swirls of
green-and-magenta college scarf, cried, "Plenty of time before they
get near here. They've been turned back at Southwark Bridge."

The emergence of these two identities, though irritating to Marcus, released him from his increasingly anxious isolation.

"It's provocation, that's all it is," a young woman said, "and the
police are with them."

"Ah! The fuckin police!"

"The Stepney boys stopped them last year."

"And we'll do it again, don't you worry."

The speakers were indeterminate to Marcus; he could hardly
"place" anyone; male and female voices, voices old and young, bodies
thin and fat, nothing to notice if it were not more bare heads than he
was used to seeing out of doors.

"Coming down and upsetting other people's business."

"Oh! There'll be plenty to do that for you in the next year or
two."

This voice was sardonic, schoolmasterly.

"Ignore them! What's that for advice?" someone asked scornfully.

"Herbert Morrison! I'd have that lot out straight away."

But the fat woman took this up: "I don't know. We've always
been Labour. My old man wouldn't ave nothin to do with it. If the
party tells us to stop away, then stop away, e said. But I told im that's
all right for you, but what if *we* was Jewish?"

"That's right. Free speech, but no filth. Coming down here with their filthy propaganda. Incitement to disorder, that's what it is, eh?"

Marcus heard himself say, "Oh, God! They'll bring order all right, if we let them. The order of death. That's why we've got to stop them."

He hardly had time to feel their responsive glow when a sudden shift of the thickening crowd pulled him away from his new-found friends. He was urged forward ten feet or more up the little street. But now he found himself so firmly wedged that he could hardly respond to the crowd's pressure as it swayed to and fro with a rhythm that had nothing to do with purpose. Like the straphangers in the tube train but without their sudden lurchings and violent sprawls, this great world of people, of which he was only some tiny lump, some senseless, unsmooth surface, kept up its determined, incomprehensible, regular motion—back, as the pressure of the heavy man in front rolled down upon him, on to the hard corners of the handbag held by the woman behind him, then rolled forward again by the pressure of her breasts on to the wadding of the heavy man's firm bum. All the cries and the talk, the snatches of singing came like the creakings of this huge world, as it swayed to and fro. He peered desperately towards the cracks of cloudy sky, the odd glimpse of a soot-thick chimney that seemed to offer the safety of dead matter in this senseless mass of life. Intent upon these patterns of sky and sooty brick that alone kept him safe from his mounting panic, his growing fear of being cut off from Marcus Matthews—ageing but still beautiful young man, friend of the Sitwells and Cocteau, part owner of Kandinskys and Braques, sole owner of Marie Laurencins and Magnasco's "Cardinals in a Crypt," lover of Jack and Ted, occasional sufferer from haemorrhoids, giver of green balls—he stretched on to his toes to complete the triangle of grey that he had carved from the visible sky and came near to losing his balance, to being sucked underfoot. By happy chance his panic reaction was cut off by a sudden distant singing out of his childhood—"Tipperary!" It must be a delusion—such as the Scotsgirl, what was her name? Jessie! at Lucknow—he saw the school history illustration before him—"Dinna ye hear them, the pipes of the Campbells?" He said it aloud and giggled for the absurdity of his new role. A woman shouted:

"Stop the bastards."

And a man: "To Tooley Street, comrades."

As if, thought Marcus, they were not going there as fast as they could. But he was wrong, for whatever barrier had blocked the crowd's way was suddenly removed, and with a rush they now swept forward, first a directionless world in flux, and then at last small groups, scattered individuals, himself, all making for the sound of "Tipperary." He had time to think that Jessie's was no illusion— Lucknow *had* been relieved—when he realized with fury that this boisterous farewell to Leicester Square came from the approaching Fascists, not from the relieving Campbells but from the enemy. Well, he had always detested all that khaki sentiment, Quentin's wounded heroism, old Bill, his mother giving herself to the boys on leave, all groups, and nations, and waving of flags, and unsought tears of emotion. From the crowd around him came an answering song, slow, solemn, creaking, yet charged with suffering and pathos: "Though tyrants frown and cowards sneer, we'll keep the Red Flag flying here." They could keep it as far as he was concerned. But then again, most insistently pathetic, it came to him: "Our cause, I fear, is dying."

He looked around him for some neutral force to save him from engulfment, to restore him to his own Sunday individual purpose— over the water to Ted? Never mind. Here, before the junction with Tooley Street, the police cordon had broken and the crowd were busy piling chairs, tables, street barrows, anything to hand to form a great barrier against invasion—of what?—a lot of paranoid, half-educated, weasel-faced vets and dentists and suburban housewives into their warm, bug-ridden slum burrows. Well, good luck to them. He summoned all his snobberies, inherited and acquired, to save him. He went up to a near-by policeman.

"I'm awfully sorry to trouble you, Constable, but is there any possibility of getting through to Devon Mansions in Tooley Street? I've come here to visit friends. I had no idea I'd run into all this."

The handsome face showed a complete blank at his question, but to face him with improbable reality in the shape of a posh, tony-voiced cissy in a grey sombrero on the battlefield of Tooley Street was perhaps to try slow wits hard.

"I mean, can you at all suggest what I had better do?"

For a moment he feared that the law would offer him all the indignity that the mob had spared him, for the policeman raised his hand —Marcus could see already the two upward-pointing fingers, or would have done if he had not wildly feared worse in the shape of a

smack on the face. But instead the officer took his arm, kindly, pater-
nally:

"If you were to go down that little street there, sir, you'd come
round to Devon Mansions the other way. And then . . . But look,
I'll . . ."

As he was about to conduct Marcus to this possible short cut, this
potential safety exit, a shout from an inspector recalled him to duty.
The marchers he was there to protect were upon them—no longer
"Tipperary," but that awful Mussolini tune that Marcus remembered dogging him and Jack from every band, every hurdy-gurdy,
two years ago in search of South Italian Baroque. The young policeman left him as abruptly as he had offered help and guidance. Marcus was once more alone. All around him the crowd had started
singing another tune. From the deep-chested contralto of a woman
near him he thought he heard, "Too long we've been the vulture's
prey." Phantasmagoria in Munch, or Ernst at a pinch, though not for
his taste; lunacy here on a simple Sunday outing was too much. He
was about to turn down the lane the policeman had indicated, no
matter what cries of "Stop the bastards," "Stop the Fascist rats," or a
sudden, improbable, clear ladylike call on "Don't let them get
through, comrades," when suddenly it was the cornet and the fife, it
was everyone rushing at high speed towards Tooley Street.

Angry, cruel, and arrogant, beyond even Marcus's wet dreams,
the mounted policemen appeared as seen from below. They did not
break the childish thrill that Marcus had felt as he rushed towards
the martial music, though they laced it with exciting physical fear.
But then the first Fascists, with no help of uniform, filled him at
once with loathing—they were so pathetic with their dreary, self-
conscious heads held high, their occasional nervous smirks, their
awful gym instructors' p.t. postures, their feigned arrogance, so ridiculous beside the arrogance of their mounted protectors. The defi-
ant faces were chalk white; why couldn't they have the decency at
least to show the natural fear they felt as they marched through this
crowd of men, women, and children all screaming their hatred?
Marcus wanted to kick them, to smack their faces in order to drive
away that silly pretence of disdain and officers' courage, he wanted
to shout at them to go, that they had no bloody right down here
where their suburban fears and graces had no place in a warm-
packed instinctual world.

"We've got to get rid of the rats," he shouted with those around him. "We've got to get rid of the rats."

And he cheered as a group of young blokes successfully made a fresh barrier of chairs and barrows farther down the street and nimbly escaped the policemen who ran to arrest them. From nowhere an old woman, some mad-moll survival from the London of Dickens, or even Hogarth, got through the police cordon to shake her fist in the faces of the Fascist marchers, to shout heaven knew what oaths or threats or obscenities at them. Marcus, with the whole vast crowd, cheered this old woman in her straw boater and shawl, who could have been the spirit of the cockney past come back to avenge this hateful, impudent invasion. And now the horses began rearing and foam spewed over their bits as crackers exploded and fizzed beneath their hoofs. As soon as a policeman broke from the cordon to pursue a cracker-thrower, the crowd would rush through the gap to chuck oranges, rotten apples, whatever was to hand at the faces now at last showing fear and hate. Marcus led the jeers as Fascist boys nervously slipped off the false Jewish noses which they had thought, as they set off from reassuring, solid Westminster, were such a good joke with which to taunt the East-End scum. And now the Fascist women, burly or petite, always ladylike and neat, marching *grande dame* to the guillotine. And here, with this monstrous regiment, the march halted as inspectors of police and mounted men and "leaders" consulted together, surrounded on all sides by heaving seas of raging men and women, now straining forward, now receding, but only held back by a tight-packed, hard-pressed cordon of police. Marcus's intense excitement, his furious sense of love for the crowd around him, his sudden loathing identification of the bestial army that in its squalid adoration of brute health threatened everything he cared for, began to ebb. What was he doing here shouting? What warmth tied him to the stinking armpits of the brawny young man under which he squinted to view the scene? What love did he really feel for the old bobbed grey-head that in her excitement or at the crowd's pressure rubbed his face with greasy, scurfy hairs? The rearing horses, the crowd's shouting, the fireworks, the rival singing, youths seized and led off jeering by the police—all this now repetitive film news— was freezing into a "still" and as it froze, so emotional tension began to relax. Had Ted been silly enough to involve himself in this mêlée? Or even generous-hearted Madge? Was this what Picasso's wonderful "Guernica" stood for, this Roman holiday? No form, no rich colour, no pale elegance. Nothing. Nothing to satisfy in this shapeless human muddle.

Then suddenly—something that made his hands tremble with rage. There, surely, in black sweater and pleated grey-flannel skirt, Dulcie, tittering and whispering with a companion marcher as the march was halted—with a weather-beaten old battle-axe with faded blond hair, come up from the country, no doubt, to show the shirking dockers true discipline and pluck. Something Dulcie said set the other cow off laughing and then, at a word from a grey-haired dragon woman, they both set their silly faces again in a noble, martyred, how-we-girls-faced-the-lions look. The silly cunts and their fucking pluck! All the bloody middle class, oh, how common, don't touch pitch, you-never-know-what-council-school-boys-may-have-in-their-hair teaching of his childhood blew over him in a foul wind of touch-me-not, smelly lady-likeness that made him want to vomit. Dulcie's distant white blob of a face seemed the very source of all his isolation from life's warmth.

"Get out, you Fascist cunt," he shouted.

A grey-haired, young-faced man with a large Adam's apple above a butcher-blue shirt and a red tie turned and said:

"Now, look here. That language isn't going to help things, you know."

But a group of delighted youths had taken it up.

"Fascist cunts! Fascist cunts!"

A Trades-Council man, with a United-Front badge, and a Party girl started up "The Internationale" again and the obscenity was soon drowned. And solemnly, oh, so decently, Dulcie and her friends tried to purify Tooley Street from this alien noise with memories of the Old Contemptibles—"It's a long, long way . . ." their nice voices told the East End air. This time Marcus answered by laughter, "Oh, God," he cried. "Silly bitches." This time he was truly the leader, for the laughter spread through the crowd and grew and swelled and lapped the more against the isolated women trying so ridiculously to sing on. At a shouted word of command, the Fascist marchers, with their mounted escort, turned off from Tooley Street, from the improvised barricades that had stopped their way, and to the crowd's cheers of derision, set off down a side street opposite to a new secret meeting place. Silly sods, they'll never get to Jamaica

Road! At last even the swagger and harshness of the mounted police looked as silly as their charges. They were strutting to Colonel Bogey, and the young kids that ran at their side parodied the blaring sounds. Laughter drove them out of Tooley Street. A right lot of charlies. And Marcus felt some freedom, some ease that he had always missed, as he let off a raspberry himself at Dulcie's retreating bum.

He found himself talking spiritedly, happily, to a small, artily dressed young woman with her black hair wrenched back into a bun.

"Oh, the heaven of victory!" he said.

"Marvellous," she answered, "they can't say it was just the Jews like they did about Stepney. It's the South Londoners, this time, who've shown what they feel."

Thinking of Ted and of Jack, he said, rather crossly:

"What's the difference?"

"Good Lord! The propaganda effect's completely different. Where on earth do you come from?"

"Hampstead. And so do you."

Something about his remark drove political contempt from her face; she laughed and said:

"Does it show so much?"

"Yes, but never mind."

As he said it he thought, My God! What on earth am I doing talking to a nut-eating, jet-earringed woman like this? She'll offer to show me her hand-loom in a minute. They edged each other a little warily, but there was no time for their friendliness to be blown away, for the crowd was suddenly turning, running, shouting. Marcus tried to stand his ground, but he was swept back down the lane, fighting all the time to keep his balance.

"It's the bastards let it loose," an old man shouted.

But an old woman said, "They oughtn't to have done it. Not even if it was our own boys. A lorry! Why, they might av killed the kids."

But all causes, enemy or erring friend, gave way before the sound of hoofs bearing down upon them. Two heavy young men, running, drove so violent a passage between Marcus and the grumbling woman that he felt himself flying through the air past the crowd to the side of them, although he could feel his feet still making contact with the road; indeed, he caught his ankle sharply against the edge of the pavement, sprawled in front of the running feet, and then dragged himself to safety in the narrow step of a doorway. Feeling, rather than seeing, the crowd hurrying past, he had a terrible fear, as in nightmares, that he would be lost if he were left behind. Yet he was too shaken and bruised to move from his half-crouching posture; he had time to think "lost?" But to whom or to what pursuer? The thumping of running feet grew less and with it his panic; at last he knew silence enough and security to examine the pain in his knee where the torn trouser cloth flapped bloodily. He staunched the wound with a handkerchief, got up, felt dizzy, imagined Madge's big-sized brown pot of tea, longed for it, and turning, saw his Hampstead young woman held kicking and screaming in the air by two grim-faced young policemen. Whether it was the pathetic way that her tight black bun, symbol of her austere superiority, had fallen in a shapeless mass on her shoulders, or the one shoeless foot waving so helplessly, or the invasion of her privacy where her skirt had ridden up to show a white thigh, he was overcome by rage on behalf of women, the poor bitch sex that had been forever pushed around by brute force, the duped victims of men's spunky idiocy. The embarrassed, self-consciously passionless faces of the two policemen were to him at that moment a mask for vicious lust. They were wrenching the poor woman's arms cruelly. Staggering into the road, he came up to them as they lifted her past him to a waiting van.

"You don't have to wrench her like that, you know. I shall report that."

He meant to sound like a commanding, substantial colonel, but, of course, it came out in high-pansy dudgeon. The younger policeman said to his mate:

"You take her, Fred. I'll just deal with Mabel here. *What* did you say?" pushing his face very close to Marcus's, showing all the fury he had concealed when handling the woman. Marcus felt from his balls a sexual battle.

"I said I should report you."

Immediately, his arm was roughly and painfully seized.

"You bastard," he cried, trying to free his arm.

"That's quite enough of that. I'm booking you for abusive language and obstructing a constable in the execution of his duty."

Marcus joined the one hundred and eleven other people arrested in Bermondsey. That evening, when he had been charged at the Borough Police Station and released on his own surety to appear at Tower Bridge Magistrates' Court on the Monday, he somehow no longer thought with pleasure of Madge's hot tea. He went back to Hampstead, where, after a long hot bath, he spent a delicious hour in showing a rich and knowledgeable Chilean their collection. And an even more delicious quarter of an hour followed when the wraith-like, mink-clad wife, who had looked lemon disdain at the abstracts, went into a narcissistic transport at his pet Marie Laurencin. Certainly, take one startled hare's eye, lose one swan's neck, it might have been her portrait. Jack, following the husband's lead, essayed an embarrassed gallantry. But Marcus said, "Oh, the bliss of someone who can like beautiful nonsense as well!" He insisted on showing her his Magnasco cardinals.

As Jack said afterwards, "You allow no human form to resist your obsessive patterns. You should have been a Moslem."

Christmas (eighty days to go from Marcus's fine of £10—"You had no business to be in Bermondsey. Your behaviour was totally irresponsible.") loomed distantly ahead that year in a flurry of questions rather than of snow, in an atmosphere of increasing fears that gnawed the guts when goodwill should have been warming the cockles. Of course a year ago there had been questions too: at 52 the Countess had demanded of the dying Regan, "Who on earth *is* she?" and it seemed too absurd, some American woman, when only yesterday she had dreamed again and again of dancing with him herself—at Ciro's. But Billy Pop had been so reassuring, "They can't afford to let him go," he'd said, "he's our chief national asset." But they had, and now he was over the water with the woman he loved. It was all too rotten. The Countess, and the waitress who always served her at Fuller's tearoom, had cried about it together. It was dramatic, and the Countess found herself often looking at the piano as though there ought to be some special music to go with the whole story.

But as this renewal of the Bethlehem theogony approached, the questions in the newspapers were all to do with unpleasant quarrels in far-away countries, all, except Austria (those enchanting waltzes), unknown to the Countess. In any case, Billy Pop reassured her again and again; he had met So-and-So, who was the real man at Something or other, and again old So-and-So, who was the fellow behind

Something else. And although all this was confidential, it did seem that there were answers. In the end the Countess decided to meet the question by refusing to read the newspapers. In any case, she was always too busy to give them more than a glance.

Gladys, too, saw a time when she wouldn't be able to open the newspapers. Unless, that was, she could answer—no, more than that —satisfy Alf's demands—was she calling him a liar then? Was this what they'd meant to each other all these years? Ringmer Development was flourishing, considering the uncertain property market and all this international tension; and Asbestos Products was expanding, no less. And now his baby, the one really sure thing he'd got on to in his life, his Cinema Hire Limited was in danger. Good God! He'd got the securities, and more than half were paid for. She'd seen young Fison's letter, as soon as the old boy had had his op, the rest of the money would be in the post. Three weeks at the most. Christ! She didn't want him to chivvy a sick man, did she? Well, if she did, no, thank you, just because the bloody auditors were chivvying *him*. My God, if he'd had ten thousand pounds by him and she'd been in a jam . . . But then she obviously didn't trust him; all right, call him a bloody liar. For three weeks, three lousy weeks, that was all he was asking her, to borrow money from an old chap who didn't even know he'd got it. He wasn't asking her to sell to Christie's or any of the posh places. No, he'd heard of a chap she could go to. A Jew, as a matter of fact. Oh, for God's sake, girlie, you don't seem to have understood me much after all these years. The best Jews are the salt of the earth and absolutely brilliant. Hadn't he always said so? All right then. Give him credit where credit was due. And as for this old boy Einstein or Twostein or Halfamostein, in three weeks she could plonk him down his ten thousand quid, they could even afford to forget the commission and she'd have saved him all the fuss of Should he take the price or shouldn't he? A decision that would probably kill him at that age with a bloody stroke. All right then, go to hell, if she preferred her ruddy principles to him.

Hoarse on the telephone hour after hour, and in American bars, his hand shaking, breathing whisky at her, so red in the face now, mopping the sweat from his brow. And at her flat once, calling her for the first time ever a straight-laced bitch, a bloody Pharisee, twisting her plump arm so that she had to bring out the ivory slave bangle she hadn't worn for years to hide the bruises. And, afterwards, two

dozen yellow roses by special messenger. But principles were principles, though his eyes looked frightened, flickered uncertainly above
his tired, baggy cheeks. But principles were principles, though his
lower lip now seemed to have a freakish life of its own. Only, at
last—they'd gone to Brighton on the new fast train from Victoria—
he'd exasperated her and also won her heart by telling her of this
greyhound he'd bought and how he called it Glad Eyes. Oh, Alf, at
this moment! But she'll win at White City, he said, and again at
Harringay! She'll be the turning point in my ruddy luck, he said.
And at kindly Doctor Brighton's clinic no business talk that day, he
said, it wasn't fair to her, just a hen lobster lunch and a blow of fresh
air along the front. And he'd tried so hard to keep to it—admiring a
pretty girl to tease her, pointing out sporting and theatrical celebrities, explaining how we'd beaten the U-boats, sketching the history of
St. Leger, describing how Lloyd's worked, predicting the weather in
the channel, and diagnosing where Bottomley had made his mistake.
And quite suddenly, sitting in the shelter, down near the Black
Rock, looking out to sea, he had burst into tears. It was Doris, he
said; if he were to be prosecuted, it would kill her. But it wasn't for
Doris that Gladys agreed; it was because of an awful vision she had
of his body, the hairy chest and legs she knew so well, the strong
thighs that had so often gripped her, covered by a ridiculously
baggy, too large, coarse canvas suit patterned with broad arrows,
like something in "Punch." She didn't know whether they dressed
convicts up like that, probably not; but the vivid picture was enough
to make her say yes. Can't help lovin that man of mine.

Questions breed questions. Stretching her thin, veined, old powdered arm out of her blue wool bed-jacket, Mrs. Ahrendt took the
cup of hot milk her husband brought her. Her voice was wheezy,
for the flatlet was draughty.

"But why don't you ask her for an answer? You are too trusting,
Hermann. Surely we have at least learned that no one is to be
trusted."

Her eyelids blinked at him, the curve of her sunken mouth was
querulous. Mr. Ahrendt, shuffling in his bedroom slippers, went into
the sitting-room through the great wide opening where the sliding
doors had once been—the landlady said how big this made the room,
their old bodies told them how cold. He carefully wound up the

ornate green marble Biedermeier clock before he spoke—they had clung to it sentimentally, since Miss Matthews had told him they would get so little for it. Then he said:

"If we have learned that, my dear, then that man really has destroyed us. But you're tired. Drink your milk. Shall I rub your chest with some camphorated oil?"

But in the morning when he brought her coffee and a roll, she asked immediately again, "Will you go to Miss Matthews this morning? Just ask her, that's all, just ask her."

"She has told me, Käthe, the experts are looking at it. Anyway, what is it? Some copy, my dear. These religious pictures were copied in hundreds." The subject, Christ's agony in the garden, annoyed him; when so much greater agonies were a commonplace today!

Perhaps it was the cold she'd caught, or perhaps it was because— after all, it wasn't her fault that they were here in this draughty hole—she was a Christian of Christian lineage and the Christian religion familiar to her—for whatever reason, she didn't know, Mrs. Ahrendt began to cry. And, since he could do nothing, Mr. Ahrendt picked up his black velour hat and his string bag and went out to Swiss Cottage to buy the week's groceries. The old lady called after him—so many years they had been together, he was her man. But no answer, and even in bed it was so cold.

Rupert asked, "Look, if I cross now, Belch won't be able to move upstage when he leaves the see-saw without masking the clown. Shouldn't I cross later on my exit lines?"

And, all right, they tried it. So, moving, he would rebuke Maria; moving, he would warn her "she shall know of it by this hand." But his thoughts were how to join this arrogant, self-righteous and with it all, favour-currying man with the pathos, no, not the pathos, something much stronger, the abominable horror of "in a dark chamber adjoining." If he could not do this, all movements were meaningless, for he would move no one. The Elizabethan conception of lunatics?—I am not mad, Sir Topas. I say to you, this house is dark. Ha, ha, ha! dark as ignorance, though ignorance were dark as hell. Ha, ha, ha! But I am not mad, Sir Topas—And if he were, he hath been most notoriously abused. Not perhaps, ha, ha, ha! but finally greeted with a gentle smile, my lady's dismissive little shrug and pitying after-glance. Puritanism? Remember the abhorrence in which the Puritans were held, but quite suddenly he *couldn't* "remember" something three centuries before he was born. Is't even so? Old Norman's voice, thick, but he hadn't really got there, simply superficially a drunken voice. He *couldn't* remember the abhorrence in which . . . Sir Toby, there you lie. Sir Toby, there you lie . . . Rupert! Rupert! I'm terribly sorry, I've dried. Do you mind then, Nigel asked in a slightly bored, almost angry voice, if we take it all again? Act 2, Scene 3, from your entrance, Rupert—My masters, are you mad? And *were* they? Was that it? To laugh at a man in hell. And again, I'm sorry I've dried. And twice again Nigel, in bored, angry voice asked, Do you mind if we take it all again? At last he said, All right, let's break for lunch. Two fifteen sharp.

And to Rupert, after explanation and exhortation and encouragement and censure that flew in and out amid the smocked waitresses and wooden soup bowls of the snack bar, "Look, love, is it Debbie?" And it wasn't, though it was clever of Nigel to have surmised, for really the shadow on the hearth was so faint that, himself, he almost thought it was his fancy. No, it was—"How do I join the two Malvolios"? he asked. "How can I make them connect?" And Nigel, who had been into all that—the "humour" of Malvolio, the anachronism of psychological unity in Shakespeare—said, with as much disguise of weariness as he could muster (for it was probably some mental blockage and would work itself out in rehearsals), "I think you can only do it, Rupert, if you give the character enough love!" Then, embarrassed by the echo of the words in this coffee-smelling shop of wooden tables, wooden spoons, and wooden-faced women, he added, "The effect of those yellow stockings alone in *this* production, my dear!" For it was to be done, save for Malvolio's stockings, in black and white. So Rupert tried giving love to the bullying and self-esteem and the pomposity. He loved himself as he averred, "infirmity that decays the wise, doth ever make the better fool" and as he announced, "she added, moreover" and as he conceded, "if you can separate yourself from your misdemeanours." And with love, it was true, he stopped "drying" and he fancied that his voice had seldom sounded better; he was, he could not help thinking, giving some real poetry to the part. Once, it seemed to him, hearing his own rich tones, that he had found a certain nobility. Anyhow, they would not reach darkness and hell until tomorrow and before that, Debbie would know, Debbie would succour him.

For it had been—and this had seemed its own reward—a red-letter day for Debbie when he told her he'd agreed to do Malvolio. She had taken over that evening from May in the kitchen and cooked specially for him as she had not done for ages, *rognons Bercy* and *omelette confiture;* she had toasted him, "May you be blessed in the Bard," which was a phrase that the ridiculous old pro whose wife was their landlady in Sheffield had used the week they became engaged. And Tanya and little Christopher had been cleared out of the way early that evening. He had read aloud to her after dinner as she sat at his feet in front of the great log fire—"O sing unto the Lord a new song; sing unto the Lord all the earth," and again, "I will lift up mine eyes unto the hills, from whence cometh my help." Not that they were religious—although since Tanya had been old enough Debbie had taken her to Sunday-school and sometimes herself went to matins. But Debbie had long thought that the Psalms were the most lovely pure language in our literature; and such a perfect vehicle for Rupert's voice. And they had drunk between them a whole bottle of her home-made sloe gin. But this evening when he returned, panting for comfort, from rehearsal, not to Sunningdale but to the Bedford Square flat, Debbie was reading aloud to Tanya and Christopher a book most suited to *her* voice.

" 'Smooth and hot. Red, rusty spot never here be seen,' Oh!" she looked up and smiled at her husband. "Mrs. Tiggywinkle, darling," she said.

"As if I didn't know."

But his smile was effaced for she put her finger to her lips and frowned. To her amusement Tanya and even little Christopher did the same. When Rupert came back from washing she had begun, at Tanya's importunate request, Jeremy Fisher.

" 'This *is* getting tiresome. I think I should like some lunch, said Mr. Jeremy Fisher,' " she read. The drollery she gave the word tiresome grated cruelly upon Rupert's actor's nerves. Later, however, when the children made a scene over Nanny's taking them to bed, she was quite firm:

"No, you've had me all the afternoon. Now it's Daddy's turn. You don't want Daddy to be forgotten, do you?" As soon as the door had closed behind them, she came up to Rupert, and, holding him by his lapels, stood back and looked at him.

"Tired?" she asked and answered herself, "Yes. Definitely tired." Kissing him, she at once mixed a superb dry Martini. At dinner she insisted that he keep most of the mushrooms for himself, though he knew that she loved them.

"Well?" she asked, when with the tangerines she could see that he was no longer hungry. "Has Nigel been tiresome?"

And he felt soothed by her putting it in this way, but then, as, taking his coffee, he sat down on the sofa, a hard, edgy object jabbed him in the small of his back. Rummaging, he took out one of Christopher's bricks, and resented her tactful approach to his mood.

"No, why should he have been?"

And now, delving deeper, he brought to light a small celluloid swan for floating in baths.

"This flat is really too small for children."

"But you always like to have me in London for the first rehearsals, darling."

"I said, the flat's too small for children."

"I'm sorry, but while Christopher has these nightmares I am not going to leave them down at Sunningdale."

"What on earth do we pay Nanny for?"

"What she can do. But she can't dispel Christopher's nightmares."

"We all had nightmares at Fifty-two. I can't remember the Countess doing a lot of dispelling."

"I don't suppose so, darling. She was probably *in* them all."

He hated her to talk of the Countess; it made her seem petty. And the Countess's hand had touched his as he had lunched her at the Ivy last Friday. "So, it's Shakespeare now," she had said. "And you could have been playing in that very funny *French without Tears* which everyone says is going to run for years. Debbie should have been a schoolmistress." She had looked extraordinarily elegant and slim; he had really enjoyed her evident delight with the whitebait. He got up and poured himself out a brandy.

"I'm not going to be able to do it. So you'd better make up your mind to that. Oh, I'll give a performance, but I just don't connect. What *is* the connection between a pompous ass and a wretch groaning in hell?"

And all her answers were Nigel's.

"After all, darling, the Elizabethans weren't exactly tender about lunatics. They thought them funny. And in a sort of way I suppose they are. Surely, Malvolio's a kind of 'humour.' He's not meant to be filled out or anything." And she went on. "Oh, no, darling, I'm sure you can't apply all that *modern* psychology to Shakespeare. You're looking for consistency, but he gives us something much more, he gives us poetry."

"You mean he couldn't create character?"

"Oh, really, darling, I'm not going to . . ."

So they read the whole play through together. And she took great trouble going over every Malvolio speech with him, trying to show how it all fused on the language level. At last:

"Well, try giving it love, darling," she said.

She was near tears, he knew, but he refused to relent. He would not now be faced with this problem if it were not for her ambitious approval.

"I don't see . . . and I don't see," he said, "that's all there is to it. How can I give love to such a self-centred, time-serving old bore? I don't have that much love in me."

When she got up from her chair the first signs of her slightly swelling belly caught his attention. By the New Year there would be swollen legs again, he thought, and her face would acquire that look of a "perpetual cold." Indeed it was so now as she turned at the door. She was crying.

"Well, why don't you try self-love?" she asked. "You've got enough of that and to spare."

And was Marcus, too, Mary Clough asked, going all political, becoming, in fact, a bore? And Rex Clough, who'd never liked him, remarked—it wasn't exactly the sort of arrest they'd all been expecting for him sooner or later, was it? Andrew Crosby-Grieves, whose Matthew Smith Marcus had refused for the exhibition, asked whether the whole thing, arrest and all, wasn't just a stunt? I mean, surely, he said, weren't his parents circus performers before Jack picked him up? I mean, isn't he the most terrific exhibitionist? I mean look at those awful baroque objects, nobody who really cared about painting in a serious way would have that Magnasco, would they? And Beatrix and Simon Dickerby, who adored the Marie Laurencin and the Cocteau drawings, asked surely the Picassos and Legers meant that he and Jack must be Communists, or were they wrong? Lady Westerton asked herself, would it be a mistake to go to this year's green ball? Jews and *tapettes* and being arrested and so on. She would hardly know how to justify her presence there to Colonel Deniston. Not, of course, that he would know—he never went into society except to address meetings. But the Ribbentrops might hear of it. Damn! Social life was gettin' less instead of more easy as she herself got older and more tired. But, perhaps, all their friends would have agreed with the Countess had they known and heard her, though some would have hesitated to use the word. "Really, Billy," she cried when she read it in *The Times* under the heading "Hooligans in Bermondsey," "I can't bear it. How could a son of mine be so common?"

This was the feeling of Ted and Madge, for they asked what did he want to get mixed up with that lot for? Black Shirts! Madge said, well, who cared about them? That was what she wanted to know. Let them march if they were so daft. But blocking up the streets, throwing crackers at poor dumb horses, shouting and screaming so that baby damn near cried herself into a fit, jostling poor old Mrs. Barnaby at No. 40 when she was coming back from the Church Hall, what sort of behaviour was that? And Ted said, too, did they think the South of the River boys didn't know how to take care of themselves? Coming in like that, a lot of foreigners. A bloke he knew had shown him where it said in the *Daily Mail*—wait a minute, he'd got the cutting—"a large number of men of swarthy complexion, some wearing clothes of obviously foreign cut"—well, all right, who asked them? Yids from Stepney and Whitechapel! As to Black Shirts, ignore the buggers. What did you do mixing up with them excepting putting yourself on a level with their lot? Well, wasn't it true? They weren't clever, Madge said, but they knew better than to behave like a lot of kids. Well, hadn't he? Honestly. Go on, own up. All right, Ted said, so the Black Shirts *did* want to clear the Yids out. Well, that was the Yids' business, wasn't it? They'll help each other right enough. Everybody knew that. Yes, said Madge, and she asked, what have they done for you, Markie, anyway? At that moment Ted gave Marcus a come-on, lustful, knowing look that changed almost at once to contemptuous hatred (were they the same look at one and the same time? was the question that remained in Marcus's mind for years to come). Yeah, answer that one. Go on, what have they done for you? He owes every bloody thing to a Jew. He'd have to lick the bloody rabbi's arse if his Jew boy pansy friend told him to. I don't know, Madge said, refilling the family teapot, that's between you and him, Ted. I won't want to hear about it. I've always been pleased to see you, Markie, you know that. And like you've said, it's a bit of warmth and home for you away from that la-di-da lot. But what I can't make out is what you think of us, making us the talk of the Mansions, with Mrs. Dyer saying that was your posh friend wasn't it that used that language? Arthur's been so good always, but what does he think of us, he said to me, when he heard, mixing us up with that lot?

"I'll tell you what I think of you," Marcus said, for he knew the answer to this one, "you're so steeped in the cosy warm fug you've made here you can't tell the smell of tea from pee."

Madge trembled, the teapot lid rattled. "You leave Dad out of this. Shame! Just because e can't hold is water." She went to the old man crouched over the cooking stove, and patted his arm, "That's all right, Dad, that's all right."

That she'd taken directly his unconscious slight gave Marcus the giggles. Ted was on his feet at once, but Marcus was nimble enough to receive only a glancing blow from Ted's fist. It was as much his fear of Ted's rage as his fury with them that drove Marcus from the room and clattering down the cold, stone stairs into the fresh, cold air of Tooley Street. When he put up his hand to pat his hair into place he realized that his ear was bleeding.

But it was only a few days before the questions caught up with him again. "Mr. Crupper on the telephone, sir," and "Mr. Crupper rang. He will ring again at six" on the bedside pad. And "Mrs. Crupper rang, sir. She seemed a little worried." And hardly legible notes, "I'm sorry, Markie, and I can't say more. You don't know how much your friendship . . ." and again, "If I'd been like some of them, but all I want is to see you. I went to the flat and saw no one had been and the man at your end says not at home." And Madge wrote, "Let bygones be bygones. Ted doesn't seem the same. Little Stanley sends this picture of Uncle Markie." And he did—yellow and red chalk scrawls on a torn piece of lined paper. And once Jack, raising his eyebrows, "Do you *have* to keep your young man on the end of the line? It makes me feel a little like the suburban father with the latch-key daughter, I think that's what they're called. I know what'll happen, it always does with suburban fathers, it will end up by my having to be 'awfully good pals' with him. And I don't at all want that. Also it is a nuisance for the servants. Also you're getting a little old, my dear, to be a latch-key or any other sort of daughter. Also it's not very kind to the young man." But Marcus said, Go to hell. And not at home, I am not at home. And indeed he hardly ever was. For the exhibition had to be arranged.

And then the Cloughs and Andrew Crosby-Grieves and the Dickerbys had not been the only voices. Of all unexpected people, two days after his appearance in court, Jane Farquhar telephoned—she and her husband Bobby kept Farquhar's Gallery in Bruton Street and although they didn't often have anything worth buying, it was there that, passing one windy, wet day three Easters ago, he'd walked in and found the greeny blue Gris still life. So that when she said, we just wanted to say how much we admired you—it was you, wasn't it, in Bermondsey?—he'd been rather pleased to say, yes. And this exchange had led to dinner at the Farquhars' little 1840-ish house off Gloucester Road, which provided surprisingly pleasant décor and food, since it turned out that they were much to the Left and rather political. When they heard how he came to be at Bermondsey, Jane said, oh, of course, I should have guessed. But his heart's in the right place, Bobby observed. Oh, so is Samuel Hoare's, no doubt. Or Ernie Bevin's. No, said her husband, not Ernie Bevin's. Shall we take on his education, Bobby? she asked. Is he educable? Bobby countered. It was, perhaps, because their little teasing act annoyed him that he determined to take up their challenge. We don't really like you very much, Jane said, but your money would be immensely useful. And then you're not stupid. As the internal contradictions of capitalism become more evident, many of the more intelligent, the less indoctrinated bourgeois recognize the inevitable outcome of the negation, she remarked. Everything she said sounded not so much angry as coldly hostile. After his warm bath of tea and pee, Marcus found such coldness cleansing. And then again to have one's emotional, impulsive actions of one afternoon placed in the perspective of world politics was flattering to the ego. He told them of this reaction as a joke against himself, as maliciously as he could manage, but Jane made no comment and Bobby commented, as often, with a loud braying laugh. So he handed himself over to their expert cleansing— expert, after all, for Jane, it seemed, was a member of the Communist Party and Bobby was only not so for some tactical, political reason difficult to comprehend. The cleansing certainly was cold—hard on the bottom in draughty halls, cruel to the feet in wet, out-door meetings, daunting to the attention with long speeches in fusty, hot rooms, yet wonderfully inspiriting. For the first time in his life people had taken him as an object, coldly, dispassionately, but with evident seriousness, and had related him and his actions to a system that comprehended the whole world, all the past and all the future. He was part now of a historic process. He was asked simply to ac-cept the very harsh, unpalatable things that historical inevitability had in store for him, his class, his money, and his interests. Every-thing, indeed, that Jane said to him was harsh. No one had spoken to him so since the Countess in the nursery; and when Marcus pointed this out to Jane, she merely tossed Freud (one of his few acquired, non-aesthetic pieces of culture) into the dust-bin with other con-temptible, idealist ideologies of a capitalist world in decline.

Middleman, home for half-term, asked, "Has violence ever settled anything? What sort of people do we make ourselves if we answer force with force?"

Hugh said, "That's all very well. But there comes a point, always has done throughout the history of civilization . . ."

But civilization seemed especially to annoy Middleman, so that, wriggling on the sofa, he upset a box of chocolates on to the floor, yet he went on talking as he gathered them up.

"Civilization! That seems to me pretty complacent, Dad. Isn't what's happening in Germany our fault as well, isn't the whole of what you call civilization smeared by it? And won't it be, so long as men can't find a non-violent technique?"

"They that perish by the sword, eh?" Hugh asked—he was puz-zled, for Middleman had shown no other symptom of the usual reli-gious phase. "Of course, I've every respect for Dick Sheppard and these chaps. Though there are other interpretations of those sayings of our Lord, you know, old man."

"I'm not a Christian!" Middleman was really irritable now.

Sukey, looking up from the writing-desk, where she was doing the overseas Christmas cards, said reprovingly, "Now, darling . . ."

"It's a question of how we're to evolve."

"As to that," Senior said grandly (he'd matured so much since he'd been articled), "I suppose you mean the survival of the fittest . . ."

"Oh, not Darwinian stuff! There's a deeper psychological level at which humanity has evolved. It's a question of techniques of supraconsciousness."

"My sainted aunt!" cried Hugh.

Senior smiled across at his father in compassionate humour over the polysyllables. Coming to the old boy's assistance, he said:

"Oh, Nietzsche and the superman!"

Middleman groaned, "Supra, not super! Oh, Lord, trying to explain in this household!"

"I'm sorry we're not high-brow enough for Your Professorship." Hugh was the schoolboy.

Hearing the tone, Sukey looked around to catch P.S.'s eye. They always shared amusement when the three big boys, or men (for it was the same thing really), got on to these discussions. But this time the small boy didn't return her glance.

"Middleman's got it all out of someone called Gerald Heard," he said. "I've seen him reading it."

"Well, Gerald Heard, whoever he may be, won't stop England acting when she knows it's necessary"—Senior, since he was articled, was no longer a conventional schoolboy, more a man of the world. "We've never hurried, you know, but then . . ."

"That's all very well," P.S.'s breaking voice in his excitement shot up to high falsetto.

Sukey was distracted from her Christmas cards. It was not like P.S. to get involved in such arguments.

"Shall I send any special message to the MacVities?" she asked. The boys went on talking, so she repeated the question, "Any message for the MacVities?"

Hugh, catching the urgency of her voice, came to.

"Christmas cards already, darling?"

"Well, my dear, I'm not sending air mail to all these abroads. I *have* to start early."

But their sons were now in full swing. Trying another tack, Sukey called to the Frau, though looking at her huddled in a fur coat on an early and warm November night almost made her too annoyed to speak—if she thought they had money to throw away on fires for show!

"Have you any friends in Australia or New Zealand, Frau Lieber-mann?"

But the woman only looked up from the Sunday paper and smiled in a vague, irritating way. Thank the Lord this temporary matron business was nearly over. Early in the New Year she was to go to a Quaker guest house as manageress. Reminding herself of how competent the tiresome woman was said to be in the school, she said, giving due, "Think of all the Quakers who are going to be more comfortable next year just because of Frau Liebermann's ministrations."

Only Hugh was left to comment.

"Yes, indeed."

For the boys were only plunged in further debate and Frau Liebermann did not look up again from *The Sunday Times*.

Matthias Birnbaum's thin lips set in an even more severe expression than usual when I asked him this question, "The 'Goat Girl' or the 'See-saw Boy' on the London stage? No, I don't think that. To begin with I don't feel that English children perhaps have the same power of fancy that our children do in Germany. Then your English theatre does not, I think, have the techniques required to present works that are not conventional. Also, to speak frankly I have no very high opinion of the English translators!" I began to feel that not much was right with this poor benighted island of ours. "But if," I suggested, "the proceeds were to go to the funds for refugees from your country." "Ah, that is a different matter. At the moment all artists must accept some sacrifices of their art so that Art may not disappear forever from the earth. Especially," and here a small twinkle came into the large, dark eyes, the gaunt features relaxed for a second into a smile, though even so rather a wintry gleam, "especially if the funds were to go to the aid of the many little children." It was clear that if anything touches this famous children's writer in his exile from his native land it is the vast audience of German children who have worshipped for so long the "Goat Girl" and the "See-saw Boy." Yet to an English eye, Herr Birnbaum is hardly the jovial Santa Claus type. But now it was time for me to go, and so he made clear. I was not to escape without one more well-aimed thrust at our way of living. "Tell me," he said, "Miss Lander, why does the famous English civilization not extend to double windows in wintertime?" and he shivered, although outside of Hampstead Heath the November sun shone with an almost springlike gentleness.

Frau Liebermann felt herself grow warmer as she read. Dear, good, Matthias Birnbaum, on whose books they had all grown up, who had left the Homeland simply in protest—for Hitler in his cunning had ignored that this great, loved man was half-Jewish—who therefore could speak some home truths to their well-meaning but arrogant, insular hosts. Tears filled her eyes as she thought of him here in England. Perhaps he would help her to get Herbert and Sigmund away. Perhaps he would shame all these people into action. She started to read the article again.

> With his piercing dark eyes, his great height, his commanding forehead, and his mane of white hair, Matthias Birnbaum is all that we English . . .

But we English made reading impossible—these stupid Pascoe boys were shouting at one another now.

"You can't be such an ass as to think that anybody wants war, can you?" Senior demanded. "We shall do everything we can to avoid it, but if we do have to fight . . ."

"Oh, by jingo!" Middleman said, "I know. Well, this time ships won't be very important and let's hope we haven't got the money. We *could* be the first civilized country in the world to contribute non-violence . . ."

"To contribute to the end of civilization, I should have thought."

She had to avoid the small, spoilt boy's eye that wished to include her in their nonsense—as a rule at least this youngest one, though Mummy's darling, was quieter than the others. But now:

"Why, if Hitler isn't stopped, it could mean a century of darkness for the world!"

"Oh, yes . . ." Middleman's voice particularly annoyed her—blah-blah-blah it went, the clever Pascoe son! "Very likely a millennium of barbarism. I quite admit it. But mankind would have begun for the first time a new technique of living."

The eldest, ugly one's braying laugh ran through her head.

"It would be the millennium if you get Englishmen to accept that nonsense, wouldn't it, Dad?"

But before that poor, feeble Mr. Pascoe could answer, the little boy had turned directly to her.

"All the decent people in Germany look to England to do the right thing, don't they, Frau Liebermann?"

His silly, well-meaning, overloved little face seemed to swell red before her until she knew that if this Pascoe balloon were not pricked the whole world would go down in a carnival of vanity and silliness. Holding her cigarette before her, she leaned forward as though to burn the excited boy. She said very deliberately and slowly:

"Perhaps you should know, my little boy, that nobody expects anything any more of England. Of course we have known always that the English talk so great about helping the weak ones and do nothing. After all, you are Great Britain. You must have something great, so let it be words. Oh! But this we are used to—the English hypocrisy. Oh, that we don't mind—all their, what do you call it? Sunday manners!"

"No, I don't think I've ever heard that." Sukey's tone was flat and conversational but it still didn't stay the throaty flood.

"But we always think—Now she is only talking, but wait until she is in danger herself, then we shall see the famous lion's claws." Frau Liebermann shouted so loudly that P.S. giggled. "Oh, yes, all this is so funny because, of course, now there are no claws. Only naughty little boys who say we must spare a little thinking for those poor damned Jews in Germany. Very naughty boys who talk about war which upsets Mrs. Pascoe. Why, think of it, if we fight Hitler Mr. Pascoe may have to move his school to somewhere that the nasty German bombs do not come to. And Mrs. Pascoe does not at all want to move. So please, Adolf Hitler, don't make your speeches and shouting, you are upsetting all the English mothers and their children. But I think you do not have to worry. Your newspapers have the picture of the Führer with the little daughters of Herr Goebbels, oh, so sweet girls with blond hair. Oh, no, we are not to worry. *Der Führer liebt die Kinder, nicht wahr?* Only I think the Pascoe boys are rather big children, so maybe he will send them to the mines or labour camps or maybe he will shoot them. Oh, I know, Mr. Pascoe, you are right to shout at me, these things are not to say, they will worry Mrs. Pascoe and she has her Christmas cards to send to Australia."

Frau Liebermann was not quite truthful. Hugh's voice had been raised, but he had not shouted. He never did so. But now, as Sukey had never heard him before, he bawled at Frau Liebermann until the veins stood out under the dark pigment of the flesh of his temples.

"Stop that. If you don't feel any gratitude, then at least spare us this exhibition . . ."

Sukey, surveying them all so grim, hysterical, excited over a tiresome woman's irrelevant words, could not help raising her eyebrows, sighing, and shaking her head in comic impatience; she hoped the comedy of it would touch P.S. and bring him back to her, to home, to the fact that half-term was too precious for all this. But her cooling comedy was cut into by Frau Liebermann, who began to cry hysterically, tears mascaraedly smearing her rouged cheeks.

"Oh, we must feel gratitude. We know that. Gratitude when the little Pascoe always sleeps here at his home but Arnold is to sleep at the school even at half-term."

"Really," Hugh said. "Now look, Frau Liebermann," and taking his tobacco pouch, he began to fill his pipe, speaking slowly and deliberately to such hysterical nonsense, "you perfectly well know that you see Arnold every day, and he comes here to Sunday lunch. And then P.S. is a prefect . . ."

"A prefect! Yes, and everybody knows he should not be. A favourite."

"That's enough of that . . ."

But Sukey, looking at the dishevelled red hair, the familiar, tiresome face all wet and spoilt, suddenly saw not just a failed talisman, but another woman bullied and wretched. She must keep to her bargain with God. It wouldn't count if she didn't live up to it, not just to the letter. God knew when He was deceived.

"Oh, shut up, Hugh," she said, but softly. Then going over to Frau Liebermann she took both her hands and began to chafe them. "No, my dear. Of course Arnold can sleep here for tomorrow night, why not?"

But Frau Liebermann seemed too hysterical to be touched by kindness. She got up, pushed Sukey aside and, teetering on her high heels, ran from the drawing-room. As she went, her squirrel coat brushed a Bohemian porcelain lamb from an occasional table; it fell to the floor and was smashed. Sukey shrugged her shoulders in despair.

"I'll go to her," she said.

Hugh levelled his pipe stem at her: "My dear girl . . ."

"No, I must."

To P.S. his mother looked so brave a figure as, all alone, she set off to comfort her own sex in distress that he got up to follow her.

"Mummy, Mummy."

"No, P.S., old chap. This is where the menfolk of the world are *de trop*. We can be most useful in picking up the pieces," Hugh said. He sent Middleman for a dust-pan and brush.

Sukey beat upon the locked door of Frau Liebermann's room to no avail.

"You'd better open to me. I shan't go away until you do."

Yet it was more than a quarter of an hour before Frau Liebermann obeyed. She still had on her fur coat, but she was carrying her suitcase and she had put on that absurd thing like a navy-blue man's homburg hat with a *diamanté* pheasant pinned in it.

"Don't be ridiculous." Sukey took the suitcase from her. "Take off your hat and sit down."

Frau Liebermann did not take off her hat, but she sank into the small arm-chair.

Sukey sat on the bed.

"Now, Frau Liebermann, it's no good letting yourself get upset. That's letting that beast win a victory. And it won't help to get Sigmund here. Or make things easy for poor little Arnold. You shouldn't have said that about P.S. But you couldn't know. He's not a boarder because he's very highly strung. Arnold will sleep here in your room for tomorrow. Just you and him. And we won't have any more tears or saying cruel things, will we?" She paused, but Frau Liebermann merely stared at her. Pressed by the silence, Sukey added, "You came here on false pretences, you know. I had some mad idea, some secret idea that if we asked you here then I'd have paid my price, that there'd be no war. Oh, of course, I didn't be-lieve it, but it stopped me worrying . . . about them, that I shouldn't lose them."

"But you will, Mrs. Pascoe. There will be war, or God help you. You must let them go. You have your husband. He needs you. To help him to make up his mind to move the school and then all the work there will be when you move to the west of England." Frau Liebermann took off her hat and shook her hair loose; she took off her shoes, and stretching her legs, wriggled her toes. "Very well, I'll stay tonight. But tomorrow I'll go to London. I've saved money. I only make trouble with you all here. I'll take a room. Arnold can join me when the holidays come."

Sukey got up. "Of course you'll stay tonight and tomorrow. We've done badly, but we've done our best. I'm not going to let you put us further in the wrong. Oh, this awful world! That two grown women who should be leading their own lives should be thrown into such intimacy."

She moved to the door. "I can't do much for you, but as you say you're going—and you're right, of course—*I* can try to be intimate for once. And though you may not believe it, it really costs me something. Do, for heaven's sake, mind your own business even with the Quakers. Probably someone had to say what you said to me. But I shan't be able to forget it. I don't think anyone can forgive things like that. We certainly can't here. We've had our own ways too long for that."

Sir,
        Your leading article last week parrots all the old cries about the crimes of Mr. Chamberlain and M. Chautemps, Mr. Attlee and Mr. Ernest Bevin and his T.G.W.U. stalwarts. The drama playing out before our eyes is not so simple as the one in which the inept and absurd Lords Plymouth and Perth are cast as villains. Non-intervention is a red herring peculiarly suited to the undiscerning palate of the English people—particularly to your mixed progressive readers from red duchesses, pink poets, Uncle Tom Cobleigh and all. To repeat de-denunciations of the crimes that the Führer and the Duce are committing against the Spanish people under cover of our Prime Minister's convenient and cowardly umbrella is too easy an indulgence. Fascism, we Socialists cannot repeat too often, is merely the undisguised brutality of capitalism in its most desperate phase. But to echo the slogans of your Communist friends in King Street is not the most helpful way to defeat Fascism or to aid the Spanish workers' cause. To anyone like myself, who has seen the Teruel front at first hand, to identify the cynical power politics of the Soviet Union with that spontaneous and extraordinary revolution of Marxists, anarchists, syndicalists, and workers of all kinds, which still has some chance of success in Spain, is itself a cynical enormity. A little hard thinking is needed. The first thing required is to ask the right questions. What part, for example, did the Russian consul play in the sad events in Barcelona last April? Who inspired the attack on the Telefonica? What was the role of Comrade Gerö, repre-

sentative of the Comintern, in the Catalonian events? How far is this suppression of all independent socialist opinion in Barcelona and Valencia only another manifestation of the fake "trials," arrests, and brutalities that have reigned in the Soviet Union over the last two years? These are just a few of the real questions that "an independent Socialist newspaper" (I quote your own description of your esteemed journal) should be asking.

But, of course, after my experience since my return from Spain, when even reactionary newspapers like the *Daily Telegraph* have been more willing to publish the truths I have tried to tell in my articles than the left wing press, so intent on preserving a United Front, I hardly suppose that you will publish this letter,

Yours, etc.,   Q. J. Matthews.

Editor's note: Q. J. Matthews is quite wrong. Our correspondence is an open forum. We do, however, reserve to ourselves the right not to publish articles criticizing the Valencia government when it is fighting for its life, especially when those articles contain the unfounded charges against the Soviet Union which are now so mechanically regular a part of this brilliant journalist's analysis of events.

Margaret, reading the weeklies in her mid-morning break from writing, did not know the answers to her brother's questions. But she thought, why is he always so cocksure? It struck somehow a false note. So Marcus had always thought, and he had a wonderful ear for the spurious.

But then she felt ashamed for herself. For really what did she know, or indeed do in these ghastly days except make occasional speeches at progressive rallies. Ill-informed nonsense too. She and all other artists probably ought to stick to their own job and get on with their art in a mad world.

The last paragraph she'd written this morning was good. The flow had come when she had remembered that opera cloak of gold thread and raised purple velvet pansies which the old woman in the royal box had worn when they went *en famille* to *Chu Chin Chow*. Mouse had smiled at its vulgarity, Granny M. had thought it shockingly "fast," but the Countess had secretly longed to possess it. It was exactly the thing Aunt Alice would have treasured from her past, and the nieces, especially sex-starved, genteel Jessica, would have hated. The effect was heightened by appearing in this Jessica-viewed section. She sat down, relaxed, to read what she had written:

When she had fixed the bed table over the old woman's knees and set down the breakfast tray, Jessica waited for the usual recriminations, the usual objections to the little cosies she put on the eggs. But it appeared that her ladyship was in a happy mood this morning for, "A real three-and-a-half-minute egg" was said with a smile. The unexpected smile irritated Jessica. Going to the huge walnut wardrobe, she opened a door. At once the old woman's expression changed. "Don't fuss in there, Jessica. I won't have it." "If *you* won't, Auntie, the moths will." She felt pleased with her condensed sentence. And, as though to approve, a small clothes moth flew out, and then another. "Damn and blast Nancy," cried the old woman, "I told her to put moth balls . . ." "Oh, don't be so selfish, Aunt Alice, my poor sister. She's rushed off her feet as it is. All this rubbish." Jessica pulled out at random an old purple-and-gold object and shook it. An opera cloak with velvet pansies: The vulgarity of it! As she shook it the room was filled with—she could only call it, a rank smell of men. "This old rag must go for a start." "Old rag! I've had very good times in that old rag, my girl," Aunt Alice's chuckle was obscene. Jessica rolled up the piece of finery into a bundle and carried it from the room.

Yes, yes, so the niece was genteel and prudish and spiteful, and the old woman had been lusty and opulent. But were liking egg cosies and having failed to attract men to count as villainy, to stand for cruelty? And was having taken so many men into you, and wearing of purple-gold cloaks with whatever pleasure, with whatever warmth, whatever extravagant finesse, to be accounted graces? And, if they were, then what was to stand for the old woman's cruel, selfish past? For if she had not been cruel and selfish then this protest against her crumbled majesty, her senile, powerless body, was mere protesting on behalf of the angels. It was the protest against powerlessness and old age itself that she sought to make, the protest against anyone, however guilty, however "deserving" of retribution, being acted upon, used, disregarded like the bed she lay in. In which case the splendid, vulgar, purple raiment with all its overtones of life and lust and saving absurdity was simply a sentimental gloss, as false and tear-jerking as that awful Lord's Prayer of Dickens that trumpeted Jo's ascent to join the angels. Oh, it was all false, false.

Here she was. Left to write in peace. Mrs. Armitage told not to come. Douglas banished to the Travellers' Club until luncheon, and down she could dig in stillness to her very self—and what had she brought to the surface but false sentimentality? She wrote on another sheet of paper:

> Elizabeth Carmichael flung her arms wide. "Oh, it's false, it's false," she cried, for she too could be poor Lady Isobel or a tragedy queen.

But the old mockeries did not somehow work. She lit a cigarette and, leaning heavily on her desk, stared out to where the bare trees of Holland Park made Chinese shapes against the skyline. Why couldn't she take on something simple, something whose outline declared itself in advance? The owls had been hooting again last night. A Gothic fable, perhaps, all elegance and self-parody about the great and wicked Lady Holland . . .

When Douglas came in, he must have seen from the dejected slump of her body that she was all but up to her neck in the slough, for he put his arms round her shoulders from behind and stroked her breasts. She could tell, as he soothed her, that he was reading what she had written.

"Well?" she asked.

"All right. Very good. Jessica's as odious as she ought to be. The garment sounds pretty revolting."

"Oh, no!" she cried, horrified that he should be so obtuse.

"Purple velvet pansies? Well, *I* don't know about these women's things."

"I assure you they used to be worn, darling."

"Really?" He didn't sound interested. "And they succeeded? You liked them?"

"Well, not *liked!* Of course not. They were preposterous. But . . ." She couldn't find words.

"I see. I don't think I really understand. I'll get you a large whisky."

As soon as he had gone from the room, she saw it all. The wretched purple cloak *was* all sentimental journalism, pride of memory, pride of eye. Journalism and worked-up righteous anger, that's all she'd written. Egg cosies and cloaks! Taste to do service for morality! And a patronizing acceptance of someone else's false taste into the bargain! The purple merely cloaked old Alice's cruelty, her vulgar tyranny. The possession loved could have splendour, but it must also once have had malice. Immediately she saw what it must be. When Douglas returned she was already making her notes, so that he put the whisky down on the desk without speaking. She gulped it down eagerly in three goes, as quickly as her fountain pen was covering the paper.

Pudding, A's beloved Persian cat, his smoke-blue hair, his *dark* amber eyes.

She underlined dark, for she could see it all now exactly.

An earlier scene in detail where he cruelly plays with a mouse. Old now. Sleeps on her bed. Mud left once. Nancy forbids it in bed. Old A., tottering to lift him on bed, falls.

As she wrote "falls" she could hear the telephone ringing and Douglas answering it.

Jessica joins to ban Pudding on bed. Doctor Malone suborned to agree cat on bed unsanitary. For A. loss of cat's warmth on bed at night is death that much nearer.

"Darling, I'm sorry I don't think I can deal. Whatever I say might be wrong."

She looked up at him with hatred for his interruption and wrote almost illegibly,

Next time they'll refuse to let him into the room and how could she know?

Standing up, she asked irritably, "Who is it?"

He laughed. "I'm sorry, darling, but you *will* involve yourself. 'The Chairman of the Victims of Fascism Appeal! A meeting at Kingsway Hall.' "

Touched by his ironic inverted commas, she kissed him.

"Damn and blast," she said.

On the telephone the man was very evasive.

"It's your brother. It seems difficult for him to appear."

"I'm not surprised. He's to be in this new *Twelfth Night* in the West End. An actor's life, you know. Anyway, the occasion's a serious demonstration against the German treatment of the Jews, not a family trapeze act."

"It's not Mr. Rupert Matthews. It's Q.J. Matthews."

"Oh, well. Quentin's horribly overworked too. But I'll try to persuade him, if you like."

"Oh, no." The man sounded aghast. "No, that's not it at all, Miss Matthews. It's that two of our speakers—I'd rather not give names —are not happy about appearing on the same platform with Q.J. Matthews."

"Good heavens! I never heard such ridiculous rubbish. Why ever not?"

"Well, you know, he's put out rather cranky notions about Spain lately, and then he's been such a violent critic of the Soviet Union."

"Whatever my brother Quentin has written, he's had a good deal of reason, I am sure. From start to finish Quentin's been concerned with getting at the truth ever since he was a boy. I can tell you this, Mr. Smalley, if your objectors won't appear with Quentin, they don't appear with me. Or with my brother Rupert. And don't quote my words back at me because the case is changed now."

"I wasn't going to. As a matter of fact I think the appeal of three related celebrities who've never appeared together before on an anti-Nazi platform is a most important draw. That—and we've got Matthias Birnbaum. I'll just have to go back to the others and see what I can do."

"I am afraid you will. My brother Quentin's been a hero to us since we were tiny children."

When she put down the receiver Douglas was looking at her with one eyebrow raised.

"Strong words."

"Well, and rightly so, Douglas. Why, Quentin and I come from the same womb."

He burst out laughing. "Wombs and purple cloaks. It's all beyond me."

"No, I won't have wombs dismissed with a little irony. Let's get lunch over. I must get back to work."

"Oh, no! This is it. This is the really big performance we all knew he had in him!"

"It was so *moving*, Debbie, that I felt quite ashamed when the everyday things like intervals happened."

"To be perfectly honest, at first I thought, No, I am not going to like this, he's playing it in too low a key. But then, of course, when the dark cellar scene came I knew why he'd done it like that. I nearly stood up and shouted for the old boy there and then."

"Of course, he won't care what a spotty schoolboy thinks, but I thought I must tell you that the first time Malvolio went from the stage Jonathan whispered to me, 'Gosh! Mummy, I didn't know Shakespeare could be *fun!*' "

The telephone had rung at the Bloomsbury flat all Thursday morning; and, at last, when Rupert had gone off to the Garrick for luncheon, it was Nigel saying:

"Is he gone, Debbie darling? Good, because I don't believe that producers should ever encourage too much, and anyway the newspapers have done it all. But it was very, very good. And specially for you, I wanted to say how did you do it? Because quite honestly, my dear, it was after you'd given him a talking to or something—yes, just about a week ago—that he stopped fudging around and made the line of his performance. Did you, darling? Well, there you are, you see, you asked the *right* question. And, of course, that gave him the right *line* which in turn gave him confidence. I'm so awfully pleased for you too, Debbie, because to be perfectly frank I had with my monster, unerring eye, unerringly wrong as it's proved, thank God, detected a tiny rift. But it's obvious that the Dunmow flitch is yours for the eating. Bless you for helping, darling."

Which bitchery, Debbie thought, showed that the little beast was furious but also admiring. It *had* been a wonderful morning because, although she'd been practically certain as she watched his performance, you can't ever be quite certain and he'd been so discouraging himself.

And now to crown all—Sunday and Jimmy Agate's review to lie in bed with down at Sunningdale, the November sun reflecting off the snow-covered garden through the huge new picture window, and Oxford marmalade and crisp bacon and skating to look forward to with the children on the pond. She stroked Rupert's cheek with the back of her little finger in nervous delight as she read the wonderful notice, now sticky with marmalade, for a second time. But before she had finished, Rupert's right hand was between her thighs and his left was taking *The Sunday Times* away from her. He nuzzled his face into her cheek and whispered:

"Put it away, darling. We've had enough of it."

And though she had intended to rise early in order to skate with the children, there was something sweet in giving herself to her clever, lauded boy. And afterwards, she thought as she sought his mouth, they would skate with the children on the pond with bright scarves and sweaters against the snow-covered evergreens. She saw the scene as brilliant, vital, and gaily familial like something out of *War and Peace*.

"You know, she is rather old, my wife, Mrs. Heathway," Herr Ahrendt said. "And she has been worrying, fretting. She has not been well. Otherwise I should not worry *you*."

But he *did* worry her, Sylvia wanted to say; he worried her very much for she could get no sense out of Gladys about the wretched business.

"But surely Christie's word was good enough," she said, "and if *they* were willing to pay . . ."

Yet gruffer with every questioning—and there had to be questioning because Herr Ahrendt rang every three days now and once came to the shop, looking sideways at her—Gladys repeated:

"I've taken it to this chap. I wanted a second opinion."

Until at last Sylvia had said, "Really, anyone would think some doctor had diagnosed cancer instead of Christie's recognizing an old master." Gladys seemed about to cry, but she went instead into their little lavatory at the back of the shop and came out again, smelling of lavender water and with her face freshly powdered.

"I'm sorry, Gladys, I certainly don't want to worry you."

But she did worry Gladys, who was already almost dead from anxiety and distress. Over four weeks had gone by now and in these last days she couldn't even get hold of Alf. The first week after she'd produced the money for him had been like a second honeymoon (if, that is, they'd ever had a first). His Home Cinemas was going ahead, old Fison was recovering, and if he didn't, young Fison was rearing to get in on the thing. She was a good girl and still the best-looking woman with the finest figure, when they supped after a show at Rules', and nothing was too good for her, as he'd have shown her before if he hadn't been worried to death. In the second week, he'd given her a cheque for a thousand pounds just to show that everything was O.K., to use a Yankeeism. And this before she had even mentioned the repayment of the money, for their bargain had been for three weeks. In the third week when she expected (well, you

could call it half expected) not the repayment in full—knowing Alf
there was bound to be a hitch, but at least enough that with her own
small capital she could at once repay, she received instead a letter
from young Mr. Fison saying that Alf had asked him, he understood
that it would be of service, since it appeared that she was an interested party, he merely wished to state his genuine and considerable
interest, etc., etc. There seemed no doubt that the delay and the
contingency were as Alfred had said—"the impossibility of discussing the negotiation with my father in his present grave state of
health." "Now," said Alfred, "you know that it's only a question of
time, a short few days, girlie." Yes, now she knew. So having given
Alfred a splendid meal at the flat and settled him with a coffee and
Courvoisier, she said:

"Alf, are you going to stand me up over this business? Because, if
you do, my dear, I shall go to prison, for I haven't got the money
myself, or not nearly enough. Not to mention that we shall have
treated two old people in a way that's vile. You are not as big a
skunk as that, are you?"

She thought, if he storms and raves, I shall know he intends to let
me down.

"Look," he said very quietly, and his flushed face seemed flabby as
ever but paler like the loose folds of colour-washed paper, "there is a
slight hitch. But I give you my word of honour that you shall have
the money in a week. In any case, I shall be the one to go to prison if
anything goes wrong. I'm to blame. No English judge or jury would
let a woman take the rap for a man. But there isn't any question of it.
I tell you what, give the old boy a couple of thousand and tell him the
auction regulations hold up the rest. He won't know."

But she wasn't really listening. He got up and took her by the
elbows. Shaking her arms to the rhythm of his words: "You'll have
the money in full within fourteen days at the outside."

She said, "Thank you, Alf," and turned the conversation to the
antique trade at Christmas.

From now half her energies had to be given to seeing that if the
worst happened he should not be involved, for if he were, then the
whole of this shameful business and misery she had suffered would
be meaningless.

The next afternoon she received a telegram at the shop. "Down
with 'flu, probably due this putrid weather. Don't ring. Doris

jumpy. Keep your pecker up. Ten days at the outside and we'll be over the top."

Recovered from 'flu (or with it perhaps, for the weather continued to be inclement) he sent the next card from Manchester, where he "was on to a good thing." She found it much easier to dismiss her fears as unworthy when he was not in London. And even easier because, at this very time, Herr Ahrendt telephoned to say that he, too, had some sort of influenza.

"Please, Miss Matthews," he said, "try to hurry up these connoisseurs. I know that the picture is probably nothing. Jesus Christ in the garden. There are thousands of such old pictures. But Mrs. Ahrendt is not at all well. She gets fancies. If you can find us some news before Christmas, please."

Well, so that was all right. Alf would have arranged things long before then. To think of someone in his absence as a monster seemed too shameful. And if luck was against him, for poor old Alf was hardly God, then the business stock would realize perhaps three thousand pounds, and a thousand pounds Alf had sent and a thousand pounds she could lay hands on—if only the shop were not rented, if only the flat . . . Sylvia asked:

"You know, Gladys, I haven't much savings, but if a thousand pounds would help, you would ask me, wouldn't you?"

The relief was enormous, to be able to talk about it, though she would have to play down Alf's part; but she'd worked out that alibi already.

"The thing is, Sylvia," she said, "I've got myself into the most appalling mess racing. Oh, I know that doesn't excuse . . ."

But she was not to know relief, for Sylvia said:

"No, Gladys. I don't want to know anything about it." She took Gladys's hand. "Well, honestly, dear. Think. Is it fair on me to tell me a lot of things I shouldn't know?" And when Gladys, ashamed that she was in danger of crying, nodded her head because she couldn't speak, Sylvia added, "But if a thousand would help, for God's sake tell me."

It did help over the week-end. And in addition, when she was sealing up the letter containing her monthly contribution to the family cheque for Billy Pop and the Countess, heartened perhaps by Sylvia's generosity that widened the world to include more than herself and Alf, she thought, I can always ask Margaret, or Marcus—al-

though it had slightly shocked her recently to realize what he was—
or even Rupert, who must be doing very well, if, as he would not be,
of course, Alf should be forced to let her down. When she came to
the shop on Monday there was a note from Sylvia to say that she was
not well; and on the Wednesday came a letter from the Capetown
Castle in Southampton Docks. "Please forgive me. But although I've
never said it, I've got more and more scared about this war business.
It seems too silly to stay in London and be blown to pieces when my
sister Gwen has been urging me for so long to go in with her at the
boarding house in Bulawayo. You'll think me mad offering to lend
money just when I'm going to need it elsewhere. Or perhaps you'll
understand. The very best of luck. Don't let him sacrifice you. He's
hopeless, I'm sure. And God bless the shop, it saved my sanity." It
had not been fair, Gladys saw, to ask Sylvia to know anything.

Quentin woke to the banging of Mrs. Ryan's dust-pan and brush
on the landing outside and the slow tuneless dirge with which she
provided a *continuo* to her loud, periodic thumps. Seeing no letters
by the crack under the door, he realized that it must be Sunday and
lateish, for she never did the stairs until she was back from Mass.
She'd given her mite, no doubt, for the Christian general. As he
thought of her, grubby, lumpy, and sodden like the clouts and mops
that she spawned wherever she swam—on the stairs, the landings, in
the close-smelling lav and in her high-smelling basement—and of her
spawned, workless grandson Terence and the bog world they'd escaped from, which no doubt made this King's Cross slum one of the
"bits of heaven" they forever droned about in their songs of Killar-
ney and Tralee, he was overcome with one of his rages—fits that
came more easily since he'd been back from Spain—so that tension
brought on cramp in the muscles of his calves and he writhed on the
narrow, lumpy mattress, grimacing and groaning. With every spasm
that shot through his legs he smashed in the face of some sneering,
tweedy landlord, some fat Spanish bishop, some smarmy Member
for Eastbourne or Bournemouth, some smirking "left" intellectual,
some hypocritical bloody-handed commissar. Grinders of faces, one
and all, he ground his heels into their porky, acorn-fed chines.

And then the bells of St. Pancras Parish Church told him just how
late he'd woken with a thick mouth and aching eyeballs. Not old
Mother Ryan's tinselly, poor-defrauding Mother of God, but the

orderly call to morning service of the bloody British bourgeoisie, God rot them! He could see that great square pile of classical decency swallowing up their silly, floral, Sunday bonnets, their sleek bowlers, their stiff upper lips, their overfed bellies, and their money-grubbing, tight-arsed buttocks. The caryatides, so decently clothed, that held up that huge barracks of an Erechtheum, became row upon row of gracious English matrons holding up the whole weight of this vast sham structure—Old Queen Mary breasting the waves, Lady Londonderry, Lady Astor, Lady Westerton, Lady Houston (poor old crank, he almost loved her), Lady Atholl (red duchesses!— makes you laugh, mate!), yes, and old Beatrice Webb (made Stalin laugh, mate), yes, and La Pasionaria, too, just to get them all together, with his own dear Mum and old Granny Matthews (God rest her soul all the same). Well, let them hold it up if they can, the cows—round and round he'd keep them going, like the treadmill, while poor old Mother Ryan and Regan and all the old girls down at The Antelope danced knees up Mother Brown or the "Carmagnole" to see the fun.

There certainly wasn't much fun here, in this room, as he tried unavailingly to turn on the gas fire and light it without getting out of bed. On the cheap, rickety chest of drawers were piled his small change, two soiled handkerchiefs, and a jumble of rejected articles with the editors' letters, bloody, insolent, or smarmy lies: "Inopportune moment," "frankly seems a stab in the back," "in view of Attlee's visit to Madrid," "without a very much more thorough documentation of what is, after all, hearsay, a rumour, suspicion, or at least generalization from personal experience." "May I say, by the way, that the passages from your Barcelona diary of April have lost nothing of the old Matthews magic" (that from the unctuous Dodo Towneley). "Look, Q.J., I can't touch this, it's too hot. But you're a housing man. Go up to Jarrow and give it to this bloody government where it hurts, we'll print it." "About some of your allegations, I can only say have you tried the *Daily Mail*, or better still Lady Houston's rag?" All right, you buggers, but I'll fight you. But looking round the room, the stained marble top of the wash-stand and its cracked blue-flowered jug, the brutally scarlet, oleographed Sacred Heart with its fly-blown glass, even the acorn of the green canvas blind, cracked so that it nipped his finger when he pulled it—he wondered with what he would fight? Christ, it was cold!

But he cheered himself, thinking of the awful, prosperous, late Sunday morning, outer suburb bedroom warmth that all that bloody arse-licking crowd of editors would be lying in now, covered by vulgar pink wadded eiderdowns or shot-silk bedspreads, with skinny sour-faced wives saying, "Not just now, darling," or fat horrors with feather negligees tickling them up the nostrils saying, "Give it to me quick." "Good fucking, boys," he said aloud. "I've got my Lena and she's got her art."

The thought of Lena levered him out of his bed, gave him the energy to dress and to make himself a cup of tea on the gas ring. As he gulped it down, he made a note to repeat all that he was determined to write for Towneley, but to disguise it all in the form of his own Spanish journal. He was determined to make the man sorry that he ever composed that little softening-up, sob stuff addendum to his rejection—"the old Matthews magic"—the bastard made you retch. Well, he'd force them to publish the truth if it took a year. A year! He began to pull his week's dirty linen out of the dressing-table's ill-fitting bottom drawer and to tie it up in a pair of soiled pyjama trousers. Lena would wash a shirt for him, with which he could shame the bastards in their offices. He believed in fighting, but first in softening up.

A whisky and a sandwich at The Antelope, then. And after a nice bit of fucky-fuck with Lena in her studio, then let her talk about her "art" while she dressed, then a drink and a meal at the French pub, and back to the studio for another slice of the cake. The prospect quickened his powers of thought and he sat down to type the notes he had made, when there floated towards him, cloud-borne like the oleographed Sacred Heart, three double whiskies, a double portion of pâté, two rolls, the wing and breast of a chicken dressed with roast potatoes and cauliflower, a hunk of bread, butter, and a piece of Camembert cheese. Lena would consume the lot that evening at the French pub—if he was lucky, that is, and she didn't ask for more. If he was going to poke up, she said, then she had to stoke up. But he just couldn't provide, he knew it quite suddenly. He could fight this battle and win if he were only one—he was used to living rough, to scrounging a bit here, borrowing a bit there, hocking anything marketable except his typewriter. Yes, with one only to keep, he could get through. But two, no. For all he saved on Lena was his laundry—she'd do that, for some esoteric, aesthetic reason, but cooking was an interference in the anarchic life necessary for her art. For her good humour, her absolute readiness in bed, her wonderful figure, her miraculous powers of availability, there was, therefore, to pay, not only the price of her zany drivel about art (that somehow made her seem more ready, more available to him, or, at any rate, took away from any guilt) but also this sheer need to consume. Facing the future quite squarely, he eliminated her. He had to. He couldn't afford her. He'd never from the first moment allowed sex to get in the way of what had to be done; and he wouldn't now. He never gave them his address, but he'd have to cut out Fitzroy and her other usual stamping grounds for a bit. It was a deprivation, almost a sadness; but when he'd beaten the bastards, forced them to print the truth, he could pick up again with her or with another. He'd had long periods of one-night stands before, even of chastity, though it drove him up the wall. All the same, when he stuffed his laundry back into the drawer, his elation had gone. The room was intolerable. He took himself off to a pub in Gray's Inn Road.

He was eating a soggy pie filled with nuggets of gut and drinking a lukewarm pint, when Towneley came in. He saw him start and turn back. He amused himself by letting him get to the door before he called:

"Dodo, what in the hell?"

So Dodo pretended to be surprised, and out it all poured—the rare Sunday office duty, the need to check an interview with a chap who lived in Bloomsbury, otherwise Sunday always saw him down at Merstham, if not, the wife cried blue murder (the skinny and sour-faced variety she'd be). Anyway, as if he cared. He listened, however, as though the boring rigmarole was a stop-press confession of Bukharin.

"Well, so you're here, anyway," he said at the end of it—he almost added, "my dear old pal." "I'm turning you in some of my diary since you liked it, Dodo." But perhaps because he smarmed in letters, Dodo Towneley turned out to be one of those chaps who could be rude to your face.

"Not if it's your usual bellyache about the Communists done up in another form, you're not, Q.J."

"I resent that, Dodo."

"Then you'll just have to resent. Have the other half?"

To control his rising fury, Quentin merely nodded, and drank silently for some minutes. Then Towneley in a voice full of old friendship, old sweats together, and a lot more hypocritical muck, "But tell us about the war itself, Q.J. Good Lord, you're one of the few that's been there who knew what war was like when he went. All these other chaps were conchies in 'fourteen."

That a so-called radical editor could talk against conscientious objectors in that sneering, hearty way, made Quentin clench his fists until the knuckles were livid. For a moment he retreated into blackness, telling himself he mustn't hit the man. When suddenly—it must be too little food, tiredness or what—he was alone, miles from anyone, the darkness hadn't left him, he was cut off into night, he would never be two again. He fought his way back, to hear Towneley say: "You all right, old boy?"

And, yes, he was; but he knew he mustn't let Towneley go, must find something to touch, to amuse him, to stop him saying "no."

"Yes, how right you are. The extraordinary innocents that one met on the Teruel front! Observers, they often called themselves. I think they gave the Spanish more laughs than annoyance. I hope so. A Danish Red Cross Liberal! Have you ever met a Danish Red Cross Liberal!" He'd got Towneley laughing already. "Well this specimen was called Mogens Mohn. Oh, that's nothing unusual in Denmark. It's just Bill Smith. But the things he said. I think the best was, 'Mr. Matthews, do you think we shall meet with a genuine atrocity?' "

He concentrated on getting a funny Scandinavian accent and let the words build up for themselves. Anyhow it had Towneley laughing in the aisles.

"Oh, marvellous! For God's sake, write *that* up for us. Have another pie? Or better still, Q.J., a spot of lunch. What about Soho?"

No, not Soho, but a spot of lunch would be very nice. Just the two of them.

Watching P.S. on top of a ladder placing a spring of holly over the John Nash downscape, her breath caught suddenly with love for him. At first she hadn't found it easy to allow him the long-trousered suit that he had worn this holidays, but now it seemed only to underline his boyish figure, his fresh, healthy, smooth boy's skin. Senior had a strange pattern of his own now—daily life at the office, regular hours—something that belonged to a world she knew nothing of, for

Hugh had always been popping backwards and forwards from class, and even old Billy Pop had worked (if you could call it that) at home. And this hols Middleman spent all his time organizing the Peace Pledge group at Ramsgate—he actually liked strangers, really. So that she'd been closer in these last ten days to P.S. than for years—long walks, afternoons shopping, cinemas, a trip up to Town, a wonderful time. He'd told her how terrific he thought it was of her to follow Frau L. that evening when they'd all sat by, manlike, and not known how to cope; he'd said that all things considered, the Frau would have a happier *Weinacht* in the boarding-house she'd gone to until the Quakers were ready for her.

"You old hypocrite! What you mean is that we shall have a jolly sight better Christmas without strangers."

He'd blushed and then squeezed her arm. Now, as she saw him self-consciously hitch his long trousers with a man's, almost a sailor's, gesture, before coming down the ladder, she thought, let the whole thing blow up so long as I don't lose *him*. Then with a shudder of her straight shoulders, she knew that she must make an act of contrition, get this straight with God.

"Look, darling, just put some over each of the pictures here. But be careful of the ladder. I'll be back in a mo. I'm just going to have a word with Daddy."

She always knocked on the door of Hugh's den; it gave him time to look busy. As a matter of fact he was. He insisted on getting the reports off before Christmas, although for some poor mothers of little idiots it would be better, she always said, to wait until after the New Year—but, then, look at beastly income tax!

"Can you spare me a few moments, darling?"

And with his usual courtesy—*that* he had handed on to the boys—he said, "My dear, my time is always yours!"

Yet she must hope that the day would never come when this was true.

She sat down: "I've been thinking . . ." she said; then she shut up, for if contrition was to be made it must be complete—God always knew.

Taking his pipe from his mouth: "Whatever you think is worth hearing."

"Before that woman . . . before Frau Liebermann left, she told me a few home truths. She said that there must be a war—if we were to survive, that is. And if that happens, of course, the boys—Senior and Middleman will have to go, won't they? And they may be killed."

He sucked in his teeth in disapproval. "My dear."

"No, Hugh, don't let's pretend. It's true, isn't it?"

"Oh, I don't know. There could very well still be peace. And with some honour."

"Precious little, I should think. Anyway, if it comes . . ."

"Oh, *if* it comes, we might *all* be blown sky high."

She frowned perplexed, for a second or two. "That's all rather newspaper talk, isn't it? But for the two boys there is real danger."

He lit his pipe again. "No more than for any others."

But she ignored this. "And the Frau implied that I make it all much more difficult for them if I try to hold them. It's true, isn't it? isn't it?"

"My dear . . ."

"Oh, of course it is. The Frau was perfectly right." She got up, and bending over his table, took up some reports.

"Aitcheson, J. M. Purkiss, Rodney, Boyle, Keith. I only faintly know who they are." She stood over him. "That house near Exeter hasn't gone, has it? Let's go down in the New Year and see it. We can take P.S. before term starts."

He looked up at her, puzzling. "Daisy's decided that if we move, they'll retire."

"She's right. But don't let that worry you, Hugh. If we go there, and I think we should—war here near Dover would be courting suiciae—then I want to be the Headmaster's wife. To get to know, to look after"—she let the reports fall from her hands on to the table— "Aitcheson, Purkiss, Boyle. P.S. will introduce me."

He took her hand. "You're sure? Purkiss has enormous red ears with chilblains." He laughed.

"Chilblains! How disgraceful! They're quite unnecessary these days! Oh, dear! What a lot of work there'll be." She squeezed his hand and left him.

Down in the hall, P.S., with cheeks swollen like a holy cherub, was blowing up balloons. She came and put her arm round his waist.

"Mrs. Pascoe," she said, "you must let them go. There must be war, or God help you." She laughed. He frowned in bewilderment above his bulging cheeks, but then she added, "Arnold, come here, *du* wicked *kleiner*."

He burst into laughter and the balloon sank.

"Oh, really, Mummy. You've got the Frau completely." And they both laughed. She mussed up his hair with her hand.

"But not you, darling, not *der kleinster* Pascoe. You'll be safe in our lovely combes, you'll like that, won't you?" She smiled at her son's perplexed face. But she wasn't really talking to him. God knew what the bargain was.

Bright and early, before the alarm, before seven thirty, Alfred rang.

"Oh, thank God," he said. Had she not known him, she would have thought fresh tragedy was upon them. "I was frightened to death you'd have gone out."

"Well, I haven't." She felt snappish.

"I just wanted to hear your voice before I go. And to tell you that it's all right, Glad. Not a moment's more worry. The cheque's in the post for you. Five weeks to the dot as I said. So perhaps you'll have a bit more faith in your old financial wizard in future."

To hear his gaiety and certainty flooded her with a relief she had not known for what now seemed centuries.

"There have got to be risks, you know."

It didn't seem worth contradicting.

"Where on earth are you off to this time?"

"I've got to run over to Holland. Bloody nuisance! And Doris is a bit seedy. But there's a man I must see there. And if he comes up with what I hope he does, there'll be no more selling of antiques for you, my darling. Caviare off golden dishes, that's what you'll have and like it." She didn't answer, so he said, "Well, there it is, your Christmas present. God bless."

She bathed luxuriously, dressed with lingering indulgence. She was agile again, hundreds of pounds of worried, anxious, stifling fat seemed to have gone from her. She put her brown tweed skirt and coat and her beaver fur away at the back of the wardrobe, they were a no longer needed disguise, as the daily racing for which she had worn them in the last fortnight had been a disguise to keep his name out if the worst . . . But now it wouldn't. She had known him long enough, with all his tricky ways, to know when he was speaking the truth. That was what partnership meant. She should have known it. Hearing Alf's voice today—confident, youthful again, cocky old Alf —made her ashamed for her fears. Well, now, with Sylvia gone and Christmas here, for some hard work; unless the "Closed" notice had put people off.

If not that, something had done so, for all the morning there was no sale, but for two fire screens to an old buffer for his daughter; however, the more time, relaxed time at last, for the neglected account books. And then, just before lunch hour—Herr Ahrendt. She knew at once from the shifting glance of his sloping goat's eyes that something was wrong.

"But what does it mean, Miss Matthews? what does it mean? No Mrs. Heathway, no Miss Matthews. Closed. What does it mean? My wife tells me they have stolen our picture. You must forgive her, please, she is quite ill and not young and then, you know, she does not like to leave Germany; she is not like me, a Jew."

"Oh, poor Mrs. Ahrendt. No, it's just that we've had illness."

To her horror Mr. Ahrendt struck a little inlaid table with his clenched fist.

"Why are you keeping the truth from me, Miss Matthews? I know that you have taken our picture to Christie and there they say that they think it is a good picture. But you have taken it away before they are sure. What does it mean, please?"

For a moment, she thought, Now it's all, all right, I shall tell him; but then he had been so badly treated that surely he could never trust people; and such people themselves were not able to be trusted.

"Oh, I meant it all to be a surprise for you. It may be a very valuable picture, worth some thousands of pounds. Perhaps by Grünewald, you know. Matthias Grünewald. But I had to have a second opinion. That's why I took it from Christie's."

Strangely the statement of its value made Herr Ahrendt more hostile. He glared at her.

"Where is the picture, please, Miss Matthews? At once."

His anger infected her.

"Mr. Ahrendt, you gave me that picture for valuation because for many years I have sold things for you and given you good prices. You told me the picture was probably of no value, but that, if it would fetch anything you would be grateful. Now you come in here . . ."

"Many years, many years. For many years bad things are happening, Miss Matthews, though you may not know in this England. My wife is ill and old. She depends upon me. Miss Matthews, this is Tuesday. I want my picture back, or a good sale, by this Sunday. Or there may happen bad things for you."

He turned, swaying slightly—he had become very frail and old— and went towards the door.

"Don't you worry, you shall have your money. And good riddance," she shouted after him—after all, if he had known worry and tension, so had she.

She saw him walking to and fro in front of the shop window for a few moments. Once he seemed about to come in. She almost went out to him—the poor old thing! There was no sense in quarrelling. But tomorrow all would be right and, with that, he too would be his courteous old self again.

The next day when she had ascertained that the letter was not at the shop, she went racing. On her return to the flat in the evening, she found a telegram: FORGOT POST LETTER LONDON. SENT FROM HERE. ALL MY APOLOGIES LOVE ALF. The telegram came from Dublin. She went racing again after that. And finally on Friday night the letter came. It contained a post-dated cheque for five hundred pounds; there was also a little note of apology from Herr Ahrendt, courteous, old world. She must forgive an old man's fussing, but Mrs. Ahrendt was ill and this was why he must insist.

I have been settled in now two weeks and all going well. Today Mr. Truscott thats the one under Mr. Roper told me I done very well and got the packin idear quicker than most and if I go on like this I will get a rise I know the letter said not to bother you and tho it makes me sad and Madge too Arthur says you did right and all for the best but I carnt let all go by without saying thank you for gettin a job was all that I wanted and like you said without it men rot. Madge and Arthur and Stanley and Baby and all send love and so does your pal with the biggest ever—Ted.

Marcus closed the letter, avoided looking at the Tchelitchew portrait, and went in search of Jack. Voices—Jack's, Mary's, and, he thought, another's—reached him from the conservatory. At first he thought to turn back, but he stimulated his own anger so that it would carry him through what would now have to be a self-consciously melodramatic entry. Speaking through great scarlet and orange sprays of bignonia, almost subdued by the heavy mingled smells of China tea and gardenias, he said, waving the letter:

"What the hell do you mean by this, Jack?"

A nervous tick of extreme irritation seized Jack's thin, papery cheeks. He leaned back in the black leather, modern rocking-chair, knotting his hands behind his head.

"Shall we battle about it later, Markie? You haven't said how do to Mary. And you don't know Hansi Münze."

Marcus grimaced at Mary and bobbed his head in the direction of a young man who immediately stood up, bowing absurdly. The creature was one of the most appalling little screamers, with a silver bracelet, a willowy figure, and large, dark, lemur's eyes—the most un-me person, Marcus thought, and to his amazement found as his eyes took in the young man's flirtatious glance that he was beginning a cock stand. He instantly turned on Jack.

"What do you mean by interfering in my affairs? Teaching me moral lessons!"

He noticed with a certain pleasure that Mary's deep-set eyes had become hooded, as they always did when there was any blasphemy or vulgarity in personal relationships.

"Oh, really!" Jack's drawl had the full arrogance that years ago would have frightened him. "The young man was most persistent. Telephoning at every hour. It's all very well for you marching behind red flags, but I was here and had to cope with it. You'd treated him very badly, so I thought he'd better have a job. I went to one of the family subsidiaries. He was told not to bother you. He deserves to be fired."

Mary was talking now to little Miss Lemur—"Do you mean that dreams have a sort of black edge around them that gives them formal coherence like a painting?"

"Oh, the dream, of course, is only one of many fruitful images for the painter."

Some bloody Expressionist rubbish. Marcus felt more angry with Jack.

"What bloody right have you to involve me in a lot of paternalistic patronage? If Ted had been left to stew in the juice all you capitalist shits had put him in, he might have acquired some sense of class solidarity."

Jack leaned back. "Oh, my Gawd!"

Mary, too, took a hand. "Horrid words, Marcus. I do think ideas must be judged a little by the words they breed."

"Well, then, Hansi," Jack said, "I'll come to the studio this evening, since you say you want them seen by electric light. You do *mean* that? All right. We could dine and go to the cinema or theatre first. Is there something you wish to see?"

"What is there of Shakespeare?"

Marcus saw that there was nothing for it but to accept the opportunity of recovering his temper that Jack and Mary had so civilizedly combined to offer him.

He said, "Well, you could see my brother in *Twelfth Night*."

"Don't be ridiculous, Markie. We couldn't go to the Old Vic."

When the lemur's eyes grew round in question, Mary explained: "It's all terribly earnest and unlovely."

"The décor!" Jack cried. "They think it's clever to do without colour or splendour."

"I think," Mary suggested, "it's because they do it all on the cheap."

"Oh, no, my dear, they like it like that. Like Heal's furniture. Do you remember, Markie, we went to *Othello*, and it was dressed in vomit colour. *Othello* and Renaissance Venice, of all things! Oh, no, you'd hate it, Hansi. We could go to Nellie Wallace at the Bedford. Or there's *Duck Soup*. Perhaps Nellie Wallace is a bit difficult for you, I think it had better be Harpo Marx."

"My God, you are snobbish," Marcus said.

"Darling Marcus," Mary observed, "I don't see why it's snobbish to go to the things one likes."

But Marcus had left the tropical scene.

Under the thickly white-painted shell that surmounted the entrance to Kingsway Hall (was it classical? was it baroque? no, eclectic), there gathered the eclectic group of speakers selected to represent a wide cultural front of opposition to the growing Fascist tyrannies. Reg Smalley, the Chairman, Free Church guardian of civil liberties, had news for each in turn, as they arrived, of the Government's repressive bill shortly to be before the House. "It's Clause ten that we've got to concentrate on," he said to each as he met them. The two Trades Council men, the comrade from the Ex-Servicemens' League against Fascism, the Co-op Guild woman, and, of course, the Labour League of Lawyers worried and fought over the clause with Mr. Smalley, eagerly, as the pack dismembers the fox. Matthias Birnbaum stood aloof in metaphysical and artistic grandeur—the great foreign visitor observing the antics of the Pytchley or the Quorn. Margaret, no hunting woman, dangerously dressed indeed in fox furs, felt it her job, as fellow writer and co-innocent, to bring life to the Olympian brow.

"Not our happiest sort of architecture, I'm afraid."

"No? I suppose it's the usual *Jugendstil* of its period."

So firm was his tone that Margaret looked around her. However, he was wrong; the building was not *art nouveau*, but argument did not appear likely to be fruitful.

"Thomas Mann's declaration was very inspiring."

"His declaration? Oh, his statement to the P.E.N. Club. You found that inspiring? He inspired also many patriotic German ladies in the Kaiser time with his new democratic faith. But as a Jew I was not so happy with his nationalism then, so I remain a little bit sceptical now."

She had the impression that he counted the minutes of silence until he felt he had adequately reproved her.

"On what will you speak this afternoon, Miss Matthews?"

"Oh, the old business, just say a word or two about the writer's inevitable commitment to freedom and his consequent implacable hatred of fascism in any form. It's mainly important that we should be seen to take a stand."

"Oh. What a great pity that John Galsworthy is not here to speak for the English writers. He was very much known and admired in Germany."

"Yes, I know. He wasn't a very good novelist, you know."

"No, I suppose not. But then the English novel is not an aesthetic novel, it is a social novel. *The Forsyte Saga* has great importance as the mirror of the British high *bourgeoisie*."

To her relief, Rupert, in a green Tyrolean hat and a camel's-hair coat, brought some glitter of the stage to dispel Herr Birnbaum's solemnity. But not for long. For even praise barely worked.

"I can hardly tell you, Herr Birnbaum, how excited my children were that I was going to meet the author of the *Goat Boy*."

No relaxation, only grim: "*Girl*. The translation is very bad."

After a pause, Rupert: "Of course our great gain in the theatre from all this wickedness has been Reinhardt's arrival."

"You admire him?"

"Well, to be honest, I was disappointed with his *Dream* at Oxford. I know it was undergraduates, but even so . . ."

"Oh, what did you expect, then?"

Margaret could tell that Rupert found such questioning unfamiliar.

"Well, the reports had been so . . . One really thought, well, here it is."

"Here is what?"

"It's rather a ridiculous expression, but what I *mean* is, the production was so old-fashioned in the spectacular manner, almost Beerbohm Tree stuff. I saw no trace of genius . . ."

"Oh, *das Genie*. That, Reinhardt has not. But I suppose he is more advanced than what you have here."

"That's what our critics had led us to suppose . . ."

"Ah! Your critics. I am right, isn't it so, that they have no training in *Dramaturgie?*"

Rupert withdrew his chin from his green-and-white spotted foulard muffler. Sniffing the air he said:

"Oh, none, I'm glad to say, none at all."

"We can't wait for Q.J. Matthews." Reg Smalley's voice broke in before the great man could react. "As people are arriving in good numbers I think we might repair to the vestry. We can go straight on to the platform from there."

Crowded into a small room of hideous yellow pitch-pine panelling, Rupert and Margaret stood disconsolately together like two flamingos with their wings cut.

"I have no training in *Dramaturgie*." Rupert was so much the awful Birnbaum, and also the old Rupert imitating Germans in the nursery, that she burst into a loud laugh. Everyone turned for a moment and stared.

"Oh, blast! Quentin is going to be late. They won't let him on the platform."

"My dear Mag, why on earth not?"

"He's in disgrace politically."

"Silly old ass!"

"Well, do be very nice to him, Rupert. I'm sure he's following his conscience."

"Oh, good heavens, yes." Rupert immediately looked stiff and pompous.

At that moment Quentin, hatless, and wearing a filthy raincoat, pushed his way into the little room. His sister and brother made to greet him. He waved to them, but before they could reach him he was deep in the conclave about Clause Ten.

"The man you want to lobby," they heard him say, "is Emrys Evans. Get him to ask questions. He's a good lawyer and he hates Simon's guts. Oh, it's an old legal story."

Once more Rupert and Margaret huddled in dishevelled isolation.

"I'm sorry I let you in for this, Rupert."

"Oh, that's all right. I suppose one had to accept."

"Yes, I think so. Though I oughtn't to, for I'm just in the middle of a new novel."

"It's not going very well, is it?"

"No. Oh, Rupert, do you mean you can still tell after all these years? And we never meet!"

"Well, yes, actually I can, Mag. But your last was good."

"As good as I could make it. But your Malvolio. Raves, Rupert!"

"Yes, I wish I . . ."

"You're not sure? *I'll* tell you."

"Oh, I wish you would. If *you* said yes . . . Come tonight. I can get you a ticket."

Margaret only had time to mouth acceptance before Reg Smalley marshalled them all on to the platform.

Marcus was late at Holborn Underground, where he was to meet Jane Farquhar. She was furious, had a cold, looked like hell as they ran across the empty Saturday afternoon Kingsway through stinging, icy rain. When they got to the entrance, ushers warned them they would have to stand at the back of the hall. A deep social instinct made Marcus greet the whole unfortunate, wet, rubber-smelling occasion by pointing out the thickly moulded shell ceiling.

"Not the happiest use of baroque. Perhaps it would be wisest to excuse it by calling it eclectic."

Jane Farquhar growled, and contrived, as they squeezed their way into the packed crowd, to give off an even more pungent smell of wet macintosh.

She sneezed violently; on the tip of the nose of the young man on his other side hung a mucous stalactite; against Marcus's ankles his trouser bottoms clung in cold, wet sogginess. The chairman's voice came through clouds of tobacco smoke and warm steam from the soaked clothing; what he said was difficult to hear, literally damp-ened, befogged; or else, Marcus thought, the fog was in his own head—no doubt the heavy beginnings of the pervasive head cold that threatened to bring a more complete unity to the meeting than anti-Fascist emotion. It was as though he was being compressed into the cheerless crowd like papier-mâché, yet he had never felt more com-pletely alone. He could see almost nothing in front of him except navy-blue raincoats. The heroic flame that had burnt within him more fiercely each day since the Bermondsey battle flickered feebly in this watery world. All his desperate determination to fight ap-proaching doom weakened into thoughts of evasion, into distaste for a last few months of peace spent in fruitless fumbling. It was all right for Jane Farquhar, her face set in militancy, for the stalactite young man, no doubt, but for . . . He forced himself to listen and was rewarded with Margaret's name (some clapping). Craning over the acres of wet wool and water he saw a dark-haired, darkly anxious-looking, befurred woman conspicuously middle-class in the setting, before he fully realized that it was Margaret. How middle-aged she looked, he thought; for all Douglas's soothing and her steady stream of well-received books, she looked haggard, fidgety, as though something were biting her bottom. Now came Rupert's name (some clapping) and he at once recognized that tall, ageing (but it had been ageing in the nursery) blond splendour with an amused but affectionate admiration which only turned to embarrassment when he took in the awful stagey clothes—camel's-hair coat and suede shoes! No doubt he played Malvolio in the dressing-gown he'd worn for *Private Lives* in repertory.

"Margaret'll be quite good, I expect, but I can't *think* what dear Rupert will say," he told Jane. Speaking of his family he talked in his usual loud, drawing-room voice. Heads turned towards him. Jane whispered, scowling:

"It doesn't matter what they say. The arts are always hopeless politically, but it's very important that they should show solidarity."

He was quite familiar with these tactical considerations by now; but he had not until then associated them with Margaret's arid honesty and Rupert's talented *blague*. He would have found it easier to accept Jane's ruling if he had not caught her looking around their neighbours to see how impressed they were by this familiarity with the platform. However, there was no mistaking the genuine delight of Jane and of all at Haldane's name (clapping, calls, and cheers). Beside this demonstration the applause for Matthias Birnbaum, though general, was formal. Nevertheless, unlike all the others, he rose from his chair—a lion surveying a group of Bank Holiday rubbernecks—tossed his mane, and looked down his long, fleshy nose. A pride of lions, Marcus thought; and then, remembering a banker cousin of Jack's, Jack's physicist sister, he thought, and a disdain of Jews. How tiresome they could be! But now it was Q. J. Matthews and more barracking than applause. He could hardly glimpse Quentin at the other end of the platform, but something in his manner must have infuriated the audience—some pipe-smoking smugness, no doubt—for there were cries of, "Get off the platform!" "Mosley's man!" "Trotskyist!" and "P.O.U.M.!"

"Pouff! They're quite wrong there," Marcus whispered to Jane, "he couldn't be more normal." Jane glared at him. "Oh, I don't defend him," Marcus went on. "He's always been a show-off. He *would* be a Trotskyist." Emboldened by the weak protestations and the Chairman, he shouted, "Trotskyist!" loudly.

Among the many protesting voices, he heard Margaret crying "Shame!" and wondered if she were addressing him personally—she'd always taken Quentin at his own inflated estimate. Indeed, the fuss and palaver on the platform were considerable as the barracking and counter-protests from the audience grew. All that Marcus could see of Quentin was his crossed legs but they appeared unperturbed, perhaps imperturbable. Now Reg Smalley was bending over Haldane in discussion and now Haldane passed a note down to a man who circulated it round the audience. A moment later the demonstration against Quentin was broken into by a small bald-headed man in the body of the hall who shouted, "Free speech, Comrades, free speech!" "We may not all agree with Q. J. Matthews . . ." Mr. Smalley began, and from all parts of the hall came shouts of "We don't," but here and there were cries of "Free speech. Let him have his say, Comrades. Let him speak. Leave him alone. Unity. Unity" that in time subdued and at last drowned the cries of "Trotskyist P.O.U.M. traitor." Marcus alone was left shouting abuse.

"For God's sake, shut up," Jane said.

He looked at her in surprise, "Why should I?" he asked.

Impatience and annoyance made Jane speak plainly: "Because we've been told to."

Again Marcus stared at her. "My God!" he said, then he let out a shrill "Traitor."

A tough red-faced Scotsman in front turned round menacingly. "Will you hush your noise, or we will have to throw you out."

But before the man had made his rebuke, Marcus was already gone.

Gladys had spent the morning first with her bank manager, then with an auctioneer, and now she set off for Herr Ahrendt's, determined to tell him the whole story. She could offer him six thousand pounds straightaway, or within days; she would ask him to give her a month or two to meet the rest. For all the disquieting, shifting glance and clenched fist of their last meeting, Gladys thought of him coming to the door, his old Santa Claus self, the thin, scholarly figure, the shy eyes, the courteous bow, the gentle smile. His difficulty would probably be to find a means of accepting her offer that wouldn't appear too abrupt—he was a great seeker for the right phrases, genuinely sensitive old thing. She imagined them exchanging compliments on a chilly doorstep, and smiled to herself. She would have to push him into acceptance of the scheme or they'd be all day salaaming at one another. Whatever happened, she mustn't let him realize that in order to pay she would be penniless, temporarily of course, until Alf— but she would not even think of Alf, his name *must* not get involved. If she didn't choose her words carefully the old boy would urge her to take her time; if anyone were to be kind to her, she might break down. She decided to try a light touch; not, of course, to make light of her own stupid wickedness; but somehow not to alarm the old boy or to encourage his pity: "Look," she would say, "I've been an abominable idiot. The story's not a pleasant one, but if you'll give me a little time, I can do the decent thing."

She had thought of the old pair as living poorly, but she was not prepared for such a collapsing house in such a mouldering terrace.

Ever since she had emerged from the lift at Kilburn Station and walked up the hill towards West Hampstead, the desolation, decay, and squalor had made it hard for her to hold on to the image of Herr Ahrendt, the courteous, neat, civilized old gentleman. Indeed, by the time she faced the broken bell-pull, under which a grubby ink-smeared card said "Ahrendt," she had reinforced him with a dandy-ish yet scholarly touch—a neat little amber velvet smoking jacket, Turkish carpet slippers, a book (no, a pile of books) under his arm, and—could it be?—a little, old-fashioned, tasselled smoking cap. No doubt his distinguished little brown head would look more *soigné*, more silky, in his own home. Much care, much sleekness would be needed if it were to counter the scabrously peeling stucco front with its green mossy-looking patches, the draped lace curtains like dirty dish cloths, the uneven steps and broken balustrade, the blistered door, the dog mess by the empty, unwashed milk bottles. Their little rooms would have to be very neat and cosy to overcome the atmos-phere of this house, not only the old boy but his wife . . . Of course, there was Mrs. Ahrendt. Gladys decided she would not in-trude on the sick room; their privacy must be very dear to them. She would just call a greeting, and conspiring with looks and finger on lips, agree with Herr Ahrendt to a little lie that would satisfy an invalid's anxious fears.

Pointless to pull the rusty bell, best get down to banging on the door straightaway, but then she thought that just because they weren't English that didn't mean this wasn't their castle—the more to be treated so since they were old, poor, and in exile. The bell when touched lightly clanged furiously, enough to waken any dead. It did, in fact, rouse a sharp-featured harridan on the top floor to throw up her window and bawl as no dead could have done. After that window had banged down again, Gladys could hear a shuffling coming towards her from behind the door—a slow shuffling—but at last the door opened and a drawn white face as wrinkled as a parrot's peered at her; the eyes, too, were parrot's eyes, hooded, small, and suspicious. From the bent old body came a stale, sour smell that made her recoil.

"I am Miss Matthews."

As though presenting a note for teacher she found herself holding out the envelope in which she had put a cheque for the three thou-sand pounds immediately available.

"Is that the money? You should have consulted us before you sold. I own that picture, you know. It belonged to my uncle. But never mind, Herrmann has been foolish, but . . ." The old creature had opened the letter by now. She held out the cheque, having peered at it angrily. "What is this? What does it mean?"

"I wanted to explain to Mr. Ahrendt . . ."

"Explain to *me*. What does it mean?"

"I can produce another three thousand pounds almost immediately. Look Mrs. Ahrendt, you'll catch your death of cold standing here. Let me come in. Anyway, I want to see Mr. Ahrendt."

"My husband is ill. You must give us all the money. I don't know what it is. Three thousand pounds? That's not very much. No, you cannot come in! Three thousand, that's not so much."

Gladys had to push with all her weight for an entry. She felt sure the old woman was mad. She looked mad, absolutely round the bend, standing in a filthy bare hall on ragged linoleum under the dismal light of one feeble, fly-blown, naked bulb, casually dismissing thousands of pounds.

"I must see your husband."

"No, no, you can't see him. You have robbed him enough, you thief!"

But now at the top of the steep flight of stairs Gladys saw Mr. Ahrendt, standing motionless, staring at her. He seemed to have cut his head, the forehead was swathed in a handkerchief. Under his old overcoat a striped pyjama jacket was open at the top to show some tufts of wiry hair at the base of his neck.

"Mr. Ahrendt, please let me tell you . . ."

But she felt now that she couldn't tell the story, explain her guilt.

"Your picture is sold. It was by the artist Grünewald . . ."

"I know," said Mr. Ahrendt, "the Christie's have told me so much. What did you get for it?"

"Nearly ten thousand pounds. I've brought three thousand now. And the rest . . ."

"The rest we want now, you thief!"

The old woman had taken her arm and was twisting it most painfully.

"Don't be absurd. I can't produce money out of a hat on a Saturday. Can I, Mr. Ahrendt?"

The old man spoke slowly—he sounded sad, but whether it was a trick of the light, Gladys could not afterwards decide, his teeth looked larger, wolfish, and his beard, far from neat, was as straggly as that awful old creature in the Dickens book.

"I don't think you can produce the money at all, Miss Matthews. I think you have robbed me. You thought, perhaps, he has been thrown out of his country; he is old and in the dust-bin; the big sharks have bitten, now let the little sharks have their chance. But I know what wicked people are, Miss Matthews. What they have done to me and Käthe and to millions more. I must not accept injustice. No! I don't want to hear any more. Bring me my money by tomorrow morning."

He disappeared into the darkness on the landing.

Mrs. Ahrendt said, "Get out, thief."

She pushed Gladys out of the door.

This is enough of all this politics, Margaret thought, this standing up emitting a lot of platitudes to people who despise the things I care for, or who, if they don't, are never going to do more than sit at meetings and wish the world was free of evil. And to have involved Rupert was unforgivable. To have made a person of talent and charm make a fool of himself—though, even with her knowledge of theatre peoples' extraordinarily feeble grasp of reality, she could hardly have guessed that he would have treated them to a sort of adolescent's anthology—Shelley: "Bliss it was in that dawn to be alive"; Milton on freedom of the press; Abraham Lincoln; and something quite inappropriate from *Julius Caesar*. Whoever had suggested it to him? Her cheeks flamed as she thought of it and she welcomed Aunt Alice, now perpetually in the wings, to take the centre stage. As the climax drew nearer—what should it be? murder? or more horribly soiled nighties? or perhaps a holocaust of all Aunt A.'s treasured souvenirs? Any rate, something Gothic she would permit herself at last—really the moment of Aunt A.'s realization that they'd cut her off from the outside world. Once that was clear to her, the ultimate outrages were infinite, and lay in her terrorized anticipation; but as this climax . . . O Lord, the awful Birnbaum was booming away; but Aunt Alice was more powerful . . . if she were to grant herself this Gothicism, it could turn out a dangerously melodramatic affair, and there were no means of tempering it with her well-known irony—for if the nieces had cut the old

woman off from the world of chars and piano-tuners, she had effec-
tually cut *herself* off in this novel from the readers who called her a
new Miss Austen—yet there must be *some* tempering. Perhaps the
pathos of Aunt A.'s position, but, if softened by pathos, where was
the mighty oak brought down? Should she go back and soften the
old tyrant? No. Oh, Lord, here she was back again at the failure of
connection—Aunt A. wicked and strong, Aunt A. pathetic and . . .
Oh, damn that old bore's pompous drone.

This chap would go on for hours, Quentin thought. At least, it
would mean Reg Smalley wouldn't get round to calling on him to
speak; probably that had been the intention. "Spirit of creation
never vanquished" *blaa, blaa, blaa;* "invincible human imagination"
blaa, blaa, blaa. Better to hear the comrades spout the gospel than
all this liberal rubbish. Margaret and "the irony of history that
will defeat Hitler," Rupert and Shelley—God help us! He'd seen
some of the comrades' faces; they were paying hard for their
solidarity with the intellectuals. Serve them bloody well right.
He picked out a young, blonde, fresh-faced girl; following the line
of her neck, he let his hand take her firm breast and between his
thumb and forefinger the nipple's stalk grew hard. But no hard-on.
He pulled up her red woollen dress to expose her flat, cream smooth
belly, but still no hard. With his arms locked together he brutally
forced her legs apart so that the panties tore but—*blaa, blaa, blaa.*
Blast all the liberals and all the other bastards who made the world
the shambles it was and then bleated to prevent others from having
any fun, from getting a hard-on. He took out a notebook and began
to write:

> Blessed are the pure in spirit. Well . . . yes, but the innocent have
> a lot to account for in the world today. This was never so much
> brought home to me as when I drove on a tour of the Teruel front
> with Mr. Mogens Mohn, Danish representative of the Red Cross. Now
> Mr. Mogens Mohn, like most Scandinavians, was a very nice chap—
> high-minded, honest, broad-minded, clean-cut, everything you could ask
> of a Dane. He had a good, sensible, modern house, too, made mostly
> of glass, in the woods of South Jutland, and a good, sensible wife, and
> two very pretty, flaxen-haired girls—I know that because he showed
> me excellent photographs of all these that he had taken himself with
> the most up-to-date camera. But even so Mr. Mogens Mohn was de-
> termined to see an atrocity. I have never known a chap so determined

to see an atrocity. Not, of course, for any morbid or even propagandist reason, but in pursuit of truth, for everyone knows that liberal Scandinavians must know the full truth about everything. So there we were bumping along in our old Ford, and every hundred yards or so, should we see an old woman sunning herself, or a chicken that had been run over, or an idiot boy, 'What do you think, my dear fellow,' Mr. Mogens Mohn would ask, in that exasperating English accent half-Etonian, half-Welsh that Scandinavians use, 'is that an atrocity?' And I always had to assure him that it was not. But the odd thing was that when we did finally come upon an atrocity and a very nasty one . . .

The odd thing was that he'd had to go behind a barn and vomit, that he could not bring himself to ask the questions that he and Mohn had devised as a method of establishing the authenticity of atrocity stories, but all the same, damn Mohn's fresh-faced seriousness, damn all liberal innocence . . .

a young girl of fifteen raped, her tongue torn out, her arms cut off, her little brother slit down the belly and left to die; Mr. Mogens Mohn recognized it at once. "This is an atrocity," he said. "We must establish the truth of the matter." And he set about it as coolly as though it were a question of faulty drainage at Odense or a badly designed play centre in Aarhus. I think his only serious grumble was that lack of tongue and arms made the girl a poor witness to establish the truth to which his readers in Copenhagen had a right as liberal Scandinavians . . .

Rupert felt glad that his moment was over—glad because it was an unfamiliar audience and then he was an actor, not a public speaker; but pleased, also, warm and pleased, for after the appalling delivery of all the others—dear, unhappy Mag should never be allowed to speak in public—and their no doubt clever but ugly words, the audience, with a rapt silence, had responded (as all audiences do) to the great language of the past well spoken. Indeed with a childlike wonder that you would not get from a sophisticated theatre audience. Looking at them, he saw suddenly what was wrong with the world, particularly with this politically active world of social conscience— it was starved of beauty. And now they must listen to this disagreeable, self-opinionated monster—for really it was monstrous that the writer of books that held thousands of children spellbound should be so vain. But he must listen all the same, if only to find some crumb to take back to an excited Christopher, a curious Tanya.

"But I have spoken enough in generalities. The creative spirit, the human imagination, the ingenuity of man, these will endure. They are stronger, more real than the false *Realpolitik*, the vulgar armed fists of maniacs and criminals. I could speak to you of atrocities, of cruel, shameful persecutions and sufferings, but these you may read in your papers, or rather in some of them. I want to speak to you of something very close to myself, for in these times we are brought up against what happens to ourselves, to the realities of the world as it touches our minds and our bodies. I have lived all my life for the language of my country, the German language. For this, and because of the great and living heritage that it gave me, I left behind altogether the language of my mother—Yiddish, and behind this Hebrew. Perhaps now I meet a punishment, though into my stories— and it is my finest boast today—there has gone much of the great story-telling tradition of the Jewish people. And I have lived to try to use the German language so that it may sweeten the minds and— how will you say?—make big, make strong the imagination of the children, of those to whom the future world belongs. To do this has been easy for me, because I have not much care for the great world, the world you say in English of grown ups; in that world I am stiff and not at ease, people say a vain man. So that such a man as I must talk to children. But to find the right language, the right words in our great tongue has been a hard lifetime task.

"And now with the coming of our Führer, I have known two hells. The one is smaller. This hell alone is for me and for the other German artists who must leave Germany or remain silent. We must speak now as I am doing in a half-tongue, in a language that is not our own. How, when Mr. Rupert Matthews was so freely breathing the words of your Milton and your Shakespeare, did I not feel that. We have too our Schiller and our Lessing—but their words are unspoken today. But there will be other artists one day and Schiller's words will be heard again. The other hell is deep and very black. To know that the language I have tried to use to give the children life of the mind is being used today, perverted, strangled, to bring to the children of my country a real and permanent death—the death of their spirit . . ."

So that he should not cry—for tears always came easily to him— Rupert deliberately switched off his attention. But shame replaced compassion. How could he have judged the man solely by his man-

ner and words in a short meeting? He should have been indulgent
from the start to such a . . . But "indulgence" pulled him up. What
appalling patronage! No, the truth was that the great story-teller
was an odious, conceited boor. But he had his vocation, his special
powers, and what Hitler had done to that vocation was odious,
wicked, and infinitely pitiable. To sweeten the man in order the better to resent the outrage upon him was unpardonable sentimentality.
Unpardonable as his . . . yes, this was it . . . it didn't matter what
they said, Debbie or Nigel or James Agate. He should have known.
But tonight he would give some thanks to Birnbaum by repairing as
far as he could his patronage of Malvolio.

> Dear Alf, I was so bucked and pleased to see the piece about Ringmer
> Development in the *Evening Standard* City Column. The financial chap
> there seems to think it's one of the best specs of the moment and I'm
> sure he's right. Well done, old dear. I know how hard you've worked
> for this, and it'll be the beginning of the great Pritchard financial em-
> pire, I know. I'm afraid I've been rather jumpy lately and I apologize,
> but the truth is I've been betting much too heavily and have got myself
> into a bad jam. I'm an incurable optimist and I'm sure something'll turn
> up, but if you do hear bad news of me . . .

The note would, if the worst came to the worst and they tried to
question him, give him a let-out. "My God, Inspector, if she'd only
come to me earlier, I could have cleared the whole thing. But this was
the first intimation I had." All the same, she hoped he wouldn't use
the note. But never say die; if she wasn't going to press Alf, there was
no reason for not calling on Margaret or Marcus. Pride's pride, but
when you're properly up against it . . . So she called at Holland Villas
where Douglas was having sherry with Spicer, the Egyptologist. He
couldn't somehow see his plump, well-groomed old bore of a sister-
in-law—he really hardly knew her, but she almost smelt of good-
heartedness and bromide utterances—talking to Spicer; besides, he
didn't get so much chance to see the old chap. Luckily she seemed
quite unwilling to come in. She was obviously in a bit of a state—
probably some trouble with that chap she lived with, but Margaret
and she could talk bosoms together about that later. "Yes, it is important. It is important. As soon as she gets home, Douglas." "She ought
to *be* home, but she's out at some stop-Hitler meeting. Do you think
that sort of thing does any good?" "It *is* important, really it is, Doug-

las." He almost said, Can I help; she looked—she usually the comfortable one of Margaret's jittery, over-the-edge family—so haggard and
scared. But these independent business-women were usually terrible
prudes; she'd have a fit if he pried into her famous, rather moth-eaten
love life. "I'll see that she phones you as soon as she gets in." Going
back to his study: "Sorry for the interruption. Did you ever know
Borchardt? . . . No, simply that there are so many questions about
Tel-El-Amarna that one would have liked to put to him."

Why was one so insincere? When she had said "rave" she should
have added that his performance sounded from the notices an atrocious sentimentalization—all that guff about a loving Malvolio. As it
was—an insincerity and then a moment's sentimental recall of the
nursery days, mutual isolation in an unfamiliar milieu, her own re-
morse at responsibility for his making a public fool of himself—and
here she was, when she should be at home writing, sitting at the
theatre, and preparing herself to see him make a fool of himself a
second time in one day.

But: "Madam, yond young fellow swears he will speak with
you . . ." the body held so stiffly, the pompous voice, the very ring
of the butler's parlour—nothing loving or sweet here—most officious
with the touch of servile, and yet the speech, yes the whole scene—
"Gentlewoman, my lady calls"—was of an odious man who yet does
his job well, loves it, and, if odious, upper servant was after all an
odious rank. Upper servant . . .

Rupert, mashing Rupert, to make himself so odiously sexless! That
was it—as in rank, so in sex, an upper servant, neither fish, flesh, nor
fowl and so on. How would he then tackle the lovesickness and the
yellow stockings? "To gabble like tinkers at this time of night" yes,
of course, a busybody and a spoilsport, but that was his job, we can't
have the mistress's sleep broken. But still, how would he wear those
stockings? Oh, this was good. Oh, darling Rupert, you've got it. The
lovesickness, of course, is as connected as the rest, an outcrop of that
firm rock of rank consciousness, of pride in his job. Oh, this *was*
Malvolio. An odious creature, all the same, for work should be the
least of life's values, when there were beauty and love to count beside it. Or was it? She ought to be writing—that was her work. Oh,
God! if only she could write as he could act. And the truth was that
he was *silly*, so *silly;* she could tell them that, she *knew* from the

nursery time. He didn't know a *thing*. Oh, how unfair that one could be so fine an actor and such a fool. Now for this last, the dark cell—he'd never manage that. Sir Topas, the curate; "Out, hyperbolical friend!"—the audience was laughing—No, it was too much; the fools to laugh, it was too cruel. And now this fool—surely court fools must have been sadists in those days—"as ever thou wilt deserve well at my hand, help me to a candle . . ." That he should be brought so low as to ask for a candle—he, the master of the house amenities. An apt punishment and the more odious for its aptness. "Believe me, I am not. I tell thee true." Oh, poor soul! But he'd done it, he had, for she was weeping. "I'll be revenged on the whole pack of you"—there was nothing lovable there. She sat in her stall as the others rose and she scribbled him a note:

> Rupert, my dear darling, it was *so* good! Don't have any doubts. I thought from the crits that you have honeyed it all over, but you haven't—he's odious and worthy and when he's brought low it's unbearable and as soon as he's up again he's odious once more. Thank you ever so much—you've solved my problem. Mag. P.S. Oh, that awful pointless black and white! It's that sort of *silly* vulgarity that keeps intelligent people out of the theatre.

She thought for a moment of going to see him in his dressing-room, but then instead she gave the note marked "immediate" to the stage-door porter, for she had to hurry home to let Aunt Alice fall apart into all the various unrelated persons that she now knew bobbed up and sank down like corks in the ocean inside that old raddled body as inside all our bodies.

"Mr. Matthews' sister on the telephone, sir. She seems a little agitated, so . . ."

"All right, Dempster. I am so sorry about this, Hansi. Please excuse me."

He wasn't sorry at all, not at all, for Hansi, filled with Martinis and faced with a tête-à-tête, had taken refuge in flirtation. To Jack, who knew that the young man hoped to sell him paintings, such a confusion of money and sex brought an access of every sort of social guilt. By the time he returned from the telephone it would be possible to order the car and whisk the little thing off to a public restaurant.

"Margaret?"

"No, it's Gladys, Mr. Pohlen. I do apologize for disturbing you, but is Marcus going to be in soon?"

"I really don't know. He should be back for dinner. I'll just ask . . ." He called to Dempster. "Yes, he's dining in. Yes, of course. I'll say it's urgent. Is there something I can do? No, no of course. I'm sure he'll ring you at once."

There had been no need for her to snub; he had only offered out of politeness. The world seemed made up of those who wish to involve one and those who bite for fear one should. He wrote on the pad: "Your sister Gladys rang. Will you telephone her urgently. She seemed in rather a fuss." Then, running for cover, he added, "Do come to Hansi Münzer's studio about eleven o'clock P.M. At 50, Rossetti Studios. G. D. de Mort" It was the sign they put out to one another when either was in sexual danger; Marcus had never let him down. He folded the note and gave it to Dempster and ordered the car.

Marcus walked around the studio, staring at each canvas in turn and passing quickly on to the next. Within the interlaced lines of thick, three-dimensional, black paint laid on with a palette knife were contained what appeared to be random forms in gamboge, acid green, magenta, and dirty mustard. Pyramids, minarets, domes, steeples were to be noted in some of the paintings; others appeared to be inadequate representations of the Fifth Avenue skyline. For the rest, the blotches of colour recalled only the most disagreeable, modern stained-glass windows. Going up close to one canvas, he saw clearly that some of the "dirty" colours were due merely to the running of one paint into another. In one place a curious pig's bristle of hairs protruded from the sticky black paint in which they were embedded.

He said, "That's an effect, certainly. Little moustaches," and sat down on a high stool, one of whose legs was propped on a pile of books. The studio was very cold; he drew his overcoat round him and held it together at his neck with one hand as though it were a woman's fur coat. Hansi, who had been explaining his work in a nervous, rapid chatter ever since Marcus had arrived, stopped for a moment when he spoke and gave him a terrified look. Marcus, interested in the pleasure this look gave him, gazed at the floor. Jack had now reached the last canvas on which a number of what to Marcus's eye could only be birds' tails—hens' perhaps—and feathers generally were picked out in thick white paint.

"Yes," Jack said, and then, standing back a few paces: "Oh, *yes.* This I like."

"Study Number Twenty-four. The buildings—all these cathedrals and so, even the skyscrapers, which in numbers fifteen to twenty-three replaced them, no longer appear. The *persona* of the dream has passed beyond this stage—what will I say?—of earthly ambitions, the soul has soared. Even the spires, the towers, the penis is no longer important."

Although Hansi's rounded eyes were quite solemn, he gave a little, apparently involuntary giggle.

Marcus said, "No more wet dreams?"

Jack quickly interposed, "And these feathers? No, of course, that doesn't matter. I like the solid construction of this. And the colour has a richness, a variation . . ."

But Hansi was not to be deflected. "We are now in the world of birds. The dream has taken the *persona* out into, I think you say, etherized regions. Many of what seem feathers are clouds. And water also. We are once more in the Beginning. In your English it is the Firmament. Before individuality and the sexual difference. The soul is now freed. The dream liberates the prisoners. Sleep has become space. Do you see I no longer have the thick line of the dream's apport? The figures fly out of the frame. The stained-glass window of the churches is no longer needed. Faith, religion, which I mock in the earth-bound dream, are dissolved in the void. Pain, too, the twisted limbs, all that is now unnecessary. The soul has been incorporated into itself, into its mass of feathers. Could you say bird time has come?"

"Bedtime, I think," Marcus said and he got up.

"Oh, so soon?"

"Look, Hansi," Jack said, "I shall want to see them again. But Study Eight, is it? Yes, and the last three studies. These particularly appeal to me. I think Rouault's influence in some of the earlier work is unfortunate . . ."

"I use the Rouault device solely as irony, you see."

"Yes, I know what you mean. But from a plastic point of view, which I'm afraid is all that really interests me . . . Anyway, in those last studies I see painterly qualities which I miss elsewhere and I'm afraid in the last analysis those are my concern. Plastic values."

"If he can't understand 'painterly qualities,' I don't suppose he'll understand the magic formula," Marcus said. "Anyway, don't lie, Jack. You know that these paintings are as good as worthless. Why do you have to lie?"

"Oh, for God's sake, Markie . . ."

"Oh, no, please, Marcus, if you don't like the paintings, you must give your reasons."

"Oh, my dear, don't worry. I shall. To begin with, all this stuff is entirely derivative—faces from Munch, buildings from Chirico, and what you call irony of Rouault is just bad, imitation Rouault. Personally, if you were another Munch or Chirico I shouldn't care a fuck because I'm not interested in a lot of modish illustrations to dreambooks. But your trouble is that you can't paint. You're simply not competent to do what in any case, I think, would be a waste of a real painter's time. It's as bad as that."

For a moment it looked as though Hansi might cry, then the yellow brown of his downy cheeks turned to crimson.

"You think because I'm a pretty boy that I can't have a vision, a soul. That I am pretending what I don't believe."

Marcus stared at him. "I did at first. But I see now that you really do believe all this nonsense. It seems a waste of a pretty face. But then think of all those pretty women who go to fake mediums. Anyhow, it doesn't matter how silly people are, they can be as uneducated and stupid as I am—kitchen-maid standard—but if they can paint, it doesn't matter what nonsense they talk. But you *can't* paint."

Jack took Marcus's arm. "Come on. You've behaved abominably enough. I am very sorry, Hansi. I'll come some other time. As she's said, she's an uneducated, silly girl and she's better in bed."

"Oh, I am sure," Hansi said, and he laughed for the first time, not coyly but scornfully.

Gliding past the coffee stall at Hyde Park corner, where the Rolls nearly ran down a sad, haunted-faced, red-nosed clubman who was cruising a guardsman, Marcus, brought out of the hostile silence by the car's jolting, said:

"All right, he's a Jewish refugee and he's h.s. and we must . . ."

"For God's sake, shut up. You queen it at charity exhibitions for refugee children like Mademoiselle Misericorde and make a fool of yourself carrying banners about God knows what and you haven't the charity to say a word of kindness to . . ."

"Look, Jack, I'm completely uneducated and, for all you've told me otherwise, not particularly intelligent, but I've got one thing I know about—painting. You've helped me to it, but I've got a much clearer eye than you have and more sense of spatial relationships. It's the only thing I've got and I'm not going to tell lies about it for any purpose whatsoever. Nor let you do so. You can give that little lemur half of all you've got if you like, but you're not going to buy even one of his ghastly canvas ruins. There are plenty of nice men with no knowledge and no taste who'll listen to all that rubbish for hours just for the sake of his *beaux yeux* but . . . Anyway, I was jealous. You know that."

Jack leaned his head back on a cushion; he still looked disdainful, but the taut muscles of his jaw relaxed. Marcus could feel the body beside him softening; he pressed his thigh against Jack's.

"Oh, I'm so sick of all this nobleness and pity and half the time one's just being taken in. Just to luxuriate in a bit of baroque nonsense before war overtakes this country of bankers' Georgian and horse brass Tudor and bungalows! But what's the good, everything luxuriantly baroque—Würzburg, Salzburg, Rome, Murcia—is in the hands of swine."

"We could go to Mexico and Brazil after we've settled the paintings in with Peggy in New York."

Marcus burst out laughing. "Oh, I should love that, darling. Once we've seen that they've 'settled down' at school. It could be a 'second honeymoon.'"

It had been so long since they had come into the house together laughing that Jack, seeing the telephone pad, did not want to break the mood by asking Marcus if he had rung Gladys. Marcus, remembering that, leaving angrily for Hansi's studio, he had not, decided to do so the next morning.

It took Quentin many whiskies—many more than he could bloody well afford—to wash the taste of all that high-minded *naïveté* at the service of all that Party bad faith out of his mouth. He had always been apart from the others, even in the old days of 52—they'd lived

and wallowed in all the parents' squalid, rubbishy dramas, while he—
well at least the old lady's solid Ladbroke Grove comfort had given
him a sense of proportion. And now there they were, Margaret and
Rupert, high-minded, artistic, "the theatre," the new interesting
novel! God! and successful, while he . . . all the same, if the Comrades had their way, or more likely when Chamberlain and the City
of London had finally done selling the pass, and Hitler's filthy mob
took over, he'd be joined with them once more—behind barbed
wire. Intellectuals all, God help us! And Marcus, too, no doubt, since
Roehm and Fräulein Heines lost the toss. All *this* muck, he thought,
looking round the King's Cross pub, will have joined the Black
Shirts. And, he supposed, his dear sister Sukey; the last time he'd seen
her she had been a proper hard-faced county cow, whose flaxen hairs
would well become a Mosley or a Hitler *Mädchen*. He felt randy as
hell but he hadn't even got the price of a quick screw in this pox-
ridden, sodding area. There was hardly an honest man in this city
that wasn't a fool—a few that the Comrades labelled Trotskyites,
perhaps: Franz Borkenau, or Eduard Konze, foreigners both of
them; all the rest were on one filthy side or the other, out to use
what could be a warm, matey, life-giving world for their own cold,
sterile ends. Well, he'd stood apart, and told the truth. And God
help him, now he hadn't even got a hole to stuff. Whisky tears, he
told himself. He'd better get back to bed before he passed out stone
cold among these bastards, who'd probably take even his gold watch
—the one the old lady had given him. God bless her shocking old
rentier soul. As he came out of the pub some fucker was singing
about Jesus and Bethlehem.

"One of the Old Contemptibles, sir. God bless you, sir. I can see
you was through it with the rest of us, back of Wipers."

Blast, he didn't know whether to laugh or cry. Very cautiously
treading the long, long trail that lay winding before him, keeping
near the railings, avoiding (*grand danger de mort*), our cause, our
poor bloody cause, I fear is dying, he turned the corner of the square
by the pillar-box. There were two of them in the darkness where the
street lamp had failed; and both spoke a thick County Cork.

"Is it you that was with the Reds today shouting for the bastards
in Spain who've blasphemed the Mother of God?"

Atrocities, he thought, I could tell them about atrocities on both
sides—poor little, red-faced Mohn trying to check human evil by his

decent little Scandinavian slide-rule. He remembered his neat little article, all finished, sealed, and addressed; something to make Dodo laugh in Dulwich or Dorking—hush, dear, that's just Daddy laughing in his den. As he pulled out the letter and pushed it into the slit, the slighter one with the choker tried to nudge his arm to make him drop it. He walked on, but they skipped round in front of him before he could reach the next lamp.

"Aren't you Q.J. bleedin' Matthews?"

"I'm Judas bloody Iscariot."

"He's Matthews all right. The dirty Red! Look now at his sodden, drunken face. And him spittin on the Host from what Terence says."

"Yes, and puking all over his room for daycent women to clear up."

"I think we'll fix him. Shall we fix him? Shall we fix you?"

They seemed such feeble little runts of unemployed, of *lumpen* rubbish, to be afraid of, but he was, for he couldn't force his arms from the grip of the slight one. And the other now smashed into his jaw, his eyes, his nose. He could feel the warm blood, oily in his throat; he spat out a tooth. But as they leaned him against the railings the stars clashed together and gave way to a swirling dark red; he vomited. He could faintly hear them cursing as they went through his empty pockets. Someone tore away his watch from its fob. Something sent waves of pain swelling up from his balls to his guts. As he slid down the railings to fall with a smack on his face on the pavement he could just hear far away running footsteps.

At the sound of her running upstairs to the bedroom, Douglas, syphoning soda into his bedtime whisky, sat down again to wait her jubilant, victorious entry. So she'd beaten Hitler! When she appeared still dressed for the street, but now carrying her dressing-case, he guessed that it was better than that.

"A breakthrough?" he asked.

She nodded, smiling. "Something in Rupert's performance tonight gave it to me."

"*That* ass?"

"He's a much better actor than we've ever realized. You won't mind being without the car for the next few days, darling?"

"Of course not. But it'll be so cold at the cottage."

"Oh, that! I'll manage."

He got up and kissed her. "I'm so awfully pleased, darling."

Then he said no more, for he thought, I know it's superstition but if I say any more it may turn out to be one of her false starts.

"Ring Mrs. Huskins tomorrow morning, Douglas, will you? Tell her I'll want feeding there for let's say a week. But not on any account to disturb me in the mornings. Just the shopping and dinner."

He suddenly remembered poor old plump Gladys—well, her loving pains would have to wait for a later occasion. Margaret's work must come first.

"No. Not every penny on horses, Inspector. Some went on the dogs."

"Look, Miss Matthews, you're not doing yourself any good by trying to be funny."

She wasn't, it seemed, doing herself any good by any of her actions—her obstinacy, her slick readiness, her hauteur, her facetiousness. Or so they said; but she knew that she was, for each day now that she was on bail, each day since her determined silence in the magistrate's court, sympathy, kindness, and pity were drying up around her. Already the inspector had a hard glint in his eye and the policewoman grew more angular and sullen. Soon, surely, as she poured out the same old lists of bookmakers, of courses, of tote bets and of runners, they would tire of the squalid story, cease to try to separate her genial person from her shabby actions, give in, leave her in peace. But now again:

"You say that on October twelfth at Uttoxeter you lost two hundred pounds placed as a bet on Navarino in the two-thirty race?"

"Yes, I've told you before, and he's still running for all I know."

"Don't be impudent to the inspector."

"That bet you say was placed with Clem Durrell, the bookmaker, on the course."

"Yes."

"Yet Mr. Durrell has no recollection whatsoever of your betting with him that day."

"I'm fat and forty, Inspector. Clem Durrell likes them frail and fifteen."

Oh, soon it would be over. But now that danger spot again— "Mrs. Heathway, in her deposition, though she clearly has no exact information to give, hints that you may have let yourself get into this situation on someone else's behalf. If that's so, Miss Matthews, you must . . ."

"Sylvia Heathway is a very dear and old friend who would hint at anything which would exonerate me from my stupid, tom-fool actions." Would he press on? No, he'd dropped it again, thank God. Two days to the trial. How she hated them all for being so kind. After all, she'd *done* the bloody thing; for whatever reason, she'd deliberately cheated an old man and an old woman out of what would have given them badly needed security and decency. She tried to think of that guilt and that guilt only, for with its support she should be able to push through her careful, unsupported story to the end. Alf turning up at the magistrate's court had nearly defeated her. She had sat in agonies, wondering whether he was about to confess, but he hadn't. When she'd left with Marcus and Rupert, who'd gone bail for her, he'd come up with a bunch of chrysanthemums. She'd taken it and presented him as a business associate. Marcus and Rupert, of course, knew who he was, and if they didn't suspect, she could tell from his eyes that he thought they did. It had given her a few moments' pleasure to feel so much in command of them all with her silence. Then she had said:

"That's very kind of you, Alf, but I want you to promise me not to associate yourself with all this. You have your . . ." she had hesitated long enough to make him wonder, "your career to think of. And it's not fair to Mrs. Pritchard. After it's all over, we'll have a laugh."

She had turned away. For the rest she had just longed to be rid of them all, their kindness, their belief in her—Margaret talking to her for hours "to keep her mind off things," Marcus suddenly blushing and saying, "My dear, I'm as keen on men as you are any day, but believe me, for God's sake, there isn't *one* that's worth going to prison for." Rupert for some reason calling her Big Sis and telling her how he played some Shakespeare part; even the Countess, on that awful visit to 52 over Christmas, cutting great thick steps of brown bread, "because you adored thin bread and butter as a girl." Only with Billy Pop had she felt free to brush off these weakening human claims. He'd heard something. "My poor little girl, if I knew who this dirty dog was who's got you into this mess, I'd knock his block off." Looking down at him and his crutches, she had said, "A little late, Daddy, aren't you? As always." And Sukey's letter, too, she had felt free to ignore—"Oh, Gladys dear, Hugh and I have thought about your coming down here to be with us while you have this beastly waiting time but I *can't* believe a school could be the right place . . ." Not that she blamed Sukey. Oh, why couldn't they leave her alone to take hot-water bottles and wallow in her comfortable bed, for though she couldn't imagine what prison was going to be like, thought of it with increasing daily terror, woke in the night determined to save herself by telling all (but she wouldn't, and that, when courage left her, kept her going), she knew at least that these were her last hot, steamy, scented baths, last silk pyjamas and linen sheets, last whiskies and praline chocolates. Oh, why couldn't they just let her alone until the frightening day?

On the day of the trial when Margaret and Douglas went to fetch the Countess and Billy Pop, they had changed their minds. The Countess in a lemon nightdress and a lilac dressing-gown explained to Margaret, "The whole thing's aged me so terribly, Margaret. I've grown overnight into a little, bent, shrunken old woman. I suddenly saw myself, dear, with your father coming into that courtroom on his crutches—a pathetic old couple. For that's what we are now. A sight like that couldn't help anyone, least of all Gladys." When they had accepted this she became more agile, more sporty with Douglas. "Now, Douglas, as soon as they've come to their senses and released that poor girl, we must all have a celebration. Something quiet, of course; Billy and I are no longer youngsters. But I rely on you to book a table somewhere nice, somewhere amusing that'll take the poor girl's mind off all these horrors. You know the West End of London today. Billy and I are so out of it."

Margaret said, "Mother, you'd better realize that Gladys may very well be convicted and sent to prison."

The Countess began to cry into a little lace-edged handkerchief.

"You've always been so hard, Margaret. You and Marcus. I don't think you can be children of mine. Oh, yes, she has, Douglas; I know her better than you. All those horrid books! Oh, you've made my head ache. I'm not at all well these days, you know."

She went back to bed. Billy Pop called to them from his study. "You've heard what your Mother thinks. I daren't tell her how poor the chances are. The vile injustice of this world, eh, Mag? Glad Eyes, the best of the lot of you."

"Yes, Father, she is."

He tapped his dictionary impatiently. "Well, the best I can do, and it's a poor best, is to get on with my work. You hear Mrs. Hannapin won't come in and cook today? Though she knows your Mother's not up to it. A sister over from Canada or something. La Rochefoucauld was unpleasantly right—'The troubles of other people sit lightly upon our shoulders.' "

The trial lasted nearly the whole day, despite Gladys's refusal to offer a serious defence. Margaret, sitting between Douglas and Rupert, heard every word that was spoken and could remember none a minute later. She went over and over that evening when Douglas had not told her of Gladys's visit, so much that when he took her hand she pulled it away. And it did not help that the idea that she had got that evening at the theatre—she couldn't quite remember now what it was—had done the trick. It only remained to kill Aunt Alice in loneliness and fear. Nevertheless, she let her hand remain in Rupert's, for this belonged to their childhood, this was part of the nightmare of 52. At the magistrate's court and in the weeks between she had felt, every time that Gladys had made some stupid, facetious joke or fooled about when she was in such danger, that they were all on trial for accepting their sister's clowning, her fat jollity, as a substitute for the pains of real intimacy. She sat tense while Gladys stonewalled in the witness box and made no compunctious noises but only once or twice bad, childish jokes until the judge rebuked her sharply—no welcoming family laughter here for the nursery Bessie Bunter. When at last the jury brought in the expected verdict, Margaret was near sick and she could feel Rupert's hand clench in hers. "Your defending counsel has laid great emphasis upon your realizing your assets in order to recompense Mr. Ahrendt. It is his job to do so. But I confess that I can see here little more than a last-minute panic, an effort to buy off the man you had so grievously wronged. Grievously, and from your conduct in court today, I fear, heartlessly, with a shameful levity. The public must be protected against this kind of fraud . . ." My God! in her fright, in the loneliness we've all condemned her to, she'll surely seek to buy him off with a somersault or a false nose. But the woman who received the sentence—"You will go to prison for four years' penal servitude, the maximum sentence for your offence, which I have no

hesitation in pronouncing"—was suddenly a very quiet, portly dignified woman, who, standing quite alone, an object in an active
world, said in a voice so low that Margaret could hardly hear it,
"Thank you, my Lord," and disappeared below. So, perhaps, Margaret noted, not, as the nieces expected, in vulgar ranting, would
the old raddled woman go out in her lonely bedroom.

Outside in the cold air they could none of them, Margaret saw,
bear the prolongation of any family play.

Rupert said defensively, "Debbie didn't feel she should come," and
looked at Douglas as an intruder.

Marcus immediately said, "Thank you for coming, Douglas," so
that Margaret felt she must come to Rupert's defence:

"Oh, Douglas! He'll do anything helpful a bit late. I'll telephone
them at Fifty-two and for the rest, we're all quite useless."

So they all felt, and went their own ways.

Quentin, recovering in hospital from broken wrist, fractured ribs,
concussion and shock, read the news in the evening paper. He could
only remember that in his comminatory catalogue of his brothers
and sisters on the fatal night, he had completely forgotten Gladys's
existence. He would write to her. Get on to Pritt about the case—
they hadn't quarrelled that much and he was a fine lawyer. Poor
Gladys—lonely, neglected, fat old dear, completely forgotten. As he
was. Not a single soul had been to see him in hospital. It was the
price you pay for telling the truth; not a soul, not even Lena, "the
good-hearted trollop." He was still very weak and he began to cry.

"Good gracious me! Whatever is wrong?" asked brisk Nurse
Evans in her sing-song.

"I'm so alone, nurse, so absolutely bloody alone."

"And so you will be if you go on like that. Nobody wants to visit
a grown man crying like that."

But he did receive visitors at five o'clock—Dodo Towneley, two
other chaps from the paper, and Muriel Lane, their famous roving
correspondent, a good-looking, bubsy, snooty bitch. He couldn't
keep his eyes off her cleavage. They said, of course, that they'd
meant long before now to comfort their hero, beaten up by Black
Shirt bullies, but they hoped to make up for it with fruit and books
and calves-foot jelly. The really important thing, however, was this
absolutely terrific article of his. Dodo showed it to him. "What

Makes the Red Cross" it was called, and was subheaded "The Dane who didn't like atrocities." It was first rate, a smash hit with everyone, all Fleet Street was laughing.

"I laughed like a drain," Muriel Lane said.

"Look," Dodo said. "This is your line—exposing all these hells with good intentions. I tell you what, you'll be out of here in a fortnight, your doctor says. We're going to send you to convalesce in Africa. There's a body of cranks—schoolteachers, nuteaters, pacifist poets, and American missionaries marching next month to the Abyssinian border to protest against Italian exploitation. Of course Musso won't let them in. But *you* must cover it. It'll be the funniest thing we've had for years."

"But what harm are they doing?"

"What harm? Good Lord! Well, even as to harm, they're deflecting attention from the important things that are being done—yes, that's the line."

"You'll be coming with *me*," Muriel said. "I'm covering the news angle."

Nigel phoned to Debbie the next week, "Debbie, darling, I'm calling a couple of rehearsals on Wednesday and Thursday. As always, the performances have gone ragged. But Rupert! Deary me! It's all broken in pieces. The line's quite gone. One minute he's a sort of sergeant-major and the next he's a lost soul in agony. I thought as you'd done so much before . . ."

"Oh, dear, Nigel. I'm afraid it's all this business of his sister. He really never saw the poor creature, but you've no idea what a 'family' family the Matthewses are in their unconventional way. But I'll work on him. Don't worry."

Munich came to most of the Matthews brothers and sisters as a horrible, long-awaited, too-predictable curtain to an exhausting play. They greeted it—most of them abroad—with the sad recognition that the nagging pain in their vitals would not now be brought to an end by any of the advertised panaceas, of which Mr. Chamberlain's "peace in our time" scrap of paper was so obvious a parody. Quentin in Somaliland doubled his evening whisky intake; Rupert, now in the Broadway transfer of *Twelfth Night,* remembered that the show must go on; Margaret at Aswan went out in a boat all day by herself and at evening had a headache from the sun; Marcus, viewing an ornate Saint Sebastian in a church at São Paulo, schemed to keep Jack from returning to Europe. Gladys, who might have been a more shocked recipient of the news, was numbed by prison.

But the effect on Billy Pop and the Countess was dramatic. The Countess was sure that it was a terrible come-down for England, but Billy Pop had met old So-and-So again, the chap who was high up in the Ministry, who said that, not at all, it was the genuine last concession to Hitler, and old So-and-So in the War Office, who said Hitler had bitten off more than he could chew, and, in any case, if it came to a scrap, most of the German forces were only on paper, whereas ours . . . But the Countess didn't feel convinced. Billy Pop had reassured her so often in life, and did old So-and-So really know? Your father's a brilliant man but he's let himself drop out of the world that counts for so long; and again, had he *really* met old So-and-So and So-and-So? It wouldn't be the first time or the last that he'd lied to her. As for the children, away from England, it just showed how little sense they had of what was happening in the world; clever enough, but with their heads in the air, ostriches with their heads in the sand. Now Billy, whatever his faults, was always alive to things, and as for herself, she'd never been a dreamer, thank God. She wrote to Sukey, since the others were unavailable. "We must pray and hope. But your father and I and a lot of informed people do feel that this is the red light. It isn't just Czechoslovakia and all that. We simply *cannot* give way any more." Sukey was so cut off, living in the provinces.

Sukey replied, "Hugh had a good idea of what was going to happen, over a year ago. Friends in high places are often useful. That's why we moved the school. If it's to come (and I'm pretty sure it must) the sooner the better, I say, and get it over. Senior and Middleman (who's recovered from his pacifist measles) are all ready for it and I don't intend to make things harder for them by holding on to them. Even P.S. makes soldierly noises, silly boy. But of couse it'll all be over before he's reached Fifth Form. Anyway, if you're worried about yourselves, you'd better let me find you a hotel down here to live in. The authorities in London will have quite enough on their hands without the elderly. Everyone says it will be comparatively bomb-free down here. There's a hotel on the other side of Exeter that might suit you well; you wouldn't want to be mixed up with a lot of grubby little boys, I know.

"We're still in a terrible pickle after the move here. And now that Hugh's sole headmaster I have to give all my time to the school. They say I'm not half bad at it, but I'm determined not to become the complete headmaster's wife. Luckily—Father will laugh—but a chap in Western Regional whose boy we've got for next term happened to see a piece I'd written about our days on the house-boat on the Nile. He liked it enormously—just the sort of thing when the news is so awful and everyone wants to think of the good old days. I'm going to do him a weekly series. They say my voice comes over with real authority. Who knows? I may outdo Margaret, especially as her sort of morbid, sarky stuff is not the thing for this moment. Of course, I'm only joking. I enclose a typed copy of 'So Many Tombs but Only One Mummy,' the piece about us on the Nile I broadcast last week. I've written another script about the car we had in 1928 that got stuck on Exmoor; you remember Winnie the Wolseley. I've got a few more in mind—all family adventures—I wonder if you can guess what they're about from the titles: 'Two Hundred Mums and One Pot of Shrimp Paste.' 'How to Climb Snowdon Without a Tin Opener.' 'When Santa Left Too Many Cricket Bats.' 'Why Can't We Take the Rhino Home?'

"Oh, by the way, P.S. is looking forward terrifically to his Easter London visit, but do remember not to mention the wretched Gladys business. I don't want him to know. I've told him she's gone to Australia (well, it's almost true, isn't it?)."

Billy Pop once again remarked on the truth of La Rochefoucauld's cynicism, but the Countess was more concerned with Sukey's interpretation of her war warning.

"As if I'd written because we were afraid! The idea!" she told Mrs. Hannapin. "Why, if war comes, Mr. Matthews will be wanted at once for propaganda. He'll be over military age this time, you know."

And Billy Pop too was angry enough to write to Sukey, "I'm afraid I shall be too busy doing my bit to get down to West Country hotels. And your Mother won't leave London if there's a war, that's certain. She'll have the time of her life."

As to Sukey's broadcast, they could neither of them read much of the script she'd sent, but then she lived such a provincial, shut-off life.

We were, in fact, very much a Swiss Family Robinson; and I, in particular, felt completely "my good wife," when Senior (then at the Awful Age) fell into the Nile, and instead of coming up a Gruesome Green was fished up a Beastly Brown by our faithful Ali, for I was able by the aid of my "magic box" (I really believe Ali thought there was magic in it) to find a soap powder (quite a new discovery in those days) that took the stains out of his little white shirt and grey flannel knickers.

Billy Pop said, almost in surprised tones, "This is muck."
But the Countess insisted on reading a little further.

I suppose it was P.S. (then, as we used to call them, a Toddler) who made the biggest hit with the servants until the awful day when he learned to imitate our Beloved Goose that swam round the boat and took scraps (mostly large quantities of rice that the Lord and Master refused to eat and I had to smuggle out in envelopes or even handkerchiefs, for dear Ali and Mohammed were very touchy about their culinary arts, which indeed, except to Lord and Master's taste, would have bid fair to outdo Escoffier). I noticed that P.S. was getting a number of what we had decided to call Egyptian Evil Eyes when I suddenly realized that his goose grunts, which so amused us, were giving offence below stairs, or perhaps I should say in "the galley." Of course I knew that the Romans had sacred geese, but I had no idea . . .

The Countess put the typescript down.
"I think, living down there, she doesn't really know what interests people."
When the war came, indeed up to the invasion of France, the Countess was most active, going around with a map of London that showed where the Zeppelin bombs fell. "That was a real war. We really went through it then." And Billy Pop, through Margaret, sold an article to a new high-brow magazine that was about to appear. The article was called, "A Day's Cricket with Enoch Soames" and contained his recollections of the poet Stephen Philips. But in August 1940 they moved from 52 to the country hotel suggested by Sukey. As the Countess said, "London has enough mouths to feed."

French Windows: An Interrupted Play

POSTSCRIPT TO BOOK THREE

(*Scene: the drawing-room of Exe Grange, a residential country hotel in Devonshire. Time: late April 1942. Arm-chairs and sofas in flowered cretonne loose covers. Curtains of the same material. A few occasional tables on which are bowls of daffodils and early species tulips. A small wood fire is burning, but through the French windows the last rays of a warm spring sun are shining. In one arm-chair,* COLONEL CHUDLEIGH, *an old, retired officer of the courteous kind, is reading* Blackwood's Magazine. *At one of the tables,* MRS. LOMAX, *a fussy but sharp-eyed old lady, is settled in a high chair playing patience. From outside the French windows voices—a man's and a woman's—can be heard.*)

MRS. LOMAX: Oh, dear, another session of "our brilliant children"! The Earl and Countess back from their evening airing.

COLONEL CHUDLEIGH: And what he did in the Great War, Daddy? It *is* a bit steep.

(*The French windows open and* MRS. RICKARD-MATTHEWS, *well preserved, well made-up, well but hardly suitably dressed, comes in. Nothing about her would betray her sixty-five years. She lifts her husband's wheel chair down the one step into the room.* MR. RICKARD-MATTHEWS *is frail and shrunken, except for his face which is still ruddy and the more cherubic for his smooth, bald head fringed with a halo of soft grey curls.*)

MRS. LOMAX: How was the sunset?

MRS. RICKARD-MATTHEWS: Oh, all right for Devonshire.

MRS. LOMAX: Don't forget Colonel Chudleigh's is one of the oldest families in Devonshire.

MRS. RICKARD-MATTHEWS: Oh, but you've travelled, haven't you, Colonel? You're not a country stick-in-the-mud. My aunt—the children's great-aunt—was quite a famous traveller. She was the discoverer of one of the original tulips. All these we have now are garden what's-its-name, you know. She used to say the loveliest sunsets of all were in Arabia. Do you remember that, Billy? How Mouse always praised the Arabian sunsets? Of course, she travelled in the days when . . .

MR. RICKARD-MATTHEWS: Speaking of Arabia, as Clara has made us do, it amuses me, Colonel, to hear all the fuss made about T. E. Lawrence these days. I met him a number of times in the middle twenties. In fact, I often think that if I'd had time to cultivate him, he might never have made an ass of himself enlisting in the Flying Corps. But I also knew F. L. Garthwaite, who was one of Allenby's right-hand men. After talking to him, the Lawrence legend can only be an embarrassment. I was arguing about it with my son-in-law Douglas Rootham just before he and my daughter left England . . .

MRS. RICKARD-MATTHEWS: Douglas is on the general staff in Cairo. He's a brilliant archaeologist, you know, and . . .

MR. RICKARD-MATTHEWS: My dear girl, they wouldn't make him a lieutenant colonel just because he can dig up fossils. No, he speaks Arabic like a native. My daughter wrote the other day . . .

MRS. RICKARD-MATTHEWS: Oh, Mrs. Lomax, you'll be excited to hear this. There's a new Margaret Matthews on the way. Margaret wrote to say she'd just sent off the proofs. Two copies this time by separate post because of the submarines—special arrangements and all that, my son-in-law is in a position and so forth, although she's famous enough in her own right . . . She couldn't say where she was, but the most fascinating thing was that she'd met her brother Rupert for a talk. He's been on a tour of all the R.A.F. stations in the Middle East. I shouldn't be surprised if Douglas hasn't packed her off to Jerusalem, Billy, with things in Egypt as they are. That could be where she met Rupert. I know he expected to go there. Of course in Douglas's position he can arrange accommodation for her anywhere at a moment's notice. Yes, it's probably Jerusalem. She mentioned cypress trees.

MR. RICKARD-MATTHEWS: Oh, the blabbing of women, eh, Colonel? Walls have ears, my dear. I wonder if you agree with me, Colonel, in thinking that air-force skills, and so on, are not quite so specialized as we've been led to believe. I'm not speaking of the bravery of these boys, of course, that's beyond question. But the sheer skill needed. I say this because my boy Rupert, who's been an actor all his life . . .

MRS. RICKARD-MATTHEWS: My dear Billy, Colonel Chudleigh knows Rupert Matthews. He hasn't lived quite out of the world. It was all they could do to stop Rupert joining up, Colonel, although he's not a boy any longer. Everyone told him how much more valuable he would be entertaining the troops. At last they got me to speak to him. I simply said, "Rupert, don't be silly. This war doesn't have any star parts. It's team work, my dear." Now, of course, he's done I don't know how many thousand miles flying keeping morale up. And of course right up to the firing line. He insists on taking the controls.

MR. RICKARD-MATTHEWS: That's just what I was about to say, dear. They say he'd have made a first-rate pilot if he hadn't been over age. I don't think it can be quite such a specialized . . .

MRS. RICKARD-MATTHEWS: Oh, nonsense, Billy, it's just that war brings out unexpected things in people. My youngest boy . . . we really thought . . .

MR. RICKARD-MATTHEWS: Oh, but Marcus was always artistic, Clara, and that's what you want in camouflage work. Though I'm surprised he makes a good adjutant.

MRS. LOMAX: And how is your *other* daughter, Mrs. Rickard-Matthews?

MRS. RICKARD-MATTHEWS: Oh, I told her not to think less of herself just because she's not in the forces. Running a school's vital war work, don't you think, Colonel Chudleigh?

MR. RICKARD-MATTHEWS: And a full-time job. We've expressly forbidden her to waste her time coming over to us. It's the youngsters that matter, not those who have got into the sere and yellow stage.

MRS. LOMAX: No, I didn't mean Mrs. Pascoe. I always see her at the Violet Tearooms when I go into Exeter. She's a great elevenses devotee. I meant your other daughter who came to you for Christmas after being away so long. Has she found war work yet? I remember there was some difficulty. I do think nothing should prevent . . .

MRS. RICKARD-MATTHEWS: Oh, that was only a temporary bother. Billy pulled strings, didn't you, darling?

MR. RICKARD-MATTHEWS: Yes, a very dry but powerful string at the War Office, to be exact.

MRS. LOMAX: As long as it's not the Treasury. We're finding it difficult enough to pay for this war as it is, eh, Colonel?

MRS. RICKARD-MATTHEWS (*losing immediately all her bright manner, fierce and aloof*): Either you're too stupid to know what you're saying, Mrs. Lomax, or you should be careful not to be slanderous.

MRS. LOMAX: Slanderous! Now, Mrs. Rickard-Matthews, what is the point in pretending? I remembered your daughter's name at once. Didn't I, Colonel? The whole case. Of course when she was here I was very careful . . . She'd paid the price. No one wanted to hound her.

COLONEL CHUDLEIGH: Now really, I don't think this is necessary, Mrs. Lomax. Mr. and Mrs. Rickard-Matthews have all our sympathies, as we said at the time.

MRS. LOMAX: But that's exactly it. It's so much better not to bottle these things up. When I think how I should have felt if my dear Isobel . . . but then of course her father was as straight as a die in money matters. . . .

MR. RICKARD-MATTHEWS: I don't know what you're insinuating, but . . .

MRS. RICKARD-MATTHEWS (*taking his hand*): Oh, Billy, dear, you don't have to explain yourself to every Tom, Dick, and Harry. My dear, you're an artist, a man of the world, don't apologize for it.

MR. RICKARD-MATTHEWS: You are right, Clara. As always. (*He presses her hand.*) Just wheel me along to our room, my dear. We may as well put on our glad rags, even if it is only vegetable pie for dinner. Dressing for dinner is an old, established, British custom when you're living among savages. (*Smiling boyishly at his joke, he is wheeled away by his proud, handsome, straight-backed wife. As they reach the door, she turns, smiling sweetly.*)

MRS. RICKARD-MATTHEWS: Colonel Chudleigh, would you please explain the laws of slander to Mrs. Lomax? I shall expect an apology, you see, when we're all dressed and civilized and in our right minds.

(*Curtain. From the darkness amid the rustle of programmes and clanking of tea cups comes a woman's voice: "Oh I think she's wonderful. That exit! She moves so beautifully. None of the young*

*ones today can do it. And they say she's almost seventy." As the
lights go up in the auditorium another woman's voice is heard:
"Her acting always seems a little hard to me. But really he is
amazing. That little chuckle and that smile, he hasn't changed
since I was a schoolgirl. And he gives such a polished, quiet performance.")*

Pop and Motor: A Catastrophe

*Later that night. Scene: a big, bare bedroom in the same hotel. The
lighting is full upon the centre stage where sits* Pop, *swathed like
a mummy, in his wheel chair. Around him prowls* Motor *like an
old caged, mangy tigress. In the darkness of the corner of the
room various articles of furniture make ever new monstrous
shapes that never quite acquire definition. A faint, sad, moonlight
coming from the window reaches the central pool of light and
dies there.)*

Pop (*reciting with dramatized nostalgia*): They are not long, the
weeping and the laughter. All is sleeping in the hereafter.

Motor (*half adapting her steps to the rhythm of her high, tuneless
singing*): Every boy in London Town is phoning.

Pop (*taking out a megaphone from the folds of the rug that covers
his legs, begins bawling*): I think they have no portion in us after
we pass the gate.

Motor (*now breaking into a slightly rusty, quick fox trot, produces
a portable radio set that accompanies her singing*): Dancing time
is any old time for me.

Pop (*shouting now as he tries another tack*): And sick of an old passion, yea, I was desolate and bowed my head.

Motor (*singing in the high little upper-class notes of Edwardian
musical*): Fates may be crossed, loves may be lost under the deo-
dar.

(*They continue to recite in competition for some minutes.*)

Pop: This has gone on long enough.

Motor: It had gone on too long the moment it began. But in for a
penny, in for a pound, I said. Laughing and looking back, my

white lace dress fell for a second from my shoulder and the geranium gleamed against it scarlet as blood! *Belle dame sans merci,* he cried. The scent of geraniums was cloying, but I ran, a young girl, back to my first ball. *Je vous félicite, Mademoiselle, de votre parfum,* and a hand pressed against my gloved hand in the lift and later at the casino, *Je vous félicite, Mademoiselle, de votre tango.* I blew smoke rings at him as we sat on the little too-correct gilt chairs. *Rauchenträumer, meine geliebte.* And then, so much later, coming home in the early hours, my stocking pinned to my drawers . . .

Pop: Suzette, Ninette, Arlette, Noisette, Poupette, Babette, Nanette, Bravo! *La gigolette.* But it was Pierrette whose troubled eyes haunt me. She lay on her tousled bed—her ruff, her pompons, her clown's cap, a touching wreckage of the evening strewn around her. Her little breasts were firm, but her little body was so thin. She arched her back like an alley cat. So "Dawn will see you gorn?" (*reminiscently*) or could it be "Don will see you gone?" The little important things like that, that we forget. Oh, she would spit, that little one. And then . . .

Motor: With a safety pin. Oh, it was crazy! But his body looked so firm and white and young as he lay there—only a week later it was to be blown to pieces, to smithereens. Be a sport, give me your garter. An amulet. He didn't want to die. They none of them did. And so, how could we women be less generous? We came waltzing home in the early hours—I don't know whether my thoughts were sad or gay, I can't remember—with our stockings pinned to our drawers with safety pins. And then after it was all over they were so restless, their safety pins had been drawn. They'd seen things they couldn't talk about. So we laughed at the all-night coffee stalls. What does it matter who one talks to? Tinker, tailor, beggarman, thief. The world's gone mad.

Pop: She looked up at me. All that you write there, you English faithless one, all that poetry and so, does it tell you why . . . why all this? The little room was pitiful with its cheap finery, but even so she wanted so much to know why . . .

Motor: Of course I wasn't just a Dance Mad Mother. Once when we were at Cromer, I was sitting under the cliffs. The children were playing on the beach, laughing, shouting, singing. Suddenly everything was silent, as though I was still a girl and yet a grown

woman, as though there was no time, and the whole world, everything beyond it, sky and all were on that beach. I felt as though I
knew then why two and two make four, what the shape of it all
was, that everything was good as it had been when I was little, as
though there might be Somebody, a Friend above the bright blue
sky. And then a great wind . . .

Pop (*bobbing up and down in his chair with pleasure*): Wind!
Wind! Farting! Belching! That's all it ever is. Don't be a mystic,
take Phystic—the only real carminative that will confirm your
doubts. Two and two don't make four; it isn't good, there isn't any
Friend, no pie, and no shape unless we make it ourselves! And
when I say we (*he raises himself in his chair with disdainful hand
extended, looking in his pride like Humpty Dumpty*) I mean we,
oui, oui. Years ago I remember, for it hasn't all been Babettes, I
was poking around my grandmother's garden—rather at a loose
end because there was no cricket—I was an athlete, you know,
close to nature, you need that, too, cricket, if it hadn't been for
water on the knee (rain stopped play, eh?) or tennis if it hadn't
been for tennis elbow—when I kicked over a stone and there was
an old wrinkled toad. Probably been there half a century. It frightened me, its squat shape, its age, its power of remaining immobile.
Another boy might have squashed it with his foot, but I couldn't
have toed it. Well, that's life, too. But I knew that wouldn't break
its power over me. I needed a spell, an exorcism, for that—a word,
not just green or brown or wrinkled or spotted, or even all those
words together, but a single word that would describe its toadness. And suddenly the word came to me. The single word laid up
for that moment to describe that toad and with him all toadness.
The word was . . .

Motor (*stopping in her tracks and shrieking*): Shit! We tried to
blame the boys. I told you to beat Marcus for it and you did. But
you had beaten him to it! It was you who wrote it on the lavatory
wall. Like a pathetic, sneaky, dirty-minded schoolboy. And it was
always the same with you—making me undress in the bathroom
and peeping through the keyhole, Keyhole Pop, the Weasel, saying my bottom's sore in front of the girls, walking about when
Regan first came to us with your hideous, puny little object showing below your vest, a knob not worth carrying. You could never
do it without sniggery, snickery. . . .

POP: And you could never take it without hiding your face. Am I your *femme fatale*, Billy, you asked, am I, am I? Meanwhile you kept your body taut and your soul empty like some schoolgirl turned tart. That's why you're so dried and withered now, all the jam licked off like a mummified girl. But I! Why even my paralysis is the fruit of my lust. My body is alive with it. I pullulate. . . .

MOTOR: But you won't for long. Doctor's diagnosis: locomotor ataxia; symptoms: disturbance of the genito-urinary functions, diminution of knee jerks, sluggish condition of the irises, paralysis of the cranial nerves, symptoms of Rombergism; prognosis: poor.

POP (*groaning and shaking his fist*): I hope loco motor attacks *yeh*. (*Pulling himself together*) But I don't believe it. I'll go to a naturopath, a homeopath, an osteopath, any old path that winds on. (*Singing*) The top of the hill hasn't room for two, be sure the one that gets there is you. (*Turns upon Motor*) But for *you*, putting your hand up to pull down the blind, running from the shop to catch the infrequent bus, taking the too-hot bath on the too-cold nights, bending to take in the scent of carnation. (*In her voice*) "Oh, what heaven," a tearing, rending pain in the chest, your legs tremble, your head swirls, all goes red, goes black. Over in a minute that seems a lifetime. But I (*propelling his chair round so that it creaks*)—creaking doors never wear out.

MOTOR (*in a more tender voice*): Never worry, my Popsie. I don't intend to let you die in or out of doors. Looking after you keeps me alive.

POP (*cheerfully*): Ah! that's better. We needed a change of tune on the trumpet.

MOTOR: *I* thought so. (*She puts her hand in his. He lifts her on to his knee.*)

POP: Let's pretend, my strumpet (*He takes her arm and puts it round his neck. He places his hand on her thigh.*)

MOTOR (*getting up*): No, no that's repulsive. Words only. (*In a shy young girl's voice*) My dearest, dearest darling, last Tuesday was so, so wonderful.

POP: Tuesday isn't a *very* likely day, my crumpet.

MOTOR: Wednesday, Thursday then, any day. (*Sound of aeroplanes in the distance.*)

POP: In these things verisimilitude has some importance. We're not *improvisatori*.

MOTOR (*in her young girl's voice*): I am only simple. I don't know
the world like you do. But I felt that evening as though we had
both learned how to live, really live life as it should be lived. Oh,
if only I had words . . .

POP: But you said this was to be in words. Oh, I can't understand it
all. I can't remember and it's too tiring. How about resting? (*Suddenly*) Supposing we rested for good. Just two old no trumps. You
could go and take me with you to that eternal rest . . .
(*As they speak the noise of the many aeroplanes grows louder.*)

MOTOR: Oh, how I should love to. But how do I know you would
follow me? You're such a liar. Anyway you ought to go first.
You're the man.

POP: Oh, no, ladies first. (*The noise of aeroplanes is very loud.*)

MOTOR: Oh, if only I could be up there with those brave boys of
ours. To let the pilot take me and do as he wills . . . or almost.

POP: Ah, there they go, my birds, my flying words, the beautiful flying words that I wrote, or rather meant to write.
(*A vast explosion. A single scream. The stage is in complete darkness. Curtain.*)

BOOK FOUR

I ⟺ 1946

Passion seized this slim-figured, balding man, so sombre and black but for his absurd dolly liquid eyes and his *démodé* ankle bracelet that glinted beneath his silk sock as he moved. He picked up a cheap wooden chair—he was clearly as strong, as agile (Could he be a window dresser? a ladies' hairdresser? a portrait photographer?)—and smashed again and again at the boxlike construction until its boards lay broken beyond repair on the worn linoleum flooring. Dust flew everywhere so that he sneezed. Looking up to the ceiling he could find nothing—no Double-hooded Crow—for where there had been damp there was now a black gaping hole and broken, protruding rafters. On the floor below, a pool of plaster lay green-mouldy like a painter's reflection of the black gap. He looked at the curtains, but thick dust had smoothed all their secret meanings. But from the broken box-bed soared minarets and domes (Byzantine? Moorish? Baroque? He checked a sentimental sigh for the ignorance of the cheap little trash-fed, snob-educated, prim-mincing, high-voiced schoolboy—*Pss, Pss,* hello, Nance, got your K.Y.? If innocence was disgusting and now not to be condoned, then surely ignorance must also be flushed away with the rest of the rubbish)—but still they surged towards him in great waves of colour-wash drawing, colours barbaric and splendid—domes, minarets, towers, campaniles, colonnades, fountains, Scheherazade, great Turkish-trousered sultans, serpentine houri-eyed sultanas, huge-bellied eunuchs in Muscovite furs, Negroes vaulting, tumblers, blazing macaws on golden rings, pretty-faced marmosets on brocaded shoulders, pretty-faced pages, dressed as this, dressed as that, running behind the cypress trees, hiding behind the cinnamon tree, the papaya tree, giggling, beckoning, here a smooth small buttock, there another, and there again the laughing, saucy, saucer eyes and . . . but that was absurd, he had never known Pirelli until many years later, and for himself, why, he judged a man by the size of his piece, no more, and, make no mistake, no less, that was well known. But somewhere the plump little buttocks persisted, and lemur's eyes, heaven knew where from, and eyes more recently seen peeping, beckoning, dark Cairene, musk-scented Ceylon, isle of spices where lovely boys are vile. If that were he, then, oh, indeed, how ignorant he'd been—fed no doubt by Oscar on Dvorak's scarlet melodies and that absurd, pathetic supping with panthers not, as they said, to have known his arse from his elbow. But now, the Bakst drawings imposed themselves on the shadowy sultans, sultanas, eunuchs, and pages—the Queen's Guard, Carabos herself, the Princess, Porphyrophores, and the pageboy of the Fairy Cherry in panniered skirt and cherry-tree headdress—the very same he had dreamed, wet dreamed no doubt as well, pressed down, hemmed in by his wooden box. There at least he could find some link with the small enuretic—he would make him a present of the Bakst drawings, indeed, of all his fun paintings—the Laurencins, too, and the Magnasco. Poor little creature! Yes, he could allow him at least one sigh in return for his luxurious dreams, a child starved of colour, of softness, of elegance, of superfluity. Time later to tell good from kitsch, enough that he'd struggled to feed himself on all the scents of Araby. Laughing kindly, he was suddenly again seized with rage—to put him in a box for all the world like a raree-show—come and see the little bed-wetter, the little pansy boy. He kicked the broken boards savagely, then turned and went out of the room downstairs to the dining-room.

The elegant, thin-faced, tall woman (London store buyer of Paris models? champion bridge player? new style headmistress?) in the next room heard him go and checked herself from calling to him. He must never know that she had heard. She picked up the seal muff that she had found among Her things and rubbed its sleekness against her cheek. Such quaint femininities were never seen now, and trailing a stifling camphor—it must be noticed, but she did not care—anything that would soothe and soften her against the hideous cold of this her native land, of this her home, of this her cruelly cramped room. Already she felt frozen, aware of her thinness, aware of her bones, drawn in, every muscle tensed, shrinking from the chest of drawers, shrinking from her brass-headed bed, shrinking most of all from the other, the iron bedstead (so *she* had been the more richly treated! Like Jane, she had played Cassandra, while to the real Cassandra the second-best bed). Yet surely some honour, some piety was due to the log cabin where it had all begun and to the long-legged tomboy (though she had hardly with her dancing class and her coral necklace been the lass of the limberlost imitating the whip-poor-will's call under the old hickory tree), the plain Jane who had started it all. From log cabin to P.E.N. Club—for she was a Great Literary Figure now. Of course it was all there in the early Carmichaels, this tension, this smallness, this snake coiled in upon itself ready to hiss—and it was just that hissing in those early stories that, for all the critics' praises, she couldn't bear. But all the same, as a saga composed to cock a snook at His thick, soupy self-content and Her endless, acid-throwing self-assertion, it had been highly creditable for a gawky girl in her teens. She tried to compose again in the old manner—surely in this room she could recapture that voice, the earliest Austen parodies of her early teens—

Elizabeth Carmichael had little reason to congratulate herself upon her fortune, which was small, her face, which was long, or her figure, which was meagre, but she had some compensation in her tongue, which was ready, and her ear, which was sharp . . .

But had she? For she had spent more than a quarter of a century since then trying to adapt the tongue to poetry, to attune the ear to deeper music than mere mimicry. The failure in human sympathy! To have grown up in that room, not noticing that hers was the brass. She had blotted out the iron bedstead and all that went with it; had remembered only sisterly confidences and giggles, had forgotten, but now they crowded in on her, the other images—long white legs, a little blue with the early morning cold, fighting their way into scruffy, crumpled, woollen stockings, the first shaping of Sukey's breasts, her desperate neatness from the start with her rags, "Which of you girls has got hares in her drawers?" (that elaborate, silly, sniggery school joke that had only said to her "Sukey"). In all those years only glimpses of her sister as a living body—for she had managed by every elaboration of movement to avoid seeing this horrible intrusion of privacy, this beastly twin flesh that kept time with her times, that disgusted her with her own.

Here had begun the Mouselike tightness, acidity, protective cattiness, sharpened claws, and all the rest of it that had led to the literary White House. If, instead, she'd gone out, Martha-like, as Sukey did, and got on with the job, perhaps her talent would not have been so thin, so acid, so poisoned at the source. But then she remembered and began laughing until she had to sit down on her bed and wipe her eyes. No, no, never Sukey, stupid, limited Sukey the butt! The Countess came up the stairs bearing the little sauce boat in her hand: "What is this revolting, pasty mess?" waving it in front of Sukey's rounded blue eyes, fortissimo dramatic. "It looks like your Father's white soggy soul." "It's bread sauce, Mother." "Bread sauce! Ill-bred like all you Matthews children. Poisoned at the source!" The Countess herself had hardly been able to finish her tirade for laughing. At least that was how the libretto ran when she and Rupert and Marcus had played it over a few times. Later, when she'd Carmichaeled it, she toned it back to what was probably the original. Laughing still, she rose from the bed. "No," she said aloud, "it was a life of desolation and I was priggish and prudish, but that was the start. Only the start, of course. But, oh, we did laugh." She joined her brother in the dining-room.

"An adjutant!" she cried. "I couldn't believe it when Douglas told me. You remember when you missed me in Cairo. An adjutant!"

"Well, the Colonel was rather a silly one. And then he liked his officers to have a lot of money and lose to him at bridge. And I *have* kept a large house and a demanding man comfortable and well fed for many years, so the mess was child's play. Also I was rather good at camouflage work. We can't all have brains, some of us must be good with our hands."

"Oh, I'm sure you were most competent, but I'd always thought you'd either go to prison as an objector or march into battle leading the attack with plumes in your helmet."

"How novelists do love to romanticize pansies . . . I can't think why you want to be so nice about us. It's a very good thing, duckie, that these clichés don't get into your books. Or do they? I haven't read a book for years. They were one of the things the Colonel didn't like."

She shrugged in apology. "Well, what next?"

"Oh, I don't know. Except that I can't bear all the dowdiness and austerity of London. It's all like this house—dust and pinched memories. Anyway, Jack couldn't possibly eat this food after what rationing's done to his proud stomach. He fire-watched, poor thing. A truly awful war. And then ate at Claridge's or the Berkeley as though rations were better there. The silly ideas of the rich! Still, as I tell him, it's better than the gas chamber. Luckily we've got the pictures in New York as an excuse, even though the monstrous government won't give us any of Jack's money there. And *they* dared to send poor Gladys to jail! Who knows, when we see the Kandinskys and the Mirós, perhaps some of the splendour'll come back? Anyway I don't want 'people,' you can imagine, after all that good talk in the mess—'I don't know whether you're religious, Matthews. I'm not, but an odd thing happened to me . . .' Oh, the odd things that happened to that Colonel. All to do with time. He was shot forwards and backwards through history like a billiard ball. No, I don't want people. Certainly not that kind. I don't really know what I want. Lucky you with your writing."

"Oh, yes, scribble, scribble, Mr. Gibbon. I shall battle on. But not in this climate, thank God. The old blue, chilblained fingers of Mrs. Gaskell or George Eliot are not for me. Douglas has been put in charge of the new dig at Saqqara, so the desert sun for me." She smiled across at Marcus as sounds came from the kitchen. "Sukey's put the kettle on, we've all come through."

Taking the clean napkin off the top of the straw shopping basket, the brisk, neatly dressed woman in the tweed suit, the little broken veins of whose cheeks showed through caked face powder (was she social worker, racehorse owner, or advocate of birth control?), unpacked two Thermos flasks, a bottle of milk, and a packet of Marie biscuits. It was lucky that she had remembered that the gas would be cut off. For the others no doubt would have been happy to pop out for snacks at all hours, but if they were ever to get through sorting out this mass of stuff they must get down to the job. Some of the furniture was all she wanted, for schools can always use furniture. As for the rest, anyone would be glad of clothing in these rationing days, and papers should always be burnt—but no doubt they would maunder, or even less appropriately, giggle, over every object that came up. They had no families of their own, of course. Or apparently, Rupert did. But theatrical families, what could they be like?

Of course, 52 had never meant anything to her. She'd been determined to get away and she had. Here in this kitchen she'd fought smells, and dirt, and grease—and won. True, her dreams had been absurd—servants and manor houses! Her mouth puckered over her dentures in a dry little smile—she must remember them for her weekly broadcast when, if ever, her adventures with the boys dried up. "Did you know that I once had a butler, two footmen, two gardeners, a chauffeur, a lady's maid, a cook, and heaven knows how many house parlour maids? Well, I did. In schoolgirl dreams. Wouldn't it be appalling if our childish dreams suddenly came true? How could an independent, modern housewife bear such servants' tyranny? How did our grandmothers survive it?" But how could she have had anything but novelettish dreams with an oddity like the Countess for a mother? She hadn't known then, of course, that it didn't matter how you married; it was the children that mattered and they could as well be of a poor man as of the lord of the manor; they were your own. Of course she *had* known; that was why there'd been all that slop about animals—crying over drowned kittens! Every woman should have children to love. That poor, dirty old Regan, always trying to tell one's fortune—dark men over the water, Prince Charmings, and all that rubbish that the lower classes soaked up in those days; though the Countess was hardly better, romantic as a shopgirl when she wasn't behaving like one of "those." They should have been married to unromantic, steady old Hugh!

Suddenly tears began to pour down her cheeks. She held her breath; she wondered if she would burst with the effort, but she couldn't stop. She had been so frightened all that time—frightened of Regan's strange hints, frightened of Aunt Mouse's tongue, always on the edge of tears. If she could have found that upright corn-haired girl going about her tasks so tensely but so determinedly in that vast ogreish kitchen, she would have taken her in her arms! But the girl would have been too proud, wouldn't have wanted it. The tears ceased now and, taking her powder puff from her handbag, she liberally covered her reddened eyelids. What a squalid lot of memories! But it couldn't all have been like that, the heredity of the boys and P.S.! Carrying the tray upstairs, she remembered Granny M. and felt a stab of conscience. *There* had been a breath of decent, orderly sanity, an old chatterbox, but steady!

"No," she said, pouring out tea for them, "there was nothing to do, really. It was a direct hit. Nothing left."

"Poor Countess!" Marcus said, "A Baedeker raid! And I'm sure she never went into the Cathedral. She hated what she called old musty things."

"A Mrs. Lomax wheeled Father round one day. He gushed about it to me a bit. I can't remember what he said. Poetic experience, or something. They rather lorded it over the other old dears in the hotel, you know. I think they enjoyed their last days."

"The throne room here had gone a little stale, certainly. A change of royal residence was overdue," Margaret said.

"My dear, yes! The Countess wrote to me. She used to look at the sunsets and pick daffodils. The last and pastoral phase."

"And then P.S. went over to see them at least once a fortnight."

The finality of Sukey's statement left Margaret and Marcus bewildered.

Margaret said, "Delicious tea! I'd no idea prep-school boys were the pampered ones in England. You must be terribly relieved, Sukey, that all yours came through unscratched."

Sukey laughed, "I simply put them into God's hands before Munich, when one knew war couldn't be avoided. And He's rewarded me. Of course, I knew P.S. would never be involved. There was an absurd moment when Hugh said they'd call him up despite his history school. But John's were very good, they got deferment. Now, of course, he'll have to do his National Service. The other two tease him about playing soldiers. Poor P.S.! He isn't a bit pleased. He's got girl trouble. Some girl at Newnham. So it won't do him any harm to occupy the awful Germans for a bit."

To prevent herself laughing, Margaret tried to exchange a glance with Marcus, but to her surprise he was staring intently at Sukey.

"Gracious, Sukey, you are *lucky*. Having a family to make do and mend for. I do hope you've spoilt them and given them every luxury and comfort. It's especially important for boys."

"What an idea! I've given them love and security; that's what all children need."

"Well, yes, of course. But I do think a bit of luxury, too, and especially to see beautiful things and to travel. I suppose, really, that's an uncle's job. Oh, I do feel ashamed. When can I meet them and take them out and spoil them?"

"My dear Marcus! You're very kind, but I don't think they'd interest you very much. They're not youths any longer, you know. They're great hulking men."

Margaret smiled at Sukey's limited conventional notions. She was going to exchange a smile with Marcus, for he'd never been reticent about his tastes to her, but he had gone red in the face.

"Oh, I shouldn't like them to hulk over me. Anyway they won't have an opportunity. I shan't be in this bloody country, thank God."

Really, Margaret thought, to take Sukey so seriously.

"And you're going to settle in Egypt, Mag, I hear. We were there in 'twenty-nine you know. A parent lent us a house-boat. I've written one or two pieces about it. Of course, you don't know that I write now. I hardly dare tell you. For broadcasting from the local station, you know. Just ordinary family stuff, of course. But I think I've caught the West Country taste. That Nile trip has been most fruitful. Are there still those hawks, Mag, that mew like kittens? I've done a piece about a special one that became quite tame and used to take food from P.S.'s hand when he was a baby—Mu Mu, he called it—and then one day I came out on deck and found it had dropped a dead rat on to his pram. I've called it 'Mu Mu's Tribute.' "

After a short silence, Marcus said, "I can't *wait* to stay *en famille* in Devon, can you?"

"And you, Mag, how was your war?"

But Margaret suddenly felt impatient. "It's no good, Sukey. I'm sorry to disappoint you, but I've never missed the patter of tiny feet. I can't bear the little brats."

The twins glared at one another across the table. Marcus was overcome with nausea from the gross smell of women. Let's put them through their hoops, he thought. Let's make the bitches purr.

"It's easy for you two to wrangle. You've always had the chance of fulfilment."

Sukey blushed, but her tense face softened contentedly; and even Margaret's thin lips parted in pleased relaxation. They both looked at him with complacent compassion.

"Oh, I know," he cried, "if the Countess had let me grow away from her, or whatever it's called. But then I shouldn't have been so stinking rich. I must say I shouldn't like not having money."

The heavily built, tall man, with flushed, jowled, handsome face and with blond hair greying at the temples (banker? Wing Co., or even A.V.M.? or perhaps a confidence trickster pretending to Air Force rank?) was thinking of money, too, as he played somewhat stumblingly "The Cobbler's Song" on the out-of-tune grand piano in the room above. He wasn't quite sure why money pervaded his thoughts, for, of course, he was in fact reflecting on women and their importance. He owed everything to them. My God, he'd only to be in this room with this absurd moth-eaten Spanish shawl, even something of Her scent still coming from it, to remember that. If it hadn't been for that love-hate battle with Her, he might have remained a good-looking, flirty clerk, a sales-manager Lothario, to this day. But She had played with him so terribly, made him so restless, so keyed up to meet the demands of any scene, that his powers had been extended to their very top note.

She'd been so completely ruthless, too, in getting rid of his Monas for him. And all for what? It was easy to say that ultimately he owed it all to the Great White Slug for not satisfying her, but that wasn't fair. He knew too much about it all now to blame the old boy for not being quite up to it. No, she was torn apart inside, ravaged by a need for power. She'd never let go. And if you asked her what she wanted the power for, she wouldn't have known. They none of them did. She'd said she needed life and air (understandable in 52. It ponged a bit today of mice and mould and general decay); Alma said it was in order to be able to give "her all"; and Debbie said it was for him and for the children. But if they'd really known what they wanted, then it would have been all up with men, for it was out of this rage, this striving in the bellies of women that men found their powers, their creative thrust. If a man found a woman who thought she had this urge herself, then he'd best wean her from it, as he had weaned Debbie.

Yes, he saluted the long, lazy, blond cad with his Hawaiian guitar who had sprawled and idled around these rooms in a haze of brilliantine and Turkish tobacco smoke and postcards of Toots and Lorna Pound. He might have been such an unutterably, underbred cad, but as it was . . .

"Well, actually, no," he told them. "I've played everything from *Hamlet*—the grave-digger scene of course, the humour still lives, you know, even for hardened old Desert Rats—to *Lady Audley's Secret* and in the most God-awful, out-of-the-way holes, so I'm off rep., even the Old Vic, off theatre altogether at the moment."

"Oh, Rupert! But your Malvolio was so unforgettable."

"Thank you, Mag darling. And bless you for that note. It happened when all that G. business came up. . . . I hope you were right. At the moment I don't feel quite sure of myself. I don't want to depend on others' opinions."

"Oh, no, you must never do that in creative work."

"I'm glad you feel that too. Anyway, the theatre hasn't found itself again after all those thunderingly good air-raid audiences. No, I want to try films for a bit. Broaden my technique. And Britain's going to have it all her own way with the cinema industry, now we've got subsidies. Hollywood's done for. I shan't go for good, mind you. The theatre's my real love. But I've got rather a handsome contract with Rank." He smiled a rueful, boyish smile. "And it won't be unwelcome. Sandra's being presented this summer, and with Christopher two years off Eton . . ." He added quickly, "Of course, we'd have sent the boys to you, Sukey, if Debbie hadn't wanted a school near enough to Sunningdale to drive over for the afternoon."

"We've never had stage people." As though to soften this, she added, "But British films have always been the best, Rupert. Look at George Arliss! Senior and I went three times to his *Disraeli.*"

Margaret said, "In Cairo we never get more than a third-class company doing Lonsdale, and the cinemas are flea pits."

Marcus said, "I adored the cinemas in Ceylon," but he didn't explain why.

"We must get on," Sukey told them. "I think I'll have to call Gladys down. And where can Quentin have got to? I've only taken at the hotel for one night. I see now that I could have saved money and stayed here."

The big-framed, gaunt-faced woman with heavy, sagging breasts and a fuzz of greying hair (ex-Resistance fighter? Labour mayor? stage star's dresser?) sat on the improvised bed on which had been piled all the mass of stuff from the lumber room and the nursery cupboard. She was so high up from the ground that her legs swung in the air and her left shoe fell off her foot on to the floor. It gave her a further excuse for remaining there, for if she bent down too far these days she suffered a giddy spell. Not that she felt happy in the little cupboard room. Really, they had had no right to stick her in a hole like this with no dressing-table and insufficient blankets;

and then to charge her rent. And a mass of housework, too, after
working at that stuffy Food Ministry all day.

She had been lodger, breadwinner, servant, everything except
daughter. Everything, or almost. She could feel Billy Pop's—what
did they call it in novels?—"hot breath" upon her now. As that
comedian who dressed up as a woman used to say, "Believe me, girls,
it wasn't *quelques fleurs.*" No, it had been disgusting, horrible. Then
a rumbling laugh came up from her stomach. Oh, fuck that for a
lark! Not after the cells at Holloway, lovey. Don't come the duchess, dear. Only one lace blouse, dearie? What about apron, dowlas
for work; badge, arm, red band; boots, ordinary; cape, serge blue,
and cap, storm, to wear with; chemise, calico; dress, blue denim;
knickers, calico; nightgown, calico; petticoat, calico; shoes, black
strap; stays, grey lace-up; stockings, black woollen? And a bucket, a
Bible, and a hard, hard bed.

As to Father's little ways, there'd been Goddard and Parker and
Darling and Avory and more girls than she could remember, who'd
been kinder to their drunken fumbling pas than she had. And
grandpas, too, in that fat girl's case—"It stood up proper lovely for
is seventy-eight years. If it adn't been for is tickly beard . . ." And
she'd laughed with the others until the tears had run and the ward-
resses gave them hell. But, it was no good, she could no longer be
honest to that nightmare world. She must judge by the standards of
her own world, of all of them assembled downstairs (Oh, how could
she face them all together?) and of the girls in the typists' pool. And
by these standards the awful parents had done very badly.

As she turned her head, something glittered for a moment on the
top of the piled-up trunks—a piece of mica. It must be the sheet that
went over Alf's photo in that old frame. She took it and rubbed it
against her cheek. The room was full of his love and her love. She
could hardly bear it, for, after she'd come out, he'd got her her job
and now he wanted it on the old footing—at her age and with her
hag's face, and he, as she'd always hoped, on his way to the top of
the tree. Take and give, take and give; that's what their lives had
been. But they couldn't go on with it now—at their age, a couple of
right Charlies they'd look. No! Marriage and a villa, that's what she
needed. Oh, what should she do? Slinging her bucket bag over her
shoulder, she went down to face them.

"Oh, no," she said, "I was terribly lucky. A friend got me an interview at the War Office. And they put me in the typists' pool. There was no money involved, you see, so nobody looked into my swimming record."

Sukey began busily to stack up the empty cups.

Marcus said, "I'm sure you floated through the whole job deliciously. Better than I could have done. All those typists! But then mixed bathing isn't for me at all."

Rupert said, "We thought of getting Tanya into the War Office, but her call-up wasn't due until two weeks after V.J. day, thank the Lord."

Margaret took Gladys's hand and said, "Darling, it is lovely to see you."

A silence so long followed that Gladys thought she would fall through the floor. Her cheeks burned, she shifted from leg to leg. At last she said, almost before she'd noticed it, "I'm going to marry a Mr. Murkins. Mr. Ebenezer Murkins. But he's called Benny, I'm glad to say. And he's my boss."

"The pool attendant?" Marcus asked.

"No, much grander! Head of Establishments, they call it. He's due to retire anyway next year. So he's not a young hot head. But then I'm not in my first flush either. His other wife—she's dead of course, he's no Turk—used to what he calls entertain a good deal in their home in Weybridge, but, as he said, all things considering, *I* wouldn't want to entertain a lot. And all things considering, he's right. So we're going to live in the country—a cottage not too far from Romsey Abbey. He likes looking at the New Forest ponies."

"You make him sound like the leech gatherer," Margaret said. "You know, very simple."

"Oh, no, he looks quite distinguished. Like a sort of colonel. But, as he says, ponies won't be enough to keep a handsome girl like me out of mischief. Yes, he honestly means it. In his eyes I'm sweet seventeen, but full in figure. It's hard to resist. And he's so kind and a good sport too. I keep him in fits. I told him it's too late to breed Murkinses, so I'd better breed dogs. And now he's got it into his head that I should. I don't know which breed easily and which don't. You're the country one, Sukey, what kind do you think I should choose. I think bulldogs, don't you? Then they'll all grow up to look like their mistress."

She stuck out her lower jaw so that her stubby teeth glared at them, and when she pushed down her head on to her chest, the baggy skin of her face and neck formed a hundred pouches. It was startlingly like, and they were in fits. Under cover of the laughter, Margaret whispered, "Darling, I *am* so pleased. I thought you might go on beating your head against a brick wall," but Gladys did not appear to hear her.

But it was all right, for Murkins reminded Marcus of the Honourable Mrs. Pitditch-Perkins. Looking down at his feet, he waved a vaguely senile hand, "*Shoo, shoo,*" he cried. Margaret got it in one, "The Honourable Mrs. P.-P.! Oh, how the Countess adored that story! Oh, Glad do!" But Regan the Podge had already begun:

REGAN THE PODGE: Cats rahnd yer legs orl the time in *this* kitchin! Mind you, the Honourable Mrs. Pitditch-Perkins knew ow to deal with *them. You* know, Mum, my little rondyvoo with the nobility. (MARCUS THE COUNTESS *gives an expectant, amused glance to the company at large.*) Poor old thing, she was as blind as a bat! And a good deal more forgetful.

MARCUS THE COUNTESS: Are bats forgetful, Billy?

RUPERT THE BILLY POP: Oh, yes, my dear. That's why they can't ever make up their minds whether they are birds or mammals. (*He laughs uproariously.*)

MARCUS THE COUNTESS: Don't be coarse. Go on, Regan.

REGAN THE PODGE: Well, down she come one evenin. Bird of paradise in er air. All spangles and uncovered mutton. But er knickers was down to er ankles. Ah—but the poor old thing was quick enough: '*You*'re heah, General, and Sir Marmaduke, on my right. Oh, *shoo, shoo,* pussy!' And then she steps out of em. I was ready for it, corse. I whips em up. 'I'll take Fluff down to the kitchin, Mum,' I says.

MARCUS THE COUNTESS: Oh, listen to that, children! Isn't it an adorable story? The aristocracy, like the cockneys, are never at a loss.

OLD GRANNY SUKEY (*her upper dentures rushing forward into the fray in innocent absurdity*): Oh, dear me! The things that happen. Will most certainly'll never forgive me. But it does remind me so of when you were a little boy. You couldn't have been more than two or three. Not tall enough anyway to reach the lock on the door for yourself. So when you went to the smallest room you used to take your knickers off and hang them outside on the door knob. (*She goes into a great gale of spluttering, spitting laughter.*)

RUPERT THE BILLY POP: And very proper, too; it showed a nice Victorian sense of privacy with a proper eighteenth-century contempt for prudery.

MARCUS THE COUNTESS: It showed very early your total egotism, Billy. Pretty it would look if everybody . . .

RUPERT THE BILLY POP: But I am not everybody . . .

MISS MARGARET MOUSE: You should have done as the Altai people do in the South-eastern Taurus Mountains, William. I employed them as bearers on my aught eight expedition. We had no sooner pitched tents than they all crouched about on the rocks performing their natural functions. When I remonstrated with the headman, he expressed great surprise. Did I not notice how they all covered their heads first. They couldn't see what they were doing, so how could it be indecent? That would be in keeping, William, with your attitude to the rest of the world . . .

But Marcus protested, "No, Margaret, you've made it up. Who are the Altai anyway? I don't believe they exist."

"They do."

"Oh, fibs, Mag," Sukey cried.

"If Mags says they do, they do," Rupert announced.

But Gladys said, "Let's take her shoes off and tickle her feet. If she yells, she's lying. If she doesn't . . ."

"No, no!" Margaret was convulsed with laughter which set all the others off.

The man with the thin, high-cheekboned, supercilious face had quite a paunch, which made him look in all like a clown stuffed with a bolster (Had he come for the rent? In plain clothes to question them? Or was he the Unknown Warrior?) He paid off his taxi irritably, walked up the front steps uncertainly, but when he heard the mixed excited voices and uncontrolled laughter from the front room, he almost turned and walked away. If there was any group from which he felt quite estranged—and, in fact, he felt so about almost all groups—it was the strident baying of an upper-middle-class cocktail party, which could make the London streets more savagely lonely to the outsider than any other sound. He pushed the half-open front door fiercely and clattered into the hall. This house, its laughter and tears, had never had anything to do with him.

They had quietened into suppressed giggles by the time he came into the room.

Sukey said, "We couldn't write to you, old man. We had no address. That's why we did it through Dumfrey and Corstall."

Gladys said, "You've grown a pot, Quentin."

"I heard your wonderful Coventry broadcast. I was in a sergeants' mess in Delhi. They all sat quite silent. Everybody up to then had been playing for easy tears over it, you know. But you, dear boy . . . Well, it made putting over scenes from Henry Five that evening uphill work, I can tell you. Did you always have that voice register?"

"Your Dunkirk description," said Margaret, "was the only thing we heard in Egypt that made it alive without patronizing. And your interviews with all those people!"

"Yes, Hugh thought of substituting the Q. J. Matthews broadcasts for the Sabatini he was reading to the boys, but then you stopped . . ."

"You didn't hear me on the Hamburg and Dresden raids, did you? And the Hiroshima tape got unaccountably burned. Those would have cheered the national morale."

Marcus, who had been squatting by the bookcase, sorting through old volumes, stood up and half turned towards his brother.

"You're among those against war?" he asked.

"War? Why the hell? A good time is had by all. We produce wars to all tastes, you know. Even the intellectuals, this time. With cultured Mr. Roosevelt and the Hutchinson Soviet novelists. Are you going to any cultural congresses in Eastern Europe, Margaret? I should move fast. The wonderful spirit's wearing a little thin. Of course, Hiroshima was a bit hard to swallow, but then, Mr. Truman's a bit of rough diamond, isn't he?"

Sukey mouthed "Drunk" to Gladys. "Well, you've got *your* government now, old man, at any rate."

"My? Oh, you mean the Woolton pie's turned pink. But a man can't live by pie alone, Sukey. Didn't you know that? Though I daresay at Pascoe's Dotheboys Hall . . ."

"Oh, stop it, Quentin!" Margaret cried. "Of course it's all a mess, but think of all the reconstruction there is to be done. Good heav·

ens, with your knowledge of housing, you could do more for this country than . . ."

"Oh, by all means give them all two-bedroomed bungalows and an Austin Ten and, if our dear allies are very kind with lease lend, who knows, perhaps to every man a refrigerator. But don't ask *me* to take part in the big swindle, Margaret. I've been four years in secret political war work. I'm not going to spend another four in open political peace work. Absolute power, my dear . . ."

"Oh, politicians, of course. But us, the ordinary people, surely we have a . . ."

"You, the ordinary people! But I find it hard to remember that the intellectuals think of Attlee's and Ernie Bevin's as their government. Anyhow you must lengthen your sights—we live in stirring times, my dear. I'm going to see Justice in person. I'm off to Nuremberg to watch the world dispose of its guilt by hanging a lot of moth-eaten crooks and psychopaths. There's nothing I like more than the spectacle of Justice. His Majesty's judges and the rule of law—it's the one thing England can still hope to export in a cold world of shrinking markets. And after that there should be unlimited fun seeing the starry-eyed fit old Uncle Joe into a new brotherhood of nations. That's going to be really good. So let's get this house sold and realize a bit of cash as soon as possible. Oh, but I forgot," he cried. "Please excuse me. You were all down Memory Lane, no doubt, judging by the laughter as I came in."

"We were playing The Game," Margaret said, "that's all."

"Some absurd old stories came back to us," Rupert explained.

"You remember the laughs we used to have," Gladys told him.

"I remember," Sukey said, "Granny M. saying that growing up meant looking back at oneself with a bit of kindly laughter. I must say I remember *her* very kindly."

"Oh, my dear, yes, that terrible day of the kittens. And Mother said that growing up meant marriage," Margaret recalled. "I remember the occasion so well. Heaven knows, strange union though it was, she kept *her* marriage going to the bitter end. So there must have been . . ."

"The old boy knocked the nail on the head there," Rupert said. "Do you remember he said growing up meant companionship? I can't imagine anyone but the Countess choosing such a companion, but then, as one gets older, one accepts other people's choices . . ."

"I think all that's a bit soft," Gladys said. "I was terrified of her, of course, but it was Aunt Mouse's advice that stuck in my mind—self-reliance!"

Marcus was sitting on the floor, his legs curled behind him, his face buried in a book. He looked up for a second.

"Regan had a piece of advice specially for me all on my own. She told me not to mix with muck. If only she'd defined what muck was. It's taken me years to learn. But she was perfectly right."

"So," Quentin said, rummaging in the sideboard cupboard, "I thought so. What a quick get-away our parents made." He brought out a decanter and poured himself a large, neat whisky. "So. Well then, wherever they may be now, the clever, ill-treated, misunderstood, sensitive young Matthewses have forgiven them. That's nice. Let me be the one to convey your verdicts, your merciful verdicts to—well, let's not paint things in unpleasant colours, let's not particularize geographically, be invidious about exact destinations—let's say, to the Judgment Seat. In fact let me sit on the Judgment Seat. Imagine me wearing the wig of one of His Majesty's Judges, the Lord Chief Justice himself, why not? and supplied with a copy of *Das Kapital* on which witnesses may be sworn and, of course—We, the People of the United States—the Court is impartial. Thus equipped, let me take the place of Jehovah himself, the Ancient of Days, with a long white beard down to my navel. William Ackerley Matthews, your sins are forgiven you. Clara Madeline Matthews, your sins are forgiven you. Maud Iseult Matthews, your sins are forgiven you. Florence Stanley Rickard, your sins are forgiven you. Henrietta Peebles Stoker, your sins are forgiven you. Give them all harps and haloes."

Sukey clicked in disapproval. Marcus quickly snatched up Sukey's fox stole that lay across the sofa back and cast it stylishly round his shoulders.

"Billy," he called, "Billy, is that God prosing away there, impertinently forgiving us all? Turn Him out of the house at once. Just because He's always been out of all the fun and games is no reason why he should bring his great self-pitying clay feet in here, ruining my carpet . . ."

Quentin stood over his young brother with his fist raised as though to smash him in the face, then lowered it and went back to his seat. Marcus fussed with the fur about his neck, but he said no more.

The silence was broken by Sukey the practical.

"Well, the sooner we get everything sorted out the better. Supposing I do the nursery. Will you do the upstairs bedrooms, Gladys?"

Gladys, the practised upon, rose with a smiling nod.

"And Mag, will you go through Her things? You know about clothes. Quentin, will you pick out any books that are too good to go in job lots? And, Rupert, will you go through His things, please? And Marcus, you must know about wine by now, will you see if there's anything special in the cellar."

But even she did not find the courage to ask for her fox fur stole to be restored to her. It was better, she thought, just to get on with things.

2 ⊂⊒ 1956

"It's all dirty pink oleanders at the moment and the dusty remains of purple bougainvillaeas. Though I *do* have a rather beautiful rare white one. You can't think how one longs for anything white here in summer. But the spring garden's enchanting, because it's all frightfully damp. Well, we can't stay outside in this heat, but I thought you'd like to see the ocean. It *is* a heavenly view, isn't it? But, Mary, why have you come here in July? It's a mad moment."

"I don't think much about moments, Marcus, nowadays. I'm so poor, you know, that when Lucy asked me to stay *abroad*, that was quite enough."

"But you should have come to *me*. Hassan would have been told to look after you like a princess. And Hamid is the most superb cook. Lucy has a dreadful cook. He serves balls of shit on skewers and calls it Tangerine delight. Oh, why *didn't* you come to me? You could have had the room with the Dufys. You always liked them. I only kept the decorative things, you know . . ."

"My dear, don't I think of it every time I go to the Tate? I can't imagine how you could have borne to part."

"Well, I've kept the Magnasco and all the Bakst drawings, and the silly Laurencins. Oh, and I've still got that embarrassing Tchelitchew of myself and two rather enchanting bad drawings Jean did of Jack with a Negro sailor at Toulon. But for the rest, when Jack died, I realized it had all been him . . ."

"But, Marcus, it was *you* who bought all the really good things and not Jack at all. I remember how I used to quarrel with you because you wouldn't let him buy all our friends."

"This is one of the spare bedrooms. Moroccan furnishing, dear, that's all you would have had. It fits so much better to these houses. Yes, I had a good eye and I loved buying, but . . . Well, anyway, it wouldn't have been right to have really good paintings in this damp climate."

"It wouldn't be any good to have me, either. I'd decline for good and all from rheumatics."

"That's one thing about living with the young, one never admits."

"He *is* very young, isn't he?"

"Are you disapproving, Mary? I expect old Lucy and her crowd spat venom."

"As if I should take notice with an old friend like you. No, and of course, he's an enchantment to look at. I was just puzzled . . ."

"Oh, you mean the change of taste. My dear, it wasn't until after the war that I did what I think they call realize myself."

"Marcus, that isn't very nice about Jack."

"Jack was a completely special person to whom I owe every-thing."

"He owed a lot to you."

"I hope so. My dear, you do tear away still at personal relation-ships, don't you? If I were in charge of you, I'd give you a rubber bone to worry at. This is Hassan's room. Very austere, you see. Those horrible scarlet and green candles are our only source of dis-sension. He comes from the South, you know. He's very simple. Tangier is the summit of worldliness for him. And now you've seen it all."

"It's a lovely house, Marcus."

"Yes. I don't suppose we'll go on living in it much longer. Hassan gets homesick. Now we must go back to the guests."

In the drawing-room Lucy was describing the ceremony.

"My dear," she was saying, "the Minister of the Interior—yes, he *was* that, Rodney; I asked—one of the little fat dark ones with mous-taches, no, not with Senegalese blood, they're the beautiful dark ones, the other kind—spoke for *quite* half an hour. Apparently in French. Not that one could hear a single word because of the dear little boy scouts—all great hulking things of sixteen or more in shorts—who were screaming and shouting, and pulling down all the flags except their own beloved starry banner. It was really rather pathetic! I felt quite sorry for some of the poor Tangerines, because

they'd looked forward to it all so. Their great Day of Independence!
The day they, too, became Moroccans. Except that they shouldn't
think they're adults when they're still small children. Anyway it will
give them some idea of the chaos to come."

Admiral Tembrick said to Marcus, "You were perfectly right to
stay away. Those of us who care for them should never see them
when they're trying to organize something. They suddenly go to
pot and lose all their poise. As Lucy says, the thing was a shambles."

Lucy seized on it: "Exactly. And these are the people who are
going to run their own country. People who've no sense of order,
honesty, or public courage. People who can't even prevent daylight
attacks in the Souk. Of course, the Administration has been to blame.
They've preferred to play in with . . ."

"Well, you can't blame them for that."

"All these years of prosperity and good administration wiped out
in a moment, *n'est-ce pas que c'est désolant*, Yvette?"

"*Oui, oui*, Lucy, *je parle à Rodney de ce qui arrive aux grands
propriétaires.*"

"Oh, my dear, even York Castle's up for sale. And who's going to
buy it with things as they are?"

Omar, walking round with a tray of drinks, showed no reaction.
Hassan sat silent and smiling; if his legs had been longer he'd have
been a twenties Bakst doll. The Moroccan restraint and mannerliness
kindled Marcus's anger.

"Old cow, fucking old cow," he muttered.

Mary, not understanding, but feeling, said, "I loved all the horses
charging and the guns firing."

"Oh, the fantasia! If things were only as they should be in the
French Zone, we'd go down to Fez and see a fantasia done properly.
It was pathetic here, wasn't it, Admiral? But then you see the poor
dear Tangerines are not warriors at all. They like to think of themselves like the Riffi or the Blue Men but . . ."

"Will there be any chance of seeing the Blue Men?" Mary asked.
Marcus's tension brought back the past unbearably to her.

"My dear, I'm afraid not. Rodney's made the journey to the desert
hundreds of times. He knows all the *gîtes d'étapes*—*and* speaks Berber. Yes, isn't he clever? He would have taken you, dear, but you
wouldn't want to go now, would you, Rodney? You see they speak

about their precious new kingdom, but they're all a lot of Bedouin bandits still, at sixes and sevens with each other. There'd be civil war at this moment if the Glaoui hadn't died so suddenly . . ."

Marcus had uncoiled his legs and risen. Taking the Martini shaker from Omar's tray, he went over to where Lucy sat. Now he filled her glass to the brim.

"Stop talking nonsense about things you know nothing about, and drink that, Lucy," he said. "Glaoui indeed! The Mahdi's more your period."

"Oh! I suppose *you're* going to be a good boy and please the nice new government, Marcus. I know a lot of people are frightened of speaking out now. But I'm not like that. I can't lie down just because someone is waving a big stick."

"My dear Lucy, if you laid down stark naked for an hour and a half in the middle of the Socco, nobody would so much as *raise* his stick at you."

After a gasping moment, Lucy gallantly led the way in uneasy laughter.

"No, but seriously," she said, "I do resent it after all we've done for them . . ."

"Lucy! Mary's tried to be tactful twice and I've been abominably rude once. Now, will you stop? Apart from anything else it's very insulting to Hassan and Omar to talk about their country like this, and I won't have it."

"Oh, of course, Hassan knows I don't mean him. Besides he's not a Tangerine at all. He's from dear little Mogador. Oh, if only I could take you *there*, Mary. You're looking so well, Hassan. Green suits you. Who is Omar, Marcus?"

"Omar has been serving you with drinks."

"Oh, I see. Oh, well, anyway, it's them I'm thinking of. Speeches and fantasies! But how do they think they're going to pay for all these schools and clinics when the foreigners have been frightened away? And they will frighten people away—look at it: two villas burgled on the Old Mountain only last week and that wretched American tourist mobbed in the Socco just because he was photographing a mosque. And their police stood by idle. Who's going to stay when that sort of thing goes on?"

"You for one, Lucy. There may be rich people whose money is needed by the new government. I hope they'll have the sense to remain here. If they don't, I shan't blame the government if it takes their property away from them. But you're not one of them, dear. You live here like the Duchess of Fartshire on what would hardly keep you in an Earl's Court bed-sitter if you went home . . ."

"I say, really, Marcus, this is too left for words . . ."

"Left of his senses, I should say."

"Just because you're stinking rich, old man . . ."

"Oh, Marcus!" Mary cried. "Oh, when we've only just met again. It's too horrid."

"I'm sorry, Mary dear. You came in on the wrong act. All right, I am stinking rich, but I'm sick of all these ill-mannered remittance people . . ."

"Oh, don't bother to answer him," Lucy cried, getting up to go. "We all know what keeps *him* here."

"If you mean that I sleep with Hassan and that you sleep alone, Lucy, that's no reason why you should come up here and abuse people who've given you hospitality and service and some sort of illusion of decency for the last ten years . . ."

When it was all over, he only could think that he should not see Mary again while she was staying with that old cow—for, of course, Mary's manners, as always, were still perfect. But now Hassan's stepfather's nephew Mohammed had arrived to tell them about the morning's celebrations, in his atrocious mixture of Spanish, English, and Arabic.

"Yes, I've heard all about it," Marcus said and he went to his room.

Later Hassan came to him with a tray of coffee. He was scowling like a schoolboy sent off the football field.

"Mohammed went away," he said. "He saw you did not want him. It was clear that our celebrations have no interest for you."

"Really, Hassan! After all I said to old Lucy just because of you!"

"Madame Lucy gives very distinguished parties. Now I shall not be asked . . ."

Marcus hit the tray so that it flew through the air. There was no noise and no breakage, for the cups fell on to cushions, but the coffee formed little soggy wet heaps of sugary grouts on the divan. He pulled Hassan face downwards on to the cushions beside him. The boy was giggling happily now. "Madame Lucy is a silly old cow," he was saying with delight.

Margaret determinedly watered the hippeastrum plants on the balcony. Looking down, she saw the legless boy on his wheeled board at his usual place by the entrance to the flats—the porter had in despair given up trying to chase him away. At the end of the road the taxis hooted ceaselessly as they careered along the riverside. In the distance she could see the scruffy black serge of her favourite local policeman—many were lounging about, for there appeared, despite everything, to be football at the stadium. Mrs. Karamazian in the flat below had put out all her mattresses and blankets. A hawk mewed. Huge crows pecked at the horse-dung on the sticky tarred asphalt. At Dr. Yousouf's someone was stumbling through "The Barcarol" on the pianoforte. She registered everything as exactly as she could, sparing time where there was none to spare, for while these landmarks were there, it was still, it must be surely, her Cairo. She never went into the city and only on occasion with Douglas into the desert; she never saw the Embassy crowd and only at great intervals people from the Institute. Her life was all here in the daily sounds and smells of Zamalek: Mrs. Karamazian's hennaed gossip; a visit over the balcony from Mr. Younan's Persian cats; cutting back the bougainvillaea; gossiping when she bought the pimentos, the eggplants, and the figs; the smell of sesame in Mrs. Shoukri's perpetual frying; the stories about the house-boat restaurant that was no restaurant; even the look of friendly complicity each day with the beggar boy—for they were both, pariah and artist, outside the law— all these, with the occasional drama—the hawk that swooped down and took the veal, the taxis in collision, the mule that died standing as it hauled the little charcoal cart—this was her Hampshire village or Sussex hamlet, but so much warmer, often deliciously hot so that she could work with relaxed nerves—a Chawton or a Rodmell set in the heart of a noisy exotic city. Well, it had worked: three novels she was not ashamed of in ten years, and this fidget now at the back of her thoughts—a schizophrenic dialogue, the gradual fissure of a coherent mind, each chapter making two out of one, or rather at first, three, for the original personality would still desperately dominate— but all that must be locked away until this absurdity was over.

She went into Douglas's room; he was sleeping now, but his face was as drawn and white as his little moustache, and his lips had that ghastly bluish shade like those horrible dyed tulips there used to be at florists'; his breathing creaked like some unoiled cradle swinging. Leila was fussing with the hot kettle and Friar's Balsam—no doctor could make her more than half-nurse, half-witch.

Farouk's flight, Shepheard's burning, all had sounded like summer thunder in her village, Zamalek's remote, daily pettiness. And now suddenly, with Douglas laid low with the worst of his asthma attacks for years, she was forced to recognize that the thunder was really threatening gunfire.

They were to leave in twenty-four hours because some hysterical, anachronistic English minor aristocrat (she knew they were mad at home to bring the Conservatives in again) couldn't come to terms with the modern world. She and Douglas, who loved Egypt, who loved every smell and colour of it, who, above all, loved its ordinary people, especially the Arabs. If this ambitious colonel was going to give a new and decent life to Ibrahim and Yussef and Ali and Leila, and millions like them, then Douglas and she were the sort of people he needed here, people who would back him through thick and thin. She was an artist, a writer, and Douglas was a scholar; they weren't arrogant service officers or greedy business-men. That the Suez Canal should be run by Ibrahim and Youssef and Ali was what she utterly believed in. She hated power and riches, always had; and arrogant colonialism. But in these dreadful times all sense seemed to be lost. Order and reason—even in art, where passion was king, they had their exalted places; but in ordinary life they were the essence of decency. She had rung or seen everyone: the silly people at the Embassy, of course, were worse than useless. Anyway, she couldn't speak to people who represented that wicked fool, and even the Institute seemed to have panicked; it was her Egyptian friends she had relied on, but to no avail. Mr. Wa'bi, so clever, so sympathetic as a rule, was almost cold; Major Barawi had been kind but quite frank; Professor Farid had even gone to some minister, but he had urged her when he telephoned again to make her arrangements as quickly as possible; Mrs. Hussain, at least, had agreed to take on Leila and Ibrahim, for Yussef and Ali would have no difficulty in getting another place.

Of course, her chief reliance was upon Dr. Ramses Rascheid; he surely could get them some stay while Douglas was so ill. But even that dear, funny old fat thing who had saved Douglas's life in his attack of '51, she was sure, seemed quite flabbergasted, flapping his hands, his protruding eyes staring, his mouth open, for all the world like a dying codfish. Professor Farid had suggested that, in view of everything, she was unwise to rely on the assistance of a Coptic doctor, so, at his suggestion, she had consulted some smart young man from the hospital, Dr. Kasim al Aziz. But really this had only worsened things, for poor old Rascheid was offended (the Copts were in a terrible state these days), and in the end the smart young doctor could do nothing. All she could contrive was full ambulance arrangements to the airfield, some English nurse who was leaving to accompany them in the plane, and a room at the London Clinic when they arrived, while she found her bearings.

And now obviously the servants, too, were anxious to see them gone, frightened of remaining in their service, though, as with all the simple people that she had known throughout her life, she had made some sort of rapport with them which even this stress could not break. They were to have all the clothes that she and Douglas couldn't take with them, and Ali, who was newly married, was to take his pick of the furniture. At least they would leave having paid their debt to the exploited, incoherent, sometimes violent, but always responsive, ordinary Egyptian people. She remembered suddenly that by the time the ambulance came her legless boy would have moved his pitch—his hours were like clockwork, like all the hours of her little world that she must leave behind, though she had the key to it all. She gathered together more money than was really right, but why not? Why shouldn't one legless boy know a sudden rain of gold from the disguised caliph's hand?

She knew every scratch on the cheap aluminum door of the lift as it carried her bumpingly down. Outside the heat was intense, the sunlight dazzled her for a moment so that she hardly knew her little intimate scene. Then, cautiously, so as not to attract the porter's attention to him, she sidled round the entrance to where the dirty, snotty little boy sat on his wooden board. She gave him a special version of her daily smile—she knew that she was near to tears, but she held them back, for what had it to do with him?

"Barraka Laofik," she said, and she put all the notes and coins into his little upturned monkey paw. He rapidly shovelled it all somewhere into his ragged blouse. She waited for that enchanting smile that always transformed a best-forgotten missing link into a Murillo urchin. He spat twice, very deliberately, on to her candy-pink cotton dress, then propelled himself at breakneck pace away on his wheels.

Coming into the entrance hall she was greeted by Mrs. Karamazian, fat, rouged, hennaed, and moustached, in a not overclean violet satin dress. Mrs. Karamazian was weeping so that her mascara ran into her eyes. She held out the official form.

"We are to go. Next week we Armenians must go. But where shall we go to? After fifty years in Cairo. Where? Tell me that. You bloody English have done this. Now where are we to go?"

All Margaret's feelings suddenly dried up within her at these oily, lachrymose outpourings. She tasted powder, dried chaff in her mouth; it was the dust, no doubt; almost choking, she said, "Orders to go? Well, you must be thankful that times have changed. At least there are to be no massacres."

"And now here to discuss the situation we have Colonel Jonathan Brown from the Conservative Central Office, John Cobmarsh Q.C., Labour member for East Dartford, and Q. J. Matthews."

Many thousands of viewers who might have turned off in face of another documentary, another dose of politics at this all too-political time, took heart at the sight of that long face, those disdainful lips, those amused eyes. There was sure to be fun with the outrageous Q. J. Matthews—a brilliant bloke; even when you couldn't understand, you could sit back and watch. Many other tens of thousands who felt shame of one sort or another over Suez, or shame of a more definite kind over Hungary, or, rather helplessly, all sorts of shame at the same time, were compelled to meet Q. J. Matthews' lazy gaze, to hear what sort of nonsense the fellow would talk, to know how far the renegade would mountebank this time. They were not disappointed. The producer angled the camera as much as possible on to him while the others were talking. As the colonel's solemn soldier tones boomed forth like an honest cannon in these days of warfare by slide rule and "stinks" (he was, they said, a peculiarly wily and ambitious politician), Q.J. stared in amused yet not unloving fascination at this mammoth brought back from extinction especially for the delectation of himself and—for he always shared his fun—the millions of viewers who, no doubt, were watching tonight the Q. J. Matthews show. As Mr. Cobmarsh talked, quick, eager, passionate, voluble (an up-and-coming back bencher, they said, if there weren't too many lawyers already in his party), one could see a more sickened recognition on Q.J.'s face, his eyes became veiled with ennui, he shuddered a little at the thought of the possible harm that might come to all those million, faithful viewers from all this stale cleverness and too often shown enthusiasm. At last, when the visitors had had their full time and more—as viewers felt and the interviewer rather implied—the question was put to Q. J. Matthews:

"Does it matter all that amount?" he asked. "Oh, granted that, as my idealistic old friend John Cobmarsh has suggested with so much emotion, had it not been for our Government's palaeolithic expedition in defence of the all-red route and the dreams of Cecil Rhodes, we might now be able to offer rather more aid than President Eisenhower's Episcopalian pieties to the insurgent government in Budapest . . ." Camera to John Cobmarsh protesting with many gestures. "Q. J. Matthews knows perfectly well that it's not just a question of rather more aid, it's a question of that extra help . . ." Camera to Q. J. Matthews.

"Very well"—Q. J. Matthews smiling at the clever child who points out the utterly irrelevant minor mistake in addition in the Chancellor's annual budget—"very well, we could have given enough to alarm our ebullient but ultimately exceedingly cautious friend from the Ukraine, Nikita Sergeyevich, and have given the worthy Dr. Nagy a year, two years, more of precarious Revisionist Socialist—let us not forget the magic language—rule." Camera to Cobmarsh.

"More, much more." Camera to Q. J. Matthews, waving his long tapering hands in liberal allowance.

"Very well. More. But our little systems, you know . . . And they are such *very* little systems! To replace the ruthless, satellite government of Mr. Rakosi, who *pretends* to govern by every word that came out of the mouth of a bearded, worthy, but misguided bourgeois gentleman of the Victorian era, now lying in Highgate cemetery, by the more insecure, somewhat less dependent government of Dr. Nagy, who really *does* believe that the words of the late and wholly irrelevant Karl Marx are gospel truth, is that such a very valuable change? Is it something for which we should risk the annihilation by radiation of man, such as he is, and his achievements, such as they are?" Camera to Colonel Brown.

"Hear! Hear!—Hear! Hear!" Camera to Q. J. Matthews, smiling with a kindly acidity all his own.

"Oh, don't mistake me, Colonel; no doubt if our left hand had not trembled so agitatedly"—camera to John Cobmarsh shaking with fury—"our right hand could have smitten the Egyptian hip and thigh with the same agility that we showed in those days when Lord Cromer and Lord Kitchener walked before the Lord. But what would that have done, Colonel? Really, what *would* that have done? Prolonged the British Empire a few more years before it inevitably goes the way of Nineveh and Tyre; and put some extra dividends into the hands of some already overweight, thrombotic shareholders and directors in the City of London. And you both ask me to take all this seriously."

On the whole it was first class Q. J. Matthews stuff. Yet only once did he rear his head and spit fiercely as viewers, above all, liked. It was when John Cobmarsh pressed about his personal friendship with Dr. Nagy, his long conversations with Professor Lukac.

"This is really abominable, Matthews. You've known both Nagy and Lukac personally. You know what sincere and courageous men they are. You also know that your voice on the television tonight, like all influential voices from the West, may make the whole difference to the Russians' attitude towards these men who are in mortal danger."

"Oh, you flatter me, my dear fellow. Quite honestly, I doubt if anything we can say here will influence Comrade Nikita and his thugs. In any case I have the greatest personal liking both for Nagy, who's a good chap, and Professor Lukac, who's a clever one. I hope they come well out of these bad times. But if you're suggesting that I have any concern for their cause, I must remind you that to me the Marxist nonsense they believe in is no more respectable than the crudest sort of Flat Earthism. And, do remember—they chose politics, and politics, like all games of power, carries its own risks." Camera to John Cobmarsh, gesticulating wildly.

"This is too disgraceful. Well, even if you won't consider the fate of your personal friends . . ."

"Oh, but I do, my personal friends are many, are . . ."

". . . perhaps you'll have some concern for the Hungarian common man."

"I have no concern for the common man except that he should not be so common." The contempt with which Q. J. Matthews looked into the camera as he spoke was the masochistic moment for which his million common viewers waited every week.

"All right, quibble if you will! Let us say the thousands of ordinary people—young men and women, many of them just beginning their lives—who are now streaming over the borders into Austria, into a Western world, sick with disappointment, sick with despair."

"Oh, my dear fellow, I have. Unlike many of my friends of the humanitarian and liberal section of our country, I am not busy telling these wretched young people to expect a paradise here. I have too much concern for man's spirit, man's real self to suggest to them that by leaving the drab earnestness of the Marxist Utopia for the glittering triviality of the affluent lollygarchy they have gained anything whatsoever but a hire-purchased Hoover and a sleeping-pill salvation."

Putting down their whiskies and sodas, their cocoas and their Cokes, a million viewers felt comfortably rebuked.

"No, we shall be living quite close. Hugh will do some of the Latin Common Entrance so long as Mr. Birkenshaw wants him."

Sukey shot the young man in question a glance that forbade him to deny his need of Hugh.

"Me? Oh, I've got so much to do, you know. Five grand-children. Then I shall go on with my weekly talks for the Western Regional. I've missed only six weeks in twenty years. And I'm on the bench now and the R.D.C. So what with that and Cathedral business *I* shan't be at a loose end. Although, of course, I shall *miss* the school. You can't shake off old habits, can you?"

"And the school will miss you," one woman said, and then another. And soon it was spreading amongst the whole group of these mothers arrived to take their boys out for half-term week-end.

"I shall try out the Birkenshaws, of course. But it won't be the same without Mrs. P."

"Mr. Pascoe was a first-rate teacher, but it was she who kept the school together."

"I remember three years ago when Jerry first came here, I was terrified of her. But she's been like a second mother to him."

"What age would she be? She looks indeterminate."

"She's looked exactly the same to my knowledge since my eldest boy came here, which must be five or six years ago. But of course she's got such energy."

Poor little Mrs. Birkenshaw, listening, thought, Oh, how will it work out? However will we undo the Pascoe legend? Oh, thank heavens, they're retiring at last. And now boys were appearing in the drawing-room to be taken off by indulgent, impatient parents. Among the fathers even this customary half-term parental impatience to be gone was drowned by the National Debate. Mr. Oldbourne, the bank manager from Taunton, had started up an argument with Wing Commander Jackley, who was stationed near Beer. It was not that either of them had any doubt about the rightness of our cause, the shame of our withdrawal, it was only that the Wing Commander was unhappy lest we might perhaps alienate the right kind of Arabs, the splendid chaps, and unhappy that we should find ourselves mixed up with Jewish politics; while Mr. Oldbourne thought all this was sentimental nonsense—the Arab world was three hundred years out of date, medieval, while Israel was a going concern. But they both rounded on Mr. Latimer, who produced childrens' programmes for Western Regional, when he said that it was we, with our gunboats and our ultimata, who were living in the past. In a few moments the political debate had engrossed all the fathers and spread to the mothers; even some of the boys in their best Sunday long-trousered suits had begun to punch and pummel one another over the rights and wrongs of the affair. Hugh and the Birkenshaws tactfully withdrew from the discussion, tactfully finding errands—boys to call, marks to show, the new Rugger XV photos to pass round. Sukey appeared to show her tact in a different way by reminiscing right through the torrent that raged around her, now indeed most fiercely, for Mrs. Latimer had quoted the *Observer* and Mrs. Oldbourne had been shocked that anyone should still read that rag—"the traitors' paper we call it."

"That was the year," Sukey was almost shouting as though to drive the general conversation from her ears, "when we had to put Winnie the Wolseley to sleep. She just wouldn't take the hills any longer, poor old girl! So despite the pleas of our Tearful Trio, Hugh the Hard-hearted sent her to the knacker's yard and we acquired a brand new Morris Oxford. It was the first new car we'd ever had. The boys were frightfully scornful, thought it was a terrible show-

off. And secretly I rather agreed. However, when the sheen had
begun to wear off we became devoted to Oxford Olga, as we called
her . . ."

But somehow, however much Mrs. Latimer and Mrs. Oldbourne
disagreed, they and the other parents clearly agreed that no tact was
permissible at this time, everyone must stand up and be counted.

"*You* wouldn't have the *Observer* in the house, would you, Mrs.
Pascoe?" Mrs. Oldbourne pressed.

And Mrs. Latimer said, "Mrs. Pascoe's much too sensible to believe in censorship of opinion."

But what was Mrs. Pascoe's opinion, they all began to ask, was she
pro? was she anti? did she care what happened to the British Empire?
to the Hungarians? did she like Jews? did she trust Arabs? Suddenly
Mrs. Pascoe, so sensible, so reliable, weather-beaten, energetic, dowdy
yet not unhandsome, began to shout at them, beating with her
clenched fists upon the back of a chair.

"Damn your Jews! And damn your Arabs! Damn the government! Haven't they done enough to us, taking everything that gave
life meaning? And don't think God's on your side! Don't make that
mistake!"

She began to cry, and taking her little handkerchief from her cardigan pocket, put it to her eyes and ran from the room. Hugh almost
collided with her as, waving a list in his hand, he came in saying,
"Yes, I was right, Oldbourne, Andrew's math marks are fifty per
cent up . . ." He stopped. "Sukey, my dear, Sukey." And he followed her.

Young Birkenshaw was able to explain: her youngest son had
been killed as a National Service Man in all that Palestine business
nine or ten years ago, after the war. But, though they dispersed with
expressed solicitude, the parents felt that the present crisis was no
time for such ghosts, perhaps, in fact, it was just that sort of living
in the past that had brought England to her present humiliations.
There was something in what Mrs. Birkenshaw, young, commonsen-
sical, and very energetic, suggested: that the Pascoes deserved,
needed, a bit of a rest.

"But that's ridiculous, Mr. Coppings," Gladys said. Catching sight
of her dull, streaky hair in the mirror, she wondered whether it

would be appropriate to have it set and blued before the funeral. Benny had always liked her to look her best. "No. That's absolutely out. I'm willing to pay any money you ask, you know. It was Mr. Murkins' special wish. You see"—and she explained all over again, for really the long, gaunt undertaker was obtuse, though everyone in the village had recommended him—"you see, Mr. Murkins's family are *all* buried in Bromley. And his first wife, too. So naturally he must be there. And then he loved the countryside, you see. Especially the New Forest and the Surrey Hills. So I promised him faithfully that he should be taken to Bromley by road, sort of passing for the last time the land he loved, and so on. So obviously we've got to do it. There won't be a lot of us to follow. Two cars will be all we shall need besides the hearse."

"If the coffin was to go by train from here, Mrs. Murkins, say to Waterloo, he'd pass through the New Forest anyway. And the Surrey Hills in a sense. And then I daresay we might get enough petrol at a pinch to take three cars down to Bromley from our London branch. Oh, yes, I think we could do that."

She wanted to explain that it wouldn't in any sense be the same by train, closed up in a goods van, no window, but, of course, that was all a bit fanciful; the thing was her promise.

"Well, if you can't arrange it, Mr. Coppings, I'm sorry. I'm afraid I shall have to go to someone else, one of the big London people. But I do want you to understand that money is no object."

"And I want you to understand, Mrs. Murkins, that I would do it for you if I possibly could. And for my usual very reasonable fee. But I just haven't got the petrol and I can't get it. Of course, we could start out and hope to pick up a little here and there on the way. But then again we might get stranded. That would be most unsuitable."

"It certainly would. Good Lord! What an idea! No. Well, I must see what someone else can do for me."

"I should hardly think any reputable firms would use black petrol."

"As if I care what colour the petrol is!"

"This is a national emergency, Mrs. Murkins."

"I am sure it can't be meant to apply to funerals. The government can't be such asses."

When he had gone she gave herself another sherry because the whole interview had annoyed her so. She wasn't pretending to herself that Benny's death was knocking her sideways, or anything like that. She would never, she knew, feel anything really deeply again since those last awful weeks of seeing Alf die at the London Clinic. What she and Doris had been through . . . She decided to ring Doris now. Doris knew how to get things done; much of Alf had rubbed off on her over the years. And she owed it to Benny, who had been so good and sweet, to see that his last wishes were carried out, emergency or no. If she rang Bournemouth she'd catch Doris before she went out for her morning coffee.

"Doris. About the funeral. The undertaker bloke here says we can't go by road because we can't have the petrol. You know—this Suez business. I promised Benny—he'd set his heart on it—so I must arrange it somehow. Yes, I know, that's what I thought immediately. Alf would have known where to go straightaway. I wondered if you could help. You know a lot of his business friends. Will you, dear? That's so good of you. Bless and bye, bye. Hope you're resting."

Doris, at the other end, replied to their usual joke.

"Of course, dear, and you've got your feet up, I hope. I'll ring you back."

Gladys even now laughed when she heard that "got your feet up." How like Alf to have kidded each of them along all those years that the other was an invalid. Only he could have pulled it off. She could see that little look in his eye as he sat up in bed there the day the new nurse had let her in when Doris was already there. He'd looked sideways at each of them to see how they'd take each other, and, when he saw it was all right, he'd winked, crafty beggar, although his eye was only set in skin and bone. And then he'd made them promise to be friends. Well, she thought, going out to meet Mrs. Palmer, who was clattering in the kitchen and singing, "Jesus loves me, that I know," but softly this morning, out of respect, I haven't regretted it; Doris is a good sport as far as women know how to be. And she was good over the legacy; not that she had to grumble with all that Alf left after years of war surplus and post-war building.

"I shan't stop on here, Mrs. Palmer, I'd better tell you now. I always prefer to be straight."

"No, Madam, of course I understand. I said to my husband, 'Mrs.

Murkins won't stop on here, I'm sure. But I wonder what she'll do,' I said."

"Oh, I don't know. I may join Mrs. Pritchard in Bournemouth. Two old girls together. Though I'm not sure hotel life is for me. Or with winter coming we might go on a cruise. Travel broadens the behind, they say. Not that mine needs it. But first I must carry out Mr. Murkins' wishes."

"There's no petrol, dear," Doris said when she rang after lunch. "It's the very first days of rationing, Glad, and they're being very strict."

"But I promised Benny."

"Well, I've tried everyone I could, dear. They all say the same. Besides, the roads are terrible. What October weather! Benny wouldn't have wanted a lot of trouble for you. He was the last man."

"But I promised him . . ."

"Glad"—Doris spoke quite sternly—"I know you've been out of things these last weeks, nursing and so on. But it's a serious time for England, dear. Very serious. It's a national emergency. Benny was very patriotic, you know. A government servant all those years. He'd have died rather than . . ."

"I don't know what to do."

"That's just what I thought. I was the same when Alf died. Well, look at all you did for me then. So I've done the same for you. Taken it out of your hands. I've been on to the people who buried Alf. Very good people. They'll arrange it all. He'll travel by train. But he won't be alone. You'll go on the same train and I'll come with you."

"Oh, I don't know. That's what Mr. Coppings . . ."

"Yes, you do, dear. It's the right thing at the moment. And Benny would have wanted you to do the right thing."

Gladys was silent; then she said, "Well, as long as he's not got his back to the engine. He couldn't bear to have his back to the engine." And she laughed so loudly that Doris had to hold the receiver away from her ear.

"Mummy, I'm absolutely sure it's the right thing for him to do." Looking at her mother across the little luncheon table at Fortnum's, Tanya wondered how to tell her not to wear that sort of Osbert

Lancaster smart hat. "You can't possibly go to Hollywood with him this winter. It'll be bad enough *his* not being at Christopher's wedding, with the ambassador there and possibly Princess Alexandra, but the profession's a sort of excuse, everybody excuses film stars. But if *you're* not there as well! Poor Christopher! Senhora Serraoẽs just won't forgive."

"But, darling, if he goes on his own he's terrified that he'll start drinking again and the studio have already said . . ."

"I think he's right. That's why I'm sure he ought to take this Len Farrer offer. You can keep an eye on him here. Anyway, it's time he did stage work again. He can't go on doing V.C.'s and diplomats and war heroes in those silly films for ever. And it isn't as if he needed all that money now. You've got all of us off your hands. Christopher's going to be terribly rich. And now Timmy's gone to Hambro's . . ."

"But, Tanya darling, it's such an awful play. No poetry, no real theatre, and all about such dreary people—mostly lorry drivers; it's all in a horrible little café on the Great North Road. And there's a girl from a reformatory, at least I think she is, and a boy who makes long speeches."

"Heavens! Daddy won't be very good as a lorry driver."

"No. Your father's to be the only gent in it—a wing commandei who's down on his luck and tries to seduce this awful girl. I can't think why. It's all terribly unreal."

"Oh, Mummy, really! Just because it isn't the Noel Coward world you grew up in or S.W.1. I think it's terribly exciting, really, his wanting Daddy to play. Because everybody's saying how these new plays could be really good if only some of the best older actors played in them. And now Daddy'll steal a march on all the Knights. Of course, a lot of it's silly show-off. But it's new, and that's what people want. Len Farrer got wonderful notices for his first—almost as good as *Look Back in Anger*. I can't think why it wasn't transferred."

"But we can't think why he wants Rupert. We gather from his agent's letter that he saw all Rupert's films in the years after the war. He must have been in arms. But then we can't tell whether he means this wing commander to be a sort of bad egg or what. He's obviously meant to be a gent, though it's so unreal."

"Well, if he's a gent you can bet he's meant to be everything that's awful. That's one of their troubles, they simply can't get class out of their heads. But then, if people like Daddy play in these plays, as Ian said—he told me, by the way, to tell you he was all for it—the whole thing will get broadened and away from all these dreary lay-about types."

"Well, I shall urge him then, darling, to see the young man."

"Yes. And tell him whatever he does not to crawl to him. They're awful, snotty little creatures, but they're terrifically keen on guts."

Rupert had suggested that they should meet at the Garrick, but Len Farrer would have none of this. He would come, with his agent, to the Salisbury. And there they met. The noise, the unfamiliarity, and the crush put Rupert at once out of ease. But he liked the young chap—he was simpler than he'd expected, with a boyish grin and a very honest North Country accent. The astonishing thing was that he really did know all those old films—*The Day the Engine Cut Out, Safe Return, Incident in Kuwait, Busted Flush,* and the rest of them —and could quote from them too. "You simply don't know the mess I'm in, Tuppence. Lying has become my second nature," "It's not very easy to believe in religion and all that when the good uns don't come back, and the bad uns like me have seven lives," "Four Kings, von Epp. Can your Führer beat that?"—these seemed to be his fa-vourites, which he repeated again and again, raising his beer glass in a toast, standing with one leg up on his chair, generally posturing and delivering them in various dialect accents but particularly in a clipped parody of Rupert's own voice in those roles. Rupert sup-posed it was all a send-up and began to tell him how they had guyed the terrible stuff on the sets. But there was something in the young man's eye that stopped him.

"Oh, Jesus," he said, "I don't think I knew what cad or gent meant, but you had me in tears in the one and nine's. I even forgot to try to get my hand up Marlene Johnson's skirt. Lovely nosh! I don't think I'd have forgotten to grope her for any man except Rupert Mat-thews. Now I can't say any fairer than that, can I?"

Rupert thought, well, even if he is tight, one can't help liking him.

It was left to the agent to ask Rupert how he felt about the part and he found it hard to answer, for Len was immediately seized with a nervous impatience that made him drum on the table, whistle pop tunes, get up and greet people at the bar. When at last he'd been persuaded to remain still, Rupert said, "I suppose this chap I'm to play is the waste stuff that gets left over when any system, any old order breaks up. Your young hero, by the way, has got a lesson or two to learn out of life, but I like his guts. And all he feels, I take it, is the sooner Lane and his type are swept under the carpet . . ."

But Len had gone to fill up their glasses. When he came back, he said, "But you've played him, man, again and again. He's Lance Graham, and Gerald Thurston, and that chap who forged the cheque in *Hotel Register*. No 'systems' and shit like that."

Rupert said, "I was working from the outside in. *He* thinks himself a chap who could have been something, if he'd had luck. Luck is his weak spot. Or rather putting everything down to luck."

Len said, "Did you ever see this done?" And he began to play the "Bolero" with a knife on his cheese plate; then he suddenly frowned and said, "Sorry, please go on."

Rupert remembered Tanya's advice. "Very well. But try not to be rude and childish." He said it with a friendly grin. "And to some extent," he went on, "the luck thing holds for those who believe it. Your play is too good to be black and white. Lane may be sweepings now, but you extend him great compassion and the actor . . ."

But Len had risen and, swaying slightly, fought his way to the gents. They waited ten minutes. Then the agent went to seek him; but it seemed that he had gone.

BOOK FIVE

1967

"And will you wear those violet trousers and that black leather coat to Gladys's?" Sukey asked.

"Shouldn't think so. Portugal will be about eighty degrees, I should think. Oh, you mean will I have a suit? Yes, I've got an absolutely super one for all the rich people we're going to cadge beds and baths off."

"Oh, Gladys isn't at all stuffy, and not really rich, only comfortably off. She's fun. Or used to be. I haven't seen her for years." Sukey crashed the gear. "These wretched gears. They just aren't any good in these new cars."

Adam, looking at her gouty little hand where the wedding ring bit into a chalky finger, made no comment.

"Adam, I expect you know all about it. But don't wear too bright colours when you go to Marcus's. In case he gets wrong ideas. You know what I mean."

The full-throttle noise he made was probably affirmative, but she was left uncertain if she had spoken out of turn. The silence was long; at last Adam, gulping, said, "Please thank Grandpa again for the money. It was super."

"My dear, I wish it had been more. I don't like you going so far on so little. Senegal, did you say? I don't even know where it is. I must look it up on the map. But do you really think you can hitch lifts all that way?"

"Oh, no. After Morocco we're joining a Land Rover party down through the Sahara. They're friends of Lucilla's. Sort of anthropologists."

"I'm surprised at Tanya letting Lucilla go. Debbie's always so correct. Or was, the few times I've met her. You know how actors and actresses are. Wanting to be ladies and gents."

She gave a little laugh that turned into a dry cough.

"Oh, Lucilla's *parents* are in Scotland. Shooting and all that. They're terribly snobbish and boring. She only had to get round her grandmother. Apparently she's a bit silly."

"But that is Debbie."

"Oh, well, I don't know. Lucilla said. Her husband's some sort of actor."

"But of course he is. He's Rupert. Your great-uncle. You must have seen his films after the war."

"Well, hardly, Gran. Apparently he isn't much good."

When they got to the by-pass Sukey had to concentrate on the traffic, so that when Adam asked if she still did her weekly broadcasts she didn't answer immediately. As they came into the city she said:

"No. Even the local rag's gone over to your kitchen sink. Some young man writes articles about the Bristol dockside pubs and the sailors' slang at Plymouth."

"Oh, *God!*"

She thought he was trying to sympathize, so she said:

"Oh, I don't mind, though I can't think who reads them. No one we know. But there are so many newcomers. Anyway I've got so much to do. I'm still on the Bench, you know. And I'm district head of the W.I. And then my religion means a lot to me."

His first "I know" was almost inaudible; repairing this, he almost shouted.

"Yes, I know, Gran."

"I wish your grandfather had more to do. He potters so. However, he's got his old Forsytes on television now."

Having seen Adam off, she drove straight to the cathedral. She felt, as always, when she entered from the sunlight into the cool, dark depths of the nave a quicker heartbeat, a feverish excitement. She passed down the north side of the ambulatory and stopped as usual to read the moving panegyric to the poor burned young mother: Rachel Charlotte O'Brien, who, "seeing the flames communicating to her infant, all regard to her own safety lost in the more powerful consideration of saving her child, rushing out of the room, preserved its life at the sacrifice of her own."

> If Sense, Good Humour and a Taste Refined,
> With all that ever graced a Female Mind,
> If the Fond Mother and the Faithful Wife
> May Claim one Tender, sympathizing sigh . . .

She smiled at the solemn words, but they were good for her pride. However long she worked at being a good wife, good mother, and a good citizen, she would never be praised in such terms.

But once in the Lady Chapel, she was oblivious to all—tombs of dead Tudor justices, modern stained glass, a woman turning over the leaves of the Prayer Book. Kneeling down she said the Lord's Prayer, then her favourite collect, and then, mouthing the words, but taking great care to be silent, she began to tell God how "P.S. and I decided to walk to Porlock that afternoon, haven't I ever told you? Well, of all the embarrassing things, I was suddenly taken short. So there was nothing to do but to ring the bell of this old dilapidated rectory—all covered in ivy, you know. Well, we waited and rang again and then we heard a scream and shuffling footsteps in the corridor and then nothing more, however much we rang. In the end I had to go in the bushes, which served me right for putting on airs. But P.S. made the most brilliant horror stories up about it. Murders and heaven knows what. I am sure he'd have been a writer. Like his grandfather or his aunt. But *really* good." She stopped for a moment to wonder perhaps if he *were* a writer now. But the whole business about afterlife was so hazy; and, to tell the truth, she was so close to P.S. that she didn't wish to think of any other reunion. Who knew what was to come? She remembered one of the absurd horror stories which P.S. had invented out of that occasion and she told it now to God . . . well, who knew really what it was all about? It was a mystery. But she felt much happier now that she spoke to God again, and much closer to P.S.

She ended by asking God to forgive her for having turned away from Him in those years after P.S. was killed, but He *had* seemed to have broken *His* side of the bargain. Then she just let herself feel at peace with P.S. again, got up, dusted her tweed skirt, put half a crown in the box, and set off hastily, for she was due at the Hospital Book Service Committee at half past three.

Debbie would have been horrified to hear herself described as silly. She had adopted a scatty manner, that was all. As she said, she

"really couldn't be expected to go on remembering everything" for
the rest of her life, and people seemed to find the manner amusing.
Rupert sometimes said it reminded him of the Countess, but only
when he intended to annoy her.

Now she said, "How is your grandmother, Adam? Still living in
caravans and picking berries? Oh, she used to, I can assure you. Once
when Rupert was playing at the Bristol Old Vic we went to see her
and she rushed us off at once on to the moors to gather those things
some people make horrid jam with. I tore a new coat on the briars
and I remember she was frightfully brave about it. Do give Adam
the drinks he wants, Lucilla. He's grown so tall since I last saw him.
And go in and see your grandfather. Remember to speak to him
about his notices. Isn't it wonderful, proper plays coming on again?
Imagine how happy the public's going to be. And all the good people, too. Rupert's playing with Ralph and darling John *and* Peggy
this time. What about *that*, Adam? Happy days are here again!
Maybe, *don't* mention the notices, unless he does, because one of the
awful critics—nobody knows their names except for funny Harold
Hobson whom I rather *love*—but one of them, not H.H., said something about Rupert's performance being all technique. Well, of
course he would, wouldn't he, Adam? I mean they've never seen
any real acting so they're dazzled. But Rupert's moping a bit. Actually I think he feels it not playing the brother again, but he's doing
the little one whose wife's unfaithful and puts on a nose, so what
could be better? I wept buckets. Go in and see him and stop him
moping."

But Rupert didn't mope. He didn't even, though Lucilla had
warned Adam, appear at all fuddled.

"Senegal? Now wait a minute. Yes! I entertained the Free French
at Dakar. Ghastly hole. We did scenes from Molière." He paused.
"It couldn't have been more disastrous. Our French was too good."
His face lit up when they both laughed. He still remembered, he felt,
what made the young laugh. "You may find my sister Margaret at
Marcus's. She wanders around those North African countries. Well,
of course, you'll know her work, Adam, as you're doing English.
Oh, you should. Her last novels have leaned a little too much on
technique for my taste, but she used to be wonderful value as a girl.
Get her to tell you some of the nonsense our parents got up to. Yes,
I suppose you'd call her a 'writers' writer' now." Then he gave Lucilla

five ten-pound notes. "Buy yourself some sun-glasses, darling. The glare at Dakar's terrible." That gift appeared to free him. He leaned back in his arm-chair and smiled at them wistfully. "I suppose your grandmother's been telling you that I'm good in *The Three Sisters*. I'm not. I am not disastrous but I'm not good. I've been away from the theatre for too long. Perhaps I could have been good once though. I don't know. It doesn't matter too much because life is kindly arranged for us. As we get older we don't distinguish very greatly between what could have been and what is."

Adam's long neck was red. Lucilla stood quite motionless in her black patent leather suit, like an unwound robot. As soon as Rupert finished, she kissed him on the cheek. He got up and held out his hand to Adam, whom Lucilla had to nudge.

"Go on," she said. "You're meant to shake hands."

They'd arrived looking like the remains of a cat's dinner, but with a bath and a change they seemed quite presentable, though like all these young people, completely weird. She couldn't tell what the Lot were thinking of them, because as a rule one of the topics along with Traitor Wilson and the terrible trippers and the filth on the stage and the rotten way the Portuguese would tax foreign cars, and how Portuguese maids, though willing enough, were so dumb, was the Young of Today and how ghastly they were. But these weren't really Beatniks—they hadn't any beards or guitars and so far as she could tell, they didn't take drugs, though what drugs looked like she didn't know, although at least three who had been inside with her were there for peddling cocaine. There had been two tricky moments: one, when old Roddy Buckell had started snickering over his handle bars at what the pretty red-haired girl's (she seemed to be Lucilla who'd written, but it was so confusing) very mini skirt revealed; and the tall, pansied-up boy (who surely must be Sukey's eldest boy's kid) had got a bit shirty. The second, when the other girl, who wore an arty skirt, suddenly began to sing—in Basque and then in Breton, it seemed, though God knew why. The Lot had just gone on shouting and helping themselves to drink. The other three kids had remained quite silent, as in church, except for producing a sort of humming chorus, but they didn't seem to care that no one listened. Actually that wasn't quite true, for luckily Fay Kingston, who fancied herself as a high-brow, had been there. She'd clapped when the girl finished and said that she had a lovely little natural voice that would repay training.

But now it was getting on for midnight; the kids looked dead beat; and the Lot were getting out of hand. Old Roddy had got Sue Barnwell against the dining-room door and Gawd knew what his hands were doing; Marian was likely to be sick as usual by the look of her; and that Polish major chap had put his hand up Fay's skirt (no less). The tall boy and the pretty girl had disappeared, but the arty girl and the boy with the gig lamps that they called Humpy (she hadn't known where to look when they'd said it, for he'd actually *got* a slight hump) were staring as though the Lot were animals behind bars. It *was* pretty sickening, for Sue was the youngest and she wouldn't see forty again. She didn't know whether to be more annoyed by the elders' exhibition before youth or by youth's supercilious gaze. Anyway, it was time to put an end to the fun.

"Come on, you Lot," she said. "Out! Off you go, boys and girls. Your elders and betters"—and she indicated the two kids—"want a bit of shut-eye."

They were all quite good, ready to go laughing and giggling, except for little Eric, who always tried to take the mickey. He came over to her.

"Come on, Glad, let me share the Great Bed of Ware." But she knew how to deal with him. "You go and get yourself some dentures, and I might give you a nice French kiss. But not on the National Health. Something posh, mind, that will match my superior ivories." And she gave them a pearly smile that sent them all into fits.

Well, as she said to the young kids after the Lot had gone, she'd made them laugh and that's what people liked.

"Now for a night-cap and a sleeping pill." She poured herself a thumb of whisky and took a red and a green tuinal capsule from the bottle. "Four of these and three of those, or three of these and four of those, I can't remember which, and you're kicking up daisies. So I keep on the safe side. Not that there aren't more than enough old girls using up the oxygen. But still, I give them all a drink and a laugh. You can't do fairer than that, can you?" With a wink she wished them good night.

"It's all awful villas like at that Algarve place where your great-aunty aunt lived. I knew we ought to have gone straight down to the desert. Just because Adam and Lucilla have relations everywhere is a frightfully poor reason for going to places." From the back of the lorry, Polly, the arty girl, complained. But then as the black-veiled, white-robed women promenading the sea edge among half-clad bathers came into view, she squealed with delight. "Oh, don't they look dignified! I can just imagine the looks they give at the awful fat tourists showing their lumpy thighs and waggy breasts."

The others groaned.

"Wherever she goes," Humpy said, "she takes local colour. She'll go sandy in the desert."

"No matter how reactionary and stinking," Adam said, "if we strike the last *slave* caravan . . ."

"The caravan that never got there," Humpy interjected in spine-chilling tones.

"When she sees it, she'll start praising manacles."

"I hate ugly, clumsy people, that's all," Polly cried.

They could all agree on this basic tenet. So that when they were set down by the town gate and could see only the long, cool, shaded streets that ran in dark symmetrical lines among the bright blue-and-white buildings—lines broken only here by a clump of white-robed men seated on the ground around a reader, and there by a ginger tom stalking a tortoise-shell queen—the exhaustion and crossness of a too-late Marrakesh night, of diesel fumes, of gritty winds blowing up into the lorry, and of bruising jolts across the desert road, all went from them in a moment.

"Isn't it super?" Adam asked.

"It's marvellous not to have to pretend," Lucilla announced.

"I pretended most at that Gladys's in Portugal, in that foul street of English villas," Polly told them.

"Oh, did you? I pretended most in that awful Tangiers, at that friend of your mother's who talked about that Barbara Hutton all the time," Lucilla countered.

"If either of you call that pretence," Humpy said, "I hope you're not going to be frank."

"Never mind. This uncle will be super rich. He gave all the Klees and Kandinskys to the Tate. It'll all be hammams and sherbet and imported caviare and dancing girls here."

"Dancing boys," Lucilla corrected. "Grandmother gave me a lecture about his tastes. She seemed to think because she used to be on the stage that she was the only one who knew of such things. Not that any actors I know are queer. It's just one of those things people say."

Humpy, pointing at the girls, said, "We'd better leave *them* behind, Adam. They can come later when we've prepared the way."

But Polly wouldn't have it. "I shall convert him," she said, imitating the awful, pious Mary Hedges. "It's what God intended me for."

Following Adam's directions read out from the plan that Marcus had sent, they were all giggling so much as they turned the corner between the high white houses that they tripped over the cables of the television unit van.

In a space where the sun cut the shaded street at a sharp angle, a young man in flowered shirt and dark glasses clicked two boards together and announced, "Should They Emerge? Morocco. Mogador. Take Four," Walking towards the camera, pressed upon from behind by a mass of ragged small children, of adolescents, of cripples, and barking dogs, Q. J. Matthews was talking with every nuance of his now famous voice:

. . . this blue-and-white paradise, built as a free city for infidels and Jews by the tolerant eighteenth-century sultan, Mohammed the Seventeenth, was designed on the model of Nancy or some other imitation Versailles of the autocratic French *grand siècle* by an architect from Avignon, a Christian prisoner and slave. What was once a small Portuguese fort—we shall see the remains of their fortress in a moment, with its Spanish and Portuguese cannon, proud trophies of a time when the Barbary pirates terrorized all Christendom in the service of the Crescent—this small Portuguese fort was transformed into a strange hybrid of the busy, teeming, muddled, intensely live soul of the Moslem world and the cold, straight verticals and horizontals of Western rationalism, of the so-called Enlightenment. So perhaps the French slave got his revenge on his Moslem master. Yet as a compromise, as a hybrid, it worked very well, resisting even the blazing cross-fires of German and British and French Imperialism, of the famous Panther incident at Agadir, even the dreary version of *la belle civilisation* that French colonialism sprinkled over its surface like those sad little villas and churches we saw coming along the *plage*—equivalents of the Peacehaven and Frinton life the British tried to impose on so much of Africa further south.

But will this beautiful little town, with its individual life, its colour, its illogicality, its poverty relieved by charity, its wealth tempered by almsgiving, survive the pressures of today? Already Mogador, under the decree of that ridiculous and competitive nationalism that now tyrannizes the Arab world, has changed its name to Essaouira. Will it, as progress descends upon it, emerge as some absurd African outpost of a misunderstood application of the totally irrelevant and mistaken economic theories of the sage of Highgate Cemetery? Or will it be granted the blessing of an equally irrelevant paradise of Coca-Cola, topless dresses, and feeble pop music?

Above the drone of Quentin's voice, on Marcus's roof, beneath a green umbrella, Margaret sat, making notes for a new novel. She had the intention to shape into a short book—it was to be a psychological duet, hardly more than a *novella*—the strange recrudescences of violent sexual passion that Douglas had shown in the last two months of his life in that furnished flat in Onslow Gardens.

To oppose the intense animality of his desires, fighting against physical weakness, to my own response so intensely motivated by love and affection but supported *physically* only by my own healthy, strong body.

The pattern of antithesis was there, and surely the emotions, the realities as she had known them, were all too powerful. Her fear only was of some *grand guignol* which would be a monstrous blasphemy, or even that she would fall into Gothic ornamentation to supply the place of remembered reality. It could emerge as decadent, too, and with Douglas, of course, it just hadn't been; there was nothing of Mirbeau's *femme de chambre* in what he had determined to have before life was wrenched away from him, or in the part she had tried to play.

Damn, she thought, the wretched young people and double damn Quentin—all their overtones of life as it was being lived today were distracting incursions into what she needed to soak in if she were to recapture that past time whole and submit it to patterned discipline. Above all, she mustn't spare *herself*: she *had* pretended, however worthy the motive. She had done the right thing but it *had* been a blasphemy. And then her making it into a story—what of that? She *must* not spare herself. Why not enclose the whole *novella* in a self-satire of the woman writer whose only passion had been feigned? No, that was too artificial and not true. She stared away across the *plage* where the black-crow women paced to and fro at the water's edge, far over to where the ruins of the vizier's palace were sinking every day a little farther beneath the sand. So had sunk Douglas's kind bones and gentle lines—and she alone, by absolute concentration of memory, absolute until the head ached, could recall them to life.

But her thoughts were distracted by a scaly place on the crook of her arm; her whole skin was scaling these days, and despite the cream Marcus had given her, had dried, over the years, in the heat, Lady into Lizard!—oh, the shame of old age when the mind could no longer keep straight ahead no matter what the hurdles.

In the vast house—three spacious houses converted into one—there were carrying and fetching and running to and fro as if some monstrous creatures—vast beetles or cockroaches—had invaded an ants' nest. Old Abdullah was directing the bedroom preparations, Omar the table laying. Leila, Hassan's wife, had come in specially from their home in the souk—rare event—to superintend, veiled, shrill, and imperious, the rolling of the *couscous*. Hassan himself, tall now and, though still slim, broad shouldered, passed majestically from room to room to see that all had been done correctly. Hangings had been beaten here, tiles washed there, silverware polished, leather wall hangings sponged and, because Marcus ordained it, all the great cedarwood chests opened to scent the air.

Hassan knew that neither Marcus nor Margaret felt as they should about this entertainment of members of their rarely seen family; but Marcus, at least, had enough of the needed sense of decorum to agree that Quentin and these young people should be received with ceremony suitable for relatives, however little they might appreciate it. The thought of this divided, incoherent, unloving family made Hassan doubly content as he went about his superintendence, for here everyone, except for the Berber gardener who watered the roof plants, was a member of his own family; and Leila, who, he could hear, was directing his cousins with energy in the cooking of the now perfectly light and separated *couscous*, was pregnant with his third child.

Mr. Hamid Bekkai, the factory manager, who had come with

some accounts for Marcus to check, darted out of a dark, cool corner, to ask if Monsieur Marcus was not yet ready to see him—he had been waiting for over an hour, the day was declining, one of the new foremen, a man unwisely hired from El Jaddidah, was not to be trusted, perhaps a thief. Hassan gave him another cup of coffee and said that M'sieur Matthews would be with him in five minutes. He did not really think this likely, for he knew the loquacity of his own great-uncle, M'Barek ben Ibrahim, who had arrived suddenly from the south and was telling Marcus of his experiences in the French Army of the First World War. Marcus, indeed, was curled up among cushions attentively inclined towards the old man's voluble story of his sergeant days, of Château Cambresis and Soissons and German prisoners, of Monsieur Le Colonel, of a visit to the Eiffel Tower and of the training camp at Melun. He plied him continually with mint tea and from time to time exclaimed loudly in interest, but in his head he was composing a letter to the U.M.T. and another to the Caid on the subject of Moroccan co-operation in his new scheme of hospital benefits for his workers. "Since Plantagenet Perfume Limited is in no sense a profit-making enterprise . . ." Even after five years he regularly repeated this phrase for which, with Hassan, he had after months found a flowery Arabic neat translation; there was still something so incredible in its actuality to Moroccan ears, whether Trade Union or Government, that the mere repetition softened them up for his requests, suspicious and minatory though they still remained about the whole affair.

But now M'Barek ben Ibrahim had ended his story of the disobedient Austrian prisoners, and the proper attention of one hour had been given to this honourable old man who had risen and was bowing his impending departure. Yes, there would be just time to see Mr. Bekkai before this tiresome, quite unnecessary family invasion came upon him; there was to be no question of the television people being entertained, he told Hassan. They could go to the hotel or to the café. The occasion was a family one.

Perhaps it was for this reason that Polly and Humpy felt a little out of it. Polly, as usual, just wandered away, so that Humpy was left to observe the strange scene while Q. J. Matthews talked on, the only addition to his television performance being some curious movements of his arms and hands that suggested a Burmese dance. Humpy lay back into a succubus of cushions and wallowed after the hardships of the last two days—everything was thick and lush and colourful, although there were none of the famous pictures—only some wonderfully living, bright drawings of Negro slaves and Turkish sultans. But the dust and the mustiness, the sense that everything —all this velvet and silk and leather and silver—had been mouldering away in a heavily perfumed caravanserai for years and leagues of camel-journeying, overcame Humpy with slight nausea. What the others must be feeling he could only guess, for he was supposed to be the untidy, dirty one of the party. And in this heavily scented dust lived or rather temporarily dwelt these three strange saurians. Q. J. Matthews, of course, was the expected iguana or gecko with his crest of hair, his long thin body, his hooded eyes; yet one could tell he was no true saurian because of his endless talk and choric— yes, that's what they were, Greek choric—gestures.

But the novelist woman, Margaret Matthews, who sat so absolutely grey and still and elongated, her dried cheek twitching occasionally, her eyelids blinking when, as rarely, she spoke, was the motionless lizard, as her other brother, their host, was the active, busy one. In and out of the room he darted, now here, now there, wearing a big fur pelisse and a scarlet cashmere shawl wound round his head, although the temperature inside was only cool by comparison with the sun's baking heat—but he was never warm, he told them. As how should he be, emaciated almost to dried skin and bone except for his huge, lively, dark eyes looking into every corner at once and his little tongue that constantly leapt out to moisten his lips. For the most part he only seemed anxious to dissociate himself from the modern world with his quick, angry little questions. That, and a kind of mad, turbulent etiquette which Humpy thought must have reigned at the Red Queen's court or that of Christina of Sweden.

In their first moments of arrival he had insisted on exact introductions and had then repeated their names to the innumerable clients, relatives, and guests who were clustered about the great room. There he presented a silent, very old man, lost in the shadows of an alcove, with the greatest show of respect, Abdullah ben Seddiq; then he silenced a knot of arguing young men standing in a doorway—"Hassan's cousins—Mohammed, Ahmed, Hamid—the same name only different, if you see what I mean—and Ibrahim and Ali." On and on it seemed to go, name after name, until at last he lost patience—either with this vast array of tea-drinking visitors or with himself—he waved one hand at two youths and said, "And those are Tiddley and Tum Tum, some cousins of Hassan's mother's cousins. I can't remember their names." And then waving his other hand, he said, "And those people I'm not speaking to." He said something in Arabic to them that sent them rapidly away. "I can't think where Hassan is. He might introduce the ladies of the party to his wife if you ask him nicely," he told Lucilla.

To his brother Q. J. Matthews he said, "Morocco emergent? What do you mean? It doesn't sound very nice. Sounds like an enema to me. If you mean the drainage isn't perfect, you're quite right. Oh, is that what they *call* us? Well, don't start pulling us too quickly into your horrid world, Beatles and beatniks: terrible creatures, they look like lady novelists with their fringes—sorry, Margaret darling, but you know what I mean—dead ones like Sheila Kaye Smith. Anyway the men here have very short hair *and* shave off the pubic. We've got enough real beetles and a horrible thing called Popsi-Cola as it is."

He didn't stay for Q. J. Matthews' lengthy statement that the concern of his programme was to avoid exactly these things, but darted out of the room to return with more bowls of pistachio nuts and sunflower seeds, with which he plied them like an old maid feeding her canaries. Then, indeed, he turned on his brother.

"Have you any idea of what the poverty is like here, Quentin? Go down and look at it. I can send you to misery that'll shock your remaining hairs off. Warmth and colour indeed! What *do* you think I started my scent factory for if there hadn't been need to relieve poverty?"

"My dear Marcus, your Robert Owen enterprise is one of the most attractive old-fashioned paradoxes of this . . ."

But Marcus cried, "Robert Owen, who's that? Never heard of him. But you're all so clever. Are you all at the University? New University! Whatever's that? Surely they have enough of them already with their old Oxford and Cambridge—terrible old things bathing naked. I'd give them all a good day's work—cleaning the streets. What do *you* study?" He turned to Humpy: "*You*, Mr., I couldn't catch your name. Do take those great glasses off. You've got very nice eyes if you'd only show them. Literature! Whatever for? Either you write naturally like my sister here or you don't. If you don't, it's a waste of time. We had enough of that with our father, didn't we, Margaret?"

"There was a wonderful lack of reality about Billy Pop's writing that has great charm in these days of kitchen sink," Q.J. began, but Marcus merely said:

"Kitchen sink? Oh, do you still have those? I thought it was all labour slaving now." And he was gone to return with great rolls of brightly coloured silks. These he presented to Lucilla.

"I expect you'll want to go into the souk. You can't possibly go in those jeans things. I dare say she *did* in Marrakesh, Adam. It's full of terrible tourists. I go to my house there for March and April because the wind's so awful here, but I never go out. Anyhow I'm not having anyone connected with me upsetting Leila and Nihal and Mrs. Bekkai and the other decent women who live in this town."

Adam protested again, "She's got an absolutely super skirt she could wear."

But Lucilla, who clearly enjoyed Marcus's draping the materials round her, said, "I don't think it would satisfy, Adam. It hardly covers my thighs."

"It certainly wouldn't," Marcus said. "What do you want to dress like Clara Bow the It girl for? It was vulgar enough forty years ago. You've got nice legs. Why not let him do some imagining instead of dressing himself up in those violet musical comedy trousers? I shouldn't think Clarkson's would take them back in the condition you've got them into, Adam. Oh, aren't they hired? You mean you *own* all this dressing-up stuff? Well!"

Margaret said, "Really, Marcus, your fancy-dress parties were the rage of London for ten years or more! He adored dressing up and gave the most wonderful parties—with themes, and acres of lights, and decor overlooking London." Seeing their incomprehension, she gave up trying to explain. "They were all in green," she added lamely.

Marcus laughed. "My dear, we had two little numbers here recently. I don't know *what* they were—chorus boys, they'd have been in my day. Travelling with a rich Australian. Anyway, the little blond one nudged the other and asked in a screaming voice who I was. 'Oh, my dear! Don't you know? She was famous for her green balls.' 'I'm not a bit surprised,' the blond said. Which, though rude, was rather one up to him." To Humpy's astonishment Lucilla and Adam were in fits of giggles, in which Marcus joined them. Q.J. smiled and moved on to the essential fidelity of young people's relationships today.

"I wish I could think that this embellishment of the male sex, repulsive though it is to my notions of manliness, spelt a return to a more gracious reverence for physical love . . ."

Marcus, who was kneeling on the ground with pins in his mouth, fixing Lucilla's skirt, got up and spat out the pins.

"Oh, lor! I'll run this up on my machine," he told Lucilla, and was gone.

Margaret said, "I think this is appalling, Quentin. He used to be the most terrific womanizer," she told them. "To preach away against sex just because it's given you up."

"We've made it the dirtiest three-letter word in the language, Margaret." Brother and sister both looked so annoyed that Humpy thought he should tactfully deflect the fire to himself.

"We don't agree with you about the pill, Mr. Matthews."

"Oh, of course, it was *you*," Lucilla cried. "Oh, that was awful!"

"Yes," Adam accused, "you spoke against the pill."

They all looked so solemn that Quentin burst out laughing.

"Blasphemy against the sacred pill."

Even Margaret had to laugh at their expressions.

"I don't think there's any way of being funny about the pill that isn't vulgar," Lucilla told them.

Margaret suddenly felt sympathy with her brother Quentin.

"I'm all for a bit of vulgarity now and again."

Hassan coming in at that moment, she presented him to them all. With perfect formality he asked them about their journey, their present comfort, their destination.

"You are welcome," he said. It was a phrase he had learned from Americans but, as Margaret could see, they took it for an old Arabic greeting. "As Monsieur Marcus's family you are particularly welcome." Then he whispered with Margaret and was gone.

"Isn't he super," Adam cried. "Who is he?"

"My brother Marcus's rather super friend, I imagine, isn't he, Margaret?"

"My dear Quentin, you really shouldn't be allowed to go on talking on television about Islam if you say things like that. Hassan's twenty-six. Naturally he's married and building up a fine family. What he may have been as a pretty boy of sixteen is long forgotten. And in any case you are not the only Matthews to leave sex behind you, although Marcus and I haven't made an ethic out of necessity."

Humpy looked to see if the other two were as embarrassed as he felt. They were. But Q.J. was on to the beauty of the calm of old age when Polly came rushing into the room.

"Oh, oh, isn't it marvellous? There's a man called Omar in there and I asked him about the Andalusian songs that survive here. And it seems they do. Of course he didn't know they were fifteenth century. And apparently it's the Jews in a place called the Mellah, but there still are some. So we must persuade him to take us. For some reason he doesn't seem very keen. And we have to do it now because apparently, to everyone's inconvenience, dinner's got to be early for some reason and he won't be here afterwards."

"I'm afraid," said Quentin, "the early dinner is because I have to leave straightaway for Casablanca. I'm flying to Cairo tonight on my way to Singapore, where emergence, alas, is a good deal more noisome than here."

Polly was scarlet with embarrassment.

"I'm terribly sorry. Anyway it doesn't matter. They can all come and talk to him now. You must be sick of entertaining them after the talking you have to do on the tele. And I know what Humpy is, he just sits. And the others aren't much better. You and Miss Matthews must have had to do all the talking."

"I don't know if it's wise to fuss Omar about the Jewish quarter," Margaret said. But the others had all risen. "I think we'd better see what Polly's been up to," Adam told her.

"All right, but before you rush away, Hassan wants to know about rooms. Would you like four? Or will some of you want to sleep together? We *have* double beds," she spoke as casually as she felt intimacy and politeness together demanded. But absurdly they appeared fussed.

"Well, couldn't we sort of sort it out ourselves . . ."

But Lucilla broke in. "No, that's not polite, Adam. You can't snub people in that way. We know you won't upset Mummy and his grandmother and everybody by telling, so yes, Adam and I will sleep together."

Margaret essayed gravity in her acknowledgment.

"And the other two?"

But at this they all burst into giggles.

"Well, really, I can't be expected to know your esoteric jokes. I quite agree with Marcus. So long as the young will go around dressed like space-travelling hermaphrodites, who's to know who sleeps with whom."

But the young had gone. A few minutes later, however, Polly came back.

"I'm afraid that seemed rather rude. Only, you see, Humpy snores so much that after two nights in tents I've been saying that the one thing I longed for was not to hear him. That's why we were all laughing."

Later again Quentin was giving Margaret more details of his Emergent series when Adam, too, returned for a moment.

"I'm sorry. All that singing makes an awful row. And don't think you have to be involved. Actually we're all sick of folk-songs, but it's the one thing with Polly, and she had a sort of breakdown last term, and so it seems important to let her find herself on this trip."

Margaret said, "Of course." And when Adam had gone: "At least they *do* have breakdowns."

"Yes. Out of that something better may build up."

Margaret felt ashamed that she'd meant something so much less disinterested.

When the stewardess took away the breakfast tray, he took out his notes for Singapore and turned his shoulder away from the cameraman, Bill Archer, to show that he wanted no conversation. How many sacred cows here to puncture in the udder that this filthy world might one day be washed clean with milk? The old Raj. The sinking of the "Hood." The Burma Road legend, perhaps; that could bring a shoal of protest letters. But all that was past stuff to stir suburban or middle-class dovecots. Mr. Lee's special brand of socialism, inappositeness and futility of. A few back bench Labour M.P.'s. might squeal. Urbanism generally—the American way of life, all that stuff. It all seemed a bit stale. Then he saw the word "Chinese." What about that?—efficiency, hard work, ambition, etc., etc. The Jews of the East. All right, why should people pretend to like the

Jews if they didn't want to, or efficiency or hard work or ambition?
That was one to try out on Bill, cynical-sentimental, Americanized
journalist Englishman.

"We'll have to touch on this Chinese problem, Bill. It could blow
up in Singapore as it has done in Indonesia. The ordinary Malay
resents the clever urban Chinese . . ."

"Yes," Bill commented, "we ought to hit that racial stuff hard in
the first round, catch it before it can get up again. Without the Chinese, the Malays couldn't survive into the next century."

"Yes," Q.J. said.

He set out in his mind to tease Bill's conventional prejudices. "Perhaps," he said over to himself, "the most central feature of this overgrown, overpopulated city today is the resentment, probably even
the hatred, of the ordinary Malays for their Chinese neighbours. The
Chinese, of course, are hard-working, efficient, ambitious. As an
Englishman said to me, without the Chinese the Malays couldn't survive into the next century." Then in his mind he practised various
pauses and various ironies of voice to mark the change. "If the next
century is going to be modelled on the collective fantasies of Wall
Street, our friends in the Kremlin, and Comrade Mao, I can only say
that I heartily sympathize with the Malayans." Or, "But why should
the Malayans wish to survive into a century of compulsory, purpose-
less visits to the deserts of the moon, sterile obligatory promiscuity,
a world where Old Mother Goose Progress has laid her golden egg
and it has turned out to be that strange idol so similar to the black
stones and marble slabs of ancient paganism—the pill?"

But now they were to land at Karachi Airport, where the loath-
somely neutralized female voice informed them that local time
would be 6:35 A.M. and the temperature 22 degrees centigrade, the
weather windy. He fastened his seat belt, then underlined "Chinese"
three times in his notes. Looking out he could see the dismal excres-
cence of the Raj sprawling among scrubby bush with endless sur-
round of rocky desert. And there was the airport waiting-room, no
doubt, where in the thick heat with pasteboard numbers they would,
in transit, await with orange juice the flight's resumption.

But now suddenly the plane began to ascend again, and round and
round they circled, bumping furiously. There was no cause for
alarm, only some delay in landing due to cross winds; they must
keep their seat belts fastened. But now the lights went out, and ab-

surdly the canned music came on—"Dance Little Lady." For a moment the Countess's dark eyes filled the plane for him. Next to him Bill Archer was mumbling, "Christ, Christ, Christ." Quentin's legs shook involuntarily, and he felt a mild not unpleasant pressure on his balls, but he had felt this so often in the war that he was proud to know that he wasn't physically afraid. Good God, he'd been too near to death in the trenches . . . As to leaving all this triviality and vulgarity for the darkness, the warm darkness, if he could take the whole human race with him into it so much the better. But he wished he had been able to love; in the darkness, warm, free from the deadening prickles of sterile reason, perhaps he would.

When they left the next morning, laden like pack mules, they asked if they could stay with Marcus on the way back. And appeared really to mean it. Margaret had to say that she would not be there.

"This is all right for Marcus, but I like real Arab country. Morocco's Berber land, really. In a few days I shall be off to Saudi Arabia."

Lucilla then said, "I liked *Divide and Rule* enormously. Of course, I've never known any schizophrenics but I was terribly impressed."

"It made a fascinating technical problem," Margaret explained.

"Oh, I see. Well, I *couldn't* put it down."

"Really, Lucilla, your language!" Adam said. "Some of your early Carmichael stories are in the Inter Wars Period English Special, Aunt Margaret."

But Margaret thanked Lucilla. "I'm awfully pleased you were held by it. That's what matters. The technique's my own affair."

"There you are. I said it was all right. But they said it sounded as though I were calling you a good read."

Humpy then got up courage to ask Marcus about the scent factory. He wasn't interested so much in the co-operative, social angle as the technical process, and the original idea.

"There wasn't much to *that*. Portuguese broom flourishes all over the dunes. It was just a question of extraction and marketing. Everyone said the English and Americans would want a French name, but I risked Plantagenet and it worked. All those old medieval queens in wimples made such wonderful advertisements. I wanted to put in Edward the Second, but business and fun don't mix. The real work was persuading the Moroccans that I wasn't going to exploit them. And that'll never really be done."

He even promised delightedly to show Humpy round the factory on their return. Polly only had an apology to make. "It seems I was rude in not staying and listening to Q. J. Matthews, but you see it was so like the tele, and part of my breakdown connects with my parents watching tele all the time."

"Oh, my dear," Marcus cried, excusing her, but he turned to Margaret. "I really *am* worried about the poor old thing, Margaret. He must be over seventy, you know. Flying about like a bat to Singapore and God knows where to keep the wolf from the door."

Margaret and all the others assured him that Quentin was very well paid both in money and in the adoration of viewers.

"Oh, perhaps! But at *that* age! Hotels and aeroplanes. I should die. Not that I *can* do much. We don't like each other, so I can't possibly offer money . . ."

When the young people had gone, Margaret, although she was really intent on her novel, felt somehow too elated to leave the conversation alone. To her surprise punctual Marcus, too, although due for a morning visit to the factory, sat down and ordered fresh coffee. They agreed about the niceness of the four young people.

"Of course, one likes being liked," Margaret said.

"They probably didn't really like us, my dear. No young generations do like their elders. But they had such good manners."

As they drank coffee she meditated. "Why are they so much nicer than we were?"

"Are they? The young are always attractive. It's like drowned people. When you're first drowned, nothing could look nicer. Look at that 'Ophelia' of Millais. There's a *nice* girl for you. Or that woman of Tennyson's drifting down to Camelot. But we've been rolled about, thrown on to beaches, dashed against rocks, and all the rest of it. You can't expect old people to be very *nice*."

"I suppose so." Margaret's mind was on her book, but she couldn't find the energy to move. "Oh, dear, what does it all mean, Marcus?"

The inanity of the question underlined the inertia Marcus wanted to resist.

"Oh, for Christ's sake! Don't let your success with youth turn your head! You can't sit there at sixty-five asking the questions of a moony girl of sixteen."

Margaret flared up, "Your malice is detestable, Marcus. All through your life it's been the same. Restless, impetuous, never stopping for thought, destroying wherever you go like a greedy hen."

He felt the attack as intolerable and unfair.

"And *you* just sit on life with your bony bottom until you've pulverized it into sand."

Margaret took her notebook away from the house; she felt too angry to work there. She walked for a while in the souk to calm down amid the familiar shouts and chatter, the smell of offal and warm blood and rotting oranges and cedar wood, the pressure of the milling crowd, until at last she had to jump out of the way of a jingling victoria. How can he say it? What nonsense when all this press of people, this living human mass is what I feed upon! Affirmed, she went up on to the fortifications to write. She sat on the white stone battlements among the baroque cannons and stared out across the ocean. A typical Mogador wind had succeeded the intense still heat of the day before. Atlantic waves were thrashing and flaying the huge boulders below. As far as she could view, great white horses leapt and were engulfed in the glaciers of green water. This sea with its constant movement and energy was as much part of her as the desert, whatever Marcus might say. She breathed in the salt wind. If she were to give herself to the ocean she would be rolled on and on until she came to the New World, to Eldorado, to the noble savages, to life renewed.

Marcus had his say at the factory—a competent, expeditious, but that day a rather "scratchy" sort of say. Yet he could not return home. He took his Peugeot out along the absurd little *corniche*, and by the cracked tarmac side road that led into the dunes. There he lay on his stomach in the hot sand among the broom bushes and pressed himself deeper and deeper into its dryness. After all these years that she should think that his farmyard hen business and good works were without any discipline, and what did they call it—pecking order? Didn't she understand anything about self-discipline? know anything of how he had let himself be measured and dried by life until he was at peace with the hot sand?

In the house the voices raised; the quarrel of M'sieur Marcus and his sister were a source of eager speculation. Omar, who was a slave of desires, thought that they had quarrelled over lust for one of the young people—who could say which? Abdullah thought that Marcus had been disciplining his sister's unwomanly ways. Old M'Barek ben Ibrahim declared that the sight of the young people had made them both ashamed of their unnatural infertility. Openly Hassan agreed with this seemly solution, but to himself he gave a more modern answer. There was no doubt that the family visit had stirred the conscience of M'sieur Marcus and his sister; but their guilt was not the old Moslem one his great-uncle thought. With the advent of M'sieur Q. J. Matthews, so famous and rich, old Margaret must have regretted that she had refused to write for the *Paris-Match*, as she had one day to his horror confessed to him. As perhaps Marcus—his good, noble, kind friend—might now see how absurd were these cooperative ideas at the factory. Perhaps he might even alter the foolish clause in his will by which the factory was to continue on these mad lines. Hassan, of course, could say nothing, for everything was left to him, so he could never speak of it. It was not as if, when he was owner, he would pay low wages or any foolish old-fashioned thing like that, if Marcus feared it; on the contrary, Miracle Germany—Stuttgart, Düsseldorf, Frankfurt—all that he admired most in the modern world, even his favourite journal, *Time* magazine, urged high wages, but also seemly ambition, high profits, and determined management.

Finished January 1967